"International tension, family secrets, and God's steadfast provision …a gripping, timely story."

> —**NANCY MOSER**, award-winning author of 21 novels, including a Christy Award-winner

"*Betrayal in Paris* is a tightly woven contemporary story of political intrigue and spiritual redemption that pumps the adrenalin and brings peace to the heart. The names and places jump out of today's headlines, but the deceit goes all the way back to the Garden of Eden."

> —**STEPHEN BLY**, Christy Award-winning author of more than 100 books and television/radio speaker

"With a plot that could well have been taken from today's headlines, *Betrayal in Paris* is a thought-provoking page-turner you won't want to miss."

> —**DEBORAH RANEY**, best-selling author of 19 novels that have won the RITA Award, HOLT Medallion, National Readers' Choice Award, Silver Angel, and been chosen twice as Christy Award finalists, including *A Vow to Cherish* (which inspired the award-winning *World Wide Pictures* film)

"A compelling and timely read! A contemporary war story that will engage readers while reminding them of battles fought beyond our normal lives. The characters are great, and the story, engaging."

> —**CINDY MARTINUSEN**, bestselling author of 10 books

"With equal parts mystery, romance, and intrigue, *Betrayal in Paris* is a book you don't want to miss."

> —**JAMES SCOTT BELL**, former trial lawyer, best-selling suspense writer of over 20 books, as well as three Christy Award-winning novels

The
Reconciled
Hearts
TRILOGY

*3 Novels of
Contemporary Romantic Intrigue
in Beautiful Europe*

Doris Elaine Fell

BARBOUR
PUBLISHING

© 1999, 2009 *Blue Mist on the Danube* by Doris Elaine Fell
© 2000, 2009 *Willows on the Windrush* by Doris Elaine Fell
© 2000, 2010 *Sunrise on Stradbury Square* by Doris Elaine Fell

ISBN-13 978-1-62836-246-6
ISBN-10 1-62836-246-4

eBook Editons:
Adobe Digital Edition (.epub) 978-1-63058-013-1
Kindle and MobiPocket Edition (.prc) 978-1-63058-014-8

Scripture quotations marked RSV are from the Revised Standard Version of the Bible, copyright 1952 [2nd edition, 1971] by the Division of Christian Education of the National Council of the Churches of Christ in the United States. Used by permission. All rights reserved.

This book is a work of fiction. References to real people, events, establishments, organizations, or locales are intended only to provide a sense of authenticity and are used fictitiously. All other characters, incidents, and dialogue are drawn from the author's imagination.

Cover photographs: Roy Rainford/Robert Harding World Imagery/Corbis

Published by Barbour Publishing, Inc., P.O. Box 719, Uhrichsville, OH 44683, www.barbourbooks.com, in association with OakTara Publishers, www.oaktara.com

Our mission is to publish and distribute inspirational products offering exceptional value and biblical encouragement to the masses.

Member of the
Evangelical Christian
Publishers Association

Printed in the United States of America.

Contents

BLUE MIST ON THE DANUBE

Dedication

For Julie Lynne,
who finished her journey early.

Prologue

Springtime

Kerina Rudzinski loved Vienna. Vienna was a tangled maze of old and new, of the ancient and contemporary, like a timeworn clock ticking away the centuries. Thrusting her back. Thrusting her forward. She had allowed the city to wrap itself around her. This was her refuge, a place of beauty and suspense, a many-sided city as complex as Kerina herself. Here she could lose herself in the music she loved. Here she was acclaimed as one of the world's most accomplished violinists. It was like a homecoming each time a concert brought her back; no audience received her more warmly than in Vienna.

~

Wednesday!

The third Wednesday in April, a balmy spring morning. Kerina awakened with the exhilaration of last evening's applause still filling her mind, her heart. It had been a spontaneous clapping of hands that began in the front row and spread within seconds through the massive music hall, up to the high balcony. The faces of those in the audience were obliterated by the stage lights, yet she remembered the whispering rustle of her blue silk chiffon gown as she stepped forward and blew them a kiss. The Viennese were on their feet at once, cheering her, begging her to play one more waltz. And she had lifted her bow and pleased them.

She stretched languorously now, feeling the smooth silk sheets against her bare skin, as smooth and supple as her bow gliding over the strings of her Stradivarius. As Kerina turned toward the open window, strands of her burnished hair fell softly across the pillows. She felt caught in a moment of timelessness. Slowly, deftly, her fingers crept over the sheet to her traveling calendar. She clasped it, her eyes focusing on the large black numbers. Her pounding heart went wild.

April.

April 15.

Another April careened into her thoughts, coloring her memory—a chilly, rainy day, gray-washed with mist that had shattered her life forever. Faces coming into sharp focus as though it were yesterday. Aloud, she quoted,

> " 'April is the cruellest month, breeding
> Lilacs out of the dead land, mixing
> Memory and desire, stirring
> Dull roots with spring rain.'"

She could not remember any more of the poem—only those haunting words and the melancholy in Bill VanBurien's voice as he whispered them to her. "The Waste Land" had been one of Bill's favorite poems, and T. S. Eliot, Tennyson, and Wordsworth the poets he quoted most frequently.

T. S. Eliot's words. Hers now. *April. . .the cruellest month.* The applause, the joy of last night faded into troubled thoughts, the past that she so carefully guarded filtering into her memories. The wasteland of her lost years plucked like lilacs out of the dead ground, out of the depths of her pain.

April. Twenty-six Aprils breeding dead memories as fragile as lilacs. She—that young concert violinist from Prague. And he—her first love. Lanky and blond and charming her with his promises. On their last good-bye so long ago, he had promised to come back, to find some way to always be with her.

"Oh Bill, even now after all these years, I cannot despise you for your betrayal; I cannot blame you for the past," she murmured.

Thrusting back the silk sheets, Kerina sat up tremulously and slipped her feet over the edge of the bed. Her thick, dark lashes were still sticky with sleep, but she allowed her gaze to follow the path of the coral sunrays filtering into her suite, highlighting the things she treasured most. Her priceless violin rested in its open case on her dresser. Diamond earrings sparkled on the bedside table beside her. Last evening's soft blue gown lay draped over the chair back, the chiffon neck scarf crumpled on the floor. Again she recalled the swishing, crinkling sweep of the flared skirt across the stage. She tried to recover the sound of the music and the thrill of last night's ovation but heard only the pounding of her own heart. Yesterday was gone. Last evening gone. A season of yesterdays plucked from dead ground.

As she fled barefooted to the luxurious marbled bathroom, a strap of her negligee slipped off her shoulder. It didn't matter. She stepped out of the gown and into the scalding hot shower, and cried for the unfurrowed ground, the dead roots of yesterday.

Swirling the lilac-scented soap over her naked body, she felt a lump in her breast, pressure. She felt again. No, nothing. Her fingers slipped quickly from it. *I'm upset this morning,* she thought. *Imagining things.* As she flicked the brass faucet off, the waterfall slowed to a trickle and then fell like the last drops of a spring rain. Blindly she reached for the Turkish bath towel and buried her swollen face in it.

Enough, she told herself, toweling down. *No need to mix memory and desire. No need to dwell on lost dreams, on the dull, dead roots of long ago. I am alive. I have my music. No one, nothing—not even this cruellest of months—can take my music from me.*

An hour later Kerina picked up her journal and left her hotel suite dressed in a trim, dusty teal sheath with cutaway sleeves and a Shetland sweater around her shoulders. Her red-rimmed eyes were shaded with dark glasses. She hurried out through the garden café, past the round, intimate tables shielded with red umbrellas.

"*Güten Morgen,* Fräulein Rudzinski," the young waiter said.

"Güten Morgen, Jorg."

He ran ahead of her to open the gate. The crisp air cooled her flushed cheeks as she walked beneath the ivy-covered arch and out into the clear spring morning, her whole life mirrorlike with echoes of the past. She felt connected, yet disconnected, a part of her surroundings and yet distant from them.

"Lovely morning," Jorg called after her and, perplexed when she didn't respond, added, "Auf Wiedersehen, Fräulein."

Yes, it was lovely, the kind of day when she wanted to touch everything, to reassure herself that she could still feel and enjoy the beauty of nature—the briskness of the air on her skin, the softness of a rose in bloom, the blueness of the sky above. At this moment, she was alive and free, in command of her own destiny. The solitary, pre-breakfast hours were her own. She was accountable to no one. Not to her manager, her publicity agent, her public. She was free to wander through the streets of Vienna and bask in the memories of strolling alone in other cities—those memorable times of brushing past petals in a storm in Paris, picking flowers in the rain in London, or catching the crystal flakes of winter's first-fallen snow in Budapest. Or simply hurrying over the leaf-strewn sidewalks of New York City, her cheeks chafed by the stinging autumn morning.

After ambling down the Karntner Strasse, she circumvented the Ringstrasse once more and made her way toward the park. But memories tripped her up at every corner. *Bill. Music. Bill.* She had not allowed herself to think of William C. VanBurien for months. Now his presence gripped her, like a cord of three strands wrapping itself around her heart and crushing her wounded spirit.

Her steps slowed as she entered Stadtpark through the ornate Jugendstil Portals and paused as she always did beneath the gilded statue of Johann Strauss playing his violin. Everything seemed to have the face of Bill VanBurien this morning. Even the sculpted features of the King of Waltz looked more like Bill's dimpled grin.

Kerina quickened her pace as she crossed the iron bridge to her favorite stone bench in the municipal park. She sank down, savoring the view of the city she loved more than any other in the world. Then she opened her journal, took out the faded snapshot from the zippered fold, and looked down at the smiling face that had once been so dear to her. *Bill.* His name as American as apple pie and ice cream or a home run at a baseball game. As American as a foot-long hot dog at Disneyland or a donkey ride down into the Grand Canyon. Bill had introduced her to all of these. Kerina had loved them, loved them because she was with Bill, and she had thought their love would go on forever.

Gently, she ran her fingers over his features, awakening the pain. Her first love with those large, smoky-blue eyes and hair as fair as the wheat fields of Kansas. One year out of her life. A thousand promises. A lifetime of memories. She thought of Bill backstage in the concert hall in Chicago, picking up her Stradivarius and running the bow across the strings. He was a tease and at times, deceptive, but he loved music, and no one who loved music could be entirely Machiavellian.

She tucked the photo back into the zippered pocket, took up her pen, and wrote:

> *April 15. Today I remembered Bill VanBurien. Remembered what might have been.*

Ahead, she saw a seagull swoop low over the distant river, watched its wings spread, felt the strength of the bird in flight. Always when the schedule was tight and the demands of her performances pressed in, she would find comfort in walking along the Danube or retreat to one of the park benches near the lake as she was doing this morning, sometimes groping in her heart for something hidden even from memory.

At the most unexpected moments, the elusive dream haunted her again. And then half awake, half asleep—while she was sitting here, or playing her violin, or resting—the picture of a country house on a hill with the quaint gazebo behind it came vividly to mind. Sometimes the house was drenched in budding spring flowers—sometimes with autumn leaves drifting across the walkway. White pillars framed the porch. Red-leafed dogwood and sumac grew in the woods behind it. Wisteria tumbled over the picket fence, and a pink rosebush grew unchecked by the corner of the house. Sometimes the fragrance of sweet gum trees and honeysuckle bushes replaced the scent of roses. And always—breaking the stillness— the sound of a baby crying.

Kerina could not recall being there. She knew that she had never gone inside the house, and yet it was part of her, that lost something she wanted to find. There was no house so vivid in her memory, none that tantalized her as this simple country home on the hill. Empty. Neglected. Sometimes she remembered the backyard gazebo with its chipped, white paint on the railing and twisted vines growing along the steps. The image sat at the edge of her mind, some truth waiting to be grasped. Each time it came, as it did now, she reached out to unlatch the gate. Rusty hinges creaked as she pushed it back. But she could not enter, could not take the winding, cobbled path up to the house. A tangle of weeds and bracken and gnarled roots scratched at her legs. She pulled back, left with only the facade of the house looming in the distance. The wind blew the frayed curtains in the windows and banged the shutters against the flaking paint.

Above the banging came the call of the whippoorwill and the cry of the baby. . . .

As Kerina sat alone in Stadtpark in this undefined state of half dream, half wakefulness, she saw again the mother and child on the wide, wrap-around porch. Madonna and child? No, an ordinary mother cradling her infant, soothing its cries. She longed to be the mother, ached to hold the child.

She stirred, then stumbled from the park bench and fled down to the water's edge, slipping and sliding on the pebbles along the embankment. In her mind's eye it was the porch steps that crumbled beneath her, but she was left staring down at the Danube—a deep chasm separating her from the house and the child as the water's blue mist veiled her elusive past.

Chapter 1

The *clippety-clop* of a horse-drawn fiacre snatched the picture from Kerina's memory and hurled her back into the heart of the city. She turned, half expecting to find the house, yet knowing it was not here in Vienna. She felt troubled without reason, the place as real as if she had just climbed the hill to its crumbling porch, to someone waiting there for her.

Without measuring her steps or noticing the street signs, she circled back and was even now within walking distance of the Sacher Café. As she reached the café, she touched her bejeweled watch with her tapered finger. *Oh Jillian. I almost forgot our appointment.*

Entering the café, Kerina gazed around the intimate cozy room at the exquisite oil paintings that graced the red velvet walls. The tall, well-groomed maitre d' hurried forward to greet her.

"Miss Rudzinski, your usual table?"

"A table for two, Karl. Jillian is joining me this morning."

"Fräulein Ingram?" He flushed, pleasure visible in his dark eyes. "This way, Fräulein."

He led Kerina to a corner table beneath a chandelier and handed her a menu. She left it closed and smiled up at him. "Tell my waiter that I'll just have coffee for now."

He flushed again as their eyes met. He was around thirty, much too young for her, but he came faithfully to her concerts. Yesterday, when her publicist was with her, his eyes spoke volumes. Karl was just the right age for Jillian, but Jillian had a mind of her own and no time at all for the young maitre d', no matter how handsome or eligible he was.

Bending down, Karl asked, "The usual, Miss Rudzinski?"

"A *pharisaer* this time. We'll order when Jillian gets here."

When her drink arrived, she sipped and found herself drawn to the whispered comments of the young woman at the next table. "Elizabeth, is that Kerina Rudzinski, the concert violinist?"

Her companion gave a quick appraisal, squinting at Kerina from beneath a wide-brimmed lavender hat. She locked her fleshy hands together. "Oh Raquel, I heard her play at the Musikverein last evening. A marvelous night of Bach and Beethoven."

Raquel's thick glasses sat perched on the tip of her narrow nose. She gave the frames a decided shove. "She is lovely."

Elizabeth's jowls slackened. "My husband and I saw her at the Opera Ball in February, looking elegant as usual. She had such a handsome escort, a distinguished gentleman. Petzold. Franck Petzold. Something like that."

She flashed an appreciative smile toward Kerina, a smile that Kerina returned with equal grace. Abruptly Kerina turned away as a blinding light shot across her right eye, the threat of another tension headache. She sat erect, her palms cupping the demitasse as the waiter refilled her coffee.

Delighted again by the public that adored her, she allowed the steaming liquid to melt the lump in her throat. She blocked out their voices now, embarrassed that she had heard them at all, but she found herself reflecting on what they had said. Franck Petzold was a handsome escort, her constant companion for years. He was always there protecting her, directing her career, waiting patiently for her to return his overtures of love.

But here in the Sacher Café, her thoughts went back to Bill VanBurien. *Where is he now?* She prayed that she would one day see Bill again. Her prayer ping-ponged to the ceiling and dropped back to the floor, her words little more than an uncertain plea to a distant God. A God that she wanted to know, but could never quite find—the forgotten link with her childhood faith that these days seemed lost forever.

As she sat fighting her headache—that miserable precursor to every concert—the mysterious dream came back. Vapors of memory rose like fleecy clouds. Through the mist she saw the country house on the hill taking shape in her mind again. Behind the ancient oaks lay the faint outline of the gazebo, the pink buds of the dogwood drifting over its blue conical roof—and out of reach, the shadow of a man walking into the woods, walking with his back to her, his thick, blond hair tousled in the breeze.

She blinked and looked up with relief to see Jillian Ingram entering the café and Karl Altridge rushing to greet her. As Kerina caught Jillian's eye, the pink petals of the dogwood drifted away. The image of the gazebo and the man faded. But those images would come back to haunt her again until she found that house and made peace with her dreams.

Kerina brushed back loose strands of hair from her forehead, long shimmering russet locks like the brilliant flecks of a sunset—her crowning glory held back with a black velvet bow. She had untold wealth and the acclaim of music lovers around the world, and yet, in this instant, she wished she could be young again. . .not forty-five but vibrant like Jillian Ingram with all of life's failures erased from the record. Jillian had the pizzazz and sparkle of a fashion model, an enviable way of stepping lightly across the room, her long, tawny hair bouncing against her narrow shoulders. She looked chic and sophisticated in her new charcoal gray suit, those black-strapped pumps making her three inches taller. The form-fitting jacket was classic and feminine, and the short skirt only served to emphasize those elegant legs as she came sashaying toward Kerina.

"Thank you, Karl," she said, brushing the maitre d' off.

She dropped her attaché case on the table and slid into the seat, her lively eyes a perceptive delft blue as she met Kerina's gaze. "The reviews were all good. Except one."

"The one who called me too solemn when I played? I no longer worry about my critics, Jillian. They're unpredictable as a sudden storm. They come. They go."

"But even that critic applauds your grace and beauty. So let's celebrate the good reviews with a Sachertorte?" She beckoned to the waiter hovering nearby and gave the order.

The matchmaker song danced in Kerina's head. "Jillian, why are you so demeaning with the maitre d'?"

"Karl Altridge? I don't like the way he gushes over me."

"You should be flattered. He likes you. I find him charming." She hummed, *"Matchmaker, matchmaker, make me a match."*

"He's yours then." Amused, Jill hummed back. *"Find me a find. Catch me a catch."* "But please, not Karl. I'm not ready to settle down, not after getting burned in Rome by Santos Garibaldi. And before him, Brian in Ireland. I'm such an easy target for a good-looking face, Kerina. Or maybe I'm just unlucky in love."

As I was, Kerina thought. "The right person will come along someday. Don't let Santos or Brian keep you from happiness."

"Once singed, caution prevails." Jillian switched her scowl to a smile. "We'd better talk business. There are several things on the docket. Franck Petzold for one."

"And what does Franck want?" Kerina asked softly.

"He wants you to have dinner with him after the concert and then take in a private showing at the art museum."

"Not tonight. Just tell him we'll have coffee and one of our evening chats in my hotel suite. He'll like that."

"Will you?"

"We're good friends, Jillian. Nothing more."

"That's good news. I don't trust Franck's romantic maneuvers any more than I trusted Santos."

Kerina gave a chuckle. "What else do you have for me?"

Jillian ticked them off with a snap of her fingers: "A hair appointment at the hotel salon today at three, your Tuesday morning fitting with your dress designer; and don't forget your luncheon with Nicole McClaren. I set that one up for next Thursday."

"I did forget."

"Nicole won't. I've marked it on your calendar. And don't worry, I'll remind you." She grinned. "Nicole loves being with the right person at the right time; she will turn your luncheon into a newsworthy event on the social page."

"She doesn't need me for that."

Jillian considered. "I think it's more this time. The McClarens are loaning another collection to the Academy of Fine Arts. Nicole wants you to attend the exhibit with her."

"Not this time." Franck would go, but she was staying as far away as she could from another art exhibit.

"Should I tell Mrs. McClaren or will you?"

"She's persistent. She'll call me."

"Kerina, you're close to Nicole. You should warn her against risking their collection like that. It's like putting a billion-dollar investment into the hands of the general public. You'd think they'd be more cautious after that last robbery." She inspected a chipped fingernail. "That Rubens painting alone would go for millions at a Sotheby auction."

"The McClarens are heavily insured, Jillian."

"What good is insurance if you lose a treasure like that?"

"My dear, I didn't know you knew so much about art."

"Perhaps your interest has rubbed off on me."

"I think not. Franck is right. You know more about the value of paintings than you let on. Even Nicole insists she read your name in a magazine from the Art Theft Registry."

Jillian took on a lighter tone. "Oh, there can't be two Jillian Ingrams on the continent. I trust that the one Nicole read about did not steal art?"

"Quite to the contrary. Nicole said she wrote knowledgeably about the Italian Renaissance paintings stolen in recent years."

Jill's answer came slowly as a faint color rose in her cheeks. "You know I lived in Italy and studied in Rome. Even took courses on the Renaissance, but I don't call myself an authority. Why does Franck insist on linking me with the art world?"

"He said it was your lifestyle. Your father with the American consulate—living abroad, going to the best schools in Europe. He feels you were exposed to art and music."

"And so I was—but I was more interested in languages and skiing. The more languages I knew, the more friends I made at the ski resorts, and the more invitations I had to party around."

Kerina disliked Jillian's flippant response and frowned. Outside of the intimate music world that they shared, what did she really know about Jillian Ingram? "Parties," she repeated. "Is that why you came to work for me? So you could travel free and attend the best social events in Europe?"

A blush of innocence touched Jillian's cheeks, giving her the sweetness of the girl-next-door appearance. She was beguiling, yet like two people in one—a resourceful, keen-witted publicity agent one minute, a shy, warm-hearted friend the next. And now this third front—this pained expression at Kerina's accusations. To cover her own embarrassment Kerina asked, "Is there anything else on that list of yours for me to consider?"

The flush in Jillian's cheeks receded. She tapped her briefcase. "Your fall tour in America."

Kerina moved her arm as the waiter returned. Her torte glistened with apricot jam and a thick, smooth chocolate coating as he set it in front of her. As he walked away, Kerina lifted her fork and said, "That schedule was finalized months ago."

"But I'm getting more requests and you have some dates available. Chicago has written three times. Faxed. Called."

"No, Jillian, not Chicago."

"Why not? That's where you made your American debut."

"Then there is no need to go back."

The crushing headache sharpened at her temples. Chicago was Bill's stomping ground, the place where he wanted his name in gold on executive row. But he was an avid concertgoer. She jabbed at the torte and dangled another gooey bite on the tip of her fork. *What if he comes to my concert with another woman on his arm?*

"What is it with you and Chicago, Kerina?"

"I hate their blizzards."

"You survived the Prague winters."

"But not the bitter cold in Chicago." *Nor the loneliness.*

The searing pain behind her eyes intensified. Even as she stared across at Jillian, the white house on the hill came back with the autumn leaves falling this time, the nip of winter on its heels. She frowned, uncertain. *No, the house does not belong to Chicago. But memories of Bill do.*

Jillian flipped open her briefcase and ran her finger down a memo. "You play two concerts in Detroit and two in New York. Then five days free. Can't we squeeze Chicago in?"

"Darling Jillian, not this time." *Not ever,* she thought.

"I hate it when you call me that, Kerina."

"But you are a darling sometimes. So, please, wire Chicago with a definite no. I am taking those extra days for myself."

"Are we going on holiday?"

"I am going alone—a side trip a long way from Chicago."

"It sounds special."

Kerina touched her fingers to her lips. "It is."

Everdale, the town that Bill had called a dot on the map. She had never planned to go back. Now she longed to go there once more. Bill's hometown, his roots. Perhaps by some miracle he would be there on vacation, strolling through the center of town, and they would meet again.

Jillian watched her intently. "Anyone I know?"

"He was long before your time."

"I'm not to ask questions? Don't you even have a picture?"

"One. A snapshot."

"Am I to see it?"

"Someday, perhaps."

Jillian pursed her lips. "What was he like?"

"I don't remember."

Yet as Kerina spooned her empty cup, she still pictured Bill as attractive, well-styled in his casual way, as rangy and straight-backed as the young waiter crossing the room to their table. With a quick smile, the waiter refilled her coffee cup and left her with her thoughts of Bill.

Jillian demanded her attention, saying, "Kerina, I'd show you a picture of Santos if I hadn't thrown them all away. Oh well, you'll need a break by the time we reach America. No matter how cold it gets there, nothing can match that three-week tour in Moscow. The hotel and concert halls were stone cold."

"But the Muscovites received me warmly."

Kerina's skin prickled with the glad remembrance of the encores in the Tchaikovsky Concert Hall and the Palace of Congresses. She still slept with the music of Tchaikovsky running through her dreams. Yet she dreaded the trips to Moscow, convinced that communism still lingered in the hearts of many politicians.

"I'm always uneasy on those trips to Russia," she said. "They remind me of my childhood under communism."

"So why do you go?"

"To please Franck. He was born there, you know. Most of his art collection is in his home on the Black Sea." Across the table she met Jillian's gaze and flashed a disarming smile. "You worry too much about me, Jillian."

"That's my job, isn't it?"

"You just worry about having everything ready for my concerts at the State Opera House in four weeks."

Jillian's eyes darkened and gleamed like sapphires. "That's Franck's baby, and I won't cross him. But he really came through arranging your solo appearance with an all-male orchestra. No ballet. No opera! Not even Wagner's *The Flying Dutchman*. How will the Viennese opera lovers like that?"

"They welcomed a female guest harpist. Why not a guest violinist?" She ran her fingers over the rim of her water goblet. "We'll know in four weeks. Whatever happens, try to get along with Franck for my sake. It took him two years to arrange this engagement."

"And all of Vienna will turn out to hear your music. It will be my first time there." A smile tweaked. "I did buy tickets for *The Cavalier Rose* once, but I went to a polo match instead."

"With a handsome escort, I trust?"

"Would you believe—with Santos?"

Kerina's laugh rippled. "And you fuss at me about Franck."

As the women at the next table glanced their way, Kerina's words softened to a whisper. "I will give the audience at the Opera House a star performance—one they will never forget. I won't cancel out, and no one cancels out on Kerina Rudzinski."

Jillian clicked her tongue. "I'm sorry, Kerina. I'm going to be a first. I hate to remind you, but in six more months, I'm out of here. The publicity gig is over."

"You still plan to leave? I thought we got on well."

"We do. I even tolerate your moods when you're practicing." Jillian took the last swallow of her torte and licked her lips. "But remember, Kerina, that's what I told you when I hired on. One year as your agent, and that was it. So. . .with Chicago on your black list, what about this request from the Czech Republic?"

Kerina kept despair from her voice. "I'll go there for a visit after the tour in America."

"Won't you get homesick before that?"

"Vienna is home now. My father says I am saving Prague for my grand finale, my final performance. But Franck thinks I'll never retire."

"If you quit, he couldn't afford all those trips to Moscow."

"Careful," Kerina warned. "Franck has been my friend for years. Far longer than you and I have known each other."

"But I don't trust his friends in Moscow, especially that man we met on the steps of the Moscow Conservatory of Music."

A regrettable encounter, Kerina thought, her skin prickling again. "Jokhar Gukganov? He is an art collector like Franck."

"He's Russian Mafia, if you ask me," Jillian muttered.

Kerina poked mindlessly at her Sachertorte, her fork tines leaving streaks of chocolate on the plate as she thought of the dark-haired Russian with the sallow face. "I don't choose Franck's friends, Jillian, and I rarely go outside of Moscow to meet any of them. I'm too anxious to get back to Vienna."

"So why do you allow him to schedule so many trips there?"

"It keeps him happy. If it weren't for the Petzolds, my family would have starved to death in Prague. If it weren't for Franck, I would never be a violinist. We're old friends."

"Childhood sweethearts? He should have given up long ago."

Not childhood sweethearts, she wanted to say. *But part of the communist takeover of my country—an acquaintance that never quite went away.* "Jillian, you are such a romantic. Franck and I, we are nothing but friends and business partners."

Jillian hummed the matchmaker song again. "That may be how you see it, but not Petzold. He'd take you to the altar in a second, given the chance."

"I won't give him the chance."

"Nor any suitor. You worry about finding me a beau, but what about you? You never leave time for love yourself."

"There is always time for love, Jillian." Kerina's words flowed like tiny ripples across the table that separated them. "I must get back to my room and rest before this evening's concert." She gave an imperceptible nod to the women at the next table. "Would you arrange for Elizabeth and Raquel to have tickets for my opening night at the Opera House?"

"You know them?"

"No, but they know me."

"Fans? I wish more people knew about your generosity."

"What I do in private is my own business."

Jillian shoved her cup aside. "What's wrong with your public knowing that you give generously to charities and children's hospitals in Prague and the Balkans? And even this—guest tickets for total strangers. Don't you see, Kerina? It would make the violinist that the world so admires more approachable, more ordinary in the eyes of the media."

Kerina touched Jillian's hand in a rare gesture of friendship. "But I am not ordinary, Jillian. And what I do with my money and my heart are private matters." *And no matter what I give away, nothing will ever erase that April so long ago.* She picked up her purse.

"Wait. There's this request from Chandler Reynolds—a music critic who wants to interview you at the Opera House."

Kerina's frown pinched her skin. "Chandler Reynolds? I don't recognize the name. Does he work for the *Standard* or *European*?"

"He works for the American army. Part of the last of the I-For forces still in Bosnia."

"A soldier! You know I'm selective with my interviews. I have a reputation to live up to. Why have you come to me with this one when you know time is precious to me?"

"Oh Kerina, don't be a snob. It's not like you." Jillian's well-shaped lips curled into a grin. "The truth is, I did throw his request into the reject pile, but I kept taking it out. I tell you I have a soft spot for a good-looking man in a uniform."

"The maitre d' wears a uniform," Kerina reminded her.

"A tuxedo," Jillian corrected.

"Did Santos wear a uniform?"

"His standard was a white polo shirt and shorts with a tennis racket in his hand."

Kerina stared down at the stains the torte had left on her platter. "Jillian, you never called me a snob before."

"I never thought about it before. But why don't you do this one for me?" The glint in Jillian's eyes brightened. "I've been checking the lieutenant out. He's in his twenties and single. I had the fax machine churning out memos on him right and left." Jillian yanked a folder from her briefcase and slapped it on the table, jarring the water goblet and adding rivulets of ice water to the chocolate stains. "See for yourself. He actually has quite an impressive résumé. Violin. Piano. Trombone."

"He plays them all?"

"Plays at them probably." She flipped the pages. "Private lessons at Juilliard. Maybe he washed out like I did at finishing school in Switzerland and saved face by joining the army."

Kerina gripped her fork again, twisting it idly. *Reynolds.*

His name played games with her. A musician named Reynolds? A violinist? A fan? No, something different. But it stayed elusive like another dream. "Jillian, I suppose you have a picture of him in that briefcase of yours?"

"Couldn't get one, but I tracked down this old copy of *Time.*" She shoved the magazine across the table, spinning it around so the young man's picture faced Kerina.

What Kerina saw looked like the face of Bill VanBurien.

She felt color drain from her cheeks; the fork tumbled from her hand. She reached for her goblet, but her hand was unsteady. What was wrong with this miserable day? Everything reminded her of Bill.

"Good-looking, don't you think? If you don't want the interview, I do. . .Kerina, are you all right?"

Kerina traced the outline of the soldier's face, but in her mind she was tracing her mental image of Bill. The young man's jaw was thrust forward by the chin strap. The camouflage helmet covered his forehead, hooding the pensive eyes that looked so much like Bill's. Wide eyes. Long lashes. Bill had long lashes and that same straight, narrow nose and Grecian cheekbones. They looked like Bill's striking features, except for the finely chiseled mouth, giving the young man a sensitivity in that otherwise manly, military face. It was like seeing Bill's handsome face on the cover of *Time*, bridging the years from Montgomery Airport to now, unleashing the memories and the pain.

"Kerina, are you ill?"

"It's just the sweet torte on an empty stomach."

Her headache was excruciating. She wrapped her hand around the goblet and swallowed thirstily. Her gaze fixed on her white-knuckled hands, her bright, manicured nails.

In that instant she remembered Everdale—saw again her knuckled grip on the side rails of her hospital bed so many years ago, felt her polished nails digging into her palms. . . .

∼

There were two beds in the small hospital room—the one by the door empty, and her own by the window that looked out toward a row of weeping willows.

A clean, dust-free room with the floors polished to a high gloss, a yellow curtain hanging between the beds, blocking her view of the corridor. It was a plain room with the walls crushing in on her and the windows too high to see much more than the trees. Her fingers slipped from the rail, and she picked at the coarse nap of the dull yellow spread. Clutching, releasing. Clutching, releasing.

The night nurse had tiptoed across her room. "Kerry, we have to remove your polish," she said as she lifted Kerina's hand and ran the cotton wads over the nails, washing away the scarlet red and leaving Kerina's fingers colorless. . . .

Chapter 2

Even here in the Sacher Café in Vienna, Kerina remembered the pungent fragrance of the polish remover. Nausea swept over her. She struggled to recall the nurse's name. She had known it back then, but like much of her past, the name had slipped away.

Shaken, she asked, "William *VanBurien*?"

"No. His name is Chandler Reynolds. The lieutenant will be in Vienna next month, by the fourteenth of May."

"The first day of my performance at the Staatsoper?"

"Yes. What should I tell Lieutenant Reynolds, Kerina?"

She took a drink, then dabbed at her lips. "No interview."

"Do I wire the soldier and tell him to stay in Bosnia?"

"No, he needs a break from the rubble of war-torn cities."

"It's not like they're still at a full-blown war. Reynolds is there protecting the peace. He may be with the reserves. He didn't say, but he's coming to Vienna on medical leave."

"A medical leave? Was he injured?"

"My guess would be he just tripped over his big boot."

"Don't be flippant, Jillian. An accident there could be serious. What about the land mines hidden there waiting for a soldier to step on them? The lieutenant will be safer coming to Vienna, but let him interview someone else."

In the silence that followed, memories of Bill paved the way for the American soldier. Bill had wanted success and found it in the lucrative business world. Yet in the back of his mind he had yearned for a place in the media as a music critic. Instead he had joined the navy. After that, it had been college. The music dream faded. No one gave him the opportunity to pick it up again.

Kerina glanced at the soldier's face one more time, her thoughts on Bill VanBurien. She ran her finger over the strap on his helmet, as though, by touching it, she could relieve the pressure. The soldier still dreamed of a music world. For Bill's sake then, Kerina recanted.

I will give the lieutenant an interview, she decided. *What he does with the article is up to him. I won't block his chance to find his way in a music career.* Her pounding headache was unrelenting as she shoved the magazine back into Jillian's hand. "You win. Tell your lieutenant I will see him for ten minutes after the concert."

"*My* lieutenant? Don't I wish. . .but couldn't you be a little more generous with your time?"

"Ten minutes is ample for any unknown music critic."

Jillian snapped her attaché case closed and glanced at her watch. "Kerina, something's upsetting you. What's wrong?"

Kerina gripped the edge of the table to steady herself against the onslaught of so many yesterdays. "It's one of my miserable headaches. It will be gone once I reach the stage this evening." She smiled to reassure Jillian. "But we need to write that letter to Sarajevo today. I want to visit that hospital and see how the new children's wing is progressing."

"The one they're naming for you?"

"Yes. That was so kind of them."

"Not half as generous as your three million."

Kerina shied away from the credit. "I'm just investing in the lives of children who have been scarred by war and land mines." She shook off her sudden depression. "They've promised to pattern the children's wing after the one in Prague."

"They should have named that one for you, too."

"In a way they did, Jillian. I asked them to name it the Kerry Kovac Center because of a little child I knew once."

"Maybe the soldier from Bosnia can put in a good word for us and get us quick passage there before the next winter sets in." Jillian's eyes twinkled. "You could do a concert for the soldiers—especially if I like the lieutenant. Luciano Pavarotti has been to Mostar with his music. If you'd like, I'll contact him."

"No, let me call Luciano and talk to him." Kerina stood and dropped some money on the table. "Take care of the bill for me—and the tickets for those two women for my performance at the Staatsoper. No, don't get up. I'll find my own way."

Jillian's words followed Kerina as she fled between the tables. "Perhaps you have done that for far too long already."

Kerina heard a baby crying as she stepped from the café into the late morning sunshine. As a woman pushed a perambulator down the street, Kerina donned her dark glasses and hurried in the opposite direction, blindly crossing against the lights and stepping off the curb unmindful of traffic.

April 15. The cruellest of months. The cruellest of days. With deep pain, she allowed her thoughts to slip beyond Bill VanBurien to encircle the memory of Bill's child. Her child. He had for years been a child without a face, a nameless little boy lost in the sea of faces she passed each day. A grown young man now with unfamiliar features, a stranger she would not recognize. At twenty-six, did he look like Bill or have his dimpled grin and charm? Was he as hungry for power and leadership as Bill had been?

Or in that mysterious way of human nature, did he inherit some of my shyness and talent, my love of music? she wondered.

She hesitated by the Giants' Doorway at the Stephansdom, not certain what one would say to the clergy inside. It was Monday, not Wednesday. But there was no rule about entering on certain days. Nothing to prevent her from going inside and taking her Wednesday pew far to the front. Still she hesitated. How could she tell the priest that without warning—without provocation—she was being torn apart by longing and memory? By rejection and guilt? By the nameless child she had left behind in Everdale?

In her pain, she wandered the narrow back streets of the city, through the parks, past the museums and coffeehouses. Seeing, yet not seeing the passing pedestrians. Aware of the street musicians, yet not hearing them.

Hours later, with her energy spent, she found herself circling the Ringstrasse once more. She was back to something familiar. Her mind cleared, her headache easing in the fresh air.

As dusk settled in, she caught a taxi to Bosendorferstrasse. A long queue of concertgoers stood in front of the theater, dressed in their evening finery, waiting to go inside to hear her music. Waiting with anticipation as she had all these years for the sound of her child, for the joy of his fingers around hers.

Even as she left the taxi, the long-ago memory of Everdale persisted—*the nurse unfolding the receiving blanket, the baby's pink toes curling, his legs kicking. She felt the grasp of those tiny fingers on her own. Gurgling, cooing sounds had filled the hospital nursery as the nurse said, "It's not too late to change your mind."*

She had hardly breathed when the nurse put him into her arms and left them alone, alone so she could cradle him for the last time. When the nurse took him from her she knew then—as she knew now—that some of the warmth of him would stay with her forever.

It was all that she had. All that she would ever have.

～

Whenever Kerina stayed in Vienna, she took one of the three spacious suites on the top floor of the Wandlsek Hotel, all of them overlooking the Danube. Her favorite was the corner suite, the one she was in now with its unobstructed view of the city from three sides. She kept her curtains drawn back, allowing her to see the star-studded sky with the moon rising above St. Stephansdom as she lay on her bed or to view familiar landmarks from the soft, winged chair in the corner of her sitting room as she was doing now. Franck's dozen red roses filled the vase beside her. She ran her finger over the velvet petals, wondering whether she could ever add up the number of roses he had given her over the years.

Moments ago she had incensed him by mentioning Bill's name. Angered, Franck had stepped out on her enclosed patio to cool down. He was there now watching the riverboats meandering along the Danube Canal, cruising beneath the bridges with their metal parapets. The banks of the Danube were buttressed with stone, the boat traffic heading toward Hungary. He turned at last, came back into the room, and, easing into the chair across from her, refused the steaming cup of black coffee that she held out to him.

He stretched his lanky legs and plucked a thread of lint from his gray flannel trousers. He was a serious man of more than medium height, his jet-black hair parted on the right, his beard well-trimmed. She thought him handsome, but he had an unsmiling mouth, his expression one of infinite sadness whenever he was with her. Tonight he was quiet. Usually in their moments together he talked passionately about art and music, of the latest painting he had acquired, or the one he coveted. He was most animated when he spoke of Cezanne and Monet, Pissarro and van Gogh. He read voraciously and often quoted from articles on art thefts and museums the world around. Yet he was a good listener, sympathetic to Kerina, patient with her. Sometimes they would sit listening to music or talk at great length about artists and musicians who had touched their lives—Franck expounding on van Gogh or Picasso, Kerina on Isaac Stern or Niccolo Paganini.

"What are you thinking about, Franck?"

"How beautiful you are. How much I still love you."

Ever since Prague, she thought.

His life was like a reversible fabric—protective and devoted toward her, yet distant to others and outright antagonistic toward Jillian. Kerina felt indebted to him for helping her escape the Czech borders with her precious violin in her hands and was endlessly grateful to him for opening the concert halls of the world to her. She treasured his friendship, but try as she did, she could not return his love. They shared music and art and the love of Vienna, but they were at odds politically, and niggling in the back of Kerina's mind were those thirteen years that separated them. They mattered to her, not to him.

Franck smiled now, relaxing in her presence, untroubled by her silence, the evening's concert safely behind them. "As always, my dear, you played beautifully this evening."

"Do you never grow tired of complimenting me?"

"I never grow tired of being with you, Kerina."

"We've known each other a long time, Franck."

"Since you were fifteen. And I've loved you all that time."

His dark eyes smiled. "Well, maybe not that first year. Not that time you hung over the fence and told me to go away."

"That was the second time you saw me. The first time I was playing my violin."

"Oh yes, and I tried to take it away from you. What a good scrapper you were."

"It seems we've known each other forever."

"A long time. You hated me in the beginning."

"I hated you being in my country. You represented everything my family had suffered. Everything they feared after the Nazis left after the Russians came." Softly she said, "Until your family took over our farmhouse, I thought my papa owned the farm. But you told me the communists were in control."

"My father's politics, not mine."

"But I grew up under your father's politics."

His solemn dark eyes held hers. "None of it was my doing."

Deny it, she thought. *Czechoslovakia! My country, the land of my birth. And you were a foreigner, an enemy on my soil.*

Czechoslovakia was a landlocked country lying miles from the sea, its countryside filled with rugged mountains and rolling hills. Ten years after the war, when she was born, trout bubbled in the streams for the taking, but many farmlands lay barren and uncultivated, ravaged by the last days of battle and deprivation. Some of the lower mountain slopes were wasted where the trees had been stripped down for fuel during the war years and seedlings had not yet been planted. She knew nothing about the Nazi rule except for her parents' bitter recollections. She had grown up during the communist domination under the watchful eye of men like Franck's father. Always she dreamed about escaping. Escaping from Franck's father, the cruel head of the secret police, his iron rule as hard as the granite of the White Carpathians to the west.

Franck toyed with his tie. "I did not like your country until I met you, Kerina."

When she met Franck, the Prague spring warmed the country and the Velvet Revolution was two decades away. The Petzolds took over the Rudzinskis' isolated farmhouse outside of Prague, forcing Kerina's family to move into the thatched building that had once housed the workhands. Even now she was proud of her father. Karol Rudzinski had defiantly farmed his own land when most farmers to the north and east were consigned to collective farms, run like everything else by the people in power.

Franck drew her attention again, saying, "Kerina, marry me. I know I could make you happy."

"It would still displease my parents for me to marry you." She lowered her voice. "Besides, I don't want to marry anyone."

His fingers locked in an iron grip. "You did once."

"Just once."

"Is there someone else, Kerina?"

She laughed. "Who would know that better than you?"

"We're not always together. You fly to Prague without me. You choose to vacation at that villa of yours alone."

"You have never wanted to go to the Riviera with me. There is plenty of room, you know. But you always tell me you need that time away from me to work on your art collection." She imagined that Franck had a mistress somewhere. "Surely there is someone else, Franck. In Moscow? You go there often enough. Or back in Prague?"

"No one that I want to spend my life with."

He had never married, but surely he had many paramours in his life. Kerina could not picture him as celibate. Under that comely, serious face and that cultured, dignified manner, he was too passionate a man to not need the love of a woman.

Morosely, he said, "You always have an admirer backstage wanting to take you to dinner. That Count from Spain always writing. The Frenchman who calls."

"Just fans, Franck."

She dared not mention the soldier from Bosnia and the scheduled interview with him at the close of the concert in May. Franck had an aversion to Americans. If he considered it the remotest possibility that the soldier had reminded her of Bill VanBurien, he would block the interview. Taking the last swallow of her coffee, she steered the conversation to the present-day art theft in Italy and to the pilfering of art treasures from the Jewish people during the German occupation.

"Franck, doesn't it bother you building your own collection from those unclaimed works of art, one piece at a time?"

"The Swiss would claim them. Why shouldn't I?"

"You never put them on display."

"And lose my collection? My grandfather lost his back during the war. I won't take that risk. I told Elias McClaren that you think him foolish for exhibiting his art treasures again."

"It is Jillian who feels that way. She says he almost lost a Rubens in the last robbery. You never told me that, Franck. But I'd rather Elias have his display at the museum under Plexiglas than hide his collection in the basement of his home."

"As you think I do?"

"Don't you? Nicole says half of their collection remains in storage. What is the value of art if you hide it away?"

"Resale value." He twirled a piece of lint in his fingers. "Keep it off the market long enough and the price goes higher."

"Hoard it? Haven't I made you a wealthy enough man?"

"Collecting art is my passion, Kerina."

"I thought *I* was. But you keep your collection hidden away from everyone. Nicole and I agree. Art was meant to be shared with the public, not grabbed up by a few wealthy collectors."

His beard twitched. "What does Nicole McClaren know of great paintings? She would still be modeling clothes in Paris if Elias hadn't married her."

"And without you, Franck, I would still be living on my parents' farm—still dreaming of the concert halls."

"Every painting I've acquired was for you. They all hang in my home on the Black Sea. Marry me, and you will see how lovely I have made it for you. Masterpieces in every room."

She would never live there with him. When she retired—years from now—she would go back to Prague, back to her family. "Franck, please don't get involved with McClaren this time. The last time you did, something was stolen."

He laughed. "And you think I took it?"

"Of course not, but someone did."

His laugh turned bitter. "I know about the concert thefts, but I was with you at the concert hall that evening."

"And this evening?"

"I was standing in the alcove as I always do, waiting with a dozen red roses when the concert ended."

She touched the rose petal nearest to her, then rearranged the flower. *You were there when the concert ended,* she thought, *but you weren't there the whole time.*

"Tomorrow on the front page of the newspaper, there will be mention of another stolen art piece. It always seems to happen when I am in concert. Please do not get involved, Franck."

His brooding eyes sought hers. "Elias McClaren is determined to buy another Josef VanStryker."

"VanStryker? He's not even that well known."

"There's renewed interest in his paintings now. He was just coming to his own at the turn of the twentieth century. He did numerous landscapes. Mountains and forests, mostly. His life and work were cut short after Hitler came to power."

"Because he was Jewish?"

He nodded, his eyes darkening. "His great-grandmother was. Enough to have Josef imprisoned. He died in Ravensbruck."

"Then his work was probably stolen or destroyed in the war."

"Five of his canvases were reportedly smuggled out of Germany in '39. Since then a couple of authentic pieces have come on the market. Elias found one at Sotheby's a year ago. I have traced another one of them. Elias is willing to go seven digits to buy the one in Moscow."

"And you will take a hefty commission?" Her stomach muscles tightened. *What if the sale he is negotiating between Gukganov and Elias fails? What if this becomes a financial disaster—for the McClarens? We can't risk the loss of their friendship.* "Franck, Elias already has a VanStryker. Stay out of it. What if this one is a fake? Let Elias deal directly with Jokhar."

"Jokhar assures me that the painting is genuine."

"How will Elias ever get it out of Russia?"

"I will arrange for shipment. You don't trust me, do you?"

"Not lately, Franck. Not when you work with Jokhar." *Not with Jillian always pointing out your shortcomings and the risks you are taking. But then, I have no right to question your friendships.*

For a moment Kerina resented Jillian for planting suspicion in her mind. But no, it wasn't Jillian who had caused her to discredit Franck. Jillian had simply awakened her own fears.

Franck's sad, brooding expression drew sympathy like a magnet from most women, but not from Jillian. She found Franck annoying, someone who needed women, needed their approval. But Jillian had discovered in Franck the harshness that few others saw. It came out in its full blast of fury against her. What existed between those two Kerina could not imagine, but she kept them apart, and, when they were forced together socially, she placed them at opposite ends of the table or at different tasks in the room.

Franck began tapping the air with the tip of his black Italian shoe. To calm him, she asked, "What about the Degas masterpiece you mentioned the last time we were here in Vienna? The one plundered by Russia at the close of World War II? Surely you would want that one for yourself?"

"Why the sudden interest, Kerina?"

Because I am frightened for you. Jokhar Gukganov cannot be trusted. Niggling doubts crept in. *Franck?* She shrank back from the idea. She shoved the fears from her mind, ashamed to even think it, to question the man she had known for so long. But she must persuade him to stop associating with Jokhar Gukganov.

"Jillian wonders why you don't look for the Degas painting. It's been listed as missing or destroyed for fifty years."

A scowl burrowed between Franck's brows. "That would be a find." He twirled his signet ring. "And what does Jillian say of Josef VanStryker's work?"

"She never mentioned VanStryker. What will you do with the Degas if you find it before Jokhar does? Sell it to him?"

"I would hide it in my own museum."

Doubts crept in again. Anguish for Franck. She owed him her loyalty for all he had done for her. She could not allow her doubts to linger, not against Franck. Franck had been her friend, her best friend since she was fifteen.

Franck ran his hand over the books on the end table, stopping as he touched Kerina's journal.

Kerina cringed as she thought of the photographs within its pages— photographs of Bill and of her newborn son.

His hand reached out instead for a small volume of poetry, the T. S. Eliot volume she had been reading when he arrived. He took it up, examined the cover, opened the book. His eyes darkened as he scanned the inscription from Bill. His face went rigid. " 'The Waste Land,'" he said, turning to the first poem.

"T. S. Eliot. I often read him."

"But not recently? 'April is the cruellest month!'" he read, and then read the words again. "Oh Kerina. You only make yourself sad thinking back to Everdale."

"That was a significant part of my life."

"No, part of your past. Leave it there." Snapping the book shut, he stood up wearily and crossed the room to her. He leaned down and kissed the top of her head. "Good night, my dear."

Even as the door closed behind Franck, the bolted chamber of her heart creaked open, drawing slowly back on its time-aged hinge, unveiling a small town and the forty-four-bed hospital with its brick facade outside and the smell of antiseptic within. From out of the past she heard a sharp-tongued nurse saying in a Southern drawl, "Why on earth do you think that girl came all the way to Everdale?"

The nurse was right. Kerina had come to the unknown, weaving dark threads into the fabric of her life in a town that could have been called Nowhere, so unfamiliar were the surroundings. . . .

Kerina felt the color drain from her face. She pressed her temple, trying to shut out that April so long ago. . .trying to block out the grating rattle of the train traveling at breakneck speed through the middle of Everdale, its whistle blaring. Bill's car squealing into the hospital parking lot. Muted voices at the nurses' station. The cry of the infant in the nursery.

Her son. No, another woman's child now.

Chapter 3

Spring came slowly to Bosnia, the ground thawing at last, the bitter cold of winter finally gone. Lieutenant Chandler Reynolds leaned on his crutches and welcomed spring, convinced that the melted snows would expose any of the land mines still hidden in the fields. Chandler's work with intelligence confined him to a crescent hunk of land east of the British sector and north of Sarajevo and the French zone. He was housed near Tuzla, locked away at a top security command post, but locating concealed mines had become a cause célébre for him. Whatever it took, he would do everything in his power to prevent another explosion from destroying innocent lives. He'd just spent the last five weeks in a hospital, injured in the same blast that had killed his best friend.

A sickening chill cut Chandler between the shoulder blades. He already regretted discarding his wool sweater and cold-weather gloves. Spring or not, it was a damp, foggy morning, a north wind sweeping across the field, sapping his strength as he waited for the armored Humvee to arrive. The mists above the mountains kept the sun at bay. Or maybe the sun didn't shine on Bosnia. He would prefer being on the Adriatic Sea, on one of those sand and pebble beaches in sunny Dubrovnik where tourists once flocked on holiday; but the American zone was far from there.

His impatience mounted as he scanned the road in both directions. "Come on, come on, before my leg gives out."

No matter which direction he turned, there was bleakness, blackness, devastation. Too much restructuring still to be done. Too little started. And ethnic discord erupting to the south. As far as he was concerned, the terms of the Dayton Peace Accord seemed more paperwork than cooperation.

What have we accomplished? Politics control the rebuilding of the land, he thought. *Too many indicted war criminals still run free. The nation is still divided ethnically. Is that what Randy Williams died for?*

Chandler saw Randy now in his mind's eye as clearly as if he were standing there, blessing the driver for being late. Randy, with his shock of flaming red hair and the freckled face that went with it, always popping peanuts as though they were candy—a big guy with a quick grin and bullying shoulders that could push their way through a crowd of defiant civilians or through government red tape. He was passionate about villagers. Yet he was hot-tempered and strong-willed with a tongue that spewed expletives, a language of his own that had never been nurtured on the front pew of a church. Still, he had been a good friend and Chan missed him.

Their friendship went back a long way. They'd met at the university, but had had little in common, until their senior year when they were thrown together in a tennis match. Randy had cussed Chandler's blunders on the court. Chandler had fought back with an inner rage that forced Randy to sweat and stretch and race to whack the ball back over the net.

Their hand grip at the end of the game was anything but cordial. Yet, in the dressing room, after they had showered and changed and looked halfway presentable, Randy had asked, "Why don't we have a beer together and talk about teaming up for the doubles?"

"Don't drink," Chandler had told him sourly.

"But you do play a good game of tennis. We'd do better playing on the same side of the net." Randy eased off. "How about a Pepsi instead?"

"You're on."

Randy had almost chucked their friendship when he discovered that Chandler came from a pastor's family. "Don't pull any of that religious stuff on me," he warned. "About the best I can offer you is my loyalty and a good game of tennis."

They had gone on to win the tournament in their senior year and afterwards competed in a stateside tennis match. Randy was like the brother that Chandler had always wanted and still wanted even as a grown man. They hit it off after that first encounter with long chats into the wee hours about politics and religion. They roughhoused like a couple of teenagers, mountain climbed on the weekends, and put their noses under the hood of Randy's '76 jalopy trying to make it run a little bit longer. Their paths parted after graduation without Chandler ever taking that visit back to Ohio to Randy's hometown.

Chandler shifted on his crutches again and nodded at an old Bosnian plodding by. He didn't get a flicker in return. *Okay, so you want NATO out of here. At least give us credit for trying to help you,* he complained silently. *At least give my buddy credit for dying for you.*

For almost a year after graduation, Randy and Chandler kept in touch with periodic phone calls. One of them had reached Chandler at Juilliard when Randy called from an Irish pub in New York City. *"Hey man, I'm in walking distance from your slave factory. But I couldn't walk a straight line to you right now. I'm thinking about giving the army three years of my life. Why not trash that music world of yours and join me?"*

"Thought you were joining the reserves, Randy."

"I want to go for the big thing. I'm signing on the dotted line in ten days with a fair chance at officer's training."

Randy's spur-of-the-moment decision appealed to Chandler. For weeks he had known he wasn't cutting it at Juilliard. He faced the daily pressure of preparing for a music career that had no end in sight and no guarantee of personal success. He had given it his best, had practiced until his arms ached. He had learned a great deal about music—about himself. Randy offered him another option, a way out, a chance to quit with a purpose. Ten days later he left Juilliard, met Randy outside a recruitment station, and signed on. After all, they were like brothers, weren't they? And brothers did things together.

They struggled through the humiliation of basic training, slithering in mud up to their ears with live bullets zooming over their heads, and locked horns on the wrestling mat. Preparation, they were told, for the possibility of another Gulf War.

But they came out looking proud and took the next eight weeks of advance training before parting ways again. Chandler was off to specialty training that would take him into intelligence work with lieutenant bars on his shoulder, and Randy was steering clear of any job that kept him behind locked doors.

Running into each other again in the officer's club in Germany was a back-pounding reunion. An hour at the bar followed with Chandler drinking water as Randy downed three beers to celebrate meeting up again. They'd caught a good duty, close to the mountains, and were soon back into hiking in the Bavarian Alps on weekend getaways that put them in top condition.

You were the picture of health, old buddy, Chandler thought. *Invincible. Strong enough to make it to a ripe old age.*

Chandler ground a deep hole in the dirt with his crutch. "Oh God, why did You let Randy die? I don't understand!"

At the end of one of those weekends in the Alps, they had finally been reassigned to the American headquarters in Tuzla, part of the second influx of I-For troops heading for Bosnia. Randy flew in weeks ahead of Chandler, landing when the visibility was almost down to zero.

Now, two rotations later, Chandler had been asked to finish out his enlistment in Bosnia, to reenlist if necessary, with the promise that it would earn him a fast promotion and get him out of the computer lab and directly into intelligence fieldwork for which he was trained. Scuttlebutt ran wild among the officers. Only single men were being tapped for a special mission—an intelligence team that would infiltrate the Serbian line. Men who might never go home again.

Randy had been tapped two weeks before his death and flat out refused, giving an inappropriate thumb swipe to his nose to confirm his refusal. Chandler's interest sparked. . .anything to remove himself from analyzing intelligence reports at the command post. He latched on to the promise of action with strict orders from Colonel Bladstone that from now on nothing they discussed would go beyond his office. That was easy. The place was like a cement vault, and Bladstone was powerful enough to silence most men.

It hadn't silenced Randy. "Bladstone isn't recruiting for the army," Randy had warned. "It's something bigger."

"Then I'm in."

"Then the CIA has a stranglehold on you."

Chandler laughed. "The CIA? Bladstone asked us to reenlist. That means three more years with the army."

"Your interpretation. Don't go in blindfolded, Chan. The Langley boys are already grabbing you by the shoulder."

They had little more than three weeks to argue about it and then Randy was blown to bits before Chandler could reach him. Reenlist? He felt torn asunder, right at the gut line, debating with himself even more since Randy's death. Somebody had to stay on as part of the team willing to put down every uprising and unearth every land mine to make Bosnia safe for its people. He knew why he wanted to stay in Bosnia. Could put a name on it. Could even hear the shrink at the makeshift hospital advising him to forget Captain Williams: *Your leg is healing. It's the guilt that is killing you.*

Guilt? Chandler had had nothing to do with Randy blowing up in a land mine. If he volunteered to stay on, he might face another bitter Christmas in Bosnia as part of an advisory team or a token army held on to quell the guerrilla activity to the south. Chandler had missed that first Christmas when the troops were deployed to Bosnia while the ink was still wet on the Dayton Peace Accord. That wasn't his choice. His training was geared toward setting up the computer systems at Tuzla, but at the last minute his unit had been kept in Bavaria in a state-of-the-art physics lab as streamlined as any in the Pentagon.

There he sat, an action man glued to his seat in a secure communications room crowded with human think tanks and physics majors—he was one himself—visualizing Bosnia from a safe distance. Massive computer-controlled maps covered what should have been windows. He spent his time at a conference table with other men and women staring down at the dregs of their empty coffee cups or at the multicolored computer screens in front of them, screens that graphically portrayed the arrival of troops in Bosnia, bound by the old adage that knowledge is military power. That's what he got for going magna cum laude at the university, a desk assignment trained to identify threats or to provide the military logistics for moving the 60,000 troops of I-For rapidly into Bosnia. Granted, it was a complex system capable of distinguishing the multinational NATO soldiers from the Serbian army holding out in the foothills. It could differentiate between a sniper and a charred telephone pole and within split seconds send a warning to peacekeepers with their boots already on Bosnian soil.

Chandler scanned the desolate road again in both directions, growing more uneasy as he waited for the armored vehicle. His leg was giving him fits, his temper rising. He saw the Humvee at last, rumbling over the rutted, muddied roadway toward him and squealing to a stop inches from the tip of his left crutch. Randy Williams' old driver was at the wheel, his face a mask, his emotions still as shattered as Chandler's had been.

As Chandler struggled for a comfortable position in the front seat, he turned for a hasty appraisal of the men behind him. Colonel Bladstone, his own unit commander, sat behind the driver, another unidentified colonel beside him.

Like the rest of them, the man was wearing his protective vest and camouflage pants, the khaki-green poly-knit shirt visible at the open neck of his parka. He was holding a British walking stick in his hands, not an M-16 rifle. The man's eyes were hard, disciplined, bluer than the cloudy sky, his face rugged and freshly shaven. His I. D. badge was pinned to his parka, but Chandler's appraisal had been too fleeting to catch the name.

As Chandler faced forward, the driver took a familiar route out of Tuzla. *Randy's road to no return,* he thought. Behind him, above the roar of the vehicle, he heard the steady beat of the walking stick in the stranger's palm. "Slow down," Chandler warned.

"I know these roads, Lieutenant."

"At this speed, you'll miss the hairpin turns."

"I can handle them."

Like the Bradley Fighting Vehicle last month? Chandler thought. *And the Abrams tank before that?* Both of them went off the road. Both of them blown with anti-tank mines.

"I only have two more weeks in Bosnia," the driver boasted.

"I thought you had three months to go, like I do."

"Somebody messed up. But who's complaining?" He swerved, then gained control again. "Ever since Captain Williams caught his, all I want to do is get out of this man's army and go home to the Puget Sound. What about you, Lieutenant?"

"I have a thirty-day medical leave coming up."

"The leg, eh? I can't wait to get out of this place. I hate the cold and the sun not shining. I hated losing the captain."

Chandler fell silent, but he understood. How old was the kid? Nineteen? Twenty? The best part of his youth wearing camouflage uniforms. At the first deployment of troops to Bosnia, *Newsweek* had called the assignment "Hell in a Cold Place."

Good description, Chandler thought. The desolation of his surroundings reminded him of those old hellfire-and-brimstone sermons of his boyhood. His father's sermons held a lighter, positive note these days, although Chandler still felt the heat of his message.

Bavaria had been like a winter holiday; Bosnia, like walking into Hades itself. Chandler found the Bosnian winters deplorable. Randy took them in stride, roaming around in defiance of caution and taking on the plight of the kids of Tuzla. He particularly liked a boy named Rasim Hovic, who had an attractive, older girl in his family. In their spare time, limited as it was, Chandler and Randy did push-ups, played pool or Ping-Pong in the officer's room, and taught Rasim how to build a snowman, Ohio style.

When the Humvee reached the Hovics' village, the driver eased to the side of the road. Here on the outskirts of town, the rubbled ruins left the farmland unproductive with nothing but scrub brush, charred gray trees, and sparse patches of new growth visible. Off to their right, a de-mining team scoured the barren fields—two eight-man teams stabbing every inch of the ground with long ice picks and Schiebel detecting sets.

"They've detonated two more land mines since Captain Williams' death," the driver said.

"And the people?" *The Hovic family,* he thought.

"Evacuated the day after the captain was killed."

They left the driver by the Humvee and moved off the road, Colonel Bladstone and his guest slowing their steps to Chandler's pace. Chandler could see the name on the visiting colonel's parka clearly now. *P. Daniels. Paul,* he guessed.

"Do you recognize the place?" Colonel Daniels asked.

You know I do, he wanted to say but said instead, "It looks like the spot, sir."

"Let me assure you, Reynolds, it is the exact location."

He stretched his arm and pointed. "About thirty or forty yards from here. Tell us about it, Lieutenant. What happened that day?"

"I've given that report at least a dozen times."

"Then oblige me. Make it a baker's dozen."

The muscles in Chandler's throat tightened. On March 25, three weeks before his twenty-sixth birthday, he had ridden along on Randy's patrol. Now he stared between the damaged houses, his thoughts marking the path that Randy had taken. The sniper's fire had come from the hills behind the village. No, that was too far away. The sniper had been closer in, hiding out in one of the homes and, afterwards, taking off for the safety of the hills.

"Captain Williams knew better than to race over those fields," Daniels said. "He knew the risks."

The picture came back—Randy sprinting over the field.

"There was a small boy in the line of fire," Chandler said.

"So Williams took off after him?"

"We were on an inspection patrol, Colonel Daniels. Just heading back toward Tuzla when the sniper attacked."

"Bladstone here tells me that's not your usual command."

"I know, sir, but we were old friends. Randy—Captain Williams— invited me to go along for the ride. I'm usually confined to an intelligence desk at the command post."

"You've ridden with Captain Williams before?"

"Three or four times. I always welcomed the chance to get away from staring at intelligence reports all day long. Even the seat of my britches is worn thin."

An amused smile touched Daniels' blue eyes, veiling his harshness. "So you rode with him without incident before?"

Chandler nodded, his gaze fixed forty yards in front of him. "We had three armored vehicles ahead of us. They'd just passed the village check-point when the sniper fired."

"And your job was to get out of there, not to return fire," Bladstone reminded him.

He swallowed. "That's what Williams said. And then he saw the boy darting between the houses. The kid was terrified."

"And Captain Williams went berserk?" Daniels asked.

"He was as clearheaded as you are today, sir. But he saw something that needed doing, and he was out of the vehicle before the driver could come to a complete stop."

And running with the speed of a jackal, his protective vest taking one of the sniper's bullets. Chandler could only hope that the driver had given the same account of the incident.

"Did you follow him, Reynolds?"

Colonel Daniels wore an army uniform. The right insignia. The right bearing. But was he really army? The colonel was trying to put words in Chandler's mouth, to blow the accident out of proportion. To trap him in lies. But why? Other men had died in accidents since reaching Bosnia. Why the particular interest in Randy's death? Was this leading to a post-humous court-martial for Randy? Or to his own for being there? But something was up, bigger than a land mine exploding. He had to hang cool, in spite of how much just standing here was tearing at his gut.

Volunteer nothing. Remember Randy's honor. His sacrifice.

"I started to follow Williams, but he ordered me to stay near the vehicle. He scooped up the kid and turned him back toward our truck." Sweat poured down Chandler's back, his knuckles white as he gripped the crutches. Standing here was bringing it all back. "I think Randy swatted his bottom and headed the boy towards me."

Colonel Daniels said abruptly, "The child's name is Rasim Hovic. Captain Williams knew the boy, didn't he?"

We both did, Chandler thought. "Did he?"

"We believe the captain was in this village on a number of occasions to see Rasim's sister, Zineta Hovic."

It was too soon to say that the Hovic family had taken Zineta in when her own family was wiped out during one of the Serbian attacks. They had found her wandering dazed in the war-torn streets of Tuzla, foraging for food in the empty stalls of the outdoor market. As Randy had described her, she was sixteen then, her dress tattered, her arms and feet bare, her sad face strangely appealing and her dark, soulful eyes unforgettable.

"We don't encourage mixing with the people," grumbled Daniels. "And courting a Bosnian woman is definitely out, Lieutenant. But from what I gather, Captain Williams rather handled things in his own way."

"They were just friends, sir. She wasn't his steady girlfriend or anything like that. Randy helped repair the Hovics' roof just before winter set in. That's how he met her."

"He was that kind of guy?" Colonel Daniels asked.

"He had his own definition of keeping peace, sir."

"It got him killed."

"The captain and Miss Hovic were just friends," Chandler repeated.

"Really, Reynolds? Just friends? The girl is pregnant."

Chandler's gut cramped. He bent at the sudden pain. *What a mess you got yourself into, Randy!* But he thought about Zineta, too. How would the people in Tuzla accept a young woman impregnated by an American army officer?

"What will become of the girl?" he asked.

Bladstone cleared his throat. "We will have to transfer her to another zone. British. French. Whichever one will take her."

"Away from the security of the Hovic family?"

"Do you have a better plan, Lieutenant?"

Chandler's thoughts churned pell-mell. Finally, he suggested, "Send her to America, where she has a chance for survival and the baby has a chance to grow up in peace."

Daniels glared at him. "Her reputation is against her. She has no relatives in America. She's penniless. Someone would have to sponsor her. Who wants to assume responsibility for an unwed mother and her newborn?"

"Or maybe someone could marry her," said Bladstone snidely. "Are you up to the job, Lieutenant?"

Chandler emitted a throaty chuckle. "Sure, why not?" he quipped. "My mom's just waiting for me to tie the knot one of these days." The words were no sooner out of his mouth when he remembered Randy's final request: *"If anything happens to me, Chan, will you make sure that Zineta gets to the States?"*

He had given his word. Of course, the oath wasn't signed in blood. Or was it? How far would he go to keep a promise to a friend? Randy had died for him—had fallen on a land mine to save Chandler's life. Didn't that make the girl his responsibility? The wheels in his mind kept spinning. It would be a marriage of convenience. He didn't love the girl, barely knew her, but he liked her, and they were already friends. And what did he have going on in his own life these days? He was footloose. Who was to say he couldn't marry the girl and give Randy's child a name? Marrying her was the quickest way he could think of to cut through military red tape.

Chandler felt a dry, humorless laugh rise in his throat. His dad would have fits over a marriage of convenience, but he would only be lending Zineta his name, gaining her a quick passage to America. You could get these things annulled, couldn't you?

"Colonel Bladstone—" he started to say.

"Don't hang yourself, Reynolds," Bladstone cautioned. "Don't ruin your career just to be noble. A dead friend isn't worth it."

"Let me be the judge of that one, Colonel." *I have to help the girl get to America. I owe that much to Randy and his child,* Chandler thought.

"Colonel Bladstone tells me you are scheduled to go on a thirty-day leave," Daniels said. "We'll want your stateside address in case we have to get in touch with you."

"I'll be in Vienna, sir."

"Vienna?" The word exploded like a land mine going off.

Chandler tapped the ground with his crutch. "I lucked out. The music in Vienna will be part of my recovery phase. But, sir, I want some time with Zineta Hovic before I fly there."

"Let's arrange that when you get back, Reynolds."

"By then you will have found her a safe place in the British sector or in Serbia. The army won't want any reminder that Captain Williams had an unborn child."

"You're right. We must avoid a clash with the Muslim faction in Tuzla at all costs. And the Hovics are Muslims."

"Zineta is Croatian." *But would that make a difference when she lived with a Muslim family?* he wondered. He rubbed his eyes, perplexed by his own concern. The void, the darkness felt like his own. "Does Miss Hovic know about Captain Williams' death?"

"We have no reason to inform her."

"Colonel Daniels, the baby should be reason enough."

The colonel slapped his stick against his thigh. "Williams' parents stirred up public opinion against us when they descended on Washington, demanding an immediate withdrawal of all US troops. Now the public is challenging our mission in Bosnia, insisting that we withdraw before our latest deadline. But our military presence is vital to our national security interests. And absolutely essential to the people of Bosnia."

Chandler despised the colonel's arrogance. "You want peace? My dad would say it's man's heart that has to change."

"And what would you suggest, Reynolds?"

Prayer popped into his head, his father's old standby. But he said, "I'm still working that one out, sir. But until these people patch up their differences, not even another Olympics would change the situation."

Bladstone looked sullen. "You sound like Captain Williams."

"We shared a lot of ideas."

"But did you share intelligence secrets?" Daniels asked.

You sleazeball. Accusing me of a lie. Robbing Randy of any honor in dying.

"The White House wants everything we can get on your friend's time in Bosnia. If the girl is pregnant—and we have no reason to doubt it— we'll force his parents to back off. The senator from the Williams' district is flying over here in ten days. He and his committee want answers."

"And you want them to think Randy was killed off-duty and off-limits from the base, under suspicious circumstances?"

"You catch on quickly, Lieutenant."

Gruffly the colonel said, "When our troops were first deployed here, the president knew there would be casualties. Every peacekeeping mission has them. Having another unexpected death like this one and the public bites into it, especially when the young woman may have been a Serbian courier during the war."

"A courier? That's crazy, sir."

Daniels scowled. "We know for certain that she served as a courier during the war, and since then, she may have carried messages to the Serb forces in Kosovo."

"She's not Serbian, sir."

"Her sympathies might be. Did you ever discuss your work with her, Lieutenant? Or with your friend Williams?"

"I told you. Never. I don't discuss classified data."

So that was it. *That's why they had interrogated him at the hospital and brought him back to the Hovics' village.* "Randy and I never discussed the work I did. Spy satellites and intelligence reports would have bored him."

Chandler's mind ran in fast-forward. *If you suspected me, I'd not be going on a medical leave. You want me out of Bosnia while the senator is here, and you're willing to risk letting me go for a month. But you will follow my every move in Vienna. So much for the pretty girls in Austria. What I need is someone with me to deflect suspicion.*

"Tired, Reynolds?" Daniels asked.

Yes, tired of the trap you're setting for me. Mad clean through at what you're doing to Randy's memory. "I'm okay, sir."

"Good." His harsh eyes glinted. "I want to know all about Captain Williams' relationship with the Hovic family right on up to the day he died."

Chandler boiled inside, but he licked his lips and began to whistle the clear notes of a Christmas carol, concentrating on the words: *"It came upon a midnight clear, that glorious song of old. . . O rest beside the weary road and hear the angels sing."*

"Feeling festive, Lieutenant?" Daniels roared.

"I'm following your orders, sir. I'm just going back to where it all began." Chandler adjusted the crutches under his armpits and swung awkwardly over the uneven ground. "This way, Colonel."

He led them toward a small house off the beaten path, a house still pocked with bullet holes and crumbling cement steps. "It all began here. Just before dusk on Christmas."

"You're certain this is the Hovic house?"

"Yes. I saw it the first time on Christmas Day and the last time on the day Captain Williams died."

The music of that first visit with the hope of Christmas in a war-torn village faded from his memory, and the sound of a land mine exploding deafened him. Refusing to be less than a man, he fought down the lump in his throat and blinked back the tears that had never flowed for Randy.

As he leaned on his crutches and stared vacantly at the Hovics' battered front door, he no longer sensed the presence of the two commanding officers. He had stepped back in time, before Randy's death, to Christmas Day. He spoke haltingly, his pain welling up from the depths of his despair, his words coming slowly like spring; and with their slowness, he felt the first touch of healing as he told them what happened.

"It was Christmas," Reynolds said, his eyes no longer on Bladstone or Daniels. "My second miserable Christmas in Bosnia."

Chapter 4

On Christmas Day four months before, the town lay smothered in snow, the ground frozen solid, a new winter storm swirling in above the mountains. Lieutenant Chandler Reynolds rolled out of the sack at dawn just in time for the chaplain's service and went away homesick for his dad's cathedral, the one he had often viewed with contempt.

As he crunched over the packed snow, the sound of carols came from the tents, the music only intensifying his isolation. At noon, he walked into the mess hall with "O Come, All Ye Faithful" blaring over a loudspeaker rigged up in one corner. A life-size Santa Claus in dyed-red long johns dangled from the ceiling, its cotton beard off-center. Reynolds gave no thought to backslapping or offering a hail-fellow-well-met salute to any of his fellow officers. He didn't even look up when Randy Williams plopped his tray on the table and dropped down beside him.

"Merry Christmas to you, too," Randy said. "Came in here thinking we could go caroling, but with a sour face like that, you'd sing off-key."

Chandler felt a slow grin coming on. "Cheers and all that to you, too. But no caroling."

Minutes later, he went back to chowing down the army's version of turkey and stuffing and chewing the cranberries and dry, overcooked turkey as though it were beef jerky—the mess hall so cold that he blew steam with every bite.

"Hey buddy." Randy's voice again. "You didn't hear a word I said. I just asked you to ride patrol with me today."

"You got the duty?"

"Someone has to do it. Are you tied up in the computer lab?"

"I'm free until six in the morning."

"Then you're on?"

As they made their way out of the mess hall, Randy asked, "What did you think of the president's visit yesterday?"

"Got to shake hands with him. Seems a nice enough fellow. He came into security while I was on duty. And you?"

"Missed him. I was out in the village."

"That's going to get you in a heap of trouble, Randy."

"Can't let my friends freeze to death. The Hovics took a lot of war damage, so Kemal and I climbed up on the roof and did a makeshift repair with some old timber."

"Was that your only reason?"

"Just checking up on Zineta. I should have sent her home to my parents for Christmas."

Chan frowned. "You can't solve everybody's problems, Randy."

"I'd like to solve hers. The president should have gone out and taken a look at her battle-scarred village."

"The army considers anything outside of Tuzla or Sarajevo unsafe for him."

"They stick us with six- and eight-month tours. Double that for us. And he pulls out after three and a half hours?"

Chan tugged on his gloves as they got into the Humvee. "Randy, you know foul weather cut his trip short."

"Just an excuse for a whirlwind holiday. I'd think more of him if he stayed on and had canteen turkey with us today."

"Something tells me you didn't vote his party," Chandler said as the driver crossed beyond the city limits.

"I don't vote any party. I vote for the man, and right now, Chan, I'd vote for anyone who got me out of this country."

"That's not what the president has in mind."

"Yeah, he rides around in a motorcade. We've got eight thousand Americans here hoofing it over frozen ground. Freezing to death. Homesick. And he wants us to stay indefinitely."

"Admit it. We don't want the peace to fail either."

"I don't call that skirmish in the south peaceful." Randy blew on his gloved hands. "I should have asked him if he had any room on board Air Force One so I could get out of here, too."

"Hey, what happened to the cheerful patriot? Take some antacid, Randy. You've got political indigestion."

"It's the bloody war. Zineta lost everything. Her home and family. Her mother killed right in front of her. If the Hovics hadn't taken her in and treated her like a daughter, she would have ended up as a beggar—or worse."

For the next three hours they skidded over the narrow, snow-crusted roads. Randy's driver took too many risks. To keep from worrying about spinning off the road into a land mine, Chandler's thoughts drifted back to his last Christmas at home. He could almost smell his mother's cooking even now, as though he were wandering into her kitchen and snatching up a turkey leg or one of her freshly baked cookies before she topped it with sprinkles or slapped his hand.

∽

That day Chandler had balanced on top of the ladder, capping the pine tree with a star. "Mom, why don't we use something different this year?" he had grumbled.

She looked up at him, biting her lower lip, that fragile smile mellowed with her soft words. "Not this year, Chandler. The star was my brother's. It must go on the tree."

He argued with her often, but not on her holiday traditions. Especially this one. An age-old star that her twin brother had made in school, a hand-me-down. Not much to treasure of a brother who died before his time.

He let the top branch swing back with only an inch to spare to the high ceiling, then scrambled down the ladder and headed for the door. "I vote for an angel next year."

"Where are you going, Chandler?"

"To watch the ball game with Dad."

"Don't forget your grandmother will be here soon."

His grandmother—the worst part of every holiday! He liked her all right, but not in the same house with his mom. Grandmother Reynolds would swoop into the parsonage, a stylish woman with silver gray hair, ready to take charge in the kitchen. He wondered why the two women were constantly at each other and why his dad, so sensitive to the needs of his parishioners, was unaware of their feuding.

After dinner, Chandler had knelt at the brick fireplace, feeding more logs on the fire and listening to the crackling and hissing as the flames wrapped around the scented logs. As they splintered, charred fragments dropped through the grate, the ashes forming burned-out ruins on the floor of the fireplace. They looked like dark, desolate holes, black and empty, the way he felt inside, as if a piece of himself were charred or missing.

Across the room his grandmother smiled at him. "Come play the piano for us, Chan."

He tossed another log on the fire and went over and sat on the piano bench with her, his fingers moving skillfully over the keys. One familiar carol after the other: "Away in a Manger". . . "The First Noel". . . "Silent Night, Holy Night."

∽

Yes, it had been a night to remember. But as touch and go as Christmas could be at the parsonage, it was more miserable here in Bosnia. Chandler turned to Randy in the armored vehicle beside him. "I wonder if we'll ever be home for the holidays again?"

Randy shot him a side glance, an amiable grin spreading across his freckled face, his bad mood on a ninety-degree turnaround. "Trust me, they may replace us with more troops if they can bluff their way through Congress, but we'll get out of here."

"Then what happens to the peace accord?"

"It's not up to us, Chan. We're just a stopgap, not a solution. Peace here is up to the Croats and Serbs and Muslims."

"But once we pack away our M-16s and move out, men like Radovan Karadzic would be in position to shell Sarajevo before our ships steamed out of the Adriatic or the C-130s had time to level out above Tuzla."

"What's the matter? No letters from home? No gifts?"

"Another tin of cookies express mail from my grandmother that took nine days to reach me. After one bite, I trashed them. I get letters but rarely send them. Since quitting Juilliard, I can't think of anything to nullify Dad's reaction to that one."

"Your dad should blame me. I'm the one who talked you into the army. What did he want—a ballet dancer?"

Chandler's deep chuckle sent his breath rising in puffy vapors. "No, he was trying to grow a concert violinist."

"No joke! Come on, Chandler. You're no Isaac Stern."

Chandler rubbed his unshaved bristles. "Tell that to my folks. They put a violin in my hands when I was four. By the time they admitted I was no Menuhin, my voice was changing, and my face was a maze of pimples. That's when Dad let me switch to piano."

"Sounds more your style."

"It was. More my thing. I already played by ear. The lessons helped. But I still enjoy a violin concert. And I can hit the notes on a trombone when I'm in a room alone."

"So you need music to cheer you up! I know just the place."

"I don't drink, Randy. You know that."

"No bars. No carousing. I'm not out to muddy the life of a preacher's kid. But I still say you're missing part of life."

"The question is, which one of us is on the missing side?"

Randy lifted an imaginary beer tankard. "Cheers!" His wide grin rearranged the freckles on his face in a pleasant, cocky way. "How did we ever get to be friends? It's like coming from the opposite side of the tracks."

"We're good for each other."

As the Humvee rumbled over a rut in the road, Randy flicked a peanut into his mouth. "Back home in Ohio, we have towns with broad, paved roads. No bombed-out conditions like we have here." He popped more peanuts. "I've given this volunteer army a good slice of my life already. Once I kiss the military good-bye, I'm going to buy me a farm along the Ohio River. My grandfather worked the old sandstone quarries and Dad was into manufacturing steel. But I want the simple life in the country." Randy tapped his temple. "Can I confide in you, Chan?"

"Why not? I've got all day."

He scratched his freckled cheek, grinning. "I've found the girl for me, Chan. If I can work through the red tape, I'm going to marry Zineta and get her out of this mess. We'll have six kids and stay so isolated we won't even know where the NATO peacekeeping missions are headed."

"You're going bonkers. Must be the turkey we had for lunch."

"Life is short. You grab at happiness when you can get it."

"Then I'll be your best man."

Randy reached over and clamped Chandler's shoulder. "I'm going to hold you to that. I'll do the same for you." Then he was silent for a moment. "If anything happens to me, will you make sure Zineta gets to the States? Make sure she's okay—ready to handle life on her own?"

"You're not even married yet."

"I will be. What about it, Chan? Will you watch after her?"

"Sure. No problem. But me...I'm going to spend some time in Vienna and Salzburg. And catch some concerts."

"You're really into that stuff."

"I considered going professional once. But about all I qualify for is writing music reviews. Nothing more."

"You do need some music to cheer you." Randy leaned forward and tapped his driver's shoulder. "Make a stop just ahead. You know the place." The Humvee slowed. "The Hovics live here. The old man's been traumatized by war, but he can still make music."

~

It was almost dusk when they pulled to a stop and parked.

In another half hour, it would be black as midnight. As Chandler followed Randy to the house, he heard the distinct sounds of a cello playing a carol. *"It came upon a midnight clear, that glorious song of old."*

They followed the music to the gutted home of the Hovic family and knocked. The door creaked open. At the sight of Randy a buxom woman in a long apron and black shawl swung the door back and gave him a shy welcome. "Captain Williams."

Her smiling eyes grew wary as Chandler stepped inside. "He's a friend," Randy said. He glanced at the man sitting on the bed. "Keep playing, Kemal. My friend is a musician."

As music filled the little house again, Randy gave a piece of candy to each child, tousled Rasim's hair, then turned, uninvited, to sit at the table beside a young woman. She was nineteen, perhaps, and pretty in a sad sort of way.

Randy took her hand. "Zineta."

As he stared into the girl's eyes and she stared back at Randy, Chandler had the uneasy feeling that Randy had indeed found his girl. Their eyes held like magnets. Randy touched her cheek, then ran his finger down her chin to loosen the head scarf. He pushed it away from her face.

Take it easy, Randy, Chandler thought. *This is a Muslim family.* As if reading his concerns, Randy said, "I told you, she's Croatian. The Hovics took her in during the war."

Randy's eyes never left the girl's face. The scarf had slipped from her shoulders now, her wan face visible in the dwindling light. Her dark hair was cut raggedly, cropped above her ears. Her eyes were dark saucers as she looked up at Randy.

"I brought you something for Christmas, Zineta."

For a moment Chandler's attention was drawn back to the haunting sounds of the cello. He patted the old man's shoulder. "Beautiful, Kemal. How did you learn to play the carols?"

"Before the war the Croats and Serbs and Muslims lived and worked together, intermarried. We learned one another's ways and music. My family even sang the carols at Christmastime."

Chandler turned again to Randy and the girl. He was slipping his college ring on her finger. *This will never work. I've got to get him out of here,* he thought. Chandler strode to the table. "This village is off-limits, Randy. Let's go. It's getting dark."

He shrugged off Chandler's grip. "My friend doesn't like the darkness," he told the girl. "But you can trust him. Chandler here is a good man."

"Chan-leer," she repeated.

❧

Chandler drew a circle with his crutch and for a moment focused on Colonel Daniels, as though surprised to see him. "That's about it, sir. Now the village is like a ghost town."

Daniels pointed to the de-mining teams. "Once it's safe, the people can move back. But why would anyone want to live here with its constant reminders of war?"

"Where else would they go?" Bladstone asked. "This is home."

"Are the Hovics coming back, sir?"

"I would think so, Reynolds."

But will Zineta be with them? Chandler wondered. Or had the army already transferred her to the British sector? Or the French zone? It had been more than five weeks since the accident. A lot could happen in that time.

"Was Christmas the last time you saw Miss Hovic?"

No, Colonel Daniels, Chandler thought. *I saw her in March—saw her peering through the plastic window covering the day Randy was blown away.* He remembered the horror on her face.

"The last time Randy—Captain Williams—and I were here in the village was late in March."

"The day Williams died? Tell us about it, Lieutenant. Are you certain that Williams didn't go inside—that he made no contact with the girl at all that day?" His lip curled. "Is there a chance he came face-to-face with the sniper? Spoke to him even? Let him escape for the girl's sake?"

"I don't think so." He had watched Randy's every move, except for those few seconds when he disappeared behind the Hovic house and reappeared. The gunfire had ceased in that moment. Had it been long enough to talk to Zineta or to confront the sniper?

❧

Three weeks before Chandler's twenty-sixth birthday, when they rode into the Hovic village en route back to headquarters, the sniper had fired at them.

"Get out of here," Randy told the driver, then canceled the order, shouting, "Stop! That's Rasim Hovic in the line of fire!"

Not even three minutes all told. Randy was out of the truck before it came to a stop—that lean body sprinting across the field toward the boy. Another sniper shot. Chandler expected Randy to fall, but he kept at his marathon, scooping the child into his arms. Turning him around. Swatting his bottom. Sending him back toward the safety of Chandler and the Humvee.

Randy had halted for a second to glance up at the Hovic house. He lifted his hand, perhaps to wave. And then he was racing in another zigzag relay back toward the Humvee.

From thirty or forty yards out, he tossed Chandler a cocky, triumphant grin. Then Chandler saw the split-second change in his friend's expression—the surprise and gritty resolution frozen on his face. As though he knew. One foot was off the ground, Randy's balance gone. Then he plunged forward deliberately, his arms outstretched as he took the full blast of the PMA-3 anti-personnel land mine.

A loud, deafening boom. A blinding, white flash.

Metal fragments exploded toward Chandler and the child as Randy's body catapulted upward and tumbled back, his legs and torso slamming back to earth in separate pieces. Chandler took up the cry where Randy left off, but he knew his friend was dead. He jerked forward in an effort to reach him, stumbling as his leg buckled, not even realizing that he had been wounded himself. He staggered a step or two more, but Randy's driver held him back.

"There may be other mines buried out there, sir."

～

Lieutenant Reynolds faced Colonel Daniels again. "I couldn't help the captain, sir." The wind swallowed his words as he turned and hobbled back toward the Humvee.

"Let him go," Bladstone called. "The lieutenant has told you everything he knows, Paul. Don't hound him another second."

Later, back in Bladstone's cramped office, Paul Daniels flipped through the files on Captain Williams and Lieutenant Reynolds. He opened them. Closed them. Opened and scanned them again, drumming his fingers on his briefcase.

"Looks like Captain Williams was a poor choice for our special operation. And even our investigation on Lieutenant Reynolds has pock holes." He slapped the folders back on Bladstone's desk. "One of the boys at Langley swears that Reynolds' birth certificate is an amended document. If it is, that leaves us with some question marks on his background."

"Trust me. Reynolds' reputation is flawless, Paul."

"Trust goes both ways, Joe. Why doesn't his army record indicate that he's adopted? If he was."

"Adopted? Maybe the lieutenant doesn't know it."

"Come off it, Joe. He's twenty-six. Been out of diapers for almost as many years. Time for him to know the truth."

"What difference does adoption make? You said you wanted to tap some of my best men for a mission before NATO pulls out of Bosnia. That's why I recommended him."

"You recommended Williams, too."

"My mistake."

"Reynolds may be another mistake. We've sent for his vital statistics. Adoption puts a new twist to our investigation. We have to know if there are any mental problems in his background. Any family history that would make us look like fools."

"Like arrests? Like a drug dealer for a father? Or some fraudulent lawyer-father who cheated on his tax form?"

"Don't judge us so harshly, Joe. Langley has to know the man's background, weed out any inferior candidates now. We're training an elite group."

"An expendable group."

"That's always a risk. But as long as we can maintain a measure of peace in Bosnia, we keep Washington happy."

"You haven't changed since Vietnam days," Bladstone said morosely. "You'd still sacrifice the cream of the crop."

"We need the best. As far as I'm concerned the old intelligence officer in the flesh is worth his weight in gold. We don't have to bring him down from some spy satellite." He thumped Chandler's file again. "I have to agree with you on one thing, Joe. Reynolds is a brilliant young man. A degree in physics. Close to a year at the Juilliard School of Music."

He tapped his fingers. "Quitting there so unexpectedly is another blot on his record; we have to check it out. But so far, everything considered, his qualifications look good as long as his background checks out. . . . As long as we find he didn't pass intelligence information to Captain Williams."

"His records in Bosnia have been excellent."

"Really? Until today we didn't know he was in contact with the Hovic girl. What if he let something of importance slip?"

"He's smarter than that."

"I trust so."

Bladstone shrugged. "I have other men to choose from."

"Until now I thought Reynolds was our best choice. A university grad. Good experience here in Bosnia. Single. No children. No family commitments."

"What if he takes Zineta Hovic seriously?"

"We can't let that happen, Joe."

"I wish I had never given you his file. You would waste him if it met your goals. I want you to keep him alive."

"No promises," Daniels said. "We have a few months' grace. Thanks to the president. No thanks to those in Congress who oppose him. But we need several months to train these men. And with this messy business with Williams' death, Reynolds worries me. He's had access to top security."

"So far we've found no cause for alarm."

I wish, Bladstone thought, *that you would pack up and head back to Washington. Back to Langley.* But Daniels was staying on at least until the senator from Ohio made his appearance.

Daniels drew him back with a question. "Do we have contacts in Vienna? I'd like to put Reynolds under surveillance. I want to know where he stays. What he does. Who he sees." The bushy brows knit together. "Every man has his Achilles' heel. I want to know the lieutenant's. If it isn't his birth certificate, it will be something else. If he causes us any trouble on his return to Bosnia, I intend to ruin his career."

"I'm missing something, Paul."

"We're trying to defend our military position in this country. Death by a land mine is a political disaster." Daniels' rugged face flushed with displeasure. "I don't like it any more than you do, Joe, but I'm only twenty-four months from retirement with Langley. Just enough time to get that elite team ready for action. I can't let Reynolds spoil that. Next thing we know, he'll want to put up a monument in his friend's memory."

Daniels ran his broad hand over his chin. "You understand, don't you, Joe? There are bigger things at stake than the death of one soldier. If we pull out of Bosnia, other NATO countries will follow. It's too soon for that. We have to stay on in one residual form or another just long enough to train a nucleus of intelligence operatives for this country."

"A little army of your own?"

"Like the president said, there's no way we can go down to zero troops. Williams's death swept the issue of land mines back into the headlines. That means public sympathy. My orders are to keep Congress from putting Bosnia on the front burner again, but I'm afraid Lieutenant Reynolds may not see it that way."

"He's lost a good friend, Paul."

"We've all lost friends. War is always costly."

"This isn't war. It's a peacekeeping mission."

"It's not just the young man's death, Joe. It's the girl. The CIA insists that Zineta Hovic was a courier between the Serbian army and Radovan

Karadzic during the civil war. And there is strong evidence that she has been running messages between the Serbs in the hills and Kosovo even recently."

Bladstone whistled. "Does the Hovic family know that?"

"What is important is whether Williams knew. Whether Reynolds knows. But if that girl is working for the opposition—we'll sacrifice Captain Williams' reputation. We'll leak word that he was working with the girl—especially if she's still a courier for Karadzic supporters or the guerrillas."

"Then pick her up."

"That was the plan, but pregnancy complicates matters. She's carrying the child of an American officer. How could we sweep that one away?" He rubbed his jaw vigorously. "We have no way of knowing whether Williams shared more with her than a bed. Military secrets or Washington diplomacy, for instance."

"The captain served under my command. I respected him. But that won't matter." With remorse Bladstone said, "The captain was an open target long before he stepped on that land mine, wasn't he?"

Paul Daniels swung around and confronted Bladstone head-on. "If he was going to die, he should have done so before he met the girl. And if Lieutenant Reynolds' use to us at Langley falls through, he might as well have been blown away with his friend."

Joe Bladstone's expression grew grave. "You've changed since our army days together, Paul. You're not the man I once served under."

"And you have turned soft. What's best for our country is what matters. We both know it costs lives now and then."

"That *was* a Serbian sniper that took Captain Williams down, wasn't it, Paul? Not one of your operatives?"

Daniels stared back at his old friend. "The records say a Serbian. Let's keep it that way, Joe."

"Do you really think the captain worked with the girl?"

"We can't take a chance. We'd have to abort the whole mission." He stood. "There's one other thing. Lieutenant Reynolds must not contact the Hovic girl again. Make arrangements to have her shipped to the French or British zone."

Bladstone frowned. He had promised Reynolds that he could see the girl again before he flew to Vienna, but he looked at Daniels and nodded. "The French agreed to take her."

Chapter 5

I t was only May but already hot as a summer day in Southern California.
Ashley Reynolds sat slouched in the lawn chair, a trowel in her hand,
her polished nails caked with soil as she surveyed her corner of the
world. Above her it looked as though someone had brushed strokes of lilac
across the heavens and added the fleecy clouds skittering through that
lake-blue sky. A pair of mourning doves had taken up residence on the
tree limb above her. She reached over and turned up the treble on her CD
player, drowning out their cooing with Schubert's *Unfinished Symphony*.

Music comforted her, but no more than her yard. Her yard, freckled
with spring flowers, dazzled her senses with sweet fragrance and splashes
of color. The showy pink azaleas and stalks of blue larkspur. Salmon and
coral impatiens in planters by the back of the house and creeping red phlox
by the water wheel. The air alternately filled with the scent of sweet peas or
gardenias. Velvety pansies still hugged the concrete walkway. She shaded
her eyes with the trowel, her gaze lingering on the rosebush by her bedroom window, already blooming with tiny yellow buds. Her backyard was
her refuge. Here she never felt totally alone.

Her yard was the one place where David seldom came; it was as
though they had drawn a silent truce to give each other space. She stayed
out of his pompous world, and David was too busy to admire her handi-
work in the garden. They no longer danced stocking-footed in the living
room, not since their son went away. And these days they rarely took time
to drive up to Lake Arrowhead for a candlelit dinner at the Seasons.

She ached for one of those evenings there with David, sitting at a table
for two overlooking the crystal blue lake, knowing that when the evening
ended they would be together, alone in one of the honeymoon suites at the
hotel—David's busy schedule left behind at the foot of the mountain. If
only they could go back there, back to where they had gone so many times.
Then it would be as it had always been, special, intimate.

But lately David was flying in every direction—too preoccupied in
being the senior pastor at the magnificent Grace Cathedral across town.
Too immersed in writing his theology books and his latest series on *Living*

in Grace and Gracefully. Ashley could no longer define the topic, had no interest in it, had no warmth toward its message.

In their frequent, self-imposed silences, David sought his study and the comfort of his books. In relaxed moments, he took one of his favorite chairs on the sun porch, backed against the expanse of windows that over-looked Ashley's garden, but he rarely took notice of her flowers. Ashley found solace in the garden or at the piano—or on the cushioned divan, her long legs stretched out, her feet bare, a good book in her hands, the CD console playing softly in the background.

Sometimes she simply closed her eyes, trying to lose herself in the music of Bach or Mozart or Rachmaninoff. She'd remain there alone, try-ing to block out her greatest rival—her husband's schedule. David was too involved in being a guest speaker up and down the West Coast. Too absorbed two days a week as a university professor expounding his love of archaeology. Too busy to know she was hurting.

They stayed together in their lovely, well-polished house, divorce or separation totally alien to David and totally unacceptable in the lofty posi-tion that was his. She no longer suggested it. If they could talk about Bill—if they could talk openly about their son Chandler—perhaps they would be happy again. Ashley wanted that. She longed for David to hold her in his arms, to make love to her again. Yet it was more than Bill and Chandler that kept them distant from each other. She had deliberately shut David out, not willing to trust him with the truth. The awful truth. Her own failures lay hidden in the coves and inlets of her heart. Now and then they resurfaced, and she'd tie a rock to them and watch them sink back into the abyss.

Ashley wiped her brow with the back of her hand, tufts of her short, honey-blond hair catching in her watchband. She tugged them free and absently examined the strands that broke off in her fingers. Dreaded streaks of gray were defiantly marching in on her fifty-four years. She dropped the hairs on the lawn and trawled them into the ground, hating even the thought of growing older.

She fought the fifties with facial creams and hormone therapy and with three days a week at the health club. And just last month she cel-ebrated retirement and spent her last paycheck on a wild shopping spree that put a wine chenille tweed suit in her closet, her first outfit with a St. John label. She didn't dare show up in it at church though; that would set the tongues wagging. No matter what she did, except for her garden, Ashley's world kept falling apart.

Above the high notes of the symphony, she heard the persistent ring of the phone. She struggled out of the lawn chair and ran, stumbling at the kitchen doorstep as she grabbed the receiver seconds before the answering machine kicked in. "Reynolds' residence," she said breathlessly.

"Mom. Mom, it's Chandler."

She grew faint, confused. It was Bill's deep voice. No, Bill was dead. It was Chandler's, their voices so much alike now. For a moment it was like an eclipse, like the moon obscuring the sun, leaving her in darkness; just as suddenly the shadows passed and her kitchen turned brilliant with sunlight again. Still she couldn't speak. Couldn't think. Months of silence. So much like Bill. Months of pain and now, as though nothing had ever put a distance between them, Chandler was calling. His voice sounded so close that he could be calling from next door or from his dorm room near the Juilliard School of Music. Eons ago.

"Mom, it's Chandler," he said again. "Are you all right?"

"I'm fine. I'm just surprised. . .pleased. But, darling, where are you? You sound so near."

"In Tuzla."

So he wasn't in the next room or in New York City, but halfway around the world, still part of the multination peacekeeping force in Bosnia. "Oh, why haven't you written or called?"

"I am calling. And I never know what to say in letters. But I get yours—and Dad's. You got my Christmas card, didn't you?"

And that was all, she thought. Six cards in one year. Bill's old trick. Bill's way. "Darling, we wanted to phone you on your birthday, but there was no way to patch a call through."

"Birthdays aren't a big thing out here unless you count it as a day closer to being a civilian."

She reveled in his deep voice, the remembered picture of the young boy becoming a tall, muscular man. Remembered his clean-cut manliness, that sharp mind, the lighthearted chuckle.

He was chuckling now. "What were you doing? I thought you'd never answer the phone."

She looked at the trowel in her hand. "I was in my garden." She whacked the trowel against her shorts, knocking away a clump of dirt. "The garden is full of spring flowers with a few summer buds breaking the ground already."

"It's that California sunshine."

She heard the sudden shiver in his voice, the wistfulness for something familiar. "So it's still cold there?" she asked.

"Bleak. It's always like winter, but the snow's gone, and I packed away my long johns."

"I am lucky the weather here lets me spend hours in my garden. I still have the lawn to mow before your dad gets home."

"Then I'll let you go."

"No, Chandler!" She fairly shouted the words, belted them out as though he were still a child, scolding him like she did when he spilled jam or broke a dish or tore his Sunday suit playing football. "Please, don't hang up."

"Okay. Okay. I'm still here."

Don't you dare let me go. Don't hang up. She tried to picture his manly face. Tried to visualize him three years older. Cold and tired in a bleak country. "The lawn can wait."

"That's one good thing about army life. No lawn to mow in Bosnia. No lawns, period. Mom, did you know I always hated mowing your lawn or picking up those slimy worms for you?"

And now you're picking through fields of land mines. Her voice tight with worry, she said, "I suspected as much, so it's a good thing I'm the family gardener, isn't it?"

"What happened to your nursing career, Mom?"

"I packed it all in a month ago—I told you that in one of my letters, didn't I? Just hung up my stethoscope and put my uniforms out in the thrift box for immediate pickup."

"No regrets?"

"None!" Did he notice the uncertainty in her voice?

"Hey, did you see that copy of *Time* magazine with my picture on the cover?"

"Yes. We loved it. It's framed and hanging on the wall in your father's study."

And we wept over it, she thought. Chandler's handsome, unsmiling face on the front of the magazine for all of America to see, for all the world to see. Just one of the army troopers in Bosnia, his auburn hair hidden beneath an olive green helmet, the chin strap tight against his jaw. She remembered thinking how boyish he looked with those pensive eyes looking straight ahead.

His father's gaze.

She had cried when she bought the magazine. Or had she wept over the clerk's words? "I don't agree with the White House," the man had said. "They should get our boys out of there, not send more troops in. A covering force? What will they call it next?"

"My son calls it a peacekeeping force," she had mumbled.

"Call it what you will, lady, but do you really think Bosnia is worth dying for?"

No, she didn't. But Chandler did.

"Chan, isn't your time up in Bosnia?"

"Long gone, but I-For isn't ready to pack it all in yet."

"Darling, don't take any risks with those land mines."

"Me?" he asked with an odd click in his voice. "Most of the time I'm stuck in a computer lab—a nice secure place. Don't fret. With any luck I'll make it out of here all in one piece."

"You're all right?"

"Fine."

"Your dad and I miss you. You're being discharged soon, aren't you? David will want to know."

He teased. "Tell him in three months unless I sign over."

"I thought they were going to rotate you home long ago."

She heard him suck in his breath, heard the distinct click of his tongue against the roof of his mouth. "That was plan A. I volunteered to stay over and finish my army days in Bosnia."

Her fingers went white around the phone. "Why, Chandler?"

"I'm still needed here."

"You're not reenlisting?"

"Nothing definite yet."

"Please don't."

"Why not? Bosnia is far from peaceful. If we all pull out—"

"It's not your responsibility."

"Whose then?" he shot back.

She felt the old floodgates opening and envisioned Chandler stubbornly piling sandbags between them. Next he would tell her not to meddle or coldly remind her that David's family pulled strings to keep him out of Vietnam. To keep David safe, alive.

"Mom, you haven't walked through these ghost towns or watched these people trying to put their lives back together again. I've seen kids without legs, without eyes. People without hope. Girls without husbands. Friends dying for no reason at all. . .and the rebuilding here moving at a snail's pace."

"Don't, Chandler."

"Don't what, Mom?" he asked huskily. "Don't think about it? Don't make friends here? Don't get involved? Don't fall in love?"

She tugged at another gray hair. "I can't imagine what it's like to live under siege."

"I can't either. But they burned their furniture for firewood. Scrounged around for a slice of bread. Saw their families marched off to concentration camps. Turned their parks into cemeteries. I've met some of these families who are trying to put their lives back together. I'd like to make a difference. I'd stay on if I thought I could do that."

"Is that why you're offering them three more years of your life? More if I know you. And if you don't reenlist, Chandler?"

"I'll stay on in Europe for a while. Maybe get married."

"You're not—you're not falling in love?"

There was a decided pause, long enough to make her heart race. *He's old enough,* she thought. *But not there. Not so far away from us.* "Is there someone special, Chandler?"

"A girl? Here in Bosnia?" He hesitated for a second time and then blurted out, "Yes, I suppose there is. A young Croatian."

"Is it serious?"

"It could be; she's pregnant."

Ashley's world spun. The sins of the father visited on the son. "Will you marry her?"

"If I can cut through the red tape."

"Chandler. . .are you in love with her? A marriage of obligation—you mustn't do that." *Don't ruin your life, son. But the baby—the girl is carrying my grandchild.*

"I'd like you to meet her, but it's impossible. No papers. And she has a name, Mother. Zineta."

"Zineta." She wrapped her lips around the word like a prayer. She sympathized with the girl, ached for her son, feared what would happen when David heard.

The officer's uniform had set Chandler apart, making him even more attractive to the girls at university and in the church choir. But three more years in uniform. She dreaded David's controlled fury when he heard his son's plans, feared even more what David would say when he learned about the girl in Bosnia.

"Mom, whatever I do, I'm staying on in Europe."

He was talking like Bill, demanding space of his own, willingly staying away from his family. But she couldn't scold him long distance, not when

Chandler was paying the bill. Not when she and David were playing the same game.

"Why do that when we miss you so?"

He kept his voice light. "Yeah, I miss you guys, too. But I've been checking into the conservatories in Bern and Vienna."

Her throat tightened. "You're going back to your music?"

"I'm considering it. If I chuck the army, I'll try my music again. Just a refresher course. I can never go professional. But maybe I can write music reviews. I'm good at that, Mom."

"A music critic?" He was sounding like Bill again. Bill when he was young and still at the university majoring in business and economics. Bill before power and profit took over. And now she sounded like Bill, saying, "That won't be very lucrative, Chan."

His tone rebuked her. "I wasn't considering the money. I just want to be happy. I just want to find myself."

"Reviewing operas and symphonies? You can do that at home."

The operator interrupted. "Reverse the charges," Ashley told her. And then she said, "Chandler, it will break your father's heart if you stay in Europe. Come home first."

"We'll talk about that later. Right now, thanks to my commanding officer, I've chalked up a thirty-day leave." She heard excitement building in his voice, excitement that hadn't been there when he spoke of the girl called Zineta.

"Mom, I'm flying to Vienna on the thirteenth if I can get a military flight out of here."

"But that's just six days from now. And Vienna! You can't afford a month in Vienna on your army pay."

"I figured my budget would cover a pension. And I could flirt with a pretty girl who would take me home for dinner."

Ashley twisted the phone cord. Flirt with a pretty girl? Had this Zineta already slipped from his mind?

"But I called Grams and hit her up for a big loan instead."

"You should have called us, Chandler."

"And have you insist on my coming home? Grams was at least reasonable. You know I'd do anything for her and she'd do anything for me. Besides, she's too old to spend it all in her lifetime. Mom, she did better than a loan—staked me to a whole month at her favorite hotel in Vienna. I'm going first class."

"The Empress Isle? You should have asked us."

"That's what I'm about to do. I want you and Dad to join me. Grams offered to pay your hotel bill as an anniversary present."

"And obligate me to her? I won't hear of it."

"You'll hear about it if you turn down her gift."

"You're too old to be taking her money."

"She takes pleasure in showering me with gifts. Always tells me—whatever I need, just call her." She heard him grind his teeth. "Come on, Mom. Money is no big deal for Grams. She's loaded. All you have to do is cover your airfare. Surely Dad will kick through for that. You do have passports, don't you, Mom?"

"Yes," she said pensively. "And the truth is, I'd love seeing Vienna again. But I could never talk your father into going abroad, not right now."

"Even to see me?"

"Oh Chandler—"

"So he's still angry about me joining the army? He's had three years to cool down."

"It was your not talking to him about it first."

"So he could change my mind? Just tell that old stick-in-the-mud to forget his busy schedule. They have plenty of cathedrals in Vienna. He can have his pick of them. You and I can do the museums and take in a special performance at the Opera House."

She gasped. "That magnificent State Opera House?"

"I've ordered tickets for a violin concert. Way up in the high balcony. But wait until you hear who's playing."

Ashley dropped the trowel and stretched the phone cord to the limit as she sank into the chair, praying to the silent house that it would not be Kerina Rudzinski.

"Kerina Rudzinski is the guest violinist, Mom."

The room spun, ceiling to floor, forcing the door of Ashley's memory back to the hospital and the beautiful young woman with a Stradivarius violin beside her.

Ashley's voice didn't sound like her own as she asked, "But why Miss Rudzinski? There are so many other performers."

"I've wanted to hear her again ever since she performed at Juilliard three years ago. You remember. I told you about her. Mom—" Urgency filled Chandler's voice. "Are you all right?"

"Just surprised. . .shocked. . .pleased at the thought of seeing you again." Her stomach knotted. "But, Chandler, it's too expensive spending money for a month in Vienna and tickets for a Rudzinski concert. Dad won't want to go to that expense."

"Tell Dad I'll pay for the extras. It won't come out of the collection plate."

"Oh honey, you can't afford the concert."

"I've saved up. You want to hear Rudzinski, don't you?"

She prayed that her words wouldn't betray her. "Of course, Chandler. You bragged about her music often enough in the past."

"I did? Must have been right after she came to Juilliard. She whipped out right after her performance before I could talk to her, but I never forgot her." He added, "She did her stateside debut with the Chicago Symphony. Back in the Dark Ages."

I know. Another eclipse passed between Ashley's eyes and the sun, blackening the kitchen once more. Her grip on the phone tightened. *Twenty-seven years ago.* It was the concert where Bill heard her play, that moment in time that had ruined all of their lives.

"I've scheduled an interview with her. Backstage after the concert." The phone wires crackled now, his voice growing distant once more. "There's a lineup behind me, Mom. Like a bunch of storm troopers. They're going to start tossing their canteens at me if I don't get off this phone."

"I don't want to let you go—"

"That sounds familiar. Gotta go, but, Mom, Vienna on the thirteenth. Okay? We're already booked at Empress Isle Hotel. Just come. I love you. And bring my birth certificate and university transcripts. I may need them while I'm in Europe."

He was gone, the telephone line disengaged, Chandler's voice replaced by the steady hum of the dial tone.

The phone fell from Ashley's hand, the receiver dangling over the end of the table. Her son was alive, well, in touch with them again. The thirteenth. The Empress Isle Hotel. He wanted them both to come. She must call David, but her momentary joy was suddenly snatched away. Chandler wanted his birth certificate. *His original birth certificate?* she wondered.

She pressed her face against the oak tabletop and wept. Give him that—unveil the secrets that she had hidden for so long—and she would lose Chandler. She would lose her son forever.

❧

Ashley was back in her garden when David came home on time, surprising them both. He had loosened his tie and was carrying his suit coat in one hand, her garden trowel in the other.

"I didn't expect you this early, David."

He tossed his suit coat over the back of the lawn chair and snapped off the CD player. "I'm ravenous."

Flustered she said, "I haven't started dinner."

"We can go out. Maybe drive up to the—"

"You should have called me."

His eyes twinkled. "The line was busy."

"Oh, I'm sorry, David. I never put it back on the hook."

"I did. Just now."

"I forgot. I came out to pick some flowers for the table."

"You usually do that when you have good news."

He was smiling down at her, looking like his old self, the crinkle lines around his blue-gray eyes relaxing. His thick, wavy hair had turned a silver gray, making him look distinguished, gentlemanly. And she thought as she looked up at him—as she always thought when he stood behind his pulpit in those velvet clerical robes—that he was a handsome man, a kind man.

He leaned down and kissed her on the cheek, a perfunctory kiss that chilled her. "What's wrong, David? Did something happen at the office today?"

"Something special. Chandler called me."

"He called you, too?" She pulled a bruised petal from one of the rose-buds in her hand. "Then you know about Vienna?"

He cleared his throat as he set the trowel in the flower bed beside her. "I won't be able to go," he said.

No, it was not the old David who had come into the house. It was the David who had rehearsed his excuses on the way home, ten miles worth of excuses. The smile was to keep her at bay.

"Another pastoral conference?" she asked acidly.

"It's a busy time of year for me. Lectures at the university and an article on archaeology due for the September issue. And, Ashley, I can't miss that appointment with my editor. We're working out a new idea for the grace series."

"You're always busy. Doesn't *Living in Grace and Gracefully* include your own son?"

"That's not fair, Ashley."

In spite of the warm evening, she shivered. "Chandler wants both of us to come."

"He told me."

And did he tell you about the girl? she wondered. No, he would not do that long distance. "David, we haven't seen Chandler for so long. Are you still angry at him?"

"About leaving Juilliard? No—just disappointed when I allow myself to think about it. He qualified for a school like that and quit. Quit before the year was over."

She stared down at a clump of pansies crushed beneath David's foot. "It was the practice rooms. Chandler hated practicing alone in those windowless, airless rooms."

"What he didn't like were the long hours. But don't worry, my dear. I am not a brooding man. I try never to let the sun go down on my wrath."

And when that fails, you let your silence beat the sun down. This wasn't the old David, not the David she had loved. This was the pulpit man again, the perfect public image that she had come to despise. The gifted orator, elegant as crystal, and lately cold as ice. The stranger she couldn't remember marrying.

"David, I find it hard to believe that you are never angry about Juilliard."

He met her gaze over the bouquet of flowers and shrugged. "We invested a lot of time and money in his music."

"It was something you wanted him to do, David."

"We both wanted it, Ashley. I don't believe in quitting once you start something. All he seems to do is mess things up."

"Don't say that. He graduated with honors from your alma mater."

"And threw it all away for the army. I didn't want that for my son. Chandler could have had honors at Juilliard, too."

Inflexible. Unbending. David had dreamed so many big dreams for Chandler. But what about Chandler's dreams? His choices? *No,* she thought, *it was that miserable promise we made to Kerina Rudzinski that we would expose Chandler to music. Music was Kerina Rudzinski's choice.*

"Juilliard was never Chandler's choice, David."

His broad shoulders stiffened. "Then wasn't it up to us to make it for him? With his background, we both saw his talent, his potential—" David bit off the words. "But as Chandler reminded me on the phone, a man has to find his own way."

"You didn't have it out with him again?"

"No, we had a good conversation. And I told him I couldn't make Vienna. He understands."

"Don't blame him, David. He wanted to go to work after the university. We're the ones who wanted him to go to Juilliard before he took a job.

Our son went there to please us."

"Our son?" His voice sounded ragged. "The boy doesn't even know who he really is. We've lied to him long enough."

"We didn't lie to him."

"No, we simply buried the truth."

"We kept our promise to Kerina Rudzinski. A closed adoption. Chandler was never to know."

His lips turned as ash gray as his hair. "And I have had to live with that every time I stand behind the pulpit. But, Ashley, you made that promise. I didn't. You'll have to go to Vienna alone. This is between you and Chandler. And please," he cried, "tell him the truth even if you have to tell him about Bill." He touched her cheek, gently, his eyes suddenly misty. "Work it out between you so we can be a family again."

The barrier between them crumbled enough for her to see the painful candor in his eyes. She longed to fling herself against those strong shoulders and feel his comforting embrace. "There's nothing to work out, David. Chan and I are the best of friends."

"Is that why he writes so often?" David's face was a mask, his words restrained. "You're so foolish, Ashley. So foolish. Chandler has an appointment to meet with Kerina Rudzinski—an interview following the concert. Yes, I can see by your expression, you already know that. How long do you think you can keep the truth from him then?"

He toed the trowel with his shiny black shoe. "You must have been gardening when Chandler called. I found that in the kitchen."

"Yes, I was. Does it matter?"

"I hoped you might ask what I was doing when he called me."

She couldn't bear the pain in David's eyes. "Tell me."

"I had just looked up the number to the Lake Arrowhead Resort—to make a dinner reservation for tonight."

She stared at him. "At the Seasons? That's a long drive."

A sardonic smile tugged at the corner of his mouth. "You know the food is worth it." The smile had reached his eyes now. "And they have our old room. They're holding a reservation for us. I thought—I thought the two of us—"

"You should have asked me first, David." She felt a mixture of anger and irritation. He wasn't willing to go to Vienna with her, but he expected her to rubber stamp his plans.

His smile faded. "The phone was off the hook, remember? And I just couldn't ask you over the phone. I was afraid you'd turn me down."

"Oh David, you know I wouldn't say no. Not usually. But now I have to start packing, making arrangements. I have a trip to plan, a plane to catch."

"Another time," he murmured, turning his back to her.

"David, it's not too late to change your mind. We could still go to Vienna together."

He didn't answer. He didn't look back but just kept walking, shoulders rigid as if deflecting her rejection. Then he disappeared into the library, his sanctuary that kept her out.

Chapter 6

Kerina stood on the port side of the *Swiss Jade*, her arms resting on the railing as the elegant river vessel slipped from its Passau moor‑ings and began the journey back toward Vienna and Budapest. She had played here in the beginning of her career and was often lured back by the city's quaint beauty. It was here she had stowed on board an old fishing vessel for her first journey down the Danube to Vienna. Passau lay on the western branch of the Danube on the border between Austria and Germany, a university town where three rivers enclosed the city. She had come back to play her Stradivarius on the open campus as part of the town's multicultural celebration.

She waved at Jillian and Franck on the dock below and watched them part ways and walk away. Jillian paused by the Italianate fountain, and Franck strolled back over the cobbled streets with the ancient fortress and cathedral towering above him. Kerina felt the vibration of the engine beneath her feet, the gentle movements of the vessel as it glided on the Danube, heard its waters lapping gently against the hull.

A river had always been part of her life—the Vltava in her childhood, the Danube throughout her career. She had grown up near the crossroads of Europe watching the Vltava winding around the bends and dividing the city into parks and gardens on the left bank and a thriving commercial center on the right. Kerina had longed to follow the river to another world, to freedom.

She leaned over the railing of the river vessel and allowed the fine mist to touch her cheeks, much as she had done along the banks of the river in her childhood. Stone embankments and dams and canals held back the flood waters, and castles and old ruins dominated the shore as they did here along the Danube. Kerina wished she could lean all the way down and put her outstretched hand into the depths of the Danube, letting the water course through her fingers like tiny tributaries, making her fingers tingle from the cold. Once when she did this in her childhood, she had tumbled into the Vltava, slipped beneath its icy, wintry surface, and came up with her skin so blue her parents thought she was dying. Her father had rescued her from certain disaster, yet she had come up sputtering and laughing because she had been part of the flow.

Standing on the deck of the *Swiss Jade*, she was reminded of springtime in Prague with the gardens bursting with color, the river meandering by them to places unknown, many of them known to her now. She had not lost that childhood love of the river, nor the spirit of celebration when spring came. Her homesickness became acute; she longed to visit her parents on their farm outside of Prague. It would be months before she could go back, but she promised herself that when she did, she would spend time on the banks of the tributary that ran below the farm where she had often run along the banks chasing the flow of the river.

Even when she had escaped into the night and fled across the Czech border into Germany, thoughts of happiness along the river went with her. The Danube was her first memory of Vienna, the river that had carried her into the city and from there to the concert halls of the world. The breeze on the river caught her laughter. She was gloriously happy in this moment. *Strauss'* Blue Danube. *And mine as well.* The river that waltzed its way straight into the heart of the people. Vienna! The Danube! Linked as one.

She braced herself against the railing of the Swiss Jade, *thinking back to the water lapping against the hull of the fishing vessel so long ago. She had been a frightened sixteen-year-old, huddled by the coiled rope and seasick on that first voyage on the Danube. Sick from the smell of fish and sick with fear. And lonely for her parents, who were no doubt wondering where in God's world their child could be. On that journey her violin lay safely beneath the smelly canvas, protected from the mist that swirled above the river. Thus she was when one of the mates came sauntering over to her—his beard straggly and his eyes twinkling as he held out a mug of tea, insisting that she drink it. And then she was violently ill again.*

By morning she had grown accustomed to the steady swell of the water, to the uneven chugging of the ancient boat. She had slept and awakened in the same place to find herself draped in the yellow oilskin of the mate and less fearful by the unexpected security of the cracked fabric against her skin.

"You will be all right," the man had said, kneeling beside her with another cup of tea. "Drink this, and then you can go below and wash up. I've set out a pair of dungarees and a sweater to warm you. The mates won't touch you. I'll see to that. But if you be running away, then go home."

"I am going to Vienna to play my violin."

She slept again after that on a berth in the pilot house, her hand resting over her violin. She slept remembering home and those last few hours on the farm outside of Prague. Even as she slept, she knew that she must prove to herself that she was born to music. She would at all costs make her parents proud. No matter how many times he probed, she did not tell the seaman about leaving home or even mention the muffled voices of her parents and Franck talking into the small hours of the morning.

∾

Prague, late 1969

In the cramped quarters of her tiny bedroom, Kerina heard her mother weeping. Her father's voice rose in despair. "Hush, woman. Hear Mr. Petzold out." His voice lowered to a grumble. "Speak your piece, Petzold; then leave."

"I won't go without Kerina," Franck said stoutly. "She can never play in concert if she stays in Czechoslovakia. Not without teachers or opportunities. I can give her both."

"She is only a child."

"Old enough to be put in work camps. Let her go while she has the strength to leave you. These days, writers and musicians are grouped with dissidents. Do you want that for Kerina?"

"Your father's doing."

"I don't follow the politics of my father."

"Do you approve the Soviet occupation? Where were you when Jan Palach burned to death protesting the Soviet occupation?"

"Your daughter is outspoken. It is unsafe for her to remain in this country. Leave her here, and she will surely follow those who are trying to crush the Soviets."

"What side are you on, Franck Petzold?"

"I declare no politics."

"Then your father will have you burned at the stake."

"That is why I wish to leave and take Kerina with me. I have money. Power. Contacts in Vienna. I promise you she will play her violin before thousands."

Kerina sank beneath her eiderdown as Franck's voice hardened. "This is not a time for creative people in your country, Karol. Playwrights are being sent to prison. Actors and musicians banned from the theater. I will take her across the German border and on to Vienna."

"And we will never see her again." Even the eiderdown tight against her ears could not shut out her mother's weeping. "I can't let my daughter go. You will corrupt her. Defile her."

"I promise you, I will not lay a hand on her unless she permits it. I will always take care of Kerina."

"She's only a child," her mother sobbed.

"She is a musician. She could be a great violinist."

During a lull in the discussion, Kerina drifted to sleep, only to be awakened at midnight with her father's work-worn hand gripping her shoulder, calling her to wakefulness.

"Get dressed. You must go with Franck. No. No. Take nothing with you but your violin." His voice caught. "It will be all you need."

He hugged her extra hard as he said good-bye.

She felt small, crunched into the front seat beside Franck, her violin on her lap, her bare legs numb in the cold, unheated car. Franck drove over the back roads, his jaw clamped tight, dots of perspiration beading his high brow. They rode with only one headlight casting eerie shadows on the narrow road. She dozed and awakened, huddling deeper into her worn sweater. Her fingers were raw from the chilled air. Still she clutched the violin case, her arms wrapped tightly around it.

"You will cross the German border as my wife. Say nothing."

"Your wife? I will not marry you."

"No," he said sadly, "but someday perhaps. You will play your first concert in Passau. And this time next week you will be in your beloved Vienna. I have arranged for lessons there."

She gave him a haughty twist of her head. "I already play well, Mr. Petzold."

"Mr. Petzold, is it now? But no harm." He reached out and knuckled her cheek in the darkness. "You are so sure of yourself, but we must polish your genius."

"What is wrong with my playing?"

"It is you," he said. "You must be groomed for the work that lies ahead. For the social world in which you will live."

"Do my parents know where I am going?"

"They have guessed. They will not oppose me."

"Will I see them again?" she whispered.

He braked so suddenly they skidded on the gravel. His fingers drummed on the steering wheel, his eyes blazing in the semi-darkness. "I have risked my safety for you. So choose well, Kerina. You begged me for the opportunity to play in the concert halls of the world. I have the power to do this for you. But if my father learns that I took you across the border—"

She feigned bravery. "Then do not cross it with me."

The moon peeked through the clouds and disappeared again, leaving misty-gray clouds whirling above them. "If there is trouble at the border, you must not be afraid."

"I will pretend that my father is with me."

"In a way, he will always be with you, Kerina. He loved you enough to let you go. He fears what I might do to you—but I have given him my word that I will always take care of you."

"Why would he be afraid of you?"

Sadly he said, "Because he says that I have a way with women. He does not know how deeply I care for you, Kerina."

When they neared the German-Czech checkpoint, he pulled to the side of the road again, edging against a forest of trees with his lights off. He left her alone in the car and walked ahead into the shadows. He was back within minutes, slipping into the seat beside her and pounding the steering wheel in his fury.

"Always before there has been one Soviet sentry here. Tonight I see three. There is no way that I can take you across the bridge in the car. And now I am the one who does not want to let you go, for you must cross alone."

"I do not know anyone in Germany."

"You will soon. Someone will be waiting for you on the other side." His hand was firm on her shoulder. "His name is Anton. He is young but wise. He will take you to his home and shelter you there for two nights. And then he will help you make your way to Passau. And from there you will take a riverboat into Vienna."

He sighed wearily. "Don't fear, little one. I would not let you go if I did not expect you to reach your destination. It would be best for me to be back in Prague before my father realizes I am gone."

Again he stepped outside and slid beneath the car. He came back reeking with oil. "In another few yards, the oil will all leak out, the car will stall. I will create a disturbance so the guards will come to me."

He lifted her face toward him. For a moment she thought he was going to lean down and kiss her. She felt his warm breath on her cheek, caught the scent of peppermint on his breath.

"While I argue with the guards, you must slip under the barricade and cross quickly. Stay low and close to the rail. I will keep the guards busy. You will have time. And remember—Anton will meet you on the other side."

He patted her hand. "Now take that violin of yours and go. Do not look back. I will see you again soon."

Halfway across, she realized it was not the bridge swaying, but her legs trembling beneath her. Ahead she heard raucous laughter and saw the German guards inside the sentry enclave drinking, oblivious to her. She slid under the rail, along a muddy embankment, around the sentry box.

"Pssst."

She stopped creeping and listened. "Pssst."

A shadowed figure moved behind the trees. A pebble landed at her feet. Another raucous laugh pierced her ears. A hand tightened around her mouth. A string of German words followed. She recognized "Anton," nothing else.

Slowly he released her, a tall wiry figure, little more than a boy himself, but confident of what he was doing, where he was going.

"Kommen Sie mit," he said, and though she did not understand the words, she knew what he wanted.

They did not speak again until they reached the safety of the farmhouse. He couldn't be more than twelve, sturdy as a rock, a visored cap shading his brooding eyes. His mother moved away from the stove to slip her arm around Anton's shoulder. And now in the light of the lantern, Kerina saw the boy's likeness to Franck, so much alike that he could be Franck's son.

But was that possible? At sixteen, these were matters that she could not reconcile, but thinking back on it, she knew there was a kinship between them and wondered where Anton might be now, and if father and son had ever recognized each other.

Chapter 7

Kerina was still standing at the rail of the *Swiss Jade* when Nicole McClaren joined her. As she turned to face her friend, the eyes of other passengers focused on Nicole. Nicole was elegantly dressed in an Italian pantsuit that emphasized her narrow waist and hips. Her slick black hair was brushed back from her forehead, highlighting that charming oval face and those luminous green eyes as cunning as a Siamese cat. But beneath Nicole's need to be noticed lay a warmhearted person, a friend Kerina had come to treasure and trust.

"Kerina, you'll end up with bronchitis in this chilly air."

"The fresh air feels wonderful. Join me. I'm just reliving my first trip on the Danube."

"Hardly as luxurious as this one, was it?"

"Quite distasteful, actually. But it's pleasant this time."

"It's still too chilly out here."

"Nicole, the only thing wrong with me is a stiff shoulder."

"Well, if it's still troubling you, I'll have you see my doctor when we get back to Vienna." She looked around. "I thought Franck and Jillian were going back with us."

Kerina tucked strands of her breeze-blown hair behind her ear. "Franck is taking a quick trip to Moscow to work out the negotiations with Jokhar Gukganov about the VanStryker painting. I wish you would talk Elias out of buying it."

She shrugged. "Once Elias sets his heart on a prize, there is no stopping him. He prides himself at the thought of owning two of VanStryker's works. So—did Jillian go with Franck?"

"As usual, they're going their separate ways. Jillian went to Munich to pick up her Saab convertible. She'll break the speed limits on the autobahn and cruise into Budapest before we do."

"She's full of surprises."

"Has been ever since I met her."

"She's such a charming girl. Where did you find her?"

"She found me when she charged into my dressing room in Berlin seven months ago and said, 'I'm looking for a job. I know you need a publicity agent, Miss Rudzinski. So here I am.'"

"You hired her! You must have liked her right off."

"There's little not to like. And I needed a new publicity agent. Jillian is never intimidated by my moods. If things are tense before a concert, she keeps everyone at bay—even Franck." Kerina squinted at the fading sun. "She promised to give me a year of her life. Told me she had the right contacts. Knew the right people. Could handle my public. She has—and well. I was sitting there wiping the bridge of my violin with a soft velvet cloth. I can still remember holding that cloth in my hand and asking her, 'And do you have any experience, my dear?'"

"Did she?"

"I don't remember. I don't think I really cared. She reminded me of myself. Impulsive. Determined. Willing to tackle any task. And she was so beguiling when she said, 'Not much experience unless you count my flunking out of charm school, Miss Rudzinski. Actually I quit. I wanted to travel with my father.'"

They faced the river now, watching the shades of blue change as the sun dipped lower: an azure blue toward the shore, a foamy blue as the bow of their vessel cut the water, a murmur of blue in the distance.

"I've always loved the Danube. More so since I play Strauss' *Blue Danube* in concert." She smiled, at no one in particular. "When I was sixteen and first arrived in Vienna, I was supposed to meet a friend of Franck's near the Danube. He was late coming, so I sat down on the stone embankment and cried. I was so afraid the police would find me there and send me back to Czechoslovakia."

"And who rescued you?"

"The waiter from one of the Bohemian coffeehouses took me inside and gave me something to eat. I looked like a peasant in my faded cotton dress, clutching my shabby violin case. I didn't look any more affluent than the clientele. One grubby guest peered at me over the brim of his newspaper and asked me whether I could play that fiddle of mine."

"And did you?"

"I was afraid not to. The buzz of voices suddenly stilled. As I played a second song, the waiter poured me a free glass of *Einspanner* with whipped cream brimming over the top. That was my first concert in Vienna. I still go back now and then to play in that coffeehouse. Even today, many of them cannot afford a black-tie performance, but no audience is ever kinder to me."

"Both the celebrities and the masses love you, Kerina."

"And I them."

"I'm so different. In some ways I don't like the crowds—just my special friends. And I could never stand living alone."

"You have your husband."

"Yes. Dear Elias. I don't mind him being twenty years older than I. He adores me. I feel safe with him. I can't think of life without him."

"You should have had children."

"He still talks about having a child. But by the time our son or daughter was in university, Elias would be an old man. Gone, perhaps."

But you would still have your child. They stared at each other for long moments. "You never regretted marrying Elias."

A tiny frown formed between Nicole's brows. "I look and tease and enjoy tennis with younger men. I flirt as Elias calls it. It never goes beyond that. Elias is my husband."

"And you love him?"

"Put that way—I believe I do. But you, Kerina. I have never understood why you stay single. Why don't you marry Franck?"

"Because I don't love him."

"I didn't love Elias when I married him." Half in jest, she said, "There must be some secret love of your life, Kerina, that you've never told anyone about."

For an instant, a crumbling ruin along the riverbank caught Kerina's attention. *Yes, there was a great love of my life and so much more.* Of late, her son and Bill invaded her thoughts, filled her waking hours, dominated her sleepless nights, thrust themselves at her in her solitary walks along the Danube. There would always be a part of her that belonged to them.

Once remembered, thoughts of Bill seemed to haunt her for days or weeks on end, as they had been doing lately. Taunting her. Swallowing up her waking hours with what might have been. Reproaching, rebuking, tormenting her. Whether it was rekindled resentment or the smoldering embers of anger that had never died out, she could not be certain. Rather, she thought it the fact that he had been her first love, her only love. For those first five years she had waited expectantly, confident that he would keep his promise to come back. During those months she remembered him with kindness, like a treasure trove that was hers alone. So strong were the recollections that she could hear him laugh, smell the woody scent of his cologne, feel his thumb passing gently over her lips.

"You should date more often, Kerina."

"I do date. My dressing room is always filled with flowers from admirers who see me as more than a concert violinist."

"That Spanish count for one?"

"Yes, Ramon." The handsome count who bore a Spanish title and family recognition whose lifestyle was lavish and unfamiliar. And the Italian tenor who sought her hand between wives. The reserved British curator in tweeds with a pipe in his vest pocket. The jocular pilot who had ferried her from concert to concert in a private jet, a quick-witted man more acquainted with the sky and mountains than with Bach and Beethoven. And always Franck. Each one seeking her hand, offering her marriage. And yet she had remained single, unwilling to risk loving again.

"Flowers are not good bedfellows," Nicole said. "They do not have broad shoulders to lean on."

"But they have pretty petals."

"Not enough."

"Really, Nicole, I am not unhappy."

"Then you'd better redefine happiness."

She met Nicole's gaze. "Music is my passion."

"Another lousy bedfellow. Music fills your world, demands all your time. Get a life outside the concert hall, Kerina."

Music energized her, brought her deep satisfaction. It remained her gift to others, her claim to recognition. But now and then a familiar sight or scent or sound stirred her memories of Bill and forced her to remember him. Like this moment. She could almost sense his presence here on the *Swiss Jade* beside her.

She turned to Nicole. "Nicole, you were right. There was someone else. It's something I have never told a living soul."

"Tell on," Nicole said lightly.

"Long ago, when I was only nineteen, I was very much in love with a man almost ten years older than I." The mist from the river sprayed her face, merged with her tears. "We had a child. A son."

Nicole's thin brows arched. "But you didn't marry him?"

"I was already pregnant when I found out he had a wife."

"I gathered as much. Did you think you would shock me, Kerina? That I would turn against you if you told me?"

"I didn't know how you would react. I only know that lately it has been an unbearable burden. I had to tell someone before I fell apart like that old castle on the shore."

"Where is he now—this son of yours?"

Kerina waved her hand toward the children racing on the deck beside them. "There. Everywhere. I don't know where. I gave him away. Sometimes I go for weeks or months and never give it a thought, never allow myself to think about him. And then at other times—on holidays and especially on his birthday in April, I cannot get him out of my mind. I grieve all over again. He becomes part of my heartbeat."

"Kerina." Nicole hesitated. "Does Franck know?"

She marveled at the calm with which she said, "Of course."

"Is that why he holds such influence over you?"

"You know he manages my career. He was always there for me, protecting me. I was sixteen when he helped me escape from Prague with just the clothes on my back. I never expected to see him again—didn't want to—but a week later he joined me in Vienna. He followed me everywhere, even to Chicago. He built my career."

"You don't owe him your life."

"In a way I do. In Chicago, when I was pregnant and frightened, with my family back in Czechoslovakia, Franck offered to marry me and give the unborn child a name. He told me he would take care of us, and I could go on with my concerts."

She gazed out at the river, remembering. That day she had looked into Franck's solemn eyes and palmed his bristled cheeks and told him he could no longer protect her. But he tried. In the fourth month of her pregnancy he had found her a place to stay, canceled her concert tours, made excuses for her. Afterward, he arranged for her to go back to the concert hall in Chicago and pick up her career where she had left it. He had stood on the sidelines, waiting for the audience to receive her. But as she lifted her Stradivarius and played the sweet music of Strauss, her thoughts were on Bill.

Now in silence Nicole and Kerina watched the *Swiss Jade* dip with the gentle swells of the river, the cobalt blue waters flowing leisurely. Far behind their vessel, the Danube wound from the Black Forest of Germany, across the plateaus and valley, around the bends that revealed the magnificent landscape and countryside of Germany and Austria. Far ahead of them, it flowed into Hungary and Romania and Bulgaria, finally emptying into the Black Sea.

"The father—does he have a name, Kerina?"

"Bill. Bill VanBurien. I loved him, but it seemed as though I had no rights. Franck and Bill reminded me that my career was at stake. That Bill's reputation would be ruined. That the child could not be raised in concert halls. I would have to raise him in shame or let him go and bear the guilt as I have done for a lifetime." Her voice went flat. "Thanks to Franck, clever man that he is, I've played in concert halls all over the world. He tells me I made the best choice for the baby, the right one for myself."

"So, Kerina, why does the choice trouble you so now?" She didn't wait for Kerina to answer but said, "Because that baby will always be a part of you. That's not wrong."

"I guess that's why I keep playing my music for him."

"You played for him in Passau last evening, didn't you?"

"Yes, out there on the open court of the campus. At least three other times when I played the Brahms 'Lullaby' this year—in the concert hall in Milan, in the Bolshoi Theatre in Moscow, in the opulent auditorium in Monte Carlo—I played my music for my son."

"Elias and I were in Monte Carlo that night. I remember how splendidly you played. We talked about it afterward."

"My son was much in my heart and in my mind that night."

"And your music was never sweeter, nor the critics' reviews more glowing. Now I know why! Kerina, when your son was born, didn't anyone ask what you wanted to do about him?"

"I was too frightened to make decisions. Everyone else decided where I would stay during my pregnancy. Where I would have my child. Who would adopt him. The lawyer chosen for me insisted on a closed adoption as he thrust the adoption papers in front of me." She bit her lower lip. "There is only one good memory in it all—the nurse who let me hold my son told me it was not too late to change my mind. I will never forget her kindness. If she had been there with me from the beginning, perhaps I would have made a different choice. The choice to keep my child."

The onset of a headache came with the remembrance of Franck's insensitive remarks. *As a single woman, you can have no ties to the baby. You must not disgrace your family in Prague. You see that, don't you, Kerina? It's for your own good. It's best for the baby.* Even his promise failed to comfort her. *"I will make you famous, Kerina Rudzinski. I will make certain that the concert halls of Europe open their doors to you."*

She had wanted Bill to hold her and tell her that they would raise their son together. All he did—all he could do was promise that he'd make certain the child had a good home; then he had driven her to the airport and said good-bye. Everyone had wanted her to go on as though she had never given birth to the child. How could she? She had left a part of herself behind in Everdale.

She spoke now, more to the wind that swept across the Danube than to Nicole standing beside her. "No one asked me to name my child. I have no idea what name went on his birth certificate."

"What would you have called him?"

"William Karol—after Bill and my father. I think of him as William. All I have of him is one tiny snapshot—the one taken after his birth at the hospital. It's stained with my tears."

Thankfully, Nicole did not ask to see it but said, "It's a good thing I wasn't there. I would have shot Franck and Bill."

Kerina smiled at Nicole's loyalty. "I kept a snapshot of Bill, too. If I ever saw my son again, I wanted to be able to show him a picture of Bill and tell him, 'This is your father.' It must be awful not knowing. I know it is for me. I'll wonder the rest of my life where he is. What has become of him? Is he still alive? Happy?"

"Other women go on with their lives, Kerina."

"I know, but the child ties me to Bill."

"The child is a grown man now."

But an infant in Kerina's mind. Tiny fingers. Tiny toes. Button lips. A warm human form held briefly against her breast, always in her heart. An unnamed child that bore someone else's name. Not Bill's. Not hers. Haunting memories possessed her, coming back to burden and disturb her quiet.

She smiled wanly. "Now you know why Franck, who knew about the child, became my refuge. My retreat. My sanctuary."

"But never your lover. Never the man you would marry. I don't know whether to pity you or Franck the most."

In the darkness that had overtaken them, the ancient castles and monasteries stood like blackened silhouettes on the craggy hillside, the medieval history of these villages veiled in the night. The women stood in silence as an eerie swirling mist rose slowly from the dark water. Five minutes. Ten.

Then, gently prodding, Nicole said, "Don't stop now. You have carried this alone for far too long. Tell me just one thing. Do you want to find your son, Kerina?"

Her headache blinded her for a moment. "It's impossible, Nicole. It was part of the Adoption Consent that my son would never know my name. I would never know his."

"Kerina, somewhere your son may be searching for you."

Sadly, she shook her head. "In the town where the baby was born, there's a ledger with an original birth certificate that bears the time and place of my son's birth and what should have been my name. Bill persuaded me to register as Kerry Kovac. And I never told the hospital the name of the baby's father."

"And why not?" Nicole asked indignantly.

"Bill begged me not to. He said he was known there in Everdale. That it might make it difficult for our son."

Nicole mumbled under her breath, something quick and explosive in French. "Something deep inside your son may be telling him that part of himself is missing. Everyone leaves a trace, some hint of where they've gone. We could find him."

She was touched by Nicole's offer. "Perhaps I will find his trail in Everdale. I never planned to go back. But when we arranged the fall tour to America with five free days, I knew that I must go back. I'm certain that a couple from Everdale adopted my baby. Perhaps by some chance, my son is still living in the town where he was born. I'd give anything to see him—to see his father. Not to interfere in their lives, but just to bring closure for myself."

"This Bill—when did you see him last?"

"Days after the baby was born."

"And not since then? No letters? No phone calls?"

"Not since he left me at the Montgomery Airport."

"In other words, he walked out on you." Another French outburst had the ring of angry words. "Then it's foolish to cling to his memory. If you won't marry Franck, find someone else."

"There could never be anyone else."

Nicole touched her lightly on the shoulder. "It's cold out here. I'm going to our cabin, Kerina. Don't be long."

As Kerina stood alone, Nicole's words thundered in the night air. *In other words, he walked out on you.*

Yes. One moment Bill had stood at the airport in Montgomery, watching her plane take off, his handsome face a blur in the terminal window. Then he was gone, walking out of her life with not another word from him all these years.

Moments before she boarded the 707, he had leaned down and said, "One day, Kerina, I will make you proud of me. I will have my name in gold on the door of my office; I'll be the president of my own company."

He did not invite her to share his success. No, he would climb alone, right to the top of the corporate ladder. She thought now of the man that she could not describe to Nicole. Bill, the go-getter, the ambitious climber; yet she had loved him. *William,* his colleagues had called him. The tennis champ of the office, an expert player in spite of that slight limp from his navy days. A man driven to succeed to surpass Kerina's success, yet a strange composite of warmth and caring, of sports and music and poetry. The White Sox and Beethoven and T. S. Eliot. Dear Bill. Living on the cutting edge, charming her with his empty promises.

As they stood in the terminal that day, he did not mention Everdale, the town they had left behind. He had gazed down at her with those solemn, smoky-blue eyes, an unruly lock of blond hair slipping across his forehead. As the boarding call came over the intercom, he gripped her hand to keep her from leaving him and quoted Noel Coward's words. Bill's spicy scent and the sound of his deep voice were so clear in her mind that it could have been just yesterday.

> " 'This is to let you know
> That all I feel for you
> Can never wholly go.
> I love you, and miss you,
> Even two hours away,
> With all my heart.
> This is to let you know.' "

Words that Bill had no right to say to her. Promises that she had no right to hear. *He must have known as he left the airport that it was over between us, that a publicized scandal with a concert violinist would have ruined his ambitions. Surely he knew he could not risk seeing me again. If only I had known then. If only. . .*

She coughed from the dampness in the evening air. Still she lingered by the rail, her thoughts turning to the family that had loved and reared her son for her. *Their son. My son.*

She had entrusted a letter to the nurse who had been so kind to her, two sheets of scented stationery with eleven wishes scrawled in her own handwriting. *Love my baby for me,* she had written to the couple who would raise him as their own. *Be kind to him. Take care of him. Let him be a happy child. Take him fishing when he is old enough and let him walk in the woods and climb mountains.* As she had done as a child, but hers had been an escape from a barren childhood ruled by communists.

Take him to baseball games, she had scribbled on the paper.

The White Sox games, she thought suddenly. *Maybe his father will see him there. . . .*

Keep him healthy, but now and then let him eat a foot-long hot dog or an ice-cream soda. And please teach him about Europe.

She dared not specify Prague or the people of Czechoslovakia. But Europe. Pointing her son toward his roots. Her roots.

With her flow of tears blurring the words, she had penned her last requests for her son. *Expose him to good music. I want him to hear music. I want him to play the violin.*

Almost as an afterthought, she had added, *And if you find it in your heart, teach him about God.*

∽

Kerina no longer felt awash with self-pity. Talking with Nicole had been liberating and left her with an unusual calm as she turned from the ship's rail and made her way to the cabin. Tomorrow when she and Nicole awakened, they would cruise the tranquil waters of the Danube, Kerina comforted as she had always been by the river. They'd visit the Benedictine Abbey on a ridge 180 feet above Melk and the next day glide into Vienna. Then overnighting on the boat, they would sail on to Budapest. With the pearl blue of the early morning sky shimmering in the blue of the water, their river vessel would pass beneath the Chain Bridge into Budapest where they would disembark. That night she would lift her Stradivarius and bring music to the people of Hungary.

Chapter 8

At Los Angeles International, Ashley scanned the overhead screen for her flight number and welcomed the sign: ON TIME. The crowded airport hummed with activity and a monotone voice warning, "Attention, all international passengers. Do not leave your luggage unattended."

Thankfully, David was there, taking charge, relieving her of the last-minute responsibility. Short of ordering a wheelchair so he could oversee her arrival inside the cabin, she was stuck with his attention. It was David's way of saying he was sorry she was traveling alone, but his not going remained a bone of contention between them. Even before leaving the house, he had irritated her more when she hurried from the shower with cream on her face and little more than a towel wrapped around her.

"You're not going like that?" he joked.

"Of course not. My jeans and sweatshirt are there on the bed." The king-size bed they had shared for thirty years.

David glanced at the open suitcase and pointed to her new wine-colored suit. "I was hoping you would wear that." His eyes were bright with pleasure. "You'd look elegant."

"I bought it with my last paycheck."

"I know. I wondered how long you'd hide it in your closet. I kept hoping you'd wear it to church and stun them all."

"You wouldn't mind?"

"I'm proud of you, Ashley. I like it when eyes turn your way. But wear what you want on the plane. Be comfortable. No matter what you wear, you are a beautiful woman."

She thought about the look in his eyes all the way to the airport. Their timing was always off. At that moment she wanted to stay home with him, and she could see by the wistful smile on his face that he shared her thoughts.

They raced to Los Angeles in a driving rain with David telling her at least three times, "Take a taxi straight from the Schwechat Airport to the Empress Isle Hotel. No matter what the cost," he insisted.

"After a red-eye flight, where do you think I would go? Out to a disco?" In her distant past, she would have.

He snapped back, "Chandler should be there to meet you, not expecting you to arrive on your own in a foreign city."

And if you were going with me, we wouldn't be having this row. "Oh David, don't blame Chandler. He's on standby. Why don't you just drop me off at the curbside check-in?"

"I'm going all the way to the boarding gate with you."

The whole route, giving one last-minute instruction after the other. Inside the lobby, he demanded, "Let me have your ticket, Ashley. I'll take care of it."

At the check-in, he handed in her ticket and passport, confirmed her first-class reservation and asked about the weather en route, about the food on board. She worried lest he'd ask whether there was a chaplain in attendance. Ashley almost walked away from the counter, but the clerk smiled and said, "I fly these planes often. It's one of the perks in the industry. Don't worry, Mr. Reynolds, our company takes care of its passengers."

David flashed a sheepish grin. "I don't like my wife traveling to Europe alone."

"She won't be. The flight is completely booked."

"I wouldn't be traveling alone if you were going with me," Ashley said in an annoyed tone.

They made it to the boarding gate without quarreling. As sleepy as David looked, she worried that he would drive too fast on the rainswept streets outside the airport. "David, go home. Don't wait for the boarding call. You'll just oversleep in the morning."

Without her there to wake him, he'd be late for his breakfast appointment with one of the elders. And then she laughed to herself. *We've been married much too long, David,* she thought. *All we do is fuss over each other.*

He stood inches from her. "Ashley, I'll miss you."

"I'll miss you, too." But would she? She could hardly wait to get away from David's commitments and crowded schedule.

"Honey, if you need more money, I can wire—"

"I'll be okay."

"Ashley, you have your ticket and passport?"

"You gave them back to me at the check-in counter. Oh David, stop hovering. You're suffocating me."

"Am I that bad?"

"You're like an old mother hen. You're making me nervous. You know

I hate flying over the ocean at night."

"Then sleep all the way."

"I'm too excited."

"About seeing Chandler?" Misgiving clouded his gaze. "Give him a bear hug for me. And the minute you get together, call me. No matter what time it is. I want to know that you're both safe."

You want to know if Chandler has changed, she accused silently. *If Bosnia or the army has changed him. He's still the same boy, David. The child you loved.* The love between them was still there if David could only express it. If Chandler would only accept it.

David touched Ashley's cheek. "I hate to see you go away."

The old David. The gentle David. They were inviting first-class passengers to board now. "That's you, Ash. My VIP."

He hugged her and gave her a long, impassioned kiss, his lips hard on hers. The old tender David. Then, his cheek against hers, he whispered, "Go, before I won't let you."

On board, she dropped into the wide, leather seat and fastened her safety belt. The fragrance of David's cologne clung to her sweatshirt as she gazed through the murky windowpane, but it was impossible to distinguish David's lanky form in the terminal window. But he was there—would be until her plane leveled out above the clouds and headed toward Europe.

She touched her lips, treasuring the memory of his good-bye, her eyes filling with tears. *We've had so much together. We can't throw all those years away. I can't—I won't let you go.*

As the aisle filled with passengers, she studied the faces of the strangers, praying that she'd have a likable seatmate, one who wouldn't snore or chat endlessly, one who wouldn't overlap onto her space or fall asleep on her shoulder. As the line thinned out, a tall man ducked as he entered the cabin, winked at the flight attendant, and gave a quick appraisal of first class before striding toward the empty seat.

He was fortyish, physically strong and attractive like David, his suntanned arms muscular and bare, his faded jeans too short for his gangly legs. A Tom Clancy paperback bulged in his hip pocket, a wedding ring glinted on his finger. He tossed his shaving kit and ribbed wool sweater in the overhead compartment, loosened his short-sleeved shirt, adjusted his belt, and slid into the seat beside her, his tangy scent crowding out David's cologne. When he turned to her, he ceased being David. His nose was crooked, his curious, dark eyes too closely set.

He gave Ashley an amiable grin, tapped his Citizens watch, and said, "Here's hoping we take off on time."

By the time the jet rolled down the runway, he had flipped open his book and was lost in a political thriller. *All you need,* Ashley thought, *is Tom Clancy's red baseball cap with USS Iowa emblazoned on the front.*

The plane lurched and leveled out as a gray, swirling cloud mass engulfed them, and they headed for Vienna.

The man ate in the same manner as he had boarded the plane, comfortable with himself and his surroundings, fingering a morsel of steak and shoving the onions aside. After eating, he sucked at a fragment of meat caught in his even white teeth and settled back against his seat as the attendant whisked his tray away.

"Wine, Mr. Gramdino?" she asked.

"Not for me. But perhaps the lady—" He turned to Ashley. "An after-dinner drink for you?"

"None. Thank you."

He crossed his legs and tightened the shoestring on his tennis shoes and was suddenly talkative, as though he had been in need of time to himself and a good solid meal to counteract a last-minute rush to the airport without dinner.

"Your first trip to Vienna?" he asked.

"Oh no, but my first one alone. I usually travel with my husband." She sounded haughty even to herself, as though this trip were a bonus accumulated from frequent flying hours and not one of those fast turnaround flights to religious conventions.

"Me—I travel on business to Geneva. Milan. Paris. Vienna." The flight attendant had called him Mr. Gramdino. Now he filled in the rest. "Joel Gramdino. Brooklyn-born. Housed in Los Angeles. My friends call me Joe. My wife calls me to dinner."

His joke fell short, but she allowed him to shake her hand.

It was a strong grip, his skin smooth, not the calloused hand of the working class. "I'm Ashley Reynolds. I'm visiting my son in Vienna. He's in the army."

"Tough—unless he likes it."

She nodded and opened her magazine to dismiss him. Long after the movie, high above the Atlantic, she sat with her reading light still on, a music magazine spread across her lap with the face of Kerina Rudzinski looking up at her. She tried to remember the youthful Kerina and quickly saw the similarities. The lovely auburn hair. The fragile, feminine features, the slight tilt of her chin. That sad melancholy look in her eyes.

The hulk beside her shifted restlessly as Gramdino stuffed the pillow behind his neck and sighed wearily. "As much as I fly, I can never get the hang of sleeping on these big birds."

"That's my problem. That's why I'm reading this article on Kerina Rudzinski. My son and I are attending her violin concert."

He handed her a business card. "I'm into art appreciation."

"An art theft registry, Mr. Gramdino?"

"It's our job to track down lost or stolen art objects and return them to the owners. Picasso. Michelangelo. All the biggies."

"Do you have much success?"

"Not as much as we'd like. We haven't found that Picasso stolen during one of Rudzinski's last concerts in Vienna."

"Stolen during her concert? You can't be serious?"

"But I am. Elias McClaren was one of the opera house patrons, a wealthy art collector with a season ticket. Had his home ransacked while he listened to Beethoven's *Fifth*."

"How tragic!"

"It was, considering its million-dollar value. But somebody probably wanted it for his private collection."

"You wouldn't be the thief, would you, Mr. Gramdino?"

"Me?" He laughed. "That would be a clever twist." He stood, grabbed his sweater from the overhead, and pulled it over his muscled biceps. "Now, tell me about you. Where are you from?"

"Southern California. Everdale, Alabama, as a child."

"The deep South? Me, I'm an Italian Yankee." He formed a horizontal line with his hand. "With some folks just the edge of the mother tongue comes off. But you now, you've almost made that complete switch between dialects—from the south to the southwest. Everdale, Alabama, eh? Never heard of it."

"Few people have."

Nostalgia swept over her. *It's just a little place on the far side of town,* she thought. *Past the railroad track, almost to the county line. To Mama's house with the wide front pillars and fresh-cut flowers on the kitchen table, and the big living room smelling of Old English furniture polish and lemon. Even more vivid was the screen door squeaking as Mania came out on the porch fanning herself with an apron, her chapped hands as bright red as the sumac bush. Mama coming outside to check on her linens air-drying on the clothesline or to delight in a dogwood tree in bloom or to sit a spell in the wicker rocker. Mama. Mama. . . .*

How quickly this stranger had sent her spinning back in time to the old family home, to the swings by the gazebo and those happy hours with her twin brother in the place where they had been sheltered and loved by the dearest mom of all.

A distinct Southern drawl crept back from her childhood as she quoted Bill. "Everdale is nothing more than a dot on the map. You have to travel miles just to reach the freeway. We haven't been back since my son was three. Twenty-three years ago."

"A long time to stay away."

She laughed dryly. "There's nothing to go back to. My parents and brother are buried there. I don't even think my friends would remember me—and those who did might snub me."

Gramdino cushioned his head against the leather seat. "Sounds like you've lost some of the good memories of Everdale?"

No, the pictures were there, as lifelike as ever. The wisteria vine, its clusters of purple flowers clambering up the fence. The sweet scent of the honeysuckle bush on a warm spring day. And then like black strokes against the canvas came the memory of a farm and barn in the neighboring town just over the county line. She forced herself to think instead of the brilliant azaleas blooming in the yard in Everdale on the day they moved away—and of her last glimpse of the swings by the gazebo where she and her brother had played. Where Chandler had played.

She sat very still, trying to recall the song of the mockingbird and hearing only the rumble of the giant jet around her. She knew the dog days of Everdale had ended forever, and the darkness of an Alabama winter were coming hard against her.

"Sometimes life's canvas gets marred, Mr. Gramdino."

He ran his hand along an imaginary line, pausing here and there like an artist dropping dabs of color on the canvas. "Going back home can be a great healer, Mrs. Reynolds. It worked like that for me when I went back to my father's birthplace in Italy. Sometimes it lets us find that missing canvas of our childhood."

He leaned over, his face close to hers, and turned off her reading lamp. "Good night, Mrs. Reynolds. Pleasant dreams."

Her dreams were frightening. Over and over, she saw a tall man in a ribbed pullover sweater and tight jeans with the face of Joel Gramdino. He was running over the blue gilded dome of the Opera House in Vienna, swinging over gold statues, a Picasso painting clutched in his hand. He slipped, tumbling to his death, as the youthful Kerina Rudzinski played her violin onstage.

When Ashley awakened from her fitful sleep, Joel Gramdino was just making his way back from the washroom, a shaving kit in his hand. As he sat down, he thumb-combed his hair the way David did early in the morning.

"Is your son meeting you, Mrs. Reynolds?"

"No, he's on military standby."

"Will you be all right alone?"

"Of course."

"You have my business card. My hotel number's on the back. If you have any problems, give me a call. I know my way around Vienna. We could have dinner—" he laughed—"at your hotel."

As the jet descended into Vienna, her stomach tightened. "I'm certain Chandler will be here in time for dinner."

∼

In Bosnia, Chandler Reynolds waited on standby to catch a military flight to Vienna. In spite of Colonel Bladstone's promise to arrange a meeting between Chandler and Zineta Hovic, Chandler had not seen her since Randy's death.

He wondered how she was; where she was. Then, as he stood by his duffel looking across the tarmac, he saw Colonel Bladstone coming toward him, a young woman by his side. It was Zineta, her woeful eyes fixed on Chandler.

When he held out his arms, she ran to him. "I thought I would never see you before I left," he said.

"Where is Ran-dee?" she whispered.

Doesn't she know? "They sent him home."

"He never said good-bye to me."

"If there had been a chance—"

"The last time I saw him, he was running by the side of the house." Her lips quivered. "I heard the land mine explode."

He took her hands and squeezed them.

"Kemal kept me in the house. He would not let me look."

"He was wise." He rubbed the top of her hand with his thumb.

"The Americans came with spotlights and trucks. They took Ran-dee away. Rasim said he died. . .is he dead, Chan-leer?"

Chandler nodded. He kept her trembling hands in his, offering her his strength. "I begged the colonel to tell you."

Tears filled her eyes. "Your colonel would not tell me." She pulled free and patted her swollen abdomen. "I have something of Ran-dee that your Colonel Bladstone cannot take away from me."

"The baby?"

She nodded and then, as if suddenly aware of the planes around her, asked, "Chan-leer, are you going away, too?"

"For a month, but I'll see you when I get back."

She shook her head. "I will not be here."

If anything happens to me, Randy had said, *promise me you will watch after Zineta.* "I want to take you to America with me. Would you go with me, Zineta?"

"To Ran-dee's town?"

"Randy won't be there." He looked beyond her to Colonel Gladstone. "Where are they sending you?"

"I do not know. Kemal says the French sector. But I have relatives in Zagreb—if they are still alive."

"I'll find you, no matter where. I promise."

He searched his kit bag, flipping past the rose-scented letter from Kerina Rudzinski's office and came up trumps. An address card for the Emerald Isle Hotel. "Take this. It's my hotel phone number in Vienna. I've scribbled my mother's California address on the back."

Her lower lip trembled. "Your mother will help me?"

"No, I will. But you have to let me know where you are. I have a plan. We'll make it work. If necessary, I'll marry you."

She shook her head. "Marry me—without loving me? That is wrong for you. I will not let you."

"But we're friends. It would get you safely to America."

"A business arrangement?" she asked sadly. "Is there no other way?"

"I don't know."

She tucked the card in her plunging neckline. "It is safe there. The colonel will not know I have it." She reached up and kissed Chandler. "Ran-dee said we could trust you."

She turned and walked back to the colonel, the palms of her hands wide, empty. Bladstone led her to the waiting helicopter, the wind from the rotor blades whipping her skirt against her thighs. She turned, waved, and climbed on board.

Chandler's eyes fixed on the chopper as it lifted and turned northwest. *They wanted me to see you leave, Zineta Hovic. Their silent warning that I am never to see you again.*

Chapter 9

Kerina awakened, feverish, with a chest cold and a stuffy nose. She stole from the comfort of her large bed and stumbled barefoot to the windows of her hotel suite. Pulling back the lace curtains, she cooled her burning brow against the windowpane. Outside it was that muggy blackness just before dawn. Dawn, the hour she loved, when the first streaks of day washed the sky with amber gold. But the sky hung like an ebony canopy over Vienna, the stars and moon bedded down now, and the familiar landmark of the South Tower of the Stephansdom a dark silhouette in the raven sky.

It had been inky black like this the last time she saw Bill, just before her jet left the runway. Incredibly, twenty-six years ago. Yet every detail remained etched indelibly in her memory: *the 707 soaring through the leaden clouds into the breaking of day, the light coming through her plane window like the promise of a rainbow. Color. Light. Hope.*

The blush of that early morning lit a tiny corner of Kerina's darkness, the shades of light bringing with it a glimmer of hope. She was homesick—a stranger in a foreign land. A young woman without the comfort of her parents in Prague. A mother without her newborn child. A musician heading back to Chicago without a song. She pictured herself, her chin nestled against her Stradivarius, on a violin that would only play off-key. She had felt like one sinking in quicksand, trapped in a marshland of sin and despair by a romance that had nowhere to go.

As she boarded that plane in Montgomery with empty arms, she was numb, her fingers icy, her body screaming at her. Beneath her navel she could feel the hard round mass of her uterus. Her swollen breasts were gorged with milk for the infant son that would never nurse there. She felt nothing inside except emptiness and guilt. She had left a divided heart—a shattered fragment in the nursery in Everdale, and the rest at the Montgomery Airport with the one person that she could not, should not, have.

High above the faceless clouds she cried out, "Oh God! Does no one care what's happening to me?"

At that moment the stewardess who had brushed past her in the terminal stood in the aisle with her beverage cart, an angel unaware in her navy blue uniform and starched blouse with its red-white-and-blue bow. Leaning down, she tucked her own linen handkerchief in Kerina's hand. "If you need me, ring."

She pointed to the button on the armrest and then, lowering Kerina's tray, placed a steaming cup of tea on it. Kerina nodded gratefully. As tears coursed down her cheeks, she turned her face to the window. Beyond the stewardess and the jet, Someone bigger than herself washed away the darkness and flooded her flight with the pastel hues of a sunrise. Yet now God seemed out of reach, distant. Unknown. Unreal. She wondered, with the psalmist, how she could find Him.

~

Standing now at her hotel window, Kerina watched the edge of the sun poke its rounded head above the horizon, brushing the carbon darkness aside as the Vienna sky went from a pelican gray to a powder blue. Morning dew was beginning to rise in a mist above the Danube. Milk-white clouds drifted across the horizon. Dawn came like a blushing begonia with ribbons of orange and gold; streaks of saffron yellow and garnet red splashed across the heavens. Sun filtered through the windows. She pressed her hands against the pane and scanned higher, beyond the clouds. Day had dawned over Vienna again, a city gloriously different. Vienna! Kerina's adopted city.

Today will be a good day, she thought.

In the distance she heard the clang of the first morning trolley, below her the *clippety-clop* of a horse-drawn carriage wending its way toward the Ringstrasse, and close by the sweet ring of the church bells. The spiraling towers of St. Stephen's Cathedral jutted skyward as though they had clasped hands with God Himself. And if God did not exist—and these days Kerina could never be quite certain—at least the Gothic architecture offered hope to those more confident of eternity than she.

In this brief moment of quiet, she was without the thundering applause that would echo through the Opera House tomorrow evening. The prospect of performing at the Staatsoper accompanied by the Vienna Philharmonic Orchestra loomed as the capstone of her career, the crowning moment, the culmination of sacrificial years of practice and devotion to hone her skill, a magnificent grand finale. If she never played again, she would have this memory, this marvelous opportunity of giving back to the city she loved some of her deep gratitude—the climax of a career in the city where it all began. It would be like giving her own standing ovation to the people of

Vienna for all they had been to her. Her thank-you. Her tears. Her applause for how warmly they had received her.

Suddenly, she remembered what she had repressed on awakening—thoughts of Bill. Ever since Jillian had shoved the copy of *Time* magazine across the table to her, the soldier's picture had stirred old, irritating wounds. Bill kept stealing into her thoughts unwelcomed, with memories of their son cascading into her heart, tumbling like a waterfall into the aching void inside her. Drenching her with the past. Depressing her with what might have been. Drowning her with what she had done. Stirring the dull, dead roots of Everdale and making even June one of the cruellest months. Each time she pushed them away by turning the music up louder or practicing more diligently.

Kerina felt shaky, her flesh tingling as she turned from the window and crossed to the telephone. She tried to remember who she planned to call. Chandler Reynolds? No, Jillian would arrange to meet Lieutenant Reynolds with the tickets before the concert. So why did he creep back into her thoughts? *Because you have awakened the loss of my own son.*

The phone? Yes, she was going to dial Nicole's doctor and confirm her appointment; then she would ring room service and order juice and a croissant. This done—and an appointment secured for four o'clock—she hurried off to shower before the breakfast trolley arrived.

Early mornings were the hours when other musicians slept or sought solitude in the quiet of their own rooms. Kerina, for want of fresh air and the sights of the city she loved most, often promenaded in the parks or browsed through the Gothic and Baroque museums on the Ringstrasse, but she reserved Wednesday mornings for her visits to St. Stephen's. This morning, though, she had a nine o'clock appointment at the Opera House where she would look out over the empty auditorium and play a Brahms lullaby—the practice run for the greatest performance of her life.

With her violin case in hand, she set out. As she passed the concierge's desk, he called politely, "Fräulein Rudzinski, I have a message for you."

Distracted, she crossed the lobby to him. He was in his late thirties, an efficient, nattily dressed man with a clipped mustache and eyes that appraised her as she reached him. She gave him her most engaging smile as he handed her the envelope.

"Fräulein Ingram left this."

Kerina slit the envelope with her thumbnail and read Jillian's familiar scrawl:

Friends in town. Having breakfast with them. Will be back to go over the day's plans this afternoon. Sorry. Jill.

Kerina turned to cross the opulent, carpeted lobby again and saw Franck Petzold cutting toward her, looking impeccable in his Italian suit, its deep charcoal complementing his thick, black hair and gray-flecked beard. As he reached her, he leaned down to kiss her cheeks and took both her hands, crushing Jillian's note as he did so.

His dark eyes never left Kerina's face. "What is this?" he asked, lifting the scented envelope and inhaling the fragrance.

"A note from Jillian."

Franck's black brows arched. "She's gone? She knows that the hours before your concert are demanding. Where is she this time?"

"Off to breakfast with old acquaintances. Don't look so worried, Franck. It darkens your eyes."

She reached up to straighten the silk paisley tie accenting his pearl blue shirt. "Jillian is free to go off on her own. You know that."

"Who is she with this time?"

Lightly, she said, "With a lover perhaps. Or a secret admirer. Or Santos Garibaldi might be in town."

"Then have her followed."

"Franck dear, her private life is her own."

"Not if it interferes with her work." He plucked at the sideburns that framed his angular face, then flashed a sly smile. "Gone, you say? Then you are free to go with me to see Elias McClaren's latest art exhibit at the museum."

She nodded at the violin case in her hand. "Franck, I have an appointment at the Opera House. I want to check out the acoustics in the auditorium."

"Wait until this afternoon and I can go with you."

"I can't."

His eyes snapped as he turned to the concierge and demanded the use of the phone. He spoke rapidly in Russian.

"I will be an hour late. . . Of course, I made the arrangements with McClaren. . . No! I must go to the Staatsoper with Kerina first."

Franck's eyes were hard as he took the violin case from her. He guided Kerina swiftly through the red-carpeted lobby, nodding curtly to the uniformed doorman as they left the hotel.

"You didn't have to change your plans for me, Franck."

"I don't want you to go to the Opera House alone, Kerina."

"But it will make you late meeting Jokhar."

"Does it matter?" He brooded in silence, his hand touching her elbow but his mind elsewhere. In muteness they crossed the wide boulevard to the ring of buildings that had replaced the ancient walls of the city. The magnificent Opera House lay ahead with its majestic arches and curving blue roof and Renaissance exterior. Beyond one of the tiered fountains, the director waited for them. He smiled down at Kerina with bright, alert eyes and shook hands with Franck, then escorted them past the box office vestibule and up the grand, marble staircase to the first floor.

The splendor of the Opera House was an artist's dream. The interior glowed, the regal oil paintings and floral motifs on the walls giving off a golden reflection. Reliefs of opera and ballet and the ivory busts of famous composers filled the panels. They climbed the stairs and walked to the center of the stage to look out on an auditorium ablaze in white and gold. Kerina glanced past the orchestra pit and the gilded chandeliers and scanned the high balcony and the frescoed ceilings. She had forgotten the opulent beauty of the auditorium.

Without even looking at the director, she said, "It's hard to imagine all of this gutted at the end of the war."

"We took a direct hit from the Allied bombings, as you know. It took months to clear the debris and shore up the walls—and years to rebuild. But that was before you were even born, Miss Rudzinski. Destruction was everywhere. London. Leningrad. Dresden. Paris."

"I was only a boy," Franck said, "but I remember the bitter cold of Leningrad, standing with my hand in my father's and hating war and weeping over my grandfather's lost art treasures."

Kerina patted his bearded cheek before turning back to the director. "Were you able to arrange box seating for my guests?"

"Elias McClaren agreed to seat them in his loge. Let me get the tickets for you."

"Guests?" Franck asked as the director walked off.

"Friends."

Frowning, he lightly touched her waist. She felt the old sadness for him and turned from those somber eyes to open her violin case. As she lifted the violin, he said, "Play something for me."

She chose his favorite and played the second movement of Mozart's *Violin Concerto no. 2*, knowing that as the music poured from her soul it would touch his. As she lowered her violin, he said, "Don't stop. Play something else for me."

She played the opening bars of a Strauss waltz, the music resounding in the empty auditorium, and then, with her eyes closed, the last few lines of the Brahms 'Lullaby.' On the last note, she opened her eyes and lowered her bow. The morose expression on Franck's face startled her.

"You didn't play that for me, did you, Kerina?"

"No—it was for my son."

His taut lips looked like rubber bands about to snap. "It does no good to remember, Kerina," he said savagely.

She placed her Strad in its case with excessive care. "Lately, Franck, I cannot forget him."

"You will make yourself sick."

"He was flesh of my flesh. I gave him away, but I will never forget him. He would be twenty-six now. Did you remember that?"

"I don't celebrate his birthday."

She tried to smile. "Please, the director is coming back. He must not hear us quarrel. And, Franck, I never blamed you."

"Didn't you?"

"As you told me, letting my son go was best for him."

Moments later, she linked her arm in Franck's and walked slowly down the stairs behind the director. At the door they thanked their host profusely and breathed in the fresh air.

"Are you all right?" Franck asked as they neared the curb.

"Of course."

"You don't mind walking back to the Empress Isle alone?"

"Oh Franck!" She laughed up at him. "If I can't get that short distance on my own, I am in trouble."

He leaned down and kissed her. "Then I will go on to the Academy of Fine Arts. Jokhar will be quite impatient by now." His eyes sought hers, moodily. "I will be back for lunch. Will you have it with me, Kerina?"

She took her violin from him. "I think not. I will just rest until Jillian gets back."

Chapter 10

Franck turned and strode off, the snapping click of his heels taking him forward, his thoughts in reverse yanking him back in time to that farm outside of Prague, Czechoslovakia, where Kerina had spent her childhood. Kerina was fifteen when Franck met her, and he, all of twenty-eight, a man about town more interested in his feminine conquests in Prague than his father's politics. But his father's politics, not the pretty women in his life, would come between the youthful violinist and himself.

He was drawn to her music at a time when he was troubled by his father's political power. Later, during one of the concerts in Vienna when Kerina was eighteen, he realized that music and soul and the girl were one. He discovered then that he had already given his heart to her and could never take it back.

~

Prague, 1969

Franck heard Kerina's music coming from the thatched cottage where the Rudzinskis lived—violin music as sweet as the song of a hundred thrushes singing. He turned to his mother. "Tell me about the girl with the violin. She makes beautiful music."

His mother patted his hand. "So did you once."

"Once, but no longer. But, Mama, the girl. Tell me about her. Her music is glorious, masterful, peaceful."

"You have already made up your mind." She shrugged. "So what is there to tell? She is Karol Rudzinski's daughter, Kerina. You be careful, Franck. She is too young for you."

He glared down at his wrist, still scarred from one of his father's beatings. "What chance does this violinist have, Mama?"

"None, unless she leaves this country."

The sound of a hundred thrushes singing stopped abruptly.

Franck strolled to the farmhouse window and saw Kerina race across the barren fields to the outhouse; a scrawny sheepdog yapped and leaped beside her. He watched the door shut, and he waited—as the dog waited until it opened again. She stepped out smoothing the long skirt against her legs, then leaned down and hugged the animal before running off down toward the river, the dog setting the pace. In that moment something stirred inside him. He was intrigued by the girl's utter sense of freedom, a freedom that eluded him. She was long-legged and scrawny like the dog, both of them jetting across the fields, her gleaming, red-brown hair sweeping across her shoulders.

The following Tuesday he sat in silence at the table with his father, his mother nervously pouring breakfast coffee for them. His father broke the stillness with a roar. "Karol Rudzinski forgot to bring the milk this morning."

"I can go for it," Franck offered.

"You? Then take this deed to the property with you. I need Karol Rudzinski's signature."

"But the land belongs to the Rudzinskis."

His father scoffed. "The country is state-owned now, and I want what is politically mine."

Franck tucked the deed into his pocket, took his jacket from the hook, and trudged over the muddy path, his eyes to the ground, his dislike for his father intense. Halfway to the cottage he thrust his hands into his jacket pockets, miserable at the task at hand. He was almost there when he heard the magical sounds of Kerina's violin again. He stopped to listen for the final note of Mendelssohn's *Concerto in E minor*. He wanted to clap, to demand that all nature give her a standing ovation.

Her music drowned out his knocking. He forced the door back and walked into a large kitchen with a woodstove smoking in one corner and sooty utensils hanging from hooks on the wall. Off to his right lay a tiny bedroom, where the girl sat leaning against an iron bedstead, her legs resting against the white, ruffled pillows as she plucked the strings of her violin.

He crossed the room to her. "Kerina."

Still she did not hear him. Her head was bent, her chin secure against the violin. She adjusted the tone, a horsehair bow in one hand, the fingers of her left hand pressed against the strings. She struck a note and listened intently at the squeal. He watched the frown crinkle between her brows. And then she powdered the bow, rubbing rosin across it.

"Kerina," he said again.

Startled, she pushed back shiny locks of hair from her face and cried out, "Who are you? What do you want?"

"I'm Franck Petzold, your landlord's son. I've come to see your father—and to collect our milk supply."

"Oh, I forgot about the milk. Papa will be furious with me."

"You're busy."

The rough board walls of her room had been painted into a garden of wild geraniums and daisies, buttercups and pink camellias. The flowers dwarfed the room. There was little space for anything but her bed, with the chamber pot visible beneath it, and a crate that held her clothes, with a washbasin on top.

He stepped closer and took the violin from her.

"Give that back," she demanded.

She was on her feet at once, not as tall as he had first imagined when he saw her sprinting across the fields on those long legs. "That belonged to my great-grandfather. Give it back."

He turned the violin in his strong hands gently, as though he were holding a newborn infant. It was marvelous craftsmanship with deeply polished grain. "It must have taken fourteen or fifteen coats of varnish to make it glow like this."

She seemed less wary. "At least that many."

He had read stories about Antonio Stradivari, the seventeenth-century craftsman, a stately, angular man with a solemn face and a cluttered workbench, the varnish from his works in progress often staining his leather apron. How many violins had come from the man's hands? At least eight hundred, Franck knew, with far fewer still in existence. But this instrument in his hands was a Strad—genuine, simon-pure.

Franck calculated its worth and saw it as money in his own pocket. "This is a marvelous piece of workmanship, an authentic Stradivarius. Worth much on the black market."

"It is not for sale." Her narrow jaw jutted forward. He saw fear in her eyes again as she said, "Please, do not take it."

"But it is worth a lot of money, Kerina Rudzinski." He twirled his tongue around her name, savoring it, teasing her.

She flicked back long strands of flaming hair from her rosy cheek, her eyes blazing as hotly. "It is more than money to me, Franck Petzold. It belongs to my family."

He knew at that moment that he would not take the violin from her. He put it back in her hands. "Play something for me, little one."

She sat down cross-legged on the bed and obeyed, her head bent toward the instrument, her loose hair falling forward and hiding those brilliant dark eyes. As her bow touched the strings, the tones came out rich and warm as the lilt of a waltz stole gently into the room. He knew as she played that he must channel her gift. He knew music and loved it and, thanks to his mother, had heard both Jascha Heifetz and Yehudi Menuhin play.

"Who taught you to play so well, little one?"

"My grandfather. My mother."

"No other teachers?"

She shook her head. "We never leave the farm, not even for school. Mother fears that one day I will flee my country and play my violin in a free world. You could help me, Mr. Petzold."

He laughed. "Why would I do that?"

"Because you like my music. And I will never give up my music— never give up my dream."

There was no future for Kerina in her own country. Stay here and her music would die with her. He could not let that happen. He could be her manager. She was worth far more to him as a violinist than the instrument itself. Again he calculated the price on the black market, marveling. "You are lucky that no one stole your Stradivarius during the Nazi occupation."

A mischievous grin filled her face. "My family wrapped it in cloth and hid it in the trap door beneath the old oak table."

"So no one found it?"

"No. But my father said no one dared play it during the war. The Nazis stole everything of value—except the violin."

"Didn't your family know what would happen if it was found?"

"My father says, 'You can only die once.'" Franck heard triumph in her voice as she added, "The important thing is that the Rudzinskis still have the violin. Even your papa agreed to let me keep it if my family farmed the land for him."

"As long as my father doesn't know its value, you are safe."

"Will you tell him?"

"No." He knew enough about music and the art world to know that he had found himself a young prodigy, a personal gold mine.

"How old are you, Kerina?"

"Fifteen. I will be sixteen in a few months." As Franck turned to leave, Kerina said, "The milk jug is by the door, Mr. Petzold."

He took the property deed from his pocket and laid it on the table.

"I will leave this in place of the milk. It is the deed to this property. Your father must sign it."

Her eyes snapped. "He won't do that. The farm has belonged to my family for generations." She slipped off her bed and followed him to the kitchen. "I will not give it to him."

She snatched it up, ran to the woodstove, and stuffed it into the crevice. It caught fire immediately.

"That was foolish," Franck said angrily.

She folded her arms against her chest as he opened the door and nodded at the stove. "Will you tell your father what I have done?" she asked defiantly.

His father would have her beaten, her hand crushed. "You would not be safe. My father is head of the secret police."

"Do you work for him?"

Wearily, he said, "No. I am trained to restore works of art. But for now, my father has me working in the office of records."

A vast room that detailed the life and statistics of every Czech in and around Prague as well as the long lists of art collections missing since the war. Paperwork that he despised.

Too many of those names had disappeared from the files—Czechs who had fought against the Germans and now resisted his father. Many had been shipped off to work the mines or fill the graves. Franck did not want to see the Rudzinskis shipped off to the mines or gunned down in the streets of Prague. He would tell his father that he had lost the deed en route to the cottage. Later he would risk eliminating the name Rudzinski from the city records and fill in his father's name as the sole owner of the farmhouse. After all it was merely logistics, paperwork. The Rudzinskis would never know what he had done.

∽

The next time Franck returned to Czechoslovakia, Kerina looked more lovely than ever, her face as sweet as her music, her hair more rusty-brown than he remembered as she crossed the fields to him. She was beginning to lose the gangly look of youth, her body flowering into womanhood and her lips soft and sensuous.

"Where have you been?" she asked.

"My father sent me to Moscow for six months."

"Did he send you because I destroyed the property deed?"

"I never told him." He smiled down at her. "Do you still play your violin, Kerina?"

"Every day. I want to play in the concert halls of the world, Franck. Can you help me?"

"How? There is little travel permitted across the borders."

"But you are free to cross them."

"My father's politics give me the freedom to come and go. Where would you like to escape to, little one?" he teased.

"To Vienna."

"I have friends there. But the borders are closed."

"You leave the country all the time."

He smiled patiently. "Because my passport is Russian."

"Then get me a Russian passport."

He took her hand and held it, and she, childlike and trusting, let him. "Perhaps I could if you married me—"

"I don't want to marry anyone. I want only to play my music around the world."

He cupped her cheeks. "And you will play before great audiences, little one. Someday soon, I will help you leave this country." *And someday I shall marry you.*

∼

When Franck reached the Academy of Fine Arts, Jokhar Gukganov, a tall, brusque, hard-faced man stepped forward. "You kept me waiting, Franck."

Franck felt the man's displeasure but said evenly, "I am here now. Shall we go in? I am sure you will find the McClaren exhibit worth your visit."

Gukganov grunted. "Have you checked out his residence?"

"Thoroughly. Elias McClaren and I are friends. We meet at the club whenever I am in Vienna. And I dine at his home often."

"You have seen his personal art collection?"

"Many times. The works of Degas and Rembrandt and VanStryker have prominent locations in his home."

"And his security system?"

Franck forced a smile. "Elaborate. State-of-the-art."

The man grunted again. "An impossible one?"

"A challenging one. But I advise against tomorrow night."

"Are you threatening me, Petzold? My only challenge is to get the Rembrandt to you at the Opera House after the concert."

"Not there. Have it delivered to me at my hotel, the day after tomorrow. I'll take it from there." *Hidden between Kerina's lovely gowns as we pass through customs at Moscow.*

"You are certain this McClaren will be occupied at the Opera House tomorrow evening?" Jokhar asked.

"He never misses Kerina's concerts when she's in Vienna. He has a private loge. And after the concert, the McClarens have asked Kerina and me to have dinner with them. That will keep them occupied until well past midnight."

"Perfect," Jokhar said, and he led the way inside the Italianate building and up the imposing stairway to the Second Gallery.

~

Later that afternoon, Kerina sat in the examining room, grasping the sheet draped over her as the physician studied her chart. As he turned to her with a benevolent smile, she focused on his narrow face where a ridge of worry lines tugged at his mouth.

"Miss Rudzinski, I can give you something to calm the cough—and a shot to relieve the shoulder pain. This should see you through the concerts at the Opera House. But I think you know you have a more serious problem."

Kerina nodded slowly as he said, "There's a mass in your left breast that must come out."

Her stomach tightened as she thought of the windowless delivery room where her son had been born. The utter loneliness, the hopelessness she had felt in that hospital. "Are you sure, Doctor?"

"I never make mistakes, Miss Rudzinski."

He seemed as cold as the metal chart he held in his hand. *You are acting like I am nothing but a number,* she thought. *A nameless person like I was in Everdale.*

She allowed her finger to touch the lump. *What if my arm is affected? What if it takes a mutilating surgery to remove the breast lump?*

"I'll have my nurse schedule a mammogram and a CAT scan on that shoulder—but even without these, I am certain you will need surgery."

"I am committed to a concert schedule—"

He smiled patiently. "We must move quickly to rule out a malignancy or the possibility of a slow-growing bone tumor in that shoulder." He consulted Kerina's chart. "I see there is no history of cancer in your family. That is in your favor."

You're talking about me. About my body. About my breast. She cut off his argument. "I have told you I cannot schedule anything right now."

She would deal with it later. She hated hospitals. Hated doctors prying into her life. A wave of nausea gripped her as she remembered the hospital in Everdale. The starchy professionalism. The silent condemnation. The doctor barking his orders and only once calling her by name. Maybe the breast lump was there for a purpose, divine retribution of some sort. Who was she to fight the dictates of nature?

She slipped from the examining table and stood there, clutching her drape around her.

His patience waned. "The biopsy is a simple procedure—"

"Later. I'll schedule any surgery later—back in Prague with my family physician." *With someone I trust.*

He stood there—his pen poised. "I'll send him my report. When will you be there?"

"In November, after my concert tour in America."

His exasperation broke. "Miss Rudzinski, five months is too long to wait. You could have a malignancy. You're risking your life. Music can't be that important."

"Music is my life."

"It is your life that I am trying to protect."

Kerina needed time to think rationally. She didn't need a biopsy or this surgeon to tell her there was a breast lump, its tentacles possibly spreading like spiderwebs to her lymph nodes. And that shoulder pain was real. More than a muscle spasm. The last few days her throbbing shoulder had made it difficult to hold her violin through long hours of practice. The doctor's words were ominous, but no darker than her fears. Kerina knew chemotherapy or radiation would follow any cancer surgery—and if surgery involved her shoulder and chest muscles, her bow arm could be damaged and useless in the future.

Her thoughts raced ahead to her fans—to the humiliation of hair loss. How could she accept baldness from chemotherapy, no matter how temporary? She had to wait until after the visit to Everdale; then she would fly home to Prague for a second opinion. No matter what happened, she could never give up her music. She had let Bill go and walked away from his child, but she could not endure that kind of agony again.

Chapter 11

As Jillian stood on the bank of the Danube, the fabled river seemed to stretch like a dull, greige fabric between the banks. Its waters were a murky gray this morning with only a murmur of blue to them; a fine, feathery mist swirled above the surface like the steam clouds on a mountain peak. As the day grew brighter, the grayness would catch reflections of the sky, and then the poet within her would see the waters as a hyacinth blue like a spring flower or as swirling pools of chambray. The rhythm of the river flowed like an unfinished symphony toward its final destination. Barges cut the waters, heading away from Vienna. She ached to go with them, to chart a new course or to find her way back to glamorous Paris or even rain-drenched London on the Thames.

Plucking a pebble from the ground, she tossed it. It dipped beneath the surface sending ripples along the embankment, little stirrings like she felt inside. For six months, she had sent her reports into the Coventry Art Theft Registry to keep Brooks Rankin appraised of Kerina's schedule. Jillian's suspicions no longer pointed to Kerina, but the more she defended her, the more she fell into disfavor with Brooks. He insisted that Kerina was behind what he called the concert conspiracy. He was like a bulldog gnarling over a well-chewed bone, snapping at anyone who differed with him.

As she made her way back up the embankment, she wished that she were meeting her dad at the coffeehouse instead of Brooks. Her father rarely told her what to do—he'd given up on that one! But she could count on him to listen to her. She felt somewhat cheered just thinking about him as she entered the smoky coffeehouse and made her way to an empty table by the window. After ordering, her thoughts raced back to her dad. She measured all men by him: Franck Petzold, Brooks Rankin, and the apron-clad waiter only came ankle high.

"It's the eyes," her dad had often told her. *"Hold the plumbline to a man's eyes. They are the window to what he is really made of."*

Her dad's eyes were a brilliant blue like her own, filled with warmth and rollicking good humor whenever they met for dinner in Paris or London or at the European racetracks. Between races, he expounded on the evils of the world and politics, pulling from memory his mother's fire-brand lectures. Theodore Ingram took his own sins lightly, counting on his political prowess and hard work to carry him through, but he warned Jillian against piling up sins of her own. He considered the racetrack a proper setting for teaching her what little he knew about God.

"After all," he reminded her once as the thoroughbreds had raced past them, *"there goes one of God's greatest creations."*

She had placed a bet on a horse three or four times from the sheer anticipated pleasure of having an opening line in her letter home. But more often she took refuge in one of the cathedrals of Europe to hash out the sin questions. She felt better for having done so, but she was uncertain of her own standing with God. She was convinced that He kept accounts, but she was not sure how the record stacked against her.

She started in on her *mohnstrudel* and mocha. Brooks was already late, reminding her of Santos. She still felt the singe marks from that fruitless romance in Rome two years ago. But she planned to marry when the right man came along. She wouldn't mind at all if he came a bit like her dad— tall and good-looking in a new Rolls Royce, someone who would literally sweep her off her feet; she wanted the man she married to be faithful, more single-minded than Santos had been.

She was two-thirds through her strudel when Brooks came puffing into the café, annoyingly late, his blowzy face bloated and red. He collapsed into the seat across from her, dropping like an overloaded sandbag. He was an obese forty-year-old with a rotund abdomen and heavy jowls. He snatched a piece of strudel from her plate and stuffed it into his mouth.

"We'll order more," he said, his mouth full.

"None for me, Brooks."

"For me then."

Surprisingly his hands were smooth and undimpled as he folded them on the tabletop and demanded of the waiter, "Black coffee and three pieces of strudel, please."

His eyes, his strongest feature, were perceptive as he checked out the room. "I have a man coming from our Los Angeles office. But Joel Gramdino won't like this crowded place one bit."

Outside, the Danube played its own whispering music. Joel Gramdino, Jillian decided, would find the coffeehouse quaint, the coffee extraordinary, and the river glorious.

"Brooks, we can chat here for hours, undisturbed. Talking politics or art theft won't even bother our neighbors. That's why we're here, isn't it?

To discuss Kerina and art and politics?"

"Why else would I fly over from London? This is Miss Rudzinski's second time back into Vienna in a short period of time. That's the pattern—that's when the thefts happen."

She disliked defending Kerina over strudel and coffee. But common sense told her that another art theft was possible. Loyalty forced her to deny it. "Kerina is not a common thief," she said.

"I'm only interested in the concert thefts. And her concert tours tie in with the statistics. She's a clever thief—plans the robberies in conjunction with her performances."

She and Brooks had been at odds from the beginning, a total surprise to Jillian, who liked people and could number her enemies on one hand, three fingers down. How brazen she had been when she had first burst into the Coventry Art Theft Registry with her perfect seven-point plan for tracking down stolen art: Know the art world, she had cut her teeth on art since she was a child. Keep contacts with the art dealers on the European scene—she knew two middle men on the Black Market, more useful to her out of prison. Recognize authenticity, suspect frauds. Acquaint yourself with the brush strokes and colors of a given artist and know the paint media he used. Trust your instincts.

Brooks stirred. "There's Joel Gramdino now."

He directed his wave toward a lanky American in jeans and a yellow sweater barreling his way toward their table. His arrogant stride annoyed her. So did his greeting.

"Hi, sweetheart. Looks like we'll be working together."

When he took the chair beside her, however, his eyes were not flirtatious but warm and kind. She knew in that instant Gramdino was a likely confidant, someone who would not destroy Kerina's career without knowing the truth.

"I was afraid you didn't get my message," Brooks said.

"Didn't get to the hotel until an hour ago."

"Then you didn't oversleep?"

"No sleep at all," Gramdino said cheerfully. "Couldn't doze on the plane, and once the plane touched down, I caught a taxi to the Academy of Fine Arts. The curator gave me a special tour before they opened the museum. Met Elias McClaren before I left."

Brooks ran his stubby fingers through his tufts of frowzy hair. "So what do you think? Is the McClaren exhibit safe?"

"No one in his right mind will touch that security system."

"So you don't expect trouble tomorrow night?"

"I'm expecting it, but not at the museum—so I promised McClaren that we could put a double guard on his home."

Brooks Rankin steamed. "Who's in charge here? We can't afford to protect all the art collectors with season tickets to the Opera House. We don't even know where the thief will strike next."

"Better to safeguard the collections than to search for stolen art. But cheer up, Rankin. In time our work will pay off." Joel turned to Jillian. "Our thief has good taste. A portrait by Joseph of Derby. A candelabra from the Nazi trove at Weimar. A black-and-white drawing by Michelangelo. And a landscape straight off the wall at Boston's Isabella Stewart Museum. Left a faded spot on the wall where it used to hang."

"And McClaren's valuable Rembrandt," Brooks mumbled.

Joel leaned back in his chair and smiled. "Tell me about you, Jillie. Brooks tells me you know the European scene."

She relaxed a little. "I should. Dad's career with the State Department allowed us to live abroad most of my life. I grew up browsing in art museums and sitting through glorious concerts—part of Mother's developmental program for her only daughter. I was lucky. Even did my university studies in Rome and Paris." She grinned at the surprise on Gramdino's face. "From Dad I learned about horse races and polo, from Mom an appreciation for the world of art and music. I admit it's a vagabond existence, but I have my father's traveling spirit. I only need a twenty-minute warning to pack up and catch a plane to somewhere new."

Joel took three sips of coffee. "And Brooks tells me you're a fair musician in your own right."

She liked his casual way of prying. "You could call it that. I learned the cello after a few effective swats on the bumpkin."

"Ouch," he said.

"It was okay. I practiced my music lessons in exchange for free ski trips to Switzerland and Italy. My language skills came in handy on the slopes. I'm really good in Italian."

Joel cocked his head. "I only know the Brooklyn version."

As they talked, Brooks ordered another cut of strudel. He looked sullen, the way he had the day Jillian sashayed into the Registry for her first interview. She had arrived fresh from a year at a university in Rome—the perfect measurements in a fashionable Italian suit. She gave him a courteous nod when they were introduced, but her side glance had taken in his size as too heavy; the state of his breathing as labored; and his facial scowl as directed at her. His art credentials were flawless, but she hadn't looked forward to working with him.

"No matter what Brooks tells you, Joel, I can handle any assignment the Registry throws at me."

"Except this one with the concert violinist?"

Her gaze lowered. She wanted to salvage her pride. "I didn't count on my friendship with Kerina."

"Trust me, Jillie. We've followed this concert conspiracy for seven years. If the statistics are correct, we can expect another theft to occur while Miss Rudzinski is in concert. So far the loss runs into the millions." He looked up from the report. "The thefts usually occur on her second visit to the city. It happened that way in Milan and Paris and Monaco. It happened in London at the Tate Gallery. And once in La Paz. Twice in New York. On Miss Rudzinski's last tour in the States, we had a theft at the Dorothy Chambers Pavilion in Los Angeles."

Rankins rasped, "It's one masterpiece at a time."

Joel's high brows arched above his bright eyes. "What Brooks insists on calling the concert conspiracy, I choose to call the Strauss Waltz." The corners of his wide mouth curled in a smile. "She plays a Strauss waltz and a painting disappears. So far we can't prove it. But there's a link somehow—a signal to the thief maybe. In the last three years, there was an occasional break in the pattern—like those times in Budapest and Rio de Janeiro."

"Break," Rankin scoffed. "The thief got bolder and got away with two paintings and laughed all the way to the Black Market."

Gramdino offset Rankin's harshness, saying, "Jillie, you know our Registry has twenty-four information centers around the world all linked to our central computer system in London. We're tapped into Interpol, sharing information. We'd be informed the moment something sold on the Black Market or went under the gavel at an auction house. So far none of the missing pieces have shown up."

Brooks shot back, "Rudzinski is masterminding this."

Gramdino stretched his long arms in a relaxed, unhurried motion. "This is where Brooks and I differ. I believe we have a thief who works alone, then uses other innocent victims to transport the stolen masterpieces." Joel took his pen and sketched a picture on the notes in front of him. "This is not an ordinary thief. No, we have a much more sophisticated gentleman, a nonviolent person. A modern day buccaneer in a tailored suit who moves in high society and makes friends with art collectors and museum personnel. Do you know anyone like that, Jillie?"

He went on sketching, his strokes sharp, definite. "He's unattached, most likely. He could not risk a wife or children betraying him." He squinted at his drawing and added another line or two and then looked up, his gaze meeting Jillian's across the table. "You may know the man and not know that you've met him."

Her voice wavered. "Do you have someone in mind, Joel?"

"Do you?"

Her thoughts fled unwillingly to Franck Petzold, who spent his free time in art museums and flying to Moscow. *A shrewd opportunist. Cunning. Resourceful. But a thief, a modern-day buccaneer? Not Franck. He is not daring or clever enough.*

Joel held up his sketch, a silhouette in black ink of a stately, well-dressed man. "Well?"

"He's faceless."

He winked at her. "But I think we have the profile of a man who loves art as you do. And steals something that will give him great pleasure in the privacy of his own home. Not a con artist."

Abruptly he said, "Many of these treasures once hung in the homes of the wealthy Jews of Europe." He scratched his nose with his uncapped pen. "Hundreds of them were probably stolen during Nazi occupation. Elias McClaren may have purchased a number of these at auction sales."

Brooks' leathery face tightened. "A VanStryker for one, but we can't confirm that without access to his paintings. McClaren and Miss Rudzinski's manager are close friends."

Gramdino said, "Jillie, do you have a problem with Miss Rudzinski's manager?"

She turned scarlet. "A personal one. I don't like him, but I doubt that he's a thief."

He nodded, not pressing her further. "Can you get me a copy of tomorrow's concert program? I must know if Miss Rudzinski has scheduled a Strauss waltz. That could be her signal—and if not one deliberately given, then one used by a very clever thief."

Bridling, Jillian nodded. "Strauss is one of her favorite composers. Of course she plays his music—especially in Vienna."

Joel referred to the list in his hands again. "Rudzinski is just back from concerts in Passau and Budapest. After Vienna, she goes to Salzburg and then to Milan for a three-day engagement at the La Scala. And in the fall she leaves for the States."

"I know her schedule. I arranged it. So put padlocks on the Metropolitan

Museum and the Getty Museum when she's in town."

"The police departments in New York City and Los Angeles have special teams to deal with art theft. We'll alert them when Rudzinski is scheduled in their cities. But if her schedule changes unexpectedly, we need to know."

Jillian felt color drain from her face. "Her manager just arranged a brief visit to Moscow before the Salzburg concert."

"Immediately after Vienna?" Rankin snapped. "She could be fencing another painting in Moscow."

"Nothing has been stolen yet," Jillian reminded him.

"Jillian, I'm pulling you off the case now."

"Don't do that. Kerina needs me. I promised her six more months of my service. I intend to keep that promise."

"And if we pull you off the case today?"

In view of her mounting frustration, she was surprised at the calm in her voice. "Then you would leave me no choice but to resign, effective immediately."

∽

As Jillian and Gramdino left the coffeehouse together, she glanced at her watch, her face still flushed with anger.

"Expecting someone?" he asked.

She hesitated, then feeling those kind eyes on her, said, "An army officer from Bosnia is due in this afternoon. A music critic. He has an appointment to interview Kerina."

"All the way from Bosnia? You have the strangest friends." He laughed as he flipped open a pocket notebook. "Let me have his name as well as any staff member working with Miss Rudzinski."

"You're putting the American soldier on your suspect list?" She felt flustered under that steady gaze. "Chandler Reynolds. If you want to see him, I'm scheduled to meet him in the lobby of the Opera House tomorrow evening to give him his loge tickets."

"Expensive seating for a soldier boy?"

"Kerina's orders. She always goes first class."

As he flicked loose strands of hair from his forehead, she thought again, *You are much younger than your silver hair indicates. Much kinder than Brooks imagines.*

"Does she do that often? Give tickets away?"

"She's very generous."

"I see," he said, and she wondered if he did.

115

Chapter 12

Ashley Reynolds checked into the Empress Isle Hotel hours before Chandler was due to arrive. Even with jet lag, she marveled at the opulent good taste in the nineteenth-century furnishings and the personal attention from the staff. The maids and the concierge, the desk clerks and the uniformed bell porters smiled pleasantly as they moved over the carpeted lobby on their soundless leather soles. She chose to walk the palatial cascade of steps rather than ride up to the third floor in the lift. Walking, she heard the music of great composers wafting through the halls and had time to gaze up at the lavish Impressionist paintings that hung on the walls: Monet, Pissarro, Auguste Renoir. The hotel was impressive and expensive and typical of her mother-in-law's lavish spending.

The bell porter led her into a capacious room with elegance beyond her imagination: a massive canopy bed, a golden oak desk where she could write to David, and a bathroom in sienna marble. Her suite was joined to the one Chandler would have, both rooms more elaborate and ornate than any hotel where she and David had stayed, even on their honeymoon.

Emptying her suitcase took forever. She stopped to glance out the windows at Vienna. Paused to run her fingers over the shiny oak bedstead. And just now she had called down to the main desk for the third time to ask whether her son had arrived.

"No. Lieutenant Revnolds has not checked in yet."

She went back to her unpacking, shook out her last garment and hung it in the spacious closet before toeing the suitcases out of sight. Reveling in the music of Mozart being piped into her room, she waltzed to the glass door, slid it back, and stepped out on the private patio. In the distance, St. Stephen's Cathedral rose from the center of Vienna, its tiled roof and tall spire brilliant in the sun.

Now she had time to worry about Chandler. She wondered if he had missed his plane. Weather would not hold him back. The clear Vienna sky was alive with fleecy clouds, puffs of white framed in the azure blue. In her childhood she had spent hours imagining the circles and polygons of the sky to be clown faces or snowmen or marbled statues napping on their backs. Now she played the childhood game again—seeing a clown face to her left, a ship with smoke stacks behind it. Another swirling mass of clouds looked like the back of David's head, his familiar face turned from her. Like the clouds, she and David were drifting apart, her secret still building a wedge between them. David thought it was Bill and Chandler. Ashley knew better.

The thick cloud swept closer, the face in her mind vivid now. It was no longer the back of David's head. It was Bill's attractive face laughing at her. How much she had loved him. He had been part of her life, part of her family. Part of her pain. How could she break through God's canopy for answers where there were none? Everything in her life was being blown away, her marriage threatened, her faith crumbling.

She was here in one of her favorite European cities with the glory of Vienna all around her—the past with its magnificent Hapsburg Empire, the present with its charming coffeehouses. But all she could think about was that day in her garden. She remembered the heat. The persistent ring of the telephone. The mad dash to reach it before the answering machine kicked in. And then Chandler's deep voice dancing over the wires.

She still heard the ring. No, it was the phone in her hotel room. She fled back inside and grabbed it. "Güten Tag."

A polite voice came back. "Frau Reynolds, this is the reception desk. Lieutenant Reynolds has arrived. He insisted on going straight up to your room."

Frazzled, she ran her hand through her hair. Not Bill coming out of her past but Chandler. She stood up straight and tall.

"It's all right," she said softly. "He's my son."

~

Ashley ran with lightning speed down the corridor to the stairwell and leaned over the hand-carved banister. Chandler had reached the first landing, his polished black boots echoless against the red carpeted steps. Her son was here safe in Vienna. Alive. Coming up to meet her. She felt enormous relief at just seeing the back of his finely shaped head, his dark hair cropped to military regulations. As short as it was, it looked a gleaming red-brown in the light of the crystal chandelier that hung above the landing. Reddish-brown like Kerina Rudzinski's.

It didn't matter as long as he was here. Pride filled her heart. As always, Chandler was straight-backed, his army olive greens trim against those strong shoulders and narrow hips. His visor cap was tucked securely in the crook of his arm. He reached out to grip the rail, propelling himself forward. He was limping.

As he reached the second landing, he looked up and saw her. Suddenly his solemn face was bathed in a warm smile. "Mom. Hi!"

She waved. "Hi, yourself."

A young couple going down the stairs moved aside to let him rush by them. As he came, double-time now, he grabbed the railing and visibly tugged himself forward.

He's favoring that leg, she thought, *limping the way Bill limped after his injury in the navy.* Bill had been a demonstrative man, but not Chandler. Chandler bear-hugged his grandmother but was standoffish with the rest of them, nursing the dark void that he sometimes felt inside.

"Something's missing in my life, and I don't even know what it is," he had told them.

Ashley knew. Perhaps her son would find his answers here in Vienna. But then the void would become hers. Once told, would Chandler ever forgive her for withholding the truth from him?

It had seemed such a simple promise when he was born.

"Don't ever tell him he was adopted," Kerry Rudzinski had begged. *"I could not bear it if he knew that I deserted him."*

Ashley braced herself, her gaze on his handsome face as she waited for him to make a move.

He stood steps from her, yet towering above her on those lanky legs. "I was afraid you wouldn't be here, Mom."

"And I was afraid you'd miss your flight out of Bosnia."

"I would have walked." He sounded like he meant it.

"Over land and sea—on that leg of yours?"

He tapped his thigh. "We'll talk about it later. Okay?"

He looked so different in uniform, his First Lieutenant bars shining on his epaulets. More mature and yet the same. Older and yet boyish. Striking and yet sad. She longed to wrap her arms around him—this son, this stranger in front of her. His face seemed thinner, making his Grecian-like features prominent. His shadowed eyes were hollow, deeper than she remembered them.

"Chandler, are you going to give me a proper hello?" she murmured. "I've been waiting for your hug for hours."

He opened his arms. "Mom," he said huskily.

The word flew airborne, straight-arrowed into her heart. She soared the three steps to him on that marvelous word and felt a surge of joy as her son's strong arms engulfed her. She stepped back laughing. "I've missed you, son. I'm so glad you're here. Why didn't you tell us you were hurt?"

"I didn't want to worry you."

"We worry anyway."

"I thought Dad preached against that."

"I don't. So you can tell me what happened."

"Just an accident."

An accident that he doesn't want to talk about. She patted his arm. "You're certain you'll be all right?"

"Good as new in a few weeks."

"Okay. I can wait."

The corridor, empty just seconds ago, now filled with people. A family with three children. An older couple—the man with a cane. A bell porter stepping from the lift with a cart full of luggage. Guests hurrying to their rooms. Doors slamming. Strangers laughing.

"Where's your luggage?" She sounded distracted by practical things, desperate not to let him read her fears about his injury.

"You're looking at it."

She saw the army duffel, the smaller kit bag, and a pair of crutches. "Your crutches, Chandler?"

His dark brows arched. "We'll talk about them later."

"Are you supposed to be using them?"

"They help," he admitted, grinning. "But I didn't want you to see me using them until we had time to talk."

He slipped his arm around her shoulder, and they turned to follow the porter. "This is my room," she said, pushing the unlocked door open. "You're in the room next to mine."

Inside, he stared in disbelief. "What a swank place."

"It is ostentatious, isn't it?"

He pumped the mattress. "This should be army issue. A king-size bed instead of a bunk."

There were autumn colors in the spread and three pillows propped against the headboard. His gaze strayed to the painting by a Flemish artist. He walked over for a closer inspection. "That's a nice scene. I always liked autumn at home."

"It was even more lovely in the town where you were born."

His head turned sharply, surprise on his face. "Everdale?"

She could have bitten her tongue. "There was a lovely woods behind Mama's place. I don't suppose you remember that?"

"Hardly. You scooped me out of there before I was three. But deer used to come through the woods to the edge of our property."

"You remember that?"

"That and not much else."

He prowled, looking at everything. Her suite had it all—an ivory soaking tub, a dressing alcove, a mirrored dresser, a bar she didn't need, a giant television she probably wouldn't turn on, and a patio with its marvelous view of Vienna.

They began their old word game. "It is grand, Mom."

"Elegant."

"Grams knows the way to go. Top hat—Chesterfieldian all the way." He laughed, but his eyes remained sad. "Army quarters were never like this." He flopped on the bed and stretched out, shoving two pillows beneath his injured leg. "All we need is a piano and Dad here so we could have a family songfest. Could even invite Grams to join us."

"Let's just leave your grandmother in Denver."

"So, things haven't improved between you two? What's the big deal, Mom? Did she have someone else picked out for her son?"

"Anyone else."

"You're the right choice for Dad as far as I'm concerned."

They talked nonstop now. "Seriously, how are Dad and Grams?"

Questions and answers back and forth for an hour. Ashley talked about planting snow flowers and glads in her garden and about David's busy schedule. Chandler asked about the new neighbors and her last days as a nurse. She admitted to tears the day she quit.

"I guessed as much when we talked on the phone."

She told him about spending her last paycheck on clothes. "I hung my new suit in the closet, waiting for just the right time to wear it, and your father knew it was there all along. He scolded me for not wearing it. Said he likes me to turn eyes."

"Dad was always pleased with how you looked."

Every time Ashley steered the conversation to Bosnia and army life, Chandler backed off or pounded the pillow to fit the curve of his neck. Finally she asked, "Chandler, what about that friend of yours from the university? Randolph. Randy something."

He'd been lying there with his arms behind his head. He sat up slowly and swung his legs over the side of the bed, his face turning ashen as he met her gaze. "Randy Williams."

"That's it. From Akron, Ohio, wasn't he?"

"He's dead."

It didn't sound like Chandler's voice. It didn't look like him. For a few seconds it seemed like he was chiseled from plutonic rock, his face harsh, unmovable, and then rage and pain flicked in his eyes.

"When?...What happened?"

He looked away and blinked. *He's not a little boy now,* she told herself. *You can't gather him in your arms and kiss away the hurts. Just listen to him.*

As she listened, he said, "Six weeks ago Randy stepped on a land mine. It was quick. He didn't suffer, Mother."

"He was only a boy."

"My age. Twenty-six. A grown man."

She accepted his rebuke without flinching. *Shall I keep questioning him?* she wondered. *Yes, don't let him escape into a pit of despair. Hear him out. Don't let him be like David now; David would want him to handle it like a man.*

Men should cry, she thought. *My son should be free to cry if he wants.* She imagined that he had not cried yet—that he had not fully admitted Randy was dead.

~

Chandler ran his thumb over his knuckles. He hadn't intended to tell his mother about Randy. This was to be a month in which he wiped the pain from his mind and heard only music and laughter. How could he have been so foolish?

He imagined her in her nurse's uniform, sitting by a patient's bedside, just listening as she was doing now. Waiting for him to crack emotionally like the doctors had waited. *Everyone is waiting for signs of my falling apart because my best friend is dead.* He glanced beyond her to the autumn painting. The storm clouds in the picture were billowing through the sky, ready to rain their fury down on him.

"Chan, did they send Randy's body back to Akron for burial?"

His body, Mom? "No, just his casket."

If she caught his meaning, she gave no indication. Softly she asked, "Why didn't you tell us? Your father and I would gladly have flown to Akron to be with them, to comfort them."

No, he thought. *Dad would have talked of heaven and peace. Of sin and salvation. Do you call it sin when a man drops on a mine and saves your life?* he wondered. Aloud he said, "It wouldn't have worked out...you and Dad going there. I don't know about his parents, but Randy was never a very religious fellow."

"All the more reason for us to show them we cared. His parents lost a son, Chandler."

And I lost a friend. Yes, you would have shown them love—the nurse in you going up to total strangers and wrapping your arms around them. "Maybe when you get home you could call them?"

"I will if you'll give me the address."

"As soon as I unpack." He hesitated. "Mom, if Dad is right—if there is a heaven and hell—"

"If he's right?"

Chandler ignored her, repeating, "If Dad is right, then I blew it with Randy. When he saw the rubble and devastation in Bosnia, he asked me where God was when the Serbs and Croats were killing each other."

He loosened the top button of his army shirt. "Randy always razzed me about being a preacher's kid. Said it was easy for me to swallow all that religious stuff. I didn't want to argue with my best friend, not when he kept telling me he had plenty of time to think about God when he got out of the army."

"Don't blame yourself, Chandler."

"Who else then?" He wiped the back of his hand across his mouth. "Randy died for me, Mom. Died in my place. Not on some cross. But in a way Bosnia was like Golgotha for both of us. We weren't in that country for the long war, or in the thick of the siege and ethnic cleansing. But in a way getting to war-torn Bosnia was like reaching hell after the long battle."

He expected her to scold him for being irreverent. But she understood. She leaned forward and put her hand gently on his arm. "You were there? You saw it happen? That's what you meant when you said he died for you. Is that when you were injured?"

The tears he had fought off for weeks burned behind his eyelids. "I still see him, Mom. He was running toward me when that cocky look came across his face—as though he knew what was happening—as though he were saying, 'Chandler, this one's on me. This is for you, buddy.' And then his foot came down and he fell forward on the mine and took the brunt of the explosion."

Her eyes coaxed him to trust her. He felt swallowed up by her love. She was not making excuses. Not saying it was Randy's time to go. Not mouthing that time was the great healer.

"Chan," she whispered, "I am so sorry."

"But I'll be all right?" *When I can sleep again. When I can stop blaming myself. When I can stop seeing Randy blown to bits.* He sighed. "I never meant to burden you with this."

"That's what mothers are for. I'm here for you. We have a month to sort out all that's happened. What's happened won't just fade away." She studied the rings on her finger, then looked up. "I knew something was wrong when you called us. I couldn't believe the army would drop a leave in your lap for nothing."

"It's a medical pass," he admitted.

"And not just for the leg?"

He gave his knuckles another jab. He would not have to pretend with her, but he would have to explain Zineta Hovic before his mom flew home. *Later! We can deal with that later.*

She grabbed his attention, asking, "Will we have time for everything? A concert in the park? St. Stephen's? The palace?"

"Everything." A month sounded like forever.

"Chandler, can we cruise the Danube?"

"Why not?" he asked lightly. "We can catch a riverboat from Vienna to Budapest and Kalocsa."

"That would be too expensive."

"You're worth it. I'll even go shopping with you on the Karntner Strasse. You can blow your traveler's checks on clothes."

Her brows arched. "I had one spending spree when I retired. I brought a suitcase full of new clothes. You won't recognize me."

"I'll be proud of you."

She tilted her head and studied him. "I wish you had someone young and beautiful to take around Vienna."

He stood and gave her a quick hug. "I do. You."

"Chandler, on the phone you mentioned a girl in Bosnia."

"Did I?"

"You know that you did. Is she off-limits right now?"

He thought about it. "No, I just didn't know when to mention her. Her name is Zineta Hovic. She was Randy's friend."

"Randy's girlfriend?" He heard surprise in her voice, more uncertainty as she asked, "Does she know what happened to him?"

"I'm afraid so."

"And now?" she asked guardedly.

"Now I'm free to marry Zineta." He ran his thumb across his dry lips. "As I told you on the phone, Mom, she's pregnant."

Ashley had taken the death of Randy calmly for his sake, but the girl's pregnancy touched a raw spot in his mother; the expression in her eyes was one of deep pain. "Chandler, are you—are you in love with her?"

"Don't worry, Mom. You'll like her."

Her voice sounded strained. "Will Dad?"

"Dad isn't planning to marry her."

"Oh Chandler, why didn't you wait? That poor girl. . ."

"It's not my baby, Mother; it's Randy's."

She twisted her rings. "Then why are you marrying her?"

"Randy's child deserves more than a war-ravaged village. But let's not argue. That's between Zineta and me." He pivoted on his good leg and headed for the door between their rooms.

"Do Randy's parents know about the baby, Chan?"

He glanced back. "I don't even know if Randy knew."

"They've lost their only son. They have a right to know about their grandchild. Aren't you going to tell them?"

He flexed his jaw as though it had frozen in place. "I'd better unpack. I'll have to buy some civvies tomorrow."

"No need. Your dad sent some of your good clothes with me. They're in your room."

"Great. But I'll need a tuxedo tomorrow at the concert."

"The concierge made an appointment for a fitting in the morning."

"Great." He paused in the doorway. "I wish Dad had come."

"There wasn't time to rearrange his schedule."

"I just wish his schedule included me."

A frown shadowed her lovely face. "I thought we weren't going to let anything spoil our time in Vienna, Chandler."

"You win." *But something's going on back home.* "Is everything okay between you and Dad?"

"Nothing that a little separation won't cure."

"He's not still mad about Juilliard?"

"Don't blame yourself for problems back home. Your dad is busy, that's all. Too busy."

"But he always found time for trips up to Arrowhead. I used to resent the two of you going off like that. I hated it when you left me home with Grams. I figured you didn't need me—or want me."

"We always wanted you, Chandler. But sometimes we needed to be alone. We still do."

"You know what? When I was a kid I dreamed of growing up and marrying someone I loved as much as Dad loved you."

"That's sweet."

She was chewing her lower lip, looking as though she would burst into tears. He couldn't let her do that. They had just weathered his news about Randy and Zineta. The slate was clear.

Still he said, "You sure nothing's wrong? I'd hate to be the one who came between you two. For whatever reason."

"Your father loves you, Chandler."

"*I know.*" *But does he still love you?* he wondered. *And if he doesn't, what right does he have to stand behind a pulpit? His whole message would be a lie.*

He started to ask if she had packed his birth certificate and transcripts, but there would be time enough to discuss his future later. "Give me fifteen minutes to shower and change, then we'll go out to dinner."

"I'd like that." Before he could protest she added, "Your father insists that I pay for all the meals. We'll cash some of my traveler's checks at the desk. You pocket the money."

He looked relieved. "I'll pay you back."

"In your civilian life? No. Our turn now. Your dad insists."

As he walked into his room, he called over his shoulder, "We should call Dad when we get back from dinner."

Her answer trailed after him. "Yes, we'd better do that. He'll be sitting up in his study waiting for the phone to ring. Or maybe we should just wait until morning."

He found his gear beside the bed where the porter had left it. He unzipped the duffel, grabbed his clothes, and started to strip down as he headed for the shower. He had the funny feeling that calling home was the last thing his mother wanted to do.

～

Fifteen minutes later Ashley slipped the pierced earring into the lobe of her ear and walked into Chandler's room. She winced at the sight of the crutches leaning against the foot of the bed, the reminder of what had happened to him in Bosnia.

She tried to visualize David standing in this room with her, his face turning purple at the casual way in which Chandler had spoken of his intention to marry a girl pregnant with another man's child. In the clash of words that would pass between them, David would say, "A marriage of convenience? I won't hear of it. You don't love her. You can't marry her out of duty to a friend."

Ashley knew what Chandler would answer. "My decision, Dad. And she has a name. Zineta Hovic. Remember that."

When had they drawn apart—these two who had been such buddies? Friends. Father and son. Inseparable. Until when?

Oh David, Chandler's friend is dead, but miracle of miracles, your son is alive. He needs you to weep with him. To sit and grieve with him. And if Chandler insists—to join him in marriage to the girl from Bosnia. Right or wrong, it is not our decision. We need to help him pick up the shattered pieces of his faith. But how can I when I am struggling with my own flaws, my own faith?

She braced herself against the doorjamb, her nerve endings all shouting at once. She would have to tell him the truth. But how could she tell her son that they had deceived him for twenty-six years? Behind the bathroom door, the shower water thundered against the glass. The floor would be sopping wet, and Chandler's towels dropped in the puddle.

What would she say as he came through the door? "Sit down, son, I have something to tell you. No, no, this is not about the mess in the bathroom. This is something that will fill the aching void you have inside. Something that may turn you against your father and me."

She groped vainly for words to describe his birth parents to him. Parents he did not know existed. "Oh Chandler, you have your father's wide, pensive eyes. Your mother's gentle smile, her musical talent. But I see David's strengths in you, too. And mine. You are our son as well."

Once started, she would say, "Look in the mirror. You are very much your birth father's son, but it is too late to know him. Your father made many mistakes—a long trail of pain that I have never forgiven. But he did one good thing, Chandler, one act of trying to right all his wrongs when he chose a country house for you to grow up in before he drove away. Whatever you do, don't ask me if he ever held you in his arms. As sensitive as you are, Chandler, you will feel that rejection."

Ashley rubbed her hands together. Would she have the courage to face her son with the truth as he came through the door, or should she wait until they came back from dinner? Wait until the midnight hour and say, "I have something to confess to you—"

She imagined Chandler too stunned to repeat the word *adopted*. She pictured him wide-eyed, disbelieving, as she said, "Try to understand. You were born to a frightened nineteen-year-old. To a successful concert violinist from Prague. She was young and beautiful. I was there at the hospital nursery when your mother held you for the last time and said good-bye. I know that she loved you. I told her it was not too late to change her mind, even knowing if she did, my heart would break. Your father and I wanted a son. We wanted you."

Ashley didn't want to go to the Opera House the following evening and give Kerina Rudzinski a standing ovation. She wanted to turn to the audience and tell them, "This is the woman who gave her son away. What right does she have to him now?"

Her vengeance startled her. "Why am I so vindictive when my own sins lie hidden just beneath the surface?"

Above the erratic thumping of her own heart, Ashley heard the shower water still running and smiled through her tears at the trail of clothes dropped on the thick red carpet. Chandler had left the regimentation of army life and slipped back in time to the carefree, careless days of his boyhood and the clutter that he always left behind. His boyhood belonged to Ashley and David, not to Kerina or the father who gave him away.

"But who does he belong to now, God?" she whispered. "Tell me quickly before I face him again."

She knew the answer, felt it tugging at her heart. Chandler belonged to himself. To God. *Let him go, Ashley. Let him go,* she cautioned herself.

She strained to hear above the sound of water and her heart raced with sudden gratitude. The problem was out of her hands. And Chandler was whistling, whistling as he turned off the shower.

Chapter 13

David swiveled in his soft leather chair, his eyes leaving the silent phone to stare out on Ashley's garden. Her flower beds were filled with brilliant colors—the cardinals and Dresden blues, the soft yellow petals on the roses. Brick paths wound around the yard past the neatly trimmed hedges and bushes. He pictured Ashley sitting on the white stone bench near the bird feeder, happily watching the humming-birds feed or the robins splash in the marble birdbath.

Through the open window, he heard the low-pitched cooing of a dove pruning its white-tipped feathers and mourning for its mate as he mourned for Ashley. His wife had been gone less than a day and he missed her desperately—missed her because of the unspoken words that lay between them. Worse were those words he could not retract. How had he dared accuse her of withholding the truth from their son? He'd been party to it for twenty-six years.

As he yanked at his tie, the top button of his shirt tore free and clattered on his desk. It rolled and then spun out as it hit the brochure of the Opera House in Vienna. The cover page featured the renowned Kerina Rudzinski, her exquisite eyes visible even in the brochure as he stared down at it.

Why did you ever come into our lives? he asked; then he laughed ironically. If she had not come, Chandler would never have been his son. *Yes, Kerina Rudzinski, I have you to thank for my son. Not the son of my loins, but no son could have brought me greater joy. So where did I go wrong? Where did I lose Chandler?*

Exhaustion frayed David's nerves. He imagined Ashley getting lost on her way to the Austrian hotel or Chandler missing the military flight out of Bosnia leaving her alone at the Empress Isle. Ashley had promised to call the minute Chandler arrived and still the phone was silent. He picked up the receiver to check for a dial tone and heard the annoying hum in his ear.

His gaze went back to Ashley's yard, her private world, and definitely off-limits whenever they quarreled. David respected her need for a private sanctuary, but he felt like an outcast barred from entry. He couldn't name the flowers growing there except for the roses and only recognized a gardenia by its smell.

He leaned forward and opened a louvered window, letting in that sweet fragrance. "Ashley. Ashley, I should hire someone to keep your garden weeded," he said aloud.

"Why, David?"

The voice was his mother's. He had forgotten her midnight arrival. She walked gracefully into his office, tightening the belt of her fleecy pink robe as she came, her pink slippers silent against the carpet. The aroma of her perfume grew stronger as she reached him, overpowering the scent of Ashley's gardenias.

"Why didn't you wake me? I told you I would cook breakfast."

He glanced at his desk clock. Almost ten. "I wasn't hungry."

His mother looked as though she had just stepped from the beauty salon. He imagined her bed unmade, her fragrances and hairbrushes scattered across the counter in the guest bathroom—every waking minute given to maintaining her perfect image. Not a strand of her salt-and-pepper hair strayed out of place. But he noticed more silver there now than on her last holiday visit and wondered why she had not dyed it.

"Why would you want a gardener?" she asked again. "Has Ashley left you, David?"

The room spun, his blood pressure surely spinning with it. His theology and archaeology books looked like they were ready to topple from their shelves. The overhead light faded in and out, and he thought vaguely that he would have to change the light globe but didn't know where Ashley kept the seventy-five-watt bulbs.

"David, does your silence mean she has finally left you?"

He fought down his anger. "You know she's with Chandler."

"Do I? When I went to bed last night—and I had to make up my own bed—you were sitting there. Right there at your desk waiting for her to call you from Vienna."

"I know."

"Obviously, you haven't heard from her yet. You look distraught—hair disheveled, face unshaven. You're waiting for something that may never happen."

David tented his fingers and rested his bristled chin against them. At times he found it difficult to think of her as the mother who had reared him through an easygoing boyhood and those tempestuous teen years. At the moment she reminded him more of one of the women in his congregation coming into the church office for counsel with complaints about marital discord. When he tried to point these women to the basic problem of the lust of the eye, they often stormed from his office. He imagined his mother doing the same if he ever confronted her with her sin nature. She tolerated his beliefs but would not accept them. She was a good woman, a good woman without a Savior. Still, for all their differences, he loved her.

But her descending on him without warning aggravated him. She had been at the house waiting when he drove back from LA International in a rainstorm. He had found her sitting in Ashley's chair, a *Vogue* magazine in her hands.

She had lowered the magazine and said, "Is Ashley gone?"

"Her plane left two hours ago. Did you fly into LA?"

"No, Orange County. I caught a taxi and let myself in."

"Why didn't you let me know you were coming?"

"I wanted to surprise you. With Ashley going off like that, you need someone to cook your meals and keep your shirts ironed."

He groaned. "I've survived on frozen dinners and eating out before. . . and Ashley sends my shirts to the laundry."

"That should be a wife's responsibility."

"You're old-fashioned," he said lightly, leaning down to kiss her proffered cheek.

"I did those things for your father for fifty years."

"I'm certain he was grateful, Mother." He kicked off his rain-sodden shoes. "If you'll excuse me, I'll run up and change. Since you think I need care, why don't you put the coffee on?"

"I already did. And I made some tuna sandwiches. Oh David, don't be sulky. I just wanted this time alone with you. You'll feel better about my coming in the morning."

She was wrong. He still felt annoyed at her coming.

"David, I thought you'd be off to work by now."

She had used that tone when he was a teenager. "You are not to see that girl again—whatever her name is."

Her name was Ashley, blond and wholesome looking, and David had fallen in love with her. He had gone to his grandparents' farm that long-ago summer, a disciplinary act on the part of his parents. "You'll be a farmhand for the summer," his father had told him. "A little honest work won't hurt you. Heaven only knows your grandparents could do with some muscle about the place."

David had flexed his biceps, mentally planning to leave the farm the minute he got there.

His mother had given her jabs as well. "Maybe it will be the making of you, David. Good preparation for going off to USC. At least it will get you away from those friends of yours." She had been on a spiel, adding, "With what it is costing your father and me, I just hope something good happens to you this summer."

Something did. Ashley happened to him.

He met his mother's gaze again. He felt responsible for her now that she was widowed, but he could not understand her lingering malice toward Ashley.

"Aren't you going to work, David?"

"I told my secretary I wouldn't be in this morning."

"You can do that as a pastor? And your university class?"

"Not until two today."

"Convenient." She sat, uninvited, in the chair across from him. "I haven't heard from Chandler since wiring the money for the hotel in Vienna. I assume the money arrived."

"You know that it did. He rarely writes letters."

"He rarely writes thank-yous. Ashley—"

"Ashley wrote thanking you, didn't she?"

"It was not the same as hearing from Chandler. I do so much for this family. Sometimes I wish you had waited for a child of your own. You deserved that, David."

"Chandler is a child of my own."

"David, you know what I mean. Instead of Ashley being in that delivery room as a nurse, she should have been there delivering your child. Not someone else's."

"That was impossible. Ashley couldn't conceive."

"Really? Sometimes I don't think you know Ashley at all."

"Ashley found Chandler for us."

"All wrapped up in a neat little package."

"I thought you and Chan were the greatest of friends."

His mother's face softened. "We are. But I can't help wishing he had been your son, David—our own flesh and blood."

He fought down his simmering rage. "From the day I held him in my arms he was my son, Mother. Surely you know that."

"Yes. Yes. I felt the same way the first time I held him. But, David, if we only knew who his parents really were."

"Ashley and I are his parents."

"I mean his birth parents, David. Can't you face the truth even now?" she asked. "Ashley comes home from the hospital at the end of her night shift and announces that you can adopt a baby. You knew nothing about the mother. Nothing about the father."

"We wanted that baby, Mother." He slid Kerina Rudzinski's brochure into his top desk drawer. "Chandler's birth mother was just a nice kid. A girl in trouble who wanted someone who would love her son. That's all she asked. That's what we did."

As Rosalyn Reynolds smiled, her lips parted, revealing her even, white teeth. "Yes, David, we have all loved him. But has it been fair to Chandler not to know that he was adopted? I would have told him the truth long ago. But tell him at this late date, and it will alienate him from all of us."

"The decision to tell him is not yours to make."

"You and Ashley made that quite apparent over the years. It didn't matter to your father. God rest his soul. But it matters to me. But to not know a thing about Chandler's parents—"

David knew the girl's name. He could take his mother to the very place where Chandler's birth father was. But the truth would only make her dislike Ashley more. He felt oddly detached, as though he were no longer talking to his mother. This person sitting across from him, judging him with her eyes, was someone who ran in social circles and spent her Sundays playing bridge or golfing, a woman who took pleasure in making the society page in Denver. At the moment they were like total strangers, yet it was his mother who had taken no part in the trail of lies that surrounded Chandler's roots. He was the pastor, Ashley was the pastor's wife, yet it was his mother—who believed in nothing beyond this life—who urged integrity. A woman who loved Chandler as her own grandson but who even now despised deceiving him.

He started to smile at her, to tell her he was glad she was on board for a few days. But as the smile formed at the corners of his mouth, she said, "I asked you moments ago—I'm going to ask you again. Has Ashley left you for good, David?"

"Is that what you want, Mother?"

"I want the best for you."

"My wife is my best—and my son."

"Oh David, it would take a blind person to miss how unhappy you and Ashley have been these last few months."

"We'll work it out."

"What if she goes away and influences Chandler to go with her? I will not be deprived of my only grandson, David."

"Moments ago you regretted that he wasn't your own bloodline. I have no control over what Chandler does. You should know that after these last three years in the army. He's even talking about reenlisting or staying on in Europe as a music critic."

"That sounds like you, David. You were always your own man."

"I was a disappointment to you, wasn't I?"

"To your father the sun rose and set on you, David."

"I never figured it that way. It was make the football squad or the basketball team. Make your old man proud of you," he mocked. "Any talk of college other than USC was out. Remember, Mother, it was law school or nothing if I wanted to please him."

"He was always proud of you."

"Even when I went off to seminary?"

"That was hard for him to take," she admitted. "But in the end, he was proud of you for standing up for what you wanted."

"I wish Dad had told me."

The midmorning sun beat against his back, coming in through the garden window and flooding the office with light. He had twelve hours until sundown, twelve hours to allow his anger at his mother to fester before he would have to be rid of his rage. As the sun touched her face, shadowed flecks of gray appeared in her eyes.

"David, do you ever tell Chandler how proud you are of him?"

The muscles along his jaw tightened. She was right. What his father had done to him, he had done in turn to Chandler. Pushing, cajoling, demanding that his son reach certain goals. David's goals. He had even taken the burden of choice for college from Chandler's shoulders. It would be David's alma mater or nothing.

"Mother, I had a thousand dreams for my son from that first day I held him in my arms."

"So like your father. Your dreams, David. Not Chandler's."

He nodded. "Chandler told me as much when we spoke on the phone last week. I exploded when he told me he was staying on in Europe as a music critic after the army. That's when he reminded me that a man has to find his own way."

"He really is like you, David. Almost like your own flesh and blood except for his love of music. He didn't get that from you." Her pupils widened, the emerald green in her eyes bright and shiny. "Ashley's brother was a music critic, wasn't he?"

She knows, he thought. "Ashley's brother was in business, investments mostly. He did music reviews in college, I think."

"I see."

Did she? She'd had twenty-six years to work out the puzzle.

"It was selfish on our part, David, but your father and I wanted so much for you. Dad wanted you to go into the law firm with him." Sadly, she said, "But once you met Ashley, the die was cast. She was all wrong for you—for us. The only good thing that came out of it was Chandler."

In spite of the hours she spent in front of the mirror, age lines framed his mother's eyes. The skin sawed at the hollow of her neck. As she sat facing him, her expression was proud—that same look of independence she had given him after his father's funeral. "Live with you and Ashley? Never. I'll make it on my own, David," she had told him. "I won't need a handout from my daughter-in-law. Good man that he was, your father has left me quite comfortable."

He tented his fingers again and rested his chin against them. "Why do you dislike my wife so, Mother?"

"I never said I disliked her, David."

"You can't be in the same room without showing your displeasure or correcting Ashley for something."

"It goes back a long time."

"Back to the summer I met her?"

"She was wrong for you. I told you that back then. How could Ashley and I be friends? We're from two separate worlds. You want the truth? Then let me tell you what I have known since the day you met her—she was never good enough for you, David Reynolds."

Mercifully the phone rang, taking with it the need to lash back. His fingered canopy collapsed as he grabbed the receiver. "Pastor Reynolds's residence."

"David! It's Ashley."

"Where are you?"

"In Vienna. Did you think I ended up in Rome?"

"I thought you were going to call when Chandler got there. I've been up all night waiting. Worrying."

"Oh David, I'm sorry. We've been so busy. Talking and laughing. It was one thing after the other—"

She sounded happy, lighthearted, distant. "It's all right, Ashley. Is Chandler there now?"

"He's here. He's fine." She hesitated. "He hurt his leg several weeks ago, but it's healing nicely. Says to tell you he looks great in the clothes you sent."

And then Chandler was on the phone. "Dad. You old rock, why aren't you here? We miss you."

"I wanted to come—but this schedule of mine. There's the church and a book deadline and—"

"What about me, Dad?"

Before David could apologize, his mother left the room. He watched her climb slowly up the stairs, his guilt mounting with her. She seemed suddenly old, as distant as his son.

"Is someone there with you, Dad?" Chandler asked.

David wanted to say, *your grandmother.* The words caught in his throat. "In the office with me? I'm alone right now. Tell me about your leg injury, son, and tell me what you and your mother have been doing."

They talked for thirty minutes, the clock ticking away until noon with every other sentence about Vienna or the violinist. Twice Chandler said, "I'm okay, Dad. Let's not talk about Bosnia." And finally, "We'd better call it quits, Dad. I think Mom reversed the charges so the call is on you. We'll call after the concert, but don't stay up all night waiting. You hear?"

"Put your mother on the line, son."

"Can't. She's back in her room taking a shower."

David hastily said good-bye, then cradled the phone and pushed it back on the desk. The silent room screamed at him. *Ashley, Chandler. My wife, my son. My whole life wrapped up in two people.*

A movement in Ashley's garden caught his attention. He shot to his feet. His mother was kneeling by one of the flower beds, work gloves on her hands. She was tugging at the weeds, trying in her own way to tell him she was sorry for what she had said. But her words kept ringing in his ears. *"Has Ashley left you, David?"*

David showered, shaved, and dressed in twenty minutes and was back down in the garden, briefcase in hand. He knelt beside his mother. "I'm off to the university, Mother."

She looked up into his face. "When will you be back?"

"In time to take you out to dinner."

"I think I'll be gone before then."

"You don't have to leave."

"I'll come back some other time when you invite me."

"Come for the next holiday?"

She pulled unsuccessfully at a weed. "If you want me to."

"It's an open invitation. You know that."

"We'll see." She removed the garden glove and touched his face with her long, slender fingers. "I love you, David. I don't mean to interfere or belittle your wife."

He pressed her hand against his cheek. She looked as if she would cry, and he wanted to spare her the humiliation. "I have to hurry, or I'll be late for class. We'll keep in touch."

Tears balanced on her eyelashes. "I learned something this morning, David. Something I didn't want to believe." He waited, glancing anxiously at his watch.

"Ashley is in your blood, and you can never let her go."

Even as he slid into the car and turned on the ignition, her words haunted him. But what if Ashley did leave him? Where would she go?

Back to Everdale, he told himself. Yes, he was certain she would go back to Everdale, back to where it all began.

Chapter 14

Even back in the 1960s, David Lee Reynolds was into politics and history. Knowing statistics pleased his father, and Clayton Reynolds's approval meant an increase in David's allowance. David kept up on the current hot spots in the world so he could engage in heated debates with his father at the dinner table. He could spiel off facts like words in a spelling bee.

John Fitzgerald Kennedy was President of the United States, Lyndon Baines Johnson his V.P., McNamara Secretary of Defense, and Premier Khrushchev in power in the Soviet Union. Concrete slabs had replaced the barbed wire along a twenty-eight-mile death trap known as the Berlin Wall—a wall that divided a city and made the Brandenburg Gate and Checkpoint Charlie names to be reckoned with. Young Prince Charles was heir to the British throne, and Beatlemania was just getting off the ground with four long-haired musicians from Liverpool taking the US by storm. And high school senior David Reynolds of Southern California was almost eighteen.

David admired the man in the White House, but the Bay of Pigs remained a blot on Kennedy's presidency. Kennedy had other problems: Air America, the CIA airline that didn't exist, was flying daring supply runs into Laos and South Vietnam, and a conflict near the Gulf of Tonkin and the Mekong River was taking shape, with American losses slowly mounting in the jungles of Laos and Vietnam. US Special Forces were serving as advisors to a poorly equipped army, ill prepared to fend off attacks by the Viet Cong guerrillas. An all-out war would force Kennedy to draft high school graduates for a military buildup that already had opposition from Congress and the Republicans. And from David.

David's real interests were the Yankee baseball scores, the latest model cars, and the conditions of the winds and surf off Hermosa Beach or Huntington Beach pier. At almost eighteen, life looked good. David intended to keep it that way. He had no intention of being one of the US troops patrolling the Berlin Wall or one of the Green Berets dying in Vietnam. He had no desire at all to wear his country's uniform, not after seeing the news photo of the bullet-riddled body of eighteen-year-old Peter Fechter trying to scale the Wall into the freedom of West Berlin.

For once David was in full agreement with his dad. Clayton Reynolds had caught the tail end of World War II and determined at all costs to keep his son from the bloodbath on the Ho Chi Minh trail.

Nor would David be out on the streets protesting the war—his mother would see to that. Let the Peace Corps circle the world and astronauts lift off into space. David's sights didn't go beyond the US border. He kept short-term goals—the prom in June and the university in the fall. Thanks to his father's legal maneuvers and David's outstanding GPA, his destination was a university campus, not the army's basic training camp.

But just before his birthday, in the last few weeks of his senior year of high school, David's defiance almost cost him his diploma. David wasn't dating much, and alcohol and smoking were out. He was saving every spare dime of his allowance toward insurance for a two-door Plymouth Fury or a Dodge Dart with heavy bumpers and tail fins.

That meant no girls. No drinks. No smokes.

He didn't have the car yet, but he expected one for graduation, a combined birthday-graduation present. It didn't even matter whether it was brand-new or not—although his dad could afford ten new ones. But as long as it was blue and shiny and souped up for speed, that's what counted. Then he blew it, and his dad pulled the dream out from under his feet. And for a few weeks David felt as if the president was breathing down his neck, waving draft papers.

It was his third straight night of breaking the family curfew. A guy almost out of high school and on his own had a right to break a few rules. Right? Wrong. That night as he turned the key in the front door, he came face to face with his father.

"I'll take that key," Clayton Reynolds said. He grabbed it and shoved it into the pocket of his plaid bathrobe.

"Why?" David shouted.

"You won't be needing it."

"Dad, I'm just a little late."

"A little later than last night," his mother said.

"An hour and a half late to be precise, Rosalyn. From now until graduation, there will be no nights out. Do you understand that, David?"

He looked to his mother to rescue him. "You can't hang this one on me. That's house arrest, Mom."

"Those are the house rules," his dad told him.

The fury in his father's face almost made David back off. "You can't do that, Dad. I'm not a kid anymore."

"You're acting like one."

"We're just hanging out at the café. Listening to the Beatles. Talking to the girls. School's almost out. The guys will all be going in different directions after that."

"Rock bands?" Clayton asked in utter disgust.

"And the girls—if they're nice girls—should be home in bed." His mother's comment only added fuel to the fire.

He glared at them both. "The two of you are too stinking old-fashioned. And I will go out if I want to."

That did it. His dad's face flushed a beet red. "There will be no car for graduation. You can count on that."

"Clayton, can't we talk about this in the morning?"

"No, Rosalyn. I've made up my mind. We'll talk about the car again in the fall when he goes to college."

David sulked in his room for a week, his grades tumbling with his mood. And then at the urging of friends on the basketball team, he struck out in the name of freedom. He took an extra set of his dad's car keys from the kitchen cupboard, waited until midnight, and climbed out the bedroom window.

His break for freedom began with drag racing on the streets of Brentwood and ended at three in the morning with an accident that left one classmate paralyzed, the town in an uproar, and his father pulling him out of school three weeks before the prom.

David wasn't driving the car, but on the next drag race he would have been at the wheel. The courts were ready to hang him on two counts: The Lincoln Continental was registered in his dad's name, and David had taken it without perrmssion.

He would become his father's hardest case, his greatest shame. David tried to remember why he had aligned himself with the daredevils in his class. Tried even now, more than three decades later, to come up with a logical reason for taking his father's Lincoln that night without permission. He still recoiled at the memory of his father's punishment—no prom and a summer away from his buddies, working on his grandparents' farm. But it was better than the punishment meted to the driver of the car. Three years' probation for the injury of their classmate.

When David tried to beg off from a summer in Alabama with his mother's parents, his father stared him down. "David, you need a summer on the farm. It will give you time to think about another young man of eighteen who will never walk again."

David's first glimpse of Everdale, Alabama, was blurry. He sat in the passenger train with his booted feet sprawled on the seat across from him and stared through the smoky windows out on the farm fields outside of Everdale.

As they pulled into the station he turned to his mother beside him and said, "I won't stay here."

"You will if you ever want to go to college. And if you don't, I think the army can use you."

USC had been his goal for years, a dream lost during those last few weeks of high school. Without his parents funding him, the dream was dead. It was dead anyway without his high school diploma. "That's out now, Mom. Dad pulled me out of school before I could graduate."

"You can be thankful he did. The scandal is hard enough on your father. It would have ruined you."

He unraveled and stood beside her. "So what do you expect?"

"There's a school in Everdale. It goes until the end of June. You can finish there. We've already arranged it."

"That's five miles from the farm. I'll need a car."

"No car. You have two good legs. That's more than your friend has now. So walk, David."

His grandfather proved less vindictive. He figured the school bus would get David home early for the chores. As it turned out, a pretty girl by the name of Ashley rode the bus for two miles each day. She lived on the outskirts of town in a large house with a big wraparound porch and a gazebo out back. And she had a mom who baked the best cookies and cooked the most marvelous dinners on Sundays.

To get Ashley's attention and to wrangle invitations to her house, David took a shine to her brother, a beanpole of a guy with an easygoing grin and a jalopy of his own. They had basketball in common and the desire to finish their sentences in Everdale. David only had to endure a summer there, but William felt he was on a life sentence if he didn't join the navy. They cruised around town in the old jalopy with David conniving every excuse to go back to the house to see Ashley. When he tired of slamming hook shots into the basket with William, he'd sit in the gazebo beside Ashley. And every time he did, he fell more madly in love.

They talked about growing up in opposite parts of the country. About their lifestyles that were so different. And they talked about the future when the war in Vietnam would be over. She wanted to be a nurse. He told her that his parents wanted him to become a partner in his father's law firm.

"Is that what you want to do, David?"

"What I want to do is stay here and marry you."

She turned scarlet. "You don't even know me."

"Then go out with me."

"Mother won't let me. She says you're going back to California for college soon, if the army doesn't get you first."

Ashley would be going to the community college in a neighboring town, three thousand miles away from USC. "Ash, I'll convince my parents to let me go to college here in Alabama."

Her laughter was musical. "I don't think they'd like that."

"You're probably right, but I want to stay here with you." That day he trusted her with the story of drag racing on the streets of Brentwood and the tragic accident that had brought him to Alabama. He looked away when he admitted that he still had nightmares thinking about his friend who would never walk again.

She had reached up and turned his face toward her. "You weren't driving the car. You can't blame yourself forever."

He could still remember the kindness and sympathy in her eyes as she looked up at him, her eyes as blue as the sky above the gazebo. He thought of the natural wave to her long corn silk hair and the sweet smile that had filled her face. Like a man trying to get everything off his chest, he had blurted, "I took my dad's car that night—and let someone else drive it."

"You stole it." It wasn't a question, but a correction of terms, an attempt to put it all in perspective. "We all make mistakes. My mama knows of only one Person who can forgive us."

"That's right," Ashley's mother said, coming up the gazebo steps just then with cookies and milk. "God forgives people who ask Him. You remember that, young man, and you'll do all right."

But he ended up doing everything wrong from the day he stole his first kiss while they sat on the swings by the gazebo until that day on his grandparents' farm. Ashley had driven out in her brother's jalopy to buy some fresh eggs. She stepped from the car with the basket in her hands.

David ran over to meet her. "I didn't know you were coming."

"I didn't know my mother would let me. But she needed some eggs, and I offered to go buy them for her."

"They have eggs in Everdale."

"But you weren't there."

He took her basket and then her hand. "Then we'd better go out to the hen house and get them."

"Where are your grandparents?" she asked as they walked along, side by side.

"Gone to Montgomery—for the whole day, I hope."

"Gone? They're never gone. You told me they were too old and decrepit to get around much."

"That's why my mother came back early. Grams hasn't been feeling well lately."

"Then it's a good thing you're with her."

"That's what Grams says. She hates the thought of my going."

"You're leaving?"

"I don't want to. Mother and I argued all last night about my going to community college here, but it ended in a nasty row. By the time she left for the doctor's this morning with my grandparents, Mother looked more in need of a doctor."

"You're here alone?"

His lips went dry, his heart pounding against his chest wall. It scared him to even think that they were alone for the first time since he'd met her three months ago. His hand tightened around hers, and he felt the dampness in her palm.

He showed her the whole farm, walking end to end, not wanting to let her go. They laughed as he showed her how to pick eggs from the hen house, and after he set the basket down, they walked down to the river. That's where he stole his second kiss, but she pulled free and ran from him.

He caught up with her and took her hand again. "I'm sorry."

She smiled coyly. "I'm not."

His chest wall was about to explode. She slowed her pace to his. On the way back they stopped off at the barn. She allowed her eyes to scan back toward the river. "It's so beautiful here."

"I hated it when I first came. I hated getting up in the half-light of early morning. But granddad treated me like a man."

"You are a man," she said. Again she flushed a cardinal red.

He struggled to keep his emotions in check. "Do you know much about farming, Ashley?"

"Next to nothing. Only what you tell me." She tucked a strand of flaxen hair behind her ear, and he longed to reach out and touch those golden waves.

"It only took me a few days to catch on to the routine," he said. "Carry oats and corn to the horses, then put them out to pasture. And take the shelled corn to the cows. But it took me awhile to get the hang of the milking machines. Now I don't mind the chores at all. Not when I'm with Gramps."

"You're happy here?"

"Because you're here. And this is the first time someone really needed me. At least that's what my grandparents tell me all the time. It's not someone planning my life for me. Gramps made me feel like part of the team. Like I'm really needed."

"I need you, too," she whispered. "Don't go away."

He tried to shut out her words as he rambled on. "I've come to love the smell of the pasture and the hay in the loft and the river running by. I don't even mind the smells in the barn—especially when the cows are out grazing like they are now. That gave me the chance to hose the place down this morning. The barn and the farm animals represent my grandfather to me. And he's pretty special."

"And your grandmother?"

"She's a sweet old thing. Frail and getting a bit deaf, but she makes me feel at home. Gives me a great big bear hug when I remember to take off my boots before going into the kitchen."

"Your grandparents do sound special."

"They are. They never mention the accident back in California. It's as though it never happened, and I'm sure my folks told them about it." He smiled. "I think the best thing every morning is going back up to the farmhouse for Gram's ham and biscuits for breakfast and the sound of the skillet sizzling. It all grows on you. And then—then I met you, Ashley. If it hadn't been for you, I wouldn't have finished high school."

"That did take a bit of prodding," she said.

He slipped his arm around her waist, the blood roiling inside him. "I don't care what my parents want. I want us to be together forever."

"But we can't, David. You're going away."

"I'll come back someday. Once I finish university."

"You'll forget me by then."

He saw tears in her eyes and reached up to wipe them away. "I love you, Ashley."

She was in his arms and he was kissing her hard, hungrily, passionately. He wanted nothing more than to stay here and be with her, but by the next weekend at the latest, his mother planned to pack up and take him home again.

Behind them, the horse neighed. Gently, David took Ashley's hand and led her into the barn, saying, "I don't expect everyone back for a couple of hours."

She pulled away from him as they reached the horse's stall.

He could still see her, holding the sugar cube in her hand for the stallion to nibble. Ashley half turned to smile at David, and every desire inside him was for her.

She lowered her eyes, the long lashes touching her cheeks. "We mustn't. We mustn't, David."

"But we love each other. Isn't that enough?"

He took her hand and led her up the ladder to the loft, where the sweet smell of hay and the scent of Ashley's cologne merged.

Later, when they heard the car coming back to the house, they made their way out the back entry of the barn and down to the creek; when they saw his mother they were approaching the farmhouse from the creek bed trail.

But Rosalyn Reynolds held up the basket of eggs and said, "Is this what you're looking for, David? You left it in front of the barn."

That night she stormed into his bedroom and said, "You are not to see that girl again—whatever her name is."

But he did, more than once walking the long distance over the country road to her house. Ten days later, David and his mother left Alabama early in the morning before he had a chance to tell Ashley good-bye. He did not see her again for five years. His letters to her came back unopened. The more she ignored him, the more he buried the guilt that he felt. He had loved her—still did—but he had in his impassioned youth demanded more of her than she should have given.

He was in his third year at the university before he remembered what Ashley's mother had told him. *"God forgives people who ask Him. You remember that, young man, and you'll do all right."*

On his own he found a church in Long Beach and sat on the back pew, listening to old-time hymns and to what he would later define as a message of forgiveness. It was an invitation to peace from a Man on a cross. David didn't know what it meant exactly, but he knew the Man hanging there had extended His arms to him. Telling his parents was the toughest job of all.

Twelve months later changing his career major from graduate studies at law school to a seminary didn't sit well either. When he faced his dad with his decision, he had said apologetically, "I'm sorry, Dad, but I think you know I was never cut out to be a lawyer."

His father had been too choked up to do much more than nod, but his mother had wrung her hands, saying over and over, "But a pastor in the family. What will we do with a pastor?"

At the end of his first year at seminary, his grandparents were forced to admit their frailty, leave their farm, and move into a nearby nursing home. David withdrew from seminary to be near them and moved back east to take up his first pastorate in the little town of Everdale. The church was an hour's drive from Grams and Gramps and a stone's throw from the house with the wraparound porch where Ashley still lived.

She was a nurse now, working the night shift at the hospital in Everdale. It wasn't hard to find her, not when she sat in his congregation, week after week. But it was months before he could convince her to go out with him again. To trust him. And that wouldn't have happened if he hadn't run into her at the nursing home visiting his grandparents.

They married a year later, Ashley refusing to come down the aisle to him in a white bridal gown. It didn't matter. She was coming to him—his wife, his bride, his love. If need be, he would take a lifetime to make up to her for those stolen moments in his grandparents' barn.

In that small church in Everdale and in the cathedral where he was now the senior pastor, his message continued to be one of hope in the Man on the cross. He continued to encourage the young people of his congregations to maintain abstinence before marriage—never admitting that it was a flawed man who stood behind the pulpit.

Even now driving toward his university class, three thousand miles from his grandmother's farm, he remembered as though it were yesterday the sweet smell of the hay and the prickle of the straw against his bare skin. And Ashley there with him. He gripped the steering wheel, his longing for his wife more intense than that day so long ago on the farm near Everdale.

Chapter 15

When Jillian opened the door to Kerina's empty dressing room, the sweet fragrance of a hundred flowers assailed her. Bouquets from Kerina's fans and friends occupied every available space. Jillian glanced at some of the gift cards as she crossed the room: the usual three dozen red roses from Franck, a variegated arrangement from Elias and Nicole McClaren, a massive pink azalea from the maitre d' at the Sacher, and a vase of yellow tulips flown in from Holland from the director of the Opera House. Almost lost among the larger arrangements was the orchid in a bud vase with a thank-you note from Elizabeth and Raquel.

But Jillian was drawn to the red carnations on Kerina's dressing table. She snatched up the card and read with surprise:

Good luck and good music, Miss Rudzinski.
Lieutenant Chandler Reynolds

Kerina's gowns for the evening's performance hung from a shiny brass pole. An elegant Valentino in a shimmering midnight blue with a tiered hem—its frills and lace scented with Guerlain from Paris. The form-fitting black silk purchased in Milan that she would wear with the diamond earrings Franck had given her. And Jillian's favorite—the low-cut, off-the-shoulder Parisian gown in a cranberry red with its spaghetti straps and long, free-flowing neck scarf.

Jillian turned her attention to the search for a white envelope marked with the lieutenant's name. She expected to find his concert tickets propped against the mirror or lying among the bottles of perfume. Instead she found Kerina's dresser drawer ajar. A sepia photo stared up at her, its reddish browns faded and yellowed with age. It lay on top of Kerina's journal—a picture of a young man, tall as a beanstalk, his hands thrust into his trouser pockets, strands of his thick hair windblown. He stood against the backdrop of the Water Tower, the stone landmark that had weathered the great Chicago fire. The Water Tower had survived. But what of this young man? Jillian picked up the photo for a closer look. It was not a handsome face, yet it was striking, winsome with its dimpled grin. She guessed his eyes to be blue, the thick hair blond. Kerina must have caught him unawares, for he had turned to look back, half smiling as she snapped the picture.

On the back in Kerina's brush script were the words, *Bill. Chicago*—and the date of her American debut in Chicago. Kerina would have been little more than eighteen. This must be the snapshot that she had not wanted to share.

Jillian's own question came back as piercing as a shard of glass. "Is he anyone I know, Kerina?"

What had she answered? "He was a long time ago." No, "He was long before your time, Jillian."

Jillian looked again at the casual pose. He wore a tie and dress shirt, dark slacks and a suit jacket. She guessed him to be a businessman meeting Kerina in the heart of the Windy City on his lunch hour. Or had they been stolen moments, a clandestine meeting at the Water Tower? His name was Bill. Bill what? Bill of Chicago—that someone special from Kerina's past? Jillian noted the high forehead and hooded brows. She bent lower, squinting. His face smiled but not his eyes. She had seen his face before. No, that was foolishness. The photo was ages old, yet those features belonged to the present as though she had faced him once, talked to him. Talked about him. Vague impressions that faded and came back. Receded and reappeared. It was that kind of a face. The face of a remembered past, of a living present.

She tried to pluck from memory the rest of the conversation at the Sacher Café. *She recalled begging, "Can't we squeeze Chicago in?" But Kerina was going on a trip alone—back to somewhere special. To someone special? Back to this man?*

Is this Bill planning to rendezvous with you? No, you would do nothing to ruin your career or your reputation.

Jillian took one final glance at the prominent features: the firm jaw, wide eyes, aquiline nose, an almost impish, devilish grin. Something in his expression reminded Jillian of the way Santos had often looked at her in Rome. She had been blinded to his weaknesses, and when their romance ended in a fit of anger, she had torn Santos's pictures into bits and thrown them at his feet. But Kerina, more gentle-hearted and coming from more sentimental times, had saved this photograph.

Impulsively, Jillian eased the sepia photo behind one of the clamps that held the mirror in place. Something lingered on the edge of memory.

"Did Kerina mention a last name?" she mumbled out loud.

"His name was Bill," Kerina said. "Bill VanBurien."

Jillian spun around. Kerina stood in the doorway looking pale and drawn, her ringed hands clasped in front of her.

"Kerina, I was looking for Lieutenant Reynolds's tickets."

"And found Bill's picture instead."

"I'm sorry. Your dresser drawer was open."

"Careless of me. I forgot to set the tickets out for you. I've—" She seemed to forget what she was about to say as she closed the door and crossed the dressing room to Jillian.

"You're late, Kerina. You'll have to hurry."

"I was talking with Franck."

"Arguing again?"

"Yes, about another trip to Moscow." She looked distraught, wisps of her hair falling over one brow. "I told him I couldn't go this time. He insists that I go."

"But you're exhausted."

Kerina rearranged a carnation and then rummaged in the drawer of her dressing table. She lifted her journal and opened it. "Oh here they are."

She handed an envelope to Jillian. "These are for Lieutenant Reynolds. But would you tell him I won't be able to keep that appointment this evening?"

"What? After we wrote and told him you would? You can't do that. The lieutenant came all the way from Bosnia."

"For an interview with me? I think not." Her eyes filled with pain. "Oh all right. Have him come backstage for just a few minutes. You be here. I'll send him off with you afterwards."

"He'll have a guest with him."

"Have his guest come, too." Kerina reached out and squeezed Jillian's hand. "It's best. You'll see. Just a quick visit. No more."

"Franck's idea?"

"Franck doesn't know about the lieutenant."

"Then why? It's not like you to break a commitment."

"Franck made dinner plans with Elias and Nicole for after the concert." Kerina sounded rattled. "Franck insists we can't disappoint them. Not when he's negotiating that art sale for Elias."

"A Degas?" Jillian asked.

"A Josef VanStryker."

"I didn't think VanStryker was that well known. Died in the thirties, didn't he, Kerina?"

"The early forties in a concentration camp. Franck is excited about the renewed interest in his work recently."

"And that makes the value go up into the thousands?"

Kerina eyed Jillian surreptitiously. "Into the millions now. And it means a sizable commission for Franck. There you go again, Jillian, showing a real interest in art. I thought you just pampered me when I wanted to browse in the museums."

"I told you. Your interest rubbed off on me. So Franck wants to get in on the ground level while he can afford a VanStryker?"

"It's for Elias—but Franck has resale value in mind, too."

"I thought he just collected art. I never knew him to sell or negotiate for it. Franck usually takes what he wants."

Color rose in Kerina's cheeks. "Go, please. Don't keep the lieutenant waiting. I have to dress for the concert. Franck will be back soon. He can zip me up."

"But he's upset you. You're flittery as a hummingbird."

"He'll come back smiling."

"He never smiles."

"And he never stays angry long. He won't want me to either. This performance is important to both of us."

"Then what's troubling you? Moscow? The McClarens? Not the concert? You've played hundreds of times before."

"Nothing is wrong."

Jillian felt a deepening sense of gloom. Kerina and Franck's evening with the McClarens alarmed her. She had no way to let Brooks Rankin or Joel Gramdino know about the dinner arrangement. *Stop fretting,* she told herself. *It's just an innocent night out. Kerina and Franck dine with kings and queens, composers, and the wealthy of the world. Why not with an art collector and his lovely French wife?*

Her worry persisted, her thoughts on an unsuspecting art collector like McClaren sitting in the loge section, thrilled with Kerina's magical touch, and going home at midnight to find that a painting was missing. The Registry's hands were tied. How could they warn any of the rich of Vienna without alerting the thief?

As Kerina slid onto the cushioned bench, she blew Jillian a kiss that reflected in the mirror; the lights above the glass caught the glitter of her rings.

"Don't be fretful, Jillian dear. Remember, I promised I would give you the performance of a lifetime tonight."

Jillian nodded toward the man in the snapshot. "Will he be in the audience this evening?"

"No," she said in a whisper. "Bill will not be here."

She watched Kerina pick up her hairbrush and in long even strokes brush her russet hair back into a shiny chignon. Suddenly Jillian felt that this moment would linger in her memory in the months ahead, long after she left Kerina's employ: the glamorous Kerina Rudzinski with her back to Jillian in the simple act of brushing her hair, a vase of red carnations from an unknown soldier on her dressing table, and a faded snapshot of someone special tucked in the mirror's edge.

~

Ashley Reynolds turned from her mirror as her son came into her suite. He looked striking in his black tuxedo, his father's Giorgio scent wafting into the room with him.

Ashley scrunched the tip of her nose. "Smells familiar."

"Dad sent it. Guess he didn't want you to forget him."

"How could I? I've known him forever—and been married to him almost as long, it seems. Son, it would take more than the absence of Giorgio to make me forget your dad."

Chandler's dry chuckle drifted off. "Thought I'd buy some Givenchy while we're here in Vienna and send it home to Dad to try. And Chanel for Grams."

"I'll help you pick them out."

"I'd like to buy something nice like that for Zineta."

She nodded. He was giving her an approving appraisal now. "Do you ever look stunning, Mother!"

"I have an important date," she said lightly.

"Is that gown one of your retirement purchases?"

"No, I've worn it on two or three occasions, but no one in Vienna will know that. Are you ready?"

He held up his black tie and cufflinks and pointed to his stocking feet. "Help."

She laughed. "Come here."

Chandler crossed the room to her. Her voice was still light, cheerful. "You are just like your father. With all the weddings he performs, he still depends on me to do his bow tie."

"He just likes being spoiled."

"And you?"

"Lack of experience," he admitted.

"It's easy—just like tying your shoelaces."

He bent down as she looped the strap around his neck.

She crossed the two ends and made a bow and gave it an extra twist to straighten it. "There, that looks perfect."

He glanced in her mirror and eyeing her from there asked, "So Dad's still in the marrying business? Do you think he'd do the honors for me?"

Her heart skipped a beat. "Zineta?" She said the name without rancor, without even a tremor in her voice, but she couldn't meet his gaze even in the mirror. "Could you handle your dad's premarital lectures?"

"I have trouble with his sermons."

"Believing them?"

"Just listening to them. Ten minutes in and I'm out."

She fussed with his bow tie again as she rose to David's defense. "He's a good preacher. Very precise. Honest."

"I just can't live up to his expectations so I tune out."

She understood. She shared Chandler's inadequacies. "You try too hard to please him; I like you the way you are."

"I wish Dad did. These last few years I feel like I'm falling short. Like a piece of me is missing." He thumped his chest, sending the tie askew again. "I've got a big empty hollow inside me, Mom. I blame it on Dad, and it really isn't his fault. No kid could have had a better father."

She forced herself to look up into his handsome face and noticed the shadowed half circles under his eyes. She longed for the freedom to say, "You have your birth mother's gift of music, your birth father's features."

But Chandler had David's strengths and integrity—and most importantly, with all of Chandler's uncertainty, he always had David's love. It was more than his birth parents had given him.

"If Dad married Zineta and me, he might like her better."

"I'll talk to him when I get home. He might agree to a simple ceremony at home but not in the church."

"Because she's pregnant? Wouldn't he bend the rules for me?"

"Would you want him to go against his convictions?"

Chandler dropped the cufflinks into her hand. "Diamond cuff links. I found them in the suitcase from home."

"They belonged to your grandfather. Your dad wanted you to wear them," she told him as she snapped the second one in place.

"Barely remember Grandpa Clayton."

"Don't tell your grandmother that."

"Never," he promised. "Rosalyn ole girl thinks I'm sharp as two ice picks. We chat Gramps every time we get together."

"Your grandmother needs that. It's all she has left."

"She has you and Dad."

"I never counted."

"I've never understood why. You bend over backwards to give her a good time."

"Not your problem, Chan." *You have enough of your own,* she thought. "Now get your shoes on and let's go, or we'll be late."

"The shoes don't fit."

"But I ordered your size."

He grinned. "But you didn't order the swelling in my foot to go down."

"Is that why you had trouble sleeping last night?" She followed him into his room and picked up his trail of clothes from the floor. "I thought I heard you tossing and turning."

"I was dreaming about Randy and Zineta and the land mines. I woke up in a sweat." He smiled reassuringly. "And then I realized I was in Vienna—and I couldn't get back to sleep."

"I'll pinch you if you fall asleep at the opera."

"Good. Will these do?" he asked, pointing to his army boots.

They were ankle boots, black and shiny. "No one will notice, Chan. And you'd better use your crutches tonight."

"No way. I'm not hobbling into Miss Rudzinski's dressing room on a pair of crutches."

∽

In spite of the crowd inside the Opera House, Jillian recognized Chandler Reynolds from his picture on the cover of *Time* magazine. He stood waiting for her near the foot of the grand marble staircase, his hand resting on the wide banister.

He was much taller than she had guessed, and she thought him handsome in his tuxedo, looking confident like a man with a purpose. He was alone and she felt hopeful. She drew his attention with a quick wave and navigated her way swiftly through the pressing crowd. She caught the masculine scent of his cologne as she reached him, a fragrance that she could not name, and yet she would in the future always associate it with this moment.

"Lieutenant Reynolds?"

His face lit with a beguiling smile, his gaze direct and friendly as he took her outstretched hand. "Chandler, please."

Even as he greeted her, she felt a touch of color reaching her cheeks. He had that fresh-scrubbed look, an all-American face too pale from the Bosnian winter; yet his profile was strong, his frame athletic, his hooded eyes shiny brown like an autumn leaf.

Those windows of his soul galvanized her. "*Hold a plumbline to a man's eyes.*" Her father speaking. Her own heart scudding, thwacking, doing crazy circular jigs inside her chest.

"I forgot to tell you I'd be out of uniform. It's packed away in the hotel closet." His voice was deep, utterly charming. "I'm just another concertgoer tonight, Miss Ingram."

"Jillian, please. And you look like one of the regulars."

"Good. I thought maybe we had missed each other."

"I'm late, Lieutenant."

"You're here now." His voice seemed to say, *Don't go away.*

As she stood there with him, Brooks Rankin and his wife and Joel Gramdino strolled past her and started up the stairs. She felt their silence, their awareness, Brooks's disapproval. Midway up the carpeted stairwell, Gramdino glanced back and saluted.

She went back to appraising the lieutenant. His hair was post military, too short to slick down. Curly strands of auburn hair fell across his fore-head as though he had just stepped from the shower before coming to the Opera House. Up close, out of uniform, he didn't look exactly like the face on the *Time* cover, yet there was something familiar about him—as though she had seen that angular face, the firm set of the jaw, the captivating smile before. She recognized him. Knew him. And yet he was a stranger.

"Do you ever get used to this opulence?" he asked, gazing around. "I can hardly wait to see the paintings upstairs."

"You're into art?"

"From the minute I walked into the Opera House."

She conjured up a romantic entanglement, a flurry of activity showing the young soldier the highlights of Vienna. She started to say, "Do you know Vienna?" and caught herself dead.

Don't go goggle-eyed over the American soldier in a sharp-looking tuxedo, she warned herself. *He's here as a well-wisher to Kerina, and after tonight, he will be gone. No dinner and dancing with this young man. No strolling through the parks of Vienna. By the time the concert is over, he won't even remember he met you.*

"Hello!" he said. "I thought I lost you for a moment."

"Sorry, Lieutenant, my mind is on a thousand things."

"Too bad it's not on me."

She held out the small envelope. "I brought your tickets for the concert."

"I have tickets—in the peanut gallery."

"Miss Rudzinski insists on upgrading you. You're in the loge with Elias and Nicole McClaren."

"Box seating? I can't accept that." He seemed serious, even when he smiled, his eyes intense and direct as he looked down at her. "What about the interview with Miss Rudzinski?"

"She can only spare a few minutes after the concert. She's sorry—"

He controlled his disappointment. "Just my luck."

"Chandler." A voice behind him. He turned, the expression on his face one of pleasure as he greeted an attractive, older woman and tucked her arm in his.

The spell had broken. Embarrassed, Jillian didn't wait to be introduced. "I must get backstage, Lieutenant. Kerina—Miss Rudzinski—always has last-minute things for me to do."

"Of course. Will we see you back—?"

She didn't let him finish but slipped through the crowd, her cheeks florid. *You are one good-looking young man, Lieutenant Reynolds,* she sighed. *But your date! She's old enough to be your mother!*

❦

A few steps from the entry to the Opera House, Jokhar Gukganov and Vladimir, his well-dressed bodyguard, awaited the arrival of a gray limousine. They were dressed in black tie and blended with the crowd, looking much like any concertgoers eager for a night of music in Vienna. A third man stood five feet from them, a smirk on his youthful face, his thick dark hair unruly, his restlessness growing with each passing second; Pierre had immigrated to Moscow from Paris with a questionable résumé, seeking quick riches. Tonight he wore the green jacket and britches of an Austrian, the outfit looking much like a uniform. It would pass as one once Jokhar gave the signal.

Jokhar Gukganov was a survivalist, fiftyish, gray-haired, his face harsh, his skin sallow. His perpetual frown formed vertical ridges between his eyes. He had left politics, his position and profit among the Russian rich secured at the fall of communism. Since then he had taken over the ownership of his father's design company, a private enterprise that paid well.

Some considered his sudden wealth stolen money, Mafia-backed cash. Jokhar never explained himself to others. He considered wealth his right, the result of wise business moves. These days he drove Cadillacs and a Mercedes with tinted windows and a chauffeur at the wheel. He drank champagne freely, not the hard Vodka of his youth, and packed a revolver and expensive tins of red caviar whenever he traveled. He dined at five-star hotels near the Kremlin and owned a villa decorated with masterpieces for his third wife. Most people did his bidding.

But lately, Franck Petzold was being overly cautious, wary of the young woman in Kerina Rudzinski's employ. Yesterday at the McClaren exhibit at the Academy of Fine Arts, Petzold had said, "Jokhar, if you want any more paintings, you must steal them yourself. But leave the McClaren paintings alone."

Jokhar had scanned the marvelous display. "Surely he has enough for both of us. And even more in his home."

"His place is heavily secured. You can't scale the walls. The only safe way in is with the McClaren limousine. There's a code system in the dash that opens the gate."

"So I would need the McClarens' chauffeur."

Jokhar shifted his weight and smiled at Vladimir, his thoughts still his own. Until recently, Petzold had worked alone. The thrill of the chase belonged to him, but tonight for the first time Jokhar would remove the painting from the wall himself and experience that personal thrill of choosing a Degas or another Rembrandt.

He needed Franck to transport the masterpiece to Moscow, but he would have the thrill of taking the prize. What was it that Franck was trying to save for himself? It had to be the Degas or Rembrandt. Petzold wanted these artists in his own collection. Threatening Franck's exposure would do no good. Outwitting him was the only way—outwitting him like he was planning to do in the sale of the fake VanStryker. Jokhar liked daring moves. Surprises. With the crowd at the Opera House bent on an evening of music, who would even notice the kidnapping of a chauffeur?

Vladimir touched Jokhar's shoulder. "That's the car we are expecting, sir."

With an imperceptible move of his hand, Jokhar signaled Pierre as the chauffeur-driven limousine slowed for a stop. Pierre's muscles flexed. Jokhar saw the excitement in Pierre's eyes, felt it in the blood coursing through his own body. Pierre sprang toward the curb, stepped out in front of the McClarens' vehicle and passed in front of it to the driver's side.

Easy, Jokhar thought. *Not yet. Give the chauffeur time to open the door for the McClarens.*

Jokhar watched with pleasure as Frau McClaren stepped from the limousine and waited for her husband. Jokhar knew women and fashion, and Nicole McClaren was elegantly dressed in a Yves Saint Laurent velvet gown that revealed her excellent figure. Her jet-black hair was slicked back from her face; her smile was bewitching, her eyes catlike. She noticed Jokhar, even flirted briefly, and then she turned with a smile and linked her arm in her husband's.

Elias McClaren took obvious pride in his wife, strutting away in his black tie, pleased with the woman by his side. *No,* Jokhar thought, *we will have no trouble from them.* A woman like that thrived on attention and would be expecting it in the crowd moving toward the Opera House. He turned to signal Pierre again.

It was too late. The McClarens' chauffeur was unaware of anything unusual until the metal object crashed against his neck. One quick blow and he crumpled without a whimper.

"You fool, Pierre. You didn't have to hurt him," Jokhar said. "We needed him alert to get us through the gate."

Pierre was thirty years his junior, jaunty and defiant and given to using his fists and not his brain. "I could not risk him putting up a fight or calling out for help," he said as he braced the injured man against the car. "Here, help me get him inside."

They were holding up traffic, but they wrangled the side door of the limousine open and shoved the chauffeur inside. He slumped to the floor. Vladimir piled in behind him.

"Too much *Krugel,*" Jokhar told the man in the car behind them. "He will be all right. He is our friend. We will take him home now and let him sleep it off."

Pierre cocked the chauffeur's cap on his own head and slid behind the wheel. "Too small," he complained.

"Your head is too big. Shut up and drive," Jokhar said.

"Fish the keys out of his pocket."

"Since when do you need keys to start a car?" But Jokhar wrestled the recalcitrant key chain from the unconscious man's hand. "A coded key," he said.

"Not if I push the right button. See—just like that."

It was a jerky start, but they were off, pulling away before the police officer who was cutting across the street could question them.

"Where to?" Pierre asked.

As they drove away, Jokhar pulled on a stocking mask and gloves. "To the McClarens', you fool."

"Just give me directions. And use my name."

Jokhar tugged a hand-drawn map from his pocket. "Right at the corner. The McClarens have an older mansion outside Vienna."

The chauffeur lying on the floor of the limousine was moaning now, struggling back to consciousness. Vladimir put his foot on the man's knee. "Move and I will crush your knee bone."

The eyes opened, stark fear in them. "Where are we going?" he asked in German.

"Home," Vladimir told him. "Just cooperate, and nothing more will happen to you. Start by telling us your name."

"Hans."

For a second he relaxed, and then, twisting his body, grabbed for Jokhar's leg. Vladimir came down hard on the chauffeur's knee, and the yelp of pain amused Pierre.

"What was that about me hurting Hans?"

"Shut up, Pierre." Right now Jokhar feared two men out of control. The revolver was in Vladimir's hand, and that familiar tick along his jaw throbbed. His face hardened as he bent over Hans and shoved the barrel of his gun beneath the man's chin.

"You understand?"

"What do you want?" Hans asked hoarsely.

"A masterpiece from your employer's library."

As Hans's frantic gaze turned to him, Jokhar said, "Do as my young friend says, Hans."

Hans's nod was blocked by the barrel of the gun. Sweat poured from his face. He lay motionless, the seat of his pants damp now.

"You will get us safely through the gate at the McClarens' residence and into the house," Jokhar said beneath his mask. "Is anyone in the house, Hans?"

The answer came back slurred. "The maid—Anna."

"She will be safe as long as you help us. Fifteen minutes, that's all we need. You will get us through the gate and turn off the alarm system."

Panic mounted in the man's eyes.

"There she is," Pierre announced. "The gate is just ahead."

Vladimir's revolver wedged tighter beneath the chauffeur's jaw, the weight of the gun pressed hard against his neck.

Jokhar put out a restraining hand. "Ease up. His lips are turning blue, Vladimir."

"Good. Then he understands us."

"Now, Hans," Jokhar said, the excitement building in him, "you must do exactly as we say. If not, you and Anna will have a long rest."

Chapter 16

As Chandler took his seat in the Opera House, he could think of no one but Jillian Ingram, the girl with the silken tawny hair and those magnificent sapphire blue eyes. Then, as the house lights dimmed, he did not think of her.

A hush swept across the audience as Kerina Rudzinski stepped onto the stage. For a second she stood there, resplendent in a cranberry-red gown, a bloodstone locket in the hollow of her throat. He watched, spellbound as she glided gracefully across the brightly lit stage, the feathery tapping of her heels and the rustle of her gown echoing in the stillness. Adjusting his binoculars, he brought Miss Rudzinski's lovely face into focus. A delicate, oval face soft as silk, arched brows pencil-thin, perfectly formed lips a glossy vermilion. For just a second, he wondered what in her life had left the tiny twist of sadness at the corner of her mouth.

She seemed to be waiting for the tap of the conductor's baton. Or was she searching her soul for that moment of calm before she played? He seemed to know her so well without knowing her at all. But he knew music and knew what drove a musician. His own fingers itched to lift the bow and glide it over the strings of her violin. His grip tightened on the binoculars. Her auburn hair was almost the color of his own, the long-lashed eyes shining as she faced her audience, her smile warm and gentle as she cradled her Stradivarius. He had not expected her to be so elegant, so breathtaking, so ravishingly beautiful.

～

Stillness thundered in Ashley's ears. She guessed that the silence was for more than the anticipated concert, more than politeness. It was for the violinist herself, a legend in the world of music.

The stage lights fell softly on Kerina's face, highlighting her cheekbones and the flawless porcelain skin. Ashley recognized the long, reddish-brown hair, not falling softly over the pillow as it did in that hospital bed so long ago but pulled back in an elegant chignon, revealing that same fragile beauty and delicate features. She knew Kerina's eyes would be pensive, full of sadness, unchanged from that first meeting twenty-six years ago when a shy, frightened Kerry Kovac had met her gaze.

Kerry Kovac. Kerina Rudzinski. One and the same.

Kerina stood center stage now. The lights caught the glitter of her glamorous Parisian gown—a low-cut, off-the-shoulder, waist-slimming evening dress with a long, flowing, berry-red train. Kerina's charisma, that magnetic smile, the perfect fit of her designer's gown delighted the Austrians. She had not played a note, yet her hold on the audience was complete. They admired, adored, respected her.

With graceful, sure movements Kerina tucked her violin under her chin, cupped her fingers over the strings, and placed her thumb on the finger board. The Vienna Philharmonic Orchestra sat poised, ready to accompany her.

The conductor tapped the music stand. All eyes turned to his gloved hands. Into the hushed auditorium flowed the magical sounds of the first violinists. The sounds grew more powerful as all the strings—the violins, the cellos, the violas, the bass—and the harpist joined together.

The conductor's baton dipped toward Kerina. She lifted her bow high in her hand, then gently, skillfully fingered the strings and guided the bow across them. The conductor raised his arms and brought them together with a gusto. The entire orchestra obeyed. The thirty-four violinists. The woodwind instruments: the bassoon and oboe, the flutes and clarinets. The brass section with its French horns and trumpets, the trombones and the deep bellow of the tuba. The glorious sounds of "The Blue Danube" vibrated through the Opera House.

The conductor's baton lowered, lowered, lowered. The orchestra played softly now, their music muted, as the violin in Kerina's hand sang out in rich, warm tones. Kerina's fingers ran over the strings like a bird taking flight, like the fine drizzle of the first spring rain, like the gentle sway of a field full of golden tulips. Heart and musician were one.

The effect of her music was hypnotic—Chandler and the audience experiencing the music, caught up in it, lost in it. Kerina's lithe body seemed to dance with the lilting waltz, her instrument dipping and rocking with her body. The Austrians around Ashley swayed to the melody. Elias and Nicole McClaren in the box seats with them linked arms. Ashley's feet tapped to the music. Her heart sang, yet she was on the outside looking in, shut out from the joy around her. But she knew from the happiness on Chandler's face and the glowing expressions on the faces of the Austrians that they had been transported back to those glorious days when Strauss and his waltzes had awakened music in the hearts of the Viennese.

A thousand acid thoughts crossed Ashley's mind. Her son was enchanted by the music of the woman who had given him away. The last time she saw Kerina she had knelt beside her in the hospital nursery in Everdale and unfolded Chandler's receiving blanket. Ashley had wanted that baby, yearned for him, and knew that he would be hers if the adoption went through. With mixed emotions and her own heart stretched to the breaking point, she had whispered, *"Kerry, it's not too late to change your mind."*

Now, once again, Ashley's heart stretched to the breaking point. If Chandler learned the truth, she might lose him forever. She glanced at Chandler sitting beside her, this attractive son of hers with his strong profile and classical features. He looked dashing in his tuxedo, his eyes glowing as he watched Kerina. Chandler was often so self-willed and restless that he could easily have been Ashley's own son.

He seemed intent—he always did when he listened to music, as though he had moved to a different realm of pleasure. Ashley loved music; Chandler felt it, lived it. He let it stir his soul.

As they sat there high above the main auditorium, Chandler's arms rested on his lap, his long fingers gripping the program, his lips smiling. She wondered if he knew or whether the mystique of the violinist had caught him unawares. Ashley could not read her son's face. He had not come from her womb, but he was more her child, her son, than Kerina Rudzinski's. And nothing—and no one—could take him away from her, not even this gifted violinist.

He remained quiet, soft-spoken during both intermissions, his thoughts far away. She could not imagine what he knew. When she returned from the powder room during the last intermission, he seemed more withdrawn. She linked her arm in his. "What are you thinking about, Chandler?"

"About music. About packing my own violin away too soon."

"Maybe you should play it again when you get home."

"Maybe. First I have to decide what I'm going to do. But I know I want to stay on in Europe at least for a little while."

"You play the piano well," she said lightly.

"How many yardsticks did you break on my butt trying to get me to practice?"

"We didn't need the yardsticks when you took piano. You were born for it. But it took a little urging for violin practice."

He sighed. "Miss Rudzinski was born to play the violin. I played classical music in Bosnia until my cassettes broke. Randy teased me about that—even threatened to trash them for me."

"Didn't he like music?"

"We knew each other for years, and I don't even know. Sometimes he played rock and roll, but he joked about classical music."

"What about his girlfriend?"

"Zineta loves music. I remember that. Kemal Hovic—he's the one who took her in when her family was killed—he plays the cello. I wish he could hear a concert like this one. Maybe he would be well again."

"He's ill?"

"Depressed. Devastated by his losses during the war. Zineta says he rarely says anything. Just sits there playing the cello."

Tears welled in her eyes. "It's good that he has his music."

"I wish I could give him something else to live for. Randy was good for him. Kemal was just beginning to take interest in life again—and then Randy was killed. Enough," he said, "or I'll have us both crying. It's time to get back to our seats. Let's not miss a note of this performance."

I would gladly run from it all, Ashley thought. *I'm afraid of where it will lead. Afraid of Kerina Rudzinski.*

Kerina was beautiful and gifted; she had the accolades of the music world and already two standing ovations in this evening's performance. She had it all—all except the child she had given away. And after the concert tonight, would she claim him back—this handsome, young man with a piece of his life missing?

"Mother."

"Oh Chandler. I was lost in thought."

"Well, I found you again." Smiling, he led her back to their loge seats in the McClarens' private box. He glanced around. The McClarens' seats were empty. "Why would anyone go home early?" he asked, incredulous.

"Shhh," Ashley said, her finger to her lips.

Kerina moved across the stage in a cloud of midnight blue—a Valentino gown with a heart-shaped bodice, its tiered skirt swirling around her narrow ankles. Under the stage lights her milky skin looked blue-white, her brushed hair like burnished gold. Dangling earrings and a glittering blue sapphire necklace sparkled as she walked.

Throughout the concert, Kerina had shown her versatility and skill as she played the glorious works of the sons of Austria, the sons of Vienna. But now as Kerina stepped to the microphone again, those sounds of

Strauss, Haydn, Mozart, and Schubert continued to form only bitter, discordant notes in Ashley's mind.

She listened in disbelief as Kerina said, "Johannes Brahms' 'Lullaby' is not on this evening's program, but I would like to play it for someone special."

Closing her eyes, Kerina lifted her Stradivarius. The high gloss on the instrument gleamed as she held it. She began to play, and as she did, the concert hall filled with the sweet notes of Brahms' "Lullaby."

Could she be playing it for Chandler? Ashley wondered. *Dear God, could anything done for Chandler out of love be wrong? Kerina, from your beauty alone,* she thought, *you could have had countless suitors or others flocking to you for your fame and fortune. Why, why then did you fall in love with my brother? And he with you?*

The romance should never have been. And yet without that short-lived affair, that stolen romance, there would be no Chandler. *My son,* Ashley thought, loving him. She had loved him from the moment she saw him in the delivery room. Nine pounds. Twenty-one inches long. Red face scrunched up; fists doubled; legs kicking. His first cry a long protesting wail as he entered the world. Then, as he was placed on the examining table, a little gurgle, a gasp as the cold stethoscope touched his chest.

Had Bill been Kerina's only love? Even back then she had loved her music, had carried her violin in a blue case into the hospital at Everdale. As she played now, it was obvious that music was still her life. It consumed her. She had sacrificed everything for it. But hadn't Ashley sacrificed, too?

Unexpectedly, Ashley's bitterness was touched with sympathy. The program slipped from her hand. Did Kerina ever think about Chandler on April 15? Did she think back on the day he was born or count the candles on his birthday cakes? Did she think of a little boy growing up without her? Did she long for him at Christmastime or wrap presents that she could never send him? Did she ever wonder what kind of man Chandler had become? Surely these were things Ashley would have done.

She reflected back to that moment when Kerry Kovac held her son for the last time. Yes, Kerry would have thought of him as a little boy at a baseball game eating a foot-long hot dog or walking in the woods, or fishing with his dad. But did Kerina, the violinist, remember those dreams for her newborn son?

The orchestra hit a high note; it resounded through the auditorium and seemed to splinter the coves and inlets of Ashley's own heart. It stirred the ripples. Her past resurfaced and refused to sink back into the abyss. The Brahms "Lullaby" collided with the remembered strands of Schubert's *Unfinished Symphony* that often came to mind. Of her own unfinished symphony. She had her own day to remember, that day when summer and fall merged back in Everdale, when her own innocence was lost. She thought of her own unborn child. Of birthday candles that would never be placed on gooey icing. Of a little boy who would never be born, never cry. Never grow up. How dare she sit here in this magnificent Opera House and condemn Kerina when she had sins of her own? Splinters in her own eye. Not splinters, giant redwoods.

Chandler reached over and brushed a tear from Ashley's cheek. She had not even felt it fall. He squeezed her hand. She focused back on the concert, on the lovely violinist. Watching her now, listening to her, even Ashley found Kerina enchanting.

For seconds as the concert ended, silence again gripped the audience before the Viennese gave Kerina a standing ovation. Chandler leaped to his feet during the deafening applause, his eyes glowing. Ashley rose reluctantly beside him, her hands barely touching.

"Come on, Mom," he said excitedly as they left the concert hall. "Let's get backstage. Miss Rudzinski promised to give me a few minutes of her time."

That is all she has ever given you, Ashley thought.

Chapter 17

Kerina sat on her cushioned bench, facing the three-way gilded mirror above her dressing table. Tiny globe lights framed the glass, reflecting the bouquets behind her and sending shadows across her face. Tonight the heady fragrance of a room filled with flowers stifled her, robbing her of her usual enjoyment. She leaned forward and outlined the quarter moons beneath her eyes with her fingers. Slowly, she touched her cheeks, her chin, her hands coming to rest on her slender throat, her elbows resting gently against her breast. That little twist of sadness at the corner of her mouth would not go away—it was as though she had been born with it.

She caught Jillian's eye in the mirror. "Should I change?"

"No, don't. The lieutenant will be here any minute. You look lovely as you are. Just freshen your makeup."

Kerina applied some eye shadow and a tea rose gloss to her dry lips. "There, that's better," she admitted.

"You must be proud, Kerina. This evening's concert was the greatest performance you've ever given."

"Then I kept my promise."

"And Vienna loved you for it. She gave Kerina a thumbs-up. "You should be up waltzing around. Singing. Dancing."

"I'm much too tired to sing and dance."

"Then call off your dinner with Franck and the McClarens, and I'll send the lieutenant away when he comes."

Kerina's laugh was brittle. "One minute you tell me I should keep my commitments, the next that I should break them." She turned and met Jillian's gaze. "This should be the happiest night of my life, yet the accolades seem so empty. Is that all I can look forward to for another twenty years? More applause?"

"I thought it was what you lived for."

Kerina reached out and touched the red carnations on her dressing table. "The lieutenant sent these, Jillian. My fans—even my critics—are so good to me. What do I give them in return?"

"Your beautiful music."

"It's not enough."

"And why not? Look—you're just tired. You have a few days between concerts. Why don't we go to your villa on the Riviera?"

That private haven in Italy. The very thought of going excited Kerina. The gated villa, high on a hill with the endless blue horizon and the silk-white sand on the beach; the olive groves and fruit trees; and her beloved housekeeper, Mia, who would fatten her up on pastas and fresh seafood and make up her bed daily with fresh, air-dried linens.

She sighed, some of her emptiness dissipating. "We haven't done that for a long time, Jillian. I was afraid to suggest it for fear Italy would remind you of Santos Garibaldi."

"I loved him once, Kerina. At least I thought I did. But now he sits on the edge of my memory so I can kick myself more often. Believe me, I won't send him an invitation to your villa."

"Why not? I might like him."

"He'd charm you all right. Can we go and not tell Franck we're going?"

"I would have to cancel my trip to Moscow."

"Oh, do."

"Franck will be furious—unless we go without telling him. But would you be happy with no one to swim with or play tennis?"

"You do both."

"Not this time. I will just sleep. Read books. Sit in the sun. And gorge on Mia's meals."

"Why don't you invite your parents to join us?"

"They dislike traveling. We might invite some friends of yours, Jillian. Perhaps the ones you met yesterday."

"They're both married. And rotten company."

"Who then?"

Jillian flipped her hair from her brow. "The lieutenant. Why don't we ask the likes of him?"

Kerina's touch of happiness faded. She turned back to her mirror and removed the hair clip, letting her hair fall loosely around her shoulders. She began brushing it with long strokes, her arm more tired than it had been in a long time. She was still untangling her hair when the knock came.

"Jillian dear, that's probably the lieutenant. Get the door for me, please."

She heard the door swing back and glanced down at the picture of Bill on her mirror. "Wish me luck," she told him.

Kerina smiled at the excitement in Jillian's voice as she said, "Lieutenant Reynolds, we've been expecting you."

"Miss Ingram, I was hoping to see you again. You rushed off so suddenly this evening—"

"Well, I'm here now. Come in. Come in, both of you."

The lieutenant came limping around the maze of flowers to the center of the room. Kerina watched him in the mirror; then her world stood still. She felt the muscles in her throat constrict. The hairbrush slipped from her hand and clattered on the dressing table; she could not move. The lieutenant stood there favoring his right leg, a strange composite of shyness and friendliness. Tall. Lean. Eyes like Bill's. Her mirror seemed to fog, leaving the tall figure veiled in a blinding mist. An apparition, a phantom of her mind, an illusion. In the mirror he was ghostlike in appearance, a shadow of her past, the image of Bill. It was Bill coming back at last, still limping. No, someone younger, young like Bill had been when they said good-bye.

Her throat locked. How could two men look so much alike? With great dignity she swung slowly around on the bench. As she looked up at her guest, her heart felt like a groggy sponge, pumping slowly, erratically. The apparition faded. His features became real. She found the strength from deep within her to meet the lieutenant's eyes. She was certain he was Bill's son. Only the set of his jaw was stronger. No one could look so much like Bill without being his child. A quizzical frown formed on his brow as he waited for her to speak.

But if this is Bill's son, he may know who I am. Perhaps he has come here to confront me, to punish me for going away.

The lieutenant smiled. Bill's smile. His piercing eyes held hers, bridging the twenty-six years from that long ago when Bill had met her gaze. "Hi," he said in a voice deep and rich. "I'm Chandler Reynolds."

No, you are my son. She found her voice at last. "I was expecting someone in an army officer's uniform."

"I left my army gear in the closet at the Empress Isle."

She felt riveted to the bench, at a loss for the right words. "I didn't know the army turned out music critics," she said.

He laughed. Bill's easy chuckle. "That's not the army's doing, ma'am. It's my personal goal—I was born into a family that loved music."

Her heart thundered in her ears. She had to know—had to be certain. "Where were you born, Lieutenant?"

He seemed surprised, the woman behind him more startled. "In Everdale, Alabama, ma'am."

"A dot on the map."

"How did you know that?"

"I guessed." She stood and stole another glance at his handsome face. *Tall and charming like your father,* she thought. Slowly, she moved toward him, her soft hands outstretched. He took them in his and lifted them to his lips. "Thank you for the flowers, Lieutenant Reynolds."

He waved his hand around the room. "You're smothered in flowers." He beckoned to the woman behind him. "Mom, come and meet Miss Rudzinski."

As she stepped forward, he slipped his arm around her shoulders. "This is my mom—Ashley Reynolds."

Kerina heard pride in his voice. But she wanted to cry out, *No, I am your mother!*

She faced the woman who had raised her son for her and was shocked. Kerina remembered that nurse who took her baby away, remembered her eyes. She was looking into them again—an attractive woman with streaks of gray in her corn silk hair and a quiet calm about her as she met Kerina's gaze.

Impulsively, gratefully, Kerina reached out and clasped Ashley Reynolds' hands and whispered in her ear, "The night nurse. I would know you anywhere."

The last time she saw her son, this nurse had knelt beside her and unfolded the receiving blanket. His pink toes curled; his legs kicked. She felt the grasp of those tiny fingers on her own. Gurgling, cooing sounds had filled the hospital nursery as the nurse said, "Kerry, it's not too late to change your mind."

It was an awkward moment as they took the chairs by the dressing table, Jillian sitting down with them. Ashley's gaze swept past the snapshot and then did a rebound; her eyes misted as she stared at Bill's snapshot. *She recognizes him,* Kerina thought. *But of course. . .they grew up in the same town.*

As Kerina looked directly at Chandler, she traced his features in her mind. *The image of Bill—pensive brow, aquiline nose, those mesmerizing eyes. But my sensitive mouth.*

"Have you made the army your career, Lieutenant?"

He glanced at his mother. "That's the big debate. Whether to reenlist or to go civilian. My best buddy was killed recently."

Kerina caught her breath. "Is that why you were in the hospital?"

His voice wavered. "Yes. A leg injury in the same accident. That's why I'm on leave. But whatever I do, I want to stay on in Europe. If I don't stay army, I want to pursue a music career."

"Jillian tells me you play a musical instrument."

"One or two."

"And very well," Ashley interjected. "The violin. The piano."

"Then your son inherited his musical talent?"

"His destiny," Ashley said. "He was born to it. My husband and I love music, but we make better listeners than performers."

"And you, Chandler?" Kerina asked.

"I started violin when I was four. But when I got to fifth grade and Mom wouldn't sign me up for a soccer team, I rebelled. By the time I reached puberty, my rebellion was in full bloom."

"We didn't want him to injure his arm," Ashley said softly. "We made a promise once to—"

Kerina cut in. "Couldn't you have both sports and music?"

"That's why I stopped playing the violin and took to piano. But I'm not professional enough for either one."

"Nor willing to practice enough?" Kerina guessed.

"Mom and Dad kept holding out for another Yehudi Menuhin or Paganini. But I was way past being a child prodigy." He shrugged, brushing off his brief push toward a musical career. "By the time I was a sophomore in high school, I buried my violin in the back of the closet. For all I know, it's still there."

Kerina's blue gown rustled as she leaned toward him. "You cannot make music that way."

"Chan studied piano for several months at Juilliard," Ashley defended. "You were a guest artist while he was there, Miss Rudzinski."

"You heard me play, Lieutenant?"

"I didn't arrive until your last number." He grinned. "I was at the recruitment office. I left Juilliard for the army."

Sadly, she said, "You left Juilliard? For lack of practice?"

He frowned, thoughtful for a moment—a look so much like Bill's. "I left because I was searching for something. For myself, I think."

Her gaze drifted to Ashley and back. "Did you find what you were looking for?"

He didn't answer. Instead he said, "What I really want to do is try my hand as a music critic. That's why I'm here."

Jillian broke her silence. "A full-time music critic! That's like throwing yourself to the sharks, Lieutenant. You'll starve to death."

Kerina smiled. *Music reviews. Like Bill once did.* "You don't want to be a concert violinist?"

"I did while you were playing this evening. My folks pinned their hopes on me being a professional musician." He looked apologetically at Ashley. "But I can never achieve my parents' goal for me. Nor play as beautifully as you do, Miss Rudzinski."

Kerina lifted her violin from its case and handed it to him.

Chandler examined it carefully. "Wow. A Stradivarius. What an instrument!"

"It's my livelihood and also my life. It has belonged to my family for generations."

"Then you must keep it in the family."

"I will." As they talked, she powdered the bow with rosin.

"May I, Miss Rudzinski?"

She gave him the bow. "Play something for me and let me be the judge as to whether you should go on with your music career."

He hesitated only a second and then tucked the violin beneath his chin and ran the bow across the strings. His eyes teasing, he made squeals and grating sounds and then clearly the first notes of a Strauss waltz filled the dressing room.

She leaned forward and repositioned his fingers. "You must take your violin from the closet, Lieutenant."

"That's what Mom and Dad tell me."

"So you're not the perfect son?"

"Hardly."

Alarmed, she asked, "You don't drink or—"

"Not with a pastor for a dad. He keeps me on the straight and narrow. And Mom here prays a house a'fire for me." Again there was pride in his voice.

He played another measure and then handed the Strad back to her. "You're the violinist, Miss Rudzinski."

"But you were born for music, Chandler."

As she placed the violin back in its case, she sketched imaginary lines over his features, outlining them in her memory. His hair was growing out, one unruly lock falling across his well-shaped forehead. His pensive eyes searched hers. "How old are you?" she asked.

"Twenty-six a few weeks ago. April fifteenth to be exact. Do you have a family, Miss Rudzinski?"

Ashley gasped. *Don't worry, Mrs. Reynolds,* Kerina thought. *I won't tell him. Your secret—our secret—is safe with me.*

"Chandler, the truth is, I do have a son your age." She felt rather than saw the shock on Jillian's face. The fear on Ashley's. Her voice grew faint. "You are very much like—my son, Lieutenant. It's strange how very much you—"

Her voice trailed, a miserable lump in her throat. She turned hurriedly back to her mirror, blinking back sudden tears.

"Miss Rudzinski, I—"

"Lieutenant, I am sorry, but I have a dinner date. I must ask you to leave. Now."

"But the interview. . ."

She began to twist her hair into a chignon. "There is no time for that now."

He stumbled to his feet. "I'm sorry, Miss Rudzinski. We didn't mean to wear out our welcome. I—"

"Please go."

Kerina caught his reflection in the mirror and winced at the bewilderment on his face. She felt like she had been swept back to Jackson Memorial—to that day when she held her infant son and heard him whimper as the nurse took him from her. Ashley was moving toward the door, the same night nurse taking her son away.

She cupped a red carnation in the vase beside her. "Thank you for sending the flowers."

"No big deal."

She put down her brush and turned to face him again. "I am sorry about the interview, Lieutenant. But you do understand?"

With a cavalier shrug, he said, "Like I said, no big deal."

Kerina forced herself to stand and walk to the door with her son. *I may never see you again. And I am sending you away.*

She glanced up into his handsome face as more tears pricked behind her eyelids. "Lieutenant." She hesitated. "Perhaps we can arrange to talk again if you still want that interview?"

The corner of his mouth twisted to Bill's half smile. "Sure. If you can find time in your busy schedule."

He smiled at Jillian, who had opened the door for them. Ashley went out first, Chandler behind her. He did not look back.

Jillian closed the door and whirled around, her face flushed. "Kerina, that was cruel. The lieutenant was in the middle of a sentence, and you cut him off and told him to leave."

"I had no choice, Jillian. Franck will be here any minute."

"Oh, forget appeasing Franck. He always fusses about your guests! The lieutenant and his mother are here for a month. Franck will be around until doomsday."

"So what do you want me to do, Jillian?"

"Invite the Reynolds for lunch on Saturday so you can apologize for your rudeness. I'll smooth it over. I'll tell him that you get on edge when you're late for dinner. That you want to make it up to him. Let him have that interview."

"Does it matter that much to you?"

"Yes. I haven't liked anyone so much since Santos Garibaldi. So please invite them to lunch. Give me a fighting chance."

Kerina fought back the tears. "Oh Jillian, I can't. That soldier is wrong for you."

"That soldier has a name, Kerina."

Kerina felt faint, grief-stricken. *Jillian is right,* she thought. *The soldier has a name. . .more than I gave my infant son.*

"Oh Jillian. . .Jillian, help me."

Jillian was at her side at once, her arm around Kerina's shoulders. "Kerina, don't sob so. What's wrong?"

"I could not go on talking to him. Knowing who he was. Knowing that his mother recognized me."

"What are you talking about?" Jillian's eyes strayed to the snapshot in the mirror, then back to Kerina's tear-stained face. "What are you talking about?"

"I can't tell you. Please, don't ask."

Jillian crossed the room and snapped up the picture. "The lieutenant looks like this man, doesn't he? You saw the resemblance between them, didn't you?"

"Yes, the moment the lieutenant entered the room."

"I thought I had seen this face before. But it didn't click until now. The *Time* magazine. This snapshot. They look like the same person, but they're not. They couldn't be."

"I know."

"But the lieutenant and this man—they're related?"

"Yes, Jillian." Kerina wrapped her hand around a rose and brushed its petals. "Yes, they are father and son."

The color drained from Jillian's cheeks. "This evening you said that the lieutenant reminded you of your son. I didn't even know you had a child. He is your son, isn't he?"

Kerina's voice quavered. "I knew the minute I saw him—and when I saw his mother, I knew for certain. She was the nurse in the delivery room the night that Chandler was born." Kerina's knuckles were bone white. "I haven't seen them for twenty-six years, not since I gave my baby away."

Chapter 18

Franck stormed into the dressing room, his bearded face flushed. "Kerina, who was that young man in the hall with an older woman? He looked familiar. Midtwenties. Wearing a tuxedo."

"Many of the guests this evening were in black tie."

Again, he demanded, "Who was he, Kerina?"

She gave him a carefree shrug. "A fan. A well-wisher. Jillian, what did he say his name was?" She didn't wait for the answer, but said, "Franck, I will be ready in a minute—here, unzip me. Never mind, I got it myself."

"Kerina, you look like you've been crying."

"Do I?"

He glared at Jillian. "Has Jillian upset you?"

"Of course not. Now, what time do we meet the McClarens?"

"Dinner is off, Kerina. Elias just called to cancel."

"Called?" She poked her head around the dressing screen. "I thought they were at the concert."

"They went home during the second intermission."

"Was I that bad?"

"No, my dear. You were magnificent as always." He paused, glancing toward Jillian again.

"I have no secrets from Jillian, Franck, so what happened?"

"McClaren's wife called their maid several times and got no answer. They always call when they're out just to make certain everything is all right at the mansion. When they couldn't even rally their chauffeur, they rushed home."

Distractedly, Franck rubbed his bony hands. "They were robbed, Kerina." She stifled her gasp. "Was anyone hurt?"

"The maid was restrained and gagged. The chauffeur beaten. But they will live."

Kerina faced him now, her voice ragged. "What did the thief want, Franck? Jewelry? Money? The McClarens' art collection?"

Franck tugged at his beard. "Three thieves. They stole two paintings. Nothing else."

"Two paintings?" Jillian asked. "Not the whole collection?"

"A Degas and a Rembrandt. Taking the VanStryker probably posed a greater risk." He paced the length of Kerina's dresser, his fingers still raking his beard. "It wasn't supposed to happen this way. The police promised to keep a guard at the house during the concert. I tried to warn Elias."

At the tremor in his voice, Kerina crossed the space between them. "Were you expecting trouble, Franck?"

"There was too much interest in the McClarens' exhibit yesterday. Strangers asking questions."

"Why would a museum complain about that? The McClarens always put on an excellent display."

"But calling off our dinner, Kerina—I'm sorry."

"We can have dinner with them another time. Why don't we drive over there and see if we can be of some comfort to them?"

As he scowled, his thick brows slid up and down. "They didn't lose a child, Kerina. Just two paintings."

She flinched, her eyes pools of sadness. "Works of art that have always interested you. Worth millions, I would suspect."

"Believe me, my dear, I didn't take them."

"I am glad." She straightened his tie and kissed his cheek. "We must talk about that soon. Now come. Be a pet and take me to the McClarens' so I can see for myself."

He gripped her wrists. "I don't want you involved. The police will have the place cordoned off. We'd be in the way."

"I know Nicole will let us in. You will excuse us, Jillian?"

"Of course. I was going to run an errand anyway."

Kerina glanced at her jeweled watch. "Wait until morning, dear. That will be time enough to invite our friends to lunch." At the door, she glanced back. "Jillian, could you do something about the flowers? Send two bouquets to my hotel suite—the rest to hospitals."

"Anything special to the hotel?"

The sad twist at her mouth tightened. "Franck's red roses and the vase of carnations from the lieutenant. And it would be best if you told no one where I went this evening."

"Then why don't you take my car?" Jillian dangled the keys. "It's fully automatic. And handy for personal emergencies."

"And you think this is an emergency?"

"Isn't it?" Jill walked over and dropped the keys in Kerina's hand. "You know the car. It will probably be the only red Saab in the hotel parking lot."

Jillian listened to the steady thud of Franck's shoes and the lighter tap of Kerina's heels until the sounds disappeared down the corridor. Something stirred in her mind. Franck was always there, protecting Kerina, so Franck would know about Kerina's son. Was this the secret that Franck wielded to his own advantage? Even art theft?

Jillian hung the midnight blue gown on the brass pole and waited around until the stagehands emptied the room of flowers. Then she switched off the lights and followed them out of the dressing room, her thoughts jumbled with unanswered questions about the robbery. Why a Degas and Rembrandt when the mansion was filled with high-priced masterpieces? Could Franck really be involved in an art conspiracy against his friend? He was shrewd, cunning, wise in the ways of the theater, but hardly one capable of plotting art thefts. She tried to remember whether Franck had left the concert hall during the performance, but she had been too busy thinking pleasant thoughts about the lieutenant from Bosnia. For weeks now, she had hotly defended Kerina's innocence. But had she defended her too quickly?

She should call Brooks Rankin and Joel Gramdino. And tell them what? She had nothing but questions. If Franck Petzold was the mastermind behind the concert thefts, she would be dragged deeper into the mess than she cared to be. She must wait, make certain. But what joy would it be if she was right? Franck was Kerina's stability, her constant companion for years. She would never marry him, but could she live without him?

Ruin Franck and Kerina's career would be over; she would never find strength to go on without him. Blow her own assignment with the Art Theft Registry and Jillian would be out of a job and taking off in a red convertible with no destination in mind.

❦

Joel Gramdino left Brooks Rankin and his wife at a *kaffeehaus* near the Staatsoper; then he hailed a cab smaller than a New Yorker, and taxied to the McClarens' with the meter rolling against the Registry's expense account.

The concert had been okay in his judgment. Highbrow stuff was out of his realm, but he recognized style when he saw it and good music when he heard it. Rudzinski lived up to the best in couture fashion and wore it well, and she surpassed her reputation as a world-class violinist. "The Blue

Danube" still waltzed in his head.

During the program, Joel had used his powerful binoculars to keep Miss Rudzinski's manager and the art collector and his wife in constant focus. Petzold stayed backstage throughout the concert, but the McClarens—decked out fit to kill—left the concert early. Joel's interest in their box seating had mushroomed when he recognized the young man who had been standing in the lobby with Jillian Ingram.

The soldier boy from Bosnia. Out of uniform, but attractive enough to make Jillian take a second look. So Miss Rudzinski had arranged special seating, had she?

As the taxi sped toward the McClarens', he wondered why the American soldier had one of the best views in the theater and with one of the most prominent art collectors in Vienna. Was the soldier messed up in the art thefts? A point of contact? Someone placed close to the McClarens by Kerina Rudzinski? If so, why didn't the lieutenant follow the McClarens when they left the theater during the second intermission?

Joel slouched in the backseat of the taxi, rehearsing the evening. The concert began with "The Blue Danube." No other Strauss waltz was listed on the program. Then Kerina returned to the stage after the second intermission and dedicated a number to someone special. Someone in the audience? Her voice cracked as she spoke. A signal? He was on alert. Once the Brahms "Lullaby" ended, she went immediately into another unscheduled waltz.

Brooks Rankin had slammed his fist into his program with a bull's-eye in the middle as Joel scanned the hot spots with his binoculars. The visible exits. The McClarens' loge seating. He spotted Franck Petzold still standing offstage. But Kerina Rudzinski had signaled someone in the audience! His binoculars swept back to the McClarens for another check. They were gone.

He accomplished nothing by replaying it all in his mind.

The concert was already a thing of the past. He paid the driver and stepped out into the shadows a half block from the McClarens' residence and took the half block with long strides. The place was flooded with lights. Police vehicles lined the street. A bad sign. He pushed his way through the crowd to the cordoned ribbon.

"I need to see Elias McClaren," he told the officer who caught him trying to duck beneath the barrier.

The officer sized him up head to toe, then made eye contact. Arguing persuasively and flashing his ID, Joel crossed the cordoned line. Reporters occupied the McClaren driveway, gaping for a look inside. He made his way past them and into the McClarens' spacious sitting room.

"What did they take?" he asked as he reached McClaren.

Elias turned, scowled. "A Degas and my best Rembrandt. And the limousine. What happened to your security guards, Gramdino?"

"I expected Brooks Rankin to handle that."

"You left me wide open for a robbery."

"I'll talk to Rankin."

I'll have it out with him, Joel thought. So what happened? He didn't have to ask. Brooks liked giving orders. He didn't like an American investigator moving in. Gramdino could pull rank, but hadn't. He'd know better the next time. "I could call Rankin from here," he offered. But how? He didn't remember the name of the coffeehouse and Rankin never hurried a good meal.

"Why bother?" McClaren asked wearily. "The three thieves—"

"Three of them? That's not the usual pattern."

"Then they changed their game plan. Three men accosted my chauffeur, Hans, at the Opera House. Tried to kill him. Ask him."

Joel's frown deepened. *Never bodily injury before, not with the concert conspiracy.* "Where's Hans?"

McClaren pointed through the glass doors that overlooked the terrace. A lone figure sat on the terrace wall, staring into space. He was hunched forward, his back to the house.

"The police blamed him. Hans offered to resign. I was willing to take his resignation." A wry smile touched his lips. "My wife insisted that he stay on."

He decided that McClaren had been this route before. The younger wife. A young employee. "Do you think Hans was involved?"

"Hans is a good man. Been with us for three years."

"I'd like to talk to him, McClaren."

"Officially?"

"Strictly as a representative of the Coventry Registry. You do plan to list the stolen objects with us?" Joel whipped out a small notepad and pen. Chewing the cap from the pen, he left it dangling from the corner of his mouth like an unlit cigarette.

"I can't list them. I'm not going public with this robbery."

"With that crowd out there and the television truck?"

"We told them there was nothing of value stolen."

"Then you won't list with the Registry?"

"Why? We are well insured. And the police say we will never get the paintings back."

"List them with us, McClaren. We can have an alert around the world in minutes. Time is your best chance for recovery."

"With a recovery rate of 5 percent?" Elias scoffed.

"Five percent back in the hands of the rightful owners is a step forward. Given time, our percentages will rise."

Joel glanced around. McClaren's wife was engaged in a conversation with a man in a tailored gray suit. Another woman stood nearby, staring at an empty spot on the wall.

"That's where the Degas hung," Elias said.

"Who's that couple with your wife?"

"You don't recognize the woman?"

"Not with her back to me."

"Kerina Rudzinski, the violinist; she gave her best performance this evening. She never played better. We've been friends for years. That's her manager Franck Petzold talking with my wife. He wants me to exhibit my collection in Moscow for a friend of his."

"You'd risk it after this? When?"

"This month." He shrugged. "Petzold is negotiating for another VanStryker for me. Not go, and I miss the opportunity to purchase that painting."

"Worth the price?" *And worth Petzold's fee?* Joel wondered.

"The portrait by Vincent van Gogh is one of his last works. I want that one before someone else bids on it and sends the price soaring. The other is a VanStryker, an unclaimed masterpiece stolen by the Nazis and then confiscated by the Russians at the close of war. That would be a bonus in my collection."

A legal sale? And what else have Franck and the lovely Miss Rudzinski been negotiating for? He pondered for a moment. *The Registry had no listing of an authentic VanStryker on the market.*

"McClaren, do you trust Petzold's judgment? And after tonight's theft, do you still trust Hans?"

His petulant grimace warned Joel to back off. "Given the position that Hans was in, I would have opened the gate, too." He went from rubbing his jaw to hand-brushing his hair, his motions jerky, disjointed. "This is not a good night for me, Gramdino. Not the time for you to question my friends. My alarm system is state-of-the-art, and look what happened."

A police officer stood at McClaren's side now, demanding his attention. Joel made himself scarce, strolling around the room to admire the pictures still on the walls. Millions in value had been left behind. But why? He glanced through the terrace doors at the despondent Hans and made his way toward him.

When Joel passed the wall where the Degas had hung, he stopped to speak to Kerina Rudzinski. "Good evening, Fräulein Rudzinski. I'm Joel Gramdino."

She turned in deep concentration, her face, even up close, lovely, well-featured. "Yes?"

"A magnificent performance this evening. Your best ever."

A smile touched her eyes, her lips. He took her icy hand and held it momentarily in his broad ones. "You surprised me with those Strauss numbers not listed on your program."

"I know," she whispered. "I like surprises."

"You were playing for someone special."

"Yes, but that was a work by Brahms. For my son," she said. "I learned later that he was in the audience."

Her hand slipped from his. "Your son?"

But she had turned from his question, her gaze fixed on the vacant spot on the wall, her thoughts far away.

"They took a Rembrandt, too," Gramdino said.

"They?" The word seemed lost in the room, in her thoughts.

"Yes, the thieves."

She glanced back briefly. "It has to stop sometime."

When he saw Franck Petzold and Nicole McClaren making their way toward Kerina, he moved off, casually, out through the terrace door. Hans jumped as Gramdino sat down beside him. His face was drawn and ashen, even in the shadows, and his hands were jammed into the pockets of his oversized Donegal tweed coat.

"You've had a bad scare, Hans," Gramdino said.

"I talked to the *polizei;* I told them all I know."

"I'm with the Art Registry. We find stolen art. We can help you—and Herr McClaren. Tell me where you were abducted."

He looked perplexed. "I drove the McClarens to the opera. That's where—in front of the Opera House. Two men—three men."

With a crowd looking on? Kidnapping the chauffeur had been carefully orchestrated. "No one tried to help you, Hans?"

"It happened so quickly that no one noticed." He touched his neck.

"I was knocked out, and when I came to, I saw they were wearing masks and carrying guns."

"An American soldier, perhaps? Anything to identify them?"

"No soldiers. No Americans. Tourists maybe, with strange accents. I think one called himself Vladimir. Another Pierre."

Not German then. "We'll find them," Gramdino promised.

"They could be hiding anywhere. Or driving south. They threatened me—that's how they got into the house. Poor Anna."

"Tell me about it, son. Tell me exactly what happened."

Chapter 19

As the Reynolds left the Opera House, Chandler hailed a horse-drawn fiacre. In the brilliant lights of the Ringstrasse, Ashley could see that the carriage was black, the wheels red. It offered a romantic view of the city that would hurl them back to seventeenth-century travel, the kind of evening that Chandler should spend with a girl like Jillian Ingram. Not with his mother.

Ashley eyed the horse, which was pawing the ground impatiently. Drawing back, she remarked, "Chandler, we could walk to the hotel. It's not far."

"Mother, let's do things the Austrian way."

She chuckled. "Most of them seem to be walking."

The coachman was a cheeky man with full gray sideburns that twisted and curled into his mustache. He wore what appeared to be traditional gear—a red jacket, baggy pants, a bow tie, and a black bowler hat that sat crunched over his balding head. His nose was bulbous, his chin double, and his carriage was ready for customers.

"Well?" Chandler asked. "What do you think, Mom?" The coachman's heavy eyelids narrowed his eyes to merry slits, but he had a friendly smile. Ashley decided that the whip in his hand was nonthreatening. She nodded, still reluctant.

Speaking German, Chandler said, "We're staying at the Empress Isle, sir, but can you take us the long way home?"

"A little ride around the inner city," he agreed.

They settled on a fare and, grinning, Chandler and the coachman helped Ashley mount the narrow step into the carriage. She stepped cautiously in her strapped heels, her elegant gown restricting her movement. She wrapped her stole around her shoulders as the driver shut the door, and with another reassuring smile, swung himself onto the high seat and took the reins in his hand. Gently he nudged his horse with the whip, and the carriage eased away from the curb.

As they turned from the Ringstrasse and merged with the Vienna traffic, Ashley rested her hand on Chandler's arm. "The concert was beautiful, Chan."

"It was great, but it was crazy thinking I could get an interview with a total stranger."

"Yes. . .a total stranger."

Ashley bit her lip and settled back in the seat to listen to the steady *clippety-clop* of the horse. *It was a simple request,* she thought. *Just an interview. Oh, you knew him all right, Kerina Rudzinski. I saw it in the way you looked at him, in the way you traced the features of his face.*

Ashley nursed her fury against Kerina. It was the one way she could bury her own guilt, her own dark secret of betrayal. The complete truth was too painful, too involved, a many-sided memory—a strange polygon.

The night air brushed against her face, cooling her cheeks. *I am angry at you. You recognized Chandler—of that I have no doubt. And you recognized me—I heard it in your greeting. I don't want you to know Chandler, yet I don't want you to reject him again. But you did when you hurried us out of your dressing room this evening.*

"What's wrong, Mother? Tired?"

"I'm fine."

But she had just lied to him. One chamber of her heart had always been off limits to her family, to her friends. The chamber of her heart where she had long harbored Kerina's secret, where she harbored her own.

Their carriage looped through the inner city, taking them back in time past Gothic edifices en route to their hotel. The midnight hour closed in on them, but the city of Vienna was awakening, coming alive to celebrate the evening. The concert crowd walked leisurely toward the restaurants and coffeehouses. In the distance Ashley could see the Prater Ferris wheel spinning around slowly. Their driver followed the flow of traffic, giving them a marvelous view of the well-lit Parliament, the City Hall, and the Palace. Chandler sat humming a waltz, musing, even smiling, but behind his dark eyes she sensed an unsettledness. Questions.

Chandler must be told the truth. For now he was still her son. But tonight, in the quiet of the hotel, she would tell him about his birth mother.

Chandler leaned down and kissed Ashley's gloved hand, his lips not quite making contact. "That's the way the Austrians do it," he said. "Thank you for coming to Vienna with me. But I'm worried about you. Are you missing Dad?"

"I should be—but we've been too busy."

He laughed dryly. "We promised to call him after the concert, but let's call in the morning. Are you hungry? We could have our coachman drop us off at a coffeehouse or at the Sacher, if you prefer."

"I'd rather go to the hotel. It's been a long day."

At the Empress Isle, Chandler helped the coachman lift Ashley from the carriage; then he paid the man, tipping him liberally.

"You shouldn't lift me, not when your leg is hurting."

"You were light as a feather."

But as they walked up the steps he was limping.

～

An hour later, Ashley tightened the belt around her robe and padded softly over the thick carpet in her blue slippers to Chandler's room. He lay in the middle of the monstrous bed, stretched out on his back, his bare arms on top of the sheets, two pillows tucked behind his head.

"Hi, Chan. May I come in?"

"Sure. Been waiting to say good night."

She pulled a chair closer and sat down beside him. "You enjoyed yourself this evening, didn't you, son?"

"Thoroughly. But I was disappointed about the interview."

"Perhaps some other time."

"We'll see."

Her heart lurched. His pensive gaze looked so much like Kerina Rudzinski's. Had he noticed the similarity? Or seen that snapshot of Bill on Kerina's mirror? No, there would be no reason for him to connect that faded snapshot with Bill VanBurien. And how long had it been since he had looked at the family photo albums with her? Three years? Five years? Why would he recognize Bill? He had never seen him.

"Miss Rudzinski liked you," Ashley said.

"I think she liked the flowers better."

"That was sweet of you to send them."

He shrugged. "I was trying to do everything right. You know, thanking her ahead of time for the interview."

"Don't dwell on your disappointment."

"I won't. It was a good evening, and she was lovely."

Ashley's clasped hands tightened. *Tell him now,* she told herself. *Let him know why he was drawn to her.* But what if Kerina Rudzinski rejected him again?

He frowned, his gaze going from the ceiling back to her face. "Miss Rudzinski said she had a son my age."

"I heard her." Ashley wanted to clap her hands over her ears to prevent him from telling her that he knew the truth already. She braced herself for the inevitable.

He stretched, made himself more comfortable, buried his head deeper into the pillows. "She didn't mention her husband."

"Perhaps there is no husband, Chan."

"I can't imagine not having a dad in the family. What kind of an upbringing did the poor kid have?"

"Tutors," she suggested. "And nannies. He would have been well cared for—provided for. The best of everything."

"But hopping from country to country? Playing cars in the dressing rooms behind the concert halls? Talking to his mother during the intermission? Probably never in one place long enough to learn how to play soccer."

"I'm sure they worked it out, Chandler."

The room was warm, the air conditioner low. Ashley felt goose bumps prickling her skin. Her spine was rigid from a nervous chill. She rubbed her hands, trying to warm them; her right hand was frigid, as though the circulation had stopped. *Stop talking in circles. Tell him. Tell him the young boy didn't play in the back rooms of a concert hall. Tell him. Tell him* he *is the young boy.*

Chandler looked sleepy, his eyelids drooping as he watched her. She must tell him now before he slept.

He reached for her hand. "What's wrong? You're cold as ice." He rubbed it between his own, laughing. "You did this for me when I was a kid coming in from the snow. There, that should do it."

"It's late, Chandler."

"Then go get some sleep. I'm about passed out myself. I think—" His words were lost in a yawn. "I think we'd better sleep in late, Mom."

"Let's do. But first, Chandler, I—your father and I—"

"Hmm?"

No, she told herself. *Leave David out of this. This is between you and your son.* She felt frost-nipped; the glacial chill paralyzed her.

She wanted to blame it on Kerina Rudzinski and did. She remembered it as it had happened and thought bitterly, *Kerina, without ever knowing who we were, you shackled us to that promise.*

The conditions had gone back and forth from Kerry Kovac to the lawyer. From the lawyer to David and Ashley. *You forced us to sign that Consent Decree. No, you signed it. But we gave you our word. Our word to the lawyer, his to you—your last hold on your son, binding David and me to silence.*

My son must never know that he is adopted, Kerry Kovac had written on the Consent Decree. *They agree to that or else—*

Or else what? You live a lie for twenty-six years.

Ashley tried again. "Chandler, I have a confession to make. But—I want you to know that I have loved you from that first moment in the delivery room."

"Good thing," he said, smiling groggily. "I came into this world on good faith. Depended on you."

She rushed on. "I never intended to hurt you—"

"No. . .problem, Mom. Go. . .get some sleep."

The room went stark still, not a sound. And then one sound. The low rumble of her son's muffled snoring.

"Chandler. . .Chandler."

His eyes were closed, his muscular arms stretched against the pillow. His lean chest moved rhythmically, up and down. His breathing became deep and even, his face untroubled, relaxed in sleep. She touched her dozing son, her fingertips grazing his forehead. *Some other time,* her thoughts whispered. *I will tell you then.*

～

Ashley went back to her own suite, closing the door behind her. She heard it click and knew that she was locked out until Chandler opened it again. She crossed to her bed in the darkness, slipped out of her dressing gown, and slid beneath the cool, crisp sheets. Even on this spring evening in May, she snuggled beneath the covers and felt as chilled as she had in Chandler's room. Sleep eluded her. She was too angry with Kerina. *You have ruined everything by coming back into our lives,* she cried.

But she knew it was her own unforgiving heart that stood in the way. She wanted more than anything to feel her mother's arms around her. Even though Mama had been dead for twenty-eight years now, she was as present in this room as she had been back in the house in Everdale. Always there singing, praying, laughing, comforting.

She thought of Mama saying, *"Remember, Ashley dear, the forgiving heart goes a long way toward happiness."*

But Ashley had forgotten how to forgive, how to be forgiven. As she tossed and turned, the luminous dial of the clock pushed the minutes ahead. One o'clock. Two o'clock. Three. When had she last been happy, peaceful? With David? Yes, joyous in the beginning, even content in these later years. She had loved him since the day she met him on the school bus. Two years ago some insidious thing had drifted between them. Memories partly. And guilt. Unasked, uninvited, she let the distance grow, shutting herself away in her garden, shutting David out.

Even in those good days with David, had she ever really been carefree as in the days of her childhood with the smell of cookies baking in Mama's kitchen and the rich fragrance of pines and cedars in the woods behind the house? Memories. Mama coming into her room to say good night. The little church that David would later pastor. The old-timers always rehashing the Confederate battles of the Civil War and casting covert glances at any Yankee who passed through town.

The miserable blunders, the sins of that year she graduated from high school, lingered in the shadows. She pushed them away, once again assigning them to the abyss—refusing to allow them to erase the enchantment of her childhood in Mama's house.

Nothing could dim that memory, not even the bleak landscapes on the frosty mornings of winter. Nothing could steal her joy of being back in that old house with its high ceilings and no central heating, yet as warm as any place could be with Mama there.

In the darkness of the Empress Isle Hotel, the memories of Everdale played across her mind. Fire logs stacked against the shed, the smell of wood smoke in the evening air, the glow of the kerosene lantern on the table when the rare ice storms short-circuited the electric wires in Everdale. Outside, the howling winds wrapped around the old pillars. Inside, Mama, Bill, and Ashley sat huddled by the potbellied stove in the living room or curled by the wood-burning stove in the kitchen—Mama drinking coffee and Bill and Ashley sipping mugs of cocoa before going to bed. She remembered that mad dash from the warm kitchen into the bedroom in her bare feet and climbing in between cold sheets. Cold like the ones she had just slipped into here in Vienna.

As a child she had shivered on her feather bed, lulled to sleep by shadows from the dying fire flickering on the ceiling. At the close of winter, spring came, her favorite time of the year. Spring pushed its way into Everdale in late February with daffodils and flowering quince. In March the azaleas and the wisteria and the dogwoods would burst into bloom in Mama's yard.

You knew it was spring when Mama put up new birdhouses for the cardinals and bluebirds and kept her windows open so she could enjoy the evening air scented with honeysuckle.

The summers in Everdale came with lush greens growing everywhere. Life slowed down. Daytime was oppressive with heat. Bill and Ashley ran barefoot, waiting for the iceman to come around the corner with a twenty-five-pound block of ice on his back. The evenings were warm with what Mama called the smell of Southern summer. She'd sit on the porch swing, a tinkling glass of iced tea in her hand. Ashley sat with her, shelling peas for her and listening to Bill mimic the frogs and crickets out by the gazebo.

When the next-door neighbor would drop in to sit a spell and swing with her, Mama bragged (it was the only time Mama ever bragged) about the butter beans, black-eyed peas, okra, and summer squash in her vegetable garden.

Sampling Mama's fresh-baked cookies and fanning herself with her apron, the neighbor would say, "I'll trade you some. A bit of your okra for a bowl of my fresh, ripe tomatoes."

For long moments, Ashley thrashed on her hotel bed, her eyes swollen from lack of sleep. And then thoughts of fall in Everdale crept in with its smell of burning leaves and dead wood. Autumn back home had filled her with sadness—the dread of everything dying, of going back to school, of the bleakness of winter coming again, and of the cemetery ghostly with its headstones in the family plot. Bill went away in the fall and Mama died in the fall—wonderful, laughable, lovable Mama. The sin of Ashley's youth came just as the seasons of summer and fall merged. But it was springtime when Chandler came into their lives and her twin brother Bill died.

In the darkness of the Empress Isle Hotel, Ashley thought about the two letters that Bill had left on the passenger seat of his car, letters that he had intended to post on the night he was killed in a traffic accident—only days after Chandler was born. One letter to Ashley. The other, addressed to the violinist, remained sealed, undelivered. It had been locked in the top drawer of Ashley's desk back home, but she had brought it to Vienna to give to Kerina Rudzinski.

Those letters were part of Everdale. Part of Ashley's unhappiness. And yet the good memories of life in Mama's house far outweighed the dread of autumn or the bitter pain of Bill's death. Bill's childhood had been happy, too. Ashley scolded herself in retrospect. What had she done leaving all that behind, running away, and taking Chandler from that magical experience of growing up in Mama's old house?

She turned on the bedside lamp and stared at the clock again. Four a.m. She crawled out of bed and jabbed her arms back into her robe and padded barefoot—like she had done as a child—to the windows. She pushed the drapes aside. Some of the night lights of Vienna were still flickering, but it was the sky that caught her attention. A bright half moon wearing a skull cap and a host of dazzling stars spattered across the night sky.

David loved the starry host. Out of all of his sermons, she remembered one. She pictured him in his clerical robe, his arms outstretched, his fingers pointing heavenward. *"Look,"* he said in his deep, rich voice. *"Look up at the heavens and count the stars—if indeed you can count them."*

Ashley could not count them. Except for the Evening Star and the Big Dipper she could barely call them by name. She left the drapes drawn and lay down once more to watch the sky over Vienna from her windows. Tears stung behind her eyes. She remembered a night much like this one twenty-six years ago with an almost full moon and the heavens bathed in brilliant stars. It was the night that Bill VanBurien had come back to Everdale for the last time.

Chapter 20

Everdale
April 13, 1973

Everdale was in the middle of nowhere, far south of Montgomery, Alabama—a sleepy place with a railroad track running through the middle of town. The stores in the business district ran down both sides of the tracks. The brownstone courthouse and bank lay on the east side, the craft store and Barney's Hardware Store with the Confederate flag still hanging on the back wall to the west. The owner of the craft store was a Yankee trying to make a go of her business, but she was as welcomed as a bad case of Asian flu in a town where few strangers ever lingered.

The town had a worn look to it, but people took pride in their place in history. Streets were kept clean, lawns mowed, historical buildings preserved. Most folks were neighborly, taking time to chat a bit over a cup of coffee and meeting at the grange for Saturday night bingo. A white, steepled church on the south side had a long list of interim pastors until David came.

Freight trains rattled through twice a day right on schedule, and a twice-weekly passenger train seldom had need to stop at the railroad depot. Except for the curious faces pressed against the smudgy train windows, Everdale remained a community turned inward, a shunning town that had no need for outsiders. Seasons came and went—hot summers, fall with bright leaves, winter with its bleakness. But this was a perfect spring day fragrant with blossoms, a snappy breeze whipping Ashley's wash and making billowy tents of the sheets and twisted coils of the towels.

The mockingbirds sang, and the wind scuttled flower petals across Ashley's path as she picked her way back toward the house. When she reached the gazebo, she set the laundry basket down and sat a spell, lifting her face up to the touch of summer that was only weeks away. A rush of tears came as she thought of Mama, Pops, and Bill. Her dad remained vague in her memory because she could not put a face to someone she barely remembered. Mama's face faded sometimes, too, but never the sound of her laughter or the sight of her peering out the window as the school bus rattled to a stop in front of the house and Bill and Ashley piled out.

Growing up, the VanBurien twins were a puzzle to everyone. Ashley was considered the good twin—*that dear sweet girl.* Bill—*that brother of hers,* the erring one. Ashley fiercely protected him. Always had. But once, when she was the erring twin, he had helped her. Ashley's roots went deep, and except for nursing school, nothing short of a disaster could pry her away from the old hometown. The deep roots trapped Bill. Once he graduated from high school, he caught the passenger train out of Everdale and headed for the first navy recruiting station he could find.

As the sun dipped low on the horizon, she picked up the laundry basket and carried it into the house and up the narrow stairs to the second floor where she dumped the wash load on the old bed in Mama's room, the room that was hers and David's now. "The master bedroom," David called their nine-by-twelve breathing space.

David was the only other Yankee living in town, if you could call him that. His grandparents had owned a farm outside of Everdale, but David had been born and reared in Southern California. He found Mama's house too cramped compared to the modern complexes going up across town. But Mama's place was good enough for Ashley, even though the creaky rafters refused to ring with Mama's old chuckle and Bill never came back anymore, not even for short visits.

Shortly after they married, they turned Ashley's old room into a nursery, painting it white with a border of colorful animals for the baby that would one day fill the room. But after those trips to the infertility clinics in Montgomery and Mobile (they were the rage now) and changing doctors, they knew they would never have a child of their own to fill the nursery.

Ashley could never bear another child. But how could she tell David when he didn't know about the one she had carried in her womb and aborted in Montgomery—the butcher job that left her barren? Someday, she had promised herself, she would talk to David about adopting someone else's child. Her arms ached from emptiness. And then six weeks ago, Dr. Nelson had announced he'd found a baby for them.

She sighed and picked up a sheet, squared it, folded it, hand-pressed the wrinkles. Absently she folded the rest of the clothes, putting them in neat, systematic piles. Sheets and pillowcases in sets. Towels and washcloths together. Underwear in separate stacks. She dumped David's socks in the middle of the four-poster bed where he would match and fold them himself. It was one of those quirks of marriage, one of their first major battles. She chuckled, recalling that first clash like yesterday.

"Ashley sweetie, these socks don't go together," he had said.

David had stood in the middle of the room, muscular and thick-browed, holding up a pair of socks for her inspection. He looked impeccable in his starched shirt and blue suit, a good-looking man who still made her heart palpitate. That morning it pounded in defiance. How dare he criticize her work! She had snatched the socks from his hand and held them up to the sunlight.

Coldly she had said, "Same color: brown. Same brand: from the Penney's catalogue, David. Same length: size 10."

"Yes, but they don't match," he had reasoned.

She had thrown them at him and made her first declaration of marital independence. "From now on, David, I wash them; you match and fold them."

She scooped up a pile of sheets and buried her nose in the air-dried bedding as she headed for the linen closet. "Oh Mama, how did you ever find time to iron sheets and towels?"

The hours had gotten away from her. Hurriedly, she laid out her uniform and shoes for the night shift at the hospital. She heard the distinct roar of a car careening along the country road and then the screeching of brakes. She ran to the windows and squinted into the shadows. A car was parked in the gravel on the wrong side of the street with its lights turned off. She saw no one hurrying up toward their porch to ask for assistance, but she did notice two figures in the front seat. As she watched, the car's engine turned over again. The driver eased the car back onto the road and, with a grating of the gears, took the first winding curve with the headlights still off.

Forty minutes later—after scouring the sinks and the toilet bowls—she ran down the steps into the kitchen where David was browning steaks and steaming garden vegetables for dinner.

"Thanks for doing dinner. Smells good," she said. "And I'm starving."

He cocked his ear. "Is that someone running on the porch?"

Someone pressed the doorbell, demanding entry. "I'll go, David. I don't want burned steaks."

She switched on the porch light, eyeballed the peephole, and could barely turn the key fast enough to swing the door open.

"Bill!" she exclaimed, her voice filled with pleasure. She was smothered by Bill's lanky arms as he stepped inside, swept her up with a spontaneous hug, and whirled her around.

"Hi, sis." Laughter rippled from him.

"Bill, what brought you to Everdale?"

"I needed the old hometown," he teased.

She stepped back so she could look at him. Six-foot-four, ramrod straight, his angular face deceptively attentive and guileless. She glanced past him. "Where's Celeste and the boys?"

"They didn't come. I drove down with a friend in my new Chevy."

"A lady friend?" she asked worriedly.

He cuffed her chin playfully. "We drove straight through from Chicago. So no lectures, sis, please. Things will work out."

"They always do for you, don't they?"

He forced a grin. "Not always, Ashley. Not this time."

As she led him into the kitchen, David lanced Bill with his intent pulpit gaze. "I threw another steak on when I heard your voice in the hall. Medium rare, if I remember right?"

"I'm hungry as a mountain lion."

"You here for long?" David asked, turning the steaks.

"A few days, if that's all right with you two."

"Would have been better if you had come sooner," David said evenly. "Like two years ago, *before* your mama died."

"I just didn't get here in time."

"Why didn't you?"

"Look, David, I can sleep in the car if you want me to."

"No, you'll stay with us," Ashley said. "In your old room." She glared at David. Let the sparks fly and Bill would walk out again. Her two favorite men had been good friends once. Now David, stouthearted as ever, saw everything in black and white. Bill was double-sided, double-minded, motivated by his own heartstrings. Bill had been brilliant in college. Successful at work. Climbing the corporate ladder, yet constantly struggling in his marriage. Everything was arbitrary with Bill, the middle line and gray okay with him, classical music his greatest relaxation.

Bill came from good stock, but he was like worsted cloth, a smooth, hard-twisted man, a rough fabric in a weave of many colors. Charming one minute. Bolting the next. Lose him and she would never know what had driven him back to Everdale at this precise time in his troubled life. She touched Bill's hand. "Let's not quarrel. Let's just enjoy our time together."

Minutes later, as they sat around the kitchen table eating steaks and sipping coffee, Ashley noticed the haggard creases that edged Bill's blue eyes. He was only twenty-nine, but graying temples added a distinctive touch to his thick blond hair He was not just lanky but much too thin. He looked more like Mama with each passing year—dimpled cheeks,

193

angular face with sensitive overtones. But he had broken Mama's heart when he married into one of the prominent Chicago families.

"How's Celeste?" Ashley asked as she warmed his coffee.

His cup rattled. "She moved back home with her parents."

"Again?" David asked. "You can't toss out nine years of marriage. Why can't you two work things out?"

Bill twisted his wedding band. "It's too late. Celeste has filed for divorce."

"On what grounds?" Ashley asked.

A crooked smile dragged at the corners of his mouth. "Infidelity. I've messed up. Blown everything this time."

Ashley rubbed the back of his hand and found it trembling. "Is that why you haven't written lately, or called? Not even one phone call in the last several months?"

"There wasn't much to say." It seemed an effort for him to lift his face to meet her gaze. "Ash, eleven months ago I thought I was going to be happy, really happy for the first time in my life. I met someone, fell in love. But even that was blown away." A bite of steak fell from his fork back onto his plate. "Don't say it, David. Another woman. Another affair. I know I'm married. I know it's wrong." He dropped his fork on his plate. "Man, I miss Mom. I knew I could always depend on her."

"David and I are here for you. You can call us anytime."

"Ash, I've been a disappointment to this family. But just once in my life I'm going to do something for all of us."

"We don't need anything. We just want you to keep in touch."

Bill's mouth turned at the corner, a pathetic twist that reminded her of his childhood when he was dreading punishment, expecting it. Ashley squeezed his hand. "I love you, Bill."

"I'm glad someone does. I hate Everdale, but when I'm away I constantly think about home. A few months ago I told my friend about my mother's home, my sister's home, my childhood home."

"And what did your friend say?"

"She said she wanted to go there someday."

"You're always welcome here, Bill. Bring your friends. Bring your boys. How are they by the way?"

Pride came into his eyes. "Skip's almost as tall as Jeff now. Eight and seven. Poor kids, they're skinny rascals."

"You should have brought them."

"They're with Celeste—staying with their grandparents."

"We'll have a son in our house soon," David said.

"Or maybe a daughter," Ashley reminded him.

Bill scanned Ashley's one hundred twenty pounds, frowning.

"Having our own child wasn't an option for us, Bill."

David sent her a reassuring smile. "When we found we couldn't have children, I wanted to adopt right away."

"And I fought it until Dr. Nelson told me he had just the right baby for us. It's a private arrangement with Dr. Nelson and a lawyer from Montgomery. The girl's coming here to Everdale."

The old cocky grin tugged at Bill's mouth. "To the middle of nowhere to have her baby? Sounds like something I'd cook up."

"A friend of Doc's referred her," David said.

Bill seemed remote again as he traced the patterns of the oilcloth with the cap of his ballpoint pen. A somber expression crossed his face. "You don't seem happy about the baby, sis. I thought that's what you wanted."

"We're not comfortable with a closed adoption. The mother doesn't want to meet us or know anything about us. I'll be right there at the hospital when the baby is born, and I won't even be able to tell her who I am."

Bill scowled. "Is that so wrong?"

David stacked his dirty dishes. "It isn't honest."

"Honey," Ashley interjected, "we've talked this out with Dr. Nelson a dozen times already. It's the girl's decision, not ours. Not yours. She doesn't even know you're a preacher."

"But did we have to agree with it? I stand behind the pulpit every Sunday, and I'm about to lie to a little baby. Someday the child will want to know more—who his parents were. All we'll be able to say to the child is, 'Your father was a businessman, and your mother was a musician.' How's that for knowing your roots?"

"We can't tell the child anything, David. The papers will be sealed." Ashley searched Bill's face. "Bill, David and I want this baby more than anything, but why is that mother coming nine hundred miles to a place like Everdale to have her baby?"

"Maybe she knows someone here, Ash."

As the grandfather clock in the living room chimed ten, Ashley shoved back her chair. "I'm on the graveyard shift, Bill. I hate leaving you two with the cleanup."

David laughed. "We could save it for you until morning."

"Do that and I'll throw the dishes at you."

Ashley reappeared thirty minutes later in her nurse's uniform. "Bill, I left towels and bedding out for you."

Bill's chair scraped as he pushed it back. He chuckled. "Dave, you make up the bed. I'll walk Ashley to the car."

He limped beside her to the door, his old navy wound kicking up a fuss. "I've never understood why you like this dreary little town, sis."

"Mama liked it."

"You and Mama were the only good things about it."

He stopped by the front pillar and stared up at the shadowed trees. A spring breeze brushed his face. "I'm glad it isn't fall. I always hated it when the old maple leaves started falling."

"Everything is beginning to bloom now. You'll see in the morning. We can go walking in the woods when I get home."

"You'll be beat."

"I like taking a walk before I go to bed."

"And crunching through dead leaves?" he asked bitterly.

"All your life, you've fought off the end of summer."

"And the barren woods and the turning of leaves to amber and burnt orange. I hated stacking logs for winter."

But most of all Ashley knew that fall reminded him of Mama. He had flown home when she was dying, but Mama—Bill's life support, his link with God—was gone before he reached Everdale.

When he'd left after the funeral, he asked, "If your God is so big, sis, why didn't He wait? Why didn't He let Mama live until I got home?" Then he gave Ashley a firm hug before limping off toward the boarding ramp.

"Bill," she had called after him, "if you ever need us—"

Turning back he'd saluted her with his boarding pass. "If I ever need Everdale or you again, I'll whistle."

Bill was whistling now. He closed her car door and leaned in the window. "You've never forgiven yourself about that abortion."

"How would you know that?"

"I see it in your face. Have you ever told David?"

"No. I can never bring myself to tell him. But, Bill, don't hold that against David. You two were friends once."

"And don't let Montgomery destroy you, Ash. Once you adopt that baby, the pain of Montgomery will slip away."

The good twin, the erring one. "And don't let Celeste slip away. You need her and the boys."

"I know. Without them—without Mom—I'm nothing."

She turned the ignition. "I'm family, too. Remember?"

He stepped back and winked. "Things will work out, Ash. For all of us. They always do."

He cupped his hands and gave the call of the whippoorwill, the way he always did when they parted as children.

～

Ashley turned down the winding street and pulled into the parking lot of the forty-four-bed hospital where she worked. The evening shift waited idly at the nurses' station, eager to be off duty. Selma Malkoski stood when she saw Ashley and handed her the key to the medicine cabinet. "I hear Bill's back in town, Ashley."

"Just for a few days. But how did you—"

Her brows arched. "Did he bring that sweet family of his?"

"No, the boys are in school now."

Selma's eyes mocked her. Selma was one of the scars that Bill had left behind with an irresponsible shrug of his bony shoulders. Selma had never forgotten. Never forgiven.

As Ashley pinned her cap in place—a habit she clung to—Beth Duran spun her chair around. "Ashley," she said gently, "Dr. Nelson told me to tell you his OB case is here now."

"Someone from town?"

Beth shook her head. "No, not Emma Garvey again. This one's a stranger, an out-of-towner from up North."

Ashley froze. *My unborn child.* "What's her name? What's the mother like?"

"The mystery girl?" Selma asked. "She's a fancy one—expensive luggage, the latest clothes. Looks like she's a violinist; at least she checked in with a Stradivarius. She calls herself Kerry Kovac but I doubt if she gave us her right name. She's as sullen and noncommunicative as they come. With her admission we have a full house. . .just three beds left for emergencies."

"Then I'm understaffed, and if the OB should deliver tonight—"

Selma patted her shoulder. "You can handle it. You may be busy, but you'll have violin music."

Beth's ebony face glowed. "Tell you one thing, if I were trying to hide my identity, I wouldn't come to Everdale. You can barely sneeze in town without someone starting a rumor. You know us; we specialize in curious eyes and quick tongues."

"The girl didn't come alone, Ashley," Selma said. "Someone drove her right to the emergency entrance in a brand new car with an Illinois license plate. Bold as you please." She gave Ashley a piercing glance. "Then he sped away so no one could identify him."

"Go easy on her, Selma," Beth said. "The poor kid is single and scared." She flipped the kardex, ready to give her evening report. "The girl intended to come here. Right smack-dab to Everdale to have her baby. So now we're the Dale Motel for unwed mothers. She should have checked into the hotel over in Spruceville, but she was so depressed, Dr. Nelson insisted on admitting her. If nothing happens by the fifteenth, he'll induce labor."

Moments later, when Ashley made her rounds, she hesitated at the girl's door—afraid to face this girl who never wanted to know her. Kerry Kovac lay on her back, her hands clenched tightly on either side of the yellow spread. A shadowed hump rose and fell with her uneven breathing. She had a porcelain, doll-like quality to her features, her dark auburn hair intensifying her pallor. She was young. Nineteen, the chart said.

Ashley walked to the bed and leaned over the side rail.

"Kerry, I'm Mrs. Reynolds, your night nurse. How are you?"

In the shadowed light, the girl's lower lip trembled; the fingers on her soft exquisite hands flattened against the spread. Ashley touched Kerry's arm. Her skin felt cold and clammy. "Kerry, do you want me to notify anyone that you are here? A friend? Your family?"

"No. No one." She turned away.

Ashley wanted to draw her back. The watch on her wrist, the clothes in her closet, the expensive violin were clues to the real Kerry Kovac. And yet she had chosen to come to Everdale, a town that was warm and friendly to those who belonged but cold and hostile to someone from the North.

"Where's your family, Kerry?"

"In Prague." A tear slid down her cheek. "They don't know about the baby. They'd be so ashamed. They think I am in Alabama on concert. But I have no desire to ever play again."

"You will—when this is all over."

"Will it ever end, Mrs. Reynolds?"

"Soon, Kerry." She quoted Bill. "Things always work out."

As the girl stared blindly out the darkened window, Ashley said, "The woods behind my house were beautiful today."

"It was too dark to see anything when we drove into town."

We? Ashley longed to take Kerry for a walk in the woods so she could get to know the beauty of Everdale where her child would live. Ashley wanted her to see the dogwoods and sumacs, the sweet gum trees, and the little leaf huckleberry. She wanted her to smell the honeysuckle bushes in front of Mama's house. She wanted Kerry to hear David's message on God's love, God's forgiveness.

"In the morning you'll see how beautiful it is in Everdale."

"It is pretty in Prague now, too," Kerry said.

~

On the night Chandler was born, Pitocin dripped steadily from Kerry's IV bottle. She lay on the delivery table, her feet in stirrups. Beads of perspiration lined her forehead, poured down her neck. Between contractions, she fell back against the pillows exhausted, panting. Crying without tears.

Ashley ached for the emptiness, for the unexpressed grieving that was tearing Kerry apart. She would deliver a child, but it would not bring joy. Only separation. Even the squirming antics of her unseen infant that she had felt in these last months of pregnancy would be gone. Kerry seemed determined to hold back her screams, but her nails dug into Ashley's hand with each contraction.

Birth should bring you happiness, Ashley thought. But there was no gladness in the room, only the clanging of the metal carts and the squeak of the bassinet being rolled into the room.

As Selma bustled around the room, Ashley dabbed Kerry's face with a cloth and reached out to steady the cold, trembling knees. "Dr. Nelson is on his way, Kerry. It will be over soon."

Kerry nodded, her eyes filling with tears. The hot, windowless room was oppressive. The skin stretched taut over Kerry's swollen, glistening abdomen.

Ashley heard Dr. Nelson's lumbering footsteps plodding down the corridor, heard the whack as his broad shoulders split the swinging doors. Kerry panicked as he barreled in. By the time Dr. Nelson settled himself at the foot of the delivery table, his gloved hands raised, she was in full-blown labor, ready to push.

"It won't be long, Miss Kovac," he said cheerily. "Your baby will soon be here. Go ahead. Push, Kerry," he commanded. "Push!"

The pungent smell of amniotic fluid filled the air. He peered at Kerry over his mask. "I see the baby's head. Hang in there, Kerry."

She cried out now as the slick, milky-wet baby slipped out between her legs.

Moments later, Nelson gave another satisfied exclamation. "We've got a little boy, Miss Kovac."

There was a gasp, Ashley's gasp, as a tiny baby filled his lungs with air and cried. *Kerry Kovac's baby. No, my baby.*

Kerry fell exhausted against the pillow as Dr. Nelson held the baby up. Tears of joy filled Ashley's eyes.

"He's beautiful, Kerry," Dr. Nelson said. "Just beautiful. You have a fine son. Would you like to hold him?"

He held the baby up with the bluish cord still attached and pulsating with Kerry's blood. For a moment, the innocent infant lay wiggling in Dr. Nelson's palm. Then he was placed on her flattened abdomen, his body small and fair, his attempt at another cry lost in a yawn.

Ashley knew that if Kerry held her baby she might want to keep him. But as she watched the girl pull back, her eyes closed, she urged, "Would you like to hold him, Kerry?"

Now the tears fell freely. Kerry reached out and stroked the infant's cheek and silky, blood-matted hair, the pain of separation intense. "Take him away," she whispered.

~

The night Kerry Kovac was to leave the hospital Ashley found her standing by the nursery window in the middle of the hall. Her suitcase and violin case were on the floor beside her; the bold name tags on both of them read KERINA RUDZINSKI.

The girl watched the baby's every move, a look that would have to last her a lifetime if Ashley didn't intervene. Ashley struggled with reality: *Her baby, my baby.*

His eyes, almost oriental in appearance, flickered. His ears were close to his scalp and his hair thick and auburn like Kerry's. The glass between them shut out the sucking sounds that must surely be coming from his rosebud mouth as he tried to chew his chubby fist.

Kerry bent down and took two sheets of scented stationery from her violin case and handed them to Ashley.

"Will you make certain that the couple who take my baby get this? Promise me."

Ashley's throat went dry. "I promise. But, Kerry, before you go, would you like to hold your baby?"

She nodded and followed Ashley, accepting the surgical gown and the rocking chair in the alcove without a word.

It was a magical moment. Kerry hardly breathed when Ashley placed the baby in her arms. There were long stretches of quiet for both of them as Kerry took in the feel of him, the sight of him. The child was warm and unbelievably alive and real as he tilted his head in contentment toward Kerry's breast.

"I am so sorry. So sorry," she whispered as she rocked him.

Ashley knelt beside her and unfolded the blanket. The baby's pink toes curled; his legs kicked. Kerry touched his tiny hands with her fingertips. Muffled joy escaped her as she felt the grasp of his fingers on her own. "You are so beautiful," Kerry said.

As Ashley knelt by the rocker, her chest muscles tightened. "It's not too late to change your mind, Kerry."

Kerry kissed her son. "If I gave up my music, Mrs. Reynolds, I would end up back in Prague. It was difficult where I grew up. I don't want that for my son." She kissed him again. "I must go back to my music. I have no choice. My family sacrificed for my career. They are proud of me, but they would be so ashamed if they knew about the baby."

Gurgling, cooing sounds filled the room. Kerry gazed up into Ashley's face. "I travel a lot and live out of suitcases. I go from concert hall to concert hall, from country to country. That is no life for my baby. I want the best for him. I want him to grow up in this country, to have a good home. To have both a mother and father."

Gently Ashley asked, "Is the baby's father married?"

Kerry's body went rigid. In a barely audible whisper she answered, "Yes, but I didn't know that at first. I was on concert in Chicago when I met him."

She cupped the baby's hand and held it. "I grew up under communism, but my parents were godly people. They sacrificed for their faith. I wanted no part of that life, Mrs. Reynolds. I kept searching for something else—someone else—to belong to." She smiled faintly. "Suddenly in Chicago, there he was—so tall he stood out in a crowd. Then he laughed that deep laugh of his as he gave me a dimpled smile and a bouquet of flowers."

"Roses?" Ashley asked, knowing they were her brother's favorite flower.

"Yes. White ones." Her tears dropped on the baby's blanket. "When we knew about the baby, I wanted an abortion. But he said, 'No, that happened to someone dear to me, Kerry. Never again. Two wrongs don't make a right. I'll think of something.'"

Kerry hesitated. "But my having a baby has changed him. Grieved him. He would keep our baby if I would let him."

Ashley felt embarrassed by the girl's honesty. Would the baby ever be truly David's and hers? Ashley was afraid and was certain that she knew why. She leaned down to take the child.

"Please, Mrs. Reynolds, could I have a few more minutes with him—before I let him go?"

Ashley left Kerry alone with her son so she could tell him she loved him. Alone so she could cradle him for the last time. Later, when Ashley took the baby from Kerry, she knew that some of that warmth of him would stay with Kerry Kovac forever.

She led Kerry out of the nursery alcove. The girl went back blindly to the hallway and picked up her suitcase and violin. "Thank you, Mrs. Reynolds."

Ashley squeezed her hand. Kerry returned the gesture.

There was nothing left to say. Ashley couldn't tell her that the baby would have a good home—that the baby would be loved.

They walked down the long corridor together, pausing at the lobby door. Kerry's face was pale, her soul in turmoil. "Where will you go, Kerry?" Ashley asked.

"Chicago for a while."

Ashley glanced at the closed door, certain that Bill was waiting on the other side for Kerry. Bill had chosen Everdale for both of them. Ashley nodded toward the lobby. "Does he know that you are going back to Chicago?"

"He knows. He keeps telling me that he will find a way for us to be together, but he needs his wife." There was a catch in her voice. "I think if he tries—I want him to try. And yet."

She put her hand to the swinging door. "He's taking me to Montgomery—to Dannelly Field."

Her narrow heels clicked as she fled through the lobby door. From out of the shadows, Bill rose to meet her. His dimples seemed like hollows in his cheeks, his eyes forlorn in the dimly lit room. He looked at Ashley without a flicker of recognition.

"Good evening, nurse," he said, forcing a smile.

He took Kerry's luggage and opened the main door with his shoulder. Kerry slipped out and stood alone in the driveway.

With one longing glimpse backwards, Bill's blue eyes seemed to say, *You're not surprised, Ash. You knew all along.* Silently he formed the words, "I love you, sis. Forgive me."

"Wait," Ashley called. "You've forgotten your raincoat, sir."

He came back in and picked it up from the empty chair.

His expression filled with torment as their eyes met. "I'm sorry, sis."

"Why, Bill? Why this way?"

"I needed Everdale, Ash. I needed you."

"Then please stay. Let David and me help you."

Kerry had almost reached the parked car. "It's over for me," Bill said. "But Kerry—Kerina has her career. What I did by coming back to Everdale, I did for you. For her."

"The baby?"

"You'll take good care of him? In Mama's house."

"I promise," she said.

Bill had come up short. There was no way out, but he had done the best he could to unravel the tangled web he'd weaved. Ashley was convinced that without Kerry ever knowing, Bill had arranged for the baby to have parents who would love him and make him a home in Mama's old house.

She opened her mouth to ask him, but Bill blew Ashley a kiss across the silent lobby and ran to catch up to the girl. He slipped into the driver's seat beside her, backed his car out of the parking space, and sped up the winding driveway, racing into the blinding rainstorm. Blasting as he had always done into the unknown.

∽

Hours later as Bill drove away from the airport, he was still speeding on a rain-drenched road when his car went out of control. Two unposted letters lay on the passenger seat beside him. One to the young concert violinist, and one to his sister, Ashley, asking her forgiveness.

∽

Ashley lay wide awake on the king-size bed. Outside her hotel windows, the sky over Vienna was still awash with stars. The heavens glowed with them, their brilliance comforting her. She still missed her brother. She knew—as she had known all along—that something of the bond between twins never died.

Remembering Kerina and Bill together as she had last seen them in the hospital lobby mellowed Ashley's heartache. Love, not anger, touched her in the semidarkness of her room. She longed to right her own mistakes, not Kerina's. Not Bill's. But Ashley had forgotten how level it was at the foot of the cross, how easy it was to go there. She ached to go home to David. David knew about forgiveness. David. David.

Chapter 21

Jillian rushed into the Empress Isle Hotel and went straight to the concierge's desk. She was accustomed to attention and second glances and was not disappointed. The impeccably groomed man blinked his dark eyes as if he had clicked a candid shot of her as she approached. Charm poured into his greeting, but a shadow crossed his face as she asked for Chandler Reynolds.

He directed her down the corridor, past the gift shops to the gym. Even at this early hour, seven hotel guests were pedaling and pumping their way back into shape, working off last evening's dinner. She was surprised to see one young man who had been standing in the lobby of the Opera House the night before, casting shifty, watchful glances toward the lieutenant.

The lieutenant lay flat on his back, his hair damp with perspiration, a determined grimace on his face as he puffed under the strain of leg weights. Instant recognition flashed in those hooded dark eyes as he gave her the same beguiling smile that had electrified her last evening. "Good morning, Lieutenant."

"You're up early." He went right on exercising. "I open my eyes and there you are. Better than any alarm clock."

She glanced around and nodded toward the man on the exercise bike. "Do you know that gentleman over there?"

"No. He followed me in here, but he hasn't bothered me."

"I'm certain he was at the Opera House last night."

"And at breakfast this morning."

"You're not in trouble?"

"Not that I know of. But it's nice to have you here to protect me. Are you staying in this hotel?"

"No, Miss Rudzinski sent me over to invite you on an all-day excursion Sunday."

"Really? Will you be there, Miss Ingram?"

She hated it when she blushed, but an embarrassing crimson crept up her neck to her cheeks, blotching the tip of her nose. "Of course; we'll be driving to the Vienna Woods—the invitation includes your mother."

"I was afraid of that."

Jillian saw teasing good humor in his eyes and Kerina's strength and strong, sculpted lines in his handsome expression. She pressed for his decision. "So what about Sunday?"

"Why the red carpet?" he asked in his deep, rich voice.

"Because Kerina was rude to you last night."

"Go, please," he mocked. "I'll just keep my distance."

"I'm not here to beg, Lieutenant. So what's your decision?"

"What I wanted was a crack at the interview."

"But the interview didn't happen," she reminded him.

He held up his hand. "I'd better accept that invitation before you change your mind. That way, I'll be with you."

She laughed. *Don't let this get out of hand,* she warned herself. *Remember Santos and the pain he caused you.*

Chandler closed his eyes and kept on pumping, a painful grimace running its course each time he bent his knee and started the rotation over again. "Do you pray?" he asked.

"I don't think much about it. Is it something like fate? Chance? Two hearts meeting and all that?"

"Better than that. A much higher connection."

"So you pray?"

"Just last night. Prayed that I'd see you again. Fat chance, I thought, when Miss Rudzinski tossed us out of the dressing room, but I prayed anyway. And here you are."

The be-careful alarm button went off. She'd been many things, but never an answer to prayer. What kind of a joker was he? But he *was* cute with that prankish grin and those eyes like pongee autumn leaves. No wedding band, she noted. No girl back home? Just a little Vienna fling and then like a quick gust of wind, he'd be back in Bosnia, forgetting her.

He sat bolt upright, flattened his bare foot on the floor, and rubbed his calf frantically. "Sorry. Another leg cramp."

Perspiration glistened on his lean body. Now she saw the jagged scar that ran from his thigh to his ankle. With a scar that size he had good reason to count on prayer.

"Picked it up in Bosnia," he said. "Nasty accident."

He seemed distant for a minute before saying, "My time there gave me a sour view on life. Especially when my friend died." His mouth twitched. "I wrestled that for a while. But God didn't make a mess of that country or take Randy's life. I don't like the duty there, but I like the people."

He was like two people himself. One teasing and lighthearted. The other sensitive, caring. Old loves passed through her thoughts. Santos again with his swarthy good looks was better looking than the lieutenant, and Brian, her sweet, hot-tempered Irishman, had been more jolly. She stole a look at Chandler's eyes. They were more open and direct than Santos's had ever been, more sensitive than Brian's. "I'm sorry about your friend."

"Not your fault. Take heart. I'm back on track now. I'll be good company. I've given prayer a fresh start since reaching Vienna."

So he was back on that and flat on his back lifting weights.

He was strong in spite of the leanness, and she wondered if he had dropped in weight lately. Wondered about that distant look when he mentioned the accident.

He distracted her with another line twenty kilometers long. "Jillian, you have the most beautiful sapphire blue eyes. Honest, every time you look at me, I go on meltdown."

She started to stomp off, but he was on his feet, blocking her way and jauntily tossing his towel around his neck. "Don't leave. I told you, you're an answer to prayer."

"You're crazy, Lieutenant."

"I don't have much time to be serious. I'm only in Vienna for thirty days. I want to spend them with you."

"I thought you were spending them with your mother."

"She won't mind sharing me."

"Sorry. I'm heading for a week on the Italian Riviera."

He cast a side glance at the man on the exercise bike. "Do you think we could shake that man if Mother and I went with you?"

"You're not invited. It's Miss Rudzinski's private villa."

"What would I have to do to score an invitation?"

This was Kerina's son. He didn't seem to have a clue about that, but as much as she wanted to get mother and son together, he didn't have a chance. At the peak of her successful career, Kerina wasn't going to risk her reputation by recognizing him. She thought of Kerina's vast fortune going to so many charities and wondered if even a dime had ever been spent on Chandler.

"You're not listening to me, Miss Ingram. I'm serious about going to the Riviera with you. Can't you put in a good word for me? After all, Miss Rudzinski promised me an interview."

"Ask her yourself on Sunday."

"My mother would have fits. So what about today and the rest of the time you're in Vienna? Let's spend it together."

"What about the man over there?" She jerked her thumb in his direction. "I hate tagalongs."

"We'll dodge him. I think he's army. Keeping an eye on me."

"I thought you said you weren't in trouble."

His facial muscles tightened. "Not in the way you think. When my buddy, Randy, was killed in Bosnia—no, don't look at the man—there were some nasty rumors. There may be those who are interested in what I'm doing in Vienna."

He mopped his face with his towel and missed her sympathetic glance. What was the lieutenant mixed up in? She was a fool for getting involved but said, "Kerina did say I could take guests. We could outrun that man in my Saab on the way to Italy."

"You're sure?"

"I'll talk to Kerina."

"Don't mention the dodgeball game I'm playing. I don't want to worry her. Now what about today? Tonight? The rest of the time you're in Vienna? Will you spend it with me?"

"When Kerina is in concert, I work twelve-hour days."

"That still leaves twelve for me."

She swung her purse strap over her shoulder. "Those are the hours on either side of midnight and just before dawn."

"I'll set my alarm. Where can I meet you? Please, Jillian, say yes. You can sleep all next month when I'm gone."

Before she could open her mouth to give him a firm forget it, he said, "We don't have all that long to fall in love."

He reminded her of a fresh gust of wind, blowing in, swirling around. She had always loved autumn when the golden brown leaves drifted with the wind. The lieutenant's eyes were like that. A brilliant, rich brown like autumn leaves. He was Santos, American style. No, Chandler was different. There were sadness and laughter, boyishness and utter charm tumbling over one another like autumn leaves. She sensed pain and loneliness—those things she saw in Kerina. She had no desire to ruin Kerina's magnificent career or bring any more sadness into her life, but could she bring the two of them together—this mother and son? Or would she only widen the wedge between them?

"So what about midnight, Jill?"

"What about a good night's sleep so you'll enjoy our trip to the Vienna Woods on Sunday?"

He dismissed sleep with the wave of his hand. "I can sleep when I get back to Bosnia. Where do I meet you?"

Her mental calculations clicked into play. "I'll pick you and your mother up for late dinner after the concert."

He looked mischievous now, his gaze locking with hers. "Mother needs her beauty rest. I insist on it. It's just you and me at midnight, Jillian. No backseat drivers."

"I'd feel safer with your mother along."

"We have that bodyguard over there. Besides, I'm harmless."

So was Santos. But as she looked at Chandler, she was confident that he was deep, more complex than Santos. "I'll pick you up in the hotel lobby, Lieutenant."

"Not very chauvinistic," he protested.

"But I have the red convertible."

She had embarrassed him. A faint flush added color to his cheeks. He was too fair, but he had wintered in Bosnia, hardly the place for a suntan. Her own brows crinkled quizzically. A shadow had darkened Chandler's eyes as he looked at her—and then beyond her to the man on the exercise bike.

~

Kerina had wandered along the winding streets in the Stephansdom Quarter since dawn but was resting now on a park bench across from St. Stephens enjoying the beauty of its high Gothic spire and glazed tile roof. She considered the magnificent cathedral the center of the city, its very soul.

Her musings were splintered by a deep voice. "Kerina."

"Franck. You frightened me."

He was wearing a gray-vested suit with a gray-striped shirt, giving his skin a sallow cast in the early morning sun. Even his eyes were a granite gray. But she had long ago come to appreciate that angular face and his deep devotion to her.

"I was looking for you, Kerina."

"In all Vienna?"

"Jillian told me I would find you here. We should have your name engraved on this bench—you come often enough."

"But usually on Wednesdays—and then I go inside."

As he smiled down at her, she made room for him. "Sit with me awhile, Franck."

He edged the seat, facing her. "I was worried about you. You shouldn't walk alone."

"Why not? This is one of the safest cities of the world."

"At least one of the most beautiful. I wanted to talk to you about our plans for Moscow, Kerina."

"I have no plans for Moscow."

He took her hand. "Let's have coffee."

"I'd like that."

He walked her to a coffeehouse near the cathedral, one of the smaller ones that lined the streets of Vienna. Kerina had tried them all—the Frauenhuber where Mozart had once performed, the Landtmann near the Burgtheater, the Kleines where she often sat and sipped a *kaffeinfreier kaffee*. No matter how elaborate or shabby the coffeehouse, it seemed a waiter always appeared in a tux as one was doing now.

"Strudel and coffee with whipped cream, Kerina?" Franck asked.

She preferred something less sweet but politely moved her arm when the waiter reappeared with a *schlagobers* topped with whipped cream— Franck's black coffee came with an egg yolk and brandy and the familiar glass of water.

"You are too pale this morning, Kerina."

"I didn't do my makeup."

He scolded gently, "You never forget your makeup, my dear."

He studied her with his perpetual sadness, plucking at his sideburns. She liked his dark beard and soft voice. But lately he had become a gruff stranger, his features distorted.

"The strudel is marvelous," she said, taking a second bite. "But what did you want to talk to me about?"

"I rescheduled our trip to Moscow. We must go after the concert in Milan."

Her thoughts raced to the magnificent paintings in Milan—to the endless theft of great works of art in Italy. She slid her hand across the table and touched Franck's. "Franck, I am going on holiday with Jillian."

Anguished, he said, "But I need your help."

"I don't know what kind of trouble you are in, but I will not let you use me. I cannot get the McClaren robbery out of my mind. I fear you are implicated somehow. Why I cannot even guess."

"Implicated? How? I was at the Opera House that night."

"I don't know the logistics. But I do know that I have made you a wealthy man, Franck. You could buy any painting you wanted. And if you needed money, you have only to ask me."

"Don't you understand? Jokhar could ruin your career."

"Jokhar Gukganov? I barely know him."

"Kerina, my grandfather lost his art collection back in the war. When he was ill and dying, he begged me to get his paintings back. Some of them were not for sale, so Jokhar helped me."

"The black market? And now it is payback time?"

He nodded miserably. "Just three or four more paintings, Kerina. Two of them for Jokhar. He won't bother us again."

"You are so foolish, Franck."

"I remodeled the house on the Black Sea. It's filled with art treasures. I did it all for you."

"Then perhaps you should move there now."

"Without you?"

She nodded. "Don't force me to betray you. The McClarens are our friends. There was no excuse for taking something from them."

"I am not a thief, Kerina."

"Then what are you?" Tearing, she looked away and saw Jillian entering the café. She caught her eye and waved. "Jillian is coming," she said, relieved.

"Why do you put up with her? She will ruin me—"

Kerina smiled as Jillian reached their table.

"Kerina, we need to talk. But it's a go for tomorrow. The lieutenant accepted with pleasure."

"What lieutenant?" Franck demanded.

Kerina hesitated for only a second. Her voice held steady. "I have found my son, Franck; he is here in Vienna."

Color crept from the edges of his beard across his cheeks. He was furious. "Not that young man outside your dressing room? That's why he looked so familiar. How? How did he find you?"

"Fate."

He glowered at Jillian. "Kerina, send him away. An old scandal will ruin your career."

"And ruin your trips to Moscow as well?"

"Don't force me to involve him in the trips to Moscow. I will," he warned, "if you don't send him away."

Her lips tightened. "Don't ask me to do that again, Franck."

"Not even for his safety?" He shoved his chair with such force that it crashed to the floor. He righted it at once.

"It was sweet of you to come here with me, Franck."

Stiffly, he said, "My pleasure, Kerina."

As he left, she met Jillian's gaze across the table. "Franck is not himself, Jill. But don't ask me about it. Now—what was so important that you had to see me?"

"I already told you. I want you to invite the Reynolds to the Riviera."

"What! I can't do that. It would never work out."

"Please. Just for a week."

"A week? For your sake or mine, Jillian?"

"Kerina, you owe the lieutenant an interview." She licked her lips with the tip of her tongue. "You owe him a lot more than that. He's your son, Kerina. It would be your chance to let him know who you are."

Her eyes filled with tears. "Do you think they would come?"

Jillian grinned. "I'm certain they will."

"Then ask them. But you heard Franck. He means what he said."

"You can put Franck out of your mind for a whole week. Don't let him go on controlling you, Kerina."

"Dear Jillian, I owe him my life, my career."

"You succeeded because you are good. If Franck hadn't been there to manage your career, someone else would have come along. Chandler is the important one now. He's your son, Kerina. You're his mother."

"No, Jillian. You're wrong. I am the person who brought him into the world. Ashley Reynolds is his mother."

～

At midnight, Chandler was leaning on his crutches in front of the hotel when Jillian's convertible careened to the curb. He was in and dragging his crutches behind him when Jillian sped away before the man standing nearby could pursue them.

Chandler peered out the back window. "We did it! The poor guy's trying to hail a taxi."

As she swerved around another corner, she shook her hair from the nape of her neck. "Did you get your mother tucked in?"

"She's a big girl now. But she's probably up on her balcony cringing at the way you drive."

He heard the soft rippling laugh well up from deep inside her. The girl in Bosnia seemed a long way away. Bosnia was Bosnia. This was Vienna. He needed someone, and right now he needed Jillian Ingram. He saw her profile reflected in the lights of the city and felt something beat wildly inside his chest.

Chapter 22

Five or six times a year Kerina slipped away to Bello la Fortezza, her gated villa on the Italian Riviera. Her bedroom and balcony balanced on a rocky promontory with an unobstructed view of the glassy sea and the sleek yachts bobbing on its smooth waters. She often arose before dawn to watch the sun rise over the sparkling aquamarine waters, but this morning she awakened to the phone ringing.

She snatched the receiver before the ring disturbed her houseguests. *"Buon giorno,"* she whispered. Then impatiently, "Santos Garibaldi? Please. You must not come here. I must warn you, my guards will turn you away." She stopped his flurry of Italian, saying, "Yes, Jillian has found someone else. I am sorry, Santos."

She jammed the receiver back in place. With Garibaldi's voice silenced, she heard the muted voices on her balcony. Tiptoeing barefoot to the window, Kerina felt the warm breeze from the Ligurian Sea brush her cheek. Outside, Chandler and Jillian stood as one, silhouetted against the iron balustrade.

The cinereous night clouds had separated, the glorious light of dawn turning the blue of the sea into rippling embers of gold. As the dawn touched Chandler's face, Kerina noticed how much his strong, chiseled features looked like Bill VanBurien's. She held her breath as Chandler bent down and tentatively kissed Jillian, and then in a warm embrace, the two of them wrapped their arms around each other.

Kerina drew back into the shadows. Her thoughts winged back to Chicago and Bill's first tender kiss. She wanted the growing bond between Chan and Jillian, yet dreaded the outcome. Would he flee back to his life in Bosnia, leaving Jill more heartbroken than she had been with Santos?

~

Ashley had dreaded coming to Kerina's private villa, but now on her sixth morning at the Bello la Fortezza, she took her breakfast on the balcony, savoring the beauty that surrounded her. The villa sat perched on a rugged cliff as white-rocked as the silk-white sands below. Beyond the harbor lay a coastline of sheltered coves dotted with tiny fishing villages, ancient castles, and steepled Romanesque churches. The sheer cliff rose from the blue-green sea up to the terraced villas where the hillsides were covered with a profusion of flowers and fruit trees, olive groves and grape-ripened vineyards. She saw Chandler and Jillian down in the vineyard, talking and laughing and carrying a picnic basket between them. She wondered if they had slept at all.

It was happening too fast; they were rushing from friendship into romance in the same quick way that she and David had rushed into their own relationship. She had no right to interfere, but she ached for the girl in Bosnia. Had Chandler already forgotten her? No, the truth was, Ashley objected to either girl.

In Vienna she had watched Chandler grab the moments with Jillian. She had known that day as they drove back from the Vienna Woods with Chandler at the wheel and Jillian stealing constant glances at him that something was happening between them. What should have brought her joy only added to her pain. Jillian was Kerina's friend. And then, as they drove along—Kerina and Ashley silent in the backseat—Chandler reached out and put his hand over Jillian's. He kept grinning at her until they almost skidded off the motorway.

After that it was breakfast the next morning at an unearthly hour, a noontime walk along the Danube, hours discovering Vienna at night, an afternoon browsing in an art museum that he had not even wanted to see the day before. Now Kerina and Ashley could not separate them. Chandler and Jillian filled their days on the Riviera enjoying each other's company—swimming in the bay, exploring the caves in the cliffs, meandering through the fishing village, climbing the ancient staircase to the castle, and listening to romantic ballads on Kerina's console into the wee hours of the night.

Ashley was forced to spend her days with Kerina, sitting on the balcony sipping hot tea or iced lemonade. It was Mia's good cooking that eased the strain between them. She fed them lunches of pasta with pesto sauce and delicately browned fish and focaccia, a salted bread that Ashley liked. With Mia's watchful eye constantly on them, Kerina and Ashley began to talk.

They talked about Florence and Tuscany, the Renaissance and Italian opera, about the Dolomites and the history of Liguria, about wine making and music, about Genoa and Christopher Columbus and the magnificent career of Michelangelo. Kerina spoke heatedly of the fascist government that once controlled these fun-loving people and with equal disdain about rich counts and countesses. She proved a wealth of information, her face animated as she spoke of the Italians who delighted her.

Kerina's lovely face was delicate, like the painting of a Madonna. Sitting so close to her these last few days, Ashley could not shake off the premonition that Kerina was not well. The fear was not clearly defined, but she saw the pallor, and saw her wince when she moved her arm.

Last night they had talked about the caves of Toirano and the concert in Milan where Kerina played Tchaikovsky's *Concerto in D major*. Kerina had played beautifully, passionately. But in five days neither Kerina nor Ashley had spoken of Chandler's birth in Everdale, or of Bill VanBurien, the other name that lay like a chasm between them.

Behind her, Ashley heard Kerina on the phone in the hall, her voice tight with anger. "Please do not call again, Mr. Garibaldi. I told you already that we have guests."

Ashley glanced up as Kerina came out onto the balcony and slipped into the chair beside her. "Buon giorno, Kerina. Is everything all right?"

"It was Santos. Twice today. I cannot let him come here and upset Jillian—not when she's on the verge of happiness." She turned sideways in her chair, shading her eyes from the sun. "Where are the children, Ashley?"

Ashley laughed. "The last I saw *the children*, they were walking off, carrying a picnic basket between them."

"At least they won't run into that man any longer."

"The one who followed us from Vienna?"

"My friends at the police station are detaining him now."

"Can they do that?"

She smiled. "When they learned that he was constantly at our gates, they took him in for questioning. Chandler will be safely back in Bosnia before the police release the man." She shaded her eyes. "Do you think Chandler and Jillian are getting serious?"

Ashley frowned. "How can they? Chandler is planning to marry someone else, someone he met in Bosnia."

Kerina's face went rigid. "A girl in Bosnia? Then why—why has he misled Jillian?"

"I don't think he meant to." She met Kerina's gaze. "I don't even know what he plans to do now. The girl in Bosnia is pregnant. It's another man's child—Chandler's friend Randy, who was killed a few weeks ago. For some reason, Chan feels responsible for the baby."

"Does he love the girl?"

"I don't think so, but he thinks marriage is the only way to sponsor

Zineta out of Bosnia."

"What a strange thing for him to do then."

"David will find the idea deplorable."

A slight flush reached Kerina's cheeks. "Poor Jillian."

"Poor Chandler," Ashley countered, "to have met someone as lovely as Jillian and to care so deeply about her."

"Is there nothing we can do?" Kerina asked as Mia set steaming cups of tea in front of them.

"Us personally? We'd have a hard time getting through military red tape. Randy's parents live in Akron, Ohio, but they know nothing about their unborn grandchild."

Kerina gazed out on the sea and said quietly, "It was that way for my parents, too. If we could get Zineta safely to my parents' farm, they would help."

"But Randy came from Ohio."

"Jillian and I have talked about going on concert in Bosnia. I have friends there, if they haven't all been killed. I could attempt to contact them—perhaps find a way to help Zineta—but I won't interfere unless you think it's right for me to help Chandler."

"I have another plan to suggest," Ashley said. She spelled it out as a backup plan and then, smiling conspiratorially, they toasted the grandparents in Akron, Ohio, with their teacups.

Kerina replaced her cup in its saucer. "Coming here hasn't been a very pleasant holiday for you, has it, Ashley?"

"The hardest part has been knowing who you are. You should know that Chandler and I argued about coming."

The trip had softened her heart. She was no longer blaming Kerina for ruining Bill's life or deserting her child for a violin. She had spent these days remembering that Mama had always said, "The forgiving heart goes a long way toward happiness."

And Ashley wanted Kerina Rudzinski to be happy. "Kerina," she said calmly, "I think it's time to talk about you and Chandler."

Kerina's eyes brimmed with tears. "I was afraid to mention Everdale— or Chandler. And what is there to tell of myself? I was born poor, but my family had a Stradivarius violin that passed down through the generations. Music became my life."

"You sent Chandler a violin when he was three, didn't you?"

A smile lit her face. "You did receive it? I played that one as a child. I sent it in care of the hospital where he was born, hoping you would receive it."

"We did. Kerina, we're leaving in the morning. You may never see Chandler again. Do you want to tell him who you are?"

Kerina's knuckles went white against the arms of the chair. "We must not spoil this time for Chandler and Jillian. It may be all they have. Right now, I have the joy of seeing him. I would lose everything if he knew I was the mother who abandoned him."

"Perhaps; you did what you thought was best."

Kerina shook her head. "For me it was always wrong. After the baby was gone, I could barely sleep or eat just thinking about him. I threw myself into my music. I had nothing else."

"You have a letter. I brought it with me, Kerina—it's from Bill VanBurien."

"You know Bill?" She laughed nervously, embarrassed. "Of course, you knew him. You grew up in the same town."

"Kerina—there is something you should know. I've been struggling to find the words to tell you ever since we arrived in Vienna. Even more since arriving at your villa. But, please, you must read the letter before Chandler comes back."

I'm going about this all wrong, Ashley thought. She took a deep breath and said, "I grew up with Bill. Bill VanBurien was my brother—my twin brother."

Kerina stared blankly, her eyes darting from Ashley's face to the sea and back again. The flush in her cheeks reappeared. "Your brother?" She was a mixture of anger and pain, her wound raw. "He arranged for you to adopt my baby. I was never to know, and he has known all these years. Why did he do that to me, Ashley? I trusted him."

Ashley thought of Bill, the man of rough fabric that had chafed so many lives. No matter how severely she judged it—no matter how much she disapproved—Kerina had loved him, too.

"You were the nurse in the lobby at the hospital the night Bill picked me up. You didn't act like you knew each other."

"Bill didn't want me to know that he was the baby's father. I just happened to be on duty that night."

"He hurt you, too."

Ashley nodded. "I worried when you left Everdale that night. You were depressed. I was afraid something would happen to you."

"I had nothing to live for," Kerina admitted.

"You had your music."

"But you had my son." Distractedly, she said, "I met Bill in Chicago.

He was charming and friendly. I was pregnant when I discovered that he was married, separated from his family. I am so sorry, Ashley. I would never have destroyed his family. I considered an abortion, but Bill said he knew someone who had done that, and he would not let me go through that pain. . . Ashley, are you all right?"

"I just felt faint for a minute."

"Bill promised to find a good home for the baby if I would carry the pregnancy to full term. He told me he knew a doctor in Everdale who would help us."

Ashley understood. Bill had chosen his childhood home as the place for his son to live. "All his life, my brother made trouble for our family, but he made certain that his son would have a good home. Dear Bill! You loved him, didn't you, Kerina?"

"With all my heart."

Ashley pulled Bill's letter from her purse and handed it to Kerina. Kerina's eyes clouded with tears as she read it, silently at first and then aloud.

"I am filled with shame, my darling, for all that has happened
to you. When you boarded the plane, I told you I loved you. I
promised that I would find a way for us to be together forever.
I think you knew that could never be—T. S. Eliot was right.
'April is the cruellest month.' I am not even certain that God will
forgive me for the twisted turns my life has taken. But if you can,
Kerina, forgive me, and may God do the same."

Kerina's voice trailed as she read,

"The baby has a good home, my darling. They will take good
care of our son. They will love him for us."

The letter slipped from Kerina's hands. "He never intended to come back to me, did he, Ashley?"

"He never had a chance to make that decision."

"Where is he now?" she asked softly.

Ashley's voice wavered. "He's dead."

"Dead? Bill—Bill is dead?" She swayed in the chair. "Tell me it's not true."

"Kerina—he was killed in an automobile accident on the freeway, two hours after he left you off at the airport in Montgomery—only minutes after he wrote that letter." *Minutes after he called his wife to ask for another chance,* she thought. "Bill's car catapulted over the guardrail into a deep gully. The back wheels were still spinning when the State Police found him. He didn't suffer."

Kerina pushed herself from the chair and stumbled across to the railing. She leaned so far over that Ashley feared she would topple. She stayed there, saying his name over and over. "Bill. Bill. Bill." At last she asked, "You are certain he is dead? You are not just protecting him?"

"He's dead, Kerina. We buried him in Everdale."

Kerina loosened her hair and let it fall softly to her shoulders, flecks of red in the gleaming gold. "No wonder I never heard from him again."

Ashley crossed the balcony to her. "The last time I saw my brother alive, he told me he had finally found happiness. That he truly loved someone. I have no doubt that you are the one Bill talked about. He loved you, Kerina."

Kerina lifted her tear-stained face and smiled. "It's good to know what happened. Good of you to have brought the letter to me. Until now I always hoped that he would come back someday. Even after all these years—" She bit her lip. "But that was impossible. Bill knew that when he said good-bye."

"It's over, Kerina. Let it rest." Gently, Ashley put her arms around Kerina, and they walked back into the villa together.

∾

The next morning as Ashley finished packing, Chandler and Jillian walked in the garden. Chandler's eyes looked like dark sockets, as though he hadn't slept all night.

"I hate to see you go," Jillian said, smiling up at him.

"I hate to go."

"You could stay on and do the three-city tour with us."

"Budapest, Berlin, and Paris? I promised Mom more of Vienna."

She felt disappointment. "Kerina and I will be in Vienna before you fly back to Bosnia. Will you call me?"

He stopped walking and faced her, looking troubled. "I don't think we should see each other again, Jill."

Her stomach churned. "But I thought—"

He ran his thumb gently across her cheek. "What did you think, Jillian?"

"That you brought me out here to ask me to wait for you."

"I wanted to. But I can't do that to you. We can't go on with our friendship. We have to break up before it goes too far."

"Friendship? Is that all you call these last few days? Last night you told me—" Her voice cracked.

He looked even more stricken. "I told you I thought I was falling in love. I was. I am."

"Then what's wrong, Chandler? Don't tell me you're another Santos in my life. A little fling and you're gone?"

"You know you mean more to me than that." He tried to grasp her hand. "The tip of your nose is turning red again," he said gently.

"Oh, don't fret, love. I've survived the best of you. So what's your excuse, Lieutenant? A girl in every city?"

"There's someone else, Jillian. A girl in Bosnia."

The pungent smell of ripened grapes and the damp soil and wild-flowers on the hillside pooled together, the sweet odor nauseating her. "Someone in Bosnia? Someone you just remembered?"

"The girl is pregnant, Jillian."

"Pregnant!" Choking, she said, "That dresses it up nicely. At least you're not leaving me that way."

"I respect you too much for that."

"Go, Chandler, before I slap you. Before I hate you."

He ran his hands through his hair. "I don't want to leave you this way. Just let me explain—"

"No, Chandler. I don't want to hear it. Just go."

He took off, running back toward the villa, favoring his injured leg. She stood in the vineyard watching him go, certain that he had taken her heart with him. She expected him to take the path around to the door, but when he reached the steep cliff beneath the balcony, he climbed recklessly up the rocky incline.

She watched, stunned at the fury at which he tugged his way up. He was almost to the balcony when he stopped abruptly.

Get over that railing, she thought, *before you fall back.*

But as suddenly as he had climbed, he was slipping and sliding franti-cally down the hillside. Her heart thumped wildly until he was safely at the bottom. He was coming back to her!

Her joy was momentary. He stood on level ground now.

Looking up. Looking away. He jammed his fists into his pockets and limped slowly around the stone-flagged path, his eyes riveted on the ground. Something had happened at the top of the cliff.

She had to go to him. But seconds later she saw him again—fighting his own demons with his head thrown back, his eyes toward the sky, his fists beating the air. He shouted angry, incoherent words, bitter words like the ones welling inside of her. Then he ran, not toward her, but on the east side of the vineyards.

Kerina and Ashley leaned over the railing waving. "What's wrong?" Kerina called.

Jillian's throat felt tighter than a drum. "Everything's cool," she cried. "It's just Chandler running off steam."

∾

Kerina went in search of Jillian and found her in the garden an hour later. "I thought you would come to see our guests off, Jill. It was embarrassing without you there. What happened?"

"I said my good-byes."

"Do you expect Chandler in Budapest tomorrow evening?"

"I don't expect him to show up anywhere. Ever."

Sharply she asked, "Why was Chan running in the vineyards?"

"Trampling grapes! No, nothing happened. That's what makes it so sad. One minute he acts like I'm the only girl for him, and this morning he tells me there's someone else. I'm afraid he's going to marry her."

"Oh Jillian, didn't you tell him how you feel?"

"I really thought I wanted to spend the rest of my life with him, and he wants to spend it with someone else. I can't fight that kind of competition."

"You needed more time together. You barely know him."

"He told me it doesn't take all that long to fall in love. Oh Kerina, if I thought he would change his mind about the girl in Bosnia, I would wait for him forever."

Like I waited, thought Kerina. "I did that once, but forever is too long. Did you tell him we'll be in Vienna this weekend?"

"He said it's over. Besides, the girl in Bosnia is pregnant."

Their eyes met. "Chandler is not the baby's father."

"He isn't? How do you know that?"

"Ashley told me. He made a promise to a friend to take care of the girl. I will try to work something out, Jillian, so we can free him from that promise. Maybe I will play for the troops in Bosnia." Her gaze traveled back to Jillian's troubled face, those long lashes still wet with tears.

"Chandler has a few more days in Vienna. Call him when we get there this weekend. Spend that time with him."

"I can't call Chandler."

"And why not? Women have been calling men for a long time."

"I don't think he wants to see me again, Kerina."

"If he loves you, he will."

Chapter 23

It was a lovely June morning in Vienna with billowy white clouds drifting lazily across the Dresden blue sky. Kerina walked along the bank of the Danube and watched the breaking dawn filter through the rising mist, the fiery embers of gold reflecting against the dark gray water. Her city, the city of Mozart and Beethoven and Haydn. Her river flowing gently, waltzing, winding its way to somewhere.

This was the day that Kerina's son was going away, waiting at some unknown airstrip for a standby flight to Bosnia. She was losing him again. An hour before, she had called his hotel only to be told that the Reynolds had checked out. In her disappointment the haunting memory of the house she longed to find came back. She captured it in her mind's eye as the rolling mist blew across the Danube. She knew that peace belonged to that country house with its heart-shaped dormer window in the attic and its narrow, wood-framed bedroom windows on the second floor. There came again the remembered scent of the sweet gum tree in the backyard, the thought of branches on the old maple hanging low to the ground, the clusters of purple flowers on the wisteria vine. She closed her eyes, trying to picture the swings by the gazebo, trying to hear the cry of the baby louder than the whippoorwill.

She felt certain that the longing for the house belonged to Everdale, to that moment in time when she sat in the nursery at Jackson Memorial and held her infant son in her arms for the last time. She had loved him then. She loved him now. The image of the house faded. Gone. The Danube flowed on. She turned from the river with her eyes to the rolling hills that surrounded Vienna. She found them beautiful at any season—sometimes a lush green, often a pale yellow, rusty-red in the fall, covered with snow in the winter. She kept walking, walking, allowing the soaring spire of St. Stephen's to guide her, the glazed roof tiles blinding in the sunshine. Shading her eyes, she glanced up where the Pummerin Bell hung high in the North Tower.

In 1945, at the close of a war she had never known, a fire had swept through the Stephansdom, plunging the bell through the burning roof into ruin. Years later, the bell that had made music was dug from the ruins and recast from the ashes. Kerina felt much like the bell, plunging into ruin, unable to make music.

Outside the cathedral, she found a discarded rosary lying on the sidewalk. Her parents' faith shouted up at her. She picked up the rosary and entered St. Stephen's through the Giants' Doorway and vestibule, her heels tapping against the marble as she went beneath the West Gallery into the nave.

Drawn by the familiar panels of the Mother and Christ Child she made her way down the narrow aisle to the front row. As she faced the High Altar, her fingers entwined around the rosary.

"God," she said tentatively, "I don't know where You are, but if you are anywhere, surely You must be here in this cathedral. If You hear me, please help me." Light from the windows reflected on the Mother and the Christ Child. "I have seen my son—as You saw Your Son and agonized for Him. Oh God, if I could only see my son one more time."

Thirty minutes of silence engulfed her and then she heard sturdy booted footsteps coming down the long aisle and wished with all her heart that it would be Chandler. Someone slipped into the seat beside her.

"Miss Rudzinski."

He wore his uniform, the lieutenant bars on his epaulets.

He looked handsome, striking in his army greens. "I was hoping to find you here. Jillian assured me that you always come here on Wednesdays. I just wanted to say good-bye."

"I called your hotel." She brushed away the tears. "But you had checked out. I thought I had missed you."

"I wouldn't leave Vienna without saying good-bye to you."

She glanced around. "Where's Ashley?"

"I took Mother to the airport early this morning. If I know Dad, he's already at Los Angeles International waiting for her."

"But, Chandler, it will be hours before she arrives."

"He's anxious to have her home. Now I'm heading out."

"Will you ever come back to Vienna?"

"It depends on what I decide to do with my future."

Again she traced his features as she had done that day he walked back into her life at the Opera House. "What do you really want to be, Chandler?"

"A music critic someday."

"And not a musician? But you were born for music, Chandler. Why did you quit Juilliard?"

"I had to face the truth. I was never going to make the grade professionally. Going there was Mom and Dad's idea."

"You had to be good to get in."

"Lucky maybe. I had an uncle who was into classical music. I always figured they wanted me to go because of him."

She felt weak, disoriented, with memories of autumn leaves sweeping across a porch. "Tell me about your uncle, Chandler."

"There's not much to tell. He died right after I was born." Chandler shrugged. "Having Dad's favor was the important thing in my life. The army was our first big clash. I can't imagine what he will do if I reenlist or take that government job."

".The one that will take you back to Bosnia as a spy?"

He laughed out loud, his laughter echoing in the quiet sanctuary. "Hardly a spy. An intelligence officer. Dad won't like it either, Kerina. He's a big influence on my life, even though I rarely please him anymore." He looked away and then came back to meet her gaze. "Did Mom tell you he's a preacher? A sought-after speaker. He'd be national if Mom didn't oppose it. And he teaches archaeology at the university. He's a smart man—makes a good professor. He's a great guy."

"But not wise enough to let you be a music critic?"

"We haven't talked that one out yet. Dad always thought he was raising a child prodigy. A violinist, no less. Now if I had the instrument that you have—"

Kerina stared down at her hands. "Someday, Chandler, when I no longer need my violin, I will send it to you."

"Your Strad? You're kidding, of course."

"I have never been more serious. Would you play it?"

"I'd be honored. But you should keep it in your own family."

"I will."

"But what about your son?" he asked unexpectedly. "Shouldn't it go to him? Surely he is musical?"

She had forgotten their conversation in the Staatsoper dressing room. They had been speaking in hushed voices; now it seemed as though her very words had reached the vaulted ceiling and echoed back like Chandler's laughter. "You remind me of him."

He grinned. "Is that why you are so kind to me?"

She patted his hand. "You remind me of someone else that I cared for deeply."

"Past tense?"

"He belonged to my past."

Now his sigh echoed through the chamber. "I have to go. Jillian is waiting for me. And so's the army."

"Jillian is fond of you, Chandler—in love with you."

"I know. But I have things to work out in Bosnia."

He stood and when he pulled her up beside him and hugged her, she caught the scent of her son's cologne, the sweet smell of peppermint on his breath. She felt the smoothness of his freshly shaven skin, the strength of his hands on her arms supporting her. Her son. Ashley's son.

"Thanks for that week on the Riviera. I still can't believe you took in strangers like that. But we're grateful."

"Jillian insisted."

"Take care of yourself, Miss Rudzinski. And take care of Jillian for me."

"I will. And you—be careful, Chandler."

She watched him striding down the long aisle, straight and tall, his finely shaped head so much like Bill's. When he reached the door, he turned and waved. She felt numb. Even her tears refused to come. Moments later, she stepped outside where a summer storm had blackened the sky. She had gone inside with the sun reflecting off the steep slanted roof. Now dark clouds hovered above the North Tower. The leaden sky blotted out the daylight. In the distance, her son strolled hand in hand with Jillian, oblivious to the rain.

Drops of rain splattered around her as she hurried toward the shelter of the café awning across the boulevard. The downpour left glittering wet spiderwebs in her tangled hair. She felt a tightening in her chest, a struggle to catch her breath as she sprinted for cover. Drenched as she was, she risked another bout with bronchitis. Nothing must stop her fall schedule. Nothing. She looked forward to reaching New York and catching a train that would carry her over the rails to Everdale—perhaps to the elusive house and gazebo that constantly filled her mind.

～

August had not changed the bleakness of Bosnia nor the isolation of long confinement behind the locked doors at the top security command post. The electricity fed into Tuzla by the burning of soft coal caused more low-hanging clouds and heavy mists. Chandler had forgotten how dreary it could be living in a town where the sun seldom shone. Even when it did shine, he was shut away in a windowless room, sifting through intelligence data and classified satellite photos of infantry training camps and the acquisition of weapons that exceeded the quotas for the Muslims and Croats.

Now after two months back from Vienna, he'd fallen into the routine where huge, brown tents still served as base camps and dissension came from American soldiers bored with bad weather, treacherous roads, and the slow reconciliation among the country's ethnic groups. Chandler stuck firmly to his belief that the separatist sympathies and guerrilla activity in the southern province was a cry for freedom. Even before his trip to Vienna, he had noted an increase in paramilitary units in the area and more Serbian helicopters and armored personnel carriers being moved in. The high command hadn't listened to him, not when the area involved was outside their military jurisdiction. Now he continued to keep his records straight, making detailed reports for his commanding officers.

He was putting in ten- to twelve-hour days. It kept his mind off Randy Williams, but it hadn't solved the problem of Zineta Hovic. Yet someone had pulled strings that permitted her return from the French sector. She was shy and reticent with him, but she was the same sweet girl whom Randy had loved, and she was definitely heavy with child. Steeling himself against thoughts of Jillian, he had filed more than one request, asking permission to marry Zineta. Two requests were tabled, the third lost, the fourth one buried under red tape.

Chandler would head home before the next Balkan winter, before the freezing cold swept over the area and hard snow made the search for land mines more difficult. It didn't give him much time to clear the military red tape that opposed Zineta leaving the country. And it didn't give him a wide margin between discharge from the military and flying to Washington regarding the government job that would eventually bring him back to Bosnia. In spite of all the plans he was making, Jillian Ingram stole into his thoughts continuously.

This morning Chandler sat in a strategy meeting as an observer, reviewing Washington's equip and train rule. The multinational group in the room was divided on the agenda. The biggest concern was not the Serbian crisis to the south but the foreign freighter sitting in the Adriatic Sea filled with weapons and tanks intended for the Muslim army and quarantined under heavy NATO guard. Chandler smothered his disgust. He was not expected to comment, but he knew why he was there. Colonel Bladstone had chosen him for the Langley intelligence team that would return to Bosnia with a new identity and a new job.

Unexpectedly, the commanding officer glowered at Chandler.

"Lieutenant, I see by your reports you predicted trouble in Kosovo long before it happened. You've been critical of NATO's response time."

"Yes sir."

"But that was outside our military jurisdiction."

"Yes sir. But does humanity have a boundary line?"

A snarl cut across the man's crusty features. "We'll pass your suggestions on to Washington, Lieutenant."

Like you passed along reports of my activities in Vienna? Chandler thought.

It was still a sore spot with him that he had been followed, a surveillance that Colonel Bladstone continued to deny. When the meeting ended, Chandler walked out of the room with Bladstone. "You see what kind of problems we're up against, Lieutenant, trying to appease a multinational force?"

"My job is to examine intelligence data, sir."

"Examine it, not interpret it." Bladstone rubbed his jaw vigorously. "That's why Langley wants a special team of operatives back in this country within the next twelve months. Separate from the military involvement. That's why we handpicked you as one of them, Reynolds."

"Is that why you had me followed in Vienna?"

"I keep telling you, if someone followed you, it was not my doing."

"Tell that to the poor devil detained in Italy. But you are the one who turned down my reenlistment."

"You're more important to us out of uniform. NATO isn't here forever. We'll leave a team of advisors when we pull out, but we want an intelligence team made up of men with no family ties."

"Is that why you ignored my request to marry Zineta Hovic?"

"What would you do with a Bosnian wife on your hands, Lieutenant? She wouldn't be welcomed back here. Besides, Miss Hovic may get a passport to America without a wedding ring."

Chandler stopped dead on the muddy trail. "What?"

"Someone advised Captain Williams's parents about the girl and his unborn child. And now Washington is on it."

"Sir, I didn't inform them."

They stood outside of Bladstone's barren office now.

"That isn't another lie, is it, Reynolds?"

"A lie, sir? I haven't been in touch with Randy's family."

"Well, there's one lie that may hold up your future. Langley tells me one of your legal documents is in question. Seems your birth certificate lacks an official signature. Langley insists you could have been adopted."

"Me? Adopted?" The colonel's words sent Chandler into a tailspin, confirming his worst nightmare. A golfball-size lump lodged in his throat. He couldn't suck in air or blow any out. He stood there, wobbly as a newborn colt, his legs so unsteady that he feared passing out like those fool recruits had done back in basic training. The pounding in his head turned explosive.

"Well?" roared Bladstone. "What do you say for yourself?"

"As far as I know, sir, I am not adopted."

But the lump in his throat grew bigger. A piece of himself was really missing. A flash of memory took him back to that last day on the Riviera to an incident he had been trying to repress for nearly two months. He had just split with Jillian and left her weeping after telling her about Zineta. On impulse, he had taken the steep cliff up to Kerina's balcony like a rock climber, tugging his way up by gripping the shrubs.

He'd been ready to swing his leg over the railing and surprise his mother when he heard her saying, *Chan doesn't even know he's adopted, Kerina. How can I ever tell him?*

He had ducked down and almost toppled backwards, as shattered by his mother's words as Jillian had been by his. He slid and stumbled back down the hillside. Once out of sight of the villa, he ran with every ounce of strength through the vineyards. Exhausted at last, he had turned back to the house, certain that he had misunderstood his mother's words.

"Reynolds, it looks like I've given you quite a shock. But I need an answer. Could you be adopted?"

Chandler forced himself to meet Bladstone's stern gaze without flinching. "What difference would it make, sir?"

He answered his own question. *All the difference in the world if the two people I trusted most in life deceived me for twenty-six years.*

Bladstone said, "I told Colonel Daniels when he was here three months ago that it was probably just a mix-up, Lieutenant. Daniels is hard to convince, so get that cleared up before you go for your interview in Washington."

The air coming from Chandler's lungs was nothing but a wheeze. "I'll try to do that, Colonel."

"And forget this business about marrying a Bosnian."

"If you guarantee me she'll get to America. If not—"

Bladstone snorted. "Why not ask that violinist who's coming in tomorrow to play for the troops? Seems like she's a friend of yours. And she's pulled some political maneuvers to get Miss Hovic to America before the baby comes."

Chandler saluted. "I'll do that, sir."

The Apache helicopter lowered and came in for a landing at the military airport in Tuzla, rotor blades whirling. Moments later, Kerina was assisted from the copter, bending low against the dust and wind, and running toward Chandler.

He took her hands, his grin widening. "Miss Rudzinski, am I glad to see you. And I've got good news."

Kerina smiled. "That was my line, as Jillian would say."

"You first," he said, walking her toward the waiting Humvee.

Her gaze met his, her wide, hazel eyes anxious. "You haven't done anything foolish about Zineta Hovic, have you, Chandler?"

He looked embarrassed. "I've filed the papers so I can marry her. My last request is bogged down in military red tape."

She touched his arm. "Marrying Zineta won't be necessary now. We found another way for you to keep your promise to your friend Randy."

"Then the colonel wasn't kidding?"

"Once your mother notified Randy's parents about the baby, they stirred up support in Washington. They are doing everything in their power to get her to Akron before the baby is born."

"The Williamses really want her? Will it work?"

She laughed delightedly. "Chandler, your commanding officer was quite pleased about my coming to play for the troops, so he offered me anything I wanted."

"And you wanted Zineta's release? How can I ever thank you?"

She blushed. "You said you had a surprise for me, Chandler."

"I do. Zineta is coming to the concert tonight to meet you."

She tucked her arm in his. "Meeting Zineta was one of the stipulations of my coming. Now—I have another surprise for you."

She turned him back toward the helicopter where a young woman in camouflage pants and parka with a helmet tilted cockily on her head was coining across the field to meet them—her sapphire blue eyes on Chandler.

Chandler's jaw dropped. "Jillian!"

Jillian waved and started running. He met her halfway, his arms wide and ready when she reached him.

The military threw out the red carpet for Kerina, receiving her warmly and whistling and cheering as she played her violin. Chandler's pride in her built with each song. The following day he escorted her to Kemal Hovic's house. Once inside the bullet-pocked home, Kerina took Zineta's hands in hers and smiled.

Zineta glanced at Chandler. "It's okay," he mouthed. She looked childlike and very pregnant. Shiny black-bobbed hair framed her flushed cheeks, but there was a brightness in those dark, soulful eyes as she looked up at Kerina.

"Are you happy?" Kerina asked her.

The girl nodded. "Am I truly going to America?"

"Soon. Your baby will be born in Randy's hometown."

Chandler swallowed hard and slipped his arm around Jillian's waist as Zineta asked, "Ran-dee's parents really want me?"

"They want you," Kerina said. "You will be happy with them."

"They want me—and my baby?"

"They have room for both of you."

Zineta's voice trembled. "But I worked for the Serbs during the war. And afterwards. Ran-dee—he never knew."

"The war is over, Zineta."

"I had to survive."

Kerina brushed Zineta's tears away. "It is over, Zineta. You don't have to be afraid any longer."

She led the girl to the table and sat down across from Kemal Hovic and his wife. "I know you feel bad about Zineta going away," Kerina said through an interpreter. She studied him earnestly. "But I have a plan, Kemal, that will comfort you. One that will bring music to this village and to Tuzla."

She outlined a detailed plan, promising to fund musical instruments and offering Kemal the opportunity to teach a few village school children how to play them. "Later you can take your program into Tuzla," she said.

He hunched forward and adjusted his skullcap. "Impossible. I have never taught anyone."

"He can do it, Miss Rudzinski," Zineta said excitedly.

"Kemal plays the cello well. He knows music."

Zineta pointed to Kemal's youngest son. "Rasim wants to play the violin like you do. He must play it. You see—he is too afraid to go outside since he saw Ran-dee die."

"I will send a child's violin for him." Kerina turned and met Kemal's worried gaze with a smile. "Kemal, are you acquainted with Luciano Pavarotti, the Italian tenor?"

He nodded.

"Pavarotti and his friends opened a music center in Mostar to unite the children of Bosnia. I have spoken to Luciano. He is sending guests from abroad to Mostar to teach the children to play and sing. Perhaps some of his guests would come here to help you get started—to show Rasim how to play the violin. We will bring music back into your village," she promised.

Chandler saw Kemal's face come alive, saw hope in the man's eyes for the first time since Randy's death.

Chan took Jillian's hand and led her outside into the breezy midnight darkness. No stars. No moon shining on them.

"Jillian, I'm not certain about my own future, but I know I want you to be part of it."

"You're sure this time? You're settled about Zineta?"

He ran his fingers across her lips. "I'm crazy about you, Jill. I'm so glad Kerina brought you with her." He paused. "I don't know why, but she has done so much for us—for me."

"You'll understand someday."

"Right now, I can only ask you to be my friend. I want more—but for now I can only offer my friendship."

"Why, Chan? Why not more?"

Huskily, he murmured, "I don't know who I really am. I'm twenty-six years old, and I just found out I may be adopted. If the army is right, I'm not really Chandler William Reynolds. But whoever I am, Jill, I don't want to lose you."

She took a deep breath. "Who told you you're adopted, Chan?"

"The colonel. And I overheard Ashley and Kerina talking about it at the Riviera."

He felt her stiffen. "Then you know?"

"For weeks I told myself it couldn't be true. But now Colonel Bladstone tells me my birth documents are messed up. It seems like everyone knew I was adopted except me."

"Have you told Kerina?"

"Kerina? No. There's really no reason." His arm tightened around her. "Why would I tell her? I'm not even sure what I'm going to say when I get back to California and see the folks."

"Don't hurt them. Your parents love you. They have done everything they could for you."

"Don't hurt them?" His throat constricted. "If I'm adopted—if I'm really adopted—they've deceived me all these years."

Gently, she said, "They must have had their reasons for not telling you. Work it out, Chan. The truth is staring you in the face—as close to you as the breeze blowing against us now. Just ask Ashley for the truth when you get home."

"No, I'm going to find my own answers, and when I do—when I know who my birth parents are—you're the first one I'm going to call." He smiled at her in the darkness. "And then when you come to Los Angeles for Kerina's concert, we can celebrate."

And we can be more than friends, he thought.

Chapter 24

Ashley sat on the white stone bench in her backyard, the weeds in her heart and garden sprouting wildly. In the early years, the three of them—she, David, and Chandler—had been a triple-braided family full of happiness and sunshine and togetherness. She'd been the envy of many with her delightful child and her attentive husband. These days they were frayed, torn apart without words.

They still made an impression on outsiders—David striking and attractive with his silver gray hair, Chandler more handsome than ever with his newly acquired California suntan, and Ashley holding her own with Lancôme facials. But inside the family cord, their facade of oneness had eroded. Ashley felt naked and exposed, the guilt of Everdale surging to the surface—up from the abyss of her own heart where she had so long guarded her secret. How dare she condemn Kerina Rudzinski when the beam in her own eye was the size of a redwood?

She heard Chandler's strong, steady steps coming down the garden path to where she was waiting. He was wearing dark slacks with a new beige pullover, his army haircut all but gone. His actions since coming home two weeks ago had been perfunctory and polite, not warm like those days in Vienna. What was going on in his mind since arriving neither she nor David could imagine. No, that was not true. She feared what had come between them and dreaded the calculated, unrehearsed questions about Everdale and his childhood that had probed their family chats in the evenings.

Ashley noticed a sharp edge to Chandler's voice as he said, "Dad tells me you're not going to the airport with us."

She waved her hand blindly over the flower beds. "I need to weed before the next storm hits."

"The weeds will be there long after I'm gone. But it's not the weeds. You're ticked off about my seeing Grams."

Irritation awakened the anger she felt against her mother-in-law. "I have no qualms about your trip to Denver, Chandler. You should spend time with your grandmother."

"You know that I won't let her criticize you, Mom. I promise."

"Would it matter? I won't be there listening to her."

He fixed his gaze on the flower bed and bent down to pull up a weed and toss it aside. "She's not a bad sort, Mom. I'll only be there a couple of days. Then I have that interview in Washington and the visit with Randy's parents in Ohio."

Ashley leaned back on her heels, brushing the dirt from her hands, wondering whether Everdale was in his plans. "Kerina will be in concert in Los Angeles in three weeks," she reminded him.

"I know. Jillian called from New York. I promised her I'd be here for the concert. Can you ask Dad to order the tickets?"

She nodded.

"So—I guess Dad will drive me to John Wayne without you."

Eyeing him sharply, she saw only that guileless smile. She took a letter from the pocket of her jeans and handed it to him. "I'm sending this instead."

He glanced down and laughed, the resentment in his eyes softening. "Are you saying your good-bye is in writing now? You do get choked up at the airports. That was quite a scene in Vienna with Jillian rushing off to find some tissues for you."

His effort to coax a smile from her fell flat. He studied the envelope, a frown forming between his brows. "Wait, this is addressed to you, Mom. It's from Uncle Bill."

"He wrote it the day he died. Twenty-six years ago."

"I can't nose into something between you and your brother."

"It's about you, Chandler. When you find time, read it."

A pulsating twitch ran the length of his jaw. He opened his briefcase and slid the letter inside. "Well, I'm off. Keep your fingers crossed about the government job."

Why? she wondered. *It will only take you away from us again.*

He leaned down and gave her a quick peck on the forehead. "No tears, Mom. Not now and not when I leave for Europe in a few months, with the government job or without it. I need to be with Jillian."

"Is it that serious between the two of you?"

"I'd like it to be. For now, we're just friends. Jill is giving me space. Time to myself. Time to thread through the past, plan out the future."

Rattled, she asked, "Will you need money? Your dad and I—"

"I'll be all right once I get a job."

"Why must you go away again, Chandler?"

"Do you mean this trip to Denver and all points east? I have to work things out for myself, Mom. To find out what's missing."

She took a gulping breath and said, "You know, don't you?"

He met her gaze. "I know. I've known for several weeks."

It was all that he said. He turned and went down the winding path. He was leaving, but for how long? In her heart of hearts she guessed that he was going off in search of himself—in search of his real roots—and as he went away she feared plunging into the cavernous pit of her own tangled yesterdays. Those days on the Riviera at Kerina Rudzinski's villa had only made Ashley keenly aware of her own shortcomings and sins. They came afresh now and weighed heavily upon her as she watched her son stroll back over the garden path.

∽

When David came back from the airport, he and Ashley roamed around the house in silence; in the end they escaped to their separate sanctuaries—David to his desk piled high with paperwork, Ashley back to weeding in her garden. At dusk he called her back into the house and sent out for pizza for supper. They ate in the living room with the gas fireplace lit for coziness, sitting at opposite ends of the sofa, nibbling cheese and anchovies, pepperoni, and thin browned crust.

David ran his hand through his thick hair dejectedly. "I can't concentrate on my sermon notes for Sunday. I hated seeing Chan go away again so soon. But it's more than that, isn't it?"

"Yes, it's us, David. No, it's me. I wish he were flying nonstop to Washington and not taking that layover in Denver."

"And skip the visit to my mother? He's fond of the old girl. Hasn't seen her since getting back from Bosnia."

"He's withdrawn since our time in Vienna."

"I know. He talks. Watches the games with me. Golfs. Helps me change the oil in the cars. Peeks over my shoulder at my book outlines. Shows an interest. But he's not communicating."

Like you, David, she thought. "I think he knows he's adopted," she blurted. "Kerina must have told him."

The muscles in David's neck grew taut. "Then why didn't he say something to us?"

"We never did."

David sat slouched against the back of the sofa, his long legs crossed, his hands clenched over his chest. Strands of his wavy hair fell across his forehead, black strands mixed with silver gray. The past, the present! His dark brows twitched and his words came out derisive as he said. "What's wrong with you, Ash? You mean to tell me you were there with him, he insinuates he's adopted, and you didn't pursue it?"

"He's waiting for us to make the first move."

She let David blame, accuse. She took another slice of pizza, and broke off bits of cheese and ate them. His expression was like a changing reel: surprise, perfection, disgust, ridicule. As he raved, she picked out slivers of anchovy and pepperoni and tossed them into the box.

"I didn't know what to tell him, David."

"The truth. You know, names like Kerina, Bill—we're sorry."

"You're the family speechmaker. You went to seminary. I didn't. You golfed together yesterday. Why didn't you tell him then?"

"I couldn't." He looked suddenly boyish. "It was the wrong time, Ash. My son and I—well, we were just getting reacquainted. I couldn't spoil our time together."

For several minutes, David went on defending himself, demanding answers. Now he looked weary, not unkind, but hopelessly unable to breech the gap between them. "Ash, I'll be in the library. When you're ready to iron this out, let me know. I don't like things standing between us. I love you—but that fact gets lost in your fury."

Ashley closed her eyes and felt the sofa cushion give as he stood, sensed him passing in front of her striding from the room. She stayed there alone, outlining the words on the pizza box with her finger and calming herself for five, ten, fifteen minutes.

Should she continue to let this wall of ridicule build between them? No. She would go to David. He wanted the truth. Demanded it. She would tell him the truth and heap her own guilt on him. Blame him as he had blamed her. Accuse as he had accused.

When she walked into the library, his Bible and theology books lay open on the desk. He glanced up. "Well!" He tapped his watch and grinned. "Only fifteen minutes this time. A record for us. I'm glad you're here, Ash." He looked sheepish. "I was just thinking about coming to find you to apologize—"

She wouldn't let him. Not now. "Stop it! You want the truth. I'm here to discuss it."

I love you, yet I'm ravaged with guilt, she thought. *And you don't even know why.* "I want to talk about Everdale, David."

He pitched his pen on the desk. "That goes back a long ways," he said stiffly, his attempt to humor her gone.

In that minute he was marvelously controlled. He had not been that way in his youth when his passions and dreams ran freely. The crinkle lines around his blue-gray eyes ridged deeper. "Are you going back to before we were married?"

"Yes, to when we first met."

"To when we fell in love?" Anxiety curled the corners of his mouth. "So that's it. That's what has come between us all these months. The past! Oh Ashley, the past is forgiven."

"How can it be forgiven if you don't even know it exists?"

He leaned forward, his gaze piercing. "In the beginning, I tried to talk to you about Everdale, and you always shut me out. But you've never forgiven me, have you? After all these years of marriage, you still hold it against me."

She let him struggle and grope for words, flinging her own pain back in his face. "I don't know what you're talking about."

His color turned pasty. "Don't you, Ashley?"

She knew. She had agonized over it many times. Often when she felt on top of the world, the ashes of the past drifted across her memory. Her chin jutted out defiantly as her impeccably groomed David fingered the papers on his desk, spread them, restacked them. His smooth hands moved restlessly as though, by the sweeping motion, he could rid himself of a damaging past.

"While you were in Vienna, Ashley, I could think of nothing else but the memories of Everdale."

"I've shouldered them often."

His voice turned bitter. "Ashley, do you hate me for that one moment in our lives? Is there no credit for the good years with you? Will you go on forcing me to bury myself in my work?"

He still couldn't bring himself to voice the truth. She wouldn't let him off the hook now. No, she was pushing him into a confessional box, almost gloating over his defeat. He sprang from his chair and gripped her shoulders. "Say it, Ash. Get it out in the open. You blame me for robbing you of your virginity before our marriage?"

"Seven years before, to be exact. And I was willing to let it go. Eager." She thumped his desk with her fists. "Do you hear me, David? I wanted you to make love to me that day on your grandparents' farm."

His hands fell to his sides. "I'm so sorry, Ashley. I've tried so hard to make it up to you."

"No, you've tried to clear your own conscience, but not for me." She couldn't stop her angry flow of words even though she knew that ridicule could destroy a marriage. "You did it for your church. For your God."

"Your God, too, Ashley." He was back in control, his words even, his gaze unblinking.

"So you could be that upstanding man to your congregation. The perfect sin-free pastor with a faithful wife by your side."

The control wavered again. "Ashley, no man is more aware of his imperfections than I am. I live with them when I stand behind the pulpit. Think about them in the classroom. I never went back to my grandfather's farm without going out to the barn and begging God to forgive me all over again."

He paced restlessly behind the desk, his face flushed, his anguish unbearable to both of them. Haggard ridges formed deep gullies by his mouth. She had gone too far and regretted lashing out at him. Regretted the whole sorry affair.

"David," she whispered, "maybe you never forgave yourself."

"I didn't give much thought to forgiveness until my life turned around—until God became both Savior and Shepherd to me; then I remembered Everdale."

"And worried that it would keep you from seminary?"

"I never told them. Never told anyone."

"What kind of an application did you fill in? No wonder the barn was your only sanctuary."

"I tried to talk to you about it. You always waved it off."

He seemed swallowed up in his own despair. "I always wanted a child of our own. Partly for Chandler. He wanted a brother."

"But I didn't want another child."

"I did. Even before the fertility clinics, I saw the doctor. I thought it was my fault that you couldn't get pregnant."

"No, it wasn't your fault, David. You were okay. But I wasn't; I couldn't have *another* child."

He seemed stunned, his eyes and mouth twitching at the same time. "Another child? I don't understand."

"I was butchered from the first one."

As the truth set in, he collapsed back into the desk chair and stared up at her. "You. . .had a baby?"

"An abortion long before we were married."

She had never seen his face fill with such rage. His voice went rigid with accusation. "Do I know the father?"

"You were the father, David."

For several moments the room was entombed in a deafening silence. He stared at her, disbelief etched in his handsome features. "Ashley, what right did you have to keep the truth from me all these years?"

David didn't wait for her to answer. He stumbled to his feet, shoved his theology books aside, grabbed his car keys from the desk, and stormed out of the room. The front door slammed shut. Car tires squealed as he backed out of the driveway.

Once again, overwhelming silence engulfed her.

$\sim$

On his second day in Denver, Chandler put the phone down and walked back into his grandmother's kitchen where the good smells of a pot roast filled the room. She stood by her shiny, white stove, stirring gravy as he entered.

"Did your call go through?" she asked.

"Straight through to New York. I put it on my phone card."

"No need."

He squeezed her shoulder. "I was afraid I'd be longwinded talking to Jillian."

"Someone special?"

"The girl I want to marry. But right now I can't."

She put the roast on a platter and shoved it toward him. "Be a dear and carve that for me."

"Grams, aren't you going to ask me why?"

He saw her hand tremble as she spooned the carrots and onions and potatoes into her best china bowl, saw again the added lines on her face since his last visit. The gravy boiled and burned as she stood there, frowning. "I forgot to make a salad."

He wanted to say, "Grams, I'm not hungry." But she had gone to a lot of effort to fix his favorite dinner. He switched off the burner. "Looks like plenty without the salad."

"But you like my salads."

"I'm more interested in spending time with you. I thought you could tell me about Everdale."

Redness crept over her cheeks. "I haven't thought about Everdale for a long time."

"Can you think about it now, Grams?"

"Please, let's not talk about it until after dinner."

Last night she had put him off with a different excuse. He had to ask his questions while he had the chance. Tomorrow or the next day he was leaving for the east coast.

Dinner was not to be hurried. On the last bite, he turned down dessert and when she attempted to clear the table, said, "The dishes can wait, Grams. We have to talk."

Again he noticed a tremor as she pushed the dishes aside and folded her ringed hands on the table. She sat stiffly in the high-back mahogany chair, a proud old woman with a handsome, stoic face and a proud tilt to her chin. Whatever religious convictions she had, she kept them to herself. But she talked for hours about the girls at the bridge club and her volunteer work at the historical society and about the library committee she chaired. She was clearly a gregarious woman.

"Who is this Jillian, Chandler? Is she good enough for you?"

"Perfect."

"Then why can't you marry her?"

"Because I don't know who I am, Grams."

"You don't know who you are! Dear boy, what's wrong?"

"Two months ago I thought I knew all my statistics. Parents. Family background—my history three and four generations back. Now I'm not certain of anything. I'm not even sure I was born in Alabama. Tell me about Everdale, Grandma. Was I born there?"

"Such a ridiculous question. Of course you were."

"Then tell me the names of my birth parents."

She steadied her hand as she covered her mouth. "I don't know much about Everdale. I haven't been there since I sold the old farm. Since my parents died. I went back then of course."

"But you were there when I was born?"

"No. A month later."

"Why? I'm the only grandchild. Grandparents can hardly wait to see their first grandchild. Didn't you want to see me?"

Tears washed the faded blue eyes. "Not at first, Chandler."

"Because I was adopted?"

"Who told you that?"

"It doesn't matter. I know now. That's why I came—because I trust you to be honest with me. I want to know the names of my birth parents. I want to know why your son and daughter-in-law have never seen fit to tell me the truth."

She slipped the rings from her right hand and placed them in a row on the linen cloth. "I don't know their names, Chan."

"Then it's true. I'm adopted. I'm somebody else's kid."

She went on the defensive. "Don't ever let your father hear you say that. He reminds me over and over that you are his son."

"His only son?"

She hesitated. "They wanted other children."

"And I always wanted a brother."

She countered, "I suspect that you had one sibling, maybe more."

"What does that mean?"

"Your birth father was a married man."

"Then you know who he was?"

"Only that he came from Everdale—that there would have been a scandal if you had been born in the city where he lived and worked."

"Mom told me she was in the delivery room when I was born."

"She was, Chandler. She was the nurse on duty that night."

"And you never came to see me because I was adopted."

"I'm a proud woman, Chandler. I thought David would have consulted me on a matter of such grave importance. Finally, your grandfather and I flew to Everdale and from the minute I held you, I loved you. And from that moment, your grandfather and I would have defied anyone trying to take you away from us."

He believed her. Felt sorrow for her. "I've got to know the truth, Grams. Why didn't—why didn't my parents tell me I was adopted? Why did I have to wait to hear it from someone else?"

"I don't know. You will have to ask them."

"I can't hurt them. I have to find my own answers. Until I know who I am, I can't ask Jillian to marry me."

Quietly, she said, "David and Ashley must have had their reasons for not telling you. Whatever happens between you and your parents, you are my grandson, Chandler. Don't ever forget that. I'll always be here for you."

"Always?" he teased, watching the tired wrinkled face across from him. "That's good, Grams, because I want you and Jillian to know each other."

"Will I like her?"

"I think so. She can charm the socks off anybody."

"Even me?"

"Even you, Grams."

"What will you do, Chandler?"

"I don't have a choice, do I? I've been on the Internet. I've checked all sorts of records. Sent for vital statistics from Everdale. Short of going there myself, I won't have the answers I need. I won't rest until I know why your son and daughter-in-law lied to me."

"Will you call your father and let him know what you're doing?"

"No."

"But as soon as you're gone, I will have to tell David."

He reached across the table and patted her hand. "You understand, don't you, Grams? I have to find my birth parents. And if I have siblings, I want to meet them."

"What if your birth parents reject you again?"

"That's a risk I have to take."

Chapter 25

For three days David nursed his grudge against Ashley, rationalizing the injustice he had suffered and finding escape in his university classes. As Thursday's class hour came to an end, Anna Weinstad pushed her way to the front of the room, her dark wiry hair bouncing against the weighted knapsack strapped to her back. She was an attractive young woman with a good mind and a quest for answers. Of all David's archaeology students, she held the most promise.

"I'm switching majors," she announced.

"You're quitting my classes?"

"No, I'm going for all the courses that will put me on an archaeology dig someday."

"That's splendid, Miss Weinstad. I'll do everything I can to help you reach that goal."

As they left the classroom and walked down the corridor, she said, "Tell me about your church, Prof. Do you do any singing over at that cathedral of yours?"

"Me? Personally?" He laughed out loud. "I'm known to bluff my way through congregational singing." *Or booming loudly and happily off-key in the shower,* he thought. "My son is the one gifted in music." Even Ashley's love of music had found its way into Grace Cathedral, her influence strongly felt, but her presence was no longer visible. *My fault,* he acknowledged.

"We have a music director at the church," he continued. "The result has been quality music. Three adult choirs. A children's choir. A string orchestra. A cellist and two violinists in the congregation always willing to play a solo in the Sunday services. And a host of music guests throughout the year."

"Impressive. Maybe I'll check it out."

"You do that." He couldn't cross the line between church and state or tamper with university policy, but he did ask, "What about next Sunday?"

"What time?"

"Take your pick. Eight, nine forty-five or eleven."

"Don't you get bored saying the same thing over and over?"

"God's Word is never boring—not when the message is based on eternal truth."

Outside, she squinted into the sun. "Maybe I will come hear you sometime. What do you talk about?"

"God's love. God's forgiveness, mostly."

"Forgiveness," she exclaimed. She rushed off ahead of him, then turned back and waved. "That's a tough one, rabbi."

He didn't correct her but headed straight to his car. He wanted to call Ashley on the cell phone and ask her to have lunch with him so they could smooth over the last three days of animosity. But no, she would be in her garden tying back the larkspurs or pruning her rose bushes. She would not thank him for disturbing her, and in these last few days—these last few months—he had forgotten how to cross back into her world.

Forgiveness. That is a tough one, he thought as he drove home. He hadn't warned Anna Weinstad that his computer file for Sunday's sermon remained a blank page. He couldn't even fall back on an old standby: "The Pilgrim's Triple-Braided Cord." How could he preach on sacrifice, truth, and trust with unforgiveness in his own heart? He had to have Ashley's forgiveness, had to break down the wall between them. He shot through the yellow light; getting home to Ashley was the most important thing he could think of.

~

At the house, Ashley made a decision. She would not let the silence go on between David and herself another day. She paraded up and down the garden path. "Oh God," she cried, "I wounded my husband when I told him the truth about the abortion. You know I love David. I want his forgiveness. I want Your forgiveness."

Twenty minutes later, she made her way into the house as she heard David's car pull into the driveway. She waited expectantly in the hallway. David was the only man she had ever loved, the only one who left her breathless. David was a jute and tartan personality, the fabric of the man tightly woven and strongly twilled, a man whose spirit was linked indelibly to family and friends. To her. Like his maternal Scottish ancestry, David was determined, self-confident, always striving for success. Ashley could not change him, yet in the quiet seclusion of their lives together he had always been a tender, compassionate lover, a faithful companion. Three days ago, she had almost torn the fabric of the man apart. In her own disquiet, she had almost destroyed him, almost broken his spirit.

She heard his key turn in the door, watched the wide, carved door swing back. "David, I have to talk to you."

He nodded. "That's what I came home to tell you." He pushed the door closed behind him, his solemn eyes fixed on her. "These last three days have been the most miserable ones in my life."

"Mine, too."

"Ash, I had to come to terms with what you told me. I had to come to accept my own guilt."

"Oh no, David—"

"Hush," he said tenderly. "I must take responsibility for putting you in an untenable situation. You were so young. We both were. I should have known when my letters to you came back unopened."

"It's all right, David."

"No—we have to put it all out in the open so we can start again." His back arched against the door. "Ash, I've made a mess of being a good shepherd. On the way home I decided to resign my position as senior pastor—"

Alarmed, she murmured, "No. You can't quit, David. You love what you're doing."

"I love you. . .and I'm afraid I'm losing you."

"I won't let you go. And I won't let you quit."

"Ash, I've prided myself in keeping short accounts. At least I thought I did. I preached it from the pulpit, encouraged it in my classroom, practiced it in my daily life."

His hand ran jerkily through his hair, tousling it like it looked when he stepped from the shower. His face twisted into a crooked half smile. "I was so certain I had a handle on short accounts. So certain that the sin of our youth was forgiven."

"And I unraveled the past and put a barricade between us. I'm so sorry, David. But, I must tell you. I never slept with another man. Only you."

"I know that now." He walked to her and ran a thumb over her chin, touched her lips. The scent of his cologne wafted in the air around them. "I don't want it to go on this way, Ash. I want us to start over again. I want you to tell me everything."

"Here in the hallway?"

He smiled and led her into the living room and stood by the fireplace, his hand resting on the mantel. "Why didn't you tell me you were pregnant? I would have married you."

"You did."

"But a long time afterwards." He buried his face in his hands, strands of gray hair slipping between his fingers. She went to him and put her hand on his shoulder, the softness of his cardigan reminding her of that day in the barn when he had thrown his clothes on top of a bed of hay for her.

"You were only eighteen. David."

"I knew right from wrong. I talk to the kids in our parish about accountability. I was of the age of accountability."

"We both were. But you were so charming, the intriguing outsider from California. You wanted me. My friends envied me."

His effort to smile fell flat. He looked grieved and ten years older than he was. His voice was very gentle, the old David reaching out for her. "You should have told me. I had a right to know. I had a right to be there for you."

"I didn't even tell my mother. Just Bill. Bill knew."

"Your brother took you to the abortion clinic?"

"He went with me. He couldn't stop me from going. I was desperate; I had my whole life ahead of me. A baby out of wedlock was a disgrace. I couldn't hurt Mama. She trusted me."

"I would have quit university. I would have married you."

She rubbed the back of his neck. "Dear David, I did what I thought was best—but I will regret it the rest of my life."

He took her hands tentatively. "My mother knew about us," he confessed. "But, Ashley, she didn't know about the baby. I swear she didn't know."

"I've never been comfortable around her."

"She never meant for you to be comfortable. If we had had a child of our own—I think things would have been different."

"We did." Her voice caught. "But I chose to wash him away."

"A boy? It was a boy?"

"That's what the doctor said."

"A son!"

"You have a son, David. Chandler is your son."

"I know. But—"

"We can't undo the past. I've tried. Oh, how I've tried."

"Must we go on suffering for our one mistake?"

"You tell me, darling. You're the theologian." Her voice wavered. "And it wasn't one mistake. We went back to your grandfather's barn four times."

"I am so sorry, Ash. I always loved you. Even back then."

She brushed her cheek against his sweater. "I wanted to hurt you for getting me pregnant—to punish you. But it never worked out that way. I only compounded our sin when I aborted the baby."

"You bore all this pain alone? Is this why you awaken in the night sometimes, crying, and won't ever tell me why?"

"I didn't want to lose you. You always comforted me. And always held me until I could sleep again—and forget."

"You've borne all this alone," he said again. "All this time? Is that why Bill made certain that Chandler came into our lives?"

"I think so. That's what he implied in his letter. But he didn't live long enough for me to ask him. And after his death, I had no one to confide in. It was too late to tell you. I kept thinking that Chandler would fill the void—and make it right."

She glanced out the window toward her garden, twisting her wedding rings over her knuckle, leaving her finger blanched.

"Put those rings back on, Ash. You're still my wife. Don't run from me now. We need each other."

Turning to face him, she said, "Chandler used to tell me a piece of himself was missing. I understood what he meant. I have a missing piece in my life—the baby that never had a chance to see the light of day or breathe the fresh air or grow up to know Chandler or us."

"Don't torture yourself, Ashley. Not when you know the One who carries heavy burdens."

"We lost one child—because of what I did. What if we lose Chandler, too?"

"He's stronger than that. Once he works through this adoption business—and we'll help him—he will come through."

"Will you tell him about my past?"

He looked surprised. "Our past. No, darling, what happened so long ago has nothing to do with Chandler. It's just between us. Let's put it to rest and go on with our lives."

"But what if Chandler chooses Kerina Rudzinski?"

Smiling down at her, he said, "I never knew anyone who could worry and fret so much. Kerina is part of his life, too. We'll work it out. Ash, let's go away for a week or two."

"But the church. Your classes. Your responsibilities."

"I've been neglecting my greatest responsibility—my family. My wife. I'd like to get away alone with you. To talk together. And laugh again. And pray together. And—"

She actually saw him blush. "But your mother is coming for a visit again this weekend, David."

"I'll call and ask her to put it off. She'll understand."

David pulled her against his broad chest, and her tears soaked the front of his shirt. "Can you ever forgive me, Ashley? I want to start over again. You and me. Only this time we'll ask for God's direction and blessing."

"And forgiveness?"

"Somehow, I think we already have that." He leaned down and kissed the top of her head, her cheek, her neck. "I love you, Ashley," he whispered in her ear. "I have always loved you."

For a long time they sat on the sofa, comfortable in each other's arms, enjoying the glow and warmth of the logs in the gas fireplace. Finally David prayed in his deep rich voice, thanking God for His mercy, speaking longingly of the son who had never been born, and gently giving him back to God. Afterwards—hours after David placed a brief call to his mother—he and Ashley talked about the days ahead and the rest of their lives together.

And long after that, David said gently, "It's past midnight. We'd better turn in, Ash."

Unrushed, unhurried, he switched off the lights, checked the locks on the doors, and smiling wryly at her, unplugged the phones from the wall. Hand in hand they climbed the stairs, the wall between them gone. They were young again.

As they reached the second floor, fragments of their wedding vows made so long ago came back to Ashley. *"For better or worse; for richer, for poorer; in sickness and in health, until death do us part."* She meant that pledge more at this moment than she had on that day when she said the words aloud to David.

Moments later, for the first time in months, Ashley slipped willingly, gladly, into David's arms, loving and being loved.

❦

At three a.m. on Friday—the very weekend they were to go away—the doorbell rang persistently. David eased Ashley out of the crook of his arm and was out of bed at once, running down the stairs in his blue-striped pajamas with his silk robe tossed over one shoulder and his slippers flapping against his heels. He unchained the door and swung it back.

"Mother!" he exclaimed. "What are you doing here at this hour? I thought you agreed to put off your visit for a week."

"Don't send me away, David."

He frowned at the desperation in her voice. "We never have."

He jammed his arms into his robe, reached for her icy hand, and drew her into the parquet entryway. He grabbed her luggage and dropped it just inside the door. "Now," he said, chaining the door again, "what's this all about? Traveling around alone at night all the way from Denver? It's not safe, Mother."

"It's Chandler, David. He's gone."

"Yes, we know that. He flew to Washington to apply for a government job. After that, he's visiting friends in Akron."

"He knows, David. He knows everything. I knew you were going away this weekend. That's why I came—to tell you he's in Everdale."

David stiffened. "You flew all the way here to tell us he went to Everdale? Why didn't you call us?"

"Because I didn't want to be alone. I'm so afraid he won't come back. David, I never saw him so distraught. He said two months ago he knew who he was—and now, he can only guess."

For a minute David said nothing. He slipped his arm around his mother's shoulders and led her into the living room. She sank gratefully into an overstuffed chair, looking lost and forlorn as he gazed down at her. He kicked the ottoman in front of her chair and sat down facing her. She looked older than her seventy-five years, her tired eyes faded and anxious, the proud face lined with wrinkles. *When did old age sneak up on her?* he wondered.

He smothered his anxiety and took her hands in his. The once smooth hands were dotted with age spots, bulging with blue veins. He hated age creeping up on her, but no more than she dreaded it herself. He massaged her fingers, warming them with his own.

"What does Chandler know?" he asked, knowing.

"About the adoption."

"It had to come out someday."

"But not this way. Not with that young woman in Europe telling him it was time to face who he really was."

"Jillian?" David asked.

"That was her name. She has him wrapped in her clutches."

He smiled patiently. "That's what you told me when I fell in love with Ashley."

"Who is this Jillian, David? What right did she have—?"

"The girl is in love with my son."

She mocked, "Whose son is he, David? Jillian seems to know—"

"Jillian works for Chandler's birth mother, but she had no right to tell him."

"I don't think she did. Not in actual words. Chandler called Jillian from my place."

"Tell me what happened, Mother," he urged. "Chandler said nothing to us before he left for your place."

"He won't. He doesn't want to hurt you, but he said it was up to you and Ashley to be honest with him—to make the first move. I assured him you had your reasons for never telling him. But Chandler is determined to find his own answers."

David wanted to lash out at Ashley again, to hide from his own responsibility. He calmed and said, "Kerina Rudzinski broke her promise to Ashley, then."

"Kerina? The violinist?" His mother's color turned ashen. She pressed both hands against her chest. "David, you will be the death of me. Don't tell me that violinist is his birth mother?"

"Yes, Mother."

"You've always known, David?"

"From the beginning."

"And his father?" she whispered.

He looked away. "Ashley's brother."

"*Chandler William.* I should have known. I guessed as much and then thought it so improbable that I pushed it from my mind. Oh David, you and Ashley have covered for Bill all these years?"

"It was a closed adoption, Mother. We were obligated to do as Kerina asked. When Bill died so soon after Chandler's birth, we didn't want Celeste and the children to be hurt anymore."

She pulled away. "All his life Chandler wanted brothers."

"And he had them. But we couldn't tell him."

"I did tell him that his birth father was a married man and that there might be siblings. As upset as he was, he will go to the ends of the earth to find them." Her voice grew shrill. "You and Ashley should have had a child of your own."

He had heard this more than he cared to remember. "Chandler is our son. How many times do I have to tell you that, Mother?"

"It was Ashley, wasn't it? Unable to bear a child."

"That's between Ashley and me. It always has been."

Arrogantly, she said, "But Ashley wasn't honest with you. She deceived you. She had an abortion; did you know that, David?" Her voice shook with remembered rage. "I had flown back to see my parents again. I heard the rumors in Everdale. I had to keep you from going back to Ashley, so I followed her to that abortion clinic. I know. I have known for years. What she did was disgraceful, a black mark against our family name."

"And you have punished her for it." He ran his hands through his silver hair, wearied by it all. "It was my child."

She gasped. "Yours? Your baby?" She looked whitewashed, frightened, old. "It was your child? You were the father? Oh no. I put all the blame on Ashley all these years! Oh David, will she ever forgive me?"

"Of course, Mother Reynolds." Ashley came quietly into the room, walked over to David's chair, and slipped her arms around his neck.

"Oh Ashley, what an old fool I have been."

"You just wanted to protect David."

"And to blame you. Forgive me, Ashley? I beg you—don't leave my son over this."

"I thought that's what you always wanted, Rosalyn."

"Not any longer. I'm sick of this family being torn apart. You have been so right for David. I just didn't like losing him."

"You never lost him. He's always been here for you. We both have. We always will be."

Chapter 26

Five days ago, when he'd arrived in Everdale, Chandler did not recognize the streets, could not put a name to a face. Rather, it was the sensation of familiarity, the feeling of having been here. Stirrings that came at the sight of goldenrod waving in the fields and the smell of burning leaves in the crisp, fall air. The feeling of going back in time to his post-toddler days. Vague impressions. Gut perceptions. His roots were here, his beginnings. More than the family photograph albums. More than the gilt-edged steeple against the Everdale skyline or the awareness of his dad carrying him in those strong arms of his or his mom pushing him on the backyard swing. Coming back was like hearing an echo of the past. Like having the missing piece of himself within grasp.

But he was convinced of one thing. As a kid, he never liked grits for breakfast, plain or mixed with eggs in the Southern way. He knew he would have spewed them out if his mom had spooned them in. He surely didn't like grits back then. He didn't like them now. And if Kyle Richardson's wife at Richardson's Bed-and-Breakfast gave him ham hocks simmered with okra and black-eyed peas for one more dinner, he'd have to plead the flu and dash for the bathroom.

Chandler awakened on Thursday morning to a rainstorm pelting the Richardsons' house, with rain coming in the open window. He showered and dressed in a cold bathroom and then used his towel to mop up the rainwater on the floor. He left the house fueled with a bowl of grits piled high with sugar and cream and set out for another day of searching for his identity.

His first stop was Dr. Malcolm Nelson's private residence, one of the older, well-preserved homes in town. The housekeeper led Chandler into the library where the doctor sat, scowling, at a large oak desk as Chandler crossed the room to him. Dr. Nelson didn't stand to greet his guest even when Chandler extended his hand.

"Thank you for seeing me, sir."

Nelson nodded, solemn and slack-mouthed. Even sitting, he looked tall and distinguished with his curly gray hair and unblinking gray eyes.

But his face was the same shade as his cream shirt, as if he had been ill and hadn't yet recovered.

"I won't keep you long, sir. I'm Ashley Reynolds's son. At least I was until a couple of weeks ago."

With effort Nelson lifted his limp arm and braced it on the desk. It was then that Chandler realized he was in a wheelchair, that the droop of his mouth was medical. The doctor couldn't be more than sixty-five, seventy at the most, but right now he was having a painful twist of an old man's body as he shifted in the chair and focused on Chandler.

"Did I come at a wrong time, sir?"

"There is no right or wrong time anymore," a woman said, entering the room. "Malcolm has few visitors since his stroke." She walked behind him and placed her hands on his shoulders. "How can my husband and I help you, young man?"

"My mother worked for Dr. Nelson some years ago."

Haltingly Nelson said, "Yes. I think I remember her."

"Of course you do, Malcolm. She married Pastor Reynolds."

"Ashley? Yes. . .yes. A good nurse."

"That's why I'm here, sir."

"I can imagine why," he said, his words slurred.

His wife's back went rigid. "Oh, no—you're not—"

"Afraid he may be, Abby. Sam Waverly over at the Court House called me. Said Reynolds here was in town, asking to meet me."

"Then you know why I'm here, sir?"

"I have trouble remembering these days, but Waverly says you're looking for your father."

"Pastor Reynolds is the boy's father," his wife said.

Wearily, Nelson cut her off. "He's not a boy, Abby. He's a grown man. Sit down, son."

And I'm not your son either, Chandler thought as he sank into the chair across from Nelson. "I can't fight the bureaucracy. I talked to the attorney involved in my adoption, but he has no files on me. I met briefly with the Probate Judge. Says he wasn't here twenty-six years ago—needs time to look over my records. I've been to the Court House three days in a row. Sam Waverly refuses to open my court papers. He says they're sealed."

"Then leave them that way," Nelson's wife advised.

"I can't, Mrs. Nelson. I have to know who I am."

Her grip on Malcolm's shoulders tightened. "Please leave."

"Not without answers."

"If the court refuses to help you, why should my husband?"

"Because he delivered me and arranged for my adoption. It was his idea. I do know that much."

"It was your father's idea," she said. "Brought some rich Yankee down here with him. But she was just another woman with an unwanted pregnancy."

Chandler's throat burned. "She was my mother."

"She had few options back then. Adoption was one."

"Hush, Abby. Hush. We both know I was fool enough to go along with it. The baby's father said nothing would go wrong."

"Malcolm, you don't owe Mr. Reynolds an explanation. You're getting upset. We both are. I don't want you ill."

"I already am."

"Why did my mother give me up, sir?"

Nelson's twisted mouth pulsated. "How does anyone know another person's reasons? She was young, frightened. Unmarried."

"I wouldn't have held it against her."

"And how would you know that, young man? From hindsight?"

Chandler pressed his case. "You took advantage of her fears. Had her come all the way to Everdale."

"We had nothing to do with her coming," his wife said.

"But your husband arranged for my adoption. I've been thinking about that. A small town. A small-town doctor. Not much money in that. Arranging adoptions could be profitable. And then along comes the opportunity to put a baby into the hands of a couple who desperately wanted a child." His words dripped with sarcasm. "You chose the right couple, Doctor, didn't you?"

A flicker of protest crossed his face. "The baby's father chose the family you would live with."

"My own father?"

"We were friends once. They were friends."

Chandler's fists doubled. He wanted to shake this man and force the truth from him. He was glad for the desk between them, for the wheelchair that kept him from hitting the man.

"Why did you choose them? Because Reynolds was a preacher, the nurse someone you worked with? People who would never tell on you. Is that the way it went, Doctor Nelson?"

What good were unfounded accusations? He'd never get his answers that way. But he worried. Had this town turned their back on wrongdoing?

Had the doctor arranged other adoptions for a fee?

Nelson leaned back against his wife's hands, a proud man defending his decision. "I did your mother a favor, Reynolds. She couldn't have any other children."

"She never had any," Chandler said.

"It seems she kept more from you than your identity."

The doctor's words were more difficult to comprehend now. He was visibly tired, his mouth sagging. His wife wiped the corner of his mouth with her handkerchief. "It was legal. We had an attorney. Rovner dealt with the courts."

"Mr. Rovner of the Rovner, Bates, and Grimwald Law Firm? I've been to his office. Like I mentioned, Rovner has no record of my adoption. It was amazing how short his memory was."

"Like mine. I have trouble remembering since my stroke. But Rex Rovner—" he laughed.

Chandler nearly lost control. "Then check your records. The law required you to record my birth parents. Both of them."

Slowly, he said, "I have no records. I sold my practice. The man who took over saw no need to keep records back that far."

"How much was I worth to you and the lawyer? Five thousand dollars? Ten thousand?"

Nelson looked smitten, as though Chandler had stolen his dignity. "Your father and I were friends. The lawyer charged a fee. I didn't."

"I wasn't worth a dime, eh?"

"Your mother was young—your father married."

"Keep still, Malcolm. He will drag us into court over this."

"I know that isn't any fun, Mrs. Nelson. I went to the courts for my answers and they are merciless."

Chandler faced the doctor again, ignoring the man's wife. "A month ago I knew who I was. I had no doubt that David and Ashley Reynolds were my parents. I could trace my family heritage back three or four generations on both sides. Back to General VanBurien on the Confederate side. Right now, sir, all I have left is the date of my birth."

"There's nothing my husband can do—"

Nelson waved her off with his good arm. "Hear the boy out."

"The courts can't tell me, but you can, Doctor. You know who my father is. I want to find him. Did he come from Everdale?"

Nelson nodded. "He did. A longtime resident." The pale gray eyes closed, opened again. "One might say he's still here."

"Please, I have to find him."

Mrs. Nelson bridled. "Sam Waverly is the one to help you."

"I've been there, three days in a row. He treated me like I was a criminal—for searching for my own roots."

"What right do you have to know?" she asked.

He thumped his chest with doubled fists. "Those records are all about me. The courts know more about me than I know myself. They won't even give me a copy of my own birth certificate."

Her face turned livid. "Your birth mother came into this town and asked my husband for help and he gave it. Don't come back here now accusing us of doing something wrong. You must leave. You're upsetting my husband."

"It was Chandler's father who asked me for help, Abby."

"How many other children did you put up for adoption, Doctor? I wasn't the only one, was I?"

Mrs. Nelson's blanched skin matched her husband's now, an ashy gray. "Leave, please."

"Mother used to trace my footprint on my birth certificate and tell me how tiny I was when she first held me. I figured it was just Mom being sentimental."

"Ask her for your answers."

His voice wavered. "I have to find my own answers, Mrs. Nelson. I've already checked the Internet. Nothing. I've gone back over my parents' tax records. I checked with the Library of Congress. Before I came to Everdale I contacted the genealogy department of a local Mormon church to see whether they could trace my roots. I've been to the newspaper office here in town."

"Why don't you hire a private detective? And leave my husband alone."

"Ma'am, I couldn't afford that until I get a civilian job."

"You don't work?"

"My army pay didn't leave much reserve."

Nelson rubbed his limp arm, a bemused smile on his face. "Your father was my friend. I can't—I won't betray him."

Chandler stood and made his way to the door. "Can you tell me one thing, sir? Did my mother want me?"

"I don't know, son. I—I don't remember."

"Good day, sir. Ma'am."

The doctor stopped him. "Where do you go from here, Reynolds?"

"I'm going to put flowers on my uncle's grave."

"Bill VanBurien?" From across the room Chandler saw the surprise on Nelson's face, saw those faded gray eyes dilate. "That uncle of yours was a good man. Shame the way he died."

Chandler nodded. "On a rain-drenched day like this."

"Heading back to Chicago that night, wasn't he?"

"Yes sir. I believe he was. That's what my mother said."

His scowl softened. "Reynolds, I'm sorry I can't help you."

Won't, Chandler thought.

"But—your mother had a friend, a nurse. . .who was in the delivery room. . .the night you were born." He struggled for each word, obviously determined to be understood. "I don't. . .I don't remember her name, but Abby, you do. Give it to young Reynolds here."

∽

Chandler guessed that Kerina was in town by now. But where? Did she have personal friends she could stay with? He'd never find her. Perhaps she had signed into the only motel in Everdale, a row of eight units chipped and timeworn, on the other side of town.

"Imagine finding you in town," he would tell her. No, he'd be up-front. "Jillian called me. Told me you'd be here. I was coming anyway. It was a good chance to see you again."

Logical. Honest. Straight to the point. He'd ask her to go to dinner, but Everdale had no fancy restaurants, no restaurants at all unless you counted the fast-food chains. With any luck she'd like the novelty of French fries, chicken nuggets, and a milk shake.

He pulled into the Everdale Cemetery where the roads were muddied by the rain. He parked near the mortuary, checked on the lot number for the VanBurien family plot, and struck out on foot, armed with the Richardsons's umbrella and two bouquets of flowers.

Perpetual care kept the plots looking good, the lawns mowed; there was serenity all around him. Something seemed familiar, a sensation of having climbed over the headstones in the VanBurien family plot when he was a child. He placed the bouquet of yellow roses on his grandmother's marker, the white ones on Uncle Bill's grave. He was doing this flower thing for his mother. He stepped back, gave the setting a proper silence, then whirled around and walked briskly away over the rain-soaked ground.

Just ahead, a woman came toward him, her eyes downcast as she walked through the cemetery. The rain fell steadily, but her head was bare. He stepped aside to let her pass by and, startled, exclaimed, "Miss

Rudzinski! Jillian told me you were taking a few days between concerts."

She glanced up, her sad eyes lighting with recognition. *Jillian was right,* Chandler thought. Kerina looked pale, thinner, a dark circle under each eye. Her clothes were soaking wet, her hair sopping. Quickly Chandler drew her under the protection of his umbrella.

"Chandler, what are you doing here?"

"I was going to ask you the same thing."

"I'm here to visit a friend's grave."

"A special friend?"

"Quite special. I didn't know he had died until a few weeks ago."

"Hold this." He shoved the umbrella into her hand, whipped off his raincoat, and slipped it around her shoulders. "You'll catch pneumonia," he scolded, taking back the bumpershoot.

"I wasn't thinking. I left my coat in the car."

"You'd better make your visit here quick—and then we'll get you back to your car. Let me go with you. Which grave?"

She consulted a map in her hand, streaked with rainwater now, and then led him to a grave with fresh flowers lying on top and placed her own beside them. It was the VanBurien family plot, and the tears that Kerina shed were obviously for his uncle.

Closure. She was looking for closure. Chandler stood back, giving her privacy for her grief. His uncle and Kerina Rudzinski? A thousand questions. Where had they met? When? What kind of torch had she carried for a man who had been dead for so long? Why hadn't his mother told him?

She turned at last. "Thank you for coming with me."

"You shouldn't wander alone in a cemetery, Miss Rudzinski."

She smiled at that. "Someone was here before me. Bill liked white roses."

"Then why did you bring red ones?" he asked gently.

"Because they are symbolic of love."

He tucked her arm in his, shielding her with his umbrella once more. "Let's get back to that car of yours."

She nodded gratefully. "Yes; then you can have your coat back. . . . Chandler, which grave were you visiting?"

He waved his hand vaguely toward a different tombstone, a different family plot.

As they reached the cars, he asked, "Would you have dinner with me this evening? We could drive over to Spruceville."

"I'm tired, Chandler. I need to be alone."

He offered her his handkerchief. "I can't let you go. Not like this. Let me take you for a drive around Everdale."

"I've been doing that all day."

He considered carefully and then said, "I know one place you didn't see—the house where I spent a brief span of my life. It's been in the family for years."

"Drive around in this weather? We'd better not."

He glanced at the drifting clouds. "These rain squalls pass over. Come back to my bed-and-breakfast. My hostess always has a pot of okra and black-eyed peas on. Or turnip greens."

"Sounds awful."

He grinned. "They're not my favorite either, but it will pass time while we wait for the sun to come back."

They were standing by her car, rain dripping down on both of them. "Let's just drive around. I'm not up to visiting anyone right now, Chandler."

"Suits me," he said. "We can leave your car here and pick it up later."

"Did you reenlist?" she asked as they drove back to town.

"No. I'm out of the army now."

"Good. Then you can take your violin out of the closet."

"Have you forgotten? Or maybe, Jillian didn't tell you. I have an interview in Washington about that Bosnian job."

"The one with the government—yes, but what happened to being a music critic?"

"That's still on. Might be delayed a bit. I asked to be assigned to London. When needed, I'd fly into Bosnia from there."

"Will Jillian like that?"

"I didn't ask her. We'll have to settle that after the interview in Washington. Now let's talk about you and your concert in Los Angeles. I hope to get done in time to hear you."

She looked surprised. "But once I get back to New York—"

"Don't disappoint me. I'm counting on seeing Jillian."

"Once we get to Europe, she's moving back to London."

"She's leaving you?"

"Her year is almost up. And Franck wants to go back to Moscow. He'll be much safer there."

"And you?"

"Back to Prague for a few weeks. I'm cutting back on my schedule. I want to leave while people are still honoring me. The accolades don't mean as much to me anymore," she said. "I want to retire my Stradivarius while people are still giving me standing ovations."

He leaned over and brushed the rain from her cheeks. Or were they tears? "Honor belongs to a power greater than a musician."

For a second she looked puzzled. "God?" she asked.

~

By the time they reached the VanBuriens', the rain had stopped. A calm swept over Kerina as she stepped from the car and took the winding path up the hill to the house. It was like coming home. She belonged. She was at peace. Surely this was Bill's home. It had that look about it. The woodsy smell. The cozy feeling. The wraparound porch. In her heart, Bill was there, walking beside her, showing her his childhood home, giving her a glimpse of that person he had wanted to be.

Wood smoke poured from the chimney on the sloping roof of the two-story house. Blue shutters framed the narrow windows and lace curtains covered the panes. Round white pillars framed the porch and straggling wet vines of the dead wisteria still tumbled over the picket fence. The flower beds had been pruned back for winter, the soil soaked from the rain.

Chandler stood beside her, saying nothing. She put her hand on his arm. "Chandler, who lives here?"

"I don't know who owns it now, but until we moved away, it belonged to the VanBuriens. Generation after generation."

"Bill's home! Bill grew up here, didn't he?"

"And you are comforted by that?"

"Yes, it is that kind of house."

"Have you been here before?" he asked.

"No, not this close. Yet I have been here a thousand times. This is the country home that I have dreamed about, thought about, searched for. There has to be a gazebo in the back."

"There is," he said in surprise. "Out by the swings. And trails lead right into the woods. You can see the trees above the roof. Pines, cedars, and the old oak trees."

Her eyes misted. "And deer come down to feed in the winter."

Chandler unlatched the gate and allowed Kerina to enter ahead of him. She waited for the rusty hinges to creak, listened for the sound of the mockingbird in the treetops or the call of the whippoorwill. Listened for the sound of a child.

A tangle of damp bracken scratched her legs as they passed the hedges. Chan urged her up the flagstone steps, through the rain puddles, along the winding cobbled path to the arched trellis. "In spring and summer, the trellis is covered with roses and bees. Funny I remember that. I was three when we moved away, but I recall running from the bees and up that porch into Mom's arms."

Touching Kerina's elbow, he urged her forward. As they crunched over the burnt orange leaves drifting across the walkway, Kerina said, "I can't smell the honeysuckle."

"Autumn is the wrong time of the year."

"There should be a rocker on the porch and a baby crying in its mother's arms—as you must have done, Chandler."

He stopped at the porch, one foot on the first step. "It's still there in the corner. See?" He laughed. "It's not the one Mom rocked me in, but it serves the purpose."

Grasping the railing, he turned to face her. "I didn't realize until I saw you at the cemetery that you knew my uncle. Kerina, why didn't Uncle Bill ever bring you here to the house?"

"We parked at the bottom of the hill once," she whispered. "On the gravel by the side of the road near where you parked. Bill said this old house was his favorite place in the world when he was a boy. Because he loved it so, it must have lingered in my memory."

She looked up at her son, wanting him to understand. "I knew if I could find this place, I would be at peace. Can you understand that, Chandler?"

"Yes. I've been looking for a missing piece in my life, too," he told her. "Mom always said the house was special because her mama was there. Once her mama was gone, her laughter went with it. But why didn't Uncle Bill take you inside?"

Tears balanced on Kerina's lashes. "Your uncle was married, Chandler. He had a wife and two children, and I was traveling with him. He didn't want to embarrass any of us. Himself especially."

"That would be my Aunt Celeste. She married again after my uncle died. I've never met my cousins. That side of the family wanted nothing to do with us after my uncle died."

"My fault," Kerina said.

"Uncle Bill had no right to hurt you."

"Love is always painful, Chandler." She sighed. "I wanted to come back and see the house in the daylight. Bill promised me that one day he would buy the place for me so I could be happy. But talking like that was wrong, and we knew it."

"Would you really be happy here? It would be filled with memories. And the townsfolk don't always take to strangers."

How well I know, she thought. She allowed her gaze to wander over the property toward a gate that led to the side of the house. It was then that she saw the FOR SALE sign propped against the railing, almost hidden behind a faded purple bush.

"Look. The place is for sale. I should buy it."

"What would you do with a house in Everdale?"

"Keep it for a summer home."

He frowned. "It's steamy hot here in the summertime, and there are lots of mosquitoes to contend with."

"I will buy much repellent."

"A house like this has to be lived in, Kerina. It's like part of the family. It needs kids running through the kitchen, poking their skates through the screen door, exploring the woods behind the house. You can't buy this place and leave it empty. It would become a thicket of weeds and disrepair."

Like the house in my dreams, she thought.

They were on the porch now, peering through the window into a room full of old-fashioned furnishings that had to be hand-me-downs. But there was warmth there, that lived-in look. They stayed for an hour while Kerina ran her fingers over the picket fence, slid her hand down the banister railing, rocked in the rocker on the porch, smelled burning leaves from the neighbor's yard, picked at chipped paint on the gazebo, and sat on the swing where Bill had spent so many happy hours. After Chandler pushed her higher and higher in the swing, they walked around the house, hiked a pace in the woods where Bill had hiked, then ran through the garden where a very young Chandler had picked a bouquet of flowers for his mother.

Kerina felt as if Bill was there. And Mama, the woman she had never met—Bill's stronghold. As she sat and rocked, Kerina imagined Mama laughing and Bill's deep voice quoting T. S. Eliot.

"You're smiling," Chandler said.

"I'm just remembering. That's all. You are right of course. There is no place in Everdale for me. I've come back. I have said my good-byes." She glanced back pensively as they walked down to the car. At the foot of the hill, her gaze went back to the house once more, sealing it in her memory. Bill and memories. Mama and her twins had made this place. But Bill and his mama were gone.

The late afternoon air was chilling, another rain squall threatening in the sky "Miss Rudzinski, do you want me to get a camera and come back and take some pictures for you?"

Her fingers grazed his arm. "No. I have seen this place in my mind and heart for years. I will never forget it. Bill used to tell me that we would share it together one day when I retired from the concert hall." Her voice filled with wistful happiness. "I knew it would never happen. Must not happen. But this house has belonged to me as far back as I can remember."

Chapter 27

The next morning, with the nip of fall pushing him on and the cold rain soaking him, Chandler took refuge under the eaves of the craft store. He wiped the rain from his face with the back of his hand and checked the street numbers against the e-mail from home.

He had hit the 300 block, a high number for a town crunched together in the middle of nowhere with a population that barely numbered 3,000. Right now, he'd settle for locating Selma Malkoski at 593 Carstone Lane. He poked his head into the craft shop and asked for directions.

"Carstone? Close enough to walk," the shopkeeper said. Chandler took the time to buy a box of candy and then plodded on, the mist-laden rain coming down harder now. *Good for the evergreens,* he thought, *but not for me.*

Ashley's friend Selma lived on a narrow residential street north of the hospital and not far from downtown. Behind her house the fields were covered with purple flowers drinking in the rain and hundreds of goldenrod—with enough pollen to send anyone into an allergy attack. As Chandler knocked on the door, a freight train rattled over the tracks in the center of town.

He knocked again. This time Selma Malkoski opened the door.

"Hey," she said.

"Hello, Mrs. Malkoski. I'm Ashley Reynolds's son. I called—"

"*Miss* Malkoski. Been looking for you. Where's your car?"

"I left it by the depot."

"And walked in the rain? I thought any son of Ashley's would be smarter than that. Come in. Take a load off those wet feet."

Selma was not the slim, trim nurse his mother had described. It was apparent she didn't need a box of chocolates, but he handed her the candy anyway.

"Bribery? Dr. Nelson warned me that you were a smooth one."

She pointed to a chair and sank down on the sofa across from him. The gift box was quickly opened and sampled, the lid left upright on her lap. "You look a bit different than the last time I saw you, Chandler. Three then, weren't you? A cute little kid."

He glanced around. It was an old-fashioned room with a high ceiling, and no visible central heating. Logs blazed in the stone fireplace, but the heat didn't reach him. His gaze strayed from the logs to the half-empty wineglass on the end table beside her and back to her face.

State your business and get out of here, he told himself.

"Dr. Nelson said you could help me locate my biological father."

"Me? Try the Court House."

"I did. But Nelson said you were my best bet. You were friends with my family."

"Don't placate me. Ashley Reynolds and I were coworkers, not really close friends."

"The doctor sees it differently. He's certain you can help me. Said he was having a bit of trouble with memory."

"Sounds like Nelson. He forgets what he wants to forget. He was an excellent physician. About the only one we had in town back then. But he is an utter coward when it comes to dealing with people. Makes it a point not to get involved."

"Meaning finding my father?"

"What makes you think I would know any more than Nelson?"

"He said you and my—birth father were close once."

"Lovers back in high school," she said bitterly. "Engaged once. That was our charming William."

William! A name at last. But he needed the last name, the whole name. He leaned forward, silently blessing the distracting box of candy. "I don't want to waste your time. Please, could you just tell me where I can find William?"

She snapped back, "I'll tell you what the good doctor was too coward to tell you. William is on the other side of town. Go dig him up."

"I need an address. Just tell me who he is—where he lives."

"Your father?" Selma's laughter trilled without mercy.

Her mouth gaped open, her tongue coated with melting chocolates. "The whole town knows who your father was. Surely you've guessed."

"I wouldn't ask if I knew."

"Beanpole. That's what we called him in high school. A scoundrel. A loser. That's what I called him. Ashley idolized him." She selected another chocolate from the box and popped it into her mouth, licking her fingers before saying, "William hated Everdale. Could hardly wait to move away."

"Did he?"

"He left town all right. Joined the navy. Nearly broke his mother's heart, I'll tell you. And that wasn't the only heart he broke. The daahling of Everdale with that charming way of his and that dimpled grin. Easy come. Easy go."

An uneasiness settled over Chandler. *You were one of the broken hearts left behind,* he thought. *One of the broken hearts that stayed single.*

Chandler felt himself drifting toward despair. *William. The navy.* No, the idea was crazy. "Miss Malkoski, have I come all the way to Everdale for nothing? The doctor who delivered me isn't talking. The attorney who arranged my adoption kept no records on it. I was told you would help me, but you're hopscotching around the facts."

"Know what, Reynolds? I think you're backing down. You're afraid of the truth." She tossed an unfinished bonbon back in the box. "If not, try the Court House."

"I told you, I already did. After being shafted from office to office, the Court House records remained sealed like some top secret at Langley. Do you know what Langley is, Miss Malkoski?"

"Central Intelligence," she said.

"For two days I've dealt with nothing but strangers. Power hungry strangers controlling the facts of my birth and spieling off state laws that forbid me to know what my own file contains. Me—my origin is top secret."

"That's not fair," she admitted. "But let it go. I can't believe that Ashley and Pastor Reynolds have not been good parents to you."

"The best until I found out we've all been living a lie."

"Do they know you've come to Everdale?"

"We've been in touch by e-mail. That's how I got your address and Dr. Nelson's name."

"Did you talk to Kyle Richardson over at the Court House? He was a personal friend of Pastor Reynolds."

"I know. I'm staying at the Richardsons' bed-and-breakfast."

"Crazy business," Selma said. "Not more than two dozen guests all year and most of them Yankees from up north."

"Richardson just referred me to someone else down the line."

"Sam Waverly?"

"He was the worst of all."

"Careful," she said, smiling for the first time. "Waverly is running for city mayor."

"I hope he doesn't make it."

"He will. He's the only one running."

"Waverly told me my birth records are none of my business. He had the paperwork right there on his desk. The files in his hands were mine, Miss Malkoski, but I couldn't touch them." Chandler indicated the size of his file with his thumb and forefinger. "Couldn't have been more than a dozen documents including a copy of the Order of Adoption and a thin form that Mr. Waverly held up and referred to as the Consent Decree."

"That would be the form your biological mother signed."

"I figured as much. A miserable piece of paper that tossed me out with the dirty bathwater."

"Try the new City Hall. Most of the records since 1970 have been transferred there. Births. Deaths. Marriages. Divorces."

"What good will it do? Waverly says my original birth certificate—if there is one—would be under seal of the court."

"Did he tell you that City Hall is closed until Tuesday?"

"Yes. Some Confederate holiday. And I'll be gone by then. I have an appointment in Washington that I can't break. I only have a couple more days in Everdale."

"Not much time to trace twenty-six years."

"Not your fault. You said my father was in the navy. If I only had a name, perhaps I could go that route. Tell me, Miss Malkoski, after his stint in the navy, where did my father go?"

She winced. "He told me he'd come back to Everdale. That's what he said in his letters. But he settled in Chicago."

Chicago? The navy? William? Chandler's uneasiness was back.

"Went to university first and then stayed on for some highfalutin job." She drummed her polished nails on the lid of the candy box, the sound like an Uzi emptying its rounds. Selma Malkoski was soured on life and men—especially William. "But he came home, all right. Back here when he needed us."

"Were you classmates in high school?"

"We all were. Nelson was ahead of us. But Ashley and her brother were in my class. Star basketball player that William."

His shirt felt clammy. He had passed the high school when he pulled into town. He'd drive there next and head straight to the library and the yearbooks mildewing there. He'd check out every William on the basketball team in the '70s. One of them would be his uncle. The greatest basketball player of all times, according to his mom.

"Dr. Nelson said my father resides in Everdale now?"

"I guess you could say that. So Ashley never told you?"

He gambled on the truth. "She never wanted to hurt me."

"Or was she too ashamed to admit the truth?"

Suddenly he didn't want to hear the truth. He stood, the chair scraping across the floor. "I have to leave. I'm sorry I troubled you."

"Where are you going?"

"I came to Everdale to find my father."

Her face twisted, a mixture of pity and pain. "It won't do any good to keep looking. You won't find him. He's—he's dead."

Chandler gripped the chair back. "Dead?" he repeated.

She nodded. "I told you he always came back to Everdale when he was in trouble."

"Was he ill?"

"He came here when you were born and was killed in an automobile accident near the airport on his way back to Chicago."

He felt absolute fury. No wonder his parents had deceived him. Uncle Bill had died in a car accident days after Chandler's birth. *During a rainstorm. A muggy, misty, rain-drenched day like this one. For twenty-six years Uncle Bill had been not much more than a name.*

His back was soaked with perspiration. "Uncle Bill?" He said the name aloud as if for no other reason than to admit the truth to himself. "My mom's brother?"

"I am sorry, Reynolds. Them keeping it from you all these years. What's wrong with Ashley?"

"I'm the one who should be sorry. Forcing your hand. I didn't have a clue when I came here. I just thought I could find him and through him find my birth mother."

"She wasn't from these parts. Not Southern at all. I've been trying to remember her name ever since you phoned me. Ashley's brother brought the girl here. To the middle of nowhere. It was foreign sounding. Kovac, I think." A scowl deepened the ridges on Selma's forehead. "Kerry Kovac—that's it. But don't go looking for someone with that name. Kerry Kovac was something she pulled from the hat just long enough to birth you."

He stared at her. "That Consent Decree Mr. Waverly wouldn't show me—that's a legal document?"

"That's right."

"But was it legal if the name she gave was false?"

She stacked the empty candy wrappers. "I'm not a lawyer. All I can tell you is that I was on duty the night she was admitted—and the night you were born."

He had passed the Jackson Medical Center out on South Main. It was an impressive, two-story hospital with a large wing. Doctor's offices, a drugstore, and a gift shop surrounded it. If he remembered correctly, it had ample parking out in the front. "Do you remember the night I was born?"

She gave him one of her trilling laughs again. "Back when you were born it was just a small forty-four-bed hospital perched on an open field. Looked like it was out in no-man's-land, but we caught the highway victims from three communities. Unlucky patients. We did well to have one R.N. on duty per shift. Back then we were rarely full. That's why I remember Kerry Kovac. The mystery girl. Figuring her out put a spark in our dull lives."

Chandler closed his eyes, trying to shut out the moment.

He had come here for two names and had them. *Kerry Kovac and Uncle Bill.* Bill VanBurien. Knowing was more painful than not knowing.

"Ashley was in the delivery room when you were born. We both were. Ashley wanted to be there to bond with you right away."

That close. Two mothers. One delivery. His mouth was dry, the taste bitter like gall. "I never knew I was adopted until recently."

"Thought Ashley might pull a fast one like that. Knew it for certain when they suddenly packed up and moved away from Everdale. She said her husband was finally going back to seminary—Pastor Reynolds always talked about doing that." Selma was on a roll, her voice rising. "But I knew better. I knew that wasn't their only reason for running out on us. I'm telling you, Chandler, it was a mean thing to do. They left us short a nurse at the hospital and the church without a pastor. Two-day notice. Just like that. Guess Ashley was going to keep her promise to Kerry Kovac or die."

"What promise, Miss Malkoski?"

"That you would never know who your biological parents were. The lawyer made Ashley and Reverend Reynolds promise. That's what the girl wanted. I was there. I heard it."

"Why would Mom and Dad make a promise like that?"

The harshness in Selma's face softened. "Bill was always in trouble—his whole life. And Ashley covered for him. Loved him. They were twins, you know. Really close. Ashley would have done anything for her brother, Bill."

Even raise his son. "Why didn't my uncle marry the girl?"

"Marry her?" She was watching him intently now, no longer interested in the candy. "Have you forgotten? Your uncle was already married. Still had a wife and two sons. Three if we count you."

Chandler's shirt suddenly felt tight. He crooked his finger at the collar and tried to relieve the burning pressure on his neck. "So I'm illegitimate."

"Not uncommon," she said kindly. "Happens a lot these days."

"Not back then. Not in a small town like this. No wonder Mom never told me the truth. Anything to protect her brother."

"And to protect you."

"Deceive me, you mean." He shook his head. "All my life I wanted a kid brother to roughhouse with. And all Dad and Mom would say was they couldn't have any more children."

"They didn't have any of their own as far as I know."

"But I have two brothers?"

"Half-brothers," she corrected. "Lived in Chicago or thereabouts. Don't know where they'd be now. They were little boys at the funeral. Be in their thirties by now."

Truth was sucking the air out of his lungs. The brutality of the word mocked him. All through his childhood, Ashley had said, *You must always tell the truth, son.*

David had preached it from the pulpit. *Talk is cheap,* he thought. Truth was to mold Chandler's life but not their own.

There was too much to swallow. Pride. Disappointment. Anger. Shame. But he kept his voice casual as he stood and said, "Thank you for seeing me, Miss Malkoski."

"No skin off my teeth. And thanks for the candy. You'll be all right, won't you?"

"I'll make it." *But how can I face Mom and Dad when I get back home?*

He was at the door when she said, "Your uncle, your father—he's buried in the VanBurien family plot."

"I know. I put flowers on his grave yesterday."

My father's grave. Bill VanBurien. Kerina Rudzinski! He knew he had found his birth mother without searching for her. Five months ago he didn't know she existed. He rehearsed everything that Kerina had said in Vienna and at the cemetery here in Everdale. Little phrases. Nugget comments. How blind he had been.

"I have a confession to make," Ashley had said in Vienna, and he had fallen asleep on her words.

He knew now that Ashley had recognized Kerina. Kerina had recognized him. He knew the truth, and he was the worse for knowing. "Miss Malkoski, what was Kerry Kovac like?"

"Quite striking, elegant. A face that you would never forget, it was so fragile. Sad eyes. Hazel, I think. It's been so many years I can't say for certain. But they were lovely. And her hair. A beautiful reddish-brown. Long and shiny." She reflected for a moment. "The girl had an accent. European, but she listed Chicago as her residence. I remember that. That's how we put two and two together and came up with Bill VanBurien."

"That's odd mathematics."

"Not odd when you consider that Bill made an unscheduled trip to Everdale after a two-year absence. He was here in town when you were born. Gone again right afterwards. To tell you the truth, I always thought his dying like he did in that car accident was justified punishment."

"It was an accident. He was driving in a rainstorm."

"That's what the police called it. But people in a small town like this have their own opinions."

"Miss Malkoski, did the girl play a violin by chance?"

"I'd forgotten that. She had one of those famous violins. A magnificent instrument and stylish clothes. She was quite young, but I think maybe your birth mother was a musician and well off financially."

She still is, he thought as he closed the door behind him. *A gifted violinist. And wealthy.*

Out on the sidewalk he stopped to take great gulps of air and realized he had not even said good-bye. But the void inside him was like a deep chasm, a black gaping hole. He knew who he was, yet he felt as if he was no one at all. For an instant he wanted to go back to the VanBurien family plot and destroy the flowers he had placed there yesterday.

He clenched his fist at the rain-drenched sky. "My uncle? No, my father," he cried. "What right did you have to die when I never even knew you?"

He set out, walking blindly toward the depot in the center of town. Back in his rental car he picked up his cellular phone and dialed the motel where Kerina was staying. "I'm trying to reach Kerina Rudzinski," he said.

He could hear the rattle of the registry and then the motel manager saying, "No one here by that name."

"Check again. It's important."

"I'm fixin' to do that." Seconds dragged. "Nope. No Robinski."

"Rudzinski," Chandler said. "You're certain she's not a guest there?"

"I swannee. . .I swear it. You got a better idea, young man? Another motel, maybe?"

"Is there one?"

"Down the road a piece in Spruceville. Twenty miles, give or take a mile—The Dale Motel—we're it for Everdale."

"She has to be a guest at the Dale. An attractive woman in her mid-forties. Reddish-brown hair. Unforgettable dark eyes."

"Ohhhh. Why didn't you speak your piece before? You mean Miss Kovac. She checked out this morning. Let me see—yes, Kerry Kovac. Said she was catchin' a plane back to New York."

"Kerry Kovac. She's gone?"

"Yep."

Chandler mumbled his thank-you and disconnected. His birth mother. Gone from Everdale. Out of his life again. Gone forever this time.

Chapter 28

Chandler tossed back the covers on the brass bed and, gripping one of the highly polished knobs, swung himself to a sitting position. He whacked the alarm button on his travel clock before it rang and was showered and packed by dawn. Outside, a glowing, rose-ribboned sky promised the first sunny fall day in Everdale since he arrived. He settled his bill with a sizable tip, refusing breakfast even though his sleepy-eyed hostess stood in the narrow hallway insisting he not leave on an empty stomach.

"Won't take but a minute to cook your grits," she told him.

No grits, Mrs. Richardson, he thought.

She stood there in a woolly, yellow bathrobe with her arms wrapped around her ample bosom. Fringes of gray peeked out from her hairnet and smudges of night cream whitened her face. She wrung her hands. "I never let my guests go away hungry," she murmured. "And my husband never starts a day without grits and coffee. Without them, he's a grumble all day."

Chandler could tell by her expression that he had offended her Southern hospitality. "I have a plane to catch, but the next time I come back, okay?" he offered.

The promise placated her. She turned the key in the front door with her red-knuckled hand and opened it for him.

He leaned down and kissed her cheek and came away with the taste of lilac face cream on his lips. The kiss was symbolic. *I have no desire to come back here,* he thought. *Everything that really matters to me lies in the cemetery.*

He strode off, the dappled sun making rainbow reflections on the wet walkway. Throwing his luggage into the backseat, Chandler slid into the car and, with a brisk wave to the woman in the doorway, roared off on his way north, racing like a speed demon through the quiet streets of Everdale, hell-bent at the wheel, like Bill VanBurien had driven.

Last night's scant sleep had left him with bitter thoughts against the man in the cemetery. Images and impressions churned over in his mind, coming at him like darts from every direction. Bill VanBurien's hometown. The high school where he led the team to a basketball championship two years in a row. His name engraved on the war monument in the park, names from every war the township could cook up. The Court House that held Bill's vital statistics: birth and death.

As Chandler's foot hit the floorboard, the car skidded. He steadied the wheel. Sweat dotted his brow as he thought of his father's car skidding out of control on a rain-drenched highway near Dannelly Field. The void inside him seemed larger than life. He had come to Everdale seeking his identity. Now what did he have? A cemetery plot. But nothing tangible.

Chandler couldn't grip his dad's hand and say, "So there you are." Or clamp his shoulder, saying, "Let me look at you."

He couldn't phone and ask, "Dad, how about the ball game tonight?" Or hear his dad answering, "Sounds like a winner, son."

Chandler felt betrayed. Cheated by his own parents. Renounced at birth. Hoodwinked by those who had adopted him. Intimidated and misunderstood at times by David's mother, the only grandmother he had ever known. The desertion was complete, as if he had been given a Judas kiss in the family garden.

He took the road that led past the VanBurien homestead and slammed on his brakes when he reached it. The engine on the rental car hiccuped. He turned the motor off and stared at the house where his dad had grown up. All his life Chandler had heard bits and pieces about Uncle Bill and had taken little interest in him. The man was dead, as dead as Randy Williams. Now it was like looking at a framed photo with the picture turned to the wall. You knew the person was there, but the face was missing. No one could fill in the features for him except his parents. His parents? In his anger, he thought of them as Ashley and David, but in his heart as Mom and Dad. What should he call them now? Who were they? Who was he?

"Dear God," he breathed, "what an ungrateful wretch I am. What a rotten Christ-follower."

What's the matter with you, man? he argued with himself. *They cradled you from the time you were born. Saw you safely from kindergarten to Juilliard. Paid every bill. Sat by your bedside through mumps and measles and an appendectomy and that fractured ankle in a skiing accident. Cheered you from every corner. Loved you all the way. So you hated being a preacher's kid. Was it really that bad? Going to church was just part of the bargain. Ashley and David were everything parents could be.*

The next move was Chandler's. Things were in his ballpark. He had two choices: split from the family forever—the choice he leaned toward— or go home and face them. Demand answers. Have it out with them and then pick up the pieces and if they could, go on from there as a family. He had no doubt that Grandmother Reynolds had told them everything he had shared with her. They knew he was seeking answers in Everdale. Why else had they sent him the address for the Richardsons' bed-and-breakfast and a check for his expenses that he hadn't cashed? When he saw them—if he did—he'd get it off his chest, give it to them straight.

"You lied to me all my life. Just tell me why," he would demand.

His conscience jabbed him. He wished that Randy were sitting here beside him. Randy always took giant-size boulders and made pebbles out of them. "So what would you do, buddy?" Chandler asked aloud.

Clear as a fast-running trout stream, Chandler knew.

Throw out the line. Take a gamble. Play the odds. Randy's philosophy.

Chandler gave it a stab. His birth mother was a musician.

He reasoned, if Ashley and David wanted to hide that one, why did they put a violin in his hands when he was four? Why expose him to good music all his life? Why encourage, even mandate, that he develop that innate ear for music? Christmas and his birthday never lacked for a new cassette or CD of one of the great violinists, Kerina Rudzinski included. By touching his life with music, they had given him part of his birth mother.

Here on a country road in Alabama, drumming his fingers on the steering wheel, he remembered Ashley giving him his first Rudzinski CD. Her voice had fractured when she said, "Dad and I thought you would like Miss Rudzinski's music."

It had gone into his growing pile of gifts—of little interest to him back then. He was into Zuckerman and Perlman. Idolized the work of Menuhin playing the Beethoven and Brahms concertos and took to Anne Sophie Mutter the first time he heard her in concert. And now, for Chandler, Kerina's work surpassed them all. But she had grown on him slowly, as though he were being drawn irresistibly to someone he should know and respect.

And what of the family trips to Europe and the wall map in his father's library, a map marked with red dots for each European country they had visited or studied together? True, David never pointed to Prague in particular, but thinking on it now, Chandler knew Czech history back for decades and had without knowing it been drawn to his mother's country. As he rested his elbow on the car's window ledge, a brisk October air chafed his skin. What pain it must have cost Ashley to withhold the truth about her brother, Bill.

A promise, Selma Malkoski had called it.

Kerina swore them to secrecy to guard her own identity, not mine, he thought. *To protect her own career, not my future. She recognized me in Vienna and Everdale and never said a word.* The cold reality of her rejection came like a slap in the face.

In their own way, Ashley and David had done their best to tie him in with his heritage. Chandler had spent these last few weeks thinking about them as liars and deceivers. Yet all they had done was love, protect, and stand by him from birth to manhood. He craned his neck and looked in the rearview mirror. "Do I look like your brother, Mom?"

Of course. She had told him many times, *"You're like the VanBurien side. Lanky and quick and ornery like Bill."*

But give me a face, Mother.

She had tried. How many times had she taken out the family albums until he was bored when he grabbed for one? To Chandler, snapshots of fraternal twins—Bill the tall, lean one with an easy smile—had been fragments that did not form a whole.

"Oh, he was a charmer, all right," Grandmother Reynolds had said, voicing her disapproval. *"A corporate climber. Definitely not a family man."*

He could recall a dozen or two references to Uncle Bill's navy days and the injury on board his ship. *"Bill wanted to go professional,"* David had told Chandler. *"But that injury in the navy cut the dream of pro basketball from the slate. A great player. I think he could have made it."*

You could have done a lot of things, Chandler thought. *Like stay alive. Like be my friend. Like admit that I was your son.* A knot of anger twisted inside him. *Mom loved you, Bill VanBurien. But I hate your guts, man.*

His life since Bosnia had become a deep, gutted chasm as though an avalanche had permanently split his yesterdays and tomorrows. He would have a thousand questions for Ashley and David when he got back to California, but all he could do was hammer away at the same one: Why hadn't they told him the truth?

In the painful silence that followed, Chandler remembered the letter Ashley had given him when he left for Denver. Grabbing his briefcase from the backseat, he snapped the locks open and rummaged through the papers. Nothing. Where was the letter? He was certain he had packed it. He sorted through the paperwork carefully this time and finally found it jammed in the fold of the lid. *"It's about you, Chandler,"* Ashley had said.

His mouth went dry as he opened it. *April 18,* Bill had written in his bold scrawl. *Three days after my birth,* Chandler thought.

Dear Sis,

There is a torrential rain outside the airport. In a few minutes I will be out there driving in it. But I had to write to you first—to try and explain. Sis, I needed Everdale. I needed you. But can you ever forgive me for my deception? It seems I've been begging your forgiveness all my life, yet you never demanded it. Never asked it. It was always there, free for the taking.

You are so much like Mama, Ash. Mama was my lifeline, and you were the hinge that always swung me back toward Mama and home. Without you two believing in me, I would never have had the courage to tackle the university and reach for the stars. Anything I've accomplished for the good is with thanks to you and Mama for standing with me. I still treasure the memory of the two of you shouting from the sidelines during my basketball games. What a lucky guy I was to have you cheering me on.

Sis, when I saw you in the doorway there at Jackson Memorial, I knew that you knew. I never wanted you to know that the baby was mine. I thought I could slip back into Everdale and make the final arrangements for my son to have a good home, a permanent one with you and David. Dr. Nelson assured me that the adoption would go through.

I have no plans to ever come back to Everdale, so I will not interfere in the way that you raise the baby. But send me pictures. Tell me about him. Ash, as we faced each other in the hospital lobby, I wanted to ask you to show me my son. To let me hold him just once. But I knew if I held him, I could never let him go. The kindest thing I could do for my child was to walk away. Celeste knew about Kerry, but she doesn't know about the baby. I've hurt her and the boys so much already that I couldn't add to their pain. Nor did I want to add to yours and David's.

When I married Celeste, Mama opposed it. She told me not to marry anyone unless I was in love. But Celeste was everything I thought I wanted. Social position. Money. Success. She was so glamorous to this small-town boy. She told me if we stayed on in Chicago, her father could open doors for me and save us years of climbing to the top. I no longer needed Everdale. I was out of the navy, doubling up on my studies at the university, determined to make it big in corporate America. Celeste offered me a chance to succeed. She was fun to be with, I was so proud of her. I figured love would come with the package.

Mama was right, Sis. It was never a good marriage. I didn't fit in. Mama was so sure I would meet someone someday that I would fall in love with. And when I did, it was too late. Celeste and I were at odds a lot, and one night I went alone to a concert in downtown Chicago to hear a violin soloist from Prague. Never had I heard such magnificent music; it stirred those old longings to work in the field of music.

Afterwards I bought a dozen white roses from the vendor outside the music hall and then pushed my way through the crowded lobby, backstage to Kerina Rudzinski's dressing room. I never intended anything more than to thank her for her concert. But I couldn't take my eyes from her face. She was beautiful and charming and, as we talked about her music, something clicked between us.

I never meant for it to go beyond my thank-you, but in the excitement of the moment, I invited her to have dinner with me. After that we were together whenever she was in town. I never meant to hurt Celeste and the boys. Never meant to hurt Kerry— that's what she wanted me to call her. When she told me she was pregnant, I worried that a scandal would ruin her career.

I was in so deep, Sis. I had nothing to offer Kerry. I was still married, even though Celeste had packed up the month before and gone back to the family mansion for the third time. She offered to call it quits, but all I could think of was Mama and her God and the way she used to get down on her knees when we were kids, night after night, and pray for us. There were the boys to think about, and I didn't need the court to tell me incompatibility with my wife was no excuse. It was up to me to make my marriage work.

Moments ago—just before Kerry's plane took off—I promised Kerry that I would find a way for us to be together forever. Ash, I cannot tell you how much I love her. I'd give anything to take her back to Mama's old house to live. But it's all wrong. I could never merit God's approval that way. It would never work out. I just walked out on my infant son. Just saw Kerry fly off. I couldn't shatter the lives of Jeff and Skip, too.

I called Celeste from the air terminal and asked her if we could try to patch up our differences—for the boys' sake. She doesn't think *so—doesn't want to—but she agreed to meet with me and talk it over with her father and the lawyer present. I'm going to drive all night, straight through to Chicago.*

When all of this is settled, I will write to Kerry again. She is young. She needs a chance to go on in her career, to find someone who will love her and care for her more honestly than I have done. But as long as I live, Sis, right or wrong, I will remember how much I love Kerry. Yet the best thing I can do for my newborn son and his lovely mother is to set them free.

For now, I know that Kerry has forced you to a pledge of silence in the adoption consent. But someday, will you tell my son that I loved him? Tell him that his mother was very young, frightened, beautiful. Tell him that I had to let him go, knowing that two of the neatest people on earth would love him as their own son and raise him in a godly home. In Mama's home. Mama would like that.

Can you ever forgive me, Ashley? Can I ever forgive myself? I will keep in touch from time to time. Ever yours, Bill

For a long while Chandler sat there gripping the letter, banging his fist against the steering wheel, too choked up to drive away. He was beginning to put a face to the man now, someone with deep emotions like Ashley. Someone who had never held him. Someone who broke his last promise.

"You didn't keep in touch," Chandler said aloud. He shook the letter in the air. "You didn't stick around long enough to tell me you loved me! All you did was fold this letter and seal it in an envelope, and an hour later you were dead. You never even saw me."

Chandler folded his father's letter with great care and put it back into his briefcase. In his anger, he longed for someone to talk to, someone who would understand. He thought of Randy Williams bullying his way through any disaster, taking a gamble on life and losing. No, Randy never lost anything that he set his hand to do. Even in that dying second, he dove facedown taking the land mine full blast to save others. *To save me,* Chandler thought. *Randy, the winner. Randy, my friend, who met problems head-on.*

Chandler pushed back his cuff and checked the hour. Avoiding grits for breakfast had given him ample time to drive the seventy-five miles to the airport. Add the rental car return and check-in at the airline counter, and time was marginal. But he could not leave Everdale this way, not without going back. He switched the engine on and accelerated. The tires spun in the gravel, spinning like his emotions and splitting his boulders into pebbles. He risked a U-turn on the country road and broke the speed limit back to the Everdale Cemetery. His birth mother had walked out of his life again, but at least he could say good-bye to his father.

The cemetery gate was locked, a caretaker just arriving.

"I have to get inside," Chandler told him.

"Sorry, don't open for business until nine."

"But you're going in, sir."

"Yep. Got another grave to dig."

Chandler's gaze glanced off the man's name tag. "Please, my dad's buried here, Rob. I'm leaving town. Won't be back."

"I'm acquainted with everybody here. Who's your dad?"

"VanBurien. William VanBurien."

Rob scratched his head. "You're new to me. You one of his younguns from Chicago?"

"No sir. They're my brothers. I'm the son from California."

"Letting you in now is against the rules."

"I just want to say good-bye."

"Have to leave your car outside the gate."

"Whatever you say."

"Hop in then," Rob said. "Bounce you over the ruts to the VanBurien plot. They've got one of the best views in town."

His truck rattled to the familiar stop, high on a quiet knoll. Two oak trees formed a natural arch over the VanBuriens. The rains had turned the lawns a forest green and washed mud over the gravesites. Autumn leaves skittered across the plots. The roses on the VanBurien headstones lay bruised and wilting.

"Be removing those later today," Rob said. "The gate's chained, but I left it ajar enough for you to slip through when you're done. Let yourself out."

Chandler slid down from the passenger side and shook Rob's dirt-encrusted hand. "I appreciate this."

Rob nodded. "Every man has to say his good-byes."

He trundled off and moments later joined his crew by the bulldozer, leaving Chandler facing the family plot, his feet leaden on the gravel path.

He moved at last, stepping over the small wrought iron rail that surrounded the VanBurien resting place. Two days ago he hadn't noticed how many VanBuriens were buried here. He counted eight of them now, two of them small children. So three of Mama VanBurien's children were buried here, not just Bill. Chandler read some of the markers. OUR LITTLE

ANGEL SLEEPS, for a child born and dead the same day. OUR SUNSHINE IN HEAVEN, for a boy of three. Mama VanBurien's head-stone said: MAMA, THE JOY OF OUR LIVES. AT REST NOW. And on his father's inscription the dates that made him twenty-nine at death—twenty-nine now—and the simple message from his family: WE LOVE YOU.

The song of a mockingbird broke the stillness. He knelt down on one knee by his father's grave and fingered the red roses Kerina had laid there. Red roses because she loved him. Then he ran his hand over the cold marble.

"I didn't know who you were the other day," he said aloud. "I'm sorry. All my life you've been just Uncle Bill. Someone who died before I knew you." His fingers traced the name. "I never shed any tears over you. You were just a faded photograph in the family album. Someone that Mom missed. Yet all my life I searched for you, trying to put a name and a face to that void inside me."

Tears pricked behind his eyes. "I never thought it would hurt so much to find you. I think you loved my birth mother. God help me, I hope you did. She sacrificed everything for you. She was here the other day, weeping for you. Still loving you."

His finger stopped on the inscription: WE LOVE YOU.

"I should hate you, having an affair like that. Ruining it for those two little boys in Chicago. Robbing me of my brothers. Breaking your vows to Aunt Celeste."

The noise of the bulldozer reached him—the ground being dug for another burial. "What hurts most is you never looked at me, Bill VanBurien. You never picked me up. You never held me. Why didn't you want me? Why didn't you hold me?"

He wept now for the father he would never know, for the emptiness he still felt—that big gaping hole lodged inside him. The white roses had wilted, but Chandler found a single red rose still in bloom in Kerina's bouquet. He tugged it free and pressed it against his father's marker.

"My—my mother left red roses because she loved you." His hand pressed against the inscription. A sob shook him. "I have to leave now. I have a plane to catch. But I had to say good-bye. David Reynolds would say that I have to forgive you. Remember him? You were good friends once."

Chandler wiped the marble free of the twigs and leaves that had blown across the family plot. "But how can I forgive you? Oh God, how can I forgive this man?"

"The way Mama would have forgiven," Ashley would say.

Mama, the joy of Ashley and Bill VanBurien's lives. The woman who knew how to love, how to forgive. Chandler felt more related to her now than he ever had. Double-barreled. Ashley's mother, the woman who had reared Bill. His birth father's mother. So Mama's ability to forgive ran in his blood. Surged there now like a spiritual renewal, like an eternal turn-around.

"I forgive you, Dad," he whispered and felt relief flood over him. He rested his head against the headstone and struggled for the courage that he needed. At last he sat back, his eyes glistening. "Dad—Dad, I just came back. . .to say I love you."

Chapter 29

Chandler's taxi careened through traffic toward his Washington hotel, jostling for right-of-way as it passed the president's residence in white-painted sandstone and the Capitol with its brilliant cast-iron dome. Here he was in that city on the Potomac River where ambitious politicians came out of anonymity and rose to power, and where cherry blossoms and scandal broke on the scene with equal flurry—a city where the laws of the country were made and the fate of the nation cemented into time, where the applause of men turned sour overnight and valor and virtue were swallowed up in a media frenzy.

In this town of monuments and war memorials from The Wall to the Eternal Flame, he kept wondering if Washington immortalized peacekeepers. If so, would Randy's name ever be engraved in marble or granite? Or was this business of applying to the CIA's Career Training Program a waste of time? He wanted to go back to Bosnia for Randy's sake and to help men like Kemal Hovic stay alive, but going back as an intelligence officer might be under false documents with a false birth certificate in his pocket. But would that be any different than the last twenty-six years of his life? He'd gone to Everdale in search of his past; he had come to Washington in search of his future.

By his third day, his eyelids were red-rimmed from hours in the lecture hall, his fingers cramped after filling in a thirty-four-page application form, his head spinning from the polygraph experience and a battery of psychological tests with their dumb questions.

Give the address of your mother-in-law. That one was easy: *not applicable.*

Employment history back to age seventeen: With all the mental gymnastics he couldn't remember the drugstore where he had clerked for six months.

Military experience: three years, US Army. Residences for the last fifteen years: the family home in Southern California, a flat near Juilliard, and army tents in Bosnia.

Are you accident prone? Yes; I swim in snake-infested rivers, walk in fields with land mines.

By the end of the first twenty-four hours, the packed-out room had thinned, some of the Ivy League candidates more interested in annual incomes and a social life than in adventures on foreign soil. What remained was the cream of the crop: ambitious, aggressive, goal-oriented men and women who had been lured in from a dozen recruitment offices across the country.

Secrecy was the key word, intelligence gathering the objective, but Chandler could see that obtaining the objective made them expendable. Before the last lecture hour, the young woman who had sat beside him permanently vacated her chair.

"No way, Reynolds," she told him. "Who wants a phony birth certificate or forged documents? I'm not living a lie the rest of my life. I've got a perfectly good birth certificate in my bank box. I don't want to be one of those memorial stars in the lobby at Langley." She seemed perfectly calm as she said, "I don't go for this remaining nameless for security reasons or dead in the line of duty with my cover blown on a covert assignment."

They shook hands and she was gone—off to seek a less demanding job that paid better. She didn't even take her yellow memo pad with her. Chandler hung in and completed the last interview. As he stood to leave, the man across from him said, "Reynolds, Paul Daniels is waiting to see you in the next room."

Colonel Daniels had dropped his army fatigues and looked like a businessman in his three-piece suit and silk tie. But his grave eyes were as unfriendly as they had been in Bosnia.

"So you've made it this far. Sit down, Reynolds."

Chandler kept it respectful. "A tough three days, sir." He wondered how long it would take Daniels to bring up Tuzla and their first visit. It took seconds. "Off the record," Daniels said, "we didn't like Miss Rudzinski pulling strings in Bosnia to get Zineta Hovic released. That woman was an annoyance."

"That woman," Chandler said evenly, "is my birth mother."

They sat in a Spartan room, the only comfortable chair the one Daniels sat in. He leaned back in it, looking like a man ready to light up a stogie, his catlike eyes triumphant. "I didn't think you'd admit that, Reynolds."

"Then you didn't check my polygraph results. They asked about my parents during the test. And I told them."

"With yes and no answers?"

"The lady turned off the equipment and demanded an explanation. It was simple. I was adopted right after birth—born to a mother who was a musician, to a father who was already married. He's dead now." He voiced the facts without shame, facing them now as one of those things in life he could not change.

Daniels remained thoughtful. "You may be useful to us after all. You've been straightforward with us, except in Bosnia."

"I didn't know I was adopted then, sir."

"Odd. We knew." Daniels exhaled, the imaginary stogie puffing away. "That girl—Zineta Hovic—worked for the Serbs during the war as one of their couriers. But according to our intelligence reports, she refused to carry any messages out of Tuzla after our peacekeeping forces arrived."

"I doubt Captain Williams knew anything about her war background. He was a today kind of guy. No yesterdays. No tomorrows. Tell me, will Miss Hovic arrive in Ohio before the baby is due?"

"I'd like to delay it, but the captain's father is pressing to get the girl out so his grandchild can be born in America. With the White House on his side, they'll make it. But what right do they have to have that child born in America?"

"Every right, sir. Captain Williams was an American."

Daniels's eyes looked dark as charred tree roots as he scanned Chandler's file. "You still have your own agenda, Reynolds. Not Langley's. If you don't come with our Career Training Program, what then?"

"London by spring or summer, and marriage to the prettiest girl on the Thames."

"Marriage? That wasn't in the picture when we talked last."

"I met her in Vienna."

"We prefer single men for the team for Bosnia. You'd be away for long periods at a time. Not healthy for a married man. If we don't take you, what then?"

"I'd write music reviews. And if I'm good—and I will be good—I'd do the European circuit. The concert scene and all. I'd still plan trips to Bosnia to help Kemal Hovic get back into his music. Miss Rudzinski arranged funding for music programs for the children. I want to be certain her wishes are carried out."

The feline eyes narrowed. "An ambitious undertaking. We're looking for single-minded candidates. Men committed to our Agency—our purpose, our goals. Not to their own agenda."

"The sacrificial lamb?"

"We prefer to call it *dedication*. We don't want wives on the phone calling to find out where their husbands are. You wouldn't consider delaying this marriage for a while?"

"No sir. I've got my dad lined up to marry us already." *As soon as my girl says yes,* he thought.

"You disappoint me, Reynolds. I thought you were serious about this job. You need to make a decision, Lieutenant. A music career or this mission in Bosnia."

"I can't have both?"

Daniels thumped his fingers together. "Perhaps you could still be useful to us in London. On a voluntary basis."

"But with no direct ties to the Agency? Right?"

"You do think quickly. We gather intelligence data from people and events worldwide—satellites, human spies, foreign broadcasts, publications of all types. Why not from music articles and reviews? If you travel the European circuit—and with your mother on the world circuit—you just might serve our purposes better in the music world." He scratched his temple. "You expressed an interest in seeing Langley the last time we met. Is tomorrow okay?"

"Not this time, sir. I leave for Chicago this evening. Save your gated buildings and barbed wire fences for another time."

Daniels' sardonic chuckle rippled through the room as he stood and held out his hand. "We are much more sophisticated than that, Lieutenant. We even have an impressive array of art hanging in our corridors that would appeal to your sensitive nature."

Chandler's brows furrowed. "I trust Langley will get back to me with the outcome of my interviews?"

"Of course, Lieutenant. In a few months. Don't look so surprised. We do a thorough check on our candidates. This is a highly sensitive mission."

Chandler kept his question friendly and lighthearted. "If you reject me, I hope you give a good reason, sir."

Daniels matched Chandler's mood. "We never give a reason for rejecting our applicants. That's classified information. But we will be in touch, Reynolds."

∾

Three thousand miles away David strolled out into the garden looking for Ashley. He saw her kneeling in the impatiens bed, patting the soil around her plants. She had that fresh, wholesome look that had drawn him to her the first time he saw her on the school bus in Everdale, pretty and long-legged even then. He had stared at the back of her honey-blond hair as he was doing now, wondering about the color of her eyes and whether she was going steady. He had saved a seat for her the next day and she took it coyly. He soon discovered her to be passionate about gardening and the war in Vietnam, a defender of women's issues and creative with a needle and thread. She was like a dark velour pattern, with contrasting shades of brightness and darkness to her personality, but tough and durable like brocade. In their marriage, though, he had seen that fine cambric quality about her—a strength of character that made her a good nurse, a good person.

He crossed the lawn to her, pleased at how sharp those form-fitting jeans looked on her. "It's chilly out here," he scolded, but he smiled as he leaned down to kiss her dirt-smudged nose.

She flashed that remarkable smile of hers—the one that said everything was fine between them again. His heart skipped a beat as her cornflower blue eyes met his. She fussed about being fifty-four, but she was still beautiful to him, her dark lashes the color of the violet pansies in her garden and her cheeks still smooth and rosy like the day he met her.

"David, I heard you drive in an hour ago."

"The house was so quiet, I thought maybe you were out shopping."

"Just gardening. My car's in the garage. How did your classes go today?"

"I have one student who drinks in archaeology like diet Cokes. But come in and have some coffee with me."

"Did you make it yourself?"

"Yes, and I want to enjoy some time with my wife."

"Hum. I baked cookies this morning."

"I found them. Chocolate chips." He swiped his teeth with his tongue, trying to make certain the evidence was gone. "I set out a plate of them on the table with our mugs from Vienna."

She dropped the trowel in the dirt bed and allowed him to help her to her feet. "Sounds good. And it is cold out here. Whatever happened to sunny California?"

"It'll be back by spring."

"Not soon enough. I'm getting the garden ready for Chandler's return. Now, don't scowl, David. He'll come. Right now he needs space."

"Three thousand miles should be enough," he said ruefully.

She paused along the path, distracted for a moment. "Look, darling, my daffodils are budding. And I pruned back the rose bushes and planted some bare roots by your office windows."

"Then I can expect bees and roses at the same time. What are these orange and yellow critters?"

"My Iceland poppies."

"Nice." He flicked at the dirt speck on her nose.

"I'm a mess, eh?" she asked as they walked into the kitchen.

"A pretty one, Ash."

"But there's a problem brewing. I can tell by the coffee and compliments. So out with it."

"I tried to call Kerina Rudzinski in New York City."

She dropped into a chair. "About Chandler?"

"Now wait—don't get upset." He poured her mocha cappuccino. "I tried to get tickets for Kerina's concert. It's been canceled. So I've been making phone calls for the last forty minutes."

He didn't burden her with the details of calling The Lincoln Center and the New York Philharmonic, the ticket agencies, the Chamber of Commerce, and Kerina's manager without success. She'd catch on when the phone bill arrived. He couldn't even remember which one gave him Kerina's hotel number.

"The hotel concierge told me she was in the hospital."

The sun freckles seemed to fade from Ashley's cheeks. She reached for a sweater and slipped it around her. "What's wrong?"

"She's at Columbia Presbyterian Medical Center."

"An accident? Is Chandler with her?"

"I don't know on both counts. We'll have to call the hospital. I wanted you with me—in case Kerina asks for you."

Ashley pushed her coffee away. "Make the call, David."

After a frustrating hold and another long delay, he was transferred to Kerina's private room at the Harkness Pavilion.

"Hello." The voice was young, sad. "This is Jillian Ingram."

"Jillian, David Reynolds here. Chandler's father. I'm trying to reach Miss Rudzinski."

"She's in radiology for X-rays. She's had pneumonia."

David felt overwhelming relief. "I was afraid it was something serious. Does Chandler know she's hospitalized?"

"He's still in Washington. I couldn't reach him. He'll be upset—they were in a horrible rainstorm in Everdale."

"Jillian, my wife wants to talk to you."

Ashley's knuckles blanched as she took the phone. "Jillian, David says Kerina has pneumonia. What's going on?"

"I'm afraid it's more serious than that. Kerina has cancer."

The thudding of Ashley's heart vibrated in her ears. "What kind of cancer, Jillian?"

"Breast. She refuses surgery. But they've done bone scans and located another slow-growing tumor. Her cancer is spreading."

Ashley glanced at David for approval as she said, "Do you want me to come, Jillian?"

"No, don't. Franck insists we leave for Europe at once."

"Is Kerina up to traveling?"

"She's gritty. Plans to see her own doctor in Prague for a second opinion. But Chandler will be so disappointed. We counted on that time together in Los Angeles."

Ashley hesitated, then found the courage to ask, "You know, don't you, that Chandler is Kerina's son?"

"I've known since Vienna."

Ashley's mouth felt dry. "Jill, does my son know who Kerina is? If he doesn't, Kerina should tell him before she leaves."

"Why, Ashley? You never told him."

She deserved that. Her cheeks felt like branding irons. "Surely Kerina wants him to know someday?"

"But not while she's ill; I am certain she wants him to remember her as he first saw her in Vienna."

Ashley recalled Kerina's breathtaking entry into the concert hall in her Parisian gown. "That will be easy to do. Chan is still talking about that lovely red dress."

"Oh Ashley, they're coming with Kerina right now. I'm sorry. I must hang up and help them."

"Keep in touch, won't you, Jill? Call us with any news. Call us collect."

❧

Kerina looked pale against the cream-washed walls and even more pallid as the orderly transferred her to the bed. But she was gracious to him and radiant with a smile for Jillian. "Jillian, you should have gone back to the hotel and not waited for me. You look as exhausted as I feel."

Jillian flipped her pillow and brushed Kerina's hair back from her forehead. "How are you?"

"Frayed and worn-out like a cloth rag. And my shoulder aches."

Jillian propped Kerina's arm on another pillow. "You don't look like frayed cloth. You're lovely. Radiant as always."

Kerina's laughter sent her into a coughing spasm. She tugged at the hospital gown. "I don't call this fashion."

"Then let's put you in a gown of your own."

"And five minutes later they'll want another X-ray. Let's put me in my clothes and get me out of here." She coughed again. "I can't stay here. Hospitals wear me out."

As the coughing eased, she gazed out the window at the towering Manhattan skyline. "The river's there. But it's not the Danube. Not the Vltava. I want Franck to take me home, Jillian."

"Back to Vienna?"

"To standing ovations and applause? They are so transitory. My dear, the doctors—if they can be believed—have just handed me a death sentence. Surgery or else." She waved her ringed hand as though to dismiss their advice. "Ever since Chandler was born, I have been afraid of hospitals and doctors and of falling asleep in surgery and never waking up. While I waited in radiology, I realized that I am a woman without hope or faith in anything eternal." Her eyes filled with unshed tears. "No surgery, dear. Two more concerts and then Franck must take me home to Prague. I want to be with my parents. I want to hear my mother pray her Rosary again."

"Do you want me to go to Prague with you, Kerina?"

"Oh, will you? Will you stay that long?"

"I'm not walking out on you while you're ill. But Vienna first. And the concert and maybe a ride on the gray Danube."

"Not gray in the song. Not in my heart. We see things the way we want to see them. And for me when I see that river, I hear the song. Strauss was right. The beautiful blue Danube."

Kerina was making an attempt to bounce back with that old stretching quality that allowed her to give her best to her audiences. But the diagnosis left her vulnerable, close to a breaking point.

"Where's Franck?" Jillian asked. "He should be here with you."

"He hates hospitals like I do. Does he think I'm wrong—refusing the surgery here? Insisting that I go home for care?"

"He doesn't like you waiting another two or three weeks."

"But I trust my family doctor in Prague."

"How long have you known?"

"For a while. I thought I'd finish this year's schedule and then take care of the problems. But it doesn't work that way."

"Kerina, you weren't punishing yourself because of Chan?"

Kerina closed her eyes and lay without moving. The television hummed. The phone rang at the nurses' station. The chair squeaked as Jillian shifted. "Someday would you tell Chandler how much I loved him?

How many times I thought about him?"

"Kerina, why not tell him yourself?"

"I can't. I am the person who plays the Strad the way he likes it played. Now—if what the doctors say is true—I'm on borrowed time."

"Borrowed. . .unless you do something about it."

She shook her head. "Jillian, please get me my lipstick—the vermilion red. I don't like the way I look." She applied it, then said, "Stop fretting. I have done the things I wanted most. Playing my Stradivarius around the world. And going back to Everdale to say good-bye to Bill." Her eyes glistened. "And finding the house that was always there in the back of my mind."

"The country house on a hill—the one with the gazebo?"

"Yes. It was just like I pictured it, with a wisteria vine growing over the fence. And the gazebo by the old swing." Her face glowed with unexpected happiness. She laced her fingers contentedly as she said, "The autumn leaves brushed across the path. I stood beneath the trellis where the roses grow in the spring and summer. And I heard the wind whistling by the porch. Have you ever heard the wind whistling, Jillian?"

"Sometimes. I think it's whistling outside now."

"Not like it did in Everdale." Another coughing spasm seized her. Jillian wiped her brow with a cool cloth.

Kerina pushed her hand away. "I'm all right. Oh Jillian, have you ever smelled wood burning in the air? The forest lies behind the house where Bill hiked as a boy. I felt like Bill was there with me—like I was a young girl again. Like maybe soon, I will see him again. Does that make sense?"

Jillian nodded as she smoothed the bed linens. "Was it Bill's house?"

"Yes. The one where he grew up. And Chandler's when he was a little boy." She turned toward the windows again. "I was there once before—when Chandler was born. I think that's why the house lingered in the back of my mind as something good and peaceful."

In spite of her pallor, her eyes glowed. She had stepped back in time, away from her hospital room. "In a way that house brought my son back to me. We sat on the porch together and watched a cloud burst and the rain pour down. And when the rain stopped, we pretended we heard the whip-poorwill. It was beautiful, Jillian, to find my son—to sit there with him. To know how well his parents have raised him. To know what a fine young man he is. He is so much like Bill."

"Then tell Chandler. Tell him how proud you are of him."

"I cannot do that. And you must not tell him as long as I am alive. I want to go on living. But in case I don't see Chandler again, I want him to remember me the way he saw me in Vienna."

"And if he calls me? Is he to know you are ill?"

"No. Just send him my love."

Chapter 30

J illian left the hospital and walked the two blocks to the subway, brushing shoulders with strangers and jumping at the sound of her own footsteps. The eerie wait in the underground and the deafening roar of the train speeding into the station rattled her nerves. She sank into the first vacant seat and dozed with her head bobbing against the grubby window until she reached her destination.

From there, it was another block to her hotel. Wearily, she unlocked the door, hurried inside, and bolted the door. A dim bathroom light cut a path across the rug. Her covers were turned back. A mint lay on her pillow. And the phone was ringing.

Not Kerina! she thought. *No more bad news today. And not Franck.* She didn't want to argue with him.

She grabbed the receiver. "Jillian Ingram."

"Jillian, it's Chandler."

For Jillian the only breath of kindness the whole day was hearing his voice. Picturing his face. Caressing him over the long-distance wires. She burst into tears.

"Honey, what's wrong?"

She couldn't tell him. She said, "It's so good to hear from you. Where are you? Are you here in New York City?"

"I'm in Washington. About to catch my plane to O'Hare."

"You're not coming to New York?"

"Can't. Too many loose ends to tie up. Don't cry, Jill. We'll see each other in Los Angeles. I can hardly wait."

She couldn't tell him the concert was canceled. Couldn't tell him Kerina was ill. "Did Everdale go all right?"

His voice changed. "I'm glad it's over."

"Did you find what you were looking for?"

"I know who my birth parents are, if that's what you mean. My father is dead, and my mother walked out on me again. So the search is over. Done with."

Kerina? Were they talking about the same person? The woman who had glowed when she said she had seen her son again?

"Now I have to go home and tell Mom and Dad what I did."

She wanted to say, "They know."

"I have to go, Jill. That's my boarding call. I love you."

Had she heard him correctly?

"Jill? I have something I want to ask you when you get to Los Angeles. It maybe rushing things a bit, but I'm sure—"

She was left with nothing but the dial tone. Her tears came in torrents. She kicked off her shoes and flopped on her bed, weeping into the pillow. It was too much with Kerina ill and Chandler expecting her in Los Angeles next week.

～

Two hours later the phone rang again. She still lay on her bed, bathed in self-pity. Perhaps it was Chandler calling from O'Hare. "Hello," she said breathlessly. "Chandler?"

"Miss Ingram, this is the concierge at the desk. You have a guest. A Mr. Joel Gramdino."

Gramdino here at the hotel? "Does he want me to come down?"

"He's already on his way up."

She leaped to her feet, splashed cold water in her eyes and rubbed them dry. The disaster in her room came into glaring focus. She swept the rumpled spread with her hand, shoved the loose items of clothing back into her suitcase.

Gramdino stepped off the elevator. He came toward her in a brisk stride, a wide grin on his face, his glistening silver hair adding its touch of dignity.

"What are you doing here, Joel?"

"Had to see you."

"Lucky for you, Franck and Kerina are not here."

His smile faded. "I know. I'm sorry about Miss Rudzinski. Will she be all right?"

"We don't know. It's very serious."

"I know that, too." He shoved the wrinkled bedding aside and sat down, his long legs stretched out in front of him. "I have two men over at Harkness Pavilion. They're keeping me informed."

"She's sick, Joel. She's not going to walk out of this country with a painting."

"Granted. But Franck Petzold might."

"What are you talking about? The rest of the concert tour is canceled. So you can call off the guards from the art museums and the hospital. We're heading back to Europe."

"Commercial line?"

"Franck arranged for a private jet from one of his friends."

"An art collector from Moscow?"

"I don't know, Joel."

"I'll alert Kennedy International."

"Don't. Franck always uses a private field in New Jersey."

"So he has all the bases covered."

"He usually does."

Gramdino whammed the mattress with his fist. "That man is constantly outwitting me. You'd think I'd be wise to it by now."

"Don't blame yourself. We had no idea we would have to fly home early. I can't remember Kerina ever canceling a performance. She's gone onstage with a raging fever and miserable migraines."

"At least it will keep some unsuspecting art collector from getting a headache. We blew it when Petzold caught the subway at Forty-Second today. Got off at the next stop. Our man lost him."

"It's not unusual for Franck to catch a train and switch destinations two stops later. Or take three taxis to go a mile. That's just Franck. But no paintings were stolen this trip."

"One." Joel turned his kind gaze on Jillian. "Petzold didn't need a concert this time, nor Kerina playing a Strauss waltz."

She looked down at her hands. "What's missing?"

"A Rembrandt etching taken from a major auction house. A flat copper plate that was about to go on the auction block for a high sum—but stolen during a blackout. It was dark long enough for Petzold to walk out the front door."

"A dozen others must have left at the same time."

"Petzold was caught on the surveillance cameras in the side room where the Rembrandt was on display."

"You can't plan a robbery based on a power outage."

"He just took advantage of it. Crazy as it seems, Jillian, I don't think of the man as a thief. He's obsessed with art."

"That's no excuse for stealing to fill his coffers now." She picked at a thread on her slacks. "Joel, he won't risk taking a painting out of this country. How could he?"

"Aboard that private jet."

"Then you'll arrest him at the airport? Think about Kerina."

"Forget her. I'm depending on you. You'll be with them the whole flight. Brooks Rankin wants Petzold back in Europe. Arrest him here, and we'll never recover the rest of the missing pieces."

"You're using me and the Rembrandt etching for bait."

"That's right, sweetheart."

～

Earlier that morning at the auction house, sweat beaded Franck Petzold's forehead as he studied a Rembrandt etching. He circled the display case. On one side was a painting of an ancient harbor by an unknown artist. On the other was the unsullied etching by Rembrandt. Desire for ownership sent an adrenaline rush through his body. As it peaked, the electricity went out. The room went black. He reached blindly into the display case, tore the plate from its base and tucked it inside his trousers, flat against his abdomen. He notched his belt and buttoned his jacket.

Panic gripped him. He wondered how he could get out of the auction house without a security guard stopping him or the copper plate tripping an alarm. Urgency forced him to feel his way in the darkness. He had only as long as it took the in-house engineer to reach the fuse box; then lights would flood the room. Or an emergency generator would kick in and the theft be discovered. He inched along the wall, stumbling through the darkened room into an auditorium filled with disgruntled clients.

"Be calm," the auctioneer shouted. "We'll have the lights back on in moments. Keep seated. Everything will be all right."

A woman grabbed Franck. He recoiled at the clammy hand clutching his and at the stench of so much perfume in one room. They were in the hall now, light from the windows making it easier to move through the lobby. The woman dashed for the door. He followed, the copper plate slipping an inch as he ran. A guard grabbed him.

"My wife. She's ill."

He pointed to the woman fleeing through the doors. The guard stepped back, and Franck was outside hailing a taxi, his shirt wet with sweat, but the thrill of escape empowering him.

Back at the hotel, he called the airfield in New Jersey and confirmed that the ultrafast business jet would be ready for departure by ten. "Do you have a nurse standing by?" he asked.

"Yes, and food on board. How many will be traveling, sir?"

"Two passengers. I won't be able to accompany them."

He called the second pilot and said, "I want to leave by eleven o'clock this evening. Midnight at the latest."

For seconds after alerting the pilots, Franck stared into space. *My plan will work,* he decided.

Separate planes. Separate destinations. The arrangement was only temporary. He would take refuge in his home on the Black Sea and find quiet and comfort surrounded by his paintings. But he refused to remain in exile. Things would calm down. Jillian had never trusted him, but to have Kerina ill and no longer believing in him, that was the worst. Stealing the Rembrandt added to his problems. He had lost the man who had followed him onto the subway at Forty-Second Street, but someone else might take up the chase.

Another plan sparked—a plan that would take the Rembrandt plate safely out of the country. Franck ordered a sandwich and a pot of black coffee from room service. He called the bell captain to arrange for a limousine at the curb by seven, a bellhop to collect the luggage ten minutes earlier. Then he dialed the concierge's desk and requested fabric glue, an X-acto knife, and thick tape to be sent to his room immediately.

Impatiently, he said, "Try a stationery store or a sewing center. Or if you have a seamstress in the hotel, ask her."

The small packet from the seamstress arrived shortly after his sandwich. He tipped generously so the tip would be remembered instead of the fabric glue. He had already opened Kerina's violin case. The Strad lay cushioned on the pillows; the bow, the extra strings, the small wrap of rosin, the mute beside it.

With the Do No Disturb sign hanging on the doorknob, he closed the room door and locked it once again. He loosened his watch, removed it, and placed it where he could keep abreast of the hour. Pouring himself a third cup of coffee, he set it on the bedside table, away from the velvet lining.

Removing the thin, lightweight Rembrandt etching from beneath his mattress, he studied it again. Touched it. Ran his hand over Rembrandt's signature. Visualized the very spot in his home on the Black Sea where the plate would one day hang. He had rescued it from the auction house, kept it from the hands of some collector who would bury it like a lost treasure.

Casting one more admirable glance at Rembrandt's work, he wrapped the copper plate in tissue paper. He, who rarely smiled, smiled to himself. He had come into possession of a masterpiece. Its worth lay in the eye of the beholder. He had felt that way in the side room of the auction house. He felt that way now.

Eyes narrowing, he bent over Kerina's violin case. He prided himself in his steady hands as he took the X-acto knife and worked the velvet lining in the lid free, each movement of his hand precise, fractional—the opening just wide enough to slip the copper plate behind it. Meticulously, he taped the plate securely in the lid, double-checking to make certain that the metal and the beautiful velvet lining did not touch.

His gaze strayed to the watch. Time was still in his favor.

He was a careful, methodical man. Still smiling to himself, he secured the torn edge with fabric glue. Pressed it gently. Stepping back, he inspected his work and was satisfied.

Genuine sorrow stirred as he picked up Kerina's violin.

The Strad and Kerina were one. Gently he lowered it into the case and locked the bow in place. He had ordered the bow for her in Paris. It had cost him thousands of dollars. He had no regrets. She treasured it as she had always treasured his friendship. Putting it down was like letting her go. She who had brought him such joy.

He closed the lid and twenty minutes later left the hotel, glancing over his shoulder and out the back window of the limousine as they drove to the Harkness Pavilion. Jillian and Kerina were waiting for him in the hospital lobby.

"You didn't forget anything?" she asked as they drove off.

"Kerina, if I forget all else, I remember your violin."

When they reached the New Jersey airfield, Franck stared out the window. No cars followed them. His confidence perked as he spotted the two jets ready for takeoff. They slid cautiously past some vintage war planes. Parked beside them was a Piper Malibu Mirage with white leather upholstery, a Cessna P210, and an old Beech Starship with its futuristic nose.

He ordered their driver toward the company jet where the pilot waited for them. The pleasant-faced young man was a capable type, his grin easy and reassuring, his leather jacket zipped midway. He escorted Kerina from the limousine, half-carrying her up the steps into the luxury and safety of the jet.

When he reappeared moments later, Franck handed the violin to him. "This is gold to Miss Rudzinski." *Gold to me.* "Would you stow this safely on board until you land in Vienna?"

"As you like, sir. I'll keep it up in the cockpit."

Kerina would rage with the violin out of her sight, but the transatlantic flight would allow time for the glue to hold securely. Once the concerts in Austria were over, he'd have Kerina ship the Rembrandt to him. She owed him that small favor.

When he joined Kerina inside the plane, her long fingers caressed his hand. "I could have flown commercial, Franck."

"You'll be more comfortable this way. Less publicity."

"Jill sent out a press release before we left."

"The publicist to the end," he said bitterly.

Kerina lay on a French daybed with stuffed pillows behind her head and a comforter tucked around her waist. "Sit with me, Franck. I don't relish flying over the ocean."

"I want you to rest. Jillian will stay in here with you. If you need pain medication or sleeping pills, just ask."

She looked around. "Franck, where's my violin?"

"It's stored safely with the other luggage."

She yawned and eased back against the pillows. "I won't need anything to sleep. What are you going to do?"

"Finalize our concert plans. Talk with the customs agent."

He wondered whether she believed him. Her fingers pressed deeper into his hand; those dark eyes searched his face. *She suspects,* he thought. *She has guessed that I am not going with her.* He wanted to hold her hand against his cheek and never let her go. Always Kerina had been the joy of his life. What right did she have to be ill? To die? To be anywhere without him?

"After the concerts, I want to go home to Prague. And then you must go away to Moscow, Franck. For your own safety."

"Go with me—"

He wanted her to understand. Every beautiful art piece had been stolen for her, displayed even now in his well-secured home on the Black Sea. His soul agonized that she thought him a common thief. How else would she describe what he had done? No display of Rembrandt and Degas and VanStryker gracing the home he had prepared for her would dim the truth of how he had obtained them.

I did it for you, he thought. *The concert halls of the world. Your success. Your acclaim—all my doing.* But now—now he accepted what she had always known. They would never be one.

As she closed her eyes, he leaned down and kissed her forehead. Her eyes fluttered open. "Where are you going, Franck?"

"I told you. To make certain everything is under control."

"And after that?" Her hand felt like ice on his as she said, "You're not going with us, are you?"

"Not this time, my dear. I'll join you later."

She smiled, knowingly. "Will you ever come back?"

"When you really need me."

He stopped at the cockpit and said, "Have a safe journey, gentlemen. And take care of Miss Rudzinski for me."

"We will," the pilot said. "We have a nurse on board. Don't worry, Mr. Petzold." He patted the instrument panel. "I've flown this baby for years. We deliver our cargo on time and safely." He reached back and shook Franck's hand. "We're ready for takeoff."

As Franck prepared to leave, Jillian caught his eye. She did not ask about the violin, nor why he was not flying with them. But she said, "Franck, the customs agent checked the luggage."

"And you passed inspection?" he asked.

"Of course. Isn't that the way you planned it?"

Outside in the cool evening, Franck watched Kerina's plane taxi and soar; then, with his eyes to the tarmac, he walked the few yards in the darkness and boarded the second private jet.

Jokhar Gukganov wore his seat belt and his perpetual frown as he watched Franck drop into the seat beside him. Jokhar was a business man who dealt in art and fraud with equal pleasure, yet maintained a successful and thriving design company in Moscow. Owning a private jet was part of his company image.

"Did you lay the groundwork for a branch company in New York?" Franck asked in Russian.

Jokhar pulled out a tin of caviar and opened it. "I don't like the American tax system. But business talks give me a legitimate reason for being here. I do not like doing business with Americans, but," he said, "I enjoy their art museums."

Their jet was safely airborne and Jokhar's eyes hard and cold as he turned to face Franck. "Did you bring it?"

"The Rembrandt etching? Of course not. It's packed securely in the lining of Kerina's violin case."

"Then you are a bigger fool than I thought you." His skin looked sallow in the dim light of the cabin. "Or do you plan to let them arrest Miss Rudzinski for robberies you committed?"

Franck would never harm Kerina. Sending the Rembrandt in her violin case was the only way to keep it out of Jokhar's hands. He closed his eyes. If he said anything, Jokhar would know how deeply he cared about Kerina.

Chapter 31

Chandler had walked away from the Everdale Cemetery at peace with his father. But he had half-brothers, brothers without faces. He wanted to touch base with the VanBuriens and bridge the gap their father had left behind. Calling Chicago from his hotel room in Washington, he blurted out his identity to the woman on the other end and asked that her family meet him when his plane touched down at O'Hare the next morning.

"Never!" she told him.

A man took over the phone. "Who is this?" he demanded.

"Chandler Reynolds—Ashley Reynolds' son."

"We don't know any Reynolds."

"Celeste VanBurien does. Ashley was Bill VanBurien's sister."

Neither name set well with the man on the other end. "I'm her son. What do you want from us?"

A better reception than I'm getting, Chandler paused. "I want to meet you. I'm your younger half-brother."

Moments later, the man demanded the flight information and, without saying good-bye, slammed the receiver in Chandler's ear.

All through his boyhood, Chandler had wanted a brother. For a while Randy Williams filled that void. Now as he stepped off the plane at O'Hare and glanced around at those in the waiting area, he had a sinking feeling that Celeste VanBurien—Sanborg now—and her sons were not coming to meet him. Just when he was ready to strike out for the gate to catch the flight to Akron, he spotted a man with sharp blue eyes and a thick blond mustache who looked like the pictures of Bill VanBurien. Their eyes locked.

"Skip?" Chandler asked.

"No, I'm Jeffrey. Jeff VanBurien."

Chandler glanced around again.

"I'm alone. Mother said she didn't know you existed until last evening's phone call. She'd like to keep it that way."

"So she didn't know about me?"

"No; my dad didn't stick around long enough to tell us. But after three glasses of wine last night, Mother was sorry, too—for you. She said Bill left too many black marks on the world."

"And Skip?"

"He doesn't know what your game is. If it's money, he'll have his lawyer meet with you."

Thanks for the welcome mat, Chandler thought. "No need for a lawyer. I just wanted to meet you and apologize."

"Apologize? For what? Not dropping in on us sooner? Believe me, we didn't know there was a little black sheep in the family."

He had been called a lot of names, but this one felt like acid tossed in his face. He braced himself for the man's darts. "All my life I thought you and Skip were my cousins. The side of the family that didn't want any part of us."

"You should have kept it that way. My mother will drink herself sick over this one." Without a flicker of warmth in his expression, Jeff said, "I know my way around O'Hare. Why don't we catch the Airport Transit System to your transfer point? That way you won't be running in the wrong direction at the last moment."

And that way, you make certain I leave town, Chan thought.

As they rode the conveyor belt, they shouted above the noisy crowd around them. Pushing their way into the Transit System, they kept exchanging barbs.

"Too bad you don't have more time, Chandler. I'd take you down by the old Water Tower. Kind of symbolic here in Chicago. It withstood the fires a hundred years ago—better than our family handled the flames that my father set."

"My birth mother had a picture of Dad standing in front of it." *Mother. Dad.* The words flowed easily.

"The violinist?" Jeff snarled. "I remember her. Young. Pretty. Played with the Elgin Symphony Orchestra here in Chicago. That's when Dad met her. And after that, our lives tumbled."

"I thought she played with the Chicago Symphony Orchestra."

He shrugged. "You may be right. Doesn't matter much with him dead now. Nothing mattered until my mother found out they were meeting at the Millhurst Inn. A limestone bed-and-breakfast in Oak Park. A romantic spot that overlooks the Fox River."

"I'm sorry."

He wanted to knock the boulder-size chip off Jeff's shoulder as he said, "You wanted to know about my side of the family. Mother lives in Oak Park in one of the fine old homes in Chicago. If Bill VanBurien had lived, we might not have fared so well."

And she might not be drinking heavily.

"I was just a kid when my grandfather hired a detective to follow Dad. Seemed to make my mother feel better somehow. Your mother," he said bitterly, "and my father had strange tastes. The planetarium. Hemingway's Museum in Oak Park. Old mansions, like the Cantigny. Sometimes they just rode the Downtown Loop."

"Were your parents in love?" Chandler asked.

"The charming Celeste and handsome, ambitious Bill from nowhere—in love? My mother thought so in the beginning. She adored him. Thought he was going places in the corporate world. That fit in with Mother's plans. She ignored the fact that he came from a little town in the South. She hadn't been around for the Civil War. Didn't think they'd end up fighting." Jeff gave his firm jaw a vigorous rub. "Sometimes I wonder how they ever got together. They had different agendas. Like my brother and I."

When they reached the boarding area, Jeff jammed his hands into his pockets and paced by the terminal windows. In the reflected glass, he looked like a blade-thin weed that had blown free from the edge of the swamp and been carried by the wind through thirty-four troubled years. If they had been kids they could kick and scream and throw their toys or wrestle each other to the ground. But they were grown men, unable to hide their smoldering resentments. Still, Chandler wanted to bridge the gap.

"You're my brother. Doesn't that count for something, Jeff?"

Jeff glared at Chandler, his slouching six-foot-four frame carrying the weight of the world. "Is it money you want?"

"Money? No, your friendship." *Your respect,* he thought.

"I don't buy that. You must want something."

As Jeff's voice rose, a woman passenger vacated her seat, not waiting to snatch up all her parcels. An older lady stayed where she was, head bobbing, her wobbly fat legs crossed at the ankles.

Chandler expected security guards on the double—an arrest instead of a boarding pass. He had to give it one last try. "I didn't plan to dump the past on you, Jeff. I just wanted to be friends. To trace my roots."

Suddenly Jeff stopped in front of the old woman and faced Chandler head-on. His fists were still jammed in his pockets, his lips tightly drawn as he fought off over thirty years of bitterness, but he said, "You're really okay, Chandler."

The woman shook her head. "Then stop making fools of yourselves in public. Hire a lawyer if you have to and settle this thing between you. You're big boys now. All grown up."

Jeff grinned down at her sheepishly. "I am a lawyer."

"The lawyer your brother would hire if he didn't trust me?"

"That's right, Chandler. One of my associates, most likely. Reynolds here is my brother," he told the woman.

"All the more reason to be friends. So shake hands."

"She's right, Jeff. And I'm not here for a cut in the insurance or Dad's stock assets. I didn't know he had any."

"It's all gone anyway. The stock money reinvested."

"I have no claims on a dead man. I just wanted to put a face to him." His own facial muscles worked overtime. "All my life, I wanted a brother, Jeff."

"Me, too." His voice was as thin as his lips. His eyes darted toward the boarding gate and back to Chandler.

"You have Skip."

"They left the wrong parcel at my house. He's like our mother. Proud. Rich. Making a mess of his second marriage. We've never been close. We're at opposite poles."

"But you're his lawyer."

"Because I'm good at it and he needs me."

Something stirred in Chandler's blood, too, a part of himself that could be redefined by knowing Jeff better. Brothers. The same blood. The same genes. "I need you, too, Jeff."

The boarding call came. "All first-class passengers—"

"I hate to see you walk through that door," Jeff admitted.

"Then let's stay in touch." Chandler scribbled his phone number in exchange for the business card that Jeff offered. "Let's give this brother thing a chance, Jeff."

He made the first move. He dropped his briefcase, stepped forward, and, awkward as it seemed, gave Jeff his first real bear hug from a brother.

❧

In Ohio, Chandler pulled the Williams's van smoothly up to the curb marked for loading and unloading only. He ignored the clamor and honking horns around him as passengers spewed out of cars, tugging their overweight luggage.

He took a deep breath and smiled at Mabel Williams, who looked even shorter than her five-two sitting beside him.

She was reticent and shy with a freckled nose—a homespun woman in a fluffy blue sweater that matched her eyes. She had welcomed him with tears and was still crying. Her husband's absence made the visit harder; Russell and their son's pregnant girlfriend wouldn't be back in Akron until the end of the week.

Chandler had come too soon, spreading Mabel Williams's wound raw again. He cut his visit down to three hours, but she had insisted on driving him to the airport. He offered to take the wheel when he realized freeway driving panicked her.

"Guess this is it, Mrs. Williams. Are you sure you're okay, driving back to your house alone?"

"I'd rather have Russell driving, but with him in Bosnia waiting to fly back with Zineta—well, I'll just have to take a firm grip of the wheel and do it myself."

"I should have taken the airport limo."

"You should have stayed on until Russell and Zineta arrived. You could have used Randy's room—except it's a nursery now."

He had seen it, a room transformed for their grandchild and highlighted in pale shades of blue with little red, white, and blue soldiers painted on the wall.

"Another time." He leaned across to the passenger side and kissed her gently on the cheek. "If I'm going to catch my flight I'd better go. Besides, we're about to be moved on."

She clutched his arm. "It's unbearable to lose a son."

"I can't imagine your grief. Randy was a great guy. I'm so sorry."

Her hand stayed firm on his arm. "Your plans to leave home for good—they're wrong, Chandler. I know we talked about it already—but I had to say it again. Your parents love you—you've told me they do. Walk out, Chandler, and it would be unbearable for them, as though you were dead. I know. Promise me—"

"I'll think about it." But she was right. It was time to go home and set things right with his parents.

He swung out of the car and around to the passenger side. She was already stepping out. "Get your luggage, Chandler, before they make me drive off with it still in the trunk."

He popped the lid and did as she told him, but he made certain she was safely back in the car and belted in. "I'm sorry about Randy. I wish it could have been different."

Her knuckles went bloodless as she gripped the steering wheel. He leaned toward her. "Drive carefully, Mrs. Williams. And remember, what you're doing for Zineta and the baby is special."

"Randy thought she was special, too. And if it weren't for you, Chandler, we would never have known about her."

The guard breathed down his neck.

"Give us another second," Chandler begged. "She lost her son recently in Bosnia, and we were just talking about him."

The guard backed off. "Try to hurry her along."

"Mrs. Williams, maybe the baby will be a boy."

"I pray so. We decorated the nursery for a boy, hoping. Randy always wanted a son."

"And if it's a girl?"

Her eyes watered. "It will still be Randy's child. Chandler, will Zineta like us? Russell and me?"

"How could she not?"

She blew her nose heartily and said through her tears, "You will come back soon? We'd like you to be the baby's godfather."

"That's quite an honor. I'll come back. That's a promise."

❧

While he waited for the flight to Los Angeles, Chandler called home. "Mom, it's Chandler."

"Chandler." Her apprehension winged over the wires to him. "When are you coming home?"

"I'm flying into LA this evening."

"We were so afraid you weren't coming."

"But I am."

"Let me grab a pencil and take down your flight number."

"It's probably there by the phone," he reminded her. "Yes. I have it. Flight 805. Dad and I will meet you." She sounded rattled, unlike herself. "I'll go to the market right now and buy some steaks for dinner. Or do you want pot roast?"

"Don't cook. I'll take you and Dad out to dinner. You know the Beverly Hills Hotel on Sunset? Join me there at eight."

"That's too extravagant!"

"Grams sent me some money. I'll even have enough for a tip."

"I'll be there, Chandler, but your father, I'm not sure—"

"Tell him we're having dinner together. My treat. So tell Dad I expect him. We have things to talk about."

And with that, he disconnected, smiling.

⁓

The jet touched down in Los Angeles, winging through a late afternoon sky rippled with layers of clouds in margarine yellow and flushed with tea rose pink streamers. The color pattern was framed with shades of gray-pelican toward the patches of blue, a familiar threatening lead gray on the horizon. The clouds would alarm Ashley but were insignificant from the pilot's report.

Chandler's upgrade to first class allowed him a speedy exodus. The prettiest of the flight attendants stood primping by the kitchenette, the same one who had smothered him with attention during the flight. He caught her flicker of disappointment as he ducked his head to exit the cabin alone.

As he strode briskly up the ramp, pain shot through his leg, reminding him that healing after all these months was still in progress. Minutes later as he waited at the baggage claim, the turnabout started spinning. He snapped up his suitcase and was out of the terminal in line for a taxi ahead of other passengers.

Chandler whistled. "Taxi!"

"Where to?" the driver asked as he flagged the meter. Chandler tossed his luggage on the backseat and tumbled in behind it. "The Beverly Hills Hotel on Sunset Boulevard."

⁓

Ashley checked her polished nails for the tenth time, biting back the desire to check the speedometer. David stayed in the fast lane, keeping with the flow of traffic, then inching above the sixty-five limit. She glanced at him, determined to warn him to slow down, but the lines at his well-shaped mouth were tight. Advice from her corner would only anger him.

She hunched in her seat. "David, I'm frightened."

"Of our son?"

"He may not call himself that any longer."

David's square jaw clamped. "He's legally ours. Has been since the day he was born. Nothing can change that."

Points one, two, three—like his disciplined sermons. She visualized him in his clerical robe, expounding boldly from the pulpit, the smooth orator preaching to others about family relationships. She saw none of this boldness in the man sitting beside her. It was the old David groping his way through a crisis. Proud and determined, yet struggling.

"David."

He shot her a glance, his heavy-lidded eyes too bright.

"I keep thinking of Chandler when he was a little boy."

His grip tightened on the wheel, his eyes catching the traffic through the mirrors. "But he's a man now."

"He was little once. He needed us then."

"We don't know what Everdale has done to him."

I know what it did to me, she thought. *It brought me my greatest joys and my deepest shame. But it was once a happy place in my childhood, and Chandler had his beginnings there.*

"He's like you, David. He'll reason things through."

"And you think that's why he asked us to drive into Beverly Hills for dinner so he can tell us everything is fine? He could have done that at home over one of your dinners."

"Maybe he likes dining out."

"Maybe he wants to tell us good-bye in a public place. What right did that woman have to come back into his life?"

She rested her hand on his arm. "Don't be bitter about Kerina. I know she regrets giving him away."

A tremor shook David's deep voice. "Oh, Ashley—how I love that boy."

"When he was little you used to tell him that. Why don't you tell him again, David?"

He grabbed her hand, his fingers locking with hers. "He should know that I love him. We've been over all of that."

He took the off-ramp at a good clip. Now he threaded his way through the traffic on Sunset Boulevard, traveling several blocks, going past the Los Angeles Country Club toward their date with Chandler.

When they saw the hotel to their left and the Will Rogers Memorial Park to their right, he said, "There's no turning back. If we want our son in our court, we have to listen to him."

Stately palms, potted plants, brightly flowered vines and lush foliage surrounded the well-lit, luxurious hotel, its blinding pink color a landmark in Beverly Hills. Ashley rummaged in her purse for her lip gloss as David stopped for valet parking. He swung around behind the car to open the door for her.

She straightened her St. John jacket. "Do I look all right?"

"You look lovely. Stop fretting."

"But we're not exactly royalty," she whispered.

"Honey, we're the famous Reynolds. We'll fit right in with the celebrities. You'll see." He took her hand. "Hungry?" he asked as they walked up the red-carpeted entry.

"Scared."

He tucked her hand in his. "Whatever happens, Ashley, we still have each other."

She took a deep breath as they stepped into the glamorous lobby. "And whatever happens, David, we must tell Chandler how much we love him."

❧

Chandler stood as the maitre d' led his parents to his candlelit table, elegantly set for three with a vase of roses in the center. A chilled bottle of Martinelli's Sparkling Cider lay tilted in the wine basket beside him. He kissed his mother lightly on the cheek, shook David's hand. Once seated, David flicked the napkin on his lap and glanced around for a waiter.

"I've already ordered dinner, Dad. To save time."

"I thought this was to be a leisurely dinner."

His mother's anxious voice intervened. "David, please."

Chandler sent her a ghost of a smile. It was not going the way he planned. He shifted uneasily. "This is a celebration."

"Really?" David asked.

"Yeah, we're celebrating our family. Mine especially. Two mothers. Two fathers. With nobody 'fessing up to the truth."

The pain on his mother's face was more than he could swallow. "Sorry, I didn't mean it that way."

"We had it coming, Chan. Not telling you before. But the longer it went, the harder it was to admit what we had done."

"What *you* did? Doesn't the finger of blame go to Kerina and your brother Bill? All you two did was pick up the pieces."

"What we picked up was the most beautiful baby boy, and we were willing to do anything to keep from losing him. We wanted you, Chandler Reynolds," Ashley said. "We still do. So what are we really celebrating?"

"The truth. I didn't ask you to come here to hurt you. I thought the hotel would be neutral ground—a place where we could start building our lives together again."

"Is that what you want, Chandler?" she asked.

"Of course, Mom." He moved his arm so the waiter could put the salad plate in front of him. "Maybe some good food will loosen your tongue, Dad. You've barely said a word."

David pushed aside his soup bowl and peppered his salad. "You've had a long journey. Do you want to tell us about it?"

"Everdale was tough, but could we talk about that later? Tomorrow. Next week. We have plenty of time to sort things out. And before you ask, I won't know about that government job for months. They do thorough checks on their applicants."

David gave a short chuckle. "We've already had the FBI at our door. I couldn't imagine what your mother had done. But don't ask us to wait until tomorrow or next week to talk about Everdale. We've already had twenty-six years of not telling you who you are. Not telling you how much you mean to us."

"Why the big secret?"

"We promised Miss Rudzinski—"

"My mother."

David's jaw jerked. "We promised—your mother—that we would never tell you that you were adopted. And we regretted it the minute she left town. And then when Bill—when your birth father—died so suddenly, well, son, we didn't know what to do."

"So you did nothing?"

"Please don't, Chandler," Ashley begged. "I'm the one who didn't want to tell you. David has always wanted you to know."

"You're a nurse. You knew the emotional impact of hiding this from me. I couldn't do much about a dead father, but it really hurt when Kerina walked out on me again." Chandler stirred his salad, thick with ranch dressing. "The only good thing that came out of this was finding out I had brothers. Half-brothers, not cousins. Why, Mom? I remember being a little kid, telling you that I wanted a brother to horse around with and grow up with."

David arched his thick brows. "Someone to bully, maybe?"

Chandler bantered back, flexing his muscles. "I would have been the big brother. King of the mountain."

"We wanted a brother for you. It just didn't work out."

"And you weren't about to bring in some other stranger—some other nameless kid without roots, eh, Dad?"

The candlelight reflected the flush in his mother's cheeks, the pain in her eyes. "You did have cousins, Chan."

"Come on, Mom. Cousins in Chicago—a family that wanted nothing to do with us." His voice cracked. "That's why Randy Williams meant so much to me. We were grabbing a little of the brotherly horseplay we missed as kids."

"Son, it seems to me that Randy was better than a brother."

"Yeah, Dad. You're right. And when he died in that Bosnian countryside, I felt like I'd lost my own flesh and blood."

Ashley twisted her watchband on her slender wrist. "Randy's child is going to mean a lot to you, isn't he?"

"Yeah. I don't want to lose touch."

"Your mother told me what you were willing to do for Randy's girlfriend."

"You mean marry her to get her to the States? That would have caused a riot in your church."

"That would have been a family matter, not something for the deacons to hash over." David flipped his fork up and down on the china plate. "Chandler, I admire you for what you wanted to do for a friend."

"You would have stood by me in a marriage of convenience?"

"I would never have counseled you that way. Marriage has a deeper foundation than that. But I would have stood by you. You are my son, no matter who brought you into this world."

He stared, disbelieving. "You blow my mind, Dad."

"The way you blew mine the first time I held you in my arms. You were the son I always wanted. You still are."

Chandler marveled at the control in David's voice as he asked, "Chan, do you think we can work through this maze of the silent years? Tomorrow we'll take out the paperwork we have in the vault. Your birth records, scanty as they are. We'll lay all the cards on the table, son. All we ask is that you forgive us."

Chandler drained his water goblet. "Jillian keeps reminding me that I owe everything to the two of you." He beckoned to the waiter for more water and drank lustily. "But it was my visit in Akron that turned me around. Mrs. Williams has a big hole in her heart since Randy died. I didn't want to do that to you."

He cleared his throat, but not the traces of anger still there. "I told her about my adoption—told her I was going to write you two off and bury our family relationship."

They sat there stoically. Not even a muscle twitched on David's jaw. "Mrs. Williams said the pain of losing a son is unbearable. She would give anything to have Randy back."

Chandler cracked his knuckles and saw Ashley's gaze slip from his face to his hands, then back to meet his eyes again. "Randy's mom said if I left home angry, I would be as good as dead to you, lost forever—so I came home to work things out."

"Will it work out for the Williams having Zineta there?"

"Mom, Zineta and the baby are exactly what the doctor ordered. They fixed up Randy's old room. It's an old-fashioned house, but Zineta will think she moved into the Hilton."

He chewed at his lip. "My showing up was rough on Mrs. Williams, but she insisted on taking me to the cemetery." He glanced at David, hesitating before saying, "Randy believed that life—like the buck—stopped here. You got on. You got off. If he believed anything beyond the exodus, I don't know what it was. And if he considered eternity or cried out for it in those final seconds, we'll never know."

David's elbows edged the table, his hands clasped.

"I know what's coming next, Dad, but don't throw words like the sovereignty of God at me. I can hardly say the word, let alone understand it."

"I don't have it all down pat either, son. That's why I spend so much time between Genesis and Revelation."

"That's why you're the solid kind of man you are." Chandler wiped his lips with his napkin. "For all of Randy's not knowing, a part of him will go on living in his child."

He felt the corner of his mouth twist into a wry grin.

"Mrs. Williams asked me to be the baby's godparent. That way my next visit won't be so hard on her."

Through soup and salad, they had skirted the real issue of what had brought them to the legendary Polo Lounge. Chandler faced it now. "What you really want to know is what happened to me in Everdale, right? You don't want to wait until tomorrow."

They exchanged guarded glances and nodded. He told them. Between bites of the rest of their five-course dinner, he choked down both the tender meat and his stretched emotions. An hour later, he said, "That covers it. I think Kerina found some of her answers in Everdale, too."

He had said Kerina's name without rancor, without revealing how deeply she had hurt him by rejecting him again.

"How was she?" Ashley asked. "I gave her quite a shock when I told her that Bill was dead. I think she always thought she would see him again one day. I don't know why."

"When she stood at your brother's grave, she seemed to let go, laying down both the memories and the red roses on his headstone at the same time. I had a feeling she was putting everything to rest. The dreams. The might-have-beens."

"She really loved him. Did she say anything about Bill?"

"She didn't say much, Mom. We were caught in a cloudburst. You know what the downpours are like in Everdale. She just took time to put the roses on the grave. How she stood the cold and rain without a coat, I'll never know." He paused, reflecting. "She didn't seem to notice even when I put my raincoat around her shoulders. She cried a little, but I gave her space, and when she turned back to face me she seemed at peace. Kind of proud, too. Head thrown back, her face washed with rain and tears. Then she clutched my arm and hung on until we reached the cars."

He peered at them over the rim of his glass. "I didn't know who she was then, but she knew that I was her son, didn't she?"

"Yes. She knew for certain backstage at the Opera House."

"Why didn't she tell me?"

Neither parent moved.

"Never mind. Right now, I have to grapple with her rejecting me again."

Ashley held him with her eyes. "I don't think you can even comprehend how much she did love you. Does love you." She lifted her hand to keep him from arguing. "I was there the night you were born, Chandler."

"So you told me. I used to think it was a dumb statement. Mothers are usually on hand when their babies are born."

David moved the vase and stared at his son. "Not every baby has two mothers there at the same time. Ashley was there for you, Chandler, from the first cry you ever made."

"I know. But why didn't Kerina want me?"

"We could give you reasons, son, but they would only be excuses. Our own beliefs. She was young. Unmarried. Frightened."

"My brother influenced her decision. Bill didn't always make good choices, but he meant well when he arranged for David and me to adopt you. It was Kerina who insisted on a closed adoption. We would have agreed to anything to have a child in our lives."

He wanted to wrap his arm around her. "It's okay, Mom. Selma Malkoski told me about the closed adoption. She said you and Dad had no choice. We can talk about this later. We'll have time to unravel the mess before I go to London."

"Chandler, what Bill did was not right, but I loved him. He was my brother, my twin—a part of me. Your father was a good man. Strong in so many ways. Fun-loving and musical—that's why he was drawn to Kerina. He was hardworking, caring, but not always dependable. In his crazy, mixed-up way he was giving us part of himself when he arranged for us to adopt you."

"I know. I finally read his letter."

"Then you know he loved you—loved Kerina. Three days after you were born—the day Bill died—he came to the hospital to pick Kerina up. I wanted to confront him, but I didn't. Bill died before I had a second chance."

"Last week when Kerina was in Everdale, she registered at the motel as Kerry Kovac."

"Oh Chandler, it was the name she used the night you were born. She went full circle—back to where she had left you. Back to the place where she held you for the only time. She loved you, Chandler."

The waiter was there with suggestions for desserts that would melt in their mouths. Chandler had no desire to add sugar to the bitter taste of bile still in his mouth. But he asked, "Mom. . .Dad—what's it going to be? Mousse? Cheesecake?"

David waved both hands and put his napkin down.

Ashley said, "It looks like no dessert for either one of us."

"Well, then!" Chandler glanced up at the waiter. "We'll just have our sparkling cider and call it an evening."

Expertly, the waiter plucked the Martinelli bottle from the wine basket, broke the white seal, popped the lid, and filled the three goblets with bubbling cider before he left the table.

"It's been a painful evening for all of us," Chandler said.

"I wasn't sure I could do this when I came here tonight. I can now. During my flight from Chicago, I thought about your sermons, Dad. Especially the ones on forgiveness. There's a lot more to say. But we have time to work out the problems before I move to London. There's just one more thing I need to tell you—"

David gripped Ashley's hand, their eyes focused on Chandler. He saw tears brimming in his mom's eyes, doubt creeping into his dad's. Chandler pushed back his chair and stood. "I'd like to propose a toast."

A romantic ballad played softly in the background. The muted lights reflected on their faces. He smiled at them, grateful for their years of sacrifice. For the trust they had placed in him. For the truth they had kept back for so long, not out of cruelty but out of their deep affection for him. He knew there would be rough days ahead. Bad moments. Disagreements. But wasn't that part of the triple-braided cord that bound families together?

Ashley and David waited, still holding hands, their eyes never leaving his face. Wrapping his fingers around the stem of the crystal goblet, Chandler saluted them. "Mom. . .Dad, thank you for loving me from the day I was born."

The lamplight behind them caught the amber glow in the glass. For a moment his mother's gaze seemed fixed on the bubbly effervescence of the cider. Slowly, comprehending, she lifted her face, her soft blue eyes wide with joy again.

Chandler brought the goblet to his lips. "Mom. . .Dad, I love you."

Chapter 32

January blew in over Southern California with wind and rain and high surf. The storms damaged many homes and toppled electric wires, putting sections of the towns in blackout and turning the hills and slopes into muddy runoffs. While the lowlands dried out, Chandler rode the ski slopes once again. His leg was nearly good as new, gaining strength as he put it to the test. His three months at home looked as pristine as the slopes. The Reynoldses had worked at settling their differences, learning to trust again as a family, disagreeing now and then, but cooling the air before sundown. They were giving each other space. David had full run of the library. The men stayed out of Ashley's garden when she was planting. And Chandler had Saturdays on the slopes at Big Bear.

He didn't know what had happened between his parents.

Whatever it was, they were back to overnighting at Lake Arrowhead and seemed at peace with each other, laughing more, loving more. If they were falling in love again and he suspected they were—his move to London would come easier. He stored up good memories for the days ahead, memories like Thanksgiving and Christmas and his grandmother contentedly baking cookies with Ashley.

The birth of Zineta's son and Thanksgiving turned out to be days worth celebrating, and Christmas rolled in with the taxi driver struggling up to the front door with his arms loaded down with Grandmother Reynolds's suitcases and holiday parcels. Chandler climbed the ladder expecting to hang the traditional star but was handed a glittering angel to hang on the top spike.

Without misgivings, Ashley had said, "We don't need the star this year."

Chandler's schedule was full. He was playing third baseman for a local team and had taken a part-time job driving for Federal Express, the temporary job stretching to thirty-two hours a week. He still had his Saturdays on the slopes and Sundays sitting beside his mother on the front pew rooting for David as he preached on forgiveness and love's triple-braided cord—sacrifice, truth, and trust.

He was not without his gray areas and bouts with hidden rage, but he was slowly coming to terms with the fact that one of the world's most accomplished violinists was his birth mother. Sometimes he awoke in a cold sweat in the middle of the night and lay in the darkened room thinking, *I am Bill VanBurien and Kerina Rudzinski's son.*

But his loyalty remained with Ashley and David, the mom and dad who had reared him, and his best days included a phone call to Jillian in London or Paris or Prague or a thick letter from her. He had no reason to think that things could be anything but improving when he flipped the calendar to February.

February coasted in with sunny days for Southern California. The worst winter storm of the season hit the East Coast. Kansas waited for meltdown from an ice storm, and the Pacific Northwest braced for the blizzard blowing in from the Gulf of Alaska. According to Jillian's last letter, London was wet and rainy, but she didn't care; she and Kerina were back in the Czech Republic watching a blanket of snow drift softly over the farm outside of Prague.

~

On the first Thursday in February, Chandler was in the kitchen drinking his morning coffee, wondering how long it would be before he would see his girl again. He folded back the newspaper to the weather report and scanned it, but his thoughts kept wandering back to Jillian. . .and, reluctantly, to Kerina.

"Are you deaf?" his dad asked, coming into the kitchen.

Chandler peeked out from behind the weather report.

"Huh?"

"The doorbell just rang."

"Did you get it?"

"Thought you would."

"Never mind, you two. I'll get it," Ashley said. She called back, "Chan, you must be moving up in your company. A FedEx truck just pulled up in front of the house."

"You expecting something, Dad?"

David glanced out the kitchen window. "Bad weather. No, looks like a sunny day this time."

"Chandler. David. Come here."

Chandler sloshed his coffee racing his dad for the door. "What's up, Mom? You okay?"

Her creamy cheeks had paled, her usually warm voice seemed too carefully articulated. She pointed to a large, well-wrapped parcel and said, "It's for you, Chandler."

"Wasn't expecting anything, Mom."

"It came from Prague."

He heard the uncertainty in her voice. Saw it in her eyes.

"Mom, Jillian didn't say she was sending anything."

"She didn't. It's from Kerina."

Chandler took three strides to the sofa and jabbed the ends of the package with his penknife. He tore away the tissue and each layer of protection and lifted a violin case from the box. He opened the lid. "It's Kerina's Stradivarius."

For a minute Kerina's words thundered in his head. *Someday, when I no longer need it, I will send my Stradivarius to you. You will play it, won't you, Chandler?*

"Is there a note with it?" Ashley asked.

Chandler pawed through the packing again, and then held out a sheet of pink stationery to Ashley. "Here. You read it, Mom."

Ashley's voice was strained as she read,

"This is for you, Chandler, with all my love. Kerina."

Chandler's gaze drifted past Ashley to his father. "It must be her way of saying, 'Sorry, kid, for running out on you.'"

Ashley shook her head in protest. "Chan, don't you remember? She wanted you to have it when she stopped doing her concerts."

"Why would she quit playing? She's still young."

Gingerly, he lifted Kerina's Strad from its case. As he cradled the violin and ran the bow gently over it—much like Kerina had done at the concert hall—Ashley said, "It took a lot of love for Kerina to let you go. She gave your dad and me everything when she gave you up."

He didn't feel strong enough for her tears. "It's okay, Mom. You don't have to explain her. I know it hurt you when she walked out on me again. Believe me, there's no love lost between us."

"She must have had a good reason for letting you go."

"Mom, she never gave me a reason for the first time." He took a deep breath and felt his ribs tighten. "Guess she didn't want to be strapped with an illegitimate kid."

"Don't," Ashley cautioned. "You're only hurting yourself."

His voice wavered. "She recognized me back at the Opera House, didn't she? And she knew who I was when we stood by Bill's grave and didn't say anything. Bet she was too embarrassed to acknowledge me."

David crossed the room to Chandler's side and pressed his shoulder. "Perhaps she thought you weren't ready."

The muscle along Chandler's jaw pulsated as he placed the violin back in its case. "What makes her think this violin will make up for twenty-six years without her?"

He felt out of control, the way he did the day Randy blew up in front of him and died. His voice was tight with anger. "Kerina didn't want me when I was born, and she doesn't want me now. She gave me as much of herself as she could when she sent this violin. Well, she can have the old thing back."

He turned from the parcel and stormed toward the front door. Chandler's hand was on the doorknob when he heard his father say, "Let him go, Ashley."

"He can't run forever, David. He has to settle this thing before she dies. Kerina needs him."

"And Chandler needs time to work it out. He'll come through. I'll talk to him."

"No sermons this time, David?"

"He doesn't need a sermon, Ash."

Chandler yanked the door open and slammed it with such force that the living room windows rattled. He took off for the beach and stared gloomily at the ocean that separated him from his birth mother. He tossed his fury back to the horizon, back to God, back to the woman across the ocean who had deserted him so long ago. What did Ashley mean, before Kerina dies? What did he care what happened to her? You live. You die. He had lived without her for a lifetime. She'd been as good as dead all those years. Big deal. She had sent him her violin. For all he knew it could be a fake. Like his mother had been.

He sank down on the sand, a hard-packed sand dune to his back. The wind whipped across the ocean, sweeping in on him like the tide. Still he sat there fighting his demons. And then he closed his eyes and saw Kerina in a beautiful red gown, crossing the stage in Vienna with the Stradivarius in her hand. And he remembered the sad twist at the corner of her mouth and groaned, his wail crashing with the waves and sweeping into shore.

It was dark by the time he went home again. He found Ashley and

David waiting for him. "Come join us, Chandler. I've made cocoa and brownies. And your father called your supervisor—told him you couldn't be in today."

"I guess I was so upset I forgot about my job."

"You did have other things on your mind, son. Have you worked them out?"

"Dad, I'm not sure. I'm angry that Kerina thinks she can buy me off with a violin."

"She's ill, son. She went back to Prague for medical care."

"Ill?"

"Seriously ill," Ashley said. "Jillian asked us not to tell you. She said Kerina had the right to be remembered as you saw her in Vienna. She was afraid of losing you if she told you who she was."

"Kerina told me that when she no longer needed the Strad—when she could no longer play it—she would send it to me. But I urged her to keep it in the family."

"She did, son," David said.

As Chandler turned and ran one knuckle gently across Ashley's cheek, she said, "Bill used to do that. You're a lot like him."

"Your mother's right. You remind us of Bill often. He had his good points, you know."

"Mom, if she had sent the violin to Bill, would he have gone to her?"

"We don't know. He wasn't free, Chandler."

"If he had been free. Divorced. Whatever. Would he have gone then?"

Ashley ran her hand along the back of the chair. "I wish things had been different for Kerina and Bill. But if they had been—and if he were still alive—Bill would already be on the plane. I'm certain of it."

"Then by not going, I'm running out on her. Is that it, Mom? But how can I possibly face her with all of this anger?"

David caught his eye. "You know the answer to that. You know the One who carries burdens."

Chandler stared out the window, seeing nothing but darkness. At last he turned back to them. "Maybe I should thank her in person for the violin. Would you mind if I went?"

Ashley and David exchanged glances. "Go to her. The trip's on your mother and me this time."

"You're not worried about my not coming back?"

Ashley shook her head. "No. You will always be our son."

Chandler's jet touched down for a brief layover in Heathrow before starting on its last ninety-minute flight from London to Prague. After a sleepless flight, he felt jet lag as the plane came in for a bumpy landing at Ruzyne Airport. The terminal looked functional and clean, its interior modern and well-lit, its customs agents polite. He showered and changed in the business lounge and stowed his dirty, wrinkled clothes in his suitcase. After cashing traveler's checks at the money exchange, he took time for roast duck and baked dumplings at a stand-up counter before hiring a red Skoda at the car rental for the last lap of the journey.

When Chandler turned on the ignition, the Skoda took a sputter or two and then rolled smoothly. In spite of the lack of sleep, he drove the nine miles out of his way for a quick overview of the city that had shaped Kerina's life.

A light snowfall capped the city in white. Ice floes churned through the River Vltava. Prague was Bohemian, medieval in architecture, historic with its jutting spires and castles. Wenceslas Square stood as a reminder of the Czechs' quest for freedom. Chandler considered Prague modern in its music and its youth.

As he drove through the city, he smiled at the young people who were strolling through the parks and crossing bridges over the Vltava with snowflakes clinging to their hair and eyebrows.

Turning west in the direction of the White Carpathians, his thoughts geared toward the farm an hour outside of Prague. Kerina had finally come home. He couldn't even guess whether they would ever be free to acknowledge each other. He passed through a charming village and on to the outskirts where the Rudzinski farm still stood. Smoke poured from the farmhouse chimney, and a worn cottage sat on the knoll toward the river. With the ground crackling under his tires, he pulled to a stop near the front door. He knocked and was surprised to see Jillian standing there when the door swung open.

"Jillian!"

He lifted her in his arms and put his frostbitten cheek against hers. "I've missed you," he said and smothered her answer with a kiss.

She pushed him away. "You're cold. Put me down," she said, but she was smiling. She took his hand and pulled him toward the warmth of the old fireplace. "I'm so glad you came. I have hardly slept since you called to say you were coming. And then I worried that you might not find the place."

He looked around. "Where's Kerina?"

"She went out an hour ago."

"Because I was coming?"

"She's uncertain how you will feel about her now."

"Am I supposed to feel some special way?"

"Don't you?"

"I'm just worried about her health."

Jillian's sapphire eyes lost their luster. "If that's your only concern, Chandler, you should have stayed at home." Jillian brushed her cheek against his sleeve. "So far, you can't get past the thought of her giving you up for adoption. I see her for who she is today. And that is someone special. Someone caring."

"Jillian, I came because she sent me her violin."

"She told you she would."

"She told me she would keep it in the family. That's how I knew she was finally acknowledging me. But I didn't want to come at first, Jill. I dragged my feet until my mom said that Bill would have already been on the plane rushing to Kerina's side."

"Wise woman that mother of yours." She squeezed his hand. "Just be kind to Kerina. Don't pretend. She wants you to be yourself." She reached up and turned his face toward hers. "Kerina is dying. That's why she sent the violin. The cancer has spread to her spine and lungs."

"Isn't anything being done for her?"

"She finally had surgery two months ago, but she waited too long."

He rubbed his gloved hands together. "Then I'd better go to her." He still sounded duty bound, as though Kerina were his project. "Where is she?" he asked.

"Out walking by the river."

"Out in this miserable weather? She'll get pneumonia."

"She doesn't care, Chandler. The prospect of dying the way she's going to die is not an easy one. You're not going out by the river to see some violinist. She's the woman who brought you into this world."

"That's the woman who gave me away. I've spent a lifetime staring in the mirror and thinking that Chandler Reynolds was staring back at me."

"He was."

"Was he? I was living a lie. I am almost twenty-seven years old and only recently found out I was born out of wedlock."

"Big deal," she snapped back. "That wasn't your doing. And it certainly didn't bother Ashley and your dad when they adopted you. You're legal. Adoption makes you legal." Her sapphire eyes were blistering hot. Sparking. "They did a good job raising you. And whatever pain and loss and mourning Kerina had to live through, you didn't. She did what she thought was best for you." Jillian tossed her head, her long, tawny hair swinging back from her angry face. "Grow up, Chandler. The fact that you were born is proof enough that Kerina wanted you from the beginning. And the fact that two of the nicest people in the world adopted you is worth a million."

He started laughing.

"And what's so funny?"

"You." He shrugged, buttoning up his coat. "I'm wondering if you will always be this hard to live with."

She looked beyond him, avoiding his gaze, her cheeks turning scarlet. "Do you want me to go with you, Chandler?"

"No. Like you said, this is between Kerina and me."

"But first there are two people who want to meet you before you go."

"Kerina's parents?"

"Your grandparents, Chan."

Grandparents!

She led him into a kitchen that was warmed both by the wood-burning stove and by the sweet smile on the face of Kerina's mother. If he had expected a plump woman in a black shawl or a tottery old man in overalls, he had guessed wrong. The man, an alert eighty-year-old, sat in a pair of jeans and a thick wool sweater with his thin legs crossed and an unlit pipe bobbing from his mouth. He scowled from under heavy brows, daring Chandler to be anything but polite to his wife. To himself.

Chandler's gaze fled back to the woman in the chair beside him, her skin tissue-thin like her body. Their chairs were inches apart, her wrinkled hand grasping for her husband's. She looked like she had weathered a long, tough journey through life and had triumphed over the fate thrown her way. As late as these last few weeks since Kerina had come home to them ill, Chandler was certain they had traveled to hell and back, agonized in the journey, and found peace on the return.

Chandler could not take his eyes from his grandmother's face. Though she looked fragile, she was strong—he saw it in her expression. Looking down at her, he felt as though he had come home, home to part of himself. Her name was Gretchen, and she was as lovely as Kerina with silver hair and kindly dark eyes and a smile of welcome on her wrinkled face.

He wondered if they knew about him, and Jillian solved that by saying,

"Darlings, this is your grandson Chandler."

He whipped off his gloves and dropped to one knee between their chairs. He felt the old man's strong grip on his arm and the tender gesture of the woman's hand on his head. "We've waited a long time to meet you," she said.

Chandler spoke apologetically in English. They seemed to understand. "I didn't realize until minutes ago that Kerina's parents would be my grandparents."

"And do you mind?" his grandmother asked.

"No. No, it's nice. Nice having more grandparents."

Odd, he thought. *I can accept my grandparents much more readily than the mother who gave me away.*

"Call me as you please," the man said gruffly. "But my name is Karol. Tell me, do your parents know that you've come here?"

"Yes sir. They sent me with their blessing."

"Young man, if you cannot love our daughter—cannot forgive her, then go. Go back home now before she knows you are here."

"Don't, Karol," Jillian said. "I told Kerina he was coming today. She wants him to stay. Let them work it out together."

Chandler heard his grandmother's stifled sob. As her hands cupped his face, he sensed more than the warmth of her skin against his cheeks. He felt loved. "Go to Kerina," she murmured. "My daughter needs you."

He nodded. "If Jillian sets me in the right direction, I'll be on my way."

He stood, shook the man's firm hand, and kissed his grandmother's cheek. "You're certain you have room for me here?"

Jillian turned to Chandler with a relieved smile. "Your grandmother told me that she's had your room ready for twenty-six years."

"I didn't know they knew about me."

"They guessed—and then Franck confirmed it a long time ago. We'll have soup simmering in the kettle when you get back."

As he put his hand on the knob, she said, "I'm sorry about Los Angeles. I couldn't tell you that Kerina had canceled the concert there. But on the phone you were going to ask me something when I got there."

"You never got there," he teased.

Disappointment shadowed her eyes. He smiled. "I told you then I might be rushing things, but—I love you. Right now with Kerina sick, it may be the wrong time to ask you."

"Go on," his grandfather said from the doorway. "Ask her."

Chandler cleared his throat. "I want you to marry me, Jill."

Jillian stood there blushing, speechless. He brushed her cheek with a kiss. "Never mind, sweetheart. I'll catch your answer later," he said and went out the door on a run.

~

Chandler found Kerina huddled on the steep embankment, wrapped warmly in her winter Burberry, a thick woolen scarf around her neck, and long, black boots snug against her legs. She seemed unaware of him as she watched great chunks of ice and time slowly floating from her. She half turned as he approached, startled when she saw him.

"Chandler." Her heel slipped on the wet concrete as she tried to push herself up.

"No, don't get up," he warned. "I'll come to you."

He slid down on the hard stones beside her and wondered why she was here alone so close to the deep, icy waters. A hazy winter mist swirled above the river, leaving frozen diamond ringlets in Kerina's hair. That sculpted, oval face was thinner now, the hazel eyes dull and hollow from illness.

"What are you doing sitting out here in the middle of winter, Kerina? You'll freeze to death."

"I've only been here a few minutes."

"Jillian said you left the house an hour ago."

"Oh yes. But I've been walking."

"Jillian said you hated the winters."

"Not anymore. It's so peaceful here. Everything so still."

Everything frozen, he thought. *Your hands like ice.*

She hugged her knees and wrapped her coat more securely around them. "I grew up along this river. Did you know that?"

"No, but we weren't talking about the river."

"I was. I like the Danube best, but this is peaceful, too, with the blue mist rising. I've always wondered where the mist went. I think it is much like life. Lifting. Drifting. Something lovely and mysterious that we can never hold on to." She turned to him. "Why did you come, Chandler?"

"I wanted to thank you for the violin."

"All the way from California just to say thank you?"

"And to see you. How are you?"

"Better—now that you're here." Her lips were turning blue. "If you've come all this way to see me, then you know who I am, don't you?"

He blew on his hands and nodded.

"Do you mind?"

"Does it matter?"

"It has always mattered to me, Chandler." She looked grieved.

Awkwardly, he reached out and put his arm around her shoulders. "Even on my birthdays?" he asked.

"Always on your birthdays. I used to wonder what you were doing. What you looked like. Whether you were happy."

Snow began to fall again, the tiny flakes melting as they drifted across her face. "Kerina, you're cold. We're both cold."

With exquisite care, he unraveled his own wool scarf and placed it around her head and tight against her cheeks, tossing the end flaps over her shoulders.

Her tears fell with the snow. "I wanted you to walk in the woods and climb mountains and play a musical instrument."

"I know."

"I wanted your parents to love you, Chandler."

"They did. I've done all those things you wanted me to do." The chill burrowed through to his spine. "Kerina, we can't stay here. We'll both freeze to death."

He pulled off his leather gloves and tugged them gently over her slender hands, making them look bulky and big, those same smooth hands that had written eleven wishes for him on scented stationery right after he was born. He moved closer, putting his arm around her again, allowing his body heat to warm her. "There, that's better, isn't it, Kerina?"

She couldn't take her eyes from him. She seemed to be drinking him in, filling memory's cup with mental snapshots of his face. "I never thought I'd see you again," she whispered.

"I didn't think you wanted to see me."

Her lower lip quivered. Perhaps from the cold.

"We can't sit here another minute," he insisted. "We'll get pneumonia. Let's go."

She didn't budge. "There's a letter in my pocket you must read."

Oh God, he prayed. *Not a suicide letter.* He pulled it free and opened it with numb fingers. *"My darling Kerina,"* it began.

"This is a personal note, Kerina. I can't read it."

"You must. It's from your father."

Chandler glanced at the date. The letter had been written three days after his birth. He felt slack-jawed as he read through the three pages, embarrassed in places, angry at others. His uncle, his father pouring out his love to a woman he had no intention of seeing again. Could not see again. How much pain she had borne for daring to love Bill VanBurien. Chandler was ready to shove the letter back in her pocket when he reached the last few lines.

Someday our son will know who you are. I can only hope that by then you will both find it in your hearts to forgive me. My mother always said that a forgiving heart goes a long way toward happiness. My dear Kerina, I want nothing more than for you to be happy again.

Chandler folded the letter and put it back in her pocket. "I didn't know he was my father when I saw you in the Everdale Cemetery. All my life, he was Uncle Bill. Nothing more. Nothing less. I didn't know him. I didn't care about him."

The gloved hand went over her mouth, leaving only the pain visible in her eyes. He drew her hand away. "Don't cry, Kerina."

"I never meant to hurt you. Can you ever forgive me, Chan?"

"I haven't thought much about it," he fibbed.

"Will you?"

"Yes." The damp cold fractured his smile. "But I'm not sure I can forgive you for not doing that concert in Los Angeles. I barely saved face with my parents."

She gave a throaty ripple. "Jillian begged me to reconsider. I didn't have the strength. But I'd give anything to play my violin in Vienna one more time—in the city I love best."

He stood and balanced himself on the slanting embankment. "Perhaps you still can, Kerina. But come. Let's get you back to the house. Jillian has some soup simmering on the stove."

Together they trudged up from the river, back toward the old farmstead, Kerina moving with a slow, painful gait.

As they crunched over the cold ground, her arm tucked in his, he said, "I didn't know I was adopted until months ago."

"But you were searching for answers in Everdale."

"Because I heard you and Mom talking on the Riviera. I had just reached the patio railing when I heard Mother say, 'He doesn't know he's adopted, Kerina. How can I ever tell him?' I figured she was talking about me."

He felt her flinch as she whispered, "That was the morning you left the Riviera. And I said, 'Then don't tell him, Ashley.' How awful that you heard it that way."

327

"There was no easy way to find out."

"I was so ashamed, Chandler. You seemed to like me as the violinist. I was afraid if you knew the truth, you wouldn't like me anymore." He strained to hear her say, "And I didn't want Ashley to tell you. Not then. Our being related might have interfered with getting Zineta Hovic out of Bosnia."

"I didn't realize—"

"Can you ever forgive me for denying you a second time?"

"A third time," he corrected, his gaze focused on the farmhouse. "You walked out on me in Everdale twice. The last time in October—I called the Dale Motel once I realized who you were. And they told me that Kerry Kovac had fled again."

She doubled forward. "My dear boy."

"Don't, Kerina."

"I wanted you when you were born, yet I deserted you. I've had to live with that for all these years."

"For me, one of the tough things was finding out I had two brothers. I tried to contact them in Chicago." Again he felt her flinch. "It didn't work out exactly."

"I am so sorry."

"Aunt Celeste wanted nothing to do with me. She said she didn't know I existed and wanted to keep it that way."

"Because you were *my* son."

The words sounded strange to Chandler. He wanted to shrug them off. "Skip wanted nothing to do with me either, but Jeff came. It was funny talking about our relationship and having nothing to say, but Jeff and I decided to keep in touch and give our friendship a chance even though we had so little in common."

"You had Bill." Frosty vapors rose in cloudy white puffs as she spoke. "You had your father," she said again, as they approached the house.

Jillian met them at the door. "I was just about to send out a search team. Why were you out so long on such a cold day?"

"I was finding myself," Kerina said. "And talking with God until Chandler came. I have these little chats now and then in case God wants to hear me."

"He does," Chandler said.

"You seem so sure."

"I am."

She touched her gloved fingers to his lips. "It's still a private matter for me."

"So you told me in St. Stephen's. Someday, if you want me to, I'll tell you about Him."

Dear God, when it comes time, help me to know what to say. I blew it with Randy. Don't let me mess up this time. Not with my mother.

"What's wrong, Chandler?" Jillian asked.

"I don't want Kerina to wait too long."

"I won't," Kerina said softly.

It wasn't until they finished supper and Chandler was feeling warm from the soup and the fire in the woodstove that he was aware of Franck Petzold's absence. "Kerina, where's Franck? No one has mentioned him all day."

"He is in Moscow."

"But you need him. When will he be back?"

"He's not coming, Chandler. It wouldn't be safe for him."

"Not coming!" She turned at the sharpness in his voice, tears brimming on her beautiful, dark lashes. The quick twist of her head sent a tear down her cheek. Gently he wiped it away. "Why isn't Franck coming back, Kerina?"

"They would arrest him for suspicion of art theft."

"Art theft!"

Jillian began stacking the dirty dishes. "He may have been involved in the theft of McClaren's Degas and Rembrandt and a host of other paintings."

"Who told you that?"

"Franck did," Kerina said. "The night he left for Moscow, he admitted that he has been stealing paintings for seven years. Taking them through customs in my luggage. The great Kerina Rudzinski. Who would do more than a cursory inspection of her luggage? I didn't know until this past year. But that night in Vienna, when the McClarens were robbed, I told him, 'Never again, Franck. Get another courier.'"

Chandler caressed her hands. "And what did he say?"

"When he realized who you were, Chandler, he threatened your safety." Her eyes were downcast. "In New York, he asked me to help him one more time, and then he would go away and never come back. That's why I had Jillian cancel my concerts. I had to protect him."

"You were ill, Kerina. That's the reason we canceled your concerts."

"That, too, Jillian, but I had to send Franck away."

"Kerina," Chandler said gently, "that makes you an accomplice."

"I told you once, if it had not been for Franck, I would never have played in the concert halls of the world. In a way, dear Chandler, your father gave me you—a very precious part of himself. But Franck gave me my music."

"And you shared it with the world. Share it with them once more, Kerina. You can't give up your music because of Franck."

She shook her head, freeing more tears. "I'm in pain when I lift my arm. I had to stop playing before people pitied me."

"Pity you? People will always love you, Kerina. But does Franck know you're ill? He'd want to be with you."

"I cannot ask him to risk arrest just to come to me."

"He'd come, Kerina, if he knew."

"Don't send for Franck," Jillian begged him. "Kerina is right. If he comes, they will arrest him."

"Not if they don't know he's here."

"I'll know," Jillian said.

He frowned, perplexed. His gaze settled back on Kerina. "Will you play in concert one more time just for me?"

"In Prague?"

"In Vienna. Here, too, if you'd like."

Jillian dropped the silverware she was holding. "Chan, a full concert is too exhausting. Wait until she's feeling better."

"What about just one song or two?" he asked. "I brought your violin back so I could hear you play again." He pulled the case out from behind the chair and opened it for her. She lifted the Strad and the bow with stiff fingers and then, with her eyes closed, slipped into the joy of her music again.

≈

That night long after the others had gone to bed, Chandler stood with Jillian by the old woodstove. The wick on a kerosene lantern burned low, the unsteady light dancing on her face.

"Jill, Kerina can't go on protecting Franck. If he's a thief, she will have to turn him in. Or you will."

"The Art Theft Registry and Interpol know about the paintings. But Franck's confession to Kerina is not proof enough."

"The Art Theft Registry?"

"They're headquartered in London. They search for stolen art. Don't worry, Chandler. Once Kerina is gone—"

"You seem so sure."

"Interpol knows that Kerina was never involved; Franck would be the first one to admit it. I've bargained with them. If they wait until Kerina's death, I will help them track Franck Petzold down to the ends of the earth."

"I think you're wrong, but you've been a good friend to Kerina. Would you do one more thing for her? Arrange a concert in Vienna so she can play her Strad one more time?"

"Chandler, she's too sick."

"I want my mother to go out with a song, Jill. That's what she wants. Let her have that chance. You heard the way she played this evening. She can do it. She'll find the strength somehow. Just think about it. That's all I ask."

"Let me sleep on it."

He reached out and ran his finger across her lips. "I love you, Jillian."

"How can you be so certain? We barely know each other."

"Falling in love with you didn't take that long. You're that special someone I've waited for all my life. You haven't given me your answer yet. Will you marry me?"

The spigot dripped, time ticking away, a new day breaking. She looked up, searching his face. Hers was shadowed in the darkness. He felt he was losing her. "It's no, isn't it?"

"For now."

"Why?"

"Kerina needs us. And I want to know whether you can accept me once you know who I really am. What I've done."

"That makes you sound more intriguing," he said.

"I had plans for my future long before I met you."

"London?" And then worriedly, he asked, "Not Santos?"

"No, that was over before I met you. But I planned to go back to London before Thanksgiving. I had an old job waiting for me. But with Kerina so ill, I couldn't walk out on her."

"Will that job still be waiting for you, Jillian?"

"My boss will hold it for me a little longer."

"You're so sure of your future."

"And I want to know what you plan to do with your life. Before it was the army. What now? That government job—the one you can't tell me about? If you take that, I'd never know if you would be home for dinner. Never know whether I would have to lie alone at night worrying about you."

"I won't know for several weeks. They do a thorough check on our background. FBI and all."

The fluttering reflection of the lantern caught the tilt of her nose, the thrust of her jaw, the softness of her lips. He touched her chin—that stubborn, jutting chin—and turned her face back to him. "I want to do the right thing with the rest of my life. To take the right job."

"Are you taking it for Randy?"

"I want to help the people of Bosnia."

"And what happened to music?"

His arm tightened around her narrow waist; her head nestled under his chin. "It's still there, Jillian. Waiting in the shadows. I know I can never play professionally as Kerina does. Doing music reviews won't guarantee a salary. Or health benefits. Or job security. And I won't have my wife supporting me."

Her eyes glistened. "What happened to that 'two shall become one' stuff? At least I'd have a husband home for dinner—even if we had to eat macaroni and cheese."

"Go lightly on the cheese, sweetheart."

"Chandler, doesn't it worry you—my not growing up in your father's church, not always believing the way you do?"

He smiled. "But you do now, don't you? I don't know how or when, but you're different somehow, Jillian."

She flushed with pleasure. "Your mother talked to me when she was in Vienna."

"Sounds like she ran interference for me."

"Ashley meant well."

"Mom didn't corner you with hellfire and brimstone, did she?"

"What's that?"

"Never mind. Dad's got the corner on that one every Sunday."

"So the two of us becoming one does worry him?"

"He's not the one proposing. So tell me what happened."

"After those glorious days on the Riviera—in spite of Santos almost showing up—I was so sure you liked me. But the day you flew back to Vienna, you told me it was over between us."

"That's when I told you about Zineta."

"Yes; I cried for four straight hours."

"Is that why you wouldn't talk to me on the phone?"

"That's why Ashley came to see me. I was a mess. I blamed her for standing in our way. She said she was pleased—my loving you—but there was something more important to settle first."

"And she gave it to you both barrels?"

"We argued. We talked. I cried. She kept me supplied with tissues and stood her ground. I almost threw her out, but before she left she gave me a little book called *The Man Called Saul.*"

"Good choice."

"I threw the book down the hall after her. But ten minutes later I went out and picked it up. No one else wanted it."

He grinned. "We've had rows like that. Mom always wins."

"I spent the next three hours drenching that book with tears. I told God I didn't want Him interfering and messing up my social life or killing my chances with you. I gave up finally and read the words your mother had underlined for me."

"About Saul seeing a blinding light?"

"How did you know?"

"She pulled the same one on me when I was twelve."

"Then it worked for both of us," Jillian said. "I was so scared, and alone in that hotel room. I was sure God was asking me the same question He had asked Saul. I figured I really didn't want to fight His Son. So I quit fighting."

He pulled Jillian tightly against him. "Did you tell Mom?"

"No. I wasn't trying to impress her. And I didn't want you to think I was trying to impress you."

"I know you better than that, Jillian. I can wait. You are dear to me. Worth waiting for."

His lips came down hard on hers, insistent, demanding. She slipped her arms around his neck, drawing him closer, her response long and passionate.

Chapter 33

Jillian stayed by the phone for the next forty-eight hours, placing calls to Vienna that would have been easy in Franck Petzold's capable hands. Exhausted, she leaned back in the wooden chair and smiled across the room at Chandler. He had such an attractive face: the well-defined bone structure, one of strength; the sensitive, finely shaped mouth like his birth mother's. He was clearly Kerina's son. His head cocked her way as he stoked the woodstove.

"Nothing?" he asked. "No invitations?"

"The concert agents can't schedule Kerina for six months. I can't tell them she doesn't have that long—that her strength would be gone by then. But everyone wants to book her."

Chandler capped the stove with its iron lid and prowled around the room. He stopped at the oak sideboard to examine the Bohemian china and crystal glasses before picking up a thin copper plate. "Where did this come from?"

"It's an authentic Rembrandt etching—perhaps a cottage where Rembrandt once stayed. Kerina found it hidden in the lining of her violin case when we came back from New York."

He inspected the plate again. "What was it doing there?"

"Stolen, we think. Franck called Kerina several times asking her to ship it to him. She refuses."

"Jill, if it's a hot item, it can't just sit here and put my grandparents at risk. If you know it was stolen, turn it in."

"No. I promised Karol I wouldn't as long as Kerina is alive. And, Chan, when she's gone, I want that copper plate."

"That sounds crass," he said. "Did you want it for a little memento? You know value when you see it. It's certainly worth more than her diamond earrings. You're not planning to hang it in our flat in London, are you?"

"When I go back to London, I'm turning it over to the Art Theft Registry. That's the agreement. I hand deliver it."

Guardedly, he asked, "You won't ruin Kerina's reputation?"

"She wasn't involved. It will go back to its owner and from there probably to the auction block. It will sell well with Rembrandt's signature and date etched there. Don't worry. No thief expects to find it sitting here with Gretchen's china."

Chandler eased into his grandfather's rocker, his long legs stretched out, his ankles crossed. Jillian forced herself to meet his gaze, dreading the questions that lingered in his sleepless, bloodshot eyes. She ached for him, thinking, *I'll marry him and put the smile back on his face. Be his comfort, companion, lover.* As quickly, she knew her love for him had to be stronger. They had to find their own peace, rake over their beliefs, and lean on the only One who could help them.

"I love you, Chandler. I want so much to help you."

His brows twisted at a rakish angle. "Does that mean things have changed since two nights ago?"

She remembered that night with a blush sitting here in this room, nestled in Chan's warm embrace, and responding to his lips on hers. "Everything is still on hold as long as Kerina needs us. You will stay, won't you?"

"FedEx is holding my job until I get back. And," he said, admitting something new, "my parents wired me two thousand dollars to help out. Not bad, eh? Guess they're crazy about me."

So am I, she thought. She studied him, loving him. She wanted to spend the rest of her life with him, but once he knew that Franck's exile to Moscow was her doing—that she had been planted in Kerina's world to take Kerina down—then he would despise her. Yet she could never marry him without telling him the truth. And once he knew, would he still want her?

She lifted the phone to dial another music agent, but felt distracted by Chandler's smile. She could not pinpoint the exactness, the likeness between Chan and his mother, but it was there in undefined lines: in the twist of his head, in the pensive, searching gaze that met hers; in the way that he smiled. Yet having met Ashley, he was clearly her son as well.

"Are there any other music halls we can try, Jill?"

"I just tried and you wouldn't let me."

"I didn't say a word."

"You didn't have to—I guessed what you were thinking."

"I will have to restrain myself or you will have to come over and sit beside me so I can show you how much I love you."

"That's a tempting offer," she said and prayed that he did not know how erratically her heart was beating.

The phone rang. She snatched it up, glad for an excuse. "Yes, this is

Jillian Ingram. Helmut, you did get my message?"

From the other end of the wire came the resolute, seductive voice of Helmut Manchurin, the tenor soloist that Kerina had helped ten years ago when his career was floundering.

He said, "*Liebling*, I just this minute picked up your message on my answering machine. How special of you to call."

She filled in his features from memory. Dark eyes. Dark hair. Five-feet-ten. A bladelike nose. At thirty-six, he swooped onto the stage these days to a thundering applause. But best of all, he was Kerina's dear friend and maybe he could help them.

"Liebling, have you decided to marry me at last? We can run off to Italy tomorrow."

"I'm busy tomorrow." She laughed. "Besides, I'm thinking about marrying someone else. An American this time."

He groaned. "My dear girl, I knew I was too late. How is my friend Kerina? Maybe she will fly to Italy with me."

"Helmut, Kerina is ill. Seriously ill."

He slipped back into his strong German accent. "What's wrong? I thought she looked unwell when we dined in Munich recently."

"But she wants to play one more concert in Vienna."

"That would not be a problem with her marvelous reputation."

"Booking soon enough would. She has terminal cancer."

The humor went out of his words. "How long does she have?"

"She may not see another summer in Vienna."

There came a long, decided pause and then, "Jillian, give me a few days. Let me see what I can do."

What Helmut did took thirty-six hours. What he accomplished was an opportunity for Kerina. He was unusually jovial when he called Jillian a few days later. "I am in concert in Vienna in ten days. There isn't much time for publicity, but my manager is arranging everything." He laughed. "One stipulation."

She held her breath, certain he would want her to run away to Italy with him. "Kerina must play at least three numbers."

Relief poured over her. "Agreed."

"This is the plan then. I am guest soloist that night, and Kerina will be featured as my special guest."

"Which won't hurt your reputation any."

"True. First I will sing 'Valencia.' Then we will do one duet. 'In All My Dreams.'" She heard the subdued crack in his words and knew suddenly that it was not a pat on the back that he wanted. He was helping a friend in the kindest way he could. Without Kerina's support, his dream of success would have died ten years ago. "The orchestra has agreed to play background for Kerina for two numbers. They'll have to know ahead of time which ones."

"Let's settle on the Brahms 'Lullaby' and a Strauss waltz. Oh Helmut, thank you. How can we ever pay you back?"

Helmut told her, laughing, "Decide on Italy someday, Liebling."

Jillian made two more calls. One a surprise for Chandler, the other a trap for Franck Petzold. She gave Ashley the dates for Vienna as quickly as she could. "David and I will be there," Ashley told her. "Could we stay at the Empress Isle again?"

"I'll book rooms for all of us there, but don't tell Chan you're coming. It's a surprise. Right now, he's out walking arm in arm with Kerina. I can see them from my window looking the picture of peace and solitude with snowflakes falling on them."

"My son is happy then?"

"It's hard to know whether he's pretending or not."

"No, Chandler is genuine. He has our blessing for whatever happiness he can give Kerina."

Jillian's second long-distance call was to Brooks Rankin at the Coventry Art Theft Registry in London. "It's Jillian Ingram, Brooks. I'm calling from Prague."

She told him about the concert, gave him the place and date. "Can you find a way to let Franck Petzold know about the concert? And will you tell him that Kerina Rudzinski is ill—dying?"

She heard Brooks chewing something and chugging down great gulps of the coffee he kept on his desk. "We'll pass the word along through the art world through the Black Market if we have to. But I thought you wanted to protect him, Miss Ingram?"

"Only while Kerina is alive."

He voiced his disapproval and then in a wheezy monotone said, "If Petzold steps off Russian soil, he's ours."

"I know. But he has a right to make that decision himself. And you must agree—Kerina is not to witness his arrest."

He accepted the bargain grudgingly. "It's Petzold the Registry and Interpol want. If he goes to Vienna, Miss Ingram, we expect you to call us and let us know he's there. That will make our job simpler. And salvage what's left of yours. If it weren't for Joel Gramdino, you would have been out the door long ago."

Thanks, she thought. *But even if Franck comes, he won't bring the paintings. So what have you gained? I will give you Franck, but it will mark the end of my career.*

⌒

Three hours before the concert, Franck Petzold arrived in Vienna in his friend's private jet. "Are you coming to the concert with me?" he asked Jokhar Gukganov.

"I have business matters to tend to—and I understand the Academy of Fine Arts has another Impressionist collection on display and—I have my caviar and vodka. I won't be lonely."

"Don't take any risks this time."

Jokhar's harsh laughter filled the cabin. "You are the one taking a risk." As they parted, Jokhar said, "You are aware that there are some lovely paintings in the concert hall? Why not make your evening there worthwhile?"

"I have no reason to build my art collection," Franck said. *Before, Kerina was my reason, and she is dying.*

"And no desire to split the profits from stolen masterpieces? Ah! I see by your face you find that distasteful. You have lost interest in life, my friend. What you need is the love of a good woman."

"I've lost the love of a good woman." Franck shook his jacket free of wrinkles and checked his watch. "I plan to take Miss Rudzinski to dinner before I come back."

Jokhar's doleful eyes narrowed. "We have filed a flight plan for one in the morning. If you are not here by then, my friend, we return to Moscow without you." A mirthless smile touched his mouth. "Which wouldn't be a bad thing. You have a number of artifacts and masterpieces in your place that should be mine."

Under his breath Franck muttered, "You have tricked me."

Forty minutes later, Franck swept into the swank, pillared lobby at the Empress Isle Hotel. He hurried past the concierge and the registration desk and avoided the busy elevators. Without even a glance up at the gilded paintings he had coveted on his last visit, he ran up the winding staircase to the second floor. For a moment he stood outside Kerina's suite listening to the sweet sound of laughter inside.

She is happy again, he thought.

She was always happy moments before a concert, drawing from a reserve deep within herself. Her troubling headaches gone, forgotten. Other musicians went tense and jittery, demanding the impossible of their managers, screaming and tossing things. But Kerina was the sweetest to him just before she lifted her violin. The brass knob responded to his gentle twist. He opened the door and stepped inside.

"Franck! Franck!" Kerina cried. "Oh Franck, you did come."

She crossed the room to him slowly, looking thinner but never more lovely in her shantung gown. A young forty-five! Elegant as ever, even in illness. Only her eyes convinced him that she was seriously ill. He held out his hands. She took them and he leaned down and brushed her cheek with a kiss.

"Dear, dear Franck, why did you come back?"

"Because you need me," he said confidently. "For almost thirty years—since you were sixteen—I have never missed your concerts. I will be safe. Don't worry about me. Just play well this evening."

"I will. I am ready." She leaned against him. "Everything is complete now. So many of those I love are here."

He slipped his arm around her waist and felt her wince. *The cancer is spreading*, he remembered. *Invading her brittle bones.*

His gaze swept the room and then more leisurely lingered on each face. The McClarens were there, and he recognized Kerina's two childhood friends from Prague. Ashley Reynolds sat in a wingback chair next to them. Surely the tall, silver-haired man in black tie was her husband. John? David? Something like that. He nodded politely to Kerina's parents sitting side by side on the bed. He had always tolerated the gruff manner of the old man and respected the benevolent smile on Gretchen Rudzinski's face. The handsome young man holding Jillian Ingram's hand had to be Kerina's son, his likeness to Bill VanBurien striking.

The stranger by the dresser said, "Güten Tag, Petzold."

Franck recognized the voice first and then the face as that of Helmut Manchurin, the tenor soloist, one of the many musicians that Kerina had befriended during her long career.

His gaze went back to Kerina. He cupped her cheeks, felt the smooth softness of her skin, looked into those kind, hazel eyes. "My dear Kerina, I missed you. Life is empty without you. But, alas, I have no ticket for this evening's concert."

"I have one for you, Franck," Jillian told him. "The seat next to mine. Fifth row back. Chandler won't be using his—he's going backstage with Kerina."

Frank's place for thirty years. Franck's position.

Jillian crossed the room toward the door. "I'll get the ticket for you.

I have things to do anyway. Phone calls to make."

Is she boldly warning me that she will betray me again? he thought. Aloud he asked, "Busy as always before the concert?"

"You know the routine."

His arm tightened around Kerina. "Give me a few hours, Miss Ingram. Just a few hours with Kerina."

Franck stepped aside so Jillian could leave. He wondered what the others in the room would make of his request. Wondered if Kerina understood. They had always understood each other.

She looked up into his face, the woman he had loved from the day he first saw her running across the fields outside of Prague. He knew as he glimpsed the sudden sadness in her eyes that she was aware he would never leave Vienna. He could flee now before Jillian completed her phone call. But, no. He had come back because Kerina needed him. Because he loved her.

~

That evening Jillian sat in the fifth row of the music hall with Franck Petzold sitting in the aisle seat beside her. She had looked forward to Helmut's concert, yet halfway through the program, she could not recall what songs had been sung. Had she done the right thing sending for Franck? He sat tight-lipped, somber, without joy. Whatever differences they had, she respected him for coming. Whatever he had done in the past had nothing to do with Kerina. She moistened her lips. Had Brooks notified the polizei and Interpol? What if they arrived during Kerina's final number? But what she dreaded most was facing Kerina afterwards.

She forced her wandering thoughts back to center stage as Helmut Manchurin belted out the last phrase of "Valencia," his body swaying with the music, his hand to his heart as he sang. The orchestra formed a semicircle behind him, some tapping their feet to the music, others swaying gently. He was backed by the triumphant sound of the horns. The pure tones of the string section. The distinct, sweet notes of the flutes. The reverberating echo of the cymbals. The rhythmic beat of the drums by a female in a chic black dress. The conductor brought them to the final note, and then, when the applause finally subsided to a ripple, Helmut half-turned to the stairs behind him and announced his special guest.

"Please welcome my friend—the lovely Kerina Rudzinski."

The Viennese stood to their feet applauding Kerina as she came down the blue velvet steps on the arm of a handsome young man in a black tuxedo. Exquisitely, courtly, one step at a time. Kerina came with a willowy gracefulness, the audience never guessing that she was weak, ill, in constant pain.

She wore her cranberry-red gown from Paris—low-cut, off the shoulder, the flaring skirt revealing her elegant ankles. Ashley and the hotel seamstress had come to the rescue with a needle and thread, taking in a tuck or two so no one could guess how loosely the gown now hung on Kerina. Franck had fastened the bloodstone pendant around her neck. Cosmetics hid the pallid skin and the dark circles under her eyes.

The stage lights highlighted the reddish flecks in her hair as Helmut stepped forward to meet her. Chandler lifted the violin from its case and handed it to Kerina. He exited the stage, leaving her with an accomplished tenor soloist and one of the finest orchestras in the world.

As Kerina raised her bow, Helmut said, "My dreams of singing all over Europe would never have been fulfilled without Kerina Rudzinski. And Miss Rudzinski tells me that all of her dreams have been fulfilled in this city that she loves so much. We join voice and violin to give you 'In All My Dreams.'"

The audience was enchanted, and from some strength deep within her, Kerina followed their duet with two violin solos: Brahms' "Lullaby" and Johann Strauss'"On the Beautiful Blue Danube." And for an encore—because her audience would not let her go—she chose selections from Tchaikovsky's *Swan Lake*, her music filling the vast auditorium, her bow gliding with the same grace as a dazzling white swan on the Danube.

As she played, the polizei strolled down the center aisle to where Franck Petzold sat. Jillian's lips went dry as one of them tapped his shoulder. Franck turned to her. "I asked you for a few hours, Jillian. For just a few hours with Kerina."

"I'm sorry. Truly I am, Franck," she whispered.

He made no effort to bolt but quietly said, "Thank God for the blinding stage lights. Kerina won't see me being led away. Tell her I had a plane to catch. Will you do that for me?"

Nodding, Jillian fought back tears. It was Franck Petzold's final performance. He stood with great dignity, stroked his beard, straightened his back, and shrugged off the manacled grip of the polizei. Jill watched him take four steps. Then he glanced back, touched his fingers to his unsmiling lips, and blew a kiss in Kerina Rudzinski's direction, saluting Kerina in his own way as he had always done.

On the last triumphant note, Helmut was the first to applaud Kerina.

As he lifted her hand to his lips, the audience rose to their feet. But Kerina, who had thrived on the adoration of her audiences—she who had always blown kisses to then, lifted her Stradivarius, one palm extended, offering praise to the One who had waited long years to receive it.

Kerina's face turned radiant. While the applause still filled the auditorium, she placed her Strad in its case and reached out her hand to Chandler, who had been standing offstage. He stepped to her side and presented her with a bouquet of red roses.

Holding them, she took the microphone from Helmut Manchurin and waited until the audience settled back into their seats. Then she said, "My dear friends, this has been a glorious evening for me. Truly this is the city of my dreams. You have given me so much. You have always welcomed me. Always loved me."

To Jillian she sounded short of breath, but she went on. "This has been such a special day—I wish it could go on forever. You have shared your hearts with me. Now, I would like to share my greatest treasure with you."

She smiled up at Chandler. "This is my son, Chandler Reynolds."

Murmurings swept through the audience. Then, as the Viennese had always done, they stood again to applaud Kerina Rudzinski—and to welcome her son.

～

Days later, Kerina collapsed in the lobby of the Empress Isle Hotel after spending the day riding through the city she loved, strolling through the park, and walking along the Danube River. She was coughing as Chandler lifted her in his strong arms, streaks of blood trickling from the corner of her mouth.

"That was silly of me," she said. "I am sorry."

"We did too much, Kerina. You're exhausted."

"Yes, Chandler. But no ambulance. . . . Please."

"All right. We'll use Jillian's car."

Hours later, she was resting in her hospital room when the doctor met with Chandler in the lobby. "Miss Rudzinski is very ill. Are there other family members to notify?"

"We're all here," Chandler said. "But I don't understand what's happening."

He smiled patiently. "Cancer has invaded your mother's body. The lungs. The bones." He shook his head. "There's been a slight hemorrhage, perhaps more blood clots in her lungs."

"Then do something about it."

"We can give her medicine to try and dissolve the clots. Or offer aggressive treatment, more chemotherapy, but she has refused."

Chandler's knees buckled. "So what happens? What are the risks?"

"A severe hemorrhage. A stroke. We have to wait and see."

"Can we take her back to Prague?"

"Don't move her, son," David said, stepping forward.

The doctor nodded. "Mr. Reynolds is right."

Jillian slipped her arm through Chandler's. "This is the city she loves more than any place in the world. The city that welcomed her and loved her. She's just come home again, Chan."

He brushed them aside and walked to the window to look out on the river flowing gently through the city. He braced his hand against the pane, felt the coolness against his palm. "She wanted to ride on the Danube. I promised her we'd do that tomorrow."

Jillian touched his arm. "Chandler, she hates hospitals. Can't we take her back to the Empress Isle and get a room that looks out over the Danube?"

The doctor had walked up behind them. "I don't recommend moving her. We have a wing here at the hospital that gets a view of the river. We can transfer her there. She'll get good medical care here."

Chandler glanced at the doctor through the reflected glass. "How long does she have?"

"Days. Weeks. Don't ask us to be heroic."

Chandler glanced at Karol and Gretchen, agonizing for them, and then he faced the doctor again. "It's happening so fast. Kerina doesn't look that sick. She's strong." And then with his throat tighter than a drum, he faced the bitter truth. "We want the right to be with her, twenty-four hours a day."

The doctor's gaze strayed around the crowded lobby.

"They're all family, sir. Her parents. My parents."

"And distant cousins, I assume." But there was a twinkle in his eyes. "I will write the order for the family, Herr Reynolds."

～

Five days later Chandler sat by Kerina's bedside as dawn broke. They were waiting for the nurse to come in and restart the IV infusion when she said, "Chandler, I want to watch the mist rise over the river one more time."

"We could push her bed to the window," Jillian suggested.

"I have another idea." He winked at Kerina, pulled back the covers, wrapped her in a fleecy robe, lifted her gently into his arms and carried her to the window. Together they watched the morning mist rise above the Danube, watched the river wind its way slowly through the city they both loved.

"An der schonen blauen Donau," she whispered.

He felt her chest convulse, knew that she was fighting off another coughing spell, "Strauss put the blueness in the water with his song," she said. "History made it a legend. And legend tells us that those who love see the blue in the river."

"Then it is a cobalt blue this morning, Kerina."

The sun formed a burst of colors on the horizon, the spires and domes of Vienna sparkling like glittering diamonds. At last Kerina rested her head on his shoulder. "I'm tired now."

He carried her back to the bed and they made her as comfortable as they could. "My violin is yours now, Chandler."

He nodded. "I'll take it everywhere I go."

She winced from the pain. "Any place in mind?"

"London with Jillian. Bosnia someday. California."

"Good." The word caught in another spasm.

As he fingered her worn copy of T. S. Eliot's poems, she said, "Read to me. *The Waste Land.*"

Chandler's voice remained deep and strong as he read, "April is the cruellest month, breeding Lilacs out of the dead land—"

She wrapped her hand over his. "Your father loved to quote those words. I felt that way for years. You were born in April, Chandler, and I lost you then. Each year as your birthday rolled around, I dreaded the coming of memory and desire." Her eyes searched his face. "I am so sorry. I always wanted to spend your birthday with you, and now I won't even be here for the next one."

"We could celebrate early."

"No." She rested and found strength to go on. "April has become special to me now. It was April when I heard from you again. Eliot should have written, April is the happiest of months, but then he did not know you." Again she rested, waiting for more strength. "The lilacs and the dull roots of my life have come together, Chandler. They have come full circle."

Kerina was dying, and she had told Chandler twice that eternal matters were a private affair. She had brushed him off when he talked of God, raising a wall between them. But could he let her go that way?

It was Friday afternoon before he found the courage to say, "God loves you, Kerina."

Her dark eyes settled on him. "How do you know that?"

He felt awkward, foolish. He was clinging to some words from his dad's sermons, hanging on for dear life like a man caught in an ebb tide and being swept out to sea. But it was his birth mother, not Chandler, drowning in her own fluids, slipping beneath the surface, dying. He was desperate to help her.

"How do you know God loves me?" she rasped.

"God sent all the proof we need. He sent His Son into the world to die for us."

"Here in Prague?" she murmured distractedly.

"Anywhere. No city limits." He didn't tell her they were still in Vienna. In the last few hours, her speech had slowed. She had drifted back to the land of her childhood and he let her. He saw no harm in it. He wondered what kind of unprepared sermon his father would call it. But he sensed how David Reynolds felt when he stood behind his pulpit in clerical garb and reached out in love to drowning people. "God gave His only Son, Kerina."

She gasped for air, struggling for each breath. Struggling to reach the surface, to come back to him, to keep her focus on him. "Gave. . .His Son away. . .like I did?"

He eased another pillow behind her back and groped for the right answer, "Gave Him up from His place of fellowship. And sent Him to earth with all the angels looking on."

Kerina's chest heaved, collapsed, did not rise again.

"Breathe," he begged her. "Breathe."

Beneath her bed linens, her chest rose again. "No flowers, Chandler. . . . No flowery words."

Her despair knocked him down a peg. He kept to the facts this time. No flowers. No flowery words. No angels thrown in.

"God loved you so much, Mother, that He sent Jesus to die for your sins. He cleans the slate if you ask Him."

"Will. . .He wipe away the guilt of giving you away?"

Chandler swallowed the rock in his throat as his gaze strayed to Jillian. She was biting her lower lip, listening. His eyes went back to his mother's face. "I forgave you. And God is a whole lot bigger than I am and much better at forgiving." His deep voice wavered. "He loves you just the way you are. Blunders and all. Just believe in Him. Trust Him."

As she sank back against the pillows, he took her cold, limp hand and held it. The tears balancing on her long dark lashes fell, rolling over her high cheeks and down the pallid skin. This time he was certain that the tears were not for him, but between Kerina's God and herself. He used one corner of the bedsheet to stem the flow. The tears came again. He let them.

At last she quit fighting and allowed her swollen eyelids to close. She looked peaceful, but he watched her breathing grow shallow, saw the dark blotches appear on her thin arms.

"Let her rest, Chandler. Go lie down yourself."

"No, Jillian, I won't leave her."

"Chan, I called Kerina's parents and left a message for them to come back as quickly as they can."

He nodded. "I know they said their good-byes this morning. But they will want to be here. I pray that they make it."

Chandler was still holding Kerina's hand and Jillian on the other side patting her arm, when Kerina's exhausted body finally relaxed in sleep.

She awoke once, her eyes unfocused.

"I'm here, Mother," he said. "Right here with you."

A smile touched Kerina's lips. Then she drifted again, this time deeply into unconsciousness. Moments later, Jillian shook her, but she would not awaken again.

"She's gone," Jillian said.

"I know."

He laid Kerina's hand gently to her side and touched her still warm, soft face.

Jillian put her lips against Kerina's cheek and kissed her. "Good-bye, sweet friend."

She slipped around the end of the hospital bed and put her arms around Chandler's neck. He made no attempt to hide his grief. His eyes brimmed with tears, the tears he could not shed while his mother was dying.

"Chandler," Jillian whispered. "Do you think they have violins in heaven?"

He clasped her hand. "Harps. Choirs. I don't know about violins."

"If they do—if she's found one, I'm sure Kerina is already playing it for God's Son."

He nodded, comforted. Jillian pressed her cheek against his, and utter stillness filled the room.

Epilogue

Chandler arrived in London in the middle of June with memories of his childhood replaying themselves in his mind, like dusty but cherished relics. *Rocking on the porch in Ashley's arms at the old homestead in Everdale. Being pushed higher and higher on the swing by the gazebo. Climbing the picket gate. His mother swooping him up in her arms and singing, "London bridge is falling down, falling down."*

Why those particular memories lingered he did not know. There was little else of those first three years of his life in Everdale that he could recall on his own, except the pungent smell of wood smoke and dead leaves burning, or the spring air scented with honeysuckle and roses. The sound of twigs snapping beneath his feet as he walked in the woods with his father. And the sound of the piano as he sat on the bench with his mother, picking out the tune of "London Bridge," one note at a time.

Jillian Ingram had awakened his longing to see London.

And now he was here with that childish rhyme running competition with the sights and sounds of London proper. He stood watching the broad sweep of the Thames, a deep blue this morning as he stood above its embankment, and watched it wind its way toward the Tower Bridge down the river a pace. Across the waters lay the historical landmarks as sturdy and steadfast as the Londoners themselves. The Houses of Parliament bigger than life, flying the Union Jack. Big Ben ticking away in the Clock Tower and booming its hour-bell. The Westminster Abbey with its High Altar and oak coronation chair. Chandler brought it down to his own generation, remembering the cadenced steps of the Welsh Guards that had borne the casket of the Princess of Wales through those massive doors.

If he crossed one of the bridges that spanned the Thames, he would be within walking distance of the Queen's Residence and have a better view of the Royal Standard fluttering from the top of Buckingham Palace. Instead he took note of the rain clouds beginning to form a canopy over the city. Chandler had ordered sunshine for his first day in London, not a cloudburst. He had planned his arrival in London three weeks early to surprise Jillian. He knew now that he had arrived three days late for the trooping of the colors on the Queen's birthday, something that Kerina would have loved. She had been like his father David with his ties to Scottish ancestry. They both liked pomp and ceremony and would have enjoyed the flying past by the R.A.F. and the gun salutes to the Queen.

Almost four months had slipped by since Kerina's death. It had been almost that long since he had seen Jillian. In her letters, Jillian boasted of her perfect view of the heart of London from her windows. He checked the address in his hand and crossed the bridge. If Jillian's flat was anywhere near here, she was right in the middle of a business district.

He checked the numbers again, and perplexed, turned to the constable with a telescopic baton in his hand. The chin strap held the policeman's helmet in place, but it didn't cut off his smile. Chandler remembered that Jillian's only run-in with the law was dating a London bobby; he sincerely hoped this was not the same man.

"I'm looking for my girl's flat. She's moved just recently." The bobby studied the address for a second. "Won't find it on these streets," came the friendly reply. "Believe that's the Art Theft Registry, two blocks on." He pointed with his baton. "If you hurry, you'll be there before the storm hits."

Art Theft Registry? An uneasy discomfiture churned inside, like the low ebb feeling he had after Kerina's funeral when Jillian refused to wear the diamond ring he bought her. She had insisted on time alone to grieve for her friend. He understood. He had gone through it after Randy died in Bosnia. But Chandler called Jillian weekly, sometimes twice a week to tell her how much he loved her.

Jillian was friendly and cheerful, but she still held back. While he despaired over what had gone wrong these last four months, he spotted her hurrying along the street in a stunning gray business suit, her tawny hair flecked with glimmerings of gold. He ran to catch up to her.

"Jillian," he cried, expecting her to break into a smile and fly into his arms.

She whirled around, looking stunned. "Chandler! What are you doing here?"

"I came over to get married."

Her cheeks turned scarlet. "I was going to send you my home address before you came—but you're here three weeks early."

"I missed you. I wanted to surprise you. Look, is this the kind of greeting you give the guy you're going to marry?"

She gave him a quick hug, brushed his cheek with a kiss.

Uncertain now, he tapped the small case under his arm. "I came in time for the London Symphony. I took in some samples of my work to the *Standard*—a review on the symphony and an article on my friend Kemal Kovic, the cellist in Tuzla."

"And?" she asked softly.

"I was hoping for a hearing—for a chance to prove myself."

She touched his cheek and ran her fingers over his lips. "And you were disappointed?"

"I didn't even get past the receptionist," he admitted. "Kemal wrote a beautiful composition during the shelling of Tuzla. I'm just trying to get it published."

"Let Kemal help himself, Chandler. Let him fly over to London or Vienna. You can't afford to worry about some musician in Bosnia. Worry about establishing yourself as a music critic."

"He's my friend, Jillian."

She wiped the raindrops from his cheek. "Oh Chandler, you can't carry Bosnia with you forever."

The corner of his mouth twisted. "I can't leave Bosnia behind either. Sweetheart, could we go somewhere and talk? Just the two of us?"

Above them the sign to the Coventry Art Theft Registry creaked on its hinges, caught by a sudden breeze from the approaching storm. It was an artistic, gilded sign with what looked like the face of a Mona Lisa engraved on it. The wind whipped around them. Raindrops started to fall.

"Chandler, if you are expecting to get somewhere in the music world, it's who you know that counts. If you weren't so proud, I could help you. We could live on my salary for a while."

"I told you I won't let a wife support me. And you know how I feel. Opportunities should come from honest hard work and because you meet the qualifications. And I do."

"Luckily for you, my father is in town."

"I wasn't expecting to meet your father today."

"Nor he you. But he insists on meeting the man who wants to marry me. Besides, he knows the people who could help you." She glanced at her watch. "I'm late for a luncheon appointment. No, Chandler, it's not what you think. I work here. It's part of my job to meet with an art collector."

The sign swayed above them, spraying water on them.

"You work here?"

"Yes. At the Art Theft Registry."

"I thought you were working as a publicist again."

"I didn't tell you that. So don't give me the third degree."

She brushed her wet hair from her forehead with quick, irritable strokes. Something was wrong. With him? With them? She looked annoyed, petulant.

"Chandler, it's not a new job. I've been working for the Registry for three years."

"But you worked for Kerina."

"Sort of. Partly. Oh, I did both."

He stared at her, trying to put it all together, but melting as he always did when he made eye contact with those sapphires.

"You're into art theft?"

"Into recovering stolen masterpieces. I'm sorry, Chandler. I was going to tell you."

"Like I was going to surprise you. It looks like we were no more ready for surprises than we were for the rainstorm that's pelting us."

He eased her back against the building, but there was no real shelter from the downpour. If they didn't shrink, their good suits would. "You worked for my mother for a year or more. And now you're telling me that this creaking sign above us—"

"That's right. It's my job. Where I do my nine-to-five every day. Except we do overtime when we're on a case."

"Was Kerina a case?"

"That was part of my job as an art investigator. I was assigned to the team working on the concert thefts. Seven years of them."

"And you thought Kerina was involved?"

"At first. I told you, you didn't really know me." Her eyes filled with tears. "I said you wouldn't like me when you did."

"That doesn't make sense. Of course I know you. Look. Look, I'm going to go back across that street, walk to the middle of the bridge and start over again. You pretend you're expecting me."

She was starting to giggle now and managed to wipe a mixture of tears and rain from her eyes. "I love you, Chandler. And I loved your mother. At first I really did think she was involved with those thefts."

"You didn't trust her?"

"I wasn't there for long before I believed in her and fought to prove her innocence."

"And Franck? Franck Petzold? What about him?"

"What about him?" she repeated.

"The concert ends and he's gone. That was tough on Kerina. He didn't really go back to Moscow, did he? You lied about that."

"I was just doing my job, Chandler. And I didn't lie. You never asked me about it." She ran her hand distractedly through her limp hair again, pushing it away from her face. "Franck was a thief; don't you understand that, Chan? A common ordinary thief."

"He was my mother's friend."

"Those stolen masterpieces were worth millions. Recovering them was my responsibility—the same way you think that all of Bosnia is dependent on you. I loved Kerina as a friend. Don't forget that, Chandler Reynolds!"

"Did my mother know who you were? What you did?"

"No. I never had to tell her. We were friends. That's all that mattered. But in the beginning we honestly thought she might be working for Franck and transporting those works of art in her luggage. Kerina was well received in Moscow—customs gave her luggage cursory inspections. After all, she was the world-famous violinist. The beloved Kerina Rudzinski."

"She wasn't a thief." He turned and strolled off in a huff.

"I told you! I knew you wouldn't like me once you knew the truth," she called after him. "I was afraid this would happen. That's why I wouldn't take your engagement ring in Vienna."

He stopped in his tracks and turned back. The half-carat diamond was burning a hole in his inside pocket. He had planned to give her the ring on the bank of the Thames and then take her to dinner. He certainly didn't plan on the rain. "You deceived me, Jillian."

"Oh Chandler, I thought you grew up on forgiveness?"

"I did, but I was never good at putting it into practice."

"Go on then. Run away from the truth."

"If I did, I'd be running away from you."

"I don't care—but I do care. I defended Kerina."

He thought about it. The rain was washing his brain clear. Jillian had given Kerina some of the best days of her life. "She never really knew about Franck, did she?"

"I think she knew. But their friendship went back a long way. She protected him. And it took courage for Franck to come back and be with Kerina. Try to forgive him. Try to forgive me."

He felt like a drowned rat, the two of them standing outside shouting at each other like peevish children as the people of London hurried around them. The rain splashed down, waterlogging his expensive tweed jacket.

He looked at Jillian and broke into sudden laughter, his anger dissipating with the rain. "You're all wet. But I still want to marry you."

She gave him a grudging smile. "It rains a lot here. I didn't want you to come early. I just moved into a new flat."

"What was wrong with the old one?"

"It wasn't big enough for two. I still have to put up the curtains. All I have now are cartons all over the place."

"I'll help you unpack."

"But I wanted to surprise you," she wailed.

"But you don't like surprises, Jillian."

"I do if I plan them. Do you like walking in the rain?"

He took a step toward her. "Did it a lot in the army."

"But did you like it?"

"It was a muddy mess. . .and you weren't there with me." He stood facing her now. "I am serious about marrying you. I don't care about the concert thefts. You can explain them to me later. And I don't care whether the boxes are unpacked. We can do it together, but, Jill, I really don't know how I'm going to make a living."

She reached out and tentatively touched his cheek. "It doesn't matter, even if you take that government job."

"Maybe I won't. Maybe I better."

"Doesn't matter. The truth is I can't imagine life without you, Chan. I love you. If the CIA sends you back to Bosnia, I'll get a dog to keep me company. And I'll sleep in the living room so I won't know you're not home."

"You're crazy. You can't coop a dog up in an apartment all day. They were meant to run free."

"So was I. So why do I still want to marry you? Maybe I'll get a house cat to keep me company when you're gone."

"I hate cats, Jillian."

He was close enough to see the tears in her eyes now. "Santos and I were engaged once," she admitted. "And he changed his mind before the wedding."

"I won't change my mind. Or hurt you like he did. I love you. You have to marry me. Mother likes you. Both of them did."

"What about your dad?"

"You're not marrying him. But he's willing to tie the knot."

"You mean go all the way to California?"

"My folks would like that."

"But *my* dad wouldn't."

"Well, it is a long way to Dad's church."

"Let me call my dad. He lives outside of London. He's a great cook.

Steaks mostly. Has a fireplace to dry us out. He wants to give his approval."

"Oh," Chan said. "You told me he checks out the eyes."

"He does, but you'll pass. I told him that your eyes are the color of autumn leaves."

"Bet that went over big."

"You'll pass inspection?"

He held out his arms and she went to him. The rain had put a sparkle in her sapphires. He brushed back the tawny wet hair from her cheeks. "You're beautiful even if you are all wet. Would you consider walking along the banks of the Thames with me?"

"Now? In this rainstorm?"

"We're already drenched, Jillian." He wouldn't let her go, ever again. He kept his arms around her. "I had it all planned, Jill. I thought it would be a sunny day, and since we don't have the Danube, I was going to take you to the banks of the Thames, give you a dozen red roses and put a diamond on your finger. . . . Could you pretend that it's a sunny day?"

"Do I have to pretend I'm holding a bouquet of roses?"

"Afraid so. Didn't have time to buy the flowers."

She leaned back her head, the rain washing over her lovely face and smiled as his lips came down on hers urgently, tenderly.

Minutes later the two of them were running, laughing, splashing through the puddles. Dancing along the streets of London, hand in hand. Dashing lightheartedly toward the banks of the Thames. Together, outstripping the wind and the rain.

WILLOWS ON THE WINDRUSH

Dedication

To Sandra
from the aunt who loves you!

Prologue

Sydney Barrington ran along the riverbank, her bare feet leaving shallow imprints on the hard-packed sand, the chilly breeze of an early spring morning snapping at her slender legs. She jogged against the wind with strong, even strides, her somber face turned to the dusky sun, her chestnut brown hair wind-tossed and tangled. Across the river, the melted snows of winter had turned into torrents cascading over the mountain cliff, the deluge crashing and thundering against the weather-beaten rocks in a vigorous display of power.

Sydney enjoyed this time of year in the Pacific Northwest—the closing of one season, the beginning of another. Even more, she sought comfort in these solitary moments by the river with the roaring waterfalls teasing her memory with shadowy images and stirring emotions both happy and sad. In her mind, one voice played out, time and again.

"You can't run away from responsibility, Sydney." Her father's voice. Always calling her back. *"You're a Barrington, Syd. Don't ever forget it."*

But she wasn't a Barrington. Not really. She was a Barrington in name only.

The memory broke. Sydney jogged on, pacing herself to the fast rhythm of the water as it roared and tumbled over the rocks. She sensed its frenzy, knew its rage, wanted its unstoppable freedom. She had everything and should be content, grateful.

But at the moment Sydney felt as though she had nothing of her own choosing. Her whole life had been designed by the couple who had adopted her. Doting parents. Dead parents. She had inherited everything from the Barringtons, even the international defense company that Aaron Barrington had started from scratch. But she didn't want to partner with a dead father for the rest of her life. She longed for a future of her own, for a purpose not inherited.

No one seeing her now would recognize her as the elegant, successful chief executive from Barrington Enterprises—envied by some for her wealth and position, feared by others for her drive and expectations. Not even her dear, charming Randolph Iverson could guess how desperate she felt competing in a global market, pouring her life into expanding Barrington Enterprises for her dead father. It was an enormous job for anyone; Herculean for a woman barely thirty. The biggest contract of her career lay at her fingertips—the bid on two British carriers. She wanted to build them and prove to the world—to her dead father—that she could live up to the Barrington name.

As she increased her pace, savoring the freedom of running alone, another memory joggled her mind: her father holding her on his lap in his leather chair on her seventh birthday.

"And what do you want to be when you grow up, little birthday girl?"

"A wife and mommy," she said, as she cradled her baby doll in her arms. "I dropped her, Daddy, so I put a bandage on her head."

"I see that."

"Maybe I'll be a nurse and take care of little children."

He took the doll from her and dropped it nonchalantly on the floor beside his chair, then tousled Sydney's hair. "Honey, when you grow up, you won't have time for babies and dolls. Any daughter of mine is going to work with me. Now, let's go get my briefcase and I'll show you some blueprints of a fighter jet—then you'll understand how important mathematics will be to you."

She had followed him, feeling belittled and ashamed, hot tears of disappointment burning behind her eyes as they were doing now.

Above the riverbank, clumps of lantana shrubs split the winter-hardened earth in a creamy carpet of tangerine swirls. How often when she was a child her mother had helped her cut their tiny flowers for bridal bouquets for her Barbie dolls.

She ached, thinking of her mom—that gentle woman who loved Aaron Barrington—who patiently tended her garden. Before the first frost of autumn, her mother always donned boots and garden gloves to tackle her perennials. Sydney could see her now, plunging a pitchfork into the knotty roots of the lantana and splitting them in two. Then, wiping her brow, she'd kneel down and replant them, patting the soil ever so gently.

"There. See how easy it is, Sydney, to dig at the tough roots and start all over again? These plants will spread and grow again in the spring and summer, and, if I live long enough, I shall enjoy the fruits of my labor."

Sydney felt like those perennials, the prongs of the pitchfork digging into her own tangled and twisted roots. The river thundered beside her, smashing into the rocks in the riverbed. Churning and spinning into whirlpools, like the whirlpools of memory sucking her into their undertow with splintered images of those last moments with her parents.

"You should go with us," Aaron Barrington had said as they stood at the boarding gate at Kennedy International. "I want you to be familiar with our foreign facilities."

"I've been abroad several times, Dad. And I know about your shipyard along the River Tyne," she teased. "I've been there."

He had poured millions into buying it. Aaron's British faux pas, his board of directors had called it. His boondoggle. Even Sydney's mother, who never questioned her husband's business moves, had considered the acquiring of an English shipyard a mistake of sizable proportion, an error in judgment.

"I'll make a go of that shipyard, Syd. Wait and see. And now just say you'll go with us, and we'll catch the next plane."

She glanced at her mother standing silently there, so short beside Aaron's towering frame. "Not this time, Dad. I'm looking into graduate courses in social work or nursing. I still want to work with children and carve out a life for myself."

Disappointment filled his dark eyes. "After all of the plans your mother and I made for you? You don't need more schooling to take over the company. I'll teach you anything you need to know."

"Your plans, Dad. Not mine."

"Honey, I thought we had an understanding. If you want to transfer to another department, just say so. But how can helping a room full of children begin to compare with building missiles and fighter jets for your country?"

For a moment she considered backing down. Then, as the boarding call was announced, he pressed his craggy cheek against hers. "You're a Barrington, Sydney. I've groomed you all your life to take over Barrington Enterprises when I'm gone."

Lightly she said, "That's a long time from now, Dad."

It was only twenty minutes before the news reached her that her parents' jet had spiraled out of the sky and plunged into the waters off Long Island. . .with no survivors.

Grief and self-recrimination engulfed her. Yet taking over the business after her father's death came with a swiftness that shocked even his closest friends. Her board of directors doubted her ability to lead, and Randolph challenged her decisions. She fought to earn their respect; the more they opposed her, the more determined she was to control the defense plants in Tennessee and California and the Barrington subdivisions abroad. And in spite of their opposition, she continued to refurbish the shipyard in England; she couldn't even give her father's botched investment away. Nor would she, not if it meant smearing his memory. But how long must she go on shoring up the loose ends of his ambitious goals before she could leave someone else in charge and move on?

Tomorrow remained an elusive vapor. No shiny, long-handled pitchfork to split the tangled roots of her father's dreams from her own. Nearing exhaustion, she stopped running and leaned against a gnarled tree to catch her breath. Her face and neck were wet with the morning dew, her clothes damp from running. Without warning, tears welled in her eyes, eyes that Randolph told her were both kind and cruel at the conference table, pensive and alluring when he was alone with her. She thrust the sleeves of her baggy sweatshirt above her elbows and brushed a twig from her faded shorts. The river rushed on, swirling, tumbling, winding around the bend in its race toward the sea, toward the open waters.

Rushing on without her.

❧

On the other side of the world, the sleek, curving hull of the HMS *Invincible* gleamed as the aircraft carrier steamed through the azure waters of the Mediterranean. Lieutenant Commander Jonas Willoughby stood on the flight deck, thrilling to the dips and swells of the sea as he headed home to England.

Tall and suntanned, Jonas made an imposing figure, the wings on the sleeve of his officer's jacket well-earned. A gusty breeze whipped against his well-chiseled face. He rubbed his jaw. A stubborn one, his father called it, but then, they were cut from the same cloth—strong, disciplined men with a certain swaggering charm that appealed to women. Jonas had his dad's thick black hair and blue eyes hooded by dark brows. His high cheekbones and wide brow were more like his mother's, but again firm, well-chiseled. Mostly, with every birthday, he was his dad all over again—ambitious, driven to succeed, energetic, loyal.

As he braced his spine against the aircraft carrier's superstructure, the song in the wind kept repeating the skipper's words, over and over. "Willoughby, I have recommended you for another promotion—and a command of your own."

"I qualified then, Captain?"

His commanding officer smiled. "Must have done. Looks like you'll make commander sooner than your father did."

At thirty-four, Jonas's career was right on course. If anything, he was ahead of schedule in his climb toward the Admiralty. Nothing short of death would stop him. But as he glanced at the row of Sea Harriers, nostalgia set in. He'd flown the Royal Navy jets from the early days of his career, the aircraft as much a part of him as his arms and legs. He knew the power of the Harrier in his grasp. The daredevil exhilaration of launching from the moving deck of the *Invincible*. The triumph and risk of flying into the wind and clouds at 600 knots.

The closer he came to the ship docking in Portsmouth to that moment when he would fly his Sea Harrier off the deck for the last time—the more reluctant he felt. His fingers lingered on his stubbly jaw. A command of his own demanded a man at peace with himself. He had learned from his father to wear a facade of calm, but his anger roiled beneath the surface, his bitterness weighing hard like rock. Three years had failed to ease his grief and that sense of unfairness at the loss of his beloved fiancée. He still carried a personal vendetta against the Irish terrorists who had murdered the woman he loved more than life itself. No matter how much he accomplished, it seemed he would never fill the void that Louise's death had left in his life.

He ducked beneath the wing of the nearest Harrier and rubbed his hand gently over the aircraft. The thought of not flying for the next eighteen months—perhaps never flying again—dug at his gut. He consoled himself with thoughts of his own ship. Not a destroyer like the HMS *Newcastle* that ran escort to the HMS *Invincible*, nor a frigate or any of the ships his father had commanded, but a 484-ton minehunter capable of operating in deep waters. Removing mines was risky, but he liked the sound of a vessel under the leadership of Commander Jonas Willoughby.

Would his father be pleased? He had a second to conjure up an image of his father's scowling gaze, dark brows puckered, slate blue eyes scornful. *"A minehunter, Jonas, not a cruiser? Wasn't flying a Harrier risky enough for you? You should have come to me. I could have put in a good word for you—"*

That was his father. James Tobias Willoughby—the proud old Admiral, respected from the Admiralty down, knighted by the Queen, reduced now to glorying in the past. And Jonas, the only son, trying for a lifetime to please him.

"Sorry, Dad," he mused wryly. "I'm going to make it to the top without you pulling strings."

Chapter 1

S ydney Barrington drove into her rain-drenched parking space at
Barrington Enterprises and ran for the cover of the main building.
At 7:00 a.m., she entered her executive suite wearing her confident
public image and a stylish suit with a designer label.

"I put coffee and pastries in the conference room," her secretary said.
"Your guests should be here by 8:00."

"Good." In her mind, Sydney rehearsed the details of the scheduled
conference. Her father's approach to landing international contracts had
been brusque. Sydney chose to use charm and feminine wiles at the conference table, along with a pot of Starbucks coffee and tempting Danish
rolls. Nail this contract to build two new aircraft carriers for the Brits, and
it would cease being her father's company. It would be hers.

Yet the minute she stepped into the room, she was struck again by
the massive dark cherry desk and the soft upholstered chair that had once
been her father's throne, his powerhouse. A tan leather chair and ottoman
stood by the window in the corner where her father often sat to read his
reports or to reread Hemingway's *The Old Man and the Sea*.

Shrugging off the weight of her father's presence, she moved swiftly
across the room and dropped her briefcase on the desk. She glanced at
his photograph and saw her father's mesmerizing eyes staring back at
her. "It's a big day ahead, Dad. The board of directors and Randolph are
dragging their feet, but I intend to be the prime contractor on this job.
I know I can take it from the design print to the blueprint to two ships
at sea."

Her father had taught her everything she knew from engineering to
yachting and always gave her credit as long as she did her best. Would he
be pleased with her now? Yes, he would want her to win the bid on the
carriers at all cost.

Through the door, she heard Randolph laughing with her secretary.
Sydney busied herself sifting through her briefcase as he peeked in. "Good
morning, darling," he said.

She looked up and met his gaze. "Oh it's you, Randolph."

He tugged at his earlobe, his expression bewildered. "Should I go out and come in again?"

"Of course not. You're right on time."

Her thoughts reeled as Randy swaggered across the room to her—tall and desirable, much taller than her own five-foot-eight. As he leaned down to kiss her, she turned her head, avoiding his lips on hers.

"Why the cold shoulder, Sydney?"

"Let's get to the conference room."

"Business! That's all you think about," he said, following her. "These last few weeks, you've had our management team working double time revising the design prints and 3-D computer images. And what for?"

"So we can win that contract with the British."

He opened the door to the conference room for her. "I don't like what's happened to you since your parents died. You're power hungry one moment, the charming girl I remember the next. You're my fiancée, but this defense company keeps coming between us. It's all business. You never show me your affection anymore."

"There's a time and place—"

"For me, it's always the right time. The right place."

Dear Randolph. She understood his frustration. Lately, he had grown impatient waiting for her to set their wedding date. She pulled away as he caught her hand and pressed it to his lips.

He frowned. "You're not wearing your diamond this morning."

She glanced at her finger. "Oh, I must have left it in my jewelry box." She wore it when the occasion demanded. . .when she remembered.

"Are you trying to impress one of those Brits?"

"Those Brits," she reminded him gently, "are all married."

"Even Nigel Tarrington?"

"Especially Nigel."

"What makes you think you'll get that contract? We're up against some stiff competition here and abroad."

Randy was undermining her again. *You don't think I can handle the job,* she thought. *But I'll prove you wrong.*

Moments later, the tweed-clad Brits filed in—no-nonsense men representing the British Defense Secretary. Peter Dykes, the retired Vice-Admiral from the Royal Navy; Graham Morrison, a barrel-chested man with a triple chin; and Nigel Tarrington, who clung to her hand long enough to bring color to her cheeks.

Her own management team came behind them—Ivy Meckerton

dressed to the nines and Kleve MacMillian with a cell phone to his ear, yakking figures. Daron Emery, her best architectural engineer, with his intelligent coal-black eyes meeting hers. And Craig Edwards and Mike Spencer, two of her computer experts.

Smiles. More handshakes. The dragging of chairs and loosening of jackets as they settled around the conference table. "We trust you had a good flight over, Admiral Dykes."

"Quite comfortable, thank you, Miss Barrington."

He was brisk and to the point as he gave them an update on the plan to combine the Royal Navy and the Royal Air Force as a single air defense unit.

Randolph interrupted. "Won't that end interservice rivalry between those units?"

"No, Iverson, it will strengthen our air fleet with pilots who can serve both on land or aboard a ship. We want those ships ready for service within the next decade." Dykes cleared his throat. "Now, let's see what you have for us."

Daron Emery unrolled the design print and spread it on the conference table for Sydney.

"Gentlemen," Sydney said, "the carrier we propose for your air fleet is a 40,000-ton ship, capable of accommodating up to fifty aircraft fighters. You'll note the slant of the flight deck—"

Admiral Dykes eyed her with amusement. "Looks good." Dykes kept that amused twinkle as they discussed the type of launchers, the speed of the ship, the cost factors—Sydney as verbal as the men.

"Admiral, your ships are much smaller than our American aircraft," Randolph interjected. "And I question your use of electric instead of nuclear power."

Sydney wanted to kick Randolph. He'd known the specs for months. If he didn't stop putting his Cincinnati foot in his mouth at every turn, she was going to order him from the conference table. She smoothed it over, saying, "Let's have a look at our 3-D computer version of the carrier."

The colored images flashed on the screen—images of pilots catapulting their Eurofighters from the flight deck. Finally she said, "Admiral, we're prepared to build those ships for you."

Dykes nodded. "But they must be built in the UK."

Sydney felt triumphant. Her dad's folly was about to pay off. "Admiral, Barrington owns a shipyard along the River Tyne."

"I personally inspected that shipyard before flying over. They were pulling a cruise ship into the dry dock when I was there. Massive place."

She gave him her warmest smile. "We're expanding so we can build those carriers for you."

"Good show, Miss Barrington. But keep in mind, we invited several defense companies to submit their bids on the new carriers." His mouth curved. "We need your complete report within the month. We'll carry it back to England with us and personally deliver it to the project manager. By the way, Miss Barrington, I hear you have a great interest in my country."

"I was born in England—to missionary parents. They were killed in a rebel uprising in Africa shortly after my birth."

He squeezed her hand. "I'm sorry."

❧

As the room emptied, Sydney gave Randy a thumbs-up. "So far, so good, in spite of your sour mood."

"Get involved in a long-term project over there, Syd, and you risk weakening our priorities at home."

"We'll keep the programs here right on course, and expand every chance we get. But I want Barrington to build those ships." She grinned. "Maybe I'll send you to oversee the project."

"You don't intend to put off our wedding date until after those aircraft carriers are built, do you?"

"Maybe not that long," she teased.

"Well, for our sake, I hope the contract doesn't come through. I'm afraid I'd lose you." At the open door, he turned back. "What did you mean about being born to missionary parents?"

She gazed out on the magnificent view from the windows.

The day had cleared. Snowcapped Mt. Rainier peeked out from the clouds, looking like a gigantic ice-cream cone with raspberry swirls. Far in the distance lay downtown Seattle with old Smith Tower dwarfed by glass-front skyscrapers and Puget Sound crowded with ships. Without turning to face him, she said, "When my birth parents were killed, the Barringtons took me in. Gave me their name. I've been a Barrington ever since."

"You were adopted?"

Now she looked at him. "Is that a problem for you, Randy?"

"I thought the Barringtons were your birth parents."

"Aaron preferred it that way. As far as he was concerned, I was his daughter."

"I don't understand."

No, you never would. The right connections matter to you. It had been a matter of pride with Aaron not to mention Africa. Not to admit that she was not his own child. "You don't understand? Perhaps that's why I never told you, Randolph."

❦

As the HMS *Invincible* plowed through the choppy waters toward the home port, Jonas Willoughby thought about Louise. Three years ago he had stood on the back of the flag deck, thinking about her. . . .

❦

The NATO flotilla bobbed in the waters all around him. The blades of a Lynx helicopter whirled above the captain's bridge, almost deafening the footsteps coming toward him.

"Jonas Willoughby?"

Jonas had recognized the ship's chaplain and remembered thinking that the man was too young to be wearing a clerical collar, too kind to be the bearer of bad news. Before the chaplain said another word, he knew it was crushing news and felt struck by the pungent smell of the sea with a rain squall building in the west.

"Would you like to go below, Willoughby?"

"No, Chaplain. Whatever you have come to say, tell me here."

He shouted above the noise of the chopper and the shore batteries, "It's your fiancée, Willoughby."

"Louise?"

"I'm sorry, sir, but—she was killed in Ireland."

Jonas's knees had buckled. The chaplain reached out to steady him. "There must be a mistake, Chaplain. Louise and I are going to Ireland on our honeymoon."

"She traveled there alone. Her car was ambushed by Irish terrorists She didn't have a chance—"

❦

Now, in spite of the clamoring noise on the flight deck, Jonas sensed the lift door opening. From the corner of his eye, he saw the Signal Communications Officer—walking toward him as the chaplain had done three years ago. The man stopped several yards from him. Their eyes locked.

Everything came at Jonas in slow motion. His fears. His blurred memories of Louise. Even the SCO's steps seemed curtailed by the twenty-five-mile-an-hour wind blowing on the deck.

As he reached Jonas, he said, "Lieutenant Commander Willoughby?"

"Yes." *You know that I am.*

The wind wafted the man's hair into unruly tufts. Blew his black tie out of alignment. Fluttered the message in his hand.

"This message came in marked *Urgent,*" he said.

Jonas took it, dismissing the man. As the SCO walked away, Jonas slit the security caveat with his thumbnail and frowned as he noted the return address: The Very Reverend Charles Rainford-Simms, M.A., Bishop of Monkton, The Vicarage, Stow-on-the-Woodland, The Cotswolds.

A lump threatened to cut off Jonas's windpipe. Rainford-Simms— Louise's father—the man once destined to be his father-in-law.

As he read, he remembered the methodical calm of the man's speech, his kindly eyes beneath white bushy brows—his annoying way of meddling.

Regret to advise you that things are going poorly at Broadshire Manor. Abigail Broderick is not well and the responsibility of caring for your father is a sizable task for her. Miss Broderick refuses to place him in a Navy residence.

Jonas stared blankly at the message. The Admiral ill? The man was a powerhouse of strength. Tall and athletic. Always in command. A man of iron will whose mettle showed in battle or crisis. Inflexible. Impregnable. Abigail was the only one who never bowed under his father's demanding ways.

He forced himself to go on reading.

Jonas, something must be done about the children as well. It needs a man's hand to settle these affairs. Once before we needed you, Jonas. . . .

What does that mean, Charles? Are you condemning me again for delaying the wedding when my ship deployed to the Gulf? I didn't know your daughter would travel to Ireland without me. I didn't know Louise would die there. What did you want of me then, Reverend? To resign my Navy commission and fly to Ireland to pick up the broken body of my fiancée? Am I to spend the rest of my life gathering up the broken threads? It was unfair thinking, and Jonas knew it. Louise's father was a kindhearted man, a forgiving man.

Jonas's fist doubled as he read of the growing problems at the manor. Go home to a sick father, to a dwindling staff? It seemed clear that

Rainford-Simms once again did not comprehend Jonas's commitment to the Royal Navy.

Don't you understand, Charles? A naval officer doesn't sacrifice his career for personal difficulties.

If the Admiral and the manor were too much for Abigail, he would sell the place. Of what value was the property to Jonas? It was riddled with memories of Louise and what might have been.

He stood rigid as though he were standing in front of the Admiral and receiving a dressing-down. *Stand easy,* he told himself. *It's just Rainford-Simms blowing dust into a storm cloud.* A few ship-to-shore messages and matters could be settled.

But Jonas felt his career hurtling to a standstill, and for what? Give up his promotion to commander because the Admiral needed him? Not likely. The distance that separated the Admiral and himself was more than nautical miles. He admired the old man, but they stayed constantly at odds. If Jonas gave in and went home, what would happen to his resolve to keep to his own course?

As he balanced against the swaying ship, Louise and his father meshed in his thinking. He'd give the world to have one more chance to tell Louise how much he loved her and how sorry he was for the way she died. Now was he man enough to make peace with his father before time ran out—to work up the courage to tell him how much he had idolized him all these years?

Charles's message concluded with,

Perhaps coming back to the Cotswolds would comfort you, son, as it did me. At last I have come to terms with Louise's absence and have become a man of peace, a man of joy by staying here. My daughter was dear to me. I daresay your whole life and mine were centered in her. And you, son—three years of silence from you. Louise would want our friendship to go on. I know that you miss her dreadfully, as I do. I think of her always. . .

Jonas smashed the message into his palm.
Miss her? He still felt dead inside without her.

∽

Twenty minutes later Jock Hollinsworth crossed the deck toward the spot where Jonas stood. He hesitated, not wanting to break into his squadron commander's solace. They'd been friends since Dartmouth, had earned their wings for fixed aircraft together. Jock had flown wingman for Jonas on more than one dangerous sortie in the Balkans and over Kosovo. He took the remaining strides and cuffed Jonas's shoulder.

"I expected to find you up here with your golf club, spinning a golf ball off the deck into the depths of the sea."

Jonas smiled. "Not after the last sounding rebuke. You know the rules. No ditching of any gash or garbage over the sides. Nothing hazardous to the aircraft. Including golf balls."

The skipper's standing rebuke was in Jonas's file, one of the few black marks there. These days Jonas kept to jogging and a regimen of exercise that kept his body trim and fit.

"The captain should ban bagpipes on board, too."

"I don't practice often," Jonas defended.

"It has to be that Scottish blood in you."

"My mother's side. You know I'm British born, but I'm proud of my Scottish heritage. So I'll take the bagpipes with me when I leave, but I'll miss flying with you when I take command of my own ship. With any luck, I'll be on patrol off Northern Ireland."

Jock's jaw tightened. "Let the government settle your problems with the IRA. Whoever set off the bomb that killed Louise didn't know her. She was just an innocent traveler."

"I should have been with her."

"It didn't work out that way. Look, old man, just stay out of the Irish waters. You've earned the promotion. You've given the Royal Navy a good return of service. Peacekeeping duties in the Adriatic. Patrolling the Scandinavian waters and the oil fields of the North Sea. Bosnia. Kosovo. Jonas, you're a climber. All I ever wanted to do was fly."

"It's been a good life—belonging to Her Majesty's Navy."

"Right on. The best of both worlds. Access to every club on land. Unbeatable camaraderie at sea. But I worry about you. Anger at the IRA could ruin your career. Focus on your future. You'll be in the Admiralty before we know it. And I count on our still being friends when you reach it."

"That goes without saying, Jock."

As the crimson of a burnished sunset glowed on the horizon, Jonas pulled the bishop's crumpled message from his pocket and thrust it at Jock. "Here. Read this. I've got problems."

After reading, Jock sputtered, "Ignore this. I don't think the Admiral is your responsibility."

"He's my father, Jock."

"Somebody should have reminded him of that long ago."

"I just had difficulty pleasing him."

"No wonder, with a distinguished career like James Tobias Willoughby's—that's like filling size twenty clodhoppers."

Jonas shook his head. "Dad earned every promotion."

"No argument there. Your dad's really switched on when it comes to the Royal Navy, so let the Navy take care of him. They have rest centers in Portsmouth, don't they?" Jock gave the paper a twist of his own. "Have Abigail Broderick look into one." He gripped Jonas's shoulder. "This Rainford-Simms; he's not—?"

Jonas's eyes turned a frosty blue. "Yes. He's Louise's father."

"Sorry, old man—but my advice still stands. Let the Navy take care of the Admiral. You deserve a command of your own."

～

Days later, after months' deployment, the HMS *Invincible* moved into home waters on a steady course toward the south coast of England. The captain ordered the Fleet Air Arm to follow standard procedure. The Sea Harriers were to leave the ship first; the Sea King helicopters would follow.

Jonas looked around the quarters he had shared with Jock and packed the last of his toiletries into his kit. Then he picked up Louise's photograph, dusted it with his sleeve, and stared at her lovely face. "Like I promised you, Louise, I'm finally coming home."

He secured the picture snugly between his shirts and underwear and zipped his kit bag. As he squared his tie, he consoled himself that he was not leaving Her Majesty's Service—just transferring temporarily to Northwood Headquarters near London.

When he opened the door, Jock was just coming back from the wardroom. "Time to fly, Jonas."

Jonas looked at his friend's nubby skin, red from the sun, and at the ginger freckles across his nose and chin. Even his scalp looked sunburned beneath the cropped sandalwood hair. He met Jock's gaze with a crooked smile. "I guess this is it?"

"Keep in touch. My wife has some pretty young debutantes in London that she wants you to meet."

"Tell her I need more time."

"You have to get on with your life."

"The IRA took my life from me when they killed Louise." He could not imagine filling the photo frame with someone else's picture, let alone allowing himself to care deeply for another woman. "No one else could take her place."

As they reached the flight deck, Jonas shaded his eyes and stared into the clouds. "I'll miss flying the Harrier."

"Sure you will—until you command your own ship. It will be Commander Willoughby the next time we meet. I envy you."

He shouted above the bedlam. "Jock—I turned the command down. My transfer to Northwood came through two days ago."

Anger turned Jock's face scarlet. "You can't be serious turning down your first command for a landlocked job? That won't set well in your record. I daresay you made the wrong decision."

"Once things are settled at home, I'll be back."

"But not in command of your own minesweeper?"

"No. But maybe back in command of my own life." They shook hands. "I'm the last one off this time. Captain's orders. I want to watch the rest of the squadron leave the flight deck one more time. We've had orders to lay over in the area until the ship docks. After that, we'll meet up in Scotland."

"Will do. I'm not lingering around Scotland long. My wife's picking me up. I'm taking a forty-two-day leave. I plan to build up my flying hours in my uncle's Learjet. You remember Rodney Christopher, don't you? Uncle Rodney keeps urging me to give up the Royal Navy and go full-time with him."

"Doing what?"

"Flying his company plane. He does country hops. Sweden. Finland. Italy. Germany. He'd pay well. But don't worry, Jonas; I have no intention of leaving the Service. I want to be around when those new carriers are commissioned."

"By then age will ground us both."

"I know. I'll be too old to fly the new planes, but at least I'd like to be on board watching the younger jocks take off."

"Don't spend too much time in that Learjet."

With a wicked grin, Jock said, "I'm spending most of my leave with my wife. We're going away. Just the two of us. We've been talking about starting a family—"

Jonas thumped Jock's arm. "Then you won't miss me."

❧

As Jonas flew above Portsmouth Harbor, the city greeted the HMS *Invincible* with a rousing welcome. The waving and cheering swept him back to the day Louise met his ship for the first time. *The piping of music had been interrupted by the order, "Attention, ship's company. All off-watch personnel to man the portside. That is all."*

He had slipped up beside Louise as she searched the faces of the men lined up on board the ship. Searching for him. He put his arms around her and kissed her.

"Jonas, you are supposed to be on that ship," she had cried.

"Honey, it's standard procedure for pilots to fly off hours before the ship reaches harbor."

"Jonas Willoughby, why didn't you warn me?"

"I wanted to surprise you."

It was then that he realized how much he loved her—this lovely, sensitive creature who had loved him back. He had been smitten by her beauty, her warmth and laughter when she was with him. He liked to remember her that way that day. The day he proposed.

In the three years since her death, she had become a veiled mist, real only in his thoughts and dreams, always out of grasp. He wondered now, with the exhilarating thrust of the Harrier in his control, whether she would have ever adapted to his long months at sea, to his love of the Royal Navy that all too often surpassed even his commitment to her.

The demands of flying drew him back. Below him, the pearl blue of the sky reflected in the water as another warship slipped from the jetty and moved out into the channel. An American supercarrier lay anchored off the Spithead, the ship too big for Portsmouth Harbor. Cruisers lay berthed at the docks, frigates and tankers by the Middle Wall. And in its permanent location stood Lord Nelson's old flagship, the HMS *Victory*.

The *Invincible* lay berthed at the South Railway Jetty now, her flight deck empty of planes. The White Ensign flew at her stern, the Union Jack on the bow. Jonas saluted with the tip of his fingers and fought the miserable lump in his throat. From the action below he knew that people were cheering. He gave the order and the squadron of Sea Harriers did another fly past, over the ship. The Sea Kings flew in formation behind them. Now some of the waving was directed toward them.

Moments later, the pilots began the return journey to their Naval Air Stations—the helicopters to their base in Cornwall and Jonas's squadron to northern Scotland. Jonas broke formation and flew once more over the carrier. He dipped his wing in salute to his ship—and to the memory of the girl who would never be on dock waiting for him again. Then he turned north toward Scotland to follow his squadron home, his future uncertain.

Chapter 2

S pring bathed itself in a glorious rainbow of pastel colors, scenting the sleepy hamlet of Stow-on-the-Woodland with wild thyme and the delicate fragrance of herbs and roses. Abigail Broderick stared out the mullion windows at Broadshire Manor, down on a quiet, unpretentious village. She had spent most of her lifetime tucked away in Gloucestershire in this English village that was rooted in the past, untouched by the passing of time.

She knew little of fame or fortune, yet her years of living in someone else's magnificent manor had made her confident, wiser. A woman of stately carriage with silver gray hair and a softly curving mouth, she had always been much loved in the village.

Her distant past remained hidden, forgotten by those who knew her best. Secrets were stowed away in the chambers of her own heart and mind, laid there like an unfinished quilt in a hope chest. Her past awakened from time to time by little things—the ringing of the church bell at St. Michael's, the rain pelting on her bedroom window, the bubbling flow of the River Windrush. And recently, by the sight of Jonas lifting his ill father in his arms and carrying him to the chair by the window. But always when those unhappy memories of the past flashed back, they were overshadowed by an arc of forgiveness. Perhaps, as her dearest friend Griselda Quigley said, it was part of growing old—this being at peace, this accepting what you could not change and garnering up instead treasures for the life that lay ahead.

These days Abigail took pleasure in her walled garden and the plump buds of her blue delphiniums or the wood lilies that lazed beneath the oak. Mostly, as she had done over the years, she found her greatest joy in the children. She shared their longing for freedom—theirs from books and schoolmasters, hers from pain and the demands of growing older. As if to mock her, a sharp jolt ran through her chest, shortening her breath. There was no time to step across the room to the safety of her chair. She groped for her medicine bottle in her skirt pocket and placed a tiny tablet under her tongue, praying that the lightheadedness would not come this time.

Gratefully, with a sudden flush, the vessels opened and the pain trickled away.

Shortly, she must call the children in for dinner. Mrs. Quigley expected them at the table on time. Abigail pressed her forehead against the window casing, waiting for her strength to return. She expected to see Jonas pushing the wheelbarrow toward the shed, his black-and-white collie at his heels and young Gregor tracking in Jonas's footsteps over the high rolling wolds. But Jonas was nowhere to be seen. Dear Jonas! Even in his few weeks back in the village, a persistent scowl had wedged between his brows. But she made no effort to send him away. Found no courage to tell him she could manage the manor alone.

Absently, she placed the medicine bottle on the dresser and selected a sweater from the top drawer. Stepping gracefully, as she always did, she made her way down the curving stairwell with her hand firmly on the rail. Then, plodding slowly down the entry hall, she felt her flagging heart set the pace, her pulse so irregular that she could not count the drumbeat of her own heart.

Taking the next step over the parquetry floor, she felt another age-old pain deepen inside her as she thought of Sir James Willoughby and the four young refugee children still in her care. The thought of permanently closing the doors of Broadshire Manor filled her with foreboding.

Above her a glittering chandelier hung from the coved ceiling, casting dancing shadows on the lovely portrait of Lady Helen Willoughby. Abigail remembered her own arrival as a young woman and the courage it took to grip the knocker seeking employment again. The door had been opened, not by Lady Helen, but by the lord of the manor—a tall naval officer with smashing good looks, thick black hair, and heavy-lidded, dark blue eyes that questioned her arrival.

The tower bell of St. Michael's chimed the hour, its sonorous tone slicing into her thoughts. Her chest constricted with pain as she hurried the last few steps and swung back the massive door as she always did at sunset to make certain all her children were in.

The sloping hills of the Cotswolds cast their golden glow in the fading twilight in a sky still lit with a murmur of blue. The air smelled sweet with the flowering shrubs and the wild English primroses that thrived against the drystone wall. It was all there—the peaceful, pastoral setting of a lifetime spreading out before her, even the small thatched cottage where she had been born. But the manor was her place of residence now—a massive three-story house built during the wool trade by Lady Willoughby's family, a commanding structure that dwarfed the rest of the village. Above the gold and emerald fields, fleecy clouds drifted toward eventide as one by one the village children were called in for the supper hour and bedtime.

Since Lady Willoughby's death, Abigail had reveled in running the manor for the Admiral and filling it with children who knew nothing of the value of the bronze statues or the art treasures in the library. Over the years, to the horror of the staff, Abigail's refugee children raced up and down the grand curving staircase and slid down the bronzed balustrade. They hid behind the brocade curtains and shouted in the lavish ballroom where Lady Willoughby's ancient pedestal clock still ticked.

A rustle in the bush at the foot of the stone steps caught her attention. "Gregor?" she called.

The nine-year-old peeked out, a lopsided grin filling his face. "Yes, Miss Abigail."

"So there you are. Have you been collecting bugs and crickets again to scare the girls?"

He stood pigeon-toed, a momentary stance with the scuffed toes of his shoes turned in, and the inside pockets of his trousers turned out. "Don't have nothing, Miss Abigail."

"Anything," she corrected.

He brushed his hands free. "See? Nothing."

"Then have you been with Jonas again?"

He nodded, his lustrous black eyes sparkling, his voice high-pitched, excited. "I helped him take the sheep in."

She could not fault him for this; he felt safe with Jonas. Still, she said, "Jonas should have sent you home sooner."

"But we saw a stranger down by the river."

She allowed her eyes to graze past the thicket of woods east of the manor to the silhouette of the bridge where so many of her children had crossed over, where so few of them ever came back.

"I see no one, Gregor."

"Me and Jonas saw him."

"Jonas and I," she corrected.

He twisted the pockets of his corduroys. "I thought my papa had come back."

Her heart lurched. "Someday, Gregor. Someday, perhaps."

But we are never going to find him, she thought. Not after months of scouring desolate towns and crowded refugee camps filled with tatter-ragged families, or checking the International Red Cross lists of missing names. No, she sensed in her heart that Gregor's village was swallowed up in rubble—his family with it.

"Gregor, you'd best come in and wash up. Your supper is getting cold. Griselda made your favorite—hot dumpling stew."

His muddy sneakers squeaked as he raced up the steps.

She cupped his smudged cheek before he could dart past her. "Did you play in the water, Gregor?"

"I was chasing Jonas's dog."

The black-and-white collie that comforted him. "You know you must not stay out when it's getting dark," she scolded softly.

"I'm not afraid with Jonas."

Would he be afraid if he knew that Jonas had flown sorties over Kosovo? Dropped missiles, perhaps, on the village where Gregor once lived? Or would Jonas still be Gregor's hero? The boy thrilled with tales of Jonas launching his Sea Harrier off the deck of the HMS *Invincible* on a mission to destroy. She shuddered even now at the thought of his plane armed with deadly Amraam missiles patrolling the skies over Yugoslavia. Trembled at the thought of Jonas's plane coming back from combat and dropping through the night clouds onto the carrier's sleek deck. It seemed to Abigail that the boy and the man had been destined to meet—that roaming the Cotswold hills together with the black-and-white collie between them offered healing to them both.

Gregor was much like Jonas had been as a boy. An intelligent child, bent on his own way. At times angelic or curious. Sometimes a rogue, straying beyond the manor to fish along the river or dawdle on the hills. She feared what would happen when Jonas went back to sea duty and the boy was left to wander alone.

"Gregor, give Griselda your wet shoes. She'll make certain they're dry by morning."

She watched him go—her boy with those solemn dark eyes and fragile smile that had tugged at her heart the day she first saw him at the refugee camp. Gaunt. Frightened. Hungry. At the peak of the conflict, she had salvaged him from the tinderbox in Kosovo—snatched him from the arms of an Albanian guerrilla in a tattered surplus uniform who held him out to her.

"There's no one else left in his village," the man had said. No one else left. Odd. Gregor, of all the children, feared darkness, yet he was always the last one in.

She lingered at the door, listening for Jonas's bagpipes. She heard only the bubbling gurgle of the Windrush as it flowed beneath the old stone bridge. The river was as dear and familiar to her as the bleating sheep in the meadows, or tea and crumpets with Jonas in the late afternoon; it was as comforting as sitting with Sir James and patting his wrinkled hand while he rambled on about matters aged as the hills around them.

She glanced at the cottage on the edge of the property and saw the light in Jonas's window flicker on, saw the plumes of smoke rise from his chimney. She loved Jonas as her own son, but was it fair to let him take on the burden of the manor and the children and Sir James? He should be finding a life's companion, settling down to his own happiness. Or going back on sea duty as a pilot—to the career he loved.

From where she stood, reluctant to close out another day, she searched the darkness again. This time Abigail saw someone crossing over the bridge—a lanky man with one child sheltered in his arms and another by his side. They came stealthily now in the shadows of the evening, making their way toward the manor.

The gate squeaked as the man thrust it open. His presence set Abigail's heart to racing erratically. She tugged her sweater against her chest. He lifted his bristly face as he neared the steps, his eyes hollow even in the semi-darkness. His shoulders hunched forward under the weight of the child in his arms.

"Abigail, I was afraid you would shut the door before we could reach you."

She recognized him now—a young man who had once lived in her home. A bleak twig of a man now.

"Conan O'Reilly," she murmured. "You've come back."

"And I brought my children with me."

The boy in his arms was three at most; the little girl clutching at his side not much older.

"Conan, the last I heard, you were hiding out in Ireland."

"Then am I not welcome, Abigail?" He climbed the steps to stand level with her. "I've come in peace. Don't turn us away."

She touched his rough cheek and felt the jagged scar that ran the length of his jaw. He was still her boy, her troubled Irish boy. She tried to remember the innocent child that he had once been, but gazing up into his hollow, empty eyes, she knew a young Irish terrorist, a revolutionary, stared back at her.

Chapter 3

Abigail's mind was awash with memories. Recollections of a boy running away from the manor fourteen years ago. And the images of headlines since then. Belfast. Northern Ireland. Sinn Fein. The Good Friday Agreement. IRA bombings in Omagh. The failure to decommission—the failure to lay down arms.

She shuddered. "Were you followed here, Conan?"

"Would it matter?"

"It might if anyone comes looking for you."

"By then, I should be some distance from here. Please, Abigail, may we come in? The children are exhausted."

"Was it wise for you to come back?" she whispered.

"Aren't you the one who always keeps the door open until all of your children are in?"

She bit her lip, and, with another cautious glance into the darkness, stepped back to make room for them to cross the threshold. She could see Conan clearly now as he bolted the door and wedged his back firmly against it. He looked older than his twenty-nine years. A week's stubble of beard marred his once handsome face. Wiry red brows failed to hide his shifty gaze. His eyes swept the room, lingering briefly on the windows that looked out on the fountain.

He was always in trouble as a boy, the outcast of the Broderick household. Conan, her firebrand, the malcontent among the other children, defending Northern Ireland's conflict with Britain. Back then, he seemed like a stormy petrel in flight, a child constantly at war with himself. A man still at war.

When Conan focused his attention on her again, his anguished expression was bedeviled, tormented, out of reach. This troubled child who had grown into a troubled man had obviously hit upon hard times. His worn tweed jacket and dark corduroys were not nearly warm enough for a man on the run. Abigail's faith in the God who looked over the woodlands wavered, yet she felt certain Conan had not come back to harm her. Whatever his sins or misdoings—and she feared they could be legion—he had taken great risks to bring his children to her. They had his red hair, the girl his intense green eyes, wide with mistrust.

"Are you alone, Abigail?"

"I never was alone. This is a big house, remember? Most of the old servants are gone, but three of the staff stayed on. Boris and my house-keeper are still with me. You remember them." She smiled thinly. "Griselda came back after you left. I couldn't run the place without her."

"You can't keep a mansion like this with three servants."

"We manage. Part of the upper floors and the east and south wings are closed off. Opened only for dusting."

"It's not like when I was a boy, is it?"

"Nor like the glory days when Lady Willoughby was alive."

"There's no one else here?"

Her heart raced. She would not mention Jonas, but she said, "The Admiral lives here now. He's old and ill, and I still have four young refugee children. The oldest is nine—a boy from Kosovo. Two are from the Gulf War, one from Bosnia."

"Then you won't mind two from Ireland?"

She glanced at the O'Reilly children again. Neither child was dressed warmly enough for the evening chill. The girl looked rumpled and mussed, her sweater shaggy. The boy's thin legs were bare, his tousled hair partly covered by a brown cap. As sleepy as he was, he clung to a toy truck. She reached out and linked her fingers with the sleeping child.

"Conan, when did your children eat last?"

"This morning. We had some hard rolls and milk."

"That was hours ago."

"We had to keep going. I had to time our arrival toward dark. I couldn't risk anyone recognizing me in Bourton-on-the-Water."

As she took a step, intending to pull the tapestry cord, he gripped her wrist. "What are you doing?"

"I was going to ring for Griselda. I want her to feed and bathe the children."

"Not yet. Not until we settle something."

She pulled free and rubbed her wrist. Tentacles of fear knotted her stomach. Long ago he had threatened to get even with Jonas over boyish quarrels. "Settle what, Conan?"

"I want you to raise Danny and Keeley for me. Will you?" Even his voice was toneless, without hope, measured by defeat, his life empty except for these children.

"Broadshire has never been a place for fugitives. I won't let it be now." She shook her head. "Look at me. Don't you understand? My work at Broadshire Manor is drawing to a close. I've grown old since you went away. Surely you've noticed."

He blew a kiss across Danny's ear. "You've never turned a child away before, Abigail."

"But I know who you are now—what you stand for."

"You have always known what I stood for."

She ran her hand nervously across her chest. "I hoped you would change. That you would want peace."

He looked perplexed. "I do. Peace for Ireland."

Outside a tree branch scraped against the windowpane.

His gaze darted from window to window and then down the long, empty corridor. He jabbed his hand into his bulging pocket, his eyes wild.

"No firearms, Conan. It's just the evening wind. Don't you remember how it would stir as darkness set in?"

"All I remember is how dark it used to be."

"What kind of trouble are you in that you want to leave your children behind?"

He rubbed his bristled chin against his son's cheek. Danny awakened with a start, his enormous eyes too large for the narrow ragamuffin face. Seeing his father, his eyelids drooped again.

"Trouble, you call it. Can't you even guess, Abigail?"

"I don't even know why you went away fourteen years ago."

"I wanted my children to grow up to love Ireland."

Her throat constricted. "That's what I wanted for you—to be proud of your country, to help bring peace to Northern Ireland."

"That's why I went away—why my people recruited me."

"You were only a boy then."

"Man enough to side with the IRA. It was my duty."

A sharp pain caught her breath. She walked unsteadily to the marble bench and sank down onto it. He went and sat beside her, balancing his son on his knee. Keeley squirmed against him.

"Abigail, what is it?"

The pain tracked along her jawbone. She grappled in her skirt pocket, but the medicine bottle was not there. And then she recalled with a certainty that she had left her pills on the dresser top when she went to call the children in. She pressed her hand against her chest. "I'm not well. My heart is giving out. Any excitement sets it to fluttering."

"Should I call Mrs. Quigley?"

"No, she worries enough about me."

She sat motionless, allowing her erratic heartbeat to ease.

Sensing Keeley's alarm, she said, "I'll be all right, child."

"It's just—I've upset her," Conan said.

His troubled gaze turned to the fountain outside the window where two carefree children were carved in marble. Water poured from the pitcher in the girl's hand and the ring jets behind her sent geysers of water back into the pool.

The changing patterns in the water spout punctuated their silence with a symphony of their own.

He broke their silence, saying, "I remember sitting here with you as a boy the night before I ran away. I didn't mean to disappoint you. I always felt safe with you."

"Then why did you go away?"

His gaze shifted back to her. "I told you—to fight for my country." He covered his son's ears, slipping from terrorist to father in that simple act of gentleness. "I wanted peace for Ireland. You must believe me."

"Peace? What about the Omagh incident? And those senseless killings? I hear you were involved."

"Please, Abigail. Not here, not in front of the children." His arm tightened around his son. "My children are not at war, Abigail. We have nowhere to go. Will you take them?" The tired lines around his eyes deepened. "Let me rest a few days, too? I could watch over you."

She patted his hand. "No, dear boy. I know this was your home once. Your running away never changed that. But I can't let you stay." She wished with all her heart that Conan could be a boy again. That she didn't have to send him away. "You see, there's something I haven't told you. Jonas came back a few weeks ago to settle the affairs at Broadshire Manor. He's staying out in the cottage, but he comes toward midnight to take care of his father."

He groaned. "So Jonas is back at the manor. No wonder you're afraid of my being here." His mouth twisted. "You were always forced to choose between us."

"That's not true, Conan." But she knew that it was.

At the sound of footsteps in the corridor, they whirled around on the bench, and stood. Abigail felt a flood of relief when her housekeeper stepped from the shadows.

"It's all right, Conan. It's Mrs. Quigley."

"Abigail, you promised to have supper with the—" Surprise lit Griselda's tired gray eyes. "So *you're* back! And what do we have here?"

"Two hungry children," Conan told her.

"Well, you know your way to the kitchen, Conan O'Reilly."

"So you do remember me?"

Her thick gray brows twitched. "Couldn't forget the likes of you. You used to steal biscuits hot from the oven. Yours?" she asked, nodding at the children.

Keeley shrank against her father. "Yes, this is my daughter, Keeley. And this boy in my arms is Danny."

Her gaze locked on Conan. "I trust Commander Willoughby doesn't know you're here. You best know now—Jonas has strong feelings about what you've been doing."

"A man has a right to defend his own country. But I'm not looking for trouble here, Mrs. Quigley. I'm just trying to find a safe place for my children."

Griselda touched Danny's cheek with her work-reddened hand. "The boy's feverish," she accused.

"And hungry, like I said."

"There's plenty of dumplings. For you, too, if you want some."

Abigail shook her head. "Conan and I will have supper in the drawing room and then he must leave. Ask Boris or Lucas if they can see Conan safely out of the village and on his way to Bourton-on-the-Water."

"Never mind, Abigail. I know my own way out of town."

"Best that way," Griselda agreed. "Besides, Lucas hasn't come in for dinner yet." The scowl on Griselda's wrinkled face deepened. "And what if Jonas asks after you, Abigail, while you and Mr. O'Reilly are in the drawing room?"

"Tell him I'm resting. I'll see him in the morning."

Griselda's eyes narrowed with disapproval. "It won't be good telling him an untruth."

"But it would be a disaster for Jonas and Conan to meet."

Griselda rubbed the back of her hand with her thumb. "The Reverend Rainford-Simms called. Should I tell him that you'll ring him back tomorrow, too?"

"Was it urgent?"

"The usual. He's distressed about Jonas not dropping in. Says there's no need for them not to be friends."

Abigail shot a guarded glance toward Conan. Only the curl of his lip suggested curiosity. "Yes, Griselda, tell the reverend I'll ring back tomorrow, would you?"

Griselda shrugged irritably. Then, as she had done over the years, she took charge of the children. She lifted Danny from Conan's arms and cradled him. "He's light as a hot biscuit." She reached out for Keeley's hand. "It's time to get you two washed up and fed."

Keeley clung to Conan. "Don't leave me, Daddy."

As he brushed back shocks of red hair from her forehead, the corners of his mouth sagged. "Your papa lived here as a boy."

Keeley's lips puckered. "I don't want to stay here."

Conan stood rock-still, sweat beading his brow. "Go with Mrs. Quigley. You'll be safe here. She will give you and Danny some supper. Later—later we can talk about it."

Griselda started toward the kitchen with a firm grip on Keeley's hand. As the child wailed, Griselda glanced back at Abigail. "Will the children be staying with us?"

"At least for the night."

Strands of wiry gray hair slipped loose as she shook her head. "That's what you always say. Should they sleep on the second floor with the other children?"

"No. Not tonight." She avoided Conan's eyes. "After their supper, you must take them to the safety of the West Wing."

Danny's head bobbed sleepily against Griselda's massive bosom.

"But the West Wing is Sir James's quarters," Griselda said.

"The Admiral will not mind, nor will he remember."

Chapter 4

Conan's iron mask dropped as a closed door silenced Keeley's sobs. Abigail put her hand on his arm. "Conan, you are breaking Keeley's heart."

"There's no other way to save her life and Danny's."

"Can't you take your children back to their mother?"

His voice rang with bitterness. "My wife, Rorie, was killed in the crossfire in Northern Ireland. If I had only known she was shopping at the market in Omagh—but I was told that the car bombing was just meant for a warning. That no one would be hurt."

"A warning? The Omagh incident broke the peace agreement. It killed twenty-eight innocent people and injured many more." Twenty-nine dead, if she counted Rorie.

"Believe me. We didn't intend for anyone to die there."

"How can you erase Omagh from your conscience? The peace won't work if any of you keep fighting. All they want is for you to lay down arms—"

He was incensed. "Give in, you mean? Sell out. Throw away everything we fought for. What we died for."

She tried to rest her hand on his wrist. He jerked free. "I belong to a fractional group—the real IRA," he boasted. "Omagh is only a taste of what will happen if they try to defeat us."

"That would ruin peace for everyone. It has become your personal war, hasn't it? Your battle against society. Do the children know about their mother?"

"They know she is dead. Keeley was with Rorie the day she died. Not a good memory for any child." The nerve along his jaw throbbed. "I never intended to bring any children into the world. Then Rorie became pregnant with Keeley. We married right after she was born." His voice mellowed. "And then our son came along."

He massaged his temples, his gaze steady. "Rorie was born in Dublin, as proud an Irish lass as ever was. Good-looking farm girl. Soft-spoken. She was a wonderful mother, but you must never tell anyone that the children came from Ireland."

She felt a faint smile touch her lips. "You don't think people will recognize their Irish brogue? Jonas will figure it out when he sees the children. Your son looks like you."

"A rough sentence for any child." He turned his gaunt face to Abigail. "You used to keep pictures of all of your children in the drawing room. Am I still there?"

She hesitated. "No. Jonas took your picture down three years ago after one of the IRA bombings."

"Why? The IRA never hurt Jonas."

"You're wrong. Jonas suffered a great loss in one of your bombings—another isolated incident where a friend of his was killed when she turned off on the wrong road. She wasn't a threat to the IRA. But it didn't matter. They bombed her car anyway."

Conan went deathly pale. "Did it happen near Belfast?"

"Does it make a difference? Nothing can change the fact that she's gone. Come, I want you to eat before you leave."

She linked her arm in his to steady herself as they walked into the library. He flicked on the light as they entered and for a long time stood looking at the photographs of the children who had passed through the manor. "When I was a boy, we could only come in here and to the gallery on guided tours."

She laughed. "Was I that strict?"

"You were just trying to preserve the Willoughby collection. We left enough imprints on the rest of the house—sliding down the balustrade, scratching the ancient furniture, and ruining the flower beds in our scuffles."

Lightly she asked, "Do you remember carving your initials C.O.W. on the family crest? Your initials are still there. I know the C.O. stands for Conan O'Reilly. But why the W?" she asked.

"Can't you guess? It was for Willoughby. I wanted to belong to someone—to have a brother like Jonas. But why did you leave my initials out on the gate?"

"They were all I had left to remind me of you."

He picked at a loose thread on his jacket. "My photo used to hang here, right beside Jonas. Tell me, why did Jonas resign his Navy commission to come back to the Cotswolds?"

"He didn't, but he had to forgo a command of his own when he transferred to Fleet Headquarters in Northwood."

His voice turned ragged. "Back at Gordonstoun, he said he would settle for nothing less than a place in the Admiralty. He won't get that by turning down a promotion."

"You were friends once," she reminded him.

"Not after Jonas discovered my father was with the IRA."

She rested her tapered fingers on his sleeve. "You were on opposite sides, but Jonas would never forget a friendship."

"Yet as an officer in the Royal Navy, he would turn me in if he found me here."

"Or be considered a traitor himself," she said softly.

"I never understood why Jonas had such a prominent spot in your life."

"The son of the lord of the manor always has a prominent place. And when his—his mother died, I gave him special care."

"So who is this hanging where my picture used to be?"

"That's Sydney. She was six when that picture was taken. An American businessman and his wife adopted her."

"Lucky girl. Someone wanted her. What about my children?"

"They can spend the night, but in the morning I'll talk to my solicitor about finding a permanent home for them."

"Don't. Abigail, I want them here with you. I trust you."

"I'm doing what's best for Keeley and Danny. I've promised myself for weeks that I would see Edmund Gallagher and make arrangements for the other children and Sir James." She gave him an ironic grin. "Now it's six children instead of four. Your coming now simply brought the need into sharp focus."

I have other legal accounts to settle, she thought. *Funds for Boris's and Griselda's old age. And I must undo what Lady Willoughby did so many years ago—I will sign the property back into Jonas's name.*

"Conan, I won't be here long enough for your children to grow up. One should not live beyond eighty, not when one's strength is failing." She tapped her chest. "Not when I could so easily become a burden for someone else."

She moved along the row of faces. "That's Santos Garibaldi. You remember him? I'm certain you were here at the same time. His father designed the fountain for us." Her voice brightened. "And over here— Sheldon Taylor and Doyle Sullivan. I fretted over those two, but they're both married now and successful."

"They're gone. Don't waste your worries on any of them."

"Sometimes, when they're in trouble, they come back. You came back, Conan. Funny, I foolishly thought that one of these boys and his wife could take up my work." She looked over the familiar faces. "But I can't expect someone else to take up my dream. Jonas tells me a dream is distinctly your own. It would no longer be mine if it slipped from my hands."

He didn't move even when Griselda came into the room with a tray of hot dumplings. "Will you hang up my children's pictures?"

"Danny and Keeley won't be here long enough for that," Abigail answered.

"Of course they will," Griselda said as she turned to leave them. "Two precious children like that. Trust me, Conan O'Reilly, I'll make certain Abigail hangs their pictures with the others. And I won't let Jonas take them down. Now, come and eat your supper while the dumplings are steamy hot."

He gulped down the chicken and dumplings, then wiped his mouth with the back of his hand. Abigail touched his arm. "I wish things could have been different for you. For all of us. But Jonas trusts me. I can't betray him. Jonas checks in on his father before midnight. James grows restless around then."

"Then I'd better leave now. You've taken enough risks for me." As they left the room, he said, "Abigail, are you all right? You look—you look not well again."

"Just another passing flutter," she assured him.

She felt the jerking of her heart. The missed beats. She linked her arm with his and leaned against him.

"Who takes care of the Admiral during the week?" he asked.

"Lucas during the daytime. The Admiral would never think of sending his steward back to Dublin. They get on splendidly. And I stay with the Admiral on the evenings when Jonas isn't here."

"I never understood your great affection for the old man. I thought the British Navy took care of its own."

"They do—but for now, I want him here with me. You used to walk along the river with the Admiral, didn't you?"

Conan's mouth twitched. "A few times."

The evening wind blew cold as she opened the door for him. "Where will you go, Conan?"

He pressed his bristled cheek against hers. "It is best that you don't know, Miss Abigail."

The familiar term of his boyhood. She choked, "I promise you, I won't fail your children. . .just stay safe."

"Don't worry. I am invincible."

A patch of moonlight shone faintly in the sky as Conan slipped out the front door. It made him even more of a blackened shadow as he darted into the thickly wooded darkness.

Twigs crackled beneath his booted feet as he edged the well-traversed footpath. She feared lest he stumble and lose his way, but he was already one of her lost ones as he forged his way toward the bridge.

A prayer for Conan stuck in her throat and remained there unuttered. For a frantic moment, she thought to ring Reverend Rainford-Simms and ask him to dash out into the night, over the pedestrian bridge, in search of her lost boy. Wasn't that the clergyman's job—to go after the lost, to rein in the wandering?

A rolling cloud drifted across the moon's path, but Conan would welcome the darkness. The night was too still, filled only with the wingbeats of owls lighting in the conifers, the churning of the waterwheel down by the old mill, and that rippling murmur of the Windrush winding through the rushes. Like the tawny owl, Conan was a creature of the night, given to darkness, his senses alert. But the owl in the woodlands was clothed in thick down; Conan had only his threadbare jacket to warm him.

The sound of his boots on the gravel faded and was gone.

She was certain he had reached the fork in the path by now. To his right, he would see a dim light flicker in the chancel of St. Michael's. Charles always left a light on for those in need. But Conan would turn left, away from the redemptive footpath, and make his way stealthily over the old stone bridge to escape from the village of his boyhood.

Without warning, gunfire shattered the stillness. She stumbled down the steps. "Conan, Conan."

A sharp pain like a knuckled fist furrowed across her chest.

She gripped the rail to regain her footing. As the sharpness eased, she cried again, "Conan, Conan!"

Only the rustling wind and gurgling river answered her.

With her heart still knocking unevenly, she forced herself back up the steps—determined to protect Danny and Keeley. She put her trembling hand on the brass knob and shoved the door open. More gunfire split the spring air. She saw Griselda running down the hall toward her, heard Gregor's cry as he ran beside Griselda.

Another explosion erupted behind Abigail. Closer this time. A crushing pain seared through her back and chest. For a second she stood motionless, stunned. Griselda's face blurred.

The tingling began in her fingers. Numbness. Utter helplessness as pain radiated into her jaw. The weight on her chest grew heavier. Unbearable. She tried to grasp Griselda's hand, to smile at Gregor. Then all awareness slipped from her as she slumped to the cold, dank floor of the manor.

Chapter 5

In Washington, time lagged eight hours behind the Cotswold clocks. Sydney awakened at dawn on Saturday with a metallic jangle blaring in her ears, her unlisted number ringing off the hook. It had to be Randolph calling at this unearthly hour to apologize—or to make excuses—for their latest lovers' quarrel.

She could hear him now, nonchalantly suggesting that he join her at the Barrington retreat in the woods for the weekend. Deliberately pretending the quarrel didn't matter. Thanks to her parents, he had always had a room of his own, had always been welcomed as part of the family. He still had a key and thought nothing of popping in at unexpected moments, more so since their engagement. At those times, when the loss of her parents seemed the most poignant, Randolph was comforting to have around. Sadly though, Randy would remain the man her parents had trusted, the one they wanted for a son-in-law. Their choice. Not hers.

Dear Randy. Tall, trim, his eyes a cold gray blue last evening. He was so much like her father. Shrewd in business, he'd earned his first million before he was thirty and now, at thirty-eight, thanks to her father's investment tips, was working on his second million. A well-groomed man, but no matter what his attire, he wore his emotions up front. Ardor. Impatience. Disappointment.

The phone rang for the third time. She ignored it, concentrating on the extravagance that surrounded her—a king-size bed, a Jacuzzi tub, and a spacious, pink dressing room only steps away. She owned her own home, held the top post at Barrington Enterprises, and traveled abroad frequently. What more could Randolph Iverson offer her?

Mother Nature flooded her room with brilliance as the sun broke through the wispy clouds. But Sydney kept rehashing the quarrel. Randolph wanted a commitment from her. She gazed somberly at his photo on her bedside table. He was an intriguing mixture of Jew and Gentile, two worlds wrapped into one man. His piercing eyes and spirited way of speaking came from his mother; the narrow, irregular nose and angular face from his dad.

In an unguarded moment, shortly after her parents' accident, Sydney had accepted Randolph Iverson's ring. But in truth, she didn't want to get married. She had everything she needed or could possibly want. Books and music and art were matters that she could share with Randolph. But not their hearts, their lives. Not her love of the woods and the river. And not that secret yearning that lingered at the edge of consciousness, tantalizing her with longings for something special, impressions that she could not identify.

On rare occasions, when she ventured to share her heart and dreams with him, he'd tug his ear and laugh uproariously. "You and your Shangri-La. Your Garden of Eden. It doesn't exist, sweetheart." But she knew he was wrong.

Love him? Sometimes she loathed him. Last night's blowup had come over her mother's sewing room. She rehearsed their bitter words, Randolph's thin lips pursed, his voice soothing, languid.

"Sydney, it's time to think about us. Get the house cleared out so it can be our house. Finish going through your mother's things and put her to rest."

"That's not fair. I can't risk the memories it will stir."

"And you're not being fair to us. You can't bring your mother back."

∼

By midmorning, Sydney took the key and unlocked the door to her mother's sewing room. As she stepped inside, she was struck with an overwhelming sense of her mother's presence. The silent room echoed with the remembered sounds of her mother's humming and the clacking treadle of the sewing machine. The brightly lit room still held the faint scent of her mother's fragrant sachets.

The shelves across the room were filled with dolls that Millicent Barrington had prepared for the children at the local hospital. The apple-cheeked china doll in a fleecy robe. The rag doll in denim overalls. And the old-fashioned porcelain one dressed in taffeta and lace—the doll that Sydney had promised to give away to someone special.

Sydney swept the room with a singular gaze. Everything was exactly as her mother had left it. The Swiss-made sewing machine faced the bay windows. Spools of thread hung from wooden spindles, their bright colors ribboned like a rainbow on the wall. A bolt of gingham leaned against one corner, and doll patterns lay strewn on the worktable. The polished armoire stood open, revealing more drawers and shelves crammed with buttons, zippers, and scraps of flannel and broadcloth. Even the rug by the sewing machine bore the imprint of Sydney's hours of sitting there watching her mother's fingers move deftly, lovingly as she formed intricate doll garments.

Her mother's pink slippers lay sprawled by the foot pedal lying in the spot where she had kicked them off the night before her flight to Europe. Sydney caught her own reflection in the mirror on the armoire. How lost she looked. A lump rose in her throat as she crossed the room to the sewing machine where a square of velour was held securely under the pressure foot—the beginnings of a doll dress that her mother never finished.

Slipping into her mother's chair, Sydney looked out on the yard and beyond toward the Olympic Mountains. Her mother had been a private person—deep, caring, sensitive. Her father she understood better—a proud, public figure concerned about his image. She was so much like him—skillful at wielding a strong arm at Barrington Enterprises, emanating his power and strength.

But she had so little of her mother's gentleness. She ran her fingers over the sewing machine, removing a layer of dust from it. Her mother had been content to stay in the background, yet at the roar of her husband's BMW into the driveway or his footsteps on the gravel, Millicent always stopped what she was doing and hurried to meet him.

The room, so much a part of her mother, brought back the last moments they had spent here together. Millicent's soft words seemed to fill the room. *"Is Randolph coming to dinner this evening?"* she had asked.

"Probably. He never waits for an invitation. This morning Daddy asked me when I was going to marry him so he could just move in permanently. Imagine!"

"Your father doesn't believe in long engagements." She laughed happily. *"Ours, as you know, was quite short-lived."*

"Randolph and I are not engaged."

"I'm certain he's asked you. So what's it going to take?"

"A bombshell."

Her mother concentrated on stitching the tiny doll dress. *"What did you tell your father, Sydney?"*

"That I cherish my independence, the freedom to come and go as I please. I just can't tie up my life to one person."

Millicent paused in her sewing. *"Is that how you view your father and me? Tied up? Without freedom?"*

Her parents—so different, so in love. *Aaron, the dashing, keen-witted businessman, silver-haired as far back as Sydney could remember. And Millicent, the beautiful and graceful wife with the soft English accent at his side. "You're different, Mom. You don't object to doing things Dad's way. You think alike. No matter what Daddy wants, you go along with it."*

Slowly, Millicent turned to face her daughter, her eyes sad. *"You have it all wrong, dear. Aaron and I do things together because we love each other. I like pleasing him, and at the end of a harried day at the office, he finds comfort in coming home to me. He still courts me with roses. A world without your father in it would be dreadfully lonely."*

"It's not like that with Randy and me. Randolph doesn't have Dad's charisma. I just can't explain him—"

"Can you explain yourself?" her mother had asked. "Do you know your own heart, know what you want?"

"Sometimes."

But how could she explain to Millicent that sometimes she found Randy charming, attentive, a comforting companion? Yet, if he left town in the morning, her world would still go on. It would never be that way with her parents. They needed each other.

"I was sixteen when Dad first brought Randy home to dinner. I guess I just think of him as a friend."

Her mother paused in her stitching and smiled. "I saw right away that he was your father's kind of man. Intelligent. A quick learner. We liked him. Your father would like him as a son-in-law." She matched a spool of thread against the material in her hand. "But I want you to be happy, so choose carefully, Sydney."

It's coming now, she thought. *The mother-daughter lecture that Sydney had outgrown long ago.* Preserve yourself for the one you love. *But what if you never fell in love?*

Her mother's foot balanced above the treadle, caught in space, caught in time. She glanced down at Sydney. "If you don't plan to marry—don't plan to give Aaron and me grandchildren—what is it you want to do with your life, dear?"

Sydney drew her knees to her chest. "Dad insists that I take over Barrington Enterprises if anything happens to him. Randolph won't like that. He thinks Dad promised the job to him."

"Aaron wants a Barrington in charge. You'll be good at it, my bright little feather. With your master's in aerospace engineering, you're a genius with figures and you understand business mergers and government contracts. You've always been your daddy's girl. He's trained you well."

She switched to a blue thread. "But promise me you won't let the position and power at Barrington destroy you."

"Destroy me? Mother, I plan to grow rich working there."

"We have already made you rich. Someday, you will own this house as well. When you're talking with Aaron about defense plants and government contracts, you're efficient. Even ruthless at times. But when you're with me at the hospital, passing out the dolls to the children, you remind me of Dulcie. You'd make a fine pediatric doctor or nurse like Dulcie was before she went to Africa."

She cupped Sydney's cheek. "More and more, you look like your mother. Dulcie was beautiful, and so are you. You have her facial features and a bit of her gentleness. And you have your father's strong points, too. He was very intelligent—as you are."

"Why do you never talk about my birth parents?"

"I am now. Aaron doesn't like being reminded that you were not our flesh and blood."

"But I am yours. You and Dulcie were sisters. And Dad shouldn't feel bad. A lot of people say I look like Aaron. I love him; he's the only father I've ever known."

Millicent held up a finished dress of taffeta and lace for inspection. Putting it on the empress doll, she said, "Won't this make some child happy?"

"It's adorable, Mother. Randolph teased me last night about having a mother who still played with dolls so late in life."

"You tell Randolph Iverson that I never had a doll of my own in those years after the war. Never." Her eyes grew misty. "Syd dear, I want you to give this one away to someone special."

"We'll do that on our next visit to the children's ward."

"I won't have time to deliver it before my trip to Europe."

"It can keep till you get back."

"No, promise me." She reflected. "When your father and I get back from this business trip abroad, let's the two of us plan a vacation. I'll take you back to England to the place where Dulcie and I were born. And to the church where she was married."

"I'd like that. Would Dad mind?"

"Very much so. But this is something I should have done a long time ago. You need to know more about your birth parents. We've given you everything, yet I feel we have let you down. I don't know what you really want to do with your life. No, that's not true. You have always talked of working with children—of leaving your position at Barrington. But I guess I just went along with Aaron's dreams for you."

Her brows puckered. "If you left Barrington, what would you want to do? Tell me and I'll try and talk to Aaron while we're in Europe. It will be hard to make him understand—he has his heart so set on you working beside him, but he loves you. . ."

Sydney knew that she was groping for something abstract, something undefined. Something she couldn't explain to her parents because it had no label. But surely it would include children. "I haven't worked out anything definite. But I think I'll recognize the right place when I find it."

"Are you thinking about God, Sydney?"

"What does God have to do with my future?"

Her mother's eyes watered. "Everything, perhaps. I really have failed you. Failed myself. Aaron has never been a very religious man—so I never pushed that part of your training."

"I've turned out all right." But even as she said it, Sydney sensed an aching void inside.

"I should stay home this time, but Aaron likes me to travel with him. I'm glad you're flying as far as New York with us, though."

"Can't miss a chance for a shopping spree. And I want to be at Kennedy International to make sure you get on that plane."

Sydney remembered that wistful look on her mother's face when she hugged her good-bye at the Kennedy boarding gate.

"Sydney darling, you'll be all right by yourself?"

"Of course. Don't be ridiculous. I'm a grown woman."

But she had wept like a little child moments later as news spread through the airport terminal that her parents' jet had just crashed in Long Island Sound, minutes after takeoff. . . .

Sydney shook off those memories and concentrated on a large black spider crawling across the floor in the sewing room. In search, she was certain, of a refuge of its own. With clarity, she knew her mother was right. She was searching for her own person, her own self. How could she discover who she really was if she married Randolph? They could never be one. Never.

~

Hours later Sydney sat curled on the floor in her white shorts and a T-shirt, her face and hands dirt-smudged, her nostrils filled with layers of dust. The fuzz from a tangle of spiderwebs curled on her bare leg as she sorted through her mother's things. A growing pile of toss-aways lay to her left: old patterns, mismatched buttons, scraps of fabric that Millicent Barrington could have turned into doll clothing. On her right, Sydney had stacked craft books and the awards her mother had won for dolls she had made.

Tearing the last carton open, she waded through a layer of yellowed newsprint before finding an old album—the pictorial record of her mother's childhood in postwar London, her mother's adult life before Aaron. In one unlabeled snapshot, her mother and three friends stood arm in arm in front of Lake Geneva. In another, they ran hand in hand over crusted snow in Austria. These were friends that her mother had lost touch with after her marriage. Aaron Quinton Barrington had not only swept into Millicent's life at a London ball, he had whisked her out of London and away from everything English, everything familiar.

Sydney studied the last picture in the album—a picture of herself as a small child standing in front of the Barringtons in the middle of an English garden. Aaron was looking into the camera—smiling, dark-haired, handsome. Her mother wore a wide-brimmed hat, her dark-lashed eyes peering out beneath the rim. On a sloping hill in the distance stood a large country house with a river winding below it. Sydney could not recall being there, but she remembered the gurgling, bubbling sound of the river.

Chapter 6

In his cottage on the Broadshire property, Jonas Willoughby crouched in front of the stone fireplace, set a match to the kindling, and watched the fire flame and crackle. Satisfied with the roaring fire, he stood and was confronted at once with Louise's photograph on the mantel.

Her lips were parted, smiling. Smiling at him when he snapped that picture. He traced the lines of her face, missing her as he did. He opened his mouth to call her name—to have her come and share the fire with him, and at once remembered that no matter how much he called, she would never come to him again.

Here in the Cotswolds, in the most peaceful place he had ever known, he couldn't shake off the uncertainty of interfering in other lives, of having them interfere in his own. He felt tormented at the thought of placing his father in a permanent residence. Undecided about Abigail and Gregor. Annoyed by Griselda's silent disapproval. His own bitterness with the IRA had almost destroyed his communion with himself and his God. And Charles—that man of peace—remained a constant reminder of what might have been. Thoughts of all of them crowded his daytime hours out on the wolds. Thundered in his ears when he played his bagpipes. Invaded his dreams at night, turning them into nightmares.

Jonas kicked off his boots and sagged into his recliner. At midnight he would cross the grounds to the manor and sit by his father's bedside until dawn. For now, it was good to stretch and close his eyes and sleep—a sleep deep and troubled as it propelled him back into the days before Louise, to the days without her. Back to the job he loved more than anything—into a sweeping panorama of the past, of flying, of launching his Sea Harrier off the flight deck of the HMS *Invincible*.

It was the same dream. The same nightmare. . . .

～

In the moonlight, the deck of the aircraft carrier gleamed like silver. The ordnance handlers had loaded the Amraam missiles. The deck crew signaled for takeoff. Jonas gave a gloved thumbs-up and with his Pegasus jet engine running full throttle, the Harrier screamed into the vast emptiness of the sky, leaving the carrier swallowed in darkness.

Squinting owlishly through the canopy toward the wingtip, Jonas saw only empty space. The hazy swirling clouds left the sky a cinereous gray. Jonas was flying blind on a combat patrol to Yugoslavia. Flying alone, his squadron nowhere in sight. He tried to rally the control tower. Silence. He felt confused, his oxygen depleted. He was totally alone. It was impossible to turn the plane back.

The menacing silhouette of the Harrier roared on toward Kosovo, rapidly closing the gap as its onboard computers scanned for a target. Gregor's village lay ahead and he must blow it into cinders, root out the Serbs who had dug in there. He had his mission, his Amraam missiles. As Jonas activated the weapons system, the cockpit screen showed TARGET ACQUIRED, then LOCKED. His thumb hovered over the firing button, just waiting for the moment.

He tried to identify the target, but the weather had turned murky. Gregor's village? He couldn't fire on Gregor's village. In the semi-darkness outside his canopy, he spotted the Serb interceptor zeroing in on him—a Russian-built MiG-29 fighter, the pilot faceless. Just then, the Serb climbed erratically. From the ground came the burst of antiaircraft guns and surface-to-air missiles. The explosions erupted around the Harrier in orange and white flames. Jonas fixed his gaze on the panel in front of him and fought for control. Pushing buttons. Twirling knobs. He was like a white knuckler, an anxious passenger in the pilot's seat.

The MiG-29 screamed toward him again, the face in the cockpit taking form now. Young like himself. A man without a face mask. For a moment Jonas knew dread, the fear of dying. Heart-pounding fear. He pressed his thumb onto the firing button. Heard the explosion. Saw more flames engulfing him. He was forced to maintain radio silence with no one but God on his wingtip.

"Abort. Abort!" he told himself.

The ejection seat jammed. He was locked in, spiraling downward. He would welcome death if he could see Louise again. No, he wanted to go on living. His skill was being tested to the limit; his survivorship training kicked in. Hope rose. He knew deep in the ship, in the operations room, seamen were monitoring his Harrier, tracking him on the radar screen— the rotating blades of radar swinging back and forth.

His arms ached as he tried to level the plane. He needed some assurance that God was flying this one out with him. " 'Our Father who art in heaven. . .'"

Was that how it went? Is that how you prayed when you were nose-diving into eternity? No, something more direct. Zero straight in. Abigail maintained that God always listened.

"God," he mouthed beneath his mask, "let me live. Take me safely back to the carrier. No, take me back to Gregor, so I can tell him that someone else destroyed his village."

Spiraling through a patch of drifting clouds, he was convinced that he was over the Emerald Island, close to the narrow road where Louise had been ambushed. He saw motion beneath him. The IRA stronghold. Not Serbs, but the IRA terrorists. His muddled brain refused to clear. With a quick maneuver, he leveled out, gained altitude. At 600 knots he seemed to creak along. Going nowhere. Unable to turn the plane back to the Adriatic Sea.

Jonas felt a rush of cold over his legs and had time to wonder why he wasn't wearing his flying boots. He reached for the zipper on his flying suit and felt instead the soft twill of his tweed jacket. As he breathed deeply into his oxygen mask, the smell of country and sheep and wild thyme filled his nostrils. Suddenly his seat shot forward, his legs extended. He tried to right himself and felt his dog nuzzling the back of his hand. . . .

~

Jonas came out of his nightmare sweating, his lanky body pressed against the back of the recliner. He was in his thatched cottage on the edge of the Broadshire property. Safe. Alive. He had been dreaming.

He blinked against the grogginess, his mind still reeling from the nightmare: Kosovo; the ship; taking off in his Harrier jet. But that was a year or two ago, part of the past. His duty. His duty to kill innocent people. He massaged his throbbing temples. When he flew the sorties, the Kosovo bombings had exploded in his ears. They still resounded in his thoughts. He glanced at his watch, surprised that he had slept only five minutes. Ten at most. A mere fragment of time in his thirty-four years. Yet he had just spent a season in hell, a torturous journey into war.

What had sent him into this mental tailspin? Thoughts of Louise? No, thoughts of Gregor walking beside him today out on the knoll, saying, *"Lucas said you bombed my papa's village. Will my papa ever come home again?"*

Gamely, Jonas had tried to explain to the boy about war.

Tried to tell man-to-boy why the Allied Forces had flown sorties over his country. Why did it matter now? Gregor had been little more than seven then, an evacuee trucked across the border into Macedonia. No, that wasn't what happened. Gregor had been forced to walk the last ten miles toward the border with one shoe gone. Somewhere between his own troubled country and the refugee camp near Skopje, the Albanian guerrilla thrust the frightened child, without kin or a tin of water, into Abigail's waiting arms.

Wood cracked in the stone fireplace and slipped in charred blackness through the iron grate. TopGun's wet nose nudged his hand again; then the dog raced to the cottage door whimpering.

Outside, an explosion shattered the stillness of early evening. Jonas's bare feet hit the floor before he realized he was standing. The explosion had been real, the dream unreal. Something out of the ordinary was happening down by the Windrush. He wiggled into his boots, stumbled out of the cottage, and ran toward the river with his collie at his heels.

Now the sound of angry voices gave him new direction.

When he came within yards of the bridge, he was convinced that the entire village had turned out. Women and children stood in the background, too curious to go back to the safety of their cottages. Men huddled in groups, staring at the ground. The gurgle of the river went steadily on, flowing down the center of town and winding peacefully over the valley.

"Jonas."

Even in the darkness, he recognized the gangly man beside him. At six-feet-two, Jonas rarely felt stunted in another man's presence, but Charles Rainford-Simms, in spite of his stooped shoulders, had two inches on him. Charles was in shirt sleeves with an unbuttoned vest, his clerical collar loose at his neck.

"Charles, I heard gunfire. What happened here?"

"A young man—a stranger in town—was shot. But he escaped."

"We rarely have strangers in town, Charles. Who was he?"

"I thought you would know."

Jonas scanned the crowd milling around in tight-knit groups. The pub owner waved his flashlight toward the thicket. "Here. Over here!" he cried. His beam of light centered on a patch of ground by the river. He lifted his hand. "Blood," he said. "We've got him. He can't be far—he's losing too much blood."

The schoolmaster took up the cry. "You women, go home. Take the children with you and lock the doors."

Lock the doors? Jonas shrugged. *How many people in the village even have locks on their doors?*

The schoolmaster thundered more orders. "Nigel, take some men with you and scour the thicket. Peter, take a group and fan out on the other side of the river. Two or three of you stay with me. We'll follow the Windrush on this side." He glanced at Charles. "No need for you to come. We younger men can take care of everything. Go back to the church in case you are needed."

Jonas started forward to join the schoolmaster. Charles pulled him back. "You heard him. The villagers can handle it." He kept a restraining hand on Jonas's arm. "Let the others go. Neither one of us should be there, not if there's more gunfire. Besides, son, I must talk to you."

Jonas spun on his heels. "We can talk later."

"No, you see, the wounded man is not the only stranger in town. Two gentlemen called on me earlier this afternoon."

Jonas rubbed the collie's head. "Visiting bishops?"

"Hardly. Intelligence officers. MI5 would be my guess."

For the first time since coming home, Jonas felt uneasy. Had three years of grieving robbed Charles of his quick wit? Or was Mrs. Quigley right? *"He seems a bit dotty at times, muttering and puttering in his garden,"* she had said.

"Intelligence officers, Charles? That's highly unlikely in Stow-on- the-Woodland. Unless—"

"Unless they were looking for you or me." Charles watched him with wise old eyes. "My boy, I know the rumors, but I have my wits about me. So don't tell me to retire and take that long-deserved rest. That long rest will come soon enough."

Doggedly, Jonas persisted. "How old are you now?"

"On my birthday three years ago I turned seventy-five; I haven't counted since then, but I'm not too old to know that those men were snooping around our village when I invited them in for tea."

"Charles, later. Please. I must join the others."

"You must not get involved. You see, when I showed the visitors my model train, they admitted that they were looking for an Irish agent living in this village. I refused to allow them to use the sanctity of the church to search for anyone. And they knew that I was Louise's father—said they expected more cooperation from me since my daughter died at the hands of Irish terrorists."

He touched the collar around his neck, pure white even in the darkness. "I am committed to helping people, not destroying them. But if they're right—if there is an Irish terrorist in the village—if this has anything to do with Louise, then those strangers may be looking for you. You must leave at once, Jonas, and go back to Northwood. Go back tonight."

Jonas jammed his hands deep into his pockets. "I'm not a man who runs. I know you believe what you're saying, but whatever is happening here this evening has nothing to do with Louise or me."

Charles rocked thoughtfully on his heels. "I was wrong to keep you from joining the search party. I'm sorry. But I've been missing you. Surely you remember your way to the vicarage? You must." His voice cracked. "Someone has been putting flowers on Louise's grave. You, perhaps? Even so, you don't stop by for a visit with me. We used to play chess together. I'd enjoy a game."

"I'll make it a point to come next weekend."

From the shadows, they saw Boris hurrying toward them. "Commander, go to the house. Miss Broderick needs you. Doctor Wallis is on his way."

$$\sim$$

As Jonas and the dog raced toward the manor, Charles heard the search party shouting in the distance. He turned in the direction of the church, an uneasiness tingling his spine. He was accustomed to long walks alone at night, roaming the Cotswold Hills. Praying. Singing. Worshipping his God. But as he moved toward the vicarage, a voice called sharply from the darkness.

"Reverend. Over here, by the trees."

Rainford-Simms stared without seeing. "Who are you?"

A whispered answer. "Lucas, Admiral Willoughby's steward."

Charles almost stumbled over the body lying on the ground.

"I need your help, Reverend. This man is badly wounded."

Charles knelt down, and with his penlight, studied the troubled young face grimacing in pain. His light trailed to the man's blood-soaked jacket and shirt. "We're here, son." And to Lucas, "He needs a doctor. All I'd have to do is ring the church bell and the men searching for him will come back."

"I daren't allow that. The crowd is merciless. I can treat a gunshot wound, Reverend. Just help me get him to safety. You must help me. He's one of Miss Broderick's boys."

Stunned, Charles asked, "Does she know he's in town?"

"Does it matter? You are a man of the cloth, and this man needs a sanctuary, sir. If we hurry, we can get him to the church before the villagers come back."

The man went limp as they pulled him to his feet. "We won't get far, dragging him like this. He'll only bleed more."

"But, Reverend, we can't let him die in the bushes." Blood splashed on Charles's clothes. Time was running short. "There's a trout stream that branches off from the Windrush. It flows just beneath the vicarage. Do you know where I mean?"

"That's a tangled mess of bracken and underbrush. We can never get through."

"There is always a way through. The vines hide a footpath from the bank to the vicarage. It's too much for an old man to climb often, but if you help me, we can make it. It is the only way to let the Windrush wash away our bloody footprints."

As they struggled up the trail, he asked, "Why do you want to help him? Are we not breaking the laws of the land?"

"I told you, he's one of Abigail Broderick's boys. And, Reverend, I am like you. I no longer bear arms or take sides. I've been the Admiral's steward for far too long."

"But you have political convictions?"

"Aye. That I do." He feigned a Gaelic twang as they stopped to catch their breath. "I've lived all my life in England, but I was born an Irishman, sir. And this man is one of my countrymen."

An icy knot formed in Charles's stomach. *The IRA? A young terrorist?* He was breaking the laws of the village, the rules of the church. Perhaps the laws of his God. Could he skim by on the Good Samaritan clause taking this man into the vicarage?

"God forgive me for getting involved," he said.

"God bless you for getting involved."

As they neared the vicarage, the door swung back, casting a bright light on their path. A young woman in an artist's apron appeared on the landing. "Oh it's you, Reverend! What is all this thrashing about in the bushes?" she scolded. "Have you gone quite mad trying to find your way home?"

Lucas stiffened. "Who are you?"

She pushed strands of hair from her cheek with a paintbrush. "Kersten. Surely you remember me, Lucas. I do light housekeeping for the reverend in exchange for room and board."

He asked gruffly, "Does your light housekeeping include helping an injured man?"

Kersten pocketed the paintbrush and rubbed her paint-smudged fingers. "So that's what all the shouting is about? Come in quickly so I can darken the windows. Who is he, Reverend?"

"One of Miss Broderick's lost boys."

"Poor man. Can't be all bad if he belongs to Miss Abigail. And, Lucas, I am good at boiling water."

She stood aside to let them enter, shock registering in her expression at the sight of the man's ashen face and bloody jacket. Then, quite calmly, she said, "He's bleeding badly—but I'm good at washing up."

"We can trust her," Charles said.

And the door closed on the darkness outside.

～

"Stay, TopGun," Jonas commanded.

The collie obeyed as Jonas sprinted up the steps of the manor and flung back the door. As he stepped inside, Gregor flew into his arms.

"Has something happened to Sir James, Gregor?"

"No, it's. . .it's Miss Abigail."

He pushed the boy aside and bounded up the curving stairs, his lanky legs taking three steps at a time. He was breathless when he reached Abigail's room. She lay on her bed, her eyes closed, her arms limp at her sides. The periwinkle blue comforter that he had given her at Christmas had been drawn to her waist. Her silver gray hair—always neatly in place—sprawled loosely on the pillow. Jonas felt like an intruder, invading her privacy.

"Abby."

She moaned, mumbling indistinct words. He felt a surge of relief that she was alive. He strode across the room and took her icy hand in his. Her lips were blue, her skin milk-white. When he called her name again, she gave him a ghost of a smile.

"Abby, what happened?"

"My heart."

He pressed his fingers to her wrist and felt her pulse. "Dr. Wallis is coming."

Tears filled her eyes. He knuckled them away. "Did he make it, Jonas?"

"Who, Abby?"

Griselda was standing on the other side of the bed now. "The gunfire upset her. You must leave at once. Go back to London."

"I can't run out on Abigail."

Abigail's eyelids fluttered open again. "Please go."

Griselda chewed her lower lip. "There's nothing you can do here.

Abigail doesn't want you involved—"

"Involved in what?"

"Just go. I will call you." He heard the sob in Griselda's voice. Saw the proud chin jut forward. "It's what Abigail wants. She wants you safe, Jonas."

"I can't leave her. . .not like this."

"And you can't do anything for her, except pray. You can do that on the way back to Northwood."

Pray? Abigail's beliefs no longer rubbed off on him. He stared down at the woman who had prayed for him all of his life—the woman who had been at the family manor whenever he went home from Gordonstoun or Dartmouth or on leave from the Navy. He choked up at the thought of her dying. She had watched him grow to manhood, had an unflinching pride in him and always words of wisdom or rebuke when he went home. She was right of course. A man couldn't travel the rough seas or fly into battle without knowing that Someone bigger than himself had charted the universe and tempered the seas. It wasn't Abigail's fault he had shelved God.

"If the Admiral were well, he'd order you to go," Griselda remarked.

Jonas leaned down and kissed Abigail on the forehead. "I'll be back next weekend—or the one after that. Get well, Abby."

Exhausted, she whispered, "Take the back roads."

He glanced at Griselda. "What is she saying?"

"She wants you to go the back roads, then join up with A-40 and on into London. With the ruckus that's going on, the police will stop anyone going through the main towns—and discover that you are from Northwood and NATO Intelligence."

Gently, he laid Abigail's hand against the comforter. When he reached the door, he heard Boris and Doctor Wallis coming up the stairs. Jonas crossed the hall and ducked into an empty room. Once they had stepped into Abigail's bedroom, Jonas went quietly down the back steps to his cottage.

Gregor was sitting in Jonas's recliner, his arms around the dog. "You're going away?" he accused.

"For a few days." Jonas threw his things into the kit bag. "Will you take care of TopGun for me while I'm gone?"

The boy nodded. "Will Miss Abigail die, Jonas?"

Jonas bent to spread the ashes in the fireplace. Picking up the daily paper, he tossed it in his case. Then, as he turned out the lights, he said, "I don't know, Gregor."

"I'm scared, Jonas."

"We both are." He put his arm around the boy and led him out the cottage door. "Go back to the house and get some sleep, son. Take TopGun with you."

"Mrs. Quigley won't let TopGun into the house."

"She will tonight. She'll understand." He tossed his luggage in the car. "Gregor, Miss Abigail doesn't want anyone to know I was here this weekend."

Gregor sniffed and wiped his nose with the back of his hand. "I know. Mrs. Quigley told me."

Chapter 7

Sydney stepped out onto the lower deck of the rustic retreat where she had come to spend the weekend. Everything she owned bore the signature of Aaron Barrington and spoke of wealth. The four-bedroom house with its knotty-pine siding and wide, wraparound porch sat high on a bluff overlooking the river. She ran her fingers over the beveled porch railing and thought of her father standing there, loving nature, loving life. . . .

~

He had stood in that very spot when she, as a sixteen-year-old, had rushed outside, exclaiming, "Dad, now that school is out, I'm going to train for the marathon."

His grip on the railing tightened. "A race? Honey, the Barringtons don't waste a whole summer running. You're going to be managing the company someday."

"But it's a benefit for children with AIDS. I talked to Mother about it. I've signed up; I've given my word."

"Your mother didn't discuss it with me. She knows I'm holding a place at Barrington Enterprises for you this summer."

"Dad, don't your employees have to be eighteen?"

"You won't be on the payroll. With your genius for math, I've arranged a special apprenticeship for you in the engineering department. You'll learn the business firsthand—"

"I'm not needed there. I'm needed in the marathon. Don't you understand? It would mean something if Aaron Barrington's daughter won the race."

He reached into his back pocket and whipped out his checkbook. "I'll make a contribution. What about five thousand? Who do I make it out to?"

She fought back hot tears. "Is it worth that much to buy my place in the race?"

"It is to me, Sydney."

Yes, worth it, *she thought,* to always have your own way.

Sydney wondered why such searing memories of her father attacked so often. She dragged one of the patio chairs over with her bare foot and sank down in its padded comfort. Her father bought everything with money, but he couldn't buy time. Now that she had his money at her disposal, she wanted only those things that wealth could not buy: solitude, peace, contentment.

From the cabin to the river, nature was garbed in spring colors. Flimsy tree branches turning a buttercup yellow. Bushes and hedges in a patchwork of holly and Kendal green on the upper cliffs. The weeping willows in shades of moss and lime, bending gracefully toward the water's edge.

Sydney had spent her whole life on the river. A privileged kid—swimming, boating, water-skiing, riding her horse along the mountain streams. Listening to the gurgling of the river, she felt as though life had turned normal again. But it hadn't. She rubbed her finger where the diamond had been a week ago.

Why had she accepted Randolph's proposal so soon after her parents' death? Out of loneliness? Because he was her father's choice? Randolph was always there to field her questions, to laugh and talk with, to dine with on quiet evenings. As her fiancé, he went on being a welcomed guest at the Barrington home and at the cabin, their long friendship as cozy and comfortable as a warm fire. But it had been a fiery good-bye.

"You're married to the job, Syd. I can't compete against that."

"Then don't," she had snapped. "The job is only a temporary arrangement until something better comes along. Someone better."

His jaw had tightened as he stared at the diamond in his hand. "Sydney, would you recognize love if the right person walked into your life?"

She didn't know.

In her mind, she saw him running down the front steps of her home on Lake Washington. She could still hear the door of his Jaguar slam. His tires squeal. She knew he loved her. But no matter how she tried, she did not love him. Why then did the thought of walking back into the empty cabin right now fill her with dread? Tonight, with so many friends a phone call away, she would be alone, with only the sounds of the river and nature to comfort her. She admitted to herself the inner longing to really belong to someone special, to love as her parents had loved. But she knew no one who could fill the void of an empty house, an empty heart.

In the midst of her dark musings, the phone rang. It had to be

Randolph. On the eighth ring she picked up the receiver.

"Hello. Sydney speaking," she said guardedly.

"Mrs. Barrington?" The accent sounded decidedly British.

"Miss Barrington," she corrected.

"This is Edmund Gallagher from the Gallagher, Blackstone, and Rentley firm in London, England."

A lawyer? A problem at one of their overseas facilities?

Solemnly, he said, "I was Abigail Broderick's solicitor."

She wanted to say, *And who is that?*

"Miss Barrington, our connection is a bit garbled."

She switched the receiver to her other hand and amused herself by counting her polished toes. "I'm still here."

With dignity, he said, "It is my sad duty to inform you that Miss Broderick is dead."

"Dead?" she retreated.

"Yes, I am so sorry."

No need to be sorry, she thought. *I don't know any Abigail Broderick.* At least she did not remember the name. Did not know whether she was a distant relative on her mother's side or one of her mother's old friends.

"What happened to her, Mr. Gallagher?"

"A heart attack. Miss Broderick died in her own manor."

In her own manner. Who would choose a heart attack? Did that run in the family? On the Barrington side? Her mother's side? No. Dulcie, her mother's only known relative, was dead.

"It was quick," the solicitor said.

The garbled distraction on the wire pierced her ear as though Gallagher had run a silver coin across the mouthpiece. The words of the man on the other end of the line sounded distorted.

"Miss Broderick had been unwell for some time, and as far as we can determine, Miss Barrington, Abigail Broderick has left everything to you."

Stunned, Sydney tried to absorb the fact that she had just inherited some stranger's possessions when she was already rich and needed nothing. In her mind, she conjured up an elegant old house on the Thames or a Tudor manor. Then curiosity took over. Why had the Barringtons not told her about this woman?

"Perhaps you can be a little more explicit, Mr. Gallagher?"

"Regarding the inheritance? It includes a house and a walled property with an English garden. Stables—"

A house and a garden. Again Sydney envisioned a lovely home on the

River Thames. Or a Chelsea residence off King's Road—a place to stay on her trips abroad. But stables in London? Ashamed of her mental wanderings, her thoughts turned back to the unknown woman with a heart too weak to keep on beating.

"Was Miss Broderick elderly?" she asked.

She heard the rattle of papers. "Quite so. Late seventies."

"Is her property in London? You said you were calling from there."

"No, the property is in the Cotswolds. It's called the Broadshire Manor. Quite a substantial place in the village of Stow-on-the-Woodland. You have heard of it?"

"No, not really. . . . The truth is, Mr. Gallagher, I don't know anyone named Broderick. I don't even know for certain whether we have relatives in England. And certainly no stranger would leave her things to me."

He raised his voice. "I am a careful man, Miss Barrington. It seems unlikely that I have the wrong number or have dialed the wrong person."

So, she was talking to a man who didn't make mistakes. He seemed so indifferent, so uncaring as he spoke of his client. Sydney pictured Edmund Gallagher sitting self-righteously at his desk, drumming his fingers on Abigail Broderick's will. As his words droned on, she wondered how well he knew Miss Broderick. Or was he simply discharging his duty as her lawyer? She imagined him well-attired in a suit tailored on Chancery Lane and decided that he no doubt took his law degree on the West End and had his plush office tucked in somewhere among England's white-wigged barristers.

Gallagher cleared his throat. For a moment there was no static on the line. "I have Miss Broderick's file in front of me. You are the daughter of Aaron and Millicent Barrington. Correct? Your father was a business icon? Known worldwide? Made his money in the defense program. Correct?"

He rattled off her birth date, her age, her educational attainments, including her summer at Oxford and those marvelous nine months studying French in Paris. Then quite cagily he said, "Perhaps you met Miss Broderick while you studied at Oxford? Or, I see from a notation here that your tie-in with Miss Broderick might go back to a missionary couple in Africa."

It was more than she wanted him to know about her. "Go on."

"Are you certain your parents never mentioned Miss Broderick?"

"If they did, I've forgotten."

The suspicion in the back of her mind intensified. She twisted the telephone cord, longing for the opportunity to ask the operator to trace the call. Gallagher could be a crackpot, someone aware of the value of Barrington Enterprises. Someone aware that she was at the cabin alone with a chilling breeze blowing up from the river. She curled her legs under her to warm her feet, but the sudden chill remained.

"I am upsetting you with news of Miss Broderick's death," the solicitor said. "Should I call back later when you have time to sort out your loss?"

"No. Tell me about her now."

"She had been ill for some months, under medication. But she constantly overdid with the children."

"Children?" Sydney gasped. "Miss Broderick had children?"

"Six of them."

"If she had children, why on earth am I her sole heir?"

For the first time he seemed amused. "It would seem for the time being that you have inherited the children as well."

A piece of land and six children! "How old are they?"

She heard him shuffling through papers again. "The oldest is nine, the youngest three. When Miss Broderick had her last heart attack, we tried to persuade her to go to the hospital. She refused because of the children. As her lawyer, I am responsible for placing them. . . . Are you still with me, Miss Barrington?"

"Of course."

"They're not her children. She was their caregiver. We will have to place them. Perhaps you wish to be consulted on this?"

She hadn't spent much time with children except for visiting those in the hospital ward. She liked children—liked their quaint way of speaking, their funny little sayings, their innocence. But whatever would she do with six of them?

Gallagher's dispassionate voice turned edgy as he asked for directions on the disposal of Abigail's remains. "As her sole heir, we need to know your pleasure."

"What is your usual custom?"

"Quite like your own. Her will calls for immediate burial in St. Michael's Cemetery. Should I go ahead with plans?"

Of course. She had no desire to arrange another funeral.

But he staved off her response when he said, "We are aware that you have a corporation to run. Your father's business."

How does he know that? she wondered.

"So there is no need for you to come," he continued. "I will be happy to act on your behalf. Sell the property—transfer the funds to you as soon as they are available. Dispose of the children. I already have a buyer in mind. I'll just send you the paperwork authorizing me—"

"A buyer for the children?"

He chuckled without humor. "The property, Miss Barrington."

No, she thought, irritated by Gallagher's brusque manner. *I will not authorize you to make decisions on my behalf. This woman could have been a flesh and blood relative, and I will not let you dispose of children as though they were rusty garden tools.*

She realized as she spoke heatedly with the man that it was not the CEO of Barrington sitting here engaged in a conversation across the world, but Millicent Barrington's offspring, ready to fight on behalf of hurting children. The thought pleased her.

Her attention was diverted momentarily to the river and her longing to get away from Randolph. But how could she think of using the death of a woman in a Cotswold village in England as an escape? Still, she said, "Mr. Gallagher, I must speak to my lawyers here. If possible, I will arrange my schedule to travel to England. I have business matters in Europe quite frequently. It will simply be a matter of adjusting my schedule."

"So you can attend the funeral?" he asked curtly.

"No. For the settling of the will—the selling of any property. And, as you said, the disposing of the children—"

Instead of static, there seemed to be silence. She imagined him covering the mouthpiece, seeking the opinion of someone else. Then he was back. "Your coming to England won't be necessary."

"But it will, Mr. Gallagher. I can't just let Miss Broderick's passing go unnoticed. You are obviously experienced at selling property—but we will not sell the children."

She heard him suck in his breath and decided that he was displeased with her decision. She didn't like what was happening on the other end of the world, but whoever this Abigail Broderick had been, perhaps she needed a friend to settle her affairs.

Sydney could spare a week or two, longer if necessary. Another inspection of the shipyard on the Tyne would be a good excuse for traveling abroad. And a dinner invitation to the manager of the carrier project would be a good investment of her time, especially if she selected one of the elegant restaurants in London. Calculating quickly, she knew she could arrange to leave within days. A week at most.

She grabbed a scrap of paper from her pocket. "Let me have a number where I can reach you, Mr. Gallagher." She jotted down his London number. "And your Cotswold listing? . . . Now, tell me, who is caring for the children at this time?"

His answer seemed indefinite, flustered. "A Mrs. Quigley. But there is no way to talk directly with her."

There is a way, Sydney thought, *but you don't want me to contact her.* "We'll be in touch, Mr. Gallagher. Perhaps we should meet in your London office."

"Yes. . .of course."

"We'll arrange that when I call back."

Suddenly she had the upper hand and knew it. Whatever was going on in Edmund Gallagher's mind, she had put him on the defensive. "You said the children were in the Cotswolds. In Stow-on-the-Woodland, wasn't it?"

"I didn't say, but that is where they are. But, Miss Barrington, they are in good hands. Trust me."

That's the one thing I won't do, she thought.

She hung up the phone and stared across at the sunlit waterfall. The tumultuous waters raged over the rock cliff and tumbled down in an ear-splitting force, yet she felt an unbelievable calm. A peace. She should be overwhelmed, confused. And she was. But across the ocean she had just inherited a piece of land and six children. Tomorrow she would make the final decision on whether to pack, close up the house, and fly to England— to a solicitor who might not delight in her arrival. And to her new responsibility: six young children who needed permanent lodging.

Chapter 8

In London Edmund Gallagher slammed his knuckled fist on his desk and glared at the younger man sitting across from him. "It didn't go the way I expected, Marshall."

"How did you expect it to go?"

"I thought Miss Barrington would allow me to handle the legal matters on this end—without her coming here."

"You lied to her. How long do you think you can deceive her into believing that Abigail Broderick is dead?"

Edmund rubbed his bruised knuckles. "My partners forced my hand. They knew Broderick was critical, and then yesterday I rushed things when I told them she was dead." He mopped his brow. "They knew the contents of her will. Rentley told me to get on the line and notify Miss Barrington. If I hadn't called her, Rentley or Blackstone would have. Blackstone is nervous enough about the problems we'll face when Jonas Willoughby discovers he's not the heir to Broadshire Manor."

He nursed his knuckles again. "I may still be able to persuade her that she is not needed on this end. She's talking to her own lawyers—that's a problem, but I'll work around it."

"Even if you persuade her to stay home, what happens when it comes time to hand over the property to her? You can't give away possessions when Abigail Broderick is still alive."

"You're the fool who said she was dying, Doctor."

Marshall escaped into a silence that infuriated Edmund.

They had known each other all their lives, played on the Cotswold Hills, took their separate degrees in London. But they had never been close friends.

Edmund, at thirty-nine, was the more ambitious man, well-esteemed in the office of Gallagher, Blackstone, and Rentley. He had grown up near Bourton-on-the-Water, but he was a Londoner at heart—a serious-looking man with thick-rimmed glasses and curly brown hair prematurely peppered with gray, a man who rarely admitted to a sheep-grazing background.

Marshall Wallis, a year younger, was content to live in the village, serving the people as a physician and spending his spare time fishing on the Windrush.

Although Edmund's firm headquartered in the heart of London, he still maintained his father's Cotswold office. He traveled to the Cotswolds two days a week with an eye to doubling profits, not from the country folk but from the growing populace of Londoners setting up holiday homes in Gloucestershire. The Broadshire property represented his ticket to independent wealth. Once he turned the manor into a hotel, it would open Stow-on-the-Woodland to tourism, a venture that would draw hundreds of tourists away from Bourton-on-the-Water.

Marshall rubbed his brow. "You've opened one of those kettles of worms, Edmund. The woman expects an inheritance now."

"I'll tell her that Abigail left heavy debts—that we must sell the estate to pay them off. I'll borrow funds from the firm—juggle a few major accounts to compensate Miss Barrington with a token amount of money. It's not as though she were a relative."

"Your partners will let you get by with that?"

"My partners will never know the money is missing. Once I take over Broadshire Manor, I'll pay them back. I'll sell portions of the property to developers. I'm not an idiot, Marshall. I don't intend to stay with Blackstone and Bentley all my life."

"You've gone too far this time. Deceiving Abigail or Miss Barrington is one thing—fraud within your firm is another. And I'll have no part of it."

"You have no choice. It's cooperate with me, or I'll destroy you. Your wife would not like that."

Marshall winced. "Keep my wife out of this. Once the people of Stow-on-the-Woodland get wind of what you're doing, they will run you out of town—if your firm doesn't send you to prison before that."

"You would like that, wouldn't you?"

"Your plans will fail, Edmund. Blackstone and Rentley started the firm long before they took you in as a partner."

"Your point?"

"They made a mistake taking you in."

"I was top in my class. High levels."

"But not an intelligent man. They'll realize that someday. Are you aware that Jonas Willoughby is home now?"

"Yes. He made two appointments with me to discuss selling the property and the legal ramifications of placing his father in a permanent residence. I promised to find him a buyer for the property. But I must put him off as long as Abigail is alive."

"Then he doesn't know that Barrington is the sole heir?"

"What difference does it make? Jonas plans to go back to sea. I'm biding my moves accordingly. Once he's gone, I would have no difficulty persuading Abigail to sell me the property—if she lives long enough to make that decision."

"I don't want to see you go down, Edmund, but if you try to take over the manor illegally, I'll stop you."

"How, Marshall? I have the law on my side and the power to ruin you. Where would the village be without a health center? Tell me—just how long does Abigail have? Days? Weeks? Hours?"

Marshall said quietly, "I have no idea. But I'd be glad if the old girl lived forever—and put a stop to your madness."

❧

Sydney awakened to a thick smog hemming the city in and thought at once of the strangers in the Cotswolds who had stepped uninvited into her life. For the first time since taking over Barrington Enterprises, she decided to work at home. Alone. She needed time to think about Abigail Broderick. Something hovered on the edge of memory, some link to this stranger who had died.

Before showering, she browsed the Internet, plugging in names and places in the Cotswolds. She found only one small segment about Stow-on-the-Woodland.

> *A quaint Cotswold hamlet along the River Windrush, fifteen miles from Bourton-on-the-Water. Noted for its fifteenth-century St. Michael's Cathedral, a historical water mill, and its trout streams.*

Her fingers flew over the keys in search of places to stay in Bourton-on-the-Water. She found hotels and inns in the center of town. The names *Mousetrap* and *Old Manse Hotel* intrigued her, but she booked her room at The Sheepfold, a bed-and-breakfast along the Windrush. She pictured herself wandering through peaceful English gardens and traipsing the footpaths into the countryside, or hiking along the streams in the village where Abigail Broderick had lived and died. Peaceful? What was she thinking? Six children would be dogging her footsteps.

Her excitement built as she turned her search engine to people.

Abigail Broderick's name did not appear on the screen. But she found a listing for Edmund Gallagher: *Edmund Gallagher of Gallagher, Blackstone, and Rentley, solicitors, London, England.*

Would it please him if she called to tell him that she was flying to Stow-on-the-Woodland within the week? An hour passed. Two. Finally, she stretched her aching shoulders and knew that she needed the rushing sound of water to help her make a decision.

Forty minutes later, she stood on a narrow stretch of beach overlooking Puget Sound, listening to the waves pounding relentlessly against the ferry dock. The wind caught the breaking rollers and swept them toward her, spraying her face. The thick swirling mist that obliterated the city at dawn had blown out to sea. Still the weather remained overcast, painting the sky and the water a dismal gray. Sand particles blew into her eyes as she walked toward the picnic benches. The surrounding sounds intruded on her thoughts about the unknown stranger who had left her everything—all of her possessions and six children.

Would going to England be Sydney's folly? Something for her board of directors and Randolph to gloat over, laugh about? Gallagher could settle everything without her presence. But again as a gentle wave washed ashore, she knew she did not trust the British solicitor. She felt certain that he did not have the best interest of these children at heart.

As seagulls skimmed across the surface of the water, other hikers jogged toward her, their voices in muffled undertones. Above came the noise of a helicopter; on the road to her left, the cranky overdrive of a battered truck on the street. Her sneakers beat a rhythmic tread to the blast of the ferry whistle and the creaking of the boat slipping from the pier.

Sydney plunged her hands into her pockets and plowed on until she came to a disposal unit, framed by a stone wall. Leaning against the wall, she tried to picture the faces of the children in the Cotswolds and could not, but she would pack toys and one or two of her mother's dolls for the trip to England.

Taking her cell phone from her jacket, she plugged in Randolph's number at the office. "Randolph, this is Sydney."

"I've been calling everyone. Your neighbors. Your caretaker at the cabin. Where have you been?" he exploded.

"I'm all right. I just needed time to think."

"About us?"

"No. I've been walking. Making plans for a trip abroad."

Hopefully, he said, "Really? Do the plans include me?"

"Not this time, Randy. I'm planning a trip alone."

"You'd better think about the work piling up on your desk."

Her thoughts winged to her father's upholstered chair and ottoman where he had read to her so long ago from *The Old Man and the Sea* and from his favorite, *For Whom the Bell Tolls.* Aaron was in many ways like Hemingway—popular, tough, scornful of other men's ideas. He loved Hemingway, but thankfully her father had not been there to scorn the toll of the church bell calling his friends and employees to his own funeral.

Randolph broke into her thoughts, "Sydney, you're not hearing a word I'm saying. What's that roar in the background?"

"The breakers. The ferries. I'm down at the beach."

It set him off again. "Barrington Enterprises is your responsibility. Have you checked on Wall Street this morning?"

"No, and I didn't have coffee either. They usually go hand in hand." This morning she hadn't thought about the ticker tape that charted the all-consuming rise and fall of her investments.

"Stock prices are down, Syd. Interest rates rising."

"Stop fussing. Our business is booming. What more do you want?"

"If I were in charge," he snarled, "I would be at my desk right now signing those new government contracts, not out walking on the beach."

"We'll talk about the contracts tomorrow."

"You're not coming in this afternoon? Great! Daron Emery has points on the carrier project to discuss with you. And your secretary has fielded your calls all day. And those defense contracts for the plant in Tennessee need your signature, not mine," he reminded her.

"That's going to change in the next few weeks. I'm leaving you in charge when I'm gone. That's what you've been wanting all along, isn't it? A chance to run Barrington?"

Her words got through to him. "You're not running out on me? It's not that quarrel the other day?"

"The other day is history."

His voice grew thick, throaty. "Am I, too?"

"We'll talk about that later. I want you to set up a meeting with the board of directors first thing in the morning. We'll discuss us—my plans for you then."

"In a room full of executives? Surely, I deserve more than that."

You deserve so much more, she thought. "Don't worry, Randolph. I won't embarrass you in front of our colleagues. Making a good impression is too important to both of us." She stretched her long legs in front of her, raking the sand with her shoe. "But I've learned something. A good impression is only temporary. It doesn't make for lasting happiness."

"Oh no. We're back to your finding your Shangri-La again. You can't fly off on some harebrained holiday, hunting for something you'll never find. Where are you going?"

She considered telling him about the children in the Cotswolds, but would he understand? He had made it clear often enough. When he married, he did not want children. The best thing she could do for both of them was go away.

"I'm going to Europe."

"Europe? Is there more trouble with the shipyard?"

"No. I'll explain everything tomorrow."

He cleared his throat. "Sydney, I must see you. Go back to the house, and I'll pick you up for a late lunch."

"Not today. I'll see you in the morning."

"Then have dinner with me?"

"Not tonight. I have to go now. It's windy down here."

She disconnected before he could argue with her and began walking back to the car. Why did he stir such mixed emotions in her? She liked him, disliked him. Cared about him, avoided him. But he was right. Barrington Enterprises with its billions invested in defense projects was her responsibility. How could she think about England when she had Aaron Barrington's empire to run?

Above her the overcast sky had lifted; billowy white clouds had blown in. Sydney came out of her own foggy mist, her decision made. No matter what Randolph thought, she must fly to England.

Chapter 9

Sydney needed legal advice, but not from her corporate lawyers or by pulling a name from the yellow pages. She wanted Jeffrey VanBurien. At the thought of him, she pictured his features vividly. Tall and blade-thin. Long-legged. Fair-haired, with a thick blond mustache that looked good on him and sharp blue eyes that glinted when he smiled.

She reached for her phone, dialed his number in Chicago, and waited for his secretary to put her through to Jeffrey. She had been exhausted and hungry when she met him at a business conference in Chicago, shortly after her parents' plane crash. The hotel dining room had been too full to seat her immediately.

"Ah! Stranded in the Windy City and hungry!" said a voice behind her. "Why don't we find another place to eat?"

She had turned and looked up into the bluest of eyes. "Sorry, I don't go running around the streets of Chicago with a stranger. My fiancé wouldn't approve."

He lifted her hand and checked the diamond. "My luck. So we'll have to eat here."

When he produced his business card, she said, "Oh, you're a lawyer."

"Jeffrey VanBurien at your service."

"I could use a good lawyer, an honest one preferably."

The blue eyes danced. "I am good. Even my brother hires me as his personal defender. And I can be honest, if I have to."

He beckoned to the maitre d'. "We were told there's an hour's wait. We don't have an hour. The lady is hungry now. Perhaps you would be so good as to get the management and tell him Celeste VanBurien's son is here with a guest."

The maitre d' was back within minutes. "This way, sir."

During dinner, he had told her about himself—born in Chicago, a mother well-known in Oak Park, his father dead and buried in Alabama.

When she confided her fears at taking over her father's business, he had encouraged her and offered his help.

On the spot, she had retained him for off-the-cuff advice. It had been a good move on her part, one that mushroomed into a warm friendship.

419

Jeff was like having a big brother to lean on, a broad shoulder to cry on, a trustworthy confidant that she could phone on a moment's notice. Whenever she changed planes in Chicago—and that was often enough— he'd be there, waiting for her with a big grin and a thermos full of coffee or a box of candy.

Now she twisted the telephone cord on her fingers as she waited for him to answer and smiled as he said, "Jeff VanBurien speaking."

She remembered his pleasant, laughing voice. "Jeff, it's Sydney Barrington. What took you so long to answer?"

"A rich client. How are you? Been weeks since I heard from you. Are you beautiful as ever?"

She glanced down at her faded jeans and brushed back her gnarled hair, windblown from the beach. "Not exactly. But I need a favor."

"You're paying me retainer's fees. Shoot."

"I'm flying to England on Wednesday. I may be running into legal problems."

"With the airline?"

"No, with a British solicitor."

"Run that one by me again."

"According to this lawyer, a woman by the name of Abigail Broderick just died and left her inheritance to me."

"I should be so lucky. Did she leave you a mansion?"

"Don't joke, Jeff. I'm pressed for time."

"Sorry. I guess I didn't know you had rich friends in faraway places. So what's up with this Abigail Broderick?"

"It's the lawyer who's troubling me. I have this uncanny feeling that he can't be trusted."

"A lot of people evaluate lawyers that way." He became more professional now. "I can't judge uncanny feelings. Is he fraudulent? Has he let you down before?"

"I haven't met him. We've just talked by phone, but there's land and children to worry about. He wanted to send me some papers to sign so he could settle everything without my being there. Said he already had a buyer for the property."

She pictured Jeff leaning forward, his elbows propped on his desk. "Don't sign a thing. When did this Miss Broderick die?"

"She isn't buried yet. I know that."

"You sound like you don't know much about her."

"I don't even know if we've met. But six children are involved, and the lawyer plans to dispose of them. At least that's the way he described it."

"Syd, if you think he's a hoax, why go over there?"

"I have legitimate reasons for checking on our European facilities. In the last eighteen months, since Mom and Dad's plane crash, I've been sending others to do my job. It's time for me to go myself."

"But you're still afraid of flying—and you're going on another overseas flight?"

"I have to for the sake of those children."

He whistled. "You always were a sucker for kids. I think you better tell me everything. And start from the beginning."

"The lawyer's name is Edmund Gallagher. I think he's anxious to sell the property before I get there." She filled in the rest of the details, choking up as she spoke of the children.

While she composed herself, he said, "Sydney, we could get married and raise those kids together. You'd have to live in Chicago, of course, and maybe you'd have to work part-time so we could support them."

For some reason his nonsense brought on a flood of tears. The crazy galoot would probably do it. "That's the sweetest offer I've had all day, but I'd rather have you as my lawyer," she said.

"Just my luck. So what steps have you taken?"

"I've made my reservation with a brief layover in New York." She gave him the flight numbers and departure time.

"Too bad you aren't transferring in Chicago. We could have dinner together. Syd, you're okay about flying over the ocean?"

"I'm trying not to think about it. And I have a meeting with my board of directors in the morning. I'll drop my bombshell then. I'm leaving Randolph Iverson in charge."

"Your call. Anything else I should know?"

"You have my arrival time in London. I'll rent a car at Heathrow. I booked a room at The Sheepfold—a bed-and-breakfast in Bourton-on-the-Water. From there, it's an easy drive to Stow-on-the-Woodland. Fifteen miles or so."

"Don't do anything rash. Just meet with Mr. Gallagher and hear what he has to say."

"I plan to look over my own inheritance."

"Look, but stay out of trouble. And we have a major problem, Syd. I'm not qualified for British law." His words sounded muffled now, and she wondered whether he was rubbing his mustache or chewing the tip of his pen.

"I understand that, but I trust your advice."

"I'll browse in my law books the minute we hang up. Don't worry, Sydney. You said you're staying at The Sheepfold in Bourton-on-the-Water? I'll contact you there." More lightly, he asked, "How's lover boy?"

"Randolph? We're not engaged any longer."

"Sorry about that." He didn't sound sorry at all.

"Jeff, all I've done is talk about me. How are you?"

"Been putting my life back together. Do you remember me telling you about my half-brother, Chandler Reynolds?"

"The music critic who works for American Intelligence?"

"The CIA is a sideline, and if he ever gets in trouble, Langley won't know him."

"What about him?"

"He's in England where you want to be. Married now. I'll fax you his number. And, Sydney, we finally decided to have that get-together. I'm taking six weeks off from the firm and flying to London myself. We're going to give this brother thing a shot."

"Then you'll be in England?"

"And we'll be in touch. It's cutting it tight, but I'll see about changing my booking and flying with you."

"Oh, you don't have to do that."

"I know. But I'd hate to miss the opportunity of traveling with a beautiful woman."

She sensed he was about to hang up. "Jeff, thanks so much."

"No problem. My legal fees come high."

"I know. Just bill Barrington Enterprises."

"I'll do that," he said cheerfully and hung up.

～

Sydney stood at the door of the conference room and surveyed the thirteen directors at the oval table. They sat rigidly, as stiff as the backs of their maroon leather chairs. Bespectacled Sam Rosman twiddled his thumbs. Max Berger twisted his tie. Randolph sat beside him—immaculate as always, his business savvy apparent in the cut of his dark suit and silk tie.

She caught Randolph's eye as she entered. He who was always confident, always putting forth his best front, looked wary. He stood as she reached the head of the table. For a moment she feared he would brazenly brush a kiss across her cheek.

He slid the chair in behind her. "Are you all right, Syd?" Ignoring his concern, she rested her wrists on the table and said, "Good morning, everyone."

Eighteen months before, it would have been, "Good morning, gentlemen."

Her father had excluded women on his executive board. In her first three months as CEO, Sydney had fired one man and replaced him with capable Ivy Meckerton. Another of her father's old cronies had died six months into her takeover. Against strong opposition, she clung to a small clause in the company policy—her father's safeguard for his own leadership—and assumed the right to choose her own replacements: another woman, three years her junior. The younger woman sat with her tapered fingers locked, her gaze straying toward Randolph.

The directors were an intelligent lot, and if they weren't loyal to her, they were loyal to the memory of her dad. Financially secure, they weren't apt to leave Barrington Enterprises, even with Sydney at the helm. Though some of them still struggled with a little girl image, they respected her business aplomb, her drive. The original dip in profits at the death of her dad had long since surged upward. Barrington Enterprises still held its firm grip in the world market.

Sydney planned to say something that would infuriate them all—but again policy gave her the right to do so. "I'm leaving town for a while on a brief business holiday to England," she announced. She glanced at Randolph, her gaze steadfast. "Mr. Iverson will be in charge while I'm away."

Max Berger quit twisting his tie, his sleepy gaze alert now. "Sydney, your father always left me in charge."

And I never understood why.

She made a mental note to offer Berger a sizable retirement package on her return, one that would allow him a graceful withdrawal and eliminate the slowdown that was obviously taking place. Max was a good man, but he should have taken his social security and pension three years ago and not hung on as the oldest member of the board. She would never fire him. She had sat on his knee as a child and delighted in the dolls and boxes of candy he had given her over the years.

"Max, Randolph will keep you apprised of what's going on."

Ivy Meckerton looked puzzled. "That trip was scheduled for next month. I thought I was handling that for you."

"Next time, Ivy. I want to see firsthand how things are going in our European divisions."

"But I know you dislike flying since—"

Sydney nodded. "It's time for me to shake off my fears, Ivy."

Randolph came out of his silence. "Foreign negotiations?" he said scathingly. "I usually handle those."

"Not this time."

He nodded to the others, his eyes unsmiling. "It would seem that Miss Barrington has already made the decision to go herself." *Without consulting me,* his voice seemed to say.

"Trust me, Mr. Iverson. This is best for all of us. I have a private matter to tend to as well. I've just been advised of the death of a friend."

Ivy leaned forward. "We're so sorry. But will you be all right flying alone? I could go with you."

"Randolph will need your help." *Your wisdom,* she thought.

A lump rose in Sydney's throat as she thought of her dad's last time at the conference table—making arrangements, handing out assignments. A handsome, silver-haired gentleman, a man who lived to make money, building success upon success. He had left the conference room and the next day flown off with his wife, not to their intended destination in Europe, but into eternity.

Sydney had flown across country several times since then, always with a knot in her stomach. But she had not flown out over the ocean since that crash off the waters of Long Island. She blinked, remembering that miserable moment when she had looked out on the bobbing pieces of the aircraft caught in the stormy swells of the water. She had turned away, tears burning behind her eyes. Her stomach tightened even now.

"I'll be all right, Ivy." She flashed her confident, executive smile. The no-nonsense, no-questions-asked variety. "Now, regarding those government contracts from Washington—"

~

As the room emptied, Randolph caught her hand. "You're running away."

"From you?"

"From life."

She pulled away from him and gathered up her papers. "I can afford to do anything I like."

"Stay. We'll work it out. We can send Ivy in your place."

"Randolph, someone really did die."

He licked his thin lips. "A close friend?"

"An older woman. I didn't know about her until—"

She couldn't speak with the lump in her throat. Why was she trying to explain the unexplainable to Randolph? She didn't even understand her own sense of loss.

"You have a business to run here."

"You can handle it. You know the company better than I do."

"Aren't you afraid I'll take control while you're gone and change every-thing your father wanted?"

"You're too honest, Randolph. Too loyal."

"You don't believe that for a minute."

"Then you're forgetting the board of directors and the company law-yers who will make certain everything runs smoothly. It's up to you. I thought you would like handling things while I'm gone. Running things—isn't that what you've always wanted?"

"What I want is to be with you. I just wish your father would stop coming between us."

"I don't understand why you dislike him so."

"Because you are so much like him. Assertive. Ambitious."

"It takes that to run this corporation."

"I wish you would just give all of this up and marry me."

"Cunning man that you are. Then you could take the helm of the ship permanently, is that it?"

"Your father promised it to me."

"No, he trained you for leadership, but he never promised that you would take over his job."

"Then delegate more of your responsibilities to me."

"I just did here at this conference table. Weren't you listening? I put you in charge while I'm gone."

"Syd, do you plan to check up on my last trips to Europe to find out whether I did everything according to Aaron's wishes? Someday you're going to wake up. Your father never did anything that didn't benefit himself."

He flipped the end of his tie. Smoothed it out again. "I'm the first one to admit that I wouldn't be where I am today without him, but he molded me to fit his own schemes. I think, my dear Sydney, he did the same for you."

"You're wrong. My father was a good man. A hard worker. He was kind to those who worked for him."

"He was more Greek myth than kindly. He was Icarian by nature, like a Greek god. But I think he flew too high with some of his bidding. And I think he had his wings clipped with that shipyard project. Someday you're going to discover another side to the man you adored, and your father's going to come tumbling down from his ivory tower. We're still trying to track down a couple of his accounts. The Broadshire account for one."

Her brows puckered at the word.

"The account records amounts of money transferred to a Swiss bank. Nothing else. No addresses. That's poor management, Syd. And the Swiss bank is tight-lipped about the recipient. Periodic transfers. In varied amounts. Was that one of your father's defense projects? Or another of his follies?"

"Stop it, Randy. My father was the most honest man I know."

"Really?" He sighed. "You're right. But he was not always fair with other men's dreams."

"Yours for instance?" she asked gently.

"I worked closely with your father. I saw the darker side. He never let another man's dreams stand in the way of his own. He was ambitious, forceful, scheming."

Like you, she thought.

"He was good at what he did. Never forget, Dad built this corporation from scratch."

"By exploiting his competitors."

"If you found him so despicable, why didn't you resign long ago?"

"Because I wanted to be near you."

She shrugged. "Randy, I feel sorry for you."

For a second she considered putting him on the streets to find his own way to the top. But she needed him at Barrington Enterprises. Sydney felt her smile coming back. He did have a handsome face, but his eyes proved his best feature—seductive, dewy-eyed, yet sad now as he looked at her. She went over to him and touched her finger to his lips. "Let's not quarrel. Not now. We need some time apart. I think all of this is just about the two of us. I don't think it has anything to do with my father."

He pressed her fingers against his mouth and kissed them. "Don't go. Stay. Marry me."

"Dear Randolph, I'll never change. I'll always be ambitious, as you call it. I think what you want is an ordinary cog in the wheel for your life's companion. A wife who will stand behind her husband and say nothing."

She started for the door of the conference room. He blocked her way. "Promise me you'll come back."

"Why wouldn't I?"

"Because, deep inside, you're searching for something and I don't think I'm part of that plan."

When they reached her private office, she wondered whether she was doing the right thing. She turned and found herself inches from him, close to that familiar scent he always wore. With her mind's eye she traced his features. Remembered the warmth of his arms. She reached out again and touched his cheek, regretting the bitter quarrel that still stood between them.

"My return ticket is open-ended."

"That's forever."

Her hand slipped back to her side. "I'm sorry, Randolph."

"Sydney, I want to be with you. Let me go home with you tonight. I'll drive you to the airport in the morning."

"No, that's not a good idea. And I'm not leaving until Wednesday. I've already ordered an airport limousine."

"You could cancel the limousine."

When she looked into his eyes again, her anger at him melted completely. He needed her, but she slipped behind her desk to separate them. She was sailing dangerously close to thin ice. Her skin prickled. The knot in her stomach doubled. She could almost taste her loneliness. What was wrong with surrendering to Randy's charms? Wasn't that what they both wanted? Wasn't that the way to put aside their quarrel?

Purposefully, she cleared her desk. The silence dragged. "Sydney, look at me."

She glanced up. He stood with his hands in his pockets, his face so familiar—so much a part of her life—that it seemed impossible to remember when their friendship had really begun.

"I'm afraid I'm losing you," he said sadly.

"You lost me last week." She didn't add, *But then I was never really yours.*

His tone, rancorous moments ago, was whipped, defeated. "I need you. Let me stay tonight? We can work things out."

Don't say another word, she thought. *Just go. Go on your own, because I might not have the strength to send you away again.*

He held her gaze, his eyes grave, mirthless, the glimmer of hope fading. She had let him down, throttled him; her leaving was the last thing he expected. She wanted to say she was truly sorry.

Sorry for him. Sorry for what might have been. But the die was cast. She was being drawn to the Cotswolds in a way she could neither understand nor explain.

He took a step toward her. His eyes said it all. *You're dazzling, beautiful, love of my life.* But where was the chemistry between them? How long could she go on pretending?

"Sydney, I need you. I love you."

"Please," she said. "Please go."

Chapter 10

Northwood Headquarters, a highly classified area, crawled with gold braid. Driving in through the security gate, Jonas stepped back into his own world, a man's world for the most part. NATO commands from several countries found posting here: the Americans and Dutch, French and Italians, the Greeks. Lunch in the wardroom allowed him to keep his language skills current. He could switch easily into German, French, or Spanish.

Minutes later, he stood outside Captain McIntyre's office, grinning to himself as he touched the three gold stripes on his uniform sleeve. As the clerk admitted him, McIntyre extended his hand across an uncluttered desk. Jonas had only seconds to survey the Spartan room. Everything looked shipshape, like quarters on board the carrier. The only personal touch in the room was the large ship's model on the captain's desk.

"Your model looks like one of the frigates from the Falklands, sir. The *Ardent* or the *Antelope*?"

"One just like them. The *Brownlee*. It was my first ship."

"Your father was CO then. Come, I have pictures over here."

Jonas steeled his shoulders and plunged in. "Sir, I would appreciate compassionate leave for a few days."

"Good grief, Willoughby. Did the Admiral die, and we haven't been informed?"

"No sir. But the friend who takes care of him is not well."

McIntyre dismissed the request, saying, "Commander, you know compassionate leave is for immediate family only. Now, come along, have a look at these old ships."

I worded it wrong, Jonas thought.

He tried again, but McIntyre led him to the far wall filled with photographs of ships that had sailed under Her Majesty's Service. His broad finger centered on the edge of one, straightening it. "This is the way the *Brownlee* looked the day I boarded her back in the Falklands. During one lull in the battle at San Carlos, your father went down to the injured and walked straight over to a dying midshipman. A lad about seventeen."

McIntyre clicked his tongue. "What a commanding officer. He came in with his cap crooked under one arm, his hair thick and black like yours, Willoughby. He took off his jacket, sat down, and took that young man's hand in his own."

The muscle in Jonas's neck grew taut. *He never held my hand,* he thought. *Ever.* His father had called it too unprofessional, too unpolished for a senior rank. *"Be a man, Jonas."*

"Your father called the lad by name. Said, 'Neil, I have a son about your age. I keep his picture on my desk.' You could hear the pride in his voice when he talked about you. Said you had gone to Gordonstoun and would go on to Dartmouth."

Jonas kept his gaze fixed on the picture of the ship, trying to see his father through McIntyre's eyes.

"He told Neil that you spent your holidays in Stow-on-the-Woodland, right along the Windrush. And quite bluntly, he asked, 'You're from that area, aren't you, Neil?'

"I was in the next bunk, injured myself, and I saw Neil's eyes brim with tears at the mention of the countryside. 'Yes sir. Gloucestershire. Winchcombe,' he said. For almost twenty minutes, your father talked to him about the Cotswold Hills. About sheep grazing and waterwheels spinning at the mill. Quite in the middle of everything your father said, 'Her Majesty is proud of you, son. Grateful for your sacrifice. You will be long remembered.'"

He squared another frame on the wall. "He made it a point to tell the boy he'd visit his parents the next time he went home on leave. He didn't tell him he was dying, but the boy knew. And I knew, and I was frightened for him. Then your father's conversation flowed quite simply into a description of heaven."

Jonas cleared his throat. "And did he tell him how to get there?"

"You would have thought he'd been there himself, speaking of the river of life and golden streams and a pain-free existence."

To Jonas, the man that McIntyre described seemed vastly different from the man he knew. He couldn't imagine his father sitting beside a dying man. The Admiral hadn't even come home for his wife's funeral. No, that wasn't fair. His father's ship was in the Far East on a crisis posting, too far away to bury the woman he loved.

Jonas's gaze slid along to other ships. A big battlewagon. A World War II submarine. The *Cavalier*, in dry dock now. He ran his teeth over his lower lip. Both the *Cavalier* and his father had followed distinguished careers. Both had been retired to inactive status—a death warrant to both the ship and the Admiral.

Captain McIntyre demanded his attention again. "Your father stayed with Neil until he died. Then he stood up, tall and wiry, put his jacket on, and squared his visored cap. I knew as they pulled the curtain around that boy, I would gladly follow your father into battle whenever, wherever. I did—twice on other ships. We never spoke of that incident in the Falklands, but he had my undying respect."

He faced Jonas. "I consider your father a great man. He deserved to be an admiral. To serve with the Admiralty. And now I have the opportunity to work with his son."

"So I'm here because of my father?"

"It influenced me, but your record is good, Willoughby." He pointed to the HMS *Invincible*. "Your last posting, wasn't it?"

"Yes, a great ship."

McIntyre's jaw tensed. "I can't say I favor the changes coming in the *Andrew*—this man's Navy won't be the same. With the reduction of ships, promotions will be hard to come by. I'm still adjusting to a combined air fleet. Can you believe it? The RN and RAF joining forces. Your father left at a good time."

"I'll miss the rivalry between the two services. But flying never appealed to my father."

"Is that why you chose it, Willoughby?" Wisely, he didn't wait for the answer. "Tell me, how is the old man? I've been meaning to get over to see him."

"He'd like that. He'd welcome your visit, but it's not likely he'll remember you."

"But he'd remember his ships."

"That he would, sir. It's all he talks about. Shouting orders from his bed. Telling us to clear the harbor at Portsmouth so we can set sail. Yes, he'd remember the ships."

"And does he remember you, Jonas?"

"Not when I first got back. But he does now."

"I'm sorry that your father's health is failing. Is that why you transferred to Northwood? A bloody shame, that's what I call it. Your not taking your own command. But the *Invincible* is due back in Portsmouth in September. By Jove, it would be splendid if you were ready to board her again."

"It depends on my father—"

"He'd never stand in your way of a promotion. Why you gave up that ship, I'll never understand. It must have shocked him, too. But it must comfort you, Willoughby, knowing your father has always been proud of you. He constantly bragged about you as you came up through the ranks."

"I wish he had told me how proud he was."

If the captain was surprised, he masked it. "Perhaps you weren't listening."

He walked back to his desk, Jonas following. "Sir, I keep hoping I'll be offered another command when things settle down."

"The best you can hope for is to go back to flying. You'd better not delay too long. Another two years and the French Dassault Rafale or the Eurofighters will replace the Harriers."

"I'd like to fly the Eurofighter—and be on hand for the maiden voyage of one of the new carriers."

The captain browsed through the folder in front of him. "Squadron commander. Naval duty in the Adriatic. On Northern Ireland patrol. Twice to the Gulf. You spoiled your record turning down the command of a minehunter. It didn't sit well with the Admiralty."

Jonas ran his teeth over his lower lip again. His father had drummed the ground rules into him.

"Never forget, Jonas, an officer is married to the Service. You marry the Navy."

McIntyre continued. "The Navy always cares for its own, Willoughby. Even in the Admiral's condition, he would be provided for throughout his lifetime. They have a great residence in South Devon. Why don't you look into it?"

He didn't have the heart to say, "I did." Nor the courage to admit that he didn't have the stomach to turn his dad out to pasture. Instead he said, "I was surprised when they let my promotion go through."

"I argued on your behalf, Commander. Besides, I had a job for you here at Northwood, no matter how tentative. So you got the promotion. And I got the man." He smiled wryly. "Once I explain, you will understand why a compassionate leave is out."

He stretched his watchband. "I'm heading up an Irish project that should interest you. We're running against the clock with the IRA. Most favor peace, but we must ward off any factional groups trying last-minute tactical maneuvers to ruin the fragile peace efforts." His gaze held steady. "I know about your fiancée. You have my sympathy. But to work with me, you must put aside any anger that you still hold against the IRA."

Jonas rubbed his chin with the back of his hand, staving off the sudden throbbing along his jaw.

"Sit down, Willoughby. I'll tell you what I have in mind." With care, he detailed his own involvement in the Irish peace process as a military advisor, the need to track any active IRA members still hiding out in England, and the urgency to prevent any unprovoked attacks on British soil. "I don't have to tell you that resuming any IRA bombings would threaten the peace efforts and be a threat to Her Majesty's ships in Irish waters."

He smiled. "For the record, you are still working under NATO Intelligence. But for the next few weeks, you will be working directly under me. And, Willoughby, I will not tolerate a man working against me, seeking his own revenge."

McIntyre was questioning his loyalty? Jonas said, "Have I stepped out of line somewhere, sir?"

"You tell me. With your transfer to Northwood, you're being vetted, checked out once again. Mostly at my request. If we are to work together, I demand your utmost loyalty, regardless of the personal cost to you."

Jonas nodded. "You still have reservations about me?"

"Your decision to turn down the command came at an odd time, Commander. Your father has been sick for months—and suddenly at the exact time when reports were coming to us about an Irish agent in the Cotswolds, your request for transfer came in."

"What would an IRA rebel be doing in Stow-on-the-Woodland?"

"I had intended to ask you that, Commander."

The muscles in Jonas's neck drew his features into a scowl. He could no more prevent it than he could his father's illness. But an Irish faction in the Cotswolds where sheep grazed peacefully and children played by the Windrush? Ludicrous. Stow-on-the-Woodland was not a town for trouble. He braced himself in the chair across from McIntyre. "Days ago, the vicar suggested the possibility of Irish problems in the village."

"But you didn't see fit to report that rumor to me?"

"The truth is, I didn't believe him. Why would I? I've known the people in the village all my life. I trust them."

"The MI5 report that reached my desk suggested the possibility of an IRA rebel hiding out in the woods near your home, Commander. Twenty-four hours later the revised report read: *Wounded, still missing.* If he's still in your village, someone has given him a place to hide."

Someone hiding a terrorist? The schoolmaster? The owner of Chutman's Pub? The parish priest? Abigail? No, not Abigail and not anyone at the manor. All of them were English to the core!

"Captain, a stranger was accidentally shot in our village the other evening. That may be the man you are talking about."

The crow's-foot lines by McIntyre's eyes deepened. "I hoped you would tell me about that. MI5's report also stated that you were in the village that night. But I find no report from you."

"Not much to tell. I heard the gunfire. There was an extensive search. I have no idea who he was or where he is now."

"But you came back to the base early. On Sunday, I believe. That's not your usual pattern, Willoughby. You usually wing in here just under the wire on Monday mornings. What happened?"

"Miss Broderick urged me to leave. She said it wouldn't sit well for the Admiral's son to be involved in a village shooting. Knowing the nature of my work here at Fleet Headquarters, I agreed. I packed and left at once."

"This Miss Broderick? Is she the Admiral's housekeeper?"

If I'm being vetted again, you already know she isn't. But he remained civil. "Griselda Quigley is the housekeeper. Abigail Broderick is more like a family member. She pretty much mothered me after my own mother died. It's hard to think of a time when Abigail wasn't there running the manor. In a way, she was always in charge. I'll never know how she talked my father into housing all those children, although my mother may have made that decision. She and Abigail were great friends. They often traveled together on the continent. I thought them inseparable."

"Housing what children, Willoughby?"

"Refugee children displaced by wars."

"A visionary. Was she too busy to marry?"

"She was engaged once to a British commando. He was killed in World War II. But she's still taking care of children."

"Would she harbor a wounded man with the children there?"

"Did he make it?" Abigail had asked. Abigail involved? Hiding someone? Urging Jonas to leave. . . .

"I say, does this Miss Broderick have Irish ties?"

"Some Irish friends. Nothing more."

"Willoughby, any Brit caught aiding and abetting the IRA would be dealt with promptly. Any senior naval officer would face immediate dismissal. And probably be tried for treason."

"Sir, are you suggesting—"

"I am just reminding you of the severity of defending an Irish rebel, even if that rebel were a former classmate or a former boarder at Broadshire

Manor. There can be no sympathy for the IRA in your village or anywhere else. The man may be wounded, but we are not dealing with some romantic freedom fighter. I trust that no one you know is embroiled in such a cause."

McIntyre leaned back in his chair. "Think about it, Willoughby. The person involved may be very close to you. Protecting an IRA terrorist means that person has lost his sense of loyalty to the Queen and the country."

Jonas felt as though Captain McIntyre saw him as the enemy. "Sir, we are on the same side."

"Good." The captain pulled a picture from the file and tossed it across the desk to Jonas. "Do you recognize this man?"

"Looks like it was taken in Belfast."

"I didn't ask for a location, Willoughby. Do you know him?"

He studied the side view of a young man caught unawares, standing on the hillside, his hair ruffled by a gust of wind. A wary countenance. A black market rifle balanced over one shoulder. He stalled. "I'd have to see a close-up, Captain."

"What about this one?"

McIntyre tossed a color photo on top of the first. A gaunt, lifelike face loomed up at Jonas. Definitely Conan O'Reilly's cold, steely eyes as green as a stormy sea. Fiery red hair. A face thinner than he remembered. A sense of déjà vu struck Jonas, a not unpleasant recollection warming him. "That's one of the lads from Gordonstoun when I was head boy. He was a superb soccer player. Gave all his classmates a run for their money."

"He's still running, Willoughby. He's an Irishman, one of the active IRA holding out on any peace agreement. Did this Miss Broderick of yours ever take in children from the IRA conflict?"

Something stirred inside Jonas. Conan O'Reilly, the crack shot on the rifle team at Gordonstoun. A rabble-rouser politically. One of Abigail's boys that she wanted Jonas to look after. Louise flashed into his mind. In that instant, his war against Irish terrorism turned personally against this old school chum from Gordonstoun.

"That's Conan O'Reilly," he admitted. "I haven't seen him for years. He was one of Abigail Broderick's boys. He stayed at the manor for several months. Longer perhaps. Our paths didn't cross much after I left for Oxford and Dartmouth. But O'Reilly was a problem at the manor, a real troublemaker."

"Would that have made a difference to Miss Broderick?"

"She would never turn a child away—even one with a violent temper like O'Reilly had. He left when he was fourteen or fifteen. I don't think Abigail ever heard from him again."

McIntyre glanced out the window. "Did you know that Mr. O'Reilly's father was involved in the early years with the IRA? He was linked with the Warrenpoint bomb and Brighton five years later. A bloody man in the beginning. Did you ever meet him?"

"No, Conan's father was like mine. Neither of them made a habit of visiting Gordonstoun."

"Willoughby, about the time of the Good Friday Peace Agreement, the older O'Reilly switched loyalties—became a strong advocate for peace. Went pro-British. I served with him at the conference table, but his political betrayal didn't sit well with his old friends. Nor with his son. Someone murdered him en route to a meeting with the British Prime Minister."

"Another case of the hunter hunted down."

"Pathetic, really. He was killed in Belfast where he was born. Just when he wanted peace, the IRA wrote him off as a traitor." He turned to the window, gazing again. "If Conan O'Reilly was involved in his father's death—in serious trouble like that—would he go back to Miss Broderick?"

"Did he make it?" Abigail had asked.

Jonas leaned forward. "About that compassionate leave, sir?"

"It's been denied."

Jonas tapped O'Reilly's picture. "Would it be if it related to this man?"

"Does it, Willoughby?"

"It could. I would recognize him."

"Are you risking another promotion?"

Jonas smiled. "I won't qualify for one as long as I'm at Northwood. The base isn't big enough for too many captains."

"Perhaps a few days' leave, but working directly under me. You won't risk your career going after this man?"

"Wasn't that part of your plan, sir, part of your Irish project for me to find out whether he's there or not?"

"Go cautiously, Willoughby. But don't rule anyone out. Whoever is protecting the young terrorist would have close Irish-Catholic connections."

"Not necessarily, sir. Religion may not enter in. It might be the least likely person, someone with a motive of his own."

"Or *her* own?" McInytre suggested.

Jonas attempted to steer his thoughts from Abigail. "Maybe someone living there had a relative shot by the British Army. Something like that.

Something he saw. Some injustice that colored his view of the establishment. What happened to my fiancée certainly colored my views. But I am a naval officer, sir. First and foremost. I have absolute loyalty to the Queen."

"I'm glad." McIntyre's attention once more focused on the view from his window. Suddenly, he whirled his chair around to face Jonas. "How much do you really know about Miss Broderick?"

"She's been part of my memories for a lifetime."

"And, as you've already pointed out, Willoughby, she would never let anything happen to any of her children. If this Conan O'Reilly is in England, I would think he would go to her."

"That's what I have to find out, sir."

"Broderick—is she British?"

"Decidedly, through and through. You don't think the Admiral would have a foreigner living at the manor all these years?"

"The children have been foreigners," McIntyre pointed out.

"Agreed. But Abigail knows no creed or nationality where her children are concerned."

"Then she might hide O'Reilly if he sought her help."

Moments later a clerk entered the room. "I've brought the folder you requested, sir."

"Good. Give it to me." McIntyre scanned it. When he looked up, he said, "Brief as it is, this is all we have for you. O'Reilly belongs to a group that calls themselves 'the real IRA.' These are men who refuse to lay down their arms for any Good Friday Agreement. They don't want peace; they want war. Conan was involved in the bombing in Omagh. Been on the run ever since." He closed the folder. "He got his just due. Lost his wife in Omagh, poor devil."

"So he married? What a mess he's made of his life."

"I'm going to clear a month's leave for you, Willoughby. I want you to go back to Stow-on-the-Woodland and find out if O'Reilly has put in an appearance." Shrewdly, he added, "Stow-on-the-Woodland is a highly unlikely place to harbor a terrorist. But if you find him, Willoughby?"

"I'll bring him in, sir."

"It might cost you Broderick's friendship."

"She knows my loyalties."

"The question is, do you know hers?"

Chapter 11

As she ran for the boarding gate at Kennedy International, Sydney was hemmed in by the vast crowd going nowhere, going everywhere. She prayed for a miracle to be on time—and for a second miracle to calm her lingering fears about flying out over Long Island, on the same route that her parents had taken.

Muffled bedlam echoed around her as she handed her passport to the attendant at the VIP counter. The agent's brow puckered. "There seems to be a mix-up. All we have left is an aisle seat."

"My window seat was guaranteed when I made my reservation."

The man behind her leaned forward. "Here—I don't mind an aisle seat. Why don't we switch?"

"You won't mind?" Sydney asked, whirling around to face the man and then exclaiming, "Jeff!"

Jeff VanBurien grinned. "One and the same. My travel agent pulled strings. We thought you could do with a friend on board."

"Then I won't have to fly alone."

"And I fly in the company of a beautiful woman."

Another tiny scowl knit the agent's brow. "We're already boarding first class, so hurry and have a wonderful flight."

"We will." Jeff scooped up his case and Sydney's carry-on and led the way. As they cleared security and walked down the long ramp, he said, "I'm here as your friend, Syd. I figured this might be your first long-distance flight. Right?"

"Since Mom and Dad? Yes."

He stooped as they entered the cabin, the light catching the amber in his hair. "Sydney, for months after we met, I studied everything about that crash—looking at the passenger list and wondering who those people were and why their lives were cut short."

"Why would you be allowed to do that?"

"My firm filed a lawsuit for one of the families."

Sydney glanced toward the pilot's cabin. "I still think it was pilot error," she whispered. "It must have been."

"No, the reports were accurate. The engine malfunctioned."

"I don't know whether to be nervous that you're on board talking like this or not."

"Just good therapy. It's bottled up inside of you. Let's get it out." He stowed her suitcase into a luggage hold. "Just consider me your guardian angel. I'll be sitting right beside you. If you need me, I'm only a hug away. Just say the word."

She fought off tears and gave an extra tug to her seat belt.

Her knuckles turned chalk white as the jet rumbled full throttle down the runway and soared into the cloudless sky. Jeff's broad hand covered hers. "Open your eyes, sweetheart, and take a look!"

She forced herself to peer through the smudged windows, down on the water sparkling in the fading sunlight. She remembered that other night. The long wait. The debris floating on top of the waves. The make-shift memorial service on the edge of the Sound days later. Suddenly that choppy sea lost its grip on her, for in remembering, the warmth of faces dear to her came back. She pictured her parents holding hands on takeoff, her dad grinning reassuringly. She knew that if they were capable of knowing, they would wish her well, loved her dearly. They'd left her a legacy of love more precious than the possessions that were hers now.

Gently, Jeff turned her face toward him. "You're okay?"

She met his gaze. "Okay."

Tweaking his mustache, he murmured, "About that problem you gave me—I've been wading knee-deep in law books on probate and British law. But your worries cost me extra money."

"How so?"

"I packed half my library in another suitcase."

Surely he joked, but she said, "Charge it to Barrington Enterprises."

His grin broadened. "Already did. Have you heard any more from that bamboozler in England?"

"Edmund Gallagher? I called to confirm my arrival time and talked to another gentleman." She used the term lightly. "He was probably another member of Gallagher's firm."

"So what are your plans when we touch down at Heathrow?"

"I have a rental car waiting. Then straight to the Ritz."

"You're going in style. My brother's meeting me. We could give you a lift to your hotel and to the Cotswolds the next day."

"I need my own transportation. I scheduled time at the shipyard, but I should be in the Cotswolds by the weekend."

An hour into the journey—safely beyond the place where her parents' jet spiraled into the ocean—Sydney leaned her cushioned seat back as far as it would go and allowed Jeff to tuck her blanket around her. She caught his hand and pressed it to her cheek. "Thanks, Jeff. You're a rock."

He kissed her ear. "I wish I could be more."

~

Fifteen miles from Stow-on-the-Woodland, wisteria climbed the face of a row of honey-colored cottages with dormer windows and brass latches on their doors. Once domestic homes, they had been converted into business establishments—a pub, a tearoom, a small postal depot, and a solicitor's office. A gold-lettered sign creaked on its hinge above the cottage on the corner: Edmund Gallagher, Solicitor.

Inside, two volatile men burned the midnight oil in another heated argument about the problems at Broadshire Manor. As the shouting grew louder, Edmund shuttered the windows and then stomped back to his father's old desk. His now.

From behind thick-rimmed glasses, he fixed his scornful gaze on Marshall Wallis. "Sit down, Marshall. I think we should deal with this like gentlemen."

Wallis kept pacing, his hands jammed into his pockets. "We have problems if you persist in laying claim to Broadshire Manor. Don't you understand that?"

"*You* have problems, my dear doctor. I'm only here two days a week—on loan from my law firm in London."

Edmund favored his lavish office in downtown London, but this country office was amply equipped with upscale furnishings that belied the ancient exterior of the building. Mentally he found himself despising Marshall for his simple tastes in life, his bent toward honesty. Edmund could take him down legally for betraying patient confidentiality; he preferred using him.

"My dear Marshall, it was your professional opinion that Abigail Broderick was on her deathbed."

"She's still running on borrowed time."

Edmund remained practical. "Then all we have to do is settle matters with the American. I'm certain I convinced her in our last phone conversation that I could handle the paperwork for her. Don't look so alarmed, Doctor. I'll make certain she receives a substantial settlement, and that will be it."

Marshall glanced at his watch. "Given the time difference between our two countries, Miss Barrington is already in flight. Her plane should reach Heathrow later this morning."

Edmund exploded. "How do you know that?"

Marshall dropped into the chair. "I answered your phone the other day while waiting for you."

"And you didn't tell me?"

"It must have slipped my mind, Edmund."

"That fool woman. I saw no need for her coming over here."

"Apparently, she did."

"We must keep her away from Broadshire Manor."

"How? Should I quarantine the place? What's happened to you, Edmund? You used to be a reasonable man."

"When I took over my father's office, all I found were promissory notes. Clients who never paid their bills. My father could have been a rich man. I intend to be one."

"Surely something good came out of your father's life."

"Yes. I learned that Abigail Broderick is the owner of Broadshire Manor. And that fit right in with my plans."

"Poor Abigail. She trusted you with her legal matters."

"She trusted my father more."

Edmund considered for a moment, tapping his thumbs together. "Perhaps the safest plan is to let Miss Barrington think that Abigail is buried in St. Michael's churchyard. We can change one of the markers. That way Miss Barrington won't be nosing around."

"You have a major problem. Abigail is not dead."

"I'm depending on you."

"You are crazy, Edmund. I'm doing my best to keep her alive. And I've lived long enough to regret our chance encounter in the London Club six months ago."

"So you keep telling me, but you're the one who broke into Lady Willoughby's sealed medical file. And you were more than anxious to share the secret that only your father knew about."

"Those were the worst forty minutes of my life. You pushing a wineglass toward me. Begging me to tell you more."

"As I recall, you enjoyed telling me everything."

"I was drunk," Marshall said. "Dead drunk."

"You never could handle wine, but you handed me what I needed to know." And what a triumph it had been. He could still hear himself saying,

"So Jonas is not Lady Willoughby's son? Marshall, you have just given me the key to Broadshire Manor. I will turn that property into a resort and open up Stow-on-the-Woodland to tourism. It will be just a beginning."

And poor Marshall, helpless as he had been that night, was right. Edmund had been scheming the way he did when they were boys. Intimidating his classmates. Bullying the younger boys. Conniving to win his way to the top. But Marshall had been guilty of sharing his father's private medical records.

"You will go on helping me, Marshall. How long do you think you would last at the health center if people knew you couldn't be trusted with their medical confidences?"

"I'll resign."

"And where would you go? Back to London? I will ruin any attempt you make to practice medicine in the city. Admiral Willoughby is still well known there. How far do you think you could go once it was known that you had ruined the reputation of the Admiral and his family?"

"Lady Willoughby is dead. Let it rest, Edmund."

"How can I? The property belonged to Lady Willoughby's family for generations, so what persuaded her to bypass husband and son and leave it to someone outside the family? Some secret? Some problem? Something more than Lady Willoughby's inability to bear a child? . . . The Admiral was a lady's man, wasn't he?"

Marshall sprang from his chair and started for the door.

"I'm not finished, my friend. Don't rush off."

Marshall paced again. "Edmund, the people in Stow-on-the-Woodland still revere the Admiral as an officer and a gentleman."

"Gentlemen sometimes make mistakes. It must have been a serious one to force Lady Willoughby to write Jonas and the Admiral out of her will." He drummed his fingers on one of his law books. "Lady Willoughby didn't live long enough to correct her error, but Abigail wants to hand over the property to a total stranger. And I must stop her. I want that property."

Tonight Marshall's ordinary features burned with resentment. "Jonas Willoughby is the rightful owner to Broadshire Manor."

"Except for this legal document, Marshall. It's called a will. Jonas is not in Abigail's will, but he was never interested in living in the Cotswolds. . . . Pacing like that, Doctor, is not good for your health. You'll end up ill like Miss Broderick."

Marshall slouched back into the chair. "Blast you, Edmund."

"Did you know she called me in London days before her heart attack?"

"We never discussed her private business."

"Not even about the children?"

"Of course, we discuss the children. I'm their doctor."

"Abigail wanted to drive into my London office to reverse her will. As she told me, she wanted Jonas to have what is rightfully his." He swiveled his chair. "I suggested waiting until I could make an appointment for her in the village. Fortunately for me, her heart prevented her from keeping that appointment. Jonas will be dumbfounded by the conditions of the will, but he won't argue with it. He's too much of a gentleman." Edmund tapped the desk. "Not too long ago, I offered to buy the place from Miss Broderick while Jonas was away at sea."

"At rock-bottom price?"

"At that time, I thought she was having financial difficulty running the manor. She should have found any offer satisfactory. The Admiral was in no condition to sign his funds over to her, and then, somehow, she received funds from a Swiss account." The drumming intensified. "After that she told me the manor was not for sale. Ever. That she did have funds to cover the necessary repairs. But that was before you told me about Lady Willoughby's past. Perhaps your Miss Broderick held something over Lady Willoughby's head."

"Abigail's not that kind of woman."

"You are a physician, Marshall. Don't you know that we all have a dark side—even your precious Miss Broderick? I'd be fair about it. I would arrange everything—have the Admiral declared incompetent, if need be, and pension off the staff. Social Services can deal with the children. You'll thank me in time, Marshall. Developing Stow-on-the-Woodland will increase your practice at the health center."

"What makes you think Jonas Willoughby will let you take control? Have you forgotten his unwavering loyalty to Miss Broderick and the Admiral?"

Edmund adjusted his spectacles. "Jonas will do anything to protect his father's reputation—even if Abigail must lose the manor over it. And I will be there with a check already written out. She'll grab at it."

Marshall rubbed the back of his neck. "You will destroy Jonas in the process. Ruin his Navy career. Abigail will give you the property before she would let that happen."

"Jonas's Navy career is of no concern to me. Nor is preserving the Admiral's unblemished reputation. Building Stow-on-the-Woodland into a bustling tourist attraction is. And I need Broadshire Manor to accomplish that."

❧

Marshall left the firm by the side door, unchained his bicycle, and started home by light of the stars and the headlamp on the cycle. Of all the villagers, Abigail brought him particular joy beyond his work at the health clinic. He admired her sacrifice, her mothering, mentoring ways with children. Telling her that she had to slow down for the sake of her heart had been received with the same philosophical approach that she tendered to any major decision. She would rest when she settled the plight of the children under her care.

As he rode the path along the Windrush, his heart thumped in beat with the pumping. A cramp started in the calf of his leg. He abandoned the ride to work the cramp from his leg and then pushed his cycle the last kilometer of the way.

At the crest of the hill, Stow-on-the-Woodland lay before him, asleep except for a light in Jonas Willoughby's cottage. So Jonas was back for the weekend? Beyond the cottage stood the manor, bleak in the darkness with only a tiny night-light in Abigail's bedroom window. He should go to her—see whether she had need of him. But what else could he do? Abigail's recovery lay in her own determination, not in the medicines he prescribed.

Marshall had only a stone's throw to go to reach the safety of his own bed, the warmth of his wife beside him. Instead he lowered his cycle to the ground, sat down on the small mound, and put his head in his hands. He never intended to betray a friend. In the quiet communing with his own soul, he had no choice but to go back in time to when he was still a lad. To when he most admired Lady Willoughby. . . .

❧

May, 1969

Marshall Wallis had just turned seven when he first saw Lady Willoughby at the village church, in a sanctuary packed to overflowing with Londoners. He swung his bare legs in the church pew, his hymnbook upside down as he watched her. She sat across the aisle from him, her wide-brimmed spring hat shading her face. Her small son was huddled beside her. Lady Willoughby sang in a voice high and crystal clear like the Windrush. In the middle of the hymn, she turned and smiled at him, her eyes as blue as the sky, her skin golden like the Cotswold Hills.

Later, as the service ended, she patted his head. "I'm Lady Willoughby. What is your name?"

"Marshall Wallis," he stammered.

"The doctor's son! Your father is a fine gentleman. Dr. Wallis has tended the Admiral for years. And now he's my doctor."

"Are you sick?"

"Sometimes." She smiled down at her son. "And your father takes care of Jonas, too."

"Was Jonas one of my father's babies?"

She shook her head, amused. "Jonas was born in the North Country. Now that you've met us, do come the next time your father calls at the Broadshire Manor."

As they walked down the aisle of St. Michael's, her frilly pink dress swished and the silk shawl around her shoulders fanned out light and breezy. Lady Willoughby smelled sweetly like the flowers on the altar; his mother smelled like cookies and greasy lamb. And there as a boy for the first time in his life, he knew that women were different, special, and he knew when he grew up that he would want to marry someone like Lady Willoughby.

Outside he stammered, "Lady Willoughby, do you have a bigger boy for me to play with when I come to see you?"

"Just Jonas. Will that matter? Yes, I see that it does. But we have horses, and Mrs. Quigley makes the best sweets in town."

They had reached the massive door of the church, and Marshall hurried past the ugly gargoyles that overshadowed St. Michael's. He looked back and saw Lady Willoughby still standing on the top step, the clergyman bending down to talk to the child beside her. Just Jonas. Just a little boy.

But Marshall did like horses and sweets and the flowery smell of Lady Willoughby as she walked past him.

On his first visit to the manor, Lady Willoughby had taken him to the stables and introduced him to her horse, Lightning. The horse had nuzzled her hand, nibbling the sugar cubes. "No one else rides him but me, Marshall," she had said.

After that, he often saw her racing across the valley, up the hills, over the glens into the woodland. He was twelve the day she died. He was riding in the car beside his father on their way back from his father's medical rounds. "Oh stop, Father. That's Lady Willoughby and Lightning. Look at them go."

Smiling, his father pulled to the side of the road and left his engine idling. They watched Lady Willoughby racing across the crest of the hill, ladylike and graceful. She turned to wave at them, and suddenly horse and rider stumbled and fell.

Marshall and his father were the first to reach her. The stallion lay neighing, helplessly trying to stand again. "We'll have to put him down," his father said.

Lady Willoughby lay crumpled beside her horse, her beautiful face twisted, the green hillside blotched with her blood. Marshall stood immobilized as his father knelt by her side and slipped his hand beneath her neck.

He shook his head. "Her neck is broken, son."

"You're not going to put her down, Dad?"

"Stay calm, Marshall. Be brave for Lady Willoughby." Even as the crowd gathered, he turned away, bent over, and vomited. He was still retching when they put the horse down.

For three days his father said nothing about the accident.

Then, the day before the funeral, he called Marshall to his side. "I am driving into Cheltenham to see the pathologist."

He put his hands on Marshall's shoulders. "Drive along with me, son. This has been a hard lesson for you, watching Lady Willoughby die. I think you want to know why your friend died."

"Lightning threw her."

"But the pathologist will tell us medically how she died."

Marshall's lips were so dry he wasn't certain he could get the words out. "The man who did the autopsy? We're going there?"

"You don't have to go, son. You know that."

Marshall had gone but not into the room with the pathologist. He stood near the open door watching his father flip through a file folder. "She was a beautiful woman," his father told the pathologist.

"Not when I saw her, Wallis."

Five minutes later, his father thumped the chart and said, "This can't be true. Lady Willoughby has a son."

"Did you deliver the boy?"

His father sounded ruffled. "No, she was in the North Country. Went there with a staff member."

"I'm telling you, Wallis, I have examined her and—"

"Hush. My son will overhear you."

The pathologist lowered his voice, but Marshall heard him say,

"I'm sorry about the boy, Wallis, but let me remind you I know Lady Willoughby's body better than anyone now. I'm telling you, it would have been impossible for her to bear a child."

"But she has a son—a young lad away at Gordonstoun. He's coming home for the funeral. She definitely has a son."

The pathologist remained adamant. "But not a son from her own womb."

Chapter 12

Anight shadow fell across the silver on Marshall's bicycle. Before he could move, an iron grip dug into his shoulder. He tried to wrench free but could only turn his head and look up. "Jonas, what are you doing here?"

The grip loosened. "Dr. Wallis! I was about to ask you the same thing. Is everything okay with you? With your wife?"

"It won't be if I don't get home."

He dropped down beside Marshall. "When I saw someone riding along the Windrush at this hour, it didn't sit right with me."

"You thought I was the intruder? He's gone by now."

"Not so. He was injured. I think someone is harboring him here in the village. A wounded man might seek you out, Doctor."

"What about you, Jonas? Why did you leave town that night?"

"Are you wondering whether the stranger rode out of town with me?" There was amusement in Jonas's voice. "I'm hardly the man to protect an Irish rebel. No, I left town alone. Abigail begged me to go back to Northwood for my own protection."

"Why would she do that?"

Jonas drew his feet across the wet dew and encircled his knees. "She said she didn't want me involved in any ruckus in town, but I think she knows more about what happened that night than either one of us. I wish I could believe that she really wanted to protect me by sending me away."

"She'd do anything to save your career and reputation." They fell silent, listening to the ripple of the Windrush.

Marshall had not fully understood as a boy, but he had guessed from the expression on his father's face that shame stalked the Admiral and his family. Now, sitting on the crest of the hill beside the Admiral's son, it came back fresh and searing: *Lady Willoughby had not brought Jonas into the world.*

"Doctor," Jonas said, "how is Abigail doing? Really? She seemed stronger this morning when I had tea by her bedside."

"Don't get your hopes too high, Jonas. Her body is worn out, battened down with a soggy heart. I'm surprised she's clung to life so long. She might have had a better chance if we had hospitalized her in the beginning, but she refused to go to Cheltenham or London and leave Sir James and the children."

"No one is blaming you, Doctor."

"She wouldn't even accept health visitors around the clock. As weak as she was, she told me Mrs. Quigley would browbeat any intruder. She seems to feel safe in Mrs. Quigley's care."

"They've been great friends for years."

The doctor heaved a sigh. "I cautioned her to slow down and give her heart a rest, but I knew she would never do so. Now it doesn't look good. What's going to become of the place when—"

Jonas's features were mere shadows in the darkness. "When I first came home, I consulted Edmund Gallagher about the legality of selling the property while Dad and Abigail were still alive. Now I have doubts about letting the place go. They have the right to live out their lives here. Abigail loves the Cotswolds. She will go nowhere else. This is her little part of England."

"Edmund won't like being crossed."

"Selling is not his decision. He's going to have to tell his buyer that the manor isn't for sale." His voice grew husky. "When I retire from the Navy, I might want to come back for good."

Marshall flattened his palm on the wet grass. "Your father and Abigail will both be dead by then. Maybe you should think of marrying and moving away."

"You know I thought about marrying. Louise and I planned to live in the manor. It will be lonely without her, but I'm going to like rambling around in that old house. It's filled with good memories. Mother. Louise. Abigail and her children. Think about it, Marshall. When Dad dies, I'll be lord of the manor. Sounds strange, doesn't it?"

Sounds complicated, Marshall thought.

With a quick spring, Jonas pushed to a standing position. "Can you spare the time to do some trout fishing tomorrow?"

"I'd like that, Jonas."

"I'll have Gregor with me. He's become my tagalong."

"Good lad, that one. He'll be lost when you go back to sea."

"I don't dare think about it." He brushed his hands. "Now that I know that it's you up here at 3:00 in the morning, I'll head back and get some sleep. Gregor tends to appear at my door at the crack of dawn."

"Take care, Jonas, and God bless."

"What?"

"I said 'God bless you.'"

He felt Jonas's eyes boring down on him. "My mother used to say that when I was a small boy and she tucked me in."

"Lady Willoughby used to say it to me, too, when I made house calls at the manor with my father. She was a good woman, Jonas. A beautiful woman."

"I was only eight when Mother died."

"I was twelve. In many ways, Abigail reminds me of her."

"How so?"

"That inner strength. Her devotion to the Admiral and you. Abigail has that same womanly grace that I admired in Lady Willoughby." *Her own measure of beauty*, Marshall thought. *A face sculpted by the hands of the gods.*

"That's good of you to say. Abigail's the one who forced me to go on riding horses after Mother's accident. I'll always be grateful to her. She's always been there for me." He reached out and gripped Marshall's hand. "Come on. On your feet, man. Go home and get some rest. Whatever is bothering you should look better in the morning. Good night."

"Good night, Jonas."

The clammy feeling came back as Jonas strolled off. A man went fishing with his friends, not with a man he was betraying.

Dawn held another dread. Before the sun bathed the Cotswold Hills in golden splendor, Miss Barrington's plane would touch down at Heathrow—a rich young woman coming here to claim her inheritance from a woman who so far refused to die.

Marshall had solved nothing by remembering the past, nothing by sitting on the hillside, yet his resolve stood firm. He would protect his friends at the manor whatever it cost him. Today he would tell his wife that his job was at stake. Yet he sensed only guilt at the thought of sharing Lady Willoughby's secret with another human being.

～

Jeff VanBurien leaned through the open window of the rental car and kissed Sydney on the cheek. "Are you certain you don't want us to follow you into London?"

"Jeff, I'll be okay. I've been here many times."

"Drive carefully."

"I won't go a kilometer over the limit. How's that?"

"Do you have a map marked out for the trip to the Tyne?"

"Right in my briefcase. And I have the trip mapped out to Stow-on-the-Woodland. You're beginning to sound like Randolph."

"And that's not good." He stepped back and stood beside his half-brother, Chandler Reynolds. Sydney turned the key in the ignition and smiled at them both. "Chan, I'm sorry I missed your wife."

"Couldn't be helped. Jillian is in Rome for a fortnight. I hope she'll be back before you leave."

"Does she always holiday alone?"

A teasing good humor settled in Chandler's eyes. "This is a business trip. She's tracking another stolen masterpiece. Lot of theft of the art masters in Italy. But you mentioned Stow-on-the-Woodland. Do you have friends there, Sydney?"

"No, but I have property. I just inherited some land when a friend died."

Chandler frowned. "It's not a big village."

"The solicitor called my place Broadshire Manor."

Chandler's answer seemed to stick in his throat. Jeff nudged him. "Something wrong, fella?"

"My wife talked about that place on the phone last evening."

"Small world," Jeff told him.

"I have to run," Sydney said. "You have my number, Jeff. I'm counting on your help."

"I can hardly forget the name *Sheepfold*. I'll leave any messages for you there. And you have Chan's number in London?"

She patted the briefcase beside her. "I have it." She blew Jeff a kiss. "Thanks for traveling with me. I mean it."

"My pleasure. Now remember. Don't sign anything. Not until you discuss it with me."

"Agreed. That's what I'm paying you for."

She backed out of the rental lot and drove off with a quick wave. As her car turned out of sight, Jeff faced his brother. "Chan, are you going to wipe that frown off your face, or are you going to tell me what's wrong? I thought you'd like Sydney."

"I do, and I'm not sure anything's wrong, but it seems unlikely that there are two Broadshire Manors in that village."

"And that bothers you?"

"What bothers me is my wife having dinner in Rome with her old boyfriend, Santos Garibaldi."

"Should I step aside and let you fly down there?"

"Jillian wouldn't thank me for that. She's in Rome on an art fraud case. But, Jeff, you didn't tell me you were traveling over here with a beautiful woman. Is it serious with this Sydney Barrington? And not a hint of it in our phone calls?"

"I'm not in her class, Chan."

"But you'd like to be?"

"What man wouldn't?"

Chandler grinned as he brushed his hand through his red-brown hair. "Me for one. I found myself when I found Jillian."

"So what about her old boyfriend?"

"Santos Garibaldi? He contacted Jillian the minute he heard she was in Rome. He lives there. Told her he needed her help."

"That's a new line."

"Jillian believed him the minute he told her he was concerned about art treasures disappearing in Stow-on-the-Woodland. Seems Santos spent part of his boyhood growing up there. As a thank-you, his father sculpted a fountain in front of Broadshire Manor. They apparently have a number of valuable paintings inside the manor."

"Then it's no small cottage Sydney's inherited?"

"Right. And according to Jillian, this Miss Broderick is ill but not dead. There's no way Sydney can inherit the place, not when it belongs to a retired Admiral in the Royal Navy who is still very much alive."

Jeff smoothed his mustache with his thumb and forefinger. "I get the feeling we're not talking about the same place."

"I think we are."

"That doesn't make sense. The lawyer who contacted Sydney said Abigail Broderick *was* dead. He wanted to settle everything by long-distance. That didn't sit well with Syd. Nor with me when she told me about it. But I'm positive there was no mention of any valuable paintings."

"The lawyer wouldn't mention them if he wanted them for himself. And if Abigail Broderick had died, I'm sure Santos would have mentioned it to Jillian. He's apparently quite fond of the old girl."

"Could we drive out there tomorrow and nose around, Chan?"

"Sure. It's only an hour and half from London. We'll make it part of our holiday."

"What's in it for Santos besides picking up a marble statue and taking it back to Rome? What is it? Another Trevi Fountain?"

Chandler laughed. "Santos appreciates art. What true Italian wouldn't?

But he has it in his head that he has to protect the art at Broadshire Manor. According to Jillian, he's kept in touch with Miss Broderick over the years and knows that she's seriously ill. He's flying back from Rome when Jillian comes home."

He clicked his remote keyless entry. "Here we are."

They had reached Chan's van and stood on opposite sides, facing each other across the rooftop. *Brothers. The same bloodline. But people would take us for total strangers,* Jeff thought. He felt even more rail-thin looking at his brother's muscular body. London and marriage had been good for Chan; he had the look of a happy man.

"We'd better go," Chan said, ducking into the van. Jeff followed his lead and fastened his seat belt. "Do you think Sydney is all right traveling alone, Jeff?"

"She's an independent lady. She'll make it. But I promised her we'd be here for her."

"You're over here as her lawyer, aren't you?"

He reached out and squeezed Chandler's shoulder. "Helping Sydney is just an added bonus. Mostly, I came to spend a holiday with my kid brother."

"I've been looking forward to your visit for months, Jeff."

"I marked it on my calendar back in January."

Jeff heaved a happy sigh as their vehicle merged with the traffic. It would be all right. They stood on a solid foundation—two brothers seeking to know each other better.

Chapter 13

As she left the Jarrow Shipyard on Saturday, Sydney wore her windbreaker as a safeguard against the unpredictable English weather. After two days of inspecting the progress at the shipyard and climbing around the construction site in a hard hat and a borrowed khaki jumper, she felt satisfied that things were moving on schedule. With a wave to the weekend foreman, she left the plant and nosed her rental car toward the Cotswolds—to the land and children she had inherited.

With her company's reputation and that deeply ingrained Barrington confidence, she had no doubt she could win the carrier contract. But she wanted someone who had worked by her side to oversee that long-term project. Her architect, Daron Emery, knew the carrier blueprints best and had been in on the initial designs. The job would be safe in Daron's hands. With that firmly settled in her mind, she was able to put the shipyard behind her and turn her thoughts completely to the journey ahead.

An hour later she pulled off the motorway and placed a call to Edmund Gallagher's Cotswold office. For the third time since arriving in England, she was forced to leave a message on his answering machine. Was he just out of the office, or had he changed his mind about their appointment at noon today?

Back in the car, Sydney decided to drive straight through to Stow-on-the-Woodland. She had no intention of meeting Gallagher in the blind or having him shove papers across the desk for her to sign for a property sight unseen. She'd drive by Broadshire Manor for a glimpse and then journey back to Bourton-on-the-Water where she was staying. That meant little more than a thirty-mile delay in her arrival time at the bed-and-breakfast. Still, she had an uncanny feeling that Jeff VanBurien would frown at this decision.

Leaving the motorway, she drove the narrow two-lane road, delighting in the scent of country air and the fragile tapestry of the hills in burnished gold. She would have known without the road signs that she had entered the Cotswolds. The evidence surrounded her: limestone slopes alive with wildflowers and grazing cattle, gardens overgrown with primrose climbers, thatched cottages and aristocratic estates that seemed to dominate each village. The road climbed and dipped into more secluded valleys, through wooded ravines, and along the banks of the river where alders and cottonwoods grew. Village after village, evoking a time gone by.

In Bourton-on-the-Water, she eased along High Street and spotted Gallagher's office. It was closed. Fifteen miles later, she came to Stow-on-the-Woodland and parked the car by the River Windrush. As she emerged from the car, the unspoiled countryside snatched her breath away. She had stepped into another time, yet it was timeless. Everything familiar stood still; everything new had been set in motion. A sweeping calm engulfed her as though some fragment of her life was coming together, some part of her future taking shape. The hills and meadows were flecked with an unending stretch of buttercups. On both sides of the river lay clusters of honey-buffed homes as ancient as her forefathers.

The past became a charming present. High-gabled buildings with dates carved into their chipped walls. Cozy shops along the narrow streets with bright metal shingles announcing their wares. A church with a fifteenth-century spire and lean, leafy trees lining the footpath to it. Seeing the high, rolling wolds, she knew she must find a horse and saddle to rent so she could explore those golden-green slopes where land and horizon met.

But there was no need to ask for directions to Abigail Broderick's place. A magnificent country home dominated the scene. If that was indeed Broadshire Manor, Sydney had come into a sizable possession that stirred more questions and concern than when she first heard about a piece of land and six children. She imagined that history had placed it there with its commanding view of the valley and that the fortunes and failures of this village were linked with the family who owned it. Was Abigail Broderick a member of an aristocratic family? Gallagher had painted her as an ordinary country woman.

Sydney retraced her steps and sat down near the water's edge, close to the village green. The crystal-clear Windrush that had been here forever rippled along through the center of town. The marvelous gurgling, bubbling of water running free. It splashed over the rocks and squeezed past the rush-tangled banks as it meandered on its way. It seemed to Sydney she had been here before, as though she had come home. She leaned down and let the river wash over her hand. Again, that simple act felt familiar.

As she drew her hand from the Windrush, a little girl as pale as the curtains in the storefront windows ran dangerously close to the water's edge, a young boy in angry pursuit. "Keeley, we must go home!" he shouted after her.

The girl stumbled to an abrupt halt in front of Sydney. Their eyes held over the grassy bank that separated them.

"Hello," Sydney said.

The child remained mute, her bright red curls falling softly around her face. As they sized each other up, shyness showed through those doelike eyes. She jerked free from the boy's grasp and ran again, this time in dizzying circles around Sydney.

Sydney understood the child's bid for freedom, the shyness. She reached out her hand to the girl. "Come. Sit with me here on the bank of the river."

Without a word, the child flopped down beside Sydney and leaned against her, trembling. Sydney drew the child closer.

Hesitating, not certain what to do with a stranger looking on, the boy said, "She's Keeley. I've come to take her home."

"Are you her brother?" They didn't look alike. His brilliant eyes were dark, his skin sun-brown.

"No. She lives with me up there."

He pointed back toward the country house at the crest of the hill. "That's a big house," Sydney said.

"It belongs to the Admiral."

Not to Abigail Broderick? Or had Edmund Gallagher already sold the land to some retired admiral and his family? But the children were still there. Still safe. The Admiral? She felt as enlightened as the peacock butterfly spreading its wings on the bush beside her. The boy reached out to rob it of its freedom.

"Don't do that," she commanded.

He pulled back, his shiny eyes staring hard at her. "I would not hurt it. I just wanted to feel it wiggling in my hand."

Her attention drew back to the manor. The property seemed to stretch on forever: a piece of land of sizable dimensions and six children. The oldest child was around nine, Gallagher had told her. This boy could easily be nine.

"Do you always come down here alone?" she asked.

"I have to. Keeley keeps running away."

"Perhaps she's unhappy."

"She's Irish."

The boy's thought process amused her. "Maybe I should walk up to the house with you," she offered.

"You coming for dinner? Mrs. Quigley don't like strangers uninvited."

His grammar was atrocious, but the English he knew had a decided British clip. Edmund Gallagher had said, *"A Mrs. Quigley is watching over them."*

A woman who didn't like uninvited guests.

"I should eat before I go up there." She glanced around at the shops and wondered where in this little hamlet she might find a hearty meal.

"Jonas goes to Chutman's Pub." His stubby finger indicated the quaint store on the corner.

Jonas? Another name, but apparently he had the boy's absolute respect and loyalty. His lustrous eyes glowed. "Or you can go to Veronica's Tea Shoppe." This time he pointed to a shop with a pink shingle. "Jonas buys me sweets there sometimes."

"Candy bars?"

He frowned, puzzled. "Chocolates. Mostly after I help him pull weeds or tend the sheep."

A hired hand for sure then, she thought. But a man well loved by this boy. "Why don't we go up to the house first?" she suggested. "I'll come back for supper later. I'd better know your name so I'll know who I'm following."

"I'm Gregor."

"And I'm Sydney."

He flashed a warm, friendly grin. "Come on."

She took Keeley's hand and felt the warmth of the child's in her own. Gregor ran ahead of them, doing leapfrogs and handstands and picking up pebbles from the ground. Still he made good mileage until he reached the twisted footpath that climbed toward the manor. He stopped and looked back. "You coming?"

"We're coming."

"We go through the woodland."

"Okay."

It was an easy climb. As Gregor rushed ahead, she thought, *There's an old beech tree just around that first corner where a clump of azaleas used to grow.* But it turned out to be a vine of musk orchids growing there. Her lips went dry. But somewhere. Somewhere back in time—

As they neared the manor, he let out a whoop. "Jonas is home!"

He was off running, in a straight line this time. Sydney set her pace to Keeley's, speaking of the beauty around them, of the shimmering Windrush behind them. They paused to touch a flower. Keeley felt the petals but said nothing. Perhaps she knew no English at all.

As they approached, the manor seemed even more imposing, the property immense and hedged in by a quaint drystone wall. It was a two-story structure, three if you counted the dormer windows on the upper level with its limited dwelling quarters. On a breezy day, it would take the brunt of the wind, its windows rattling and its eaves bending.

A flowering vine with ruby-red fronds climbed the face of the building, close to where another wing had been added. Off to the side of the house, Sydney could see the edge of the stables and a high water tower. A thatched cottage stood on the far corner, a car parked beside it. But most intriguing was the marvelous fountain in front—a boy and girl in marble spewing a steady flow of water that turned to ribbons of color as the sun reflected through it. In the back of her mind, Sydney felt certain she had seen the statue before—as though she had actually heard the water cascading over the bare feet of the children a long time ago.

Her thoughts raced. Inherit this immense acreage, and she would have to hire a large domestic staff and gardeners and someone to maintain the stables and plow the land—a more formidable task than being CEO at Barrington. As much as she disliked Edmund Gallagher, his plan could well be the better choice. She could parcel out the land to developers as he wanted to do. Or would pride force her to take it on as another opportunity to prove to Randolph Iverson that she could handle anything? Or would this become Sydney's folly—only a driving distance from the shipyard still known as Aaron's faux pas?

Gregor shoved open the gate and bounded to the gardener. Sydney caught the gate with the palm of her hand as it swung back and noticed the family crest embedded in it. BROADSHIRE MANOR: THE WILLOUGHBYS. On the other side of the drystone wall, the gardener was pruning the roses. She was struck by the strength of his broad shoulders, his suntanned skin. He yanked off his sun shades, further revealing his handsome, unsmiling face. But the second Gregor flung himself at the man, he tossed his spade in the wheelbarrow and gathered the boy to his side. He glanced over at Sydney and Keeley and nodded brusquely; there was no warm welcome for Keeley, only question marks in his frosty blue gaze.

"When'd you come, Jonas?"

"Two hours ago," he said. "You'd best take your guests inside and then get back and help me. Later we can bring the sheep in for Boris."

The boy raced back to Sydney, grinning. "I'm going to help Jonas. He just got home."

"I see that," she said. "Was he off buying garden supplies?"

"Boris does the shopping. Jonas was at Northwood." Sydney felt the gardener's eyes still on her as she walked up the steps with Keeley dogging her heels and Gregor bounding up ahead of them. Twelve steps. She counted them. Twelve steps closer to possessing this land. She thought of the gardener's frosty blue eyes meeting hers; perhaps she would keep him on to man the flower beds. She reached over Gregor's head for the knocker, but he swung the massive door open for her.

"So there you are, Gregor," said a gravelly voice. "I sent you to get Keeley—not go on a picnic that took all morning."

"Keeley didn't want to come, Mrs. Quigley." He pointed his thumb backwards. "This lady helped me."

At the sight of the woman fanning herself with a makeshift apron, Keeley pressed against Sydney. "I thought Gregor needed help," Sydney apologized.

Mrs. Quigley was a tall, buxom woman. Wrinkled ridges cut deep into her face. The top button of her housedress lay open, revealing the sagging skin folds at her neck. Her eyes were stern, a faded green, but alert, not missing a thing as her ample body blocked the doorway. She was obviously a country woman, a member of the staff, yet overpowering with her grim expression.

But she gave Gregor's head an affectionate pat. "Go on with you. And take Keeley. I want you both washed up and back in the kitchen right away."

"Can I take the Admiral's tray up to him?"

"Not today, Gregor. Lucas came for it."

He glanced up at Sydney, his thumb pointing back at her again. "What about her? She's hungry."

"No, I only walked the children up here," explained Sydney. "Actually, I was looking for Broadshire Manor when I came to town."

"You found it. But you already know that. I saw you reading the family crest on the gate," Mrs. Quigley said accusingly.

"Yes: *The Willoughbys*. Somehow that wasn't what I expected."

"What were you expecting?"

"Abigail Broderick's name. Has the place already been sold?"

A shadow darkened Mrs. Quigley's face. "You're the American woman looking to take over the land?"

Sydney blushed at the accusation. "I'm Sydney Barrington."

"That's the name Dr. Wallis gave us. He was here today. Said you were to see the solicitor from Bourton-on-the-Water. We weren't expecting you to put in an appearance at the manor."

"I'm sorry. Everything was so beautiful, I just kept driving. I did call Mr. Gallagher, but he wasn't in."

"Odd. If he had an appointment, he'd be there. He thinks in terms of pounds and more pounds. He won't like it; you coming here first." But Mrs. Quigley flashed a whimsical smile as though she were delighted with Sydney's defiance.

"It's Saturday. Maybe he forgot our appointment."

"Dr. Wallis thought you were to see him in London."

Sydney wondered who Dr. Wallis could be. "No, yesterday Mr. Gallagher definitely said his Cotswold office. I had an appointment to meet with him at noon today, but his office was closed."

"It sounds like he's avoiding you." It was Mrs. Quigley's turn to look puzzled. "Well, you are here now, so come on in." She shot a glance at Keeley as Gregor led her away. "Getting that one to move is worth a cup of tea. Getting her here without a tantrum is worth some stew and dumplings. That's what the rest of us are having. So come on in, Miss Barrington."

"I really should go back to the village tea shop."

"You think that's better than my cooking?"

"I really don't know. I haven't tried either one. I know this is an awkward time for me to put in my appearance. Truly, I'm sorry about Miss Broderick."

The cagey eyes narrowed, a tear brimming on the eyelash. "She spent too much time taking care of the children and the Admiral—and not that old heart of hers. Nobody could stop her."

As Sydney stepped inside, she said, "Mrs. Quigley, I thought the Admiral was—maybe the new owner?"

"New owner? This place has been in the Willoughby family for generations. And if I get my way, it will stay in this family. Actually, it belonged to Lady Willoughby, the Admiral's wife. I've been here for years, and there's never been a "For Sale" sign in front of Broadshire Manor. Never. I suppose you've been listening to that Edmund Gallagher and all his fancy ideas for expanding Stow-on-the-Woodland?"

The Admiral's property? Not Abigail Broderick's?

"I haven't met Mr. Gallagher yet. We've just talked on the phone. That's how I knew about the place—and the children. I think I don't really understand what's going on."

"Then you didn't fly over to buy the place?"

"Right now, I'm not sure why I'm here. I reserved a room at a bed-and-breakfast in Bourton-on-the-Water. I really should be getting back there."

"Wait. We need to talk first. Get some understanding between us. I'll make up a room for you. You can try phoning Mr. Gallagher again on Monday."

"Stay here?" Sydney was thrilled at the prospect. "I'd have to get my car. I parked it down by the war memorial."

Mrs. Quigley snorted. "Left down there unattended it could become another war casualty. Coming here first won't sit well with Edmund, but I rather think Dr. Wallis will be pleased."

"I don't know Dr. Wallis."

"He runs the health center. Comes by here every day. But never mind. Boris will go for the car and bring it up. This is the last place Gallagher will be expecting to find you. You get a good night's rest—you'll need it before you talk to him."

～

The stranger did not go unnoticed by Jonas. He had watched her coming up the footpath from the center of town. He liked her easy, unhurried stride, but who was she? Why was she here? Would she and her little girl interfere in his search for the wounded man? She seemed to be soaking up the beauty of the Cotswold Hills as she paused to cup a flower in her fingers and to pluck a tree leaf for the child.

The thick foliage had shaded her features as she approached, but as she stepped through the gate, their eyes met briefly, curiosity in her gaze. She had an elegance of her own—beauty and stature, poise and gracefulness. She was lovely to look at with her chestnut brown hair drawn back from her oval face. Brilliant brown eyes shone beneath arched brows. She was fashionable even in the slacks and blue sweater she was wearing—a successful-looking woman. A woman with a little girl of her own.

So busy was he watching her that he snipped his finger with the pruning shears. He grabbed a rag from the wheelbarrow to stem the flow of blood, but as Gregor ran back to the stranger, she had looked at Jonas once more. Their gaze locked across the primroses. Her skin was soft. Her lips full. A hint of laughter at her mouth. In that split second, Jonas sensed something familiar about her—as though she had stepped from his past to brighten his life again.

He watched her until she reached the top step, and then he turned away, embarrassed. He tossed his tools in the wheelbarrow and broke off a rose in full bloom. A rose for Louise. A rose for the stranger.

Chapter 14

Jonas marked the restless night by tossing on his bunk until 2:00 in the morning with his thoughts on the possibility of Abigail harboring a fugitive. Niggling doubts crushed the image he held of her. She was in his memory, his mother's closest friend, the woman who had stepped in to comfort him when his mother died. Without her, his mailbox at Gordonstoun would have been empty, his holidays lonely. When he was older, she smothered her disappointment when he spent his holidays in the homes of his classmates and fellow officers. But even then, Abigail boasted about his career and defended him in front of the Admiral.

At Gordonstoun parental visits rarely exceeded three times a year. Jonas's Uncle Ian assumed this responsibility, not his father, and certainly not his mother's friend. She was too busy with her refugee children. Yet that day when he was only eight, he marched into the headmaster's office feeling small and insignificant in his gray jersey and corduroy trousers and found Abigail waiting for him.

"I have come to take you home, Jonas."

"I can't leave midterm."

The headmaster cleared his throat. "It is all right, Mr. Willoughby. You have permission to leave with Miss Broderick."

She had come to take him home for his mother's funeral, but even then she said, "Jonas, something has happened to Lady Willoughby and Lightning."

He thought it odd afterward that she had not said, "Something happened to your mother and her horse." But with Abigail, it was always *Lady Willoughby*.

As far back as he could remember, Abigail Broderick had surrounded herself with children, yet she always had time for him. She taught him respect for Margaret Thatcher and an unwavering admiration for the monarchy. She could trace the monarchy back for decades and considered the Queen a peer, so close were they in age. She spoke movingly of Princess Elizabeth making her first broadcast in 1940 to the children being evacuated from the London Blitz. Jonas knew little of Abigail's past except that she had been engaged to a British commando, a man she had met on the beaches of Dunkirk. What had become of him, why she had never married, why she had never loved anyone else were matters that she kept to herself, making the mysteries that surrounded her even more intriguing.

But Abigail work against the British crown? Never. She would not betray the Queen. But would she risk hiding one of her children and consider it nonpolitical? He honestly did not know. One thing he knew with searing accuracy, however. Her prayers had followed him everywhere.

He had come back from Northwood yesterday with the full intention of taking Lucas into his confidence and enlisting his help. He felt a tie-in with any man who had served with the Royal Navy, a man loyal to his own father. Together they could search out Stow-on-the-Woodland cottage by cottage and comb through Broadshire Manor floor by floor, room by room. Corridor creeping at midnight, if need be. But did Jonas really expect to find Conan O'Reilly hiding out in some closet in the manor?

~

Jonas piled his tools into the wheelbarrow and took them with him so he could get back to the primroses after breakfast. When he wheeled his equipment into the front yard, he spotted Gregor with the small red-headed girl in tow.

"Good morning, Gregor. Where are you going?"

"To the kitchen."

"Griselda has enough to do without children underfoot before breakfast. Where's the child's mother?"

"She didn't come with a mother. Just with her brother over there."

The girl turned her enormous eyes on the front door as a small boy propelled himself over the threshold and tumbled down the stone steps. Before he reached bottom, he was screaming.

Jonas scooped the boy up and covered the torn shin with his bare hand. Blood spurted through Jonas's fingers as he carried him up the steps and into the kitchen.

"Griselda, call Dr. Wallis. This child needs stitches."

She held a cooking pan in her hand, her eyes bulging. "The poor darling. What did you do to him, Jonas?"

"Do? I picked him up. Here, give me a towel. I've got to stop this bleeding."

She pushed him aside. "No need to bother Dr. Wallis. Let me look. I've been dealing with skinned shins for forty years."

"Who is he anyway?" Jonas asked.

"A guest at the manor."

"I saw a woman arrive yesterday—"

"A pretty woman never passed your notice." Immediately she murmured, "I'm sorry, Commander. It's just all the excitement lately. Cooking for the children. Caring for—"

"That woman should be down here taking care of her own children. I didn't realize she had two children. Has the whole family moved in? All this company is too upsetting for Abigail."

"Hush, or Miss Barrington will hear you," Griselda said as she cleaned the wound.

Miss Barrington? A name from his boyhood. He remembered the crush he had on the little girl from America. "That woman is Sydney Barrington? Did Abigail send for her?"

"No. Edmund Gallagher did. And she came alone."

"What about these children, Mrs. Quigley? Two little redheads. What are they doing here? Who are they?"

Gregor volunteered the answer. "Keeley and Danny O'Reilly."

"Jonas, they're Conan O'Reilly's children."

For a second Jonas stood immobilized. Speechless. Then anger rose and spilled over. "Conan O'Reilly's children? That's why you were so anxious to send me back to Northwood that night. You took a terrorist into this house? How dare you!"

"Calm yourself, Jonas. The children—"

"Where is he?"

"I don't know what you're talking about."

"Their father. Where is he?"

"He went away the night he left the children here."

Jonas saw Keeley's lip quiver, but he raged on. "Was that the night Abigail had her heart attack? I see by your silence that it was. Griselda, you can't keep the children of Conan O'Reilly in this house. I won't allow it."

"You don't expect me to throw them out, do you?"

"Where is Conan?"

"Gone."

"I intend to find him."

Griselda drew Danny into her lap and held him against her. "You're frightening this child."

"The accident frightened him. Have Boris take him to the doctor."

"No. Dr. Wallis comes later this morning. I'll have him check the leg then—once the American woman leaves."

Gregor murmured, "You said she's staying for the weekend."

"Oh, so I did. I invited her myself." Flustered, she reached out and patted Keeley's cheek. "It is all right, Keeley. No one will harm you. Gregor, get some sausage and scones for the children, will you?"

"When did you start serving sausage and scones for breakfast? You never served them to me."

"You didn't cut your leg, Jonas."

He was outraged. He looked at the injured child. Glared at the frightened sister. He felt sudden remorse as Keeley trembled uncontrollably. Above their heads, his gaze turned back to Griselda. "That child needs comfort too."

"She doesn't like sitting on my lap."

Gregor placed a bowl of sausage and scones on the table beside Griselda. "I think I'll go out, Mrs. Quigley."

"Why don't you take Keeley O'Reilly with you?" Jonas snapped.

But Keeley darted past him, tears streaming down her face, and ran toward the East Wing.

"Now see what you've done, Commander."

They endured a five-minute silence, and then Jonas stomped to the stove and poured himself a boiling cup of tea. Without wincing, he swallowed and then turned his full rage on the woman who had nursed him through his childhood. "I think you'd better pack up, Griselda, and leave—"

~

Sydney stretched contentedly on her bed, enjoying the old-fashioned luxury of her room with furnishings of English oak dating back to the seventeenth century. The high headboard and four posters were carved with peacocks and floral buds. Above Sydney, the ceiling was designed with rosettes. *Her room.* She already thought of it as her own. She contemplated how she could rearrange the furniture and soften the colors with a pastel spread and curtains instead of the thick mauve drapes that had gathered dust into their folds. She would push her bed closer to the windows for the view and the fresh air of the country. And perhaps the gardener—and she flushed thinking of his handsome face—would cut her a fresh bouquet of flowers for her room.

Stop, she told herself. *You haven't seen Edmund Gallagher. The settling of a will takes time. The children. Yes, they would come first. They would have to take priority over remodeling.*

She was so engulfed in her own thoughts that she almost missed the clamor of voices outside and the sudden cry of a child in distress. Thoughts of Keeley sent her racing across the room. She leaned out the window and saw only the beauty of the landscape, the hills just as glorious as yesterday. The air was scented with intoxicating herbs.

As she watched, Gregor walked down the front steps with his hands jammed in the pockets of his short trousers, his head downcast. A picture of gloom on a sunny morning.

"Gregor, I heard someone crying. Is everyone all right?"

He shaded his eyes. "Danny fell down. Mrs. Quigley has him."

"Then he'll be all right?"

"Everybody is all right with Mrs. Quigley."

"Where's the gardener, Gregor?"

He shrugged. "The gardeners come on Monday."

"I mean the man who was pruning the roses yesterday. Jonas, you called him. I see his wheelbarrow out there."

"He's in the kitchen. He's mad at Mrs. Quigley."

And you're driving me mad, she thought, smiling. "But I wanted him to pick me some wildflowers to take with me when I leave."

"Come down. I will help you pick them."

"I'll be there in fifteen minutes."

She bathed in an old tub with claw feet in a room with no lock on the door. After she dressed, she went back to her bedroom and found Keeley buried under the pillows. "What's wrong, sweetheart?"

"Danny fell down. And that man is mad at me."

The child had actually spoken. Sydney dropped onto the bed and encircled her. "Who's Danny?"

"My little brother. He's bleeding."

She panicked at the thought of any of the children hurt, unattended. "Honey, isn't Mrs. Quigley with him?"

"Yes, but I want you to come."

Keeley tugged at her hand and led her from the East Wing, down the long corridor to the kitchen. They stopped short of the open door, Keeley shrinking against her. Sydney listened, shocked at a man's angry voice saying, "I think you'd better pack up, Griselda, and leave."

Sydney burst into the kitchen and stared at the rangy gardener lording it over Mrs. Quigley. "How dare you speak to Mrs. Quigley like that! Go back to your garden and take your anger out on the weeds and the rosebushes."

As he spun to face Sydney, a lock of dark hair fell across his broad forehead. He swept it back, revealing a pinched frown wedged between his brows.

"You heard me. You can't talk to Mrs. Quigley that way. Just go back to your flowers and cool down."

For a moment, his frosty blue eyes seemed like dark circles. He looked as though he would turn his tongue-lashing on her. Instead the frost in his eyes melted, and a bemused smile formed at the corners of his mouth. He took his teacup and deliberately poured the contents into the sink, then glancing briefly at Griselda, said, "We'll finish this later."

Jamming his hands into his pockets, he left the kitchen, but he was whistling.

"Who does he think he is?" Sydney asked when he was out of earshot. "A gardener talking to you like that!"

Mrs. Quigley's hand shook as she pulled Danny closer to her. "Everything will be fine, Danny," she said, but her voice trembled. "And I've got to get the rest of the children up and fed. And breakfast upstairs to—"

More gently Sydney said, "What right did he have to talk to you that way?"

"He has every right, Miss Barrington. He is the lord of the manor—at least he will be someday."

"Lord of the manor? The owner? He's—he's not the gardener?"

"No, he is Jonas Willoughby—the Admiral's son."

The admiral that Gregor had mentioned yesterday.

"But what about Miss Broderick? Oh, never mind—" She had blown it. If she was up against an admiral and his son, she felt certain the carrier bid would slip through her fingers. "I guess I just don't understand what's going on."

"None of us do. Right now, with the Admiral ill, Jonas isn't himself. He has too much responsibility. On top of that, he's stationed at Northwood."

"That Navy base near London?"

"Yes. Jonas is a serving officer in Her Majesty's Royal Navy. A Navy pilot really, but stuck on land now. I know the poor boy hates it. He had to give up so much when he found out about the Admiral and Abigail."

Sydney patted Griselda's shoulder. "It's all right. I'll apologize to Jonas. I'm so sorry for coming in the way I did. But he still doesn't have any right to talk to you that way."

"In a way he did. You see, he didn't know Danny and Keeley were staying here. He thought Keeley came with you."

"With me? He didn't know about these children?"

"Not about the O'Reilly children. He came back from Northwood just an hour or so before you saw him. He's been gone a couple of weeks. We wanted him to stay away from the excitement in Stow-on-the-Woodland."

"Excitement in this quiet little hamlet? It doesn't look like anything exciting ever happens here. It's so peaceful—"

Mrs. Quigley gave an indiscernible nod toward Keeley. "I'll let Jonas explain things to you. You said you were going to apologize to him. I think that's best. Otherwise he will send these children away."

"That sounds like Edmund Gallagher."

"He's nothing like Mr. Gallagher," she defended. "It has to do with being in the Navy. His patriotic duty—oh, just ask him."

"Does he really plan to send *you* away, Mrs. Quigley?"

"He just might do that. Except—well, I think he still needs me to help with these children. Poor Jonas. He's been holding so much anger inside for so long."

"Anger at his father? At what happened to Miss Broderick?"

Griselda nuzzled her chin against the sleeping child. "You'd better ask Jonas."

Sydney moved slowly across the room and peered into a kettle. "Porridge? May I have some? I'm hungry. And maybe Keeley would enjoy some, too. And while we eat, maybe you can tell me what happened to—" She couldn't bring herself to mention Abigail Broderick's name. She nodded toward the child on Griselda's lap. "He looks like Keeley."

"This is Danny, Keeley's brother."

"I gather that. Maybe you can tell me a little bit about them and why Keeley keeps running away. Perhaps I can help."

Griselda eased the sleeping child more comfortably in her arms. "I guess I owe you that much. You see, their father was one of Abigail's boys. He brought them to us a couple of weeks ago—that's the night when everything went wrong."

"The night Miss Broderick had her heart attack?"

"How did you know that?"

"Mr. Gallagher told me. That's why I flew over."

"That's right. Your mother and Abigail were old friends. No wonder you came."

Friends? More links to the past. "Yesterday when I arrived, you said you thought we needed to talk. I think this is as good a time as any."

Chapter 15

When Sydney opened the front door, a stranger stood on the top step. "Good morning," she said. "I was just going out."

"Then you won't mind if I come in?"

Appearing to be in his thirties, he was a pleasant-faced man and held a medical kit in his hand. He stepped inside the corridor. "I'm Dr. Wallis. How is my patient today?"

Puzzled, she said, "Your patient? I guess I didn't know anyone was ill. Well, Danny did hurt his knee, but I'm certain that Boris took all of the children down to the stables, and I'm just going out to look for Jonas."

"He won't be hard to find. He's across the river playing his bagpipes. I knew it was Jonas the minute I heard the music."

"By the way, Doctor, I'm Sydney Barrington. Would you mind telling Mrs. Quigley I won't be gone long?"

A noticeable twitch pulsated along the doctor's jaw as he returned her smile. "Are you staying at the manor?"

"Yes, and unexpectedly for several more days. I had a reservation at The Sheepfold, but when I didn't show up, they gave it away. They promised to find me a room early next week—that will make it easier to make an appointment with the solicitor in town."

"Edmund Gallagher?"

"Yes. You know him?"

"Since boyhood. Have a good day, Miss Barrington." She stood in the doorway, expecting him to turn toward the West Wing where the Admiral lived. Instead he climbed the magnificent stairs with his medical kit still in his hand. An uncanny feeling stirred inside her, leaving her certain that she already knew the answer.

Sydney left the manor and made her way back over the path she had taken yesterday. Crossing the River Windrush she climbed the hills toward the keening wail of the bagpipes. She longed to hear a march or a reel, but it was a lament that the wind carried toward her. She saw Jonas now, a towering picture of strength against the backdrop of emerald hills. She cut through a patch of wildflowers, pressing on toward the Admiral's son.

The collie lay near his master's feet, both the man and dog looking peaceful. The sudden lurch inside her was a heartbeat out of sync with Barrington Enterprises. *I could be happy here,* she told herself, and wondered where the thought had been born.

Jonas turned as she approached. The music died in the middle of the dirge. He smiled. "I wasn't certain we would meet again."

"I came up to apologize."

His sea blue eyes twinkled. "No need."

"But I thought you were the gardener, Mr. Willoughby."

"And I thought you brought your daughter with you."

"I'm not married."

"That could be good news."

"It was foolish of me thinking you were the gardener. I had no right to interfere in your quarrel anyway."

"A man out of control needs to be checked."

Jonas, she noted, had a full, sensitive mouth, a firmly set jaw, and the tantalizing scent of a woody cologne. The pinched frown still wedged between his brows as he talked to her. In spite of their snap judgment animosity, his features lit with an amused smile. "I garden, but I'm not a gardener. And I'm certain Griselda has told you that I'm the Admiral's son?"

"She takes a good bit of pride in that." Sydney averted his probing gaze. "Now that I'm here, I'm not sure what else to say."

"You've come too far to turn around and leave." He bent down and placed his bagpipes on a soft quilt. "I have no chair to offer, but the grass is like velvet to the touch up here."

"I can't stay long."

He pointed toward the ground. "Then be my guest for as long as you can stay. Or even longer."

Once seated, he faced her. "I'm glad you came, Miss Barrington. I was embarrassed once Griselda told me your name. I should have recognized you when you first arrived."

"Recognized me?" Surely if she had seen Jonas before, handsome as he was, she would have remembered.

"Abigail often talked about you."

"But I never met her."

"But you did. A long time ago. I didn't like it when your parents took you away—and Abigail was heartsick. You don't remember being here, do you?" he asked.

She had a feeling of floating, of drifting back in time. She tried to remember his face, his voice from the past. "I'm not sure. Vaguely, maybe. The fountain was familiar when I saw it. And walking up to the manor yesterday, I expected to see a beech tree around the first corner, with a clump of azaleas by its roots—I was wrong. I found musk orchids instead."

He smiled. "One of the gardeners dug up the azaleas after a rather nasty storm. The orchids grew wild." He tugged at a blade of grass and blew it away. "I was ten when they took you away. I thought I would never see you again."

She turned and looked into those mesmerizing eyes. "You seem so certain I was here before. Was I one of Abigail's children?"

"Only briefly—until the Barringtons took you to America. They brought you back twice when you were a little girl."

In a flash, it was clear in her mind. "I wore a pink bow in my hair. A ponytail, I think. And I blew out birthday candles."

"Yes. You were six that day."

She touched his hand. "But I don't remember you, Jonas. I don't remember Abigail."

"Your mother and Abigail were friends. You stayed here with Abigail for several weeks until the Barringtons adopted you."

"Then I've come back—I've come home?" She looked back toward the stately manor where the property stretched out for miles. The immensity of it struck her. "Have you always lived here, Jonas?"

He nodded. "My parents kept a London home, but mostly in the summers and on holidays we lived here in Stow-on-the-Woodland."

"I thought the property belonged to Miss Broderick."

He laughed. "No, it belonged to my mother. It's been in our family for generations. Several hundred years at least. My people made their fortune in the wool trade, but I don't think I would have liked my forefathers lording it over the village people, riding their hunts, eating off the fat of the land. My mother was not like that. She was warmhearted and kind; people loved her. When Mother died, I thought Dad would move us back to our London home. But I think he came to see the land as a good thing."

Her mind reeled. "Then *you* are next in line?"

"Of course. I'm the only child. My mother's brother never wanted the place. He took over the family estate in Scotland and is content there. So, with Dad ill, the burden of care is mine."

She broke off a tiny yellow flower and stared down at it. "What will you do with the property?"

"When I first came home, I talked to our family solicitor about selling it and placing Dad and Abigail in senior residences. It's much more land than we can tend to as a family. I even agreed to give the solicitor, Edmund Gallagher, the option of parceling off the land to developers if I'm away. He told me he had a buyer in mind."

Himself, she thought. "Why won't you be here, Jonas?"

He rubbed his knuckles. "I'll be back at sea. Some people think I followed in my father's footsteps, but by the time I was nine I wanted a Navy career myself." His fingers glided over his knuckles. "Now that I'm here, I realize I can't sell the place out from under him. He's an old man. He was old when I was born."

"Would you give up your Navy career?"

"The sea is my life. Yet I've spent my life trying to please my father. Selling what belonged to Mother would only hurt him."

"You should preserve the land for your own children."

He smiled. "It seems unlikely that I'll have a family."

"You're still a young man."

"But my fiancée is dead."

"I'm sorry. What happened to her?"

"An accident. A terrible accident."

Sydney envisioned a plane crash or a car careening off the motorway at a reckless speed.

"If we had married, she would have overseen the care of Broadshire Manor. Now I have to make other arrangements. The taxes are unbelievable—more than Dad or I can handle now."

She thought of Edmund Gallagher. Of the illegal maneuvers he had in mind. "Have you decided what to do, Jonas?"

"I've considered turning most of the property over to the National Trust. They acquire ancestral homes like mine. I can donate the property in lieu of taxes, maybe continue to live here if I open part of the manor to the public."

"Is that what you want to do?"

"I want to keep a piece of the land to build on. But since coming home this time, I realize it is wrong to keep this vast property for one family. My solicitor would like to own the land himself. Or sell it. But too much of the money would go into his pocket, and the Willoughby name would soon be forgotten. But the government would preserve our name and the integrity and beauty of this place for generations to come."

"Then you have real problems," Sydney said, picking another small flower.

She longed to be honest with him and tell him that she had come to claim her windfall from Abigail Broderick. But the manor belonged to the Willoughby family. Or had some quirk in the law left it in the hands of Abigail Broderick? If so, the Admiral's son faced the shock of his life.

"Sydney, if the National Trust takes over, I wouldn't have to worry about a staff large enough to run the manor. In the early days it took shepherds, gardeners, plumbers, domestic staff, stable boys. World War II brought a lot of changes. Some of the property was divided up, farmed by locals. The staff dwindled once Mother died. But I still remember chauffeurs driving my mother and me back and forth to London."

He faced her, looking chagrined. "I'm sorry. All I've done is talk about my land and my family. What about you? Why have you come back after all these years?"

She couldn't tell him the whole truth, but she said, "I'm here on business."

"A businesswoman! Then tell me, what would you do with the manor?"

"I'd use my money to maintain the gardens, keep a place for the children, and restore the manor to its former glory."

"A rich businesswoman. A noble aim but an impractical one. Better for the National Trust to assume the care and restoration. I think that would please my mother. But you sound like Abigail. Is that why you came? To take up her work with refugee children?"

She didn't answer him but looked off at the distant hills.

Sitting high on a wold gave her a sense of splendor and grandeur, a view of the sweep and breadth of the land. She felt part of the magnificent landscape and a deep sense of security with solid earth beneath her feet, the heavens above her.

"It's beautiful here, Jonas, with the sun on the hills, the wildflowers flourishing, the sheep grazing. I'm overwhelmed with the unending beauty of the Cotswolds. Maybe that's why I came back—to soak up the beauty again."

He said solemnly, "Abigail always said this place gave her an awareness of the sovereignty of God. I tend to agree with her. The hills are always here. The color changes. The seasons change, but the hills are everlasting."

"I'm glad I came back, Jonas."

Her words pleased him. He leaned forward. "You think it is lovely now. You should see our fiery autumns. We're ablaze with color. London seems drab then."

"Perhaps I'll come back then."

"Promise?"

She flushed at his casual remark. Yes, she would come back if she knew Jonas Willoughby would be here.

~

Jonas liked the sensuous curve of Sydney's mouth, the teasing ripple in her laughter, the intelligence that sparked in her eyes as she listened to him. It surprised him how easy it was to talk to her, how effortless to hold her attention without turning on the old Willoughby charm. He thought of that crush he had on a little girl when he was ten. Had anything changed? Yes, she had grown into a beautiful woman, and he felt suddenly as uncertain as he had when they were children. He wanted to pursue their friendship, to delay her leaving Stow-on-the-Woodland. But did he dare allow her presence to lure him from his true purpose in the village? Could he really trust her?

She drew her legs up and encircled them with her arms.

Slender wrists. Slender ankles. "It's peaceful here, like my cabin by the river. I look at a place like this and think I could stay forever."

"Stay. I'd like that."

"Randolph teases me about finding my castle in the sky."

"Competition?" he teased. "I might be a jealous man."

She laughed. "He's my right-hand man at Barrington."

"As long as he doesn't bother your left hand," he said, noting the blanched skin where a ring had been. *Stop it,* he told himself. His quick, easy way of flirting had irritated Louise. A charm he had learned from his father. But this woman—like Louise—deserved more than a brief flirtation.

He pointed back toward the West Wing. "My father stays there. He's ill and frail; that's why I've come home."

"He didn't come down for breakfast this morning."

"He never comes for breakfast. Lucas—the steward who takes care of him—thinks he rests better away from others."

"And what do you think?"

"That my father will never change."

"And now you're not talking about breakfast. But why do you have him locked away in a room of his own?"

His tone sharpened. "We don't have him locked away. I told you, the Admiral's steward is with him."

"I haven't met the man, and already I don't like Lucas. Your father is a retired admiral. That means he's spent a lifetime with people. How sad to have no friends now."

Jonas rubbed his moist palms. "Dad's a bit dotty. Confused."

"And you're ashamed of him? Don't be, Jonas. Even someone with memory loss needs to be among friends."

"Lucas takes him out on the balcony each morning. Gregor pops in once a day. More if we let him. And Abigail and I used to take turns staying with him at night. But it's up to me now." He looked directly at her. "Would you like to meet my father?"

"Yes. It sounds like Gregor adores him."

"Most people are afraid of him."

Jonas rallied the dog and hoisted his bagpipes to his shoulder. When they reached the West Wing, the Admiral was sitting by the window, his steward standing beside him.

"Dad, I brought company. She's a friend of Abigail's."

The old man went on gazing out the window. "The tide's coming in. We've got to get the ship underway."

"Right-o, Admiral," Lucas said.

Lucas was an unpretentious-looking man. Tall, authoritative, visibly showing concern for the Admiral. His hair was cut short, poking up with a reddish glow. Sydney wasn't certain which man was dotty. Or were they playing a game?

Whatever they were doing, the Admiral went on with his orders. "Let's take the HMS *Barham* out today."

"Very good, sir."

"Dad," Jonas said sharply.

His father turned his hoary head to acknowledge them, suddenly aware of their presence. The Admiral's face was lined with sea wrinkles, his eyes wide, curious.

"Is that you, Willoughby?" the Admiral said. "You going with us? You don't have a command of your own. When I was your age—"

Jonas winced. "Not this time, sir. You have company."

At the scold in Jonas's voice, the old man's eyes settled on Sydney. Even at eighty he was still handsome with strong chiseled features. Thinning fluffs of black hair framed the bald spot. "Is she a snotty? And I don't want any women on my ship."

"That's a midshipman," Jonas said, embarrassed. "That's what they called them when Dad first entered the service."

"I wouldn't be very good at sea, sir. I'd be seasick."

He laughed, pleased. "I've been with the Royal Navy all my life. Did Willoughby tell you I entered the service as a cadet at Osborne in the midthirties? Joined the fleet as a midshipman eighteen months later." The dull gaze in his eyes brightened. "I was on one of those big battleships in time to give that war a run for its money. Do you remember that war, snotty?"

"I wasn't born then, sir," Sydney said.

"It's a shame you missed that war. I was given a command of my own. I wasn't like Willoughby here—turning down a ship."

"He's right on both counts," Jonas said. "Dad never turned down anything—for anyone. By war's end he was in command of a warship on escort duty in the Atlantic."

"Hunting U-boats," the Admiral said proudly.

"A remarkable career," Sydney told him.

"Lucas, we have guests. Should we have tea?" the Admiral suggested.

"Don't bother, Lucas. We won't stay long, Father."

"Stay long enough to make this young snotty welcome. We should show her my medals and ships."

"Another time, Dad."

"Yes, I will come back. You can show me your ships and medals then," Sydney said reassuringly.

"Keep her to that promise, Willoughby."

The whole time the Admiral talked, Lucas kept his piercing gaze on Sydney. His face was full, his eyes provocative as he studied her. His shirt sleeves were rolled up, his collar open at the neck. His jeans were tight, his feet bare in their loafers. A man's man and he knew it. And he knew she was aware of him.

Sydney stepped back as Lucas wheeled the old man back to his bed. With strength visible in those muscled arms, he lifted the Admiral and settled him on top of the bedding. He fluffed the old man's pillows and braced him in a sitting position.

"That's good, Lucas. I was getting tired on my watch. Now where was I, young woman?" And without a pause, he went right on commanding ships from his four-poster bed.

"He's getting excitable. Should I give him his medicine early, Commander?"

"No. Wait until bedtime, Lucas."

Sydney liked the gruff old man, but she questioned his mental status. Had he been overmedicated? Or was he simply losing his memory?

Rambling in the past? Lucas seemed protective enough, but was he smothering the Admiral?

She flushed when she realized Lucas was watching her.

Lucas seemed charming enough in his own way, yet shifty-eyed. She felt uncomfortable in his presence, wondering whether he was a double-minded man in all his ways.

She was relieved when Jonas dismissed the Admiral's steward. "We'll take over now, Lucas. Give us another ten minutes."

"Very good, sir. It will give Miss Barrington more time to hear about the Admiral's ships. The walls are lined with them." He cast a sly smile Sydney's way. "I'll get the Admiral's tray."

"Jonas," she said when Lucas had gone, "you look tired. Do you plan to sit up all night with your father?"

"I have no choice. Boris filled in for me last evening. I can't ask him to do it again."

"Then let me do it. I'd feel like I was earning my keep."

"Would you really mind? What about midnight until three? I could get some good sleep that way."

"It's a done deal, Jonas."

❧

At midnight Sydney went back to the West Wing and tapped lightly on the Admiral's door. It swung back so swiftly that it startled her. Lucas stood in the shadows glaring out at her.

"I've come to sit with the Admiral."

"I could have spelled the Commander, taken his place. But you're here now."

He led her to the Admiral's bedside where the old man lay with his eyes closed, his hoary head resting against the pillows. His breathing seemed uneasy, not that of a man asleep.

"I've given the Admiral his medication. He should be fine, but if you need anyone, pull that cord. That will bring Mrs. Quigley at once. If he grows restless—or seems out of sorts—push this buzzer. It's wired to my room in the stables."

He stared down at the Admiral with an expression that could only be a mixture of respect and disdain. She had no doubt that there had once been a close friendship between the Admiral and his steward. But now? Or was Lucas fighting the loss of an old friend through illness and old age?

"Good night, sir," Lucas said. "I will be back in the morning to help you bathe and dress."

The inert man on the bed remained motionless with his eyelids closed, but Sydney had discerned a slight increase in the rise and fall of the Admiral's chest. *He's awake,* she thought. *He knows exactly what is going on in this room.*

For a second she panicked at the thought of being left alone with him and then, regaining her composure, asked, "Lucas, did Dr. Wallis think the Admiral was better this morning?"

"Dr. Wallis?"

"Yes, I met him when he came this morning."

"Dr. Wallis," Lucas said coolly, "does not take me into his confidence. Besides, he wasn't calling on the Admiral."

Her unease grew. "Should I sit by the Admiral's bedside?"

"That's what Miss Broderick always did. I don't know how the Commander spends his time here." The words implied doubt, scorn. "The Admiral likes a cup of hot chocolate at one in the morning. At least he did when Miss Broderick sat with him."

"I can do that. Should I awaken Mrs. Quigley?"

"No. I keep a hot plate in the bathroom and all the fixings. I have a tin of sweet breads there as well."

With a quick nod he was gone, closing the door emphatically behind him. She listened, waiting for the echo of his footsteps to fade. Satisfied that he had gone, she reached for a chair and pulled it to the bedside.

"Abigail." The old man's eyes fluttered. He glanced around, his gaze vacant for a moment, then he focused on her. "Where's Abigail?"

Hadn't they told him what happened? Or did he forget and ask the same question over and over? "I've come in her place. Your son will be here later."

He waved his veined hand in disgust. "He should be back on the *Invincible* flying those planes of his, not here with me."

The words of a rational man, a concerned father. "He wants to be with you while you're ill."

"Ill?" he roared. "I'm not sick. I'm just an old man stuck with all the appendages of old age. Give me a cloth, girl. Whoever you are."

"I'm Sydney Barrington. I visited you earlier today."

"I don't remember. Just give me a cloth."

She handed him her handkerchief. He lifted his head from his pillows and spit into it. Pills spilled from his mouth. She took the hanky and dabbed his lips.

"It looks like you didn't take your medicine."

"A man can't think for himself with all of that forced on him. Abigail doesn't make me take that stuff when she's here. We just sit and talk." A faint twinkle touched his eyes. "And we hold hands when Lucas leaves."

Abigail's name again. Was she alive, or only alive in the old man's mind?

He looked at her with a piercing gaze. "You're an attractive young woman. Like Abigail and my wife. Did you know my wife?"

"Only through the portrait on the wall. Lady Willoughby died when I was a child. But she and Abigail were great friends."

His eyes mocked. "Were they?" he asked. "I'm tired. I'll rest now before my son gets here. And when I wake up, Miss—"

"Sydney Barrington."

"Well then, Miss Sydney, we will talk then, and you can tell me why you're here."

He sank back against his pillow and five minutes later snored peacefully. Sydney glanced again at the three pills and decided on the spur of the moment not to leave them for Lucas to discover. She wandered around the half-lit room trying to tie the enigma of the man together. She found the pill bottles in the Admiral's top dresser and made her way to the table lamp to read their labels. She matched the pills. Two sleeping pills and another medication if the Admiral became combative. She tried to make out the doctor's name, but it was not Dr. Wallis.

Anger rose inside her. A man who had been in command of ships should not be reduced to a shell of a person, in constant stupor from medication. She folded her handkerchief over the pills and tucked them into her pocket. Moments later, changing her mind, she walked into the bathroom, poured the pills into the bowl, and watched them swirl into oblivion. But she would nose around and find out why he was so heavily medicated.

"Abigail," came a voice from the dark.

She turned and hurried back into the bedroom. From the doorway she saw the outline of the Admiral's frail body lying on the monstrous four-poster bed. He was tall, but he appeared frail and uncertain in the shadows. He lifted his hand.

"Abigail," he called again.

"I'm coming," Sydney said. "And we'll have hot chocolate together."

Chapter 16

Sydney reached the solicitor's office before Edmund Gallagher arrived and stood with her back against the buff-colored building waiting for him. Above her, the green shingle swayed and creaked. Another half hour passed before a smartly attired man strode purposefully toward her.

She stepped forward. "I'm Sydney Barrington."

Gallagher's cool expression never wavered. He was younger than she had expected, perhaps still in his thirties, and looked smooth and professional in his tailored suit.

"I'm sorry I missed our appointment on Saturday, but an emergency kept me in London. I hope you didn't wait long," he said nonchalantly.

He unlocked the door and walked in ahead of her, taking precise steps. His office looked modern except for an old cloak rack where he tossed his Burberry coat. He opened the windows as he passed them, put his briefcase on the floor beside him, and pressed the button on his answering machine. "Edmund, this is Cora Churchill. Please return my calls."

Sounds familiar, Sydney thought.

The second caller said, "This is Dr. Wallis returning your call, Edmund."

She smothered her surprise when Jeff's cheerful voice echoed in the room. "Mr. Gallagher, this is Jeffrey VanBurien. I'm trying to reach a client of yours—Sydney Barrington. I'm on holiday at the St. Michael's vicarage in Stow-on-the-Woodland. Trust we can make contact with her there. Tell her we have some surprises for her."

Behind his thick-rimmed glasses, Edmund's cold eyes met hers. "You didn't leave a number for him to reach you?"

"I guess not. Isn't Miss Broderick buried at St. Michael's?"

"It's the only cemetery in the area. Will you be going on to Stow-on-the-Woodland today, Miss Barrington?"

She didn't tell him she had already been there. "I really should. Imagine friends from home being here at the same time."

"Imagine," he agreed. "It's not exactly a tourist spot."

"But why would they be staying at the vicarage?" *Unless they had discovered something—or someone—buried there.*

"There are no hotels. The vicar tends to take in strangers. The St. Michael's church tower will be the first thing you see from the road when you drive to the village." His eyes narrowed. "Ask for directions to the Very Reverend Charles Rainford-Simms. The church is centuries old, the cleric there not much younger."

Waving his hand at the seat across from him, he sank down into his leather chair and folded his ringed hands on the desktop. "I conclude you are here regarding Miss Broderick's will and your inheritance? I have a full schedule this morning, so we need to set up a regular appointment time. Preferably in London."

She decided to play his game. "No, preferably here where it is convenient for me. I came for the burial of my friend, Mr. Gallagher. There's no point in driving back to London."

"You are rather late for a funeral. I was unable to attend myself. I believe they cremated—"

"You said she was to be buried, per her own wishes. So it's not too late to place flowers on Miss Broderick's grave once I know where it is."

"I may have rather disturbing news for you. There have been some legal problems. Some unexpected debts. You do remember I told you everything could be handled by my office?"

"I was coming to Europe on business anyway."

He whirled in his seat and reached for a folder from his file. "It looks now as if we must sell the property to pay the sizable debts. I'm not certain what will be left for you—perhaps a few thousand in American currency. That's one of the problems, Miss Barrington."

"What about the other six problems? The children?"

A tic twisted the corner of his mouth. "We will find proper homes for them when the time comes. And I told you on the phone that we have a prospective buyer for the property."

She challenged him. "So you still plan to sell the property and send the occupants away? Were you going to consult me first?"

"I thought we agreed on the phone—"

"I don't think we settled on anything. That's why I'm here."

"Then I assume you would like me to go ahead with that offer? It's a private arrangement, Miss Barrington."

I'm certain it is. "I would like to meet with the buyer."

He opened his mouth to speak and wiped his lips instead. "I told you, it is a private arrangement. If you can wait until Wednesday, I will arrange to drive you out to Stow-on-the-Woodland. That way we can inspect the property together."

"I have my own car. I can meet you there, but let's meet tomorrow. And I want to see the children and Mrs. Quigley. That was the house-keeper's name, wasn't it?"

"Stay away from the manor. Mrs. Quigley is a cantankerous old woman. I don't think we should trouble her right now. I need time to work out the arrangements with the buyer. He's already signed a tentative agreement with me."

You're talking about Jonas, the Admiral's son, the rightful heir. There were obvious distortions and lies in what he told her, but it was too soon to mention Jonas. She tried to guess Jeff VanBurien's counsel and said, "The buyer signed an agreement with you, Mr. Gallagher? Not with me?"

"I am Miss Broderick's solicitor. I was the obvious contact. With all the debts piling up, the final settlement could be months away. Perhaps years. There's no need for you to stay."

No need to come? No need to stay? According to Jonas, the story was different. She was certain that she had inherited nothing. Not a parcel of land, not a child. But how could she pack up and go home? How could she walk out on Keeley O'Reilly? Again this morning, the child had popped into her room, tugging at her sheet and her heartstrings. Or how could she walk out on Commander Willoughby? Wasn't it her responsibility now to make certain he inherited the property that was rightfully his?

"Will anyone else contest the will?" she asked. "According to your phone calls, I am the sole heir."

"But if there's nothing left—"

I've seen the property, Mr. Gallagher, she thought. *It's immense. And somehow I don't believe that the bill collectors are lined up at the door.*

She pitied the man sitting across from her, digging himself in deeper. Was greed driving him? Or would that legal document sitting in his folder ban Jonas from falling heir to the Willoughby property? She fixed her gaze on Gallagher's hands—large, smooth hands, the nails finely clipped. Then she met those sharp eyes again and wished she could look into his mind and heart. He was backing himself into a corner of lies.

"May I see the will?" she asked.

"It would be best—"

"Mr. Gallagher, I have only recently gone through the settlement of my parents' estate, a complicated one. I realize that wills take time, that problems arise, that debts must be paid. But as sole heir, I do have a right to review Miss Broderick's will. And I will have a right to be advised of all claims against her estate."

The tic started again. He slid the paper across the desk and tapped the place where Sydney's name was entered. "I hereby will, give, devise, and bequeath all the rest, residue, and remainder of my estate. . ."

Her name leaped from the page. Before she could read further, he pulled the file away. "Now do you believe me?"

Edmund Gallagher had told the truth. But something was still wrong. What quirk of the law had passed Broadshire Manor from Lady Willoughby to her lifelong friend Abigail—and on to Sydney?

"I want to have a copy of that will. And perhaps you have a copy of Abigail Broderick's death certificate there in your file. I'd like a copy of that as well."

Edmund's skin blanched. "Just now I cannot do as you ask. For reasons already explained, the settling of the estate has been delayed."

She wanted to laugh. What had she walked into? "Another excuse, Mr. Gallagher." *A time-out to change your game plan?*

His face remained ashen. He spoke with subdued rage. "I have no control over the barrister's decision. You see, you may not be the rightful heir."

The truth at last. Or more lies? "Who then?"

As Edmund contemplated his next words, a smirk touched his lips. He took great pleasure in his announcement. "You may not be the sole heir. Miss Broderick may have a child of *her own*."

Had one of Abigail's hidden children laid claim to her estate? *She had a dozen sons. Perhaps more.* Sydney felt flushed. "I didn't know Abigail Broderick was married."

"I don't know the particulars. I just wanted to settle this business and not get you involved."

"But I am involved, Mr. Gallagher. And I'm more concerned than you know. Would you mind telling me again about her? About her illness? Her history? Her death? Her burial?"

Gallagher put his hands to his temples. "I need time, Miss Barrington. Don't you understand?"

"I haven't understood anything since you first called me. Something tells me that all I have inherited is trouble. But I won't run away from it. I intend to see this one through."

He bristled. Color came back to his face. The tic twisted the corner of his mouth even more. "Are you questioning my integrity?"

"Don't make the situation any worse. If Miss Broderick has a child, then I am obviously not the sole heir." Again she felt pity for Gallagher and the web he had drawn around himself. "Put your plans for developing Stow-on-the-Woodland on hold. I want to see Miss Broderick's grave before we make any decisions at all. And when we meet again, my lawyer will be at my side."

He hit the repeat button on his answering machine and listened to Jeff VanBurien's voice echoing through the room again. "Somehow I believe it will be this Mr. Jeffrey VanBurien."

"Perhaps. But don't put the manor on the selling block. I'm certain my lawyer will insist that you locate that child first, if such a child exists."

He grabbed another excuse. "It's possible that he's deceased now. No one in the village has ever heard of him."

"But you have! So make certain."

He picked up his pen. "Where are you staying?"

Sidestepping his question, she said, "I'll be in touch, Mr. Gallagher. And most definitely, the next time we meet, I will ask my lawyer to join us."

❧

As she stepped from his office, Edmund dialed the health center. "I don't care if Wallis is seeing a patient," he said gruffly. "Get him on the line."

He didn't have to wait long.

"Edmund, don't upset my nurse like that again."

"That Barrington woman is here. She's going to be a problem for me. I can't lose that Broadshire property. You've got to help me stop her. Did you change one of the grave markers for me?"

"Of course not. And I know she's here, Edmund. In fact, I've met her. She's staying at Broadshire Manor."

Edmund cleared his voice three times before he could mumble, "Has she seen Abigail? Does she know—"

"I don't think so, but it won't take long for her to figure it out."

"I've gone too far."

"I've been telling you that, Edmund. You need to know. Miss Barrington has met the Admiral. But you have a bigger problem than the Admiral. Miss Barrington has met the Admiral's son."

❧

When Sydney reached the village, she parked the car near the center of town and walked through the tree-lined path to the Church of St.

Michael's. She found the vicar and his two guests wandering through the church cemetery.

Sydney felt an immense relief at the sight of them. Jeff was his lean, beanpole self. Her ally, her friend. She fought off the urge to run up and throw her arms around him. His brother Chan, long-legged and pleasant, was just another link to home. Chandler was the better looking of the brothers with shoulders broad enough to cry on if things got rough for her. As tall as the brothers were, the vicar towered above them; he looked like he'd bent forward most of his life—out of awkwardness in his boyhood, out of hearing loss in his older years. Yet he turned at the sound of her footsteps behind him and smiled.

"Well, here's the young woman you've been expecting. Miss Barrington, I believe. I've heard a good bit about you from Mrs. Quigley. And from Gregor. And, of course, from these friends of yours. You must visit me in the vicarage while you're here."

She was struck by the kind eyes that looked down at her and felt an immediate warmth toward Charles Rainford-Simms. For a second, the joy in the cleric's eyes dimmed. "I was just showing the boys where my youngest daughter is buried."

Sydney glanced at the tombstone. It was old-fashioned and cut of stone but not tilted or cracked like the older monuments that lay in uneven rows. Fresh flowers had been placed on the grave.

Louise Rainford-Simms, it read.

Sydney subtracted quickly. "She was very young."

"Too young to die the way she died," her father said.

Uncomfortable at the catch in the vicar's voice, she turned to Jeff. "Jeff, I was shocked when I heard your message coming over the answering machine at the lawyer's office."

He slipped his arm around her. "And don't think we weren't surprised when you didn't show up at the bed-and-breakfast."

"We were downright worried," Chandler agreed. "If we hadn't gone back to The Sheepfold after breakfast this morning, we wouldn't have known you were safe."

"Chan's right. The owner told us she gave away your reservation when you didn't show up. We stayed there last night."

Sydney chuckled. "She probably gave you my room, but why did you leave that crazy message at Gallagher's office?"

"To let you know we were still here for you. The lady at The Sheepfold did us another favor when she steered us to the vicar."

The vicar smiled patiently, "It seems like I've had more guests lately than I've had parishioners. It will be nice to have you swell the congregation on Sunday."

"Count me out," Jeff told him.

Chan kicked him. "We'll both be there, Reverend."

Charles seemed a kindly sort with his bushy brows knit together. "It's tea time. I'll go in and ask my housegirl to make a spot of tea for all of us."

He strode off with a young man's gait, his snowy white hair thick and unruly.

"Likable old guy," Jeff said. "He knows this village well and everyone in it. I even asked him about Edmund Gallagher. He said Gallagher doesn't attend the worship services. And it seems that Gallagher's father was much more liked in the village."

"Well, after my visit with Gallagher today, I wasn't too impressed," Sydney added. "Something funny is going on. But I got a glance at the will. My name really is there."

"It can't be, Syd. That's what we wanted to tell you. Seems like the owner at The Sheepfold knows the Willoughby family well. She said Jonas will inherit the property when his father dies. And when I mentioned about Abigail Broderick dying, she just stared at me and said, 'Dead? She's a fighter, that one.'"

"The woman's exact words," Chan agreed. "She filled us in on the night Broderick had her heart attack. She said nothing about her dying."

Sydney wasn't certain she wanted to hear any more. Here it was the middle of spring, in an idyllic place, and a cold chill engulfed her. "What is Edmund Gallagher trying to pull?"

"His own program, probably. That's another reason I called and left a message on his answering machine. I wanted him to know you had friends here in town who were looking out for you."

She gave them a quick rundown on the visit and said, "I told him that I won't return without my lawyer at my side."

"Good girl. One other thing," Jeff said. "We heard rumors about an IRA terrorist being shot—maybe dying—here in Stow-on-the-Woodland the night Broderick had her heart attack. We picked that little nugget up at The Sheepfold, too."

Sydney laughed it off. "What would an IRA rebel be doing in a peaceful village like this?"

Jeff glanced at Chandler, then back to Sydney. "They believe he was one of Miss Broderick's boys."

"When we heard that, we decided to drive on to Stow-on-the-Woodland even if we had to camp out on the hills. Of course, I'm glad the vicarage turned up."

The vicar stood in the doorway now, beckoning them in.

"We've been here less than three hours," Chan said.

"I like the vicar, but I don't like the sounds that come from the wall of that parsonage. It's a spooky place. Maybe it's just the housegirl banging around in the kitchen."

"Chan's right again. She doesn't really look like someone who would take up cooking and cleaning for a living. Cute, though," Jeff said, grinning. "She's a poverty-struck artist, so the vicar took her in. He certainly didn't take her in for her cooking."

"I'm sure Jeff told you I'm a music critic by profession. But the notes that are playing in these Cotswold Hills, and particularly here in Stow-on-the-Woodland, are out of tune. We really want you to pack up and leave, Sydney."

She thought of Keeley and Jonas. Of the unanswered questions about Abigail Broderick and the lawyer who wanted to betray her. "I can't leave. Not yet. Not without knowing what's going on."

"I told Chan that you'd say that. That's why we're digging in at the parsonage. You stay. We stay."

Chapter 17

Sydney sat at Griselda's kitchen table, her mind on anything but the chatter of the children. For those few short hours on arrival, she had gloried in the prospect of taking over the manor. Now she knew the only thing she had inherited was trouble. Everything else belonged to the Admiral's son: the magnificent manor house and its gardens, the well-kept stables, and even the housekeeper who seemed lost in her own black mood this morning.

Did she dare draw Griselda into a conversation about the missing Abigail Broderick and the solicitor who hedged with the truth? Or was Abigail Broderick really dead and buried?

Sydney glanced at Keeley. Strands of the child's red hair dangled in the porridge. Her juice sat on the table untouched. Woeful eyes met Sydney's. What was behind the unhappiness there?

"Honey, you need to eat," she said.

Keeley slapped the porridge with her spoon, her lower lip trembling. "I'm not hungry."

"Do you want me to help you eat?" Sydney offered.

"Leave her alone. She knows the rules in Griselda's kitchen."

Keeley's tears fell into her porridge bowl.

Sydney tried again. "Mrs. Quigley, after Keeley finishes eating, I could take all of the children for a walk down by the Windrush."

"That'd be good of you."

It looked like a long standoff between the housekeeper and Keeley. Sydney kissed the top of Keeley's head. "Finish your breakfast, sweetheart, and then we'll go for a walk."

Griselda glared at them both. "Promise her a ride on that pony Lucas keeps for her and you'll get further. You do ride, don't you?"

"Yes, and well. Is there a horse I could ride?"

"Of course. Ask Lucas."

As she left the room, Sydney wondered whether the children would consider it a game if they explored the cemetery in search of names. She wanted to find the Willoughby and Broderick family plots. Gregor would know exactly where to take her, but finding Abigail's gravestone, if one existed, had to be casual.

She closed the kitchen door behind her and almost bumped into Lucas carrying an empty tray back to the kitchen. "Good morning. How's the Admiral?"

"Getting ready to ship out as usual. This morning he thinks the bedroom is the bridge of the *Queen Elizabeth*. He sailed on that great lady once."

"Lucas, I'd like to go riding with Keeley tomorrow."

"Boris can saddle the horses for you if I'm busy. I'll mention it to him."

She stood in the corridor for a few seconds as he entered the kitchen. Except for the room where she was staying, the other rooms on the East Wing were ghostly apparitions shrouded in dustcovers. She would like to search them all, but she would have to wait until everyone retired. Last evening she had gone to the elegant dining room and later to the library to browse through the hundreds of books on the shelves. There was grandeur to every room, and the library held art treasures and portraits of Abigail's children.

Now she felt drawn back to the library where the narrow windows looked out on the hills and the Windrush. She imagined that this room was one where Abigail Broderick spent many of her hours. She saw again the quaint desk with its pigeonholes stuffed with envelopes. The day planner lay open on the desk as though Abigail had just this moment been called from the room.

Leaving the library, Sydney climbed the elegant stairwell to the second floor—and just in time to avoid Lucas's watchful eye, for she heard his booming voice as he left Griselda.

The hallway on the second floor was wide and carpeted with an Oriental runner. She tried doors and peered in. One was obviously the schoolroom where Jonas and the others had sat at the tiny desks. She wondered whether Jonas had ever gone to the primary school in the village, or had he always been sent away to boarding schools? But there were toys here, too. Books and games. Perhaps they once belonged to Jonas.

Four doors led off from the schoolroom. She tried each one, finding the children's bedrooms as she did so. One had to be Gregor's, with model planes on the worktable and boys' things cluttering the bed. The next room had pink comforters and frilly dolls on both beds. The third room lay empty; the fourth was obviously set up for the three smaller boys with pillows marked with their names: Danny, Yasmin, Philip.

Sydney went on prowling, room after room, delighting in the old furnishings and the thirteenth-century frescoes that reminded her of the artwork from the town of Assisi. As she stepped from one room, she saw an elderly woman inching along the hallway in bare feet. The woman was clothed in a sheer dressing gown and was bracing herself with her tissue-thin hands on the wall.

"Who are you?" Sydney asked, fairly certain that this was Dr. Wallis's patient.

The older woman's response was peppery. "I'm Abigail Broderick. Who else?"

Sydney's eyes opened wide. "Abigail Broderick? I don't know what to say. I was going down to the St. Michael's Cemetery in a few minutes to look for your grave. I thought you were dead."

"Not exactly, my dear." She poked at the shimmering gray hair hanging loosely at her neck. "I may look a wreck, but I'm quite alive. So, who are you?"

"I'm Sydney Barrington."

A sparkle lit the lined face. "You did come! I wanted you to come, dear girl. Prayed that you would." She began to chuckle, then sobered at once. "Did someone tell you I was buried at St. Michael's?"

"Someone wanted me to believe that."

Miss Broderick smiled. "Mr. Gallagher, no doubt. He's always so solicitous about my welfare. Give me your hand, dear, and take me back to my room before I fall." She leaned hard against Sydney. "Let's not tell Edmund that you've seen me. The poor man is counting on me dying." She started to chuckle again. "If I go on living—and right now I must—he will be so disappointed."

"You don't seem to trust him—so why are you laughing?"

Miss Broderick sighed as she sat on the bed. "He thought I wouldn't live long enough to change my will, and I intend to fool him."

"Where were you going, Miss Broderick, when I found you?"

The smile turned sad. "I was foolish enough to think I could get down the stairs without Griselda catching me."

"You're too weak to manage the stairs alone. Please don't try that again. If you want something, I'll go get it."

"You're right. My heart is fluttering, but I wanted to see the Admiral and check on Conan's children to know they were all right. No one tells me a thing. They think my heart will go wild with knowing. It's almost quit beating with not knowing."

Conan's children? Keeley? Danny? "Abigail, they're all well. Let me go down to the kitchen and get you something hot to drink. Then we can talk about a visit to the West Wing."

"And you can tell me why you came back."

Sydney did a light dance down the stairs and burst into the kitchen, where a smoky haze rose from the oven.

Griselda stood with a hot baking dish in her hands. "Is something wrong, Sydney?"

"There's someone upstairs who needs a hot bowl of soup."

"And who might that be?"

"Miss Broderick."

The dish in Griselda's hand crashed to the floor. "What were you doing up there?"

"Snooping around. I came here because I was told Abigail Broderick was dead. And, Mrs. Quigley, I have no intention of leaving until I know what's going on—and who these children are."

"You had no right to go up there."

"Didn't I? I've been lied to and brought over here on false pretenses. Did you know I was told I had inherited this property? That would give me every right to wander through it. But the woman hasn't even died yet. And Jonas has no idea why I'm here. He expects to take over this property when his father dies."

Griselda plopped down in a chair. "I know. The whole sorry mess is too much for all of us. Give me a minute, and I'll heat some chicken broth. Abigail likes little biscuits with her soup and hot tea, so I'll send those along. But don't forget, you promised to take the children for a walk. They're waiting for you in the primrose garden."

"Oh, I had forgotten. Give me another twenty minutes." She crept back up the magnificent stairway, walking slowly so the soup wouldn't spill. Before she touched the knob to Abigail's room, she felt a restraining grip on her wrist.

Jonas Willoughby towered above her, his face clouded. "What do you think you're doing here?"

"I'm taking a tray to Abigail—and you're hurting my arm."

He released her. "Dr. Wallis doesn't encourage visitors."

"Abigail shouldn't be cooped up here all alone."

"I plan to visit her. And Gregor comes. And Griselda spends the evenings with her after the children are in bed."

"And do you laugh with her?"

Jonas glared back. "We try not to excite her. She had a heart attack recently."

"I know. I heard she was dead, and she isn't. Now, Jonas, the soup is getting cold."

"Wait. I've just come from talking to Edmund Gallagher."

"That must have been an enlightening visit."

"He says you're trying to buy the property while Abigail is ill so you can parcel it out to developers. You can't do that."

"So now Gallagher is spinning lies about me. Jonas, I own a defense empire. I don't need this property—or want the headaches that go with it."

He still blocked her entry. "Do you deny meeting Edmund?"

"I don't deny anything, nor am I obligated to explain anything to you. Besides, Commander Willoughby, I understand you're back in town to track down an Irish terrorist. And they tell me he's one of Miss Broderick's children. Is Abigail aware of what you're doing?"

The smile began at the corner of his mouth. "I live here, remember? And yes, there are rumors in the village. You are well informed."

She shrugged. "Why don't we start over and work together?"

He turned the knob and pushed the door open.

Abigail sat propped in her bed, her silver hair shining. She put down her hairbrush. "Jonas dear! When did you get back from Northwood?"

"A few days ago."

"And you've been ignoring me? At least you met Sydney. Oh dear, I can see by the pair of you that the rich American executive and the country squire have marked their battle lines. But hold off on the war. Come in. Sit with me."

"I'll come back. I'll go see how Dad is while you eat."

A sparkle came into her face. "Give him my love."

"You'll soon be well enough to see him yourself."

"Not if she has to climb up and down that staircase. Jonas, why can't we move Abigail downstairs to the room next to mine? Then she can see everyone. She could even have her meals with the rest of us."

He scowled. "I want to keep the East Wing closed off."

Abigail protested. "It's been far too long, Jonas. Tell Griselda that I want to be moved down there beside Sydney. You'll do that, won't you, Jonas? The first room is the nicest."

"It was intended for someone else."

"I know. For Louise—someone who can never occupy it. Louise wouldn't want that room to remain unoccupied forever."

An hour later Sydney gathered the children to her and walked leisurely down the hillside to St. Michael's. She half-expected to find a grave with Abigail's name on it, perhaps a crude marker—one more attempt on Edmund's part to deceive her.

When she opened the gate to the churchyard, Gregor made faces. "What'cha going in there for?"

"To look around. I thought we could play a little game and then we'll go on to Veronica's Tea Shoppe and have some treats."

"All of us? Philip and Danny always make a mess."

"I don't think Veronica will mind." She herded them into the cemetery and led them along the crooked rows. "Gregor, I want to find where the Willoughbys and the Brodericks are buried, so let's see how many names we can find."

"The little ones can't read," Gregor said.

"But you and I can. So let's do it!"

"That's no fun."

"I agree with the boy," Jeff said, coming up behind them and startling Sydney. "Hey, kids, see that far wall? I want you to run for it, and the first one back gets some sweets."

"I'll win!" Gregor announced.

"Then we'll give the small fry a running start."

As Gregor dashed after Danny and Philip, Jeff pulled Sydney aside. "Cancel your game with the kids. We've already checked it out," he said cheerfully. "We've been over every tombstone and know the people of Stow-on-the-Woodland for decades back. There are several unmarked graves or stones where the lettering has been worn thin with the years— but no fresh graves. If your Miss Broderick is dead, she isn't buried here."

"You're right, and I'm not looking any longer, Jeff. I found her."

"You mean—" he cleared his throat—"you mean she's buried somewhere else?"

"She's not buried at all. She's been ill, but Abigail Broderick is very much alive." Sydney laughed. "Oh, close your mouth, Jeff. I'm not making it up. It's true."

He shook his head. "You mean, the woman's really alive. Then we've been taken for a ride!"

"And I'm fighting back. Now I'm trying to find out how far Edmund Gallagher would go to deceive me."

He cocked his head. "You mean some extreme measure like replacing a grave marker so he could pretend it was Miss Broderick's?"

"Something like that."

"There are some Brodericks buried here. Abigail's parents, perhaps. Syd, I've talked to Reverend Rainford-Simms. He won't openly condemn the lawyer. It's not in him to run another man down. But he assures me there have been no fresh graves here in the last month."

"I just wish I knew what Gallagher is up to—and whether Miss Broderick is safe."

"I intend to find out, Sydney."

The children were flying back to them, Gregor doing leapfrogs over the crumbling stones. Danny tried desperately to mimic him.

"We'll end up with another scraped knee," she said.

Keeley slipped her hand in Sydney's.

"Cute kid," Jeff said.

"Too young for you."

Chandler came over the cobbled walk, smiling. "Jeff is waiting for you to discover what a great guy he is, Sydney. In the meantime, he has his eye on Kersten. He thinks all artists are romantics."

"Like you, I have good taste, little brother."

"Any word on your wife, Chandler?" Sydney asked.

"She's still in Rome—although I couldn't reach her by phone last night. But I'm certain she'll be home soon."

Chapter 18

Days later, Abigail smiled as she sat down on the white bench beside Sydney. "I've been watching you, my dear. Day after day. I see you are drawn to this fountain as I have always been."

"Abby, I feel so peaceful sitting here."

"The father of one of my boys sculpted it for me—his thank-you for caring for his son during a crisis time in his own life."

"There's such simplicity, such beauty to it."

"I know. Whenever I am tired or discouraged I come here and find comfort in this marble fountain with its two carefree children carved in ivory. It reminds me of all of my children. The ones who still keep in touch. The ones who never call anymore. At one time or another, every one of the children sat here with me."

"Were they in trouble?"

"Sometimes just troubled. We'd sit together and talk and pray. It's peaceful with the water spewing in ribbons of color."

"It seems sad to have such a magnificent work of art out here in this tiny hamlet where so few ever see it."

"But the few who do find great pleasure. Santos's father is a well-known Italian designer. I met Victor at Dunkirk and owe my life to him. Later, when he needed someone to care for his son, he turned to me. The fountain was a gift of gratitude for taking care of Santos and, perhaps, for what might have been."

"Was Victor in love with you?"

"He was charming, but I did not love him. Later he married a beautiful Italian girl from Rome who saw his creative genius. And that was best. He would never have been happy here. Sydney, you may not remember it, but you met Victor when the plans for the fountain were drawn up." She placed her thin hand over Sydney's. "Victor chose you and Jonas as his models because he knew how special you both were to me."

"You knew me that long ago? Did you know my birth parents?"

"Just your mother, Dulcie. She was a sweet girl—beautiful and visionary. And once she met Joel, her destiny was settled."

Abigail sat pensively for a moment, then she went inside to the hall table and rummaged through the drawer. With sudden recall, she pulled a photo from beneath the blotter. She waved it triumphantly as she walked slowly back to Sydney. "Here. This was taken at Mont Blanc. That's Millicent beside me. And Kathryn—and Dulcie."

"I have that exact same picture. You were lovely, Abigail."

"Were?" she teased. "The four of us had wonderful times that summer before Dulcie met your father. We were all so young, out to conquer the world." Abigail blew the dust from the photograph and touched each face. "One of the last times I saw Dulcie was a week before they left for Africa."

"Sometimes I think I remember my parents crying and screaming as the rebels ran them out of town, down to the river. I think my mother thrust me into the arms of someone else for safety. And then the quiet. The terrible quiet."

"How could you know that, my dear? You were ten months old."

"Maybe I just want to remember."

Or maybe, Abigail thought, *you overheard that heated discussion between the Barringtons and myself when you were six.*

Aaron had insisted that the past be done with. That Sydney was his child. He would raise her without ever telling her that her parents gave up promising careers for missionary endeavors. Did she know that Aaron condemned the foolishness of missionaries dying as martyrs, the foolishness of risking a baby's life?

Sydney broke their silence. "We, the Barringtons that is, were never a religious family."

"Aaron wanted it that way. He and Millicent were raised differently. I worried about it when they married. Later, when they adopted you, I argued with Aaron. I told him your parents would want you raised in the church. He didn't agree."

"Dad always did what he wanted to do, patterned his own life, set his own rules, and his rules included Mother and me."

"Sydney, they didn't come back to visit me often, but your parents were generous. They set up a Swiss account for my work with the children. That Broadshire Account proved a lifesaver so many times. I was able to have the whole electrical system here rewired and the plumbing repaired."

Sydney thought of the file marked BROADSHIRE ACCOUNT and the controversy it had stirred back home with Randolph. Now she felt a warmth toward her father. A pleasant surprise. "Abby, after Dad died, we tried to identify the Broadshire Account and never could. The Swiss banks are notoriously tight-lipped. It particularly irritated Randolph Iverson, one of my staff."

"The gentleman who calls here?" Abigail noticed Sydney's embarrassed nod and glanced back at the photograph. "Sydney, Millicent was one of my best friends when we were younger. I hated losing touch with her. I think the money was her way of saying 'I still love you.' If only she had brought you back to see me again—"

"Mother talked about bringing me back to England. She wanted me to see where Dulcie was born and baptized. Where she married."

"Then she did plan to come back. Dulcie and Joel were married at St. Michael's. You'll find their names in the registry there." Abigail spanned her fingers. "Charles is good about maintaining the church records. Marriages and baptisms. Births and deaths. It won't be long before he records my name there."

"Don't talk like that."

"If I don't, I'm only pretending. But what will happen to the children after I'm gone? Jonas won't want the responsibility. I was surprised when he came back to help his father. Sir James—Tobias—was a good man, but his mind-set and plans for his son were unwavering. He wanted to mold Jonas in his own likeness."

"They should be friends. Jonas followed in his footsteps."

"Like Tobias, Jonas grew up on the River Thames, cut his holiday time along the Windrush, and battled the angry sea off Cornwall." She rubbed her eyes. "I don't think the Admiral ever realized how much his son did to try to gain his love. Poor Jonas. He knew from the time he was six that Tobias expected him to carry on the family tradition as a Navy officer. But Jonas came to want it for himself by the time he was eight or nine."

"So he's married to the Royal Navy," Sydney said.

"That's part of the tradition. But he was engaged once."

"I know, but he won't talk about his fiancée."

"He's not been the same since her death. Did he never tell you her name or how she died?"

"No—just that it was a terrible accident."

"Louise is buried in St. Michael's Cemetery."

In a whisper, Sydney asked, "Reverend Rainford-Simms's daughter?"

"Yes. She was killed three years ago in an IRA bombing in Ireland. Now you can understand why Jonas is struggling with how deeply he feels about you. Wondering whether he should. The thought of getting close to someone again is too threatening."

Down the hillside, the chortling Windrush whistled through the rushes. "I used to take you and Jonas down there and let you wade in the water and chase the swans. You made such good playmates. Jonas was protective of you because he knew what had happened to your parents. Now, perhaps, it is time for you to help him."

∾

That evening Sydney found solace on the bank of the Windrush, listening to the rippling river. Coming to the Cotswolds had become part of her search for herself, part of her search for peace. But she was pleased when Jonas came to sit with her.

"I wondered where you were, Sydney. Do you come here often?"

"Yes, with Keeley."

"I'm glad she isn't with you this time."

"Would you send her away?"

"No, but I'm glad for the chance to be alone with you." He tugged at a weed. "Don't bother with her, Sydney. She's trouble."

"She's troubled. That's what matters to me. Why does she annoy you so? She's only a little girl, Jonas."

"A little girl with an IRA terrorist for a father."

"Is he the man you're searching for? I don't think of Conan as a terrorist, Jonas. I think of him as Keeley's father."

"He's much more dangerous. I want to be with you, yet when we talk, we don't understand each other, do we?"

"I'd like to hear your side of the story."

"And I wish I understood why you spend so many hours on phone calls and take so many trips to the Tyne. Now Abigail tells me you've bid for another shipyard in Italy."

"I have. But if I win that bid on the British aircraft carriers, I'll build them at the Jarrow plant. And I expect to build them. You might sail on one of my ships someday, Jonas."

She saw his profile in the shadows—strong, determined, introspective.

"The fleet has slimmed down," he said. "That means the ships afloat have to be the best, Sydney."

"If my company wins, they'll be the best. I do a good job the first time around. It's what my father expected of me."

"It sounds like we both had strong-willed fathers. All my life, I had everything, except my father's approval. The best schools. The best training at Gordonstoun and Dartmouth. I was good in sports. Excelled academically. But always I sought to escape the shadow and displeasure of my father."

She pictured a dark-haired boy growing up along the Thames, holidaying in the Cotswolds. Risking his life off the shores of Cornwall. Going to boarding schools. A lonely boy; a distant father; a dead mother. "My parents adored me," she said. "They gave me everything. Even the things I didn't know I wanted."

"We were both fortunate. Gregor, on the other hand, has nothing. Everything he once had is gone. I have plans for Gregor. Boarding school at Gordonstoun. Then Dartmouth and the Navy."

"Is that what Gregor wants?"

"Gordonstoun is a good boarding school, if he can qualify. I went when I was eight."

"It's tradition with you. But you didn't have your life torn apart by a war. You didn't lose your whole family."

"My mother died when I was young."

"Yes, I know, but there was always someone here for you. You were never totally alone. Jonas, don't think by arranging for his financial needs and schooling that you've discharged your duty. You made a pact with that child the day you put your arm around his shoulders and allowed him to walk to the river with you and to bring the sheep in."

"I think it best to send him to my school. Prince Charles went there. So did I. I can sign Gregor up for Gordonstoun. The Navy may be more difficult since he wasn't British born. Gregor tells me if I adopt him, he won't be foreign born. But he would need a mother, too."

In the distance, the church bell rang. "Do you attend the services there at St. Michael's, Jonas? Gregor does."

"I did as a boy. But not lately."

She had stirred something deep inside of him and veered away. "I shouldn't pry—but I must ask about your father. Why is he on so much medication? He falls asleep in his soup bowl."

"He was eighty his last birthday."

"It doesn't mean he has to sleep all the time."

"Lucas insists that the medication keeps him calm. He goes into London every three weeks to pick up Dad's refills."

"Why don't you have Dr. Wallis check him over?"

"Are there any other problems you'd like to solve? I moved Abigail down by your room. Now you want to play doctor with Dad."

She blushed and was glad that in the dark he didn't know. "I'm sorry.

I'm like my father—good at giving orders. Dad was a blustery, outgoing man. My mother was mellow, but after thirty years of marriage she still blushed when Dad kissed her."

"And now you're alone in the world."

"You're alone when you fly in your Sea Harrier."

"But Abigail tells me that God flies with me. What about you, Sydney? Does God fly with you?"

"I guess so. I made it safely to England this time." Quickly she said, "Jonas, tell me more about your life as a pilot. Abigail says you have every opportunity to aim for the highest rank in the Navy. Is that true?"

"Anything's possible."

And he was off, telling her about his plans for the Admiralty. She competed with him, boasting about the aircraft carriers that she would build for him.

"Sydney, never have I met a woman like you—blessed with all the feminine wiles yet so abreast with the defense industry and its needs. So many women are interested in the glory of the ships coming into port— the excitement of them setting out to sea. But you want to build them. I just wish you didn't take so many trips to that shipyard. The children miss you when you're gone."

But do you? she wondered.

She couldn't tell in the semidarkness whether he was mocking her or pleased with her. Was he comparing her to someone in his past? Someone who had not measured up? He grew animated as he spoke of flying at high speeds and landing on a moving deck. She sensed something else. He was saying words, but from his expression he seemed more aware of her eyes. Her lips. Her nearness.

"Why are you here?" he asked.

"I have my father's international corporation to run."

"But why are you *really* here?"

She wanted to be honest, totally honest with Jonas Willoughby. "Because I feel at home in England, Jonas."

"Then stay."

Suddenly she was in his arms and he was kissing her softly, there by the Windrush. When he released her, she said breathlessly, "What was that for?"

"Because I really want you to stay."

Chapter 19

Sydney couldn't remember when the decision was made to cancel her reservation at The Sheepfold and accept Abigail's invitation to stay on as a guest at the manor. So comfortable had she become that she went freely into the kitchen for tea with Griselda. They sat there now by the old oak table with steaming cups of tea in their hands watching the children play outside.

"Keeley never plays with the others," Griselda said. "All she wants to do is go horseback riding with you."

"I promised her we'd go for a longer ride today."

"You'll be using Jonas's horse, then? Maybe you and Jonas should go horseback riding together. You could pull him back into the world of the living. He knows those hills better than anyone."

"Oh Griselda, Jonas is too preoccupied for pleasure."

"You know why, don't you? He has his mind set on finding him a terrorist. Prowls around here like as though Abigail and I have hidden the man here in Broadshire Manor. Jonas grew up under my thumb. I don't like him acting that way toward us."

"You don't make being with Jonas very appealing."

She hadn't fooled Mrs. Quigley. Griselda snorted in her impatient way. "That's up to you, Sydney Barrington. I thought you were more of a fighter. You like those Cotswold Hills out there? So did Jonas's mother. So we all do. Jonas should be showing you around. After all, you're our guest."

"I'm more of a bother to Jonas."

"Then it's up to you to make yourself visible. He can't go on grieving for Louise the rest of his life."

Griselda glanced out the window again and smiled as Gregor tossed the ball to Danny. "Gregor is good with the younger children. It's hard to remember how frightened he was when Abigail brought him here. He wouldn't let her out of his sight. Then Jonas came home, and the boy was drawn to him like a magnet." She turned her troubled gaze back to Sydney. "What do you suppose will become of Gregor once Jonas goes back to sea?"

"Jonas plans to send him to Gordonstoun."

Griselda's cup clattered as she put it back on the saucer. "Gregor isn't ready for the rigors of boarding school. Jonas even has it in the boy's head to join the Royal Navy someday. I hope Jonas gets some sense in that handsome head of his. He thinks Her Majesty's Navy is the answer to everything."

"Isn't it?" Sydney teased.

"If he wants to treat him like a son, he'd likely have to adopt the boy, and that's best done with two parents," she said with a twinkle. "I'm sure you'd be interested in that, Sydney."

Before Sydney could blame the blush on the hot tea, someone put a heavy hand on the door knocker. "I'll get it, Griselda. I was going outside to join Abigail anyway."

"I'll bring you both some tea and crumpets—we just have to get some weight back on that dear woman."

Sydney's heart beat in tune to the tapping of her heels on the long corridor. She swung the door back and looked up into the face of an attractive stranger. Everything about him seemed daring, from the disheveled strands of shiny black hair falling over his forehead to his generous mouth with its full fleshy lips. His jacket and shirt were obviously Italian, as he was.

He arched his brow at a rakish angle. "Buon giorno, pretty lady. I'm looking for Miss Abigail. Are you her nurse?"

"No, a friend. But Abigail isn't well enough for visitors."

"But I have come from Rome just to be with her."

She expected piercing black eyes, but when he whipped off his dark glasses they seemed more hazel, almost transparent.

"I am Santos," he announced. "Son of Victor Garibaldi. Tell her I am here. I am certain Abigail will see me. Where is she?"

"In the front garden by the fountain."

"My father's fountain! Let me surprise her."

"The excitement may be too much for her heart, Santos."

"I won her heart a long time ago." He was swiftly past her, making his way toward the glass doors. She followed and reached the garden in time to see Abigail's face bathed in a smile.

Abigail held out both hands. "Did Victor come with you?"

He took her hands and kissed her on both cheeks. "You can only take one Garibaldi at a time. But Father will come if you need him. He has just married again, for the third time, a much younger woman so she will not die on him this time. But, alas, I think he still searches for someone like you."

"Dear man. But why your surprise visit, Santos?"

"Boris called me. He said you had a second heart attack."

"The first one was only a flutter."

"Boris was afraid someone would steal the art treasures if something happened to you. That's why I am here."

"Sit down. Let me look at you."

"I am as handsome as ever. And you, dear lady, are still beautiful. Father will be pleased."

They sat sideways on the bench, their faces animated, intense. Talking. Laughing. Going happily back to the days when Santos was a child. Sydney sat near them, invited to do so, and wondered whether Abigail was aware of Santos's extraordinary charm. Or was she simply remembering the boy he had been?

They spoke of happier, lighter times. "Abigail, I think the fountain is one of my father's best works of art."

"I have few to compare it to. Sydney was one of his models."

"Ah," he said, his tantalizing gaze back on Sydney. "My father will be delighted to know that you have grown so lovely." He took Abigail's hands again and held them. "When I was a boy, I was spoiled. But you took my hands in yours—as I hold yours now—and told me that one day I would do great things."

"Have you, Santos?"

"I cannot sculpt with my father's skill. And for years, in spite of the education my father gave me, I took life lightly. But three years ago, the girl I loved would not have me. I let her go, thinking she would come running back to me. She didn't. She married someone else."

"I'm sorry."

"Don't be. Jillian is extremely happy, and I am happy for her. Because of what happened, I began to grow up. I renewed my interest in art restoration and went back as an apprentice. And, Abigail, I am good at it. That's why I'm here."

She eyed him curiously. "Something tells me you want to restore the paintings in the library?"

"Would you let me start there? Father will send others to work with me."

Her sparkle faded. "I'm not certain what will happen here. Jonas speaks of putting the property under the National Trust."

His dark face clouded, then brightened at once. "Then you will put in a good word for me with the National Trust?"

"Go, let Griselda know you are here. She can get your room ready and set a place at the table for you. I know you're anxious to go to the library and the drawing and tapestry rooms. And don't slide down the banister and break your wrist again. You'll need both hands if Jonas wants you to stay and help out."

"Father says I can work for a shingle over my head and pasta in my stomach. He will support me. It is his way of paying you back for taking care of me."

"Wasn't the fountain enough?"

"Father doesn't think so. He was so afraid I would not get here in time. And here you are in our favorite spot."

There was a fresh glow on her face as he left.

"I have never seen you happier, Abigail," Sydney said.

"I am always happy when I see one of my children succeed."

And to hear about his father, Sydney thought.

As they sat there, Keeley ran up to them and rested her head on Sydney's arm. "You promised to take me riding on my pony."

"Oh Abigail, will you be all right alone?"

"Go, dear. I won't be alone for long. Santos will be back, once he prowls through the manor and sees his art treasures."

"Do you think he can restore luster to the paintings?"

"If he's half as gifted as Victor, yes. He lacked confidence as a boy. But he's changed. I can see that already."

A spark of Abigail's enthusiasm rubbed off on Sydney. "It will be good for you to have Santos here when Jonas leaves."

"And when you leave. You are both growing restless."

I'm restless all right, Sydney thought. *But it's Jonas who has caused my unrest.* "You're certain it's all right if Keeley and I leave? We could wait with you until Santos gets back."

"Run along, dear. You worry too much about me. I've spent many hours alone just sitting here thinking about my children."

About Santos and Jonas. And Conan O'Reilly and his children. And all the others that Sydney didn't know.

Keeley peered around Sydney. "You can watch us ride." She pointed toward the hills, far beyond St. Michael's. "We're going up there today. Sydney promised me."

"Don't let anything happen to her," Abigail cautioned Sydney. "I—I promised her father that I would take good care of her."

Impulsively, Sydney leaned down and kissed Abigail's cheek and tasted the salty tears falling there. "You're all right?"

Abigail turned away. "Go, please. The child needs you."

Keeley chatted happily as they left the garden and made their way to the stables. As they walked, Sydney said, "Keeley, I wish you would spend more time with Miss Abigail. She's very fond of you and Danny."

Keeley's eyes grew wide. "No, she sent my papa away."

Chilling thoughts gripped Sydney. Did Abigail send Keeley's father away? Or had she risked hiding him within the walls of Broadshire Manor in one of the closed wings or in the old keeper's cottage out by the water tower? She'd been ill for almost a month now, not well enough to hide anyone. But would she ask someone else to hide one of her boys? Boris or Mrs. Quigley, or Lucas perhaps? Sick as Abigail had been, she was still mistress of the manor. The one who gave the orders. The one who made decisions.

Or had she turned to Reverend Rainford-Simms? They often chatted about the children over cups of tea and freshly baked scones. And she always sought his advice about the cleansing of her soul, if for nothing else. Hadn't he spent a lifetime reaching out to the lost? But Charles, dear man that he was, moved about in his own world—tending his garden, enjoying his train set, wandering over the golden hills of Stow-on-the-Woodland, singing, praying. A man of the cloth! An honorable man. Would he really break his vows to the church and his parishioners and take in a castaway even for Abigail?

She felt a nudge.

"Are you sad, Sydney?"

"Just a little. But it's a wonderful day for riding."

"Can we go every day?"

"We'll see, but someday soon I have to pack up and go home."

Pack up? Leave? Go back to her responsibilities at Barrington Enterprises? How could she run out with so many things unsettled here? Randolph Iverson constantly phoned and wrote, begging her to come home, insisting that there were decisions that only she could make. Randolph rarely gave her breathing space, but it was Jonas Willoughby who took her breath away.

She felt the warmth of Keeley's hand tugging her own.

"When you go, Sydney, will you take me with you?"

In her busy workaday world, there was no room for a child. "You need to stay with Danny. He's happy here. He needs you."

"I want to be with you."

She touched the child's cheek. "I won't be able to take you with me. I'm sorry, Keeley."

She pulled back the doors to the stables and Keeley ran ahead, crying. Sydney stopped at Windstar's stall to wipe her own tears dry. She wondered if Jonas had named the stallion for a battleship, since the horse was so feisty; her own thoughts were as wild and unsettled as the stallion's.

The creaking of steps snapped her attention back to the moment. She glanced to the top of the wooden staircase that led to Lucas's quarters and saw Keeley with her hand on the doorknob.

"Keeley O'Reilly, what are you doing up there? Come down this instant. We're going riding."

"I want Lucas to put me on my pony."

"I can do it this morning. Please."

"No, Lucas smells like my papa."

And what was that supposed to mean? Did Lucas smell like horses or a long day at work in the barn? She tried to recall whether he wore cologne, or did that enigma of a man with his muscular physique and brawny chest ever bother with scents?

Keeley stood on tiptoe, turning the high knob into Lucas's room. "Keeley, Lucas has gone into London to buy the Admiral's medicine. You must not go into his room when he isn't here."

"Dr. Wallis has medicine. He brings Abigail's."

Sydney tried to squash her own doubts about Lucas. "Lucas likes time away from the manor to meet with old shipmates."

The Admiral's last posting had been to the Admiralty in London where Lucas had continued as the Admiral's steward. Surely he had numerous friends in the city, even the wrong friends.

Sydney started up the wooden steps, listening to them creak, feeling the wobbly instability of the handrail. "Honey, you can't go in there when he's not home. He'll have fits if he finds you."

"What's a fit?"

"Oh never mind. Just come down." She extended her hand, the riding stick in the other.

Keeley shrank away from her.

"Oh Keeley, I'm not going to use the stick on you. Don't you understand? I love you."

The words startled them both. Still the red curls bobbed in defiance, but when she reached the top step, Keeley flung her arms around Sydney's neck. "I want my papa," she wailed.

"I know you do. I'm glad that Lucas is good to you."

"He smells like rain."

Rain on a tweed jacket or woolly sweater? A familiar odor to Keeley. A remembered closeness to her father. Her father must have held Keeley tightly, as she was doing now, protecting her from the fear of a storm. So Lucas didn't smell of spice or a woodsy cologne but of nature's fury drenching his clothes leaving them smelling of mildew, a scent familiar to the child.

"Was it raining the day your daddy went away?" she asked.

"I don't know."

She must ask Mrs. Quigley if it rained the day of Abigail's heart attack. That way Conan's name would be kept out of the conversation. She rocked the child, sitting on the top step and not wanting to let her go. Ever. Had they both been brought to this village for this purpose, for this moment in time to comfort each other? Sydney couldn't rock away the hurts that were deep inside the child. She couldn't even shake off her own. She missed her parents and felt a sudden rage at Conan O'Reilly and then a mixture of pity and concern. What had driven him away? What foolishness had forced him to leave his children behind?

"Let's go riding, Keeley, before it gets too late."

She set Keeley down, and the child kicked the door open and bounded into Lucas's room. A faint musty odor assailed Sydney as she followed her into the cold, cluttered room. She stared at the elaborate computer system on the L-shaped desk, a scanner, and two printers attached to it. The personal furnishings seemed insignificant in comparison: a narrow, unmade bed; a chest of drawers and television set; an easy chair and a rack with socks and undershirts drying on it. The bookshelves were stocked with printer paper and boxes of computer discs.

Keeley flew to the corner of the room. "Sydney, come look at Lucas's radio."

It was not an ordinary radio. There were numerous dials and a transmitter and sending set. Earphones lay on top. A cryptic code book lay wedged in the crevice of the desk, and beneath the desk sat an emergency power system. It looked much like a wireless model of war vintage, like the type carried in rucksacks onto the battlefields of Europe.

On closer scrutiny, Sydney decided it was more sophisticated. She could see at a glance that the whole system could be rolled back into a boxlike alcove in the desk and the louvered doors locked over it. Secrecy. Security.

Antennas protruded from the top of the communication system. She followed the thin wire to the murky window and pressed her face against the pane. The wire extended to the roof. Once she and Keeley were saddled and riding, she would look back to see whether outdoor antennas were attached to the stables. If so, this was a radio set capable of sending and receiving messages for thousands of miles. An amateur radio operator used codes that untrained listeners would never understand.

Sydney knew that Mrs. Quigley tolerated Lucas Sullivan because he had no family and few friends. She always excused him, saying, "He is committed to the care of the Admiral." But there had never been a word about Lucas's electronic skills. Now questions lurked at the back of Sydney's mind. What had lured the man to give up a full pension and medical benefits to care for one retired admiral? Wasn't the hamlet of Stow-on-the-Woodland a quiet, sleepy village? Yet Lucas had said he sat up late at night—a perfect time to be sending messages. But where? To whom?

She glanced around for signs of a second occupant. Lucas's quarters could only serve one person. If a terrorist was harbored somewhere in the village, he wasn't hiding here in the stables.

Keeley watched her intently. "Do you like Lucas's radio?"

"Yes, but he won't like my being here and seeing it."

"I won't tell him."

Sydney felt both pleased and sad for the child. How many times had her father pledged her to silence? Young as she was, she already knew how to keep silent. Suddenly alarmed, she tilted Keeley's chin toward her. "Has Lucas—did Lucas ever touch you?"

A frown knit between the child's thin brows, a look of bewilderment. "He doesn't like children. He only lets me in his room to tell me about my papa."

"Has Danny come here with you?"

"Once. But he doesn't like the rickety stairs."

Sydney didn't either. She wondered whether he kept the stairs in disrepair to warn him of someone approaching.

"Did Gregor ever come up here?"

Her frown deepened. "Lucas doesn't like Gregor."

Sydney could understand. Gregor would not miss the contents of this room and would report back his findings to Jonas or Mrs. Quigley. No, Lucas would not trust the boy.

As they prepared to leave the room, Keeley took her hand and led her to another built-in closet. She pouted at the stubborn door, but Sydney reached up and unbolted the lock.

"See," Keeley said, "Lucas likes guns."

Sydney's spine tingled as she looked at a row of rifles. Three pistols hung on hooks above them. On one shelf lay boxes of ammunition. "You must never touch these, Keeley, promise me?"

Before Keeley could promise, they heard Lucas's truck gunning up the driveway and squealing to a stop outside the stables. She had only seconds to wonder whether he had any radio equipment installed in his old truck and felt certain that he did. She grabbed Keeley's hand and fled down the wobbly steps. They were inside the pony's stall when Lucas found them.

He glared suspiciously at Sydney. "What are you doing?"

"We're going riding."

"Did you forget your riding stick, Miss Barrington?"

She shivered. She had left it in his room.

"Here, let me help you, Miss Barrington. You can't put the saddle on with trembling hands."

His smile was little more than a sneer as he helped her onto the saddle. He handed her the reins and went at once to lift Keeley on the pony. He was surprisingly gentle with her, a mask of incongruity. He led Keeley's pony out of the yard.

As they rode off, Sydney was afraid to glance back at the antenna wires. Cirrus clouds hovered high above them like a wispy ribbon of rainbows. The joy of the ride was gone. Sydney still felt Lucas's cold gaze on them. His trips to London took on new meaning, new possibilities. She felt convinced that he was contacting someone besides the pharmacist at the Navy exchange. But what was worse, once Lucas reached his apartment, he would find Sydney's riding stick.

He would know she had been in his room.

Chapter 20

Jonas stood on the rain-drenched slope behind the manor and allowed his eyes to look over what was once a bottom story. In the early decades, his forefathers had built servants' quarters right into the hillside; and, if memory served him right, a tunnel lay beneath the stables and the main house, passing just to the left of the water tower. Jonas had searched the stables, but unless he mucked out every stall, he could not be certain that such an opening still existed.

In those early days—if he were to believe the ramblings of his father— the staff had been housed down here along with a secret gun gallery that hid the weaponry from the Cornwall forces. Then a hundred years ago, a flood almost washed the village away, and eventually those rooms had been cemented off.

Now tangled vines climbed the back walls and prickly brambles covered what had once been windows. Try as he did, he could not remember where the back entry had been. He often explored this area as a boy; now it looked hopeless.

Somewhere behind that cement there was a perfect hiding area for a man on the run, but only if he had someone supplying him sustenance. Boris was too loyal a Brit to hide anyone and too unsteady on his feet to wander behind the manor on this uneven, slippery ground. Nor was it likely that Griselda would join forces with anyone to befriend Conan O'Reilly. She would care for his children, but there she would draw the line.

But what if Conan remembered that a refuge lay beneath the manor? Conan would be clever enough to find it. Whichever way Jonas's search led, he risked betraying someone, and it kept boiling down to three people: Danny and Keeley O'Reilly and Abigail. One thing was certain. There were ample rooms in the manor to hide a dozen men. He had covered every inch of paneling on the second floor, and no hollow sounds indicated a space behind them. Plowing through furnished rooms on the West Wing, ghostlike under their dustcovers, he found the original blueprints with proof that a bottom floor had once existed.

Jonas stepped forward in his muddy boots and began tearing at the bramble with his bare hands, searching for cracks in the masonry. He tore at the vines and trampled them with his boot. He brushed angrily at the damp strands of hair straying over his brow and kept tearing at nature's barricade. Thirty minutes later his hands were bleeding, his clothes sopping with rain and sweat.

Wiping the sweat and hair from his brow, he scanned the back of the manor once more, his gaze settling on the West Wing. Lucas stood in the Admiral's window watching him. As their eyes locked, Lucas let the curtain fall in place.

~

Jonas's hands stung as he walked around the manor and came face-to-face with Sydney on the front steps.

"You're hurt," she said.

"Just a few scratches."

She took his hands in hers and turned them palms up. "Those are more than scratches, Jonas. What have you been doing?"

"I was trying to break through some bramble."

"Without your gardening tools? Come inside and I'll wash those wounds for you."

She led him into Abigail's room, past the sleeping woman and straight into the washroom. He winced as she scrubbed the wounds and poured antibiotics on the deepest cuts. In spite of the stinging pain, he could not take his eyes from her face.

"You've been gone the last two days," Sydney said.

"So have you."

"I flew to Germany to visit our associate plant there, and then I went back up to the shipyard."

"What a busy woman you are."

She smiled. "I'm getting everything ready in case we win those carrier bids. Where were you?"

"I was on business, too. Griselda probably thought we stole away together. She's a romantic at heart, you know."

Sydney felt a crimson flush on her cheeks. "So, where were you, Jonas?"

"I drove into Northwood to meet with my commanding officer, but he was called away unexpectedly. So I checked some files."

"Files on your Irish terrorist?"

"You know things like that are classified."

"At least off limits to me?"

"Jonas!" Abigail called, stirring from her sleep. "I forgot. Gregor said you have company at the cottage. The gentleman is waiting for you."

He held up his bandaged hands. "Thanks, Sydney."

Sydney sighed as he left.

"Missing him already?" Abigail asked.

Sydney propped herself on the edge of Abigail's bed. "I definitely missed him while I was gone. I thought things would be different when I came back, but I still feel as though his dead fiancée keeps coming between us. Abigail, why did she go to Ireland alone?"

Abigail squeezed her hand. "A woman in love does foolish things. Their wedding was delayed. Their honeymoon canceled. Rather than face her friends, Louise took the trip alone."

"What was she like?"

"Are you asking me whether she was anything like you?"

"I guess I am."

"You're two completely different people, but both lovely. To answer your question, though, Louise was sweet-tempered, sweet-scented as a bouquet of roses, as fresh and pure as the Windrush. And shy. She was six years younger than Jonas, but it wasn't just the age. It was Louise. She grew up in the shelter of the parish, living under the pressure of being the daughter of the Bishop of Monkton. With Jonas she experienced a new sense of freedom—a stretching of her personality."

"Were they happy?"

"They were in love. I don't know if they were happy—that's something different. She never adjusted to Jonas being gone so many months at a time. I think she wanted him to give up the Service and settle down in Stow-on-the-Woodland."

I would never ask him to do that, Sydney thought. *Give up his dream. Give up his career.*

"And she was afraid of his flying. She never flew herself."

"Did you like her?"

"Most assuredly. Perhaps because she was so in love with Jonas. So transparent. Totally honest. And yet sometimes she wasn't honest about what she really wanted. They were refurbishing the East Wing for their own quarters—"

"No wonder he was shocked when Mrs. Quigley put me in the East Wing. And why he fussed even more when we moved you down beside me. If Griselda had only said something."

"I think she did it deliberately—so Jonas would let go of memories. But once when Louise was decorating the East Wing, I found her hanging up new curtains and crying. She wanted a cottage of their own. Just a small place. No extra rooms. Just a place for the two of them."

"But there would have been children."

"Childbirth frightened her. Her own mother died when Louise was born. I don't think there would have been children."

"How sad. Watching Jonas with Gregor, I think he would make a wonderful father."

Abigail's mouth curved into another smile. "Jonas doesn't see himself as a family man. But there are so many positive things about him. He's a skilled pilot, an excellent horseman, an avid sportsman. He helps take care of Sir James and tends the sheep and works in the garden."

"I don't hear him complain."

"No, bless his heart, he does what he does without rancor, but he must be longing for the day when he can return to his Navy commission on board ship. I pray for that return. I have prayed for all my children. For you, too. But mostly I prayed for Jonas, even before his birth. I'm so proud of him." From her window, they watched Jonas and Gregor pushing through the gate, Jonas towering above the boy. "Right this moment, seeing those two, I have everything to live for—and I have everything to die for."

To Sydney's startled frown, she said, "Don't look so worried, dear child. I am not afraid of dying, for when this old heart of mine gives out for the last time, I will simply leave the Cotswolds and be in heaven. I've roamed these hills since childhood. I can't think of any place more beautiful, yet heaven will be more glorious. I will have a new heart. A new body. One of the first things I'm going to ask is, 'Dear Lord, why did You forgive me so much? Why did You love me so much?'"

Her voice grew unsteady. "There's a poem of someone asking that question of Jesus. He answered by stretching out His arms as He died on the cross."

"Abigail, I could never believe the way you do. I've messed up so much of my life."

She chuckled. "Oh my dear child, no one could have marred the clay more than I did. Think about it. One day soon I think you will understand what I am saying about God and forgiveness."

"You sound like Reverend Rainford-Simms."

"He's the one who taught me the extent of forgiveness."

"I think Jonas feels the same way, but he seldom says anything."

"He's carrying bitterness against the IRA. When he lets that go, God will heal him. Maybe if he went to Ireland and saw the place where Louise died, then he could put it all to rest."

"Have you told him that, Abigail?"

"No, that's between himself and his God."

"Does it worry you that he will go back to sea soon?"

"I try not to think about it. But sometimes I think Jonas is itching for an act of war that will thrust him back to sea duty—and free him from the responsibility of everything here. More action in the Gulf or anywhere that would lead him to another promotion and eventually to the Admiralty."

"He has such big dreams."

"No, only one. To finally attain his father's approval."

"Abigail, I find his father charming."

"Most women do. But as a father, he's not a very warm man. The Admiral's wife, on the other hand, was sophisticated and gracious. They rather went their separate ways. She loved the Cotswolds. James loved the city. So she brought their London friends to the manor for glorious parties and dances." She reflected for a moment. "The parties ended when she died out on the wolds while horseback riding. Soon after the accident I took the train to Gordonstoun to tell Jonas. I think he knew when he saw me. I opened my arms, and he just flew into them."

"Have you always been close?"

"Lately he's been avoiding me. But he's always in my heart. I've loved him for a thousand reasons."

"Special to you?"

"More than special. But you asked me about Louise. I must tell you she was delightful, but no more so than you. You're more guarded with your affections. Less sure of yourself that way. With Louise, there was never any question about how she felt about Jonas."

"I feel uneasy around him as though we are always a party of three. Louise comes silently between us."

Abigail smiled sympathetically. "I think what you see as uneasiness, Jonas sees as self-assurance, independence. The other day he told me that he might end up sailing on a ship that you built. Louise didn't have your confidence or your business strengths. Nor your sophistication. But she was lovely. Dear to all of us. And so terribly young to die that way."

Keeley burst into the room and flung herself at Sydney. "I looked everywhere for you!"

"I've been right here with Abigail."

"Gregor said you were with Jonas."

Abigail touched the child's hand. "I see you've brought a book with you. Would you let me read it to you?"

"You never read to me before, Miss Abigail."

"I was sick right after you came."

"Did I make you sick?"

"No, dear child." She patted the bed. "Climb up here with me, and I'll read to you."

"Read, Abigail," Keeley cried impatiently as she settled against the pillows. Abigail opened the book and flattened the first page. By the time they reached the last page, Keeley had fallen asleep.

"Well, I haven't lost my touch," Abigail said. "Sydney, when I saw how quickly you took to Keeley, I prayed that you would take up my work. But I won't thrust my burden on your shoulders. There comes a time when we must finish our own course when the work is complete. And there must come a time when *you* follow your own heart."

"Are you talking about Keeley or Jonas now?"

Their eyes met across the sleeping child. "Both."

"Abigail, were you never in love?"

She laughed. "Many times. But only twice with all my heart. Once when I was young—and once when I was foolish."

"Did neither man want to work with you and the children?"

She answered in riddles. "One did. It was forced on the other one." Abigail tucked her blanket around the sleeping child and settled more comfortably against her pillows. "You know Santos Garibaldi now. I wish you could meet his father. Remember, I told you Victor and I met on the beaches of Dunkirk."

"Then you were in love with him?"

"No, but in true Italian fashion he thought himself in love with me. Our friendship began when Victor found me weeping along the roadside during the evacuation of Dunkirk. You'd have to know him to know how sweet he was. Even with the Germans swooping overhead, Victor promised that we would both reach safety."

Her voice softened, saddened, as she retreated into the past. "It was the spring of 1940. Czechoslovakia and Poland had already surrendered, and the German scout cars were speeding toward the Luxembourg frontier. Vice Admiral Ramsay sat in his command post in Dover, and what was left of the British Expeditionary Forces were fleeing toward Dunkirk, hoping, praying that there would be ships there to rescue them. Nine days

of deliverance for some, captivity for others, death for the unfortunate."
Abigail's voice became softer still.

"The sea was littered with mines and the shattered remains of rescue
boats. Vessels of every size zigzagged across the English Channel in the
darkness, some colliding with the mines." Her fingers plucked nervously
at a stray thread. "I have tried to forget the bodies in the water and the
dead along the road to Dunkirk. But I will always remember Victor
Garibaldi and Neil Irwin, because I owe my life to them.

"In spite of the darkness looming over the continent, I had insisted on
going to Belgium to visit a school friend. Now we were stumbling along
the road with thousands of civilians fleeing toward the coast, the younger
pushing the elderly and injured in wheelbarrows. The burning city and the
harbor lay ahead.

"An hour into the march, I lost sight of my friend when we dove for
cover. When the sound of the planes faded at last, I climbed from the
ditch. 'Gabrielle. Gabrielle!' I called.

"My friend never answered. Smoke curled from the cart in front of
me. Slowly the living began to stand. There was no time for weeping for
the dead; all of us fell into line and moved toward the burning city."

Sydney touched Abigail's trembling hand. "Abigail, I didn't mean to
bring back so much pain. You don't have to go on."

"It's all right, child. That road to Dunkirk lives in my memory." Her
smile grew faint. "Strange as it may seem, Sydney, Dunkirk led to my life's
work, for it was after the third Luftwaffe attack that I saw two small children standing against a fence, crying. When I pushed my way to them,
they cried out in German and I recoiled. They were the enemy. The older
boy's lip trembled. He was as afraid of me as I was of him. *Mütter? Väter?*
I asked, unable to touch them. He shook his head and pointed to a woman
lying motionless facedown a few yards from us.

"I forced myself to read the name tags pinned to the boys' tattered sweaters. Hermann. And Isaac—the younger one with the dirt-smudged face and
cavernous eyes. I knew by their names that they were the hated Jewish children. The German army must not overtake them. There would be no mercy.
I held out my hands. They took them, and without looking back at their
dead mother, went with me through the deserted towns of Flanders, stepping around broken windows, tripping over suitcases with broken straps,
and worse, climbing over lifeless bodies. Somewhere along the way, we came
across another dead German soldier whose belt buckle read: 'God is with us.'

"I almost gave up then. Where was God in all of this? With the enemy? I lay down with the children and wept. Victor Garibaldi found us there. In broken English, he said soothingly, 'I will protect you and your sons. So young. All of you so young.'

"He was young himself and handsome. An artist, I would learn later, a young man fleeing from the fascist regime in his own country. 'No family. You will be my family now,' he said as he tapped his chest. 'Twenty. I am a man.'

"I held tightly to the boys. As our world exploded around us, Victor, Hermann, Isaac, and I pushed along in the throng like a family of four. We were just one more family of evacuees fleeing toward the burning city of Dunkirk. Then the rumors reached us. Only British soldiers would be evacuated. Everyone else would be turned away—even the French and Belgians who had fought beside them.

"That's when we met Neil Irwin, a bewhiskered British Tommy with sun-blond hair who had not lost spirit and who was hurrying his unit along. But the strafing kept on, and some of the men in his unit died. 'There's no point in going on,' I told him. 'We'll die before we get there. And they're not evacuating civilians.'

" 'You'll never know until we get there, mate,' he told me, 'but if it's just soldiers, then we'll make soldiers out of you and your husband. Get yourselves kitted up.' He clamped his jaw as he stripped the uniforms from two of his dead comrades and handed them to Victor and me. 'Quick,' he commanded us.

"As he shoved the steel helmet on my head, it slipped down over my ears. The Lee-Enfield rifle was too heavy for me to carry and the khaki greatcoat swept my ankles, but I managed a faint smile for his efforts. I asked him what we should do about the children. With gunfire exploding behind us, he winked and put khaki undershirts and sweaters on the boys. 'We'll find a way, mate,' he assured me."

Abigail paused. "When we reached the port, it was true. They were only evacuating British soldiers. Everyone else was being turned back. Pushed aside. I put my finger to my lips to silence the children. One word in German, and there would be no mercy. Victor begged the soldiers passing by in canvas-covered trucks to let us ride, but angry men shoved us away. In despair, he said, 'But these are children. And this woman—she is British.'

"They turned a deaf ear, but not Neil. He looked at the mass of troops standing silently on the sands, waiting their turn for evacuation. 'I'm not leaving unless you go with me, Abigail,' he said.

"He boosted Hermann to his shoulders and ordered Victor to carry Isaac. With the determination of a man bent on living and taking his friends with him, Neil led us over the bloody beaches of Dunkirk to the water's edge—

"A dinghy was loading, ready to carry more evacuees back to the waiting ships. 'Soldiers only,' the helmsman said.

"Neil took a firm grip on the man's arm. 'If you want to get back to your vessel, take this family on board. Or I will keep you here with me and you can wait it out with my men, but this family goes.' Within twenty minutes we reached a pleasure yacht, part of Admiral Ramsay's cockleshell navy. 'Sir,' the helmsman said, 'I told them we're not to take women and children.'

" 'This is my ship, Smithers,' the captain said, smiling at me. 'And I'm not a man to leave a woman and children stranded. Bring them on board.'"

Abigail brushed a tear from her eye. "Neil lifted Hermann into the captain's arms. Then he held out his hand to me, smiling, as he shielded me from the whistling crash of the German shells. 'Don't worry, my love. I'll catch the next vessel,' he said."

She wiped her dry lips. "I was sick all the way across the Channel but so grateful to reach Dover safely. We were greeted by volunteers passing out strong tea and sandwiches and meat pies. We were treated like royalty, and then one of the volunteers told me that Admiral Bertram Ramsay had been informed that a ship of odds and sods had come ashore with a woman and two Jewish children and an Italian artist.

"She quoted the Admiral as saying, 'That's bloody marvelous. Sounds like a nice family.'

" 'Should we send them back, sir?' the helmsman asked. 'The food is intended for the soldiers.'

"But the volunteer told me that Admiral Ramsay lowered his field glasses. 'Let them come ashore. No soldier who reached the safety of English soil will turn that family away. There will be plenty of apples and sweet biscuits and chocolate for the children. And have the women rally up some warm clothing and blankets for the children. This is England, young man. Welcome them.' "

Abigail's voice choked with emotion. "It was days before I saw Neil Irwin again. But he was my first love. We fell in love quickly and were engaged shortly after Dunkirk, but my family wanted me to wait until after the war to marry him. And there were the children—I had nowhere to send them. After a short rest, Neil went back to battle—as a British

Commando. Before he left he put his helmet on my head again and said, 'Well, mate. We'll have to wait until after the war to keep your parents happy. But never forget, Abigail, how much I love you.'"

Her eyes grew misty. "I waited for him to come back all through the war."

"But you never married him?"

"No, he was killed in Normandy. After that it just seemed like I was meant to go on mothering the hidden children of wars. I loved Neil, and I've always thought he would have wanted me to go on taking care of children."

"Abigail, you mentioned two loves. What about the *foolish* one?"

"Another time, child. Perhaps we can talk about it then." She placed her hand on Sydney's. "But follow your heart, Sydney, as I did with Neil, and you will have no regrets."

Chapter 21

Jonas found Captain McIntyre waiting for him in front of the cottage. He wore his full dress uniform, making no secret of his presence in the village.

"I've just come from seeing your father, Willoughby."

"Then you know the state of his health?"

"I know he is a man still to be admired. He was commanding his ship right there in the West Wing. We talked about the Falklands. He remembered everything clearly."

"It's only the present that's lost, sir. Dad spends most of his time in the past, standing on an imaginary bridge giving orders. He rarely takes an interest in the Navy News anymore."

He took the captain inside. "Tea? Biscuits?"

"Not necessary. The Admiral's steward served me tea. But, Commander, your father is not happy with you on board here. He tells me you gave up your future with the Navy when you turned down the minesweeper. You didn't change your career course with your father's approval."

"That's something I've never had."

The captain let it pass. "Perhaps your father is more aware of what's going on around him than any of us know."

"He's more lucid since Dr. Wallis took him off narcotics. The only thing he's on now is heart meds. But he doesn't have much of a life anymore."

"I take it you're still angry with the Navy for retiring your father?"

"You put him down like an old ship. Even the HMS *Cavalier* fared better. At least they attempted to salvage the *Cavalier* from the scrap pile. My dad gave his best to the Navy, too."

"The final duty is never easy, Commander."

Now that the steam was blowing, he couldn't stop it. "I still say the ship ended up with more recognition and a permanent berth. What did my father get for his long career?"

The captain snapped off his answer. "Your dad was knighted by the Queen. He had every honor a man could earn. He had a long career. An excellent service record. And he had 250 acres to come home to; Broadshire Manor is no small final docking."

Jonas glanced out the window where the sheep grazed. "But you put Dad out to pasture long before he planned to retire."

"Commander, there's something you don't know. Toward the end of his career, he failed to keep appointments that were on his schedule. He rambled when he gave reports. He was found wandering at the wrong tube station carrying high priority briefs."

Stunned, Jonas asked, "Why wasn't I notified?"

"The Admiral's doing. You were not to know. Nothing was to interrupt your career. That was the Admiral's stipulation. He'd go quietly with that promise. The Admiral was one of the most respected men in the Service. He was no quitter. He went out with his head high. In full uniform. I can still see him walking away and getting into the car provided for him. He never looked back."

Jonas ran his hands through his hair. "I don't know what to say. I suppose I did disappoint him by not taking that promotion."

"With your fine record, something else will come along." He turned to the business at hand. "Did you take the Admiral's steward into your confidence?"

Jonas's stomach took a dive. "I'm afraid so, sir. I tried to enlist his help in finding O'Reilly, but Lucas told me not to dirty up Stow-on-the-Woodland with Navy rumors."

"Be careful whom you trust. I know Lucas Sullivan has been with the Admiral for twenty years, but without polishing the Admiral's boots, he might not have made it in this man's Navy." He rested his elbows on the arms of the chair. "Tell me, how is your assignment going, Commander? Give an accounting."

Jonas knew better than McIntyre how little he had accomplished. "I spend most of my evenings at Chutman's Pub, meeting old neighbors, being introduced to new ones. They all have legitimate reasons for living in Stow-on-the-Woodland."

Jonas knew everybody in the hamlet by name. He knew which men found employment out of the village and which ones played darts left-handed down at Chutman's. He could name the men who had searched the woods and combed the riverbank the night of the shooting. Many had strong opinions about the negotiations on the Northern Ireland conflict; none had an Irish connection strong enough to want the conflict to go on. And none of them cared whether the Irishman was found or not.

"So you haven't accomplished anything except to improve your dart game at the pub? I don't believe that for a minute, Willoughby. Have you checked out the women who live here, too?"

That was a stab in the dark at Abigail Broderick again. "I did locate the O'Reilly children. Here at the manor."

Not a muscle twitched in the captain's face. "And you're just now reporting that to me? So where is Conan O'Reilly?"

"The men here stand to a man that Conan left the village alive. As far as they're concerned now, Stow-on-the-Woodland is a long way from Ireland. I've known most of these men all my life. I can't believe any of them is aligned with the IRA movement."

"Or you refuse to believe it? We'll take the children in."

"Captain, that will create a disturbance we don't want. Their father left them on the doorstep the night Abigail Broderick had her heart attack. Abigail is highly respected in this village for her work with the children and her fairness with others. The entire village would rally if you tried to take the children." He hesitated. "Abigail is getting better each day. Sooner or later, she will tell me where Conan is, if she knows."

McIntyre stood and squared his cap. "We've taken the peace agreements as far as we can, Willoughby. The only thing standing in the way of a permanent peace would be the IRA factional groups still holding out. Even Sinn Fein can't tell us where they are, but men like O'Reilly could ruin it for all of us. I trust that your loyalty to Miss Broderick is not standing in your way?"

"Politics have never been important to her. Conan came here just to bring his children to her. His boyhood memories are here in the village, but not his Irish ties."

McIntyre leaned forward. "Don't be too sure. Conan is not a man to work alone. I have to give him credit. He wanted his children safe and took a risk coming here. You're not close to airports or train depots. But O'Reilly must have had help coming in—and he needs help going out."

"So he's locked in, Commander. And so am I." Jonas stood, his palms together, his forefingers to his lips. As he processed the last few days, he knew he was fighting for his career and his reputation. "We were friends once until we disagreed politically. But I can't ignore his children, sir. I understand where Abigail was coming from when she took them in. But keep in mind, she sent Conan away. Whether she knows where he is now, I don't know."

He glanced up and found Captain McIntyre watching him sympathetically. "The Admiral told me there's a lovely young American staying here at the manor. The Admiral was never one to miss a beautiful woman. He said quite lucidly that it's a shame for you to find someone again and not be able to make a commitment to her. Tell me, how does she feel about O'Reilly?"

"She thinks of him as the father of Keeley and Danny."

"And she is influencing you?"

"She calls it a cat-and-mouse game. She suggested that the village is a perfect place for an IRA encampment."

"She's right. They could blend right in with this community while planning for the future. Whether you believe it or not, Willoughby, they may have been here for months or even years. When the time comes, violence could erupt again."

"Then finding Conan becomes secondary, sir."

"Explain yourself, Commander."

"Those who are sheltering him become more important. If he is hiding somewhere here in Stow-on-the-Woodland, I'd be forced to look at the men in this household and find excuses for them. As it is, I look at the schoolmaster—a single man who travels a lot and is an expert shot—and I think, are you the one protecting Conan? I challenge the Irish owner of Chutman's Pub to a game of darts and find myself drawing a web around him, wondering whether he was planted here. He's lived here for twenty years, and I no longer trust him. Last night I awakened in a sweat, accusing Rainford-Simms of Irish connections. Do you know who he is, Captain?"

"The name sounds familiar."

"He's the rector. He would have been my father-in-law."

"And I've put you in the middle, scrutinizing your friends?"

"You've put me to the test, sir. Whoever it is—whoever took Conan in—I will find it difficult to end an old friendship."

The captain shook Jonas's hand warmly. "I'm flying back to Belfast for another go at the conference table. The end is definitely in sight. But if you need me, call me on the red-alert line. Someone on my staff will plug you through without delay."

❧

Jeff VanBurien walked into the tiny kitchen in the vicarage and startled Kersten. The tray in her hand crashed to the floor, the tea and a soft-boiled egg curling together on the tray.

"Are you eating in your room?" he asked as he bent to help her clean up the mess.

"Don't ask."

He touched her wrist. "Kersten, I know from watching that this isn't the life you want. Why don't you think about going back to Maine and getting a job? If you're unhappy there, I'll help you find employment in Chicago."

"Even if they needed artists in the Windy City, I couldn't leave the reverend. Not right now."

"I've seen you out on the hills painting. May I come and watch the next time?"

"If you want." She sniffed as they stood. "Jeff, I'm an awful cook. I hope I'm a better artist."

"Who was the tray for, Kersten? Chan and I get our own breakfast, and Reverend Rainford-Simms can't be ill. I saw him out walking in his garden a few moments ago."

"He prays out there or something."

"Is he praying away some kind of trouble?"

"Please, Jeff. Don't ask. He's a good man."

"I think he could be breaking the laws of the land—especially if there's another guest staying in this house."

Kersten's chin jutted forward stoutly. "I know he's troubled about what's happening, but he feels it's his duty as a man of the church to deal kindly with everyone who comes to him."

She thinks I know more than I do. "When are you going to paint again?" he asked.

"This afternoon if I can get away."

"I'll do up the dishes for you. Will that help?"

Her tears spilled over. "Can you boil eggs, too?"

He laughed. "For you, yes. Here, take my handkerchief. I can't stomach a woman crying."

She grabbed the linen cloth and blew lustily. "Now go, please, before the reverend comes in and finds me crying."

He left her and went straight to his room and closed the door. "Chandler, we have a bigger problem than Edmund Gallagher. We can settle that one legally. But I think the rumors about an Irish terrorist are real. I think he's holed up in this parish."

Chan gave an amused wave of his hand. "Well, he's not in any of the shops or the pub or in those cottages nearby."

"So you have been thinking about it, too? The missing man can only be in one of two places big enough to hide him. That manor where Sydney is staying—or here in the old rectory."

"You're dead serious, big brother?"

"Quite serious. Have you pawed through the trash lately?"

"I don't make a habit of it."

"You should. Kersten has been carrying out trash bags filled with bloody bandages. Take my word for it, Chan. We'll have to wait a couple of days for a good look around the vicarage when Charles is gone and Kersten is out as well."

"Charles will be at the church for at least an hour and a half on Sunday. That's when Kersten escapes to the hills to paint so she doesn't have to go to the service."

"We'll check this place out on Sunday. One of us better go to church. Chan, you're more into this God business than I am."

Chan studied his brother. "Sunday it is then. But I doubt you'll find anything. Charles isn't going to break the law."

"We'll know more on Sunday."

~

Behind the secret Jacobean wall in a windowless room, a weakened Conan O'Reilly lay on his narrow cot with his sweaty face close to the panel. He smothered his cough until he was certain the Americans had left their room. Shortly, Kersten or Lucas would come to redress his festering wounds. He must remember to warn them to destroy the old dressings at once. He had no desire to put harm in the reverend's path. The man had been good to him. Kind, benevolent.

Conan longed to be gone by Sunday, but the Americans had no way of finding him here. He was safe in this airless room that smelled of his own rotting body. How many of his IRA comrades had died in even less favorable conditions? With great effort, he turned on his back. The motion increased the throbbing in his gut. Lucas had assured him four men in the village waited to take up arms when the time came—the schoolmaster for one. Other strong men were in close proximity. But in Conan's confusion, he tried to define the loyalty of the schoolmaster, so convinced was he that the schoolmaster had shot him.

Conan coughed again and winced from the pain. *Will I ever be well again?* he wondered.

Could Lucas really get him out of here alive? Or had his usefulness run its full course? He wished the priest would come in for his daily visit. Priest? No, he had that wrong. That was from his boyhood. The vicar was Protestant. But he wore a white clerical collar as the priests back home had done, and he carried a prayer book when he came. Charles was a mild-mannered man, ducking low to enter the Jacobean room. He had strange beliefs and firm convictions. He'd sit on the only chair available and visit. Never condemning. Always insisting before he left to open that little book and read its comforting words.

Conan tried to tell him that there was a place in hell—if hell existed—for men like himself. Yesterday Conan tried to convey to Reverend Rainford-Simms that it was too late. That his soul was already condemned to eternal damnation.

Charles had stood, a very tall man towering above Conan's cot, an old man with gentle eyes. *"Son, there's still time,"* he said.

Conan closed his eyes and drifted into an empty void, then fought for consciousness again. He ached to go outside and breathe in the fresh air. Longed to stand facing the golden hills that he had loved as a boy and glance up at the manor where he had once lived. Tonight, when the Americans and the cleric slept, he could inch his way outside and crawl on his hands and knees back to the manor. Keeley. Danny. Rorie. No, Rorie was dead. Keeley and Danny, his own flesh and blood, were still alive. He ached even to whisper their names. The dankness of the room could not blot out the sweetness of their faces. Rorie, his fiery redhead. Danny, the image of Rorie. Keeley, too much like himself.

Danny. Keeley. You are safe, he thought. *Safe with Abigail.*

He drifted, and this time he could not rally himself but fell into a deep slumber that numbed his mind and took away the pain, the fear of dying—at least for a little while.

～

On Sunday Sydney walked up the narrow aisle of St. Michael's while the church bell was ringing and squeezed into one of the hard pews, two rows behind Jonas. As the organ played, she studied the stony interior with its tall pillars and high vaulted ceiling. The sun poured through the stained-glass windows. The names of the Archbishops of Canterbury were etched in marble on the back wall, the life of Christ recorded in the windows.

The songs and message were unfamiliar. She kept her eyes on the back of Jonas's head and wondered if he understood what Charles was saying. Her thoughts wandered again, her eyes straying to the window behind Reverend Rainford-Simms. Was it possible that she was the lamb that Christ was carrying?

As the sermon ended, she focused on the white baptismal font that stood to her right. She tried to visualize Lady Willoughby with Jonas in her arms and the Admiral in full uniform—proud man—standing beside her. Neither approving nor disapproving, simply lending his powerful image. And Abigail—where was she when the bishop touched Jonas and said, "In the name of the Father and Son and Holy Ghost"?

The service was over. Jonas slipped out of the church and strode briskly toward the manor. Had he seen her? How could he miss her in such a small congregation? Saddened by his rejection, she made her way to the vicarage where Jeff waited for her.

"Good morning, Miss Sunshine. Was the sermon that bad?"

"If you had been there you could judge for yourself."

He tilted her chin up and looked down into her eyes. "You were there for both of us. But I hope you didn't attend just because Jonas Willoughby was going to be there. I see what's happening—and you're only going to get hurt."

"Am I that obvious?"

"Only to another man who fancies himself in love with you. Don't get me wrong. I like Jonas. But he has an ongoing love affair with the Royal Navy. In the old days they were discouraged from thinking about marriage until after they were thirty. That's obstacle enough, but Jonas is still picking up the pieces from his fiancée's death. Chan and I don't want you hurt."

She straightened her shoulders. "Why aren't you off with the young artist? She's pretty enough to take your fancy."

"She does. And she's in trouble enough to need my help. But I had something else to do while Charles was otherwise engaged."

"You didn't confront Edmund Gallagher?"

"I can't get past a phone call with him. He's probably digging into his law books to come up with answers for us. Just don't make any appointments with him, Syd. We'll keep Gallagher guessing that way. I've called Gallagher's London firm. I don't think they will like what he is doing to the doctor in town."

"Marshall Wallis? He's a good man. He's guarded around me but kind to his patients. Abigail adores him."

"Gallagher is holding something over his head. A breach of confidentiality is my guess. I told Wallis I have no legal claims in this country, but if he's honest with me, I think I can help him. But that's not what I wanted to talk to you about. I'm on to something different this morning. The harboring of a terrorist here in Stow-on-the-Woodland is no longer a joke to me."

She started to tell Jeff about Lucas's radio system. But accuse him falsely? No, she would wait until she was certain.

"I gave the rectory a once-over, but the whole property needs a more thorough search, including that domed-roof dovecote," Jeff said.

"It's boarded off."

"Then tear those boards down when Chan and I drive Charles into London for his meeting with the Archbishop of Canterbury."

"The senior cleric? Is Charles in trouble with the Church of England?"

"He doesn't say. If they wanted to retire him, they'd do so. If he harbored an Irish fugitive, then he's heading to Lambeth Palace for a dressing-down. It's up to you and Jonas to check this place out while we're gone. Chan plans to see his wife, and I made an appointment with the senior member at Gallagher's firm."

"You're going to talk to them about Edmund?"

"They can't conduct a reputable firm with a dishonest lawyer on their staff. Blackmailing Wallis or destroying Broderick are no more acceptable here than in our own country. I'll be careful. And I'll be back to keep a watch on you a few more days."

"So what do you have in mind for me to do?"

"It regards Charles. I have to admit I'm not always certain that Charles is with the whole program. But down at the pub, Chan and Jonas take offense if anyone calls him dotty. At least he's smart enough to know what's going on. That's where you come in."

He leaned forward and lowered his voice and mapped out a plan, daring in its possibilities, threatening in its outcome. And it put Sydney and Jonas in the thick of the battle.

"Oh Jeff. You can't expect me to confront Charles here at the vicarage? And Abigail? I'm not sure I can accuse them—"

"See how things go. They both trust you."

"And I'm about to break their trust."

～

Sydney stood on the flower-lined path between the church and the vicarage and waited for Charles. She saw him at last. He had discarded his clerical robe and was returning to the vicarage with a tiny kitten cradled against him. Charles came the rest of the way toward her tall as timber, yet his shoulders bent forward like the branch of an old oak. His wise eyes counseled her without a word; the bluish gray threads of his Shetland sweater enhanced their silvery blue. "My dear, if I had known you were waiting for me, I would have come right home."

She murmured, "I didn't mean to intrude. Or come uninvited."

"Intrude, my child? Hardly; I keep the doors of the church open at all hours for those who come to reflect and pray."

"I didn't come to pray, Charles."

"Thinking and sorting life out are permissible here, too." His eyes twinkled, and she felt comforted in his presence. Though his thick head of hair was as white as snowfall, aging him, Sydney did not find him dotty at all.

He put the kitten on the ground. "She's my most faithful parishioner. She comes every day. Of course, a saucer of milk tempts her." He smiled. "Sydney, I watched you in the service this morning. I think you are quite close to the Man of peace."

"God, you mean?"

"God's Son."

"Did you know my parents were missionaries?"

"Abigail told me. They were married here at St. Michael's—and your mother baptized here. You had a godly beginning, child."

Sydney looked into his kindly face. She had never known anyone so peaceful, and she was about to take his peace away.

He smiled again, the warm smile still ministering to her as he grasped her hand. "Now then, how can I help you?"

The direct approach was best. "Reverend, the night of the explosion down by the bridge—were the church doors open then?"

"Of course. The doors are never locked." He sighed. "They were barred shut for too many months before I came. But it wasn't an explosion that night. It was gunfire."

"If you heard gunfire, would you go to help the injured?"

"That would be my pattern." He peered intently over his rimmed glasses. "I'm an old man, but I did my fair share of stumbling in the dark that night."

"Jonas would argue that your purpose of coming to this hamlet was to light the darkness."

"So Jonas does speak of me?"

"Often. He's fond of you."

"He avoids me. Jonas is too busy for a cup of tea with an old friend. I think he's forgotten the way to the vicarage."

"He's been busy settling the affairs at the manor."

"Tell him, if he needs my help, I'm available seven days a week. But at least he found his way to the service this morning."

Sydney was running in circles, avoiding the crucial topic. "You remind Jonas of Louise." Her throat tightened at the word.

"It's his bitterness against the way she died that keeps us apart." She saw the tremor in his hand. "Louise was killed in an IRA bombing, perhaps by one man. We will never know for certain. Jonas's war is against anyone who bears allegiance to the IRA. I understand his bitterness—I struggled with it myself. But vengeance will only destroy him."

He had steered her from the night in question. "Do you think that terrorist was wounded the night of the shooting, Charles?"

"Such is the rumor."

"Conan O'Reilly was in town that night."

The bushy brows arched with amusement. "You've obviously been looking into matters. And you have a theory?"

"My friends and I think Conan stumbled into the church that night. Wounded, perhaps. If he did, you would never turn him out of the church. Was he here, Charles? Is he still here?"

"Conan is one of Abigail's boys. If he went anywhere, wouldn't he go to her for protection?" He pointed to the door that led into his study. "We'd better sit down and talk."

"Only if you're honest with me."

Again the bushy brows arched. "If I am a man who lights the darkness, as you say, then I must be honest."

He turned abruptly, walked into the room, and went to his model train. He seemed distracted as though he had forgotten that she had followed him inside.

"Charles, the Windrush flows behind the church, doesn't it?"

His shoulders stiffened. "You seem to know for certain. But it's only a small stream that branches off there."

"Yesterday, the children and I were out walking. Gregor ran ahead of us as he always does. He's the one who found the trail that leads from the water up to the brow of the hill where the church stands. I think Conan could have reached the church that way after he was shot trying to leave Miss Broderick's."

He turned. For the first time, there was coolness in his eyes. "Miss Broderick is not a violent woman."

"No. I didn't mean that. Someone else shot him. But I think he found refuge with you."

"Could one terrorist outwit all the men in this village?"

"He was that kind of man, Reverend. He's been on the run since Omagh. His little children miss him."

"Such a long time to keep running," he reflected. "And you really think I am harboring a fugitive?"

"You spoke on the prodigal coming home this morning. To you, Conan would seem like a prodigal coming home. Home to Abigail. Home to the manor. Home to the village."

"Home to the church. To the Shepherd," he said.

"Sir, you're the only one in the village that no one suspects."

"But, Miss Barrington, you suspect me? It would be quite difficult for me to harbor a fugitive with Jeff and Chandler staying with me."

"If not in the vicarage, then perhaps in the church? Or in that old roundabout dovecote out behind the parish?"

He flipped the switch. The train chugged along the track, its whistle blowing. "Why would I protect someone when my daughter was killed in an IRA bombing? She was the child of my old age. The delight of my life."

"You are one of the few people who would find the strength to do so. Or maybe you did it to protect Jonas from himself."

"Louise went on that trip to Ireland with my blessing. I sent her to her death. We don't know why she strayed into that thickly wooded valley. There was concern at first—because she was engaged to a naval officer. . . . The terrorists never gave my daughter a chance. She was just in the wrong place at the wrong time. . . . But if she had to die, it was good that she died there. She loved Ireland. Loved the people."

Your thoughts aren't scattered, she thought. *You have your wits about you.* "Charles, you still haven't answered me. Are you hiding Conan O'Reilly in your home or in the church?"

"If I did something like that, may God forgive me." He smiled wearily. "I'm tired, Sydney. I must go and rest now."

Chapter 22

S ydney's global ambitions as a young executive slipped into second gear as her call with Randolph Iverson ended. These days her waking hours were peppered with thoughts of a British pilot and a motherless child. She dared not mention them to Randolph.

Randy called daily, hour-long calls. He threatened to fly over to conduct business in person, to help her pack. She vetoed each offer. One minute he vowed that he loved her, begging her to come home. The next he gloated on his position, making certain that Sydney knew he was handling the job well.

In between, he questioned what was delaying her return.

"Is there someone else?" he had asked. "Are you chasing your rainbows? . . . What would your father say about neglecting your responsibilities at Barrington Enterprises?" With a breath barely taken, he had asked, "Are you planning to move Barrington's headquarters to the English countryside?"

Sydney swung Abigail's desk chair around and looked out on the Windrush. She was at home here—as comfortable in her leather pumps as she was in her bare feet by the river. A country girl, a city girl, all in one, her father had called her.

But more and more Randolph sounded like the professional side of her father: arrogant, assertive, superior. Through her new image of Randy, her father was toppling from his pedestal. She dangled the receiver between her thumb and forefinger and dropped it in its cradle, severing the connection completely.

Still she heard her own words echoing in the empty room: "All right, Randy. I'll see to a reservation this week. I'll be home soon. Just go ahead with the government contract for more jet fighters. You're authorized to sign in my absence."

"I already did," he had announced as the call ended. Randy knew how to hit and hit hard. She had not shirked her job by conducting the business of Barrington Enterprises from her makeshift office in the Broadshire library. Never had she been happier than in this temporary control center in the heart of the Cotswolds. But were her decisions linked to the presence of Commander Willoughby in Stow-on-the-Woodland?

Yes, dear Randolph, in my wild fantasies, I have considered moving the main office to England.

She sat for another ten minutes before wandering outside where she found Abigail and Keeley sitting by the fountain. In that moment, she saw herself as a six-year-old, crying because she was going back to America. The sound of the water stirred another memory. Jonas had not wanted her to go away back then.

Keeley fled to her side. She sat down and felt the comfort of the child against her, much as she had felt comforted on Abigail's lap so many years ago. "Abigail, just this moment, I truly remembered being here as a child. I'll have so many memories to take home with me."

"Must you go?"

"Soon. Randolph insists."

"Is Mr. Iverson that important to you?"

"We were engaged once."

"And did you love him?"

"I don't think so. Not really. He was good to me when my parents died. He was their choice. But he is so like Aaron. Strong willed. Dominant."

"Jonas is strong willed."

"Not in the same way. Jonas, tough as he is, is tethered with kindness. He set aside his career for you and the Admiral."

"He'll go back on sea duty soon. And we'll all miss him, especially you, Sydney. But, dear child, you come from separate worlds. Different backgrounds. Different beliefs."

"So did Millicent and Aaron, but they loved each other."

"Yes, I disapproved of Aaron, but he did love her."

"And, Abigail, your children all came from different backgrounds and beliefs. And you loved them."

"Yes," she said, "from my very first boys. Hermann and Isaac are grown men now. Fathers and grandfathers themselves. They're living in Israel. I hear from them at Hanukkah and on my birthday. Now and then, Hermann surprises me with a phone call."

"They were a big responsibility."

"But never a burden. They were like my own. I always had the hope of Neil coming home and the four of us being a family. Just knowing they are well now pleases me." She laughed, a deep, bubbling chuckle. "By the end of the war, I had five more children in my care—five evacuees from the London Blitz."

"You were only a child yourself."

"Yes, not quite twenty-three when the war ended. Neil was gone by then, so Edmund Gallagher's father helped me through the legal battle of sending Hermann and Isaac to a kibbutz in Israel. Emigrating to Israel was what the boys wanted, but I hated sending them away. Within weeks, three of the other children went home to London, and Social Services sent the other two to orphanages in Cornwall. For a time I had no children at all."

Keeley had listened in silence. Abigail patted her knee. "Keeley, little children have always come to live with me."

Sydney hugged the child on her lap. "Abigail, I can't imagine how you supported all of them in wartime."

"Lady Willoughby's parents came to my rescue. Helen was still a child herself—Helen Broadshire back then. Her parents made certain that my children didn't go hungry. I never asked how they managed ration cards for us. Helping us seemed to be their bit for the war. I was given the task of a parlor maid; it meant beds and food for the boys and girls even though we had to live in the servants' quarters beneath the South Wing. The boys liked being close to the gun gallery. Helen liked coming down for visits. We became great friends—at least we were friends then."

A gray cloud swept across her face, an undefined sadness. "I left their employ after the children were gone and went back to school. But I was old for my years." She laughed, the same soft ripple. "I think war and motherhood does that to you."

She rested and went on. "When I finally went back to the manor, the older Broadshires had died and left the place to Lady Helen. I had seen little of her in those intervening years. She went to boarding school and finishing school and did a season or two in London. That's where she met the Admiral. He was several years older, but once Helen set her eyes on him, that was it."

A faraway smile touched her face. "It was Sir James who opened the door when I went back to the manor looking for a job. A tall, handsome naval officer. A commanding man even then. He never lifted an eyebrow when I told him I had children with me."

"And you stayed on ever since?"

"Yes. Griselda was part of the kitchen staff then—the same gruff yet warm and caring woman that you know. The children have been a bond between us. She saw me through great difficulties. I shall always be grateful to her for that."

Abigail gazed off toward the hills. Still curious, Sydney asked, "Is it true that you own Broadshire Manor now?"

Abigail's clasped knuckles turned white. "Yes, the manor and all the property surrounding it are legally mine."

"But Jonas has no idea my name is on your will. Edmund Gallagher called me at my summer retreat and told me I had inherited this property. It was all a lie. Why, Abigail?"

Tears balanced on her thick lashes. "I can't tell you what happened. Someday perhaps I will. Edmund is so unlike his father. He has used my deception to his advantage. He doesn't know exactly how I obtained this property, but he is digging for answers. The truth is, I was fighting for my rights. Poor Lady Willoughby! None of us thought she would die so young. But you are right to be concerned. I must rewrite my will before this fluttering heart of mine gives out altogether."

"And will you remove my name?"

"Yes. I know how much you've grown to love this old place, but it belongs to Jonas. I fear not living long enough to rewrite my will. I don't have the strength to face Edmund alone, nor the courage to tell Jonas how I deceived his mother so long ago."

"Changing your will won't please Edmund. He wants to parcel out the land to developers and turn the manor into a showcase."

Her knuckled hands trembled. "That's why I refused to sign the papers on my last appointment just before my heart attack."

"I have a lawyer friend," said Sydney. "He doesn't know British law, but he won't let Edmund coerce you into signing anything. Jeff might suggest that you settle your affairs right here at the manor. He could make the arrangements."

"A deathbed repentance?" Abigail asked. "Your lawyer friend might put Edmund on the defensive."

"They're already at odds." Sydney scooted Keeley off her lap. "Go tell Griselda I'm coming for tea. Then Abigail can go to her room and get some rest before supper."

As Keeley left them, Abigail said, "I invited Jonas to have supper with me in my room. I plan to tell him what happened the night I had my heart attack. You won't mind eating without us, will you? He thinks I'm hiding Conan here on the property. I don't even know where Conan is." She closed her eyes, her color as gray as it had been moments ago. "Regardless of how Jonas feels, Conan is one of my boys. I'll never forgive myself for sending him away."

"Come, Abby, I'll walk you to your room."

Moments later, relieved to be in her own bed once again, Abigail reached under her pillow and retrieved a medicine bottle. "Tell Griselda that I want her to call Edmund in a few days when I'm feeling stronger. Oh Sydney, Edmund has caused you great trouble, hasn't he? But I'm glad it brought you to us."

Her eyelids fluttered. "I'd like to take communion before I meet Edmund. Do you think Charles would come and pray with me?"

"I'll ask him while you're sleeping."

Her uneven breathing eased. "When all of these things are settled, I want to spend time with the Admiral again. It takes such a long time to get one's house in order."

~

At midnight Sydney sat propped on her bed, too pent up for sleep as she listened to the muffled voices of Jonas and Abigail in the next room. A few minutes later a knock came on her door. She pulled her robe around her. "Come in."

Jonas poked his head in. " 'I saw the light under your door. I'm leaving tomorrow, and I wanted you to know."

"Are we at war again? Abigail said it would take a war to send you back to sea."

He smiled wanly. "I'm flying to Ireland tomorrow afternoon. I'm going back to the place where Louise was killed." His words meshed together. "I have to bring closure to that part of my life—because I care about someone else."

Someone else? Sydney could hear the faint lopping sound of the Windrush. "Jonas, this is not something you should do alone."

"That's how Louise took the trip."

"That was different. She didn't know what would happen. And I don't know what will happen to you if you go alone."

"I can take care of myself. The negotiations in Northern Ireland are coming to a close. We don't expect any more trouble."

"Then why are you so anxious to find Conan O'Reilly?"

"Conan is still trying to prove his own worth by holding to the principles of the IRA. Regardless of the bloodshed."

"Do you go to Ireland with the Navy's blessing?"

"No, but I go with Abigail's. Abigail told me you would want to go with me. Will you go, Sydney?" he asked.

◇

As the jet lowered for a landing, Sydney gazed down on a blue-green lake and the verdant Celtic hills. At the departure gate, Jonas held out his hand to her and led the way through the terminal to the car rental. Driving toward the place where Louise had made the wrong turn, Sydney studied the firm set of his jaw and wondered how long this ruggedly handsome man with his sea- and suntanned face could go on wearing a facade of strength. She was there for him. Perhaps in the end that would be enough.

They rode through a countryside carpeted in emerald green, past wet meadows, monastic ruins, and around mist-veiled farmland. In the shadow of the glen where cattle and sheep grazed, they came to a whitewashed farmhouse. Jonas maneuvered the car over a rough road toward a woodsy area with charred undergrowth.

As he stepped from the car, he unfolded a crudely sketched map. "This is it, Sydney. I'm going on alone."

She watched him trudge several feet before stopping beneath an old shade tree with drooping limbs. He stood—a tall, proud man, facing his grief. He was wearing dark slacks and a Shetland sweater, but she pictured him in his uniform, his officer's cap in the crook of his arm, offering a final salute to the woman he had wanted to marry.

Tufts of his raven hair caught in the gentle breeze, and the emerald hills engulfed him. In a way this was a memorial service to his dead fiancée as he worked out his good-bye and fought his unending battle against unknown assailants. At sea—in the midst of a major crisis and as squadron leader—he had not flown home for her funeral. She wondered now whether he ever cried for Louise. Or would the Admiral frown at tears coming from his son?

She saw his shoulder jerk. Once, twice. She went to him and slipped her arm in his. The leaves in the tree rustled. A bird's clear sweet notes mocked their silence.

Sydney heard the rickety, donkey-drawn cart before she saw it barreling over the field toward them. The driver with a weather-scarred face pulled to a stop near them. The cart wheels blew an unexpected cloud of dust from the ground, the breeze wafting the smell of a wagon load of peat toward them.

"A good day to you. I'm Sean Callahan." He squinted down at them from beneath his battered straw hat, a man perhaps in his late sixties. "You're on my property, so I ask you to be leaving."

Sydney tugged at Jonas's arm. "Let's get out of here."

He studied their faces. "No need if you be needing help."

"I'm Jonas Willoughby. My fiancée was killed here three years ago, Mr. Callahan."

"In that car bombing?" Unexpected sympathy shadowed the faded gray eyes. "You're the first ones to come asking after her. A clergyman's daughter according to the news accounts."

As Callahan climbed down from his cart, Sydney pulled at Jonas's arm again. "Let's go, Jonas."

The Irishman removed his hat and beckoned them to follow. He led them through a grove of trees to a cleared space of land. A bouquet of wilted flowers lay propped against a charred tree.

"It happened yonder. Blew the trees out. Blew the car apart. Killed the lass instantly. . . . Not likely she knew." He rubbed his forearm across his eyes. "My daughter died the same way in that bombing in Omagh, so we know how you be feeling."

"No one knows how I feel," Jonas said, but he was in control. "Were you here when it happened, sir?"

"I was at my wife's bedside at the hospital. I refused to trust her life in the hands of Protestant doctors in Belfast."

Jonas nodded toward the farm. "Then the house was empty?"

The battered hat shaded his solemn eyes again. "No, I left my son-in-law and his friends in charge of the farm. Never should have done that. Thought I could trust them for that long."

Jonas winced. "Was your son-in-law involved in the bombing?"

"No proof," Callahan said. "But I know how his mind works. We never wanted Rorie to marry him. But our Rorie was going to have his child, and my wife couldn't stand the shame."

Keeley, Sydney thought. *He's talking about Keeley O'Reilly's mother.*

He gave a feeble sweep of his hand. "It was days before they cleared the mess away. The grass has grown back, but I'll be dead before we can replace the trees and see them grow tall like they were. Mrs. Callahan puts those flowers there—for your fiancée and for our daughter. So senseless, these killings."

Say something, Jonas, Sydney thought. *Mr. Callahan is reaching out to you. He's hurting, too.* She pressed his arm.

"Thank your wife for me. Sir, is your son-in-law here now?"

The wrinkled face hardened. "I ordered him off the property after the accident. Told him to be gone, to never come back." His mouth twisted.

"His friends were responsible for your fiancée's death. They fled before the police arrived. The police found my son-in-law up at the farm, napping with his two children."

Jonas glowered. "He slept through the explosion?"

Another twisted grimace cut through the Irishman's wrinkles. "Would you have slept through it, Mr. Willoughby?"

"No. Never."

"Don't know why I ever took them in. Guess I thought my son-in-law would reform for the sake of his children."

"I'd like to get in touch with him."

"He's not worth the search. He laughed in my face the day he left. Told me they'd be hiding out in various places until the last peace agreement is signed—and then they will strike again." He rubbed his eyes once more. "The peace we prayed for could be destroyed. We won't even know who they are or where they are. I'd like the hatred to end in my lifetime."

"Sir, it's apt to get worse before it gets better."

"I know," he said wearily. "There's a song in my country that only our rivers run free. But I'd like things settled in my lifetime so my daughter's death will have some purpose. So my poor wife can have some peace."

"The conflict will come to an end someday, sir."

"I wish I shared your confidence, young man. Better if I had turned in my daughter's husband when I had the chance. If I had to do it over, I would have shot him myself."

"Revenge never works, sir. I should know."

The wrinkles in the old man's face seemed permanently embedded by pain and weather. "He's out there somewhere, still looking for a home for his children. He wanted my wife to raise them. I wouldn't hear of it. Didn't need any reminders of my Rorie."

He walked back to the donkey cart and pointed toward the end of the road. "I told my daughter's husband to get out and to take his children with him. They looked like him. The youngest only an infant then. If only they had looked more like Rorie." He shrugged helplessly. "My wife has never forgiven me for sending our grandchildren away."

Someday, Sydney thought, *I'll bring them back and let you hold them again. You'll see how much like Rorie they really are.* She patted his hand. "There's still time for your grandchildren to grow up without bloodshed. Maybe your son-in-law will realize that. Maybe he will change."

"No. Not that lad. I told Rorie he was no good when she ran off with him. But I have to give the devil his due. He loves those children of his." Callahan went back to pick up the wilted flowers. "I'll have my wife replace these. It's all we can do. We still feel responsible for that poor lass turning off on the wrong road—getting herself killed like that."

Jonas looked gaunt. "Louise always had trouble reading maps and often made the wrong turns on the motorway."

"Pity. You can't see them now, but there were tire tracks where she tried to turn the car around. My son-in-law's friends were too quick for her. I knew when that happened that they had used my place for an arsenal—a place for building bombs."

Sydney shuddered. "The police never arrested anyone?"

"Been three years. They wouldn't be looking now. Even the local police aren't wanting to stir up trouble. We're a peaceful people here. All my wife and I ever wanted to do was raise crops and make a home for our grandchildren."

"But you sent them away."

His voice turned gravelly, belligerent. "Had to. Keeping them spelled trouble. We're a Catholic neighborhood. A few kilometers over, the Protestants settled in. We want no disfavor with them."

"How old are your grandchildren?" Sydney asked. She felt Jonas's eyes turn on her, but she kept her face averted.

"Danny would be about three. The girl two years older."

Jonas stiffened.

The farmer nodded toward his cart filled with peat. "I need to be getting this fuel back to the house. Would you be liking to come in for some Irish beer?"

"No thank you. No beer of any kind," Jonas told him.

"Then some Irish coffee?" he said with a twinkle.

"We'll pass on that one, too. We have a plane to catch."

"The papers said the girl was engaged to a Harrier pilot."

The muscles in Jonas's jaw grew taut. He stretched out his hand to the farmer. "The newspapers don't always get their facts straight. Thank you for taking time to talk to us. I could never bring myself to come before this—"

"Aye, I see. Too busy flying those jets."

"Busy," Jonas acknowledged. "It was good to see that the ground cover is growing in again. I don't think I could have faced it if the ground were still charred."

The man took his battered hat off again. "With your fiancée's father being a vicar, would he want us to pray here? You likely belong to them

Protestants, but maybe you'd like to say a little prayer here for your fiancée."

When Jonas hesitated, Sydney said, "That would be nice."

The farmer's craggy face lit with understanding. "Maybe you're a bit rusty along those lines. No matter. I think we all have a hook in the Lord's Prayer." He twirled his old cap and closed his heavy lids. "Our Father," he began in a tremulous voice.

Jonas joined him. "Hallowed be thy name. . .forgive us. . ."

Unsure of the words, Sydney kept her own prayer to a soft murmur. "Deliver us from evil—" *Deliver me from evil.*

She heard the farmer's footsteps as he left, heard the labored breathing as he climbed back on the donkey cart loaded with smelly peat. When they opened their eyes, he lifted his battered cap to them and was gone.

Jonas took her hand. "I thought I was bearing the weight of the world until I met that man. He's a giant, isn't he?"

"But he turned his grandchildren away."

"He did what he thought was best for his community."

"When he turned that cart toward the farmhouse, he was telling us it was time to leave. He wanted us to go away and not come back. But, Jonas, I should like to come again and meet his wife. We must bring Danny and Keeley back someday."

"So you know who he is? You can come back, Sydney, but don't ask me to come with you. You see, I knew who Callahan was before we came. Captain McIntyre traced Conan's family ties here. I came here to say good-bye to Louise, but I also came on that slim chance of finding Conan O'Reilly hiding out here."

At the car, he took another glance back at the place where Louise had lost her life. The emerald island never seemed more peaceful. "If Louise had chosen a place to die, it would have been here. She loved Ireland and wanted to share it with me."

"She just did."

Sydney glanced up, half expecting the sky to reflect the green of the Irish hills. But it was a powdery blue, with broken patches of wispy clouds drifting lazily above them.

"Sydney, it would have pleased Louise that you came here with me. She never wanted me to be alone."

Chapter 23

Gregor sat on the ground, hugging his bare knees to his chest. As Jonas placed flowers in a tin of water, Gregor asked, "Are they for Louise?"

Jonas nodded. He glanced down at the freshly cut flowers. Primroses with their buds still tight, the brilliant clump of green-winged orchids, the last of the sweet-scented jasmine that Louise had always loved. It struck him that he should be cutting flowers for Sydney Barrington. Courting the living, not still mourning the dead. He faced the boy again.

Gregor's shoes pointed inward, toeing the grass—a sure sign that he was upset, warding off rejection.

"May I go down to the cemetery with you, Jonas?"

"Not this time. I want to talk to Reverend Charles on a personal matter."

"About Miss Sydney?"

The boy's perception annoyed him. Jonas snapped off one more orchid. "She might come into the conversation." More kindly, he added, "Charles and I often speak about you."

Gregor's eyes brightened, lustrous dark circles in a childish face. "Why?"

"He wants you to sing in the choir when school begins."

"With Tesa and Keeley? I'd rather go to boarding school."

"I told him we're planning a trip to Gordonstoun so you can visit my school. I went there when I was eight."

He watched Gregor's boldness vanish. Was Gregor at nine too young, too vulnerable to send away to boarding school?

"We'll wait until you see the place before we decide. And then we'll have to convince Miss Sydney that you are man enough to go away."

"Sydney was looking for you."

"She was?" He automatically gave his corduroys and shirt a once-over. Brushing the soil from his hands, he glanced toward the front door. "When?"

"When her and Keeley went horseback riding."

"She and Keeley," he corrected. "I don't think you like Miss Barrington much, do you?"

"Mrs. Quigley says she wants to sell Broadshire Manor."

"It's not for sale, Gregor."

"But if she does, you will go away?"

"You know I'm going back to sea someday. We've talked about it." He ruffled the boy's hair and grabbed up the tin of flowers. "I'll be back in an hour. This afternoon we can gather the sheep in. Maybe walk out on the knoll. You'd like that, wouldn't you?"

"Just the two of us, Jonas?"

He had thought to ask Sydney, but he said, "Of course. Just the two of us. Come on. Walk me to the gate and that's as far as you go. Tell Mrs. Quigley I'll be back for the noon meal."

"Will you take a tray to the Admiral when you come back?"

"If you go with me. He eats better for you, young man." He left Gregor at the gate and strolled off without looking back. Why had the boy latched on to him, making going back to sea more difficult? Even this morning, Griselda had told him, "I don't take kindly to what you're doing to that boy. Having him eat out of your hand. Following you everywhere. I don't understand the likes of you, Jonas Willoughby. Coming home like you did. Taking over. Gregor will fall apart when you go away."

Life seemed muddied enough. Why did it have to include an orphan boy from Kosovo? *How could I even think to court Sydney Barrington with the boy on one heel and TopGun on the other?*

He knew that Griselda's snarl was a cover-up. It was her feeble defense at the thought of him turning over the manor to the National Trust and going back to sea. Didn't she understand? He would make provisions for her and the children. But she wanted life to go on as it always had. The running of the house was her realm. She rarely welcomed anyone in her kitchen even to boil a kettle of water for tea. Not even when the tea was for Abigail.

Life on board the carrier had been far simpler.

When Jonas reached the Church of St. Michael's, he found Charles walking in the churchyard and humming one of Louise's favorite hymns about angels guarding and defending us. He marveled at the man, still singing even with all of his losses. Jonas had long ago laid aside his own melody.

"Good morning, Charles."

He turned, not seeing for a moment, and then the song on his lips died. "Jonas, you came early today."

"I brought flowers." He felt as though the flowers for Louise were merely an offering to pave the way for other things.

They took the few steps to the grave site together. Jonas stooped down and arranged the flowers in the tin of water.

Charles knelt on one knee. "She would have liked those, but I think you are here with something else on your mind."

For a second time within a half hour, Jonas found himself brushing soil from his hands. "I wanted to talk to you about Sydney Barrington. You see, lately, I just can't get her out of my mind."

If the announcement shocked Charles, he hid his reaction. "Sounds like matters of the heart from the look on your face."

They stood, the older man almost losing his balance.

"Should we talk out here, Jonas, or do you wish to go inside the church?"

"Not in the sanctuary. This is not a spiritual matter," he blurted. "Not a confession." And yet as he said the words, it was both. "I only need a moment of your time."

He had talked to Charles about growing older, had thought of him as living in the twilight years. Suddenly the man aged before his eyes. His face seemed a maze of wrinkles, the tired eyes without merriment. His mouth sagged, aging him even more. But Charles reached out and put his broad hands on Jonas's shoulders. They felt strong and manly, the grip ageless.

His voice remained steady. "Are you in love with her?"

"I don't know, Charles." He stared down at the tombstone.

Louise Rainford-Simms
Beloved daughter
Lost in Ireland; alive in Jesus

His gaze veered off toward the hills and slowly back to Charles. "I thought there would never be anyone after Louise."

"Surely Louise would understand," Charles said, his voice quivering. He turned abruptly and strode into the house.

Jonas caught up with him in the sitting room and found Charles bending over his electric trains. The train set had been built from scratch and run by a generator so the diocese would not complain of needless costs at the vicarage. The hobby had always been a source of pleasure to Charles, a great comfort to him at Louise's death. Now in Stow-on-the-Woodland, it was the chance for the children of the village to come to the vicarage to hear about the Shepherd.

Charles examined the caboose on the freight train and placed it back on the track. As he did so, a tear splashed on the rails.

"We could talk about this another time," Jonas said quietly.

"No, it's long past time to bare our thoughts to each other. You've avoided me since you came home. Perhaps I have been avoiding this meeting."

He repositioned the railroad crossings and the depot and gave a little twist to the toy church with a steeple. "I call it St. James after my last parish." He looked up at last. "I've been watching you and Miss Barrington strolling over the knolls and walking together by the river. When I shut my eyes, I imagine that it is Louise and you again. Pretending what happened didn't happen. It's just—seeing you come with the flowers and knowing now that you won't be doing that any longer."

His eyes misted with more unshed tears. "Forgive me, Jonas. These are just the rambling thoughts of an old man. I long ago came to terms about my daughter's death. I realize now that I had not come to terms with having the man she loved fall in love again." He held up his hand. "No, Jonas. Let me go on. I thought for years that this might happen. But I thought you would be away somewhere. At Portsmouth or in Paris. And you'd post me a letter saying you had married. I could have wept in private then."

"You're Abigail's minister. I thought I should come to you."

"You were part of St. Michael's parish when you were a boy and even when you were courting Louise. It's good that you came to me. Sit down. I'll have Kersten bring us some tea."

Jonas sat and crossed his lanky legs.

The reverend's skin turned red above the clerical collar. "After we lost Louise, you changed, Jonas. I saw it in your eyes. In the set curve of your mouth. I couldn't see your heart, but I knew it was hardened. Mine was like that for weeks after her death." He smiled, his watery eyes brimming. "You have been like a son to me since the day my daughter brought you here. Do you remember what she said that first Sunday afternoon?"

"I remember. I was shocked, in fact."

He mimicked his daughter. " 'Father, this Navy boy may be an old reprobate, but I love him. I'm going to marry him when he gets around to asking me.' What a wicked little charmer she was. You were a happy pair. And then—Ireland came between us. I want you to be happy again, but you must understand. Louise was my daughter. The one who brought me my greatest happiness after my wife's death."

Jonas allowed his gaze to sweep the familiar room. A smoke-blackened kettle dangled over the stone fireplace. The painting of the

Garden of Gethsemane hung above the mantel, its frame warped on one corner. The ancient chairs felt uncomfortable, as though sitting stiffly in them brought humility to the shepherd of St. Michael's. He allowed himself the pain of stealing a glimpse of the portrait of Louise that sat on the console table.

Jonas's attention was drawn back to Charles as Kersten poured tea for them. She smiled sweetly at Jonas, a young woman around Louise's age with rose-colored lips that looked good on her and brows finely plucked above those curious dark eyes.

"It's safe to try the biscuits, Commander Willoughby. Mrs.Quigley made them." She sashayed from the room, her long hair bouncing on her narrow shoulders.

"I see what Mrs. Quigley meant now. Kersten doesn't look the part of a housekeeper, Charles."

"There's plenty of space in the old vicarage for lonely people to wander around. She hasn't made many friends since coming to the village, and it's hard for me to keep a smiling face seven days a week when people only come by on Sundays."

"And hash out your sermons the rest of the week?"

"Is that what you do, Jonas?"

"Sydney asks a lot of questions. Last week you talked about the sympathizing Jesus—and Sydney kept asking me who he was."

Charles tented his fingers, a faint smile finding its way to his lips. "That's from a hymn."

"I know, but Sydney didn't. This past Sunday, you worried her about the spotless Lamb. She said she doesn't know Him. You should talk to her."

His fingers remained tented. "Jonas, you must tell her about the Lamb. I practice my sermons on Kersten—that way she hears them. She finds herself too busy on Sundays to worship with us."

Most of the village finds something else to do, Jonas thought. But he asked, "Is she busy cooking?"

"Mercy no. She's a much better artist than cook. Of late, though, she's been learning some recipes in Mrs. Quigley's kitchen." He patted his stomach. "So things are tasting better now."

A resounding thump startled them both. "What was that?"

"Perhaps Kersten dropped the kettle again."

But Jonas knew the thumping sounds did not belong to Kersten. "Do you have a guest, Charles?"

"The two friends of Miss Barrington. You've met them at the pub. It

545

means more work for Kersten, but she has taken an interest in the young man from Chicago." Charles leaned his head back, hands clasped. "Kersten came from America. She sees herself as an artist. She's good, too. Ought to be," he chuckled. "She paints the same scene over and over. Mostly the golden hills with the Windrush winding through."

"So she won't stay forever?"

"Few of us do, Jonas. She has free room and board for as long as she needs it. She does light housekeeping for me. And now and again, I phone her family to reassure them that she is well."

He switched gears abruptly. "Jonas, have you told Miss Barrington how you feel? One usually goes to the woman he loves, not to the parish priest."

"How can I? We come from two separate worlds." He wiped the palms of his hands on his corduroys. "I can't give up my world."

"Do you expect her to give up hers?"

"That wouldn't be fair either. I remember how lonely my mother was with Dad always away at sea."

"I would not worry too much about Miss Barrington giving up her own career. She is determined to carry on her father's defense company until she can turn it over to a reliable staff. But I think she came here as much to find herself as to lay claim to Broadshire Manor. She's found her way into the hearts of several of us."

Mine mostly, Jonas thought.

"Has she considered basing her company here in Europe? Other corporations have done so. If she wins the contract for the carriers, she'd have more of a reason to remain in England."

"I can't ask her to do that."

"You won't have to. She's untangling the threads of her life. Give her time, Jonas. Louise would be happy for you."

The silence dragged as Charles refilled their cups.

"I came here about something else, Charles. Something I haven't had the courage to face before. You see, I feel responsible for what happened to Louise."

"How could you? You weren't even there."

"Charles, why in the name of heaven—"

"Be careful, son."

"What possessed her to go on our honeymoon trip alone?"

Charles looked up, his bushy white brows arching. "Son, she loved you, but it humiliated her to cancel the wedding plans. She had to get away."

"My ship was going right out—a quick turnaround with deployment back to the Adriatic. There was no time to bring in another pilot. I thought Louise understood."

"I think she realized that day that your career would always come first with you. That you would never give up the Service. She was like her mother, God rest her soul. Louise needed someone to be with her. All she really wanted was a home, a hearth, a fireplace. She wanted to curl up beside you."

His cup rattled as he put it on the saucer. "As you know, about the time of your engagement, the diocese offered me a choice between retirement or taking a much-neglected parish in Stow-on-the-Woodland. And so I came here. I wanted to be here for Louise during those lonely months when you were at sea."

"Forgive me for failing your daughter."

"You didn't fail her. I did. I fed into her fancies. I thought that once you were married—once you had a child—you might resign your commission and come home to stay."

"I never told her that."

"I know. But she believed in her own charms. She was convinced the Admiral had influenced your choice of the Navy."

"I wanted the Navy for myself. I had to fly. I remember the first time I watched a ship sail from Portsmouth. The first time I flew solo. It's in my blood."

"When you had to cancel the wedding, she knew that the Navy would always come first with you. That's why she went ahead with the trip to Ireland. She wanted to work things out for herself."

"The day I heard—" Jonas tried again. "The day I heard she had been killed, my world fell apart. She meant everything to me, Charles."

"If she had given me the choice, I would have chosen you for a son-in-law. You're trustworthy. Hardworking. And what pleased me most was that you genuinely loved my daughter."

Jonas choked out the words. "I never meant her to go to Ireland without me. I should have been with her."

"And then I would have lost both of you in that bombing."

Heavy footsteps resounded on the other side of the parish wall.

Jonas frowned. "I'm telling you, it sounds like that noise is coming through the paneling."

The reverend's expression turned anxious. "That's the way it is in this old vicarage. Dank and cold and full of ghosts."

Jonas was certain he was not teasing. "I should go and let you get some rest."

"Yes, do that."

He stood and watched Charles rise wearily in front of him. Again the cleric planted his broad hands on Jonas's shoulders. But this time his hands trembled. "We shall talk again, Jonas. And you have my blessing, whatever decision you make."

                      ~

Charles stared into empty space for several minutes, then slid back the panel and stepped into the Jacobean chamber with his prayer book in his hands. The stench of decaying flesh filled his nostrils. Old dressings stained with blood and pus lay on the floor. He had come into the room to confront the young man lying helplessly on the cot and felt only pity as Lucas sponged the feverish body.

"Lucas, the boy needs a doctor."

"And ruin my position with the Admiral? No. It won't be long. One way or the other, I will have him out of here."

Conan's words seemed strangled as he said, "We heard you talking, Charles. I didn't know about your daughter. I didn't know she was Jonas's fiancée."

"Her death almost destroyed him. After my daughter died, his career was all that mattered to him."

Conan's shallow breathing turned raspy. "That sounds like Jonas. Unblemished commitment and loyalty to the British crown. And those bloody bagpipes? Is he still playing them?"

"Sometimes, out on the hills. Conan, it's been three years since Louise was killed—on a farm not far from Belfast."

"My wife died the same way." Conan struggled to go on speaking. "I didn't know your daughter died in an IRA ambush. I'm sorry. You've been so kind to me—" He thrashed on the bed, fought for coherence again. "I heard the bomb go off, sir."

Stunned, Charles gripped the boy's shoulder and shook him. "What are you saying?"

"Careful, Reverend," Lucas warned.

"Conan, what are you saying?" Sudden rage consumed Charles. He gripped Conan's arm. "Were you there when my daughter died?"

The red-flushed eyes opened again as Lucas left the room. "My wife's father owned the farm. I went there to ask him to make a home for my children. But when that girl was killed, even their grandfather turned my children away."

Charles's grip tightened. "Did you kill my daughter?"

Conan blinked his bloodshot eyes. "My friends did."

Charles fought his rage. "Why, Conan O'Reilly? She never did a thing to you. What a fool I have been offering you refuge."

"It's your job, isn't it? To help the sick and dying."

The prayer book almost slipped from his hand. "Get out. You're nothing but trouble, Mr. O'Reilly."

Conan tried to pull himself to a sitting position. "Lucas promises to get me out of here soon. We told you all along that once I could walk, I'd be gone. Now Lucas plans to fly me out."

"Fly you out? He has no access to a plane."

"He promises to find one."

"Lucas has no intention of risking his own safety for you, Conan. Let me go for Dr. Wallis. Let me turn you in for the sake of your children." His anger was a mixture of mercy and pain. "Don't ruin the peace negotiations by taking up arms again."

"I'm sorry about your daughter. You have to believe me. Just give me a few days, Reverend. I want to see my children one more time before I leave."

"If I arrange it, will you go away?"

"Yes. I'll leave on my own if I have to—if I can just see my children one more time."

"Miss Barrington takes the children for walks every day, usually before the noon meal. You can see them then."

He swayed on the narrow cot. "If I'm caught doing so, it could ruin you, Reverend."

"Yes, I would have to resign."

～

For hours after he left the Jacobean room, Charles roamed the hills and searched his own soul. It would be so easy to call Jonas back—to take him to the narrow room and tell him, "There. There's the man who watched your fiancée die."

Out on the wolds, he talked to the sympathizing Jesus, begging for understanding and mercy and knowing that he must show mercy to the dying man. At midnight he came to terms with his own pain. He would not—could not turn a man from the church.

St. Michael's is Your house, dear God, he reasoned, *and the young terrorist is a prodigal who fears dying and longs for peace.*

Chapter 24

As Sydney tossed on her canopy bed, the urgency that had sent her flying to England invaded her subconscious, forcing her into sleeplessness. Abigail Broderick needed her. The undefined cry for help exploded in Sydney's ears. It echoed louder than the rumble of the Windrush. Blew in stronger than the breeze rustling the curtains of her open window. Cried out full-throated like the screech of the night owl.

Thumping her pillows and shifting her tired body, she tacked the demands of her life on an imaginary clipboard. Her staff at Barrington Enterprises was capable of carrying out her orders. But if she wiggled her toes in Aaron Barrington's shoes, he would expect her to take the brunt of leadership—not allow someone else to do it. These demands weighed against the needs in the Cotswolds; the unsolved problems at Broadshire Manor; the handsome pilot who wanted nothing more than to go back to sea; the five-year-old who had wrapped her very existence around Sydney's heartstrings; Abigail's failing health and her unswerving loyalty to the Admiral and to the Irishman who had come to her for help and left his children behind.

The choice was Sydney's. She could stay on in this quiet hamlet of Stow-on-the-Woodland or return to the chaotic rush of life back home. She flung back the bedcovers and pulled on her warm khaki slacks and university sweatshirt to ward off the chill of the predawn hours. Opening her suitcase, she found her mother's dolls tucked in with her heavy socks and running shoes. The rag doll in denim overalls and the empress doll dressed in taffeta and lace. The doll she was to give to someone special.

She put the dolls against the pillows on the side where Keeley would crawl in and wait for her return. Then she crept past Abigail's room, felt her way safely to the massive front door, and let herself out. The gate creaked as she slipped through, jangled as it swung closed again. She felt no fear in the predawn mist, no apprehension at being alone. The light drizzle of rain that had tapped against her windows during the night had left the fresh after-scent of a spring rain on the meadows. Within minutes she was on the footpath, making her way through the woodland down to the Windrush.

As dawn began to break, she dropped to the bank, hugged her knees to her chest, and sat there thrilling to the river tumbling beneath the bridge. The verges along the riverbank swayed back and forth. The cottonwoods and weeping willows dripped the dew of morning. The cottages became more than shadows until inch by inch the glow of dawn turned the hills golden and night disappeared completely. With it came the awakening of the birds and the sweet scent of flowers opening their buds to the morning.

Now she saw St. Michael's through the trees and two men walking there together. She recognized Charles at once but not the other man. He was leaning heavily against the vicar and was almost carried by him into the parish.

~

Charles saw Sydney and took a steadying grip on Conan's arm. "Come, Conan. We must get you back inside."

"Why?" His speech slurred. "I need air. I'm having more difficulty breathing. I don't want to go back in there."

"The minute you stepped into the vicarage, you became my responsibility."

"Would your archbishop see it that way, Reverend?"

He chuckled. "We do have a difference of opinion from time to time."

"Is that what landed you here in this little village?"

"My age did that. My usefulness to the diocese ran thin."

Conan stopped his halting steps. "You won't get in trouble because of me?"

"I trust not. But each man must live by his conscience."

"I have none, Reverend."

"Perhaps it is just asleep for now."

"I don't understand you forgiving me when your daughter—"

"I'm in the business of forgiveness. You will have to trust me, Conan. That young woman down by the Windrush saw two of us."

"Does it matter?" he asked wearily. "I will never be well enough to leave. Never free enough to see my children again."

"There is one way to see them."

Conan coughed, his chest sounding even more congested this morning. "I couldn't even pick Danny up now. And Keeley saw her mother die in Omagh. She must not see me. I look terrible."

"Conan, you have an infection. You're burning up. Let me send for the doctor or drive you to the hospital. Lucas doesn't have to know."

"Lucas will get me out of here as soon as I can walk."

"You can't even stand alone."

"I will soon." But he went up the steps and through the door leaning hard against the vicar, his body too weak to walk alone. "Reverend, don't send me behind those walls again. I am sick of that dark room."

"I have no other place to hide you, son. We have guests. The church of the fifteenth century must have planned that room for you."

Charles felt the burning of the young man's body resting against his arm.

"Reverend, give me a little longer. I can't stand it behind those walls. This isn't the Chastleton House. Cromwell's men aren't storming the place."

Charles eased his charge down on the couch in his study. "Son, you are a fugitive in this village. I can't guarantee your safety until you go back into the Jacobean room. But rest here for now until Kersten can make you some tea and boil you an egg. She can help you back to your room after you eat."

"No food. I'm not hungry."

"But you must eat."

Conan shivered, his fever rising; Charles pulled a blanket over his legs. "I'm going to leave you here. You must stay quiet. My guests are not to be disturbed."

"Where are you going, Reverend?"

He smiled. "To see another prodigal."

Sydney was still sitting by the Windrush when he reached her and sat down beside her. For several minutes they were silenced by the gentle flow of the river. He stretched his legs toward the water, bracing himself with his palms against the ground.

Finally, he said, "You're up early, Miss Barrington."

"And you?"

"I am accustomed to walking these hills early each morning. I feel closer to God when I do."

"Who was that walking with you?"

He crooked the corner of his mouth. "A young man in need."

"In need of shelter?"

"We all have need of shelter. You have come to the river early this morning. You must have big problems. How may I help you?"

"Is that another one of your morning chores?"

He snuggled into his warm sweater and looked toward the hills. "My parishioners are not always in the pew. This is a peaceful place—an outdoor cathedral. I think that is why you came down here at dawn."

"I'm leaving soon. I came here with so many questions. Now that I'm here, I have a thousand more. I'm worried about the children, particularly the O'Reillys. If something happens to Abigail, Danny and Keeley will be even more lost than they are now. I could take Keeley home with me, but how? Danny would be left behind. They don't even have passports."

"As I said, you have big problems." His attempt to smile was surely mirroring her own unhappiness.

"Do you know what I think, Reverend Rainford-Simms? I think Keeley's father didn't just vanish."

"We discussed that once before, didn't we?" *I have sleepless nights over that,* he thought.

"I still think someone is hiding Conan O'Reilly right here in this village. So it wouldn't be right for me to take Keeley away. It wouldn't be right for me to separate the children."

"Do you not have room in your heart for both of them?"

"Keeley's the first child who ever—oh, if only I knew who was hiding their father, I would persuade him to turn O'Reilly in for the sake of Danny and Keeley."

"Do you have someone in mind?" he asked guardedly.

"Do you want the truth?" She didn't wait for his answer. "I still think you know exactly where he is. This morning—a few moments ago, I had every reason to believe that I was right. Maybe you and Abigail planned this together. Or maybe you helped out because she was so ill. Abigail is gaining some strength—but for how long? But it's the children whose lives are being torn in so many directions."

Charles felt drawn to this sensitive young woman. Felt concern for the turmoil and search that goaded her. From all she had told him during their times together, she seemed to see herself as one living with a handful of memories, a large bank account, and the position of CEO in an ever-expanding global market. All it had done for her was make her feel old at thirty. Here in the Cotswolds she was on the verge of happiness. Yet he found himself wanting her to leave. Not because she was getting close to the truth, but because she obviously was falling in love with Jonas. He fought their friendship, screaming in protest that it was unfair. Jonas belonged to Louise.

What a selfish man you are, Charles, he told himself. *Louise would want Jonas to be happy again.* He couldn't meet her eyes as he said, "If you are so anxious to go home, you must regret coming here?"

"No. I've been peaceful here, as though the answers for which I've searched all of my life lie just beyond the next hill. But I feel like one of those sheep grazing aimlessly, unable to find my way back without someone to guide me."

He reached up and felt his clerical collar, the symbol of his ministry. He felt as if it were choking him. He should call this hillside a pulpit and tell her of a greater Shepherd. His voice sounded unreal as he said, "I think the answer you want is closer than the next hill. Christ went the distance for you, Sydney Barrington. Why don't you consider Him?"

"I don't want to bother Him with so many things happening. My old fiancé keeps calling and begging me to come home. My engineers are finalizing the blueprints for the carriers so we can bid on that job. And I've scheduled a dinner meeting in London with the British Defense Secretary as my guest. Jonas was shocked when I told him about the dinner."

"What Jonas Willoughby thinks matters to you. I think you see some of the qualities in Jonas that my daughter saw. He's a good man. I'm going to ask you what I asked my daughter a long time ago. Have you told Jonas what's on your heart?"

"And make a fool of myself?"

"Isn't that better than losing him altogether?"

"I think he's worried about everything at the manor, particularly about Abigail. They're quite close, you know."

"Have you ever wondered why?"

"He told me she's always been there for him, especially after his mother died. He really respects her."

"And rightfully so," Charles said.

"They're much alike. Even his smile reminds me of Abigail."

The sun cast its shadow across her cheeks. "So you've noticed the likeness between them?" he asked.

She looked at him sharply. But he knew she saw only innocence in his expression.

"I think she would have liked children of her own, Reverend. Taking in all of those hidden children like she did."

"Yes." Charles tugged at a blade of grass on the riverbank.

The sun was higher now, the weather warmer. The Windrush crystal clear. A swan and her ducklings swam across the water.

"Mothers tend to protect their young, even when they grow up, Sydney."

"That's the way Abigail has been with all the children. Especially with Jonas. She always jokes and says she has a thousand reasons to love him."

He sat taller and brushed the palms of his big hands. "Have you ever considered the one reason why she really does? The answers are there for you; they are there for Jonas as well. But first Jonas must rid himself of his bitterness against the Irish Republican Army. And you, my dear, must remember that Christ went the distance for you. Once you settle who this Christ is, then everything else will fall into place."

"And then I'll know whether to go home or whether to stay on here in Stow-on-the-Woodland?"

"One answer at a time. I found my greatest happiness here. I always took pride in having a large parish. Did you know? I used to be the Bishop of Monkton in the best of my days, but now I am content to be the Vicar of Stow-on-the-Woodland."

"Oh, I didn't know. I thought you were always here."

"Like the hills?"

She glanced at her watch. "I promised Abigail that we'd spend the day together. She's getting up more each day. Her favorite spot is sitting outside by the fountain."

Without asking permission, Charles breathed a quick prayer for Sydney; then he stood and helped her spring to her feet. "We both have a busy schedule today. Tell Abigail I'll try to come by this evening. I've been missing our good visits."

"I'll tell her." She looked up into his face. "Reverend, if that was Conan O'Reilly walking with you this morning, tell him his children miss him. Tell him I'd like to see him."

The lump in his throat was too big to answer her. He watched her sprint away on those long legs in a graceful motion, her chestnut hair bouncing at her neck. *She knows, and this time she did not accuse me. She is bearing the weight of Broadshire Manor on her shoulders, and she's giving me time to make amends. For the sake of the children? Or Abigail? Or?* And this time the sight of her blurred and the collar at his neck seemed unbearably tight as he watched the young American. Miss Barrington had fallen in love with Jonas, and all he could think about was Louise.

"Oh, God," he prayed. "Forgive me. I have broken faith with You—and with those who need my help."

～

As Sydney hurried back to the manor, she tried to sort through what Charles had said. The prayer that he had prayed on parting was more glowing than the sunrise. It struck her as she reached the gate that he was trying to tell her something about Abigail and Jonas. Something that would help her decide whether to stay a little bit longer.

They looked alike. They smiled alike. No, Jonas looked like his father with his thick black hair and blue eyes and that stubborn jaw. But he smiled like Abigail.

No, that wasn't it. Abigail had a thousand reasons to love Jonas. No, only one reason, the vicar had said. The thoughts were still troubling Sydney when she found Keeley asleep on her bed, an arm around each doll.

She leaned over and kissed the sleeping child. "Keeley sweetheart, we're going to have breakfast with Abigail."

Keeley snuggled deeper into the pillow. She could not be roused, so Sydney showered and dressed and went off to find Abigail. At breakfast, at lunch, in the garden, and later as they walked outside and took their places on the bench near the fountain, she searched for words to question Abigail.

One reason. A thousand reasons.

They chatted for long hours. About Jonas. About Lady Willoughby. About Edmund Gallagher and about what Griselda planned to do to him. Abigail spoke, as she always did, gently about the Admiral. In the last few days Sydney had begun to link Abigail Broderick with the frail old man in the West Wing. But when Sydney mentioned going home, back to America before another week slipped by, Abigail begged her to say no more.

By late afternoon a southwesterly breeze stirred behind them. Sydney glanced at Abigail. "Would you like to go back in? I don't want you to catch a chill out here."

Abigail shaded her eyes with her rail-thin hand and studied the landscape as the sleepy hamlet waited for the close of another day. "No, let's stay here awhile. It's one of my favorite places. I want to watch the sunset."

"Griselda won't like supper getting cold."

"That's one of the good things about my last heart attack. She is letting me set my own pace. We used to keep such a rigid schedule. Besides, I want to be here when Gregor comes home."

"Waiting until all of your children are in! Are you watching for Gregor—or for Jonas?"

She twisted sharply in her chair. "All of my children?"

"That's what you always say, isn't it?" Sydney risked another bold step. "So are you watching for Gregor, or for Jonas?"

"I worry about them both." Her words seemed to carry on the wind.

"Gregor will be lost when Jonas goes back to sea."

"Did he tell you the HMS *Invincible* is due to dock in Portsmouth next month?"

"I saw the notice in the *Navy News*. And this time I won't try to stop him. He's done so much for us already."

They saw them coming on the high knoll in the distance. Over the rolling hills. Through a patch of wildflowers. Past the winding goat path. Man and boy and TopGun racing ahead of them.

Abigail smiled. *The same smile.* "I must capture that picture of the two of them," she said.

"You must have a hundred such pictures in your mind."

"At least a thousand of Jonas."

So do I, Sydney thought. *And I've only known him for such a little while.* "Jonas is special to you."

"Yes."

Jonas, Abigail. Defined by some invisible cord. Tied together as one. But that could only happen if—if Abigail were his mother. She loved him for a thousand reasons. . . . And I have finally guessed the most important one.

Their voices echoed over the hills. The man's deep chuckle. The boy's shrill laughter. TopGun barking to hurry them along.

"I might not be here when Jonas comes home next time."

Nor I, Sydney thought. "Don't even think that way, Abby."

"If you could feel the uneven flutter in my chest, you would understand why I say such things. But your leaving troubles me. Are you running away from Jonas, Sydney?"

"I've left a business unattended far too long."

"Not with all those phone calls and your trips to the Jarrow Shipyard. Didn't I hear you ring long-distance this morning?"

She flushed, admitting, "Several times to the States."

"Have you considered keeping your main office in England?"

"Why would I do that?"

"For Jonas, for one."

Jonas unlatched the gate, and he and Gregor walked through together. They stood there companionably, Jonas looking down and smiling at the boy. Even TopGun seemed aware that they were about to part, for he licked at Gregor's hand.

"If you settled in Southampton, you'd be close to Portsmouth when his ship came in."

"But the Harrier pilots fly off before the ship docks."

"You can work those details out between you. And from the practical standpoint, didn't you win that contract on the aircraft carriers? If so, Southampton is a perfect location."

"The shipyard is on the River Tyne."

"So it is. Then Southampton is not quite perfect."

Not half as perfect as here, Sydney thought. *Here I could be happy with the sound of the birds singing, with early autumn flowers budding, and trees shading the footpaths down to the river.* How often at home she had watched the river and wondered where it led and felt now that it had led to the Windrush.

"You did win that contract?" Abigail asked again.

"Phase one only. Now Barrington is required to submit detailed drawings. We have months of work ahead, Abigail. So I—I have to get back to America."

"And after that, my dear?"

"After that," she said excitedly, "once we turn in those drawings and propose alternate designs to reduce costs, we will beat our competitors. We will win the job. I expect to win, Abigail."

"You sound like Aaron Barrington did when he built his empire for himself."

"What he did, he did for Mother and me."

"What he did was leave his dreams for you to fulfill. I understand that now. I wanted someone to take up my work, to carry on my work with the children. I know now that we can only fulfill our own calling. Except for Millicent I used to wonder whether your father thought of anything but making a profit."

"He loved working. Loved proving himself."

"I'm afraid you are too much like him." She glanced toward Jonas. "I don't know whether anything can come for you and Jonas. I would like it to. But I can't make any promises. Don't leave unless you are certain that you must do so."

Abby caught Jonas's eye and waved. He waved back, smiling. *The same smile.* Still grinning, he leaned down and whispered in Gregor's ear. Gregor broke into a run toward the house as Jonas veered off toward the cottage, TopGun at his heels.

"Abigail, how can I know for certain?"

"Only you will know the answer to that. But don't miss out on happiness, Sydney. Don't let your father's death rob you of your own place in life. You're an intelligent woman; you could choose someone else to be CEO, if necessary. This Randolph for one."

Sydney felt herself flush, her anger rising in behalf of her father, in opposition to Randolph taking over. But Gregor bounded up the steps, cutting off any sharp comeback.

He came to a running stop by Abigail's chair. She cupped his chin and wiped a dirt smudge from his cheek. "You'd better go wash for supper."

He lingered. "You coming?"

"In a few minutes," she assured him.

He sent a shy glance toward Sydney. "Jonas is coming to supper. He'll be here in thirty minutes. Is that okay?"

"Of course," Abigail told him.

"But I get to sit by Jonas."

"He has two sides," Abigail said good-naturedly. "Now run along and tell Griselda to set another place at the table."

With the boy gone, something besides the southwesterly breeze stirred between them. Sydney felt uneasy at the thought of leaving this magical world and going back to her father's world. Her father's dreams. But something troubled her even more. Abigail Broderick and Jonas Willoughby might not be here when she came back.

Chapter 25

As Sydney and Abigail waited for Jonas to come back, they were caught in the timelessness of the never-ending beauty around them. The rolling limestone hills were rich with wildflowers, dotted with sheep grazing on grassy knolls, and ridged here and there with a goat path winding up from the valley. Early touches of autumn had already speckled the higher slopes in copper and burnt orange. Below them, the Windrush flowed lazily beneath the bridges, past a bank overhung with alders and cottonwoods and weeping willows.

"I heard you go out before dawn this morning, Sydney."

"I tried to tiptoe by your room. I ran into Reverend Rainford-Simms down by the Windrush. We sat on the riverbank and watched the burst of dawn reflecting on the water."

"Charles is comforting to be with. At least I find him so."

"He plans to come by this evening with communion for you and the Admiral." Sydney paused. "We talked about you and Jonas. About how close you are and how much alike you are."

"And did you find the answers you were looking for?"

"Some, but the more we talked, the more questions arose."

"You know, don't you?" Abigail asked calmly.

Sydney focused to where the tower of St. Michael's jutted toward the clouds. Clusters of buff-colored cottages lay on the sloping hillsides, their drystone walls overgrown with primrose climbers. She said at last, "Jonas is *your* son, isn't he?"

"Yes."

Sydney faced her. If she had expected to threaten Abigail with her past, she had misjudged the strength of the woman beside her. Abigail's smile, when it came, was composed, a smile so much like Jonas's. Warm. Friendly. She had obviously come to terms with whatever agony had haunted her over the years. In spite of the lingering pallor, hers was not a face of old age, but one of lasting beauty.

"How long have you known?" Abigail's voice held amazing calm. "Was it something I said—or did—that gave me away?"

"It was the way you always look at Jonas—with such love. Does he know, Abigail?"

"No."

"Then you must tell him. You've waited far too long."

"It is because I waited that it's too late to tell him."

"I don't agree with you. He has a right to know."

"Dear child, in the maternity clinic where he was born, Lady Willoughby admitted me under her name. Lady Willoughby's name is on the birth certificate, and Lady Willoughby chose to take that secret to the grave. For Jonas's sake—not Lady Willoughby's—I kept my silence. A scandal now could still ruin his career."

"But the Admiral? The doctor who delivered him? Surely they know? Surely Sir James knows that Jonas isn't his son."

"But Jonas *is* his son."

Sydney gasped. "You mean—you and the Admiral?"

"Put that way, it sounds crude, scandalous. I must tell you, it took a long time for me to find my way back to peace. I have known God's love for forty years, but only since Charles came to Stow-on-the-Woodland have I fully comprehended God's forgiveness—and how to forgive myself as well."

Sydney thought of her own relationship with Randolph Iverson, the miserable blunders she had made. Forgiveness? Yes, it had made a difference in Abigail Broderick's life. But what price silence had cost her. Her son didn't even know the truth.

Abigail interrupted Sydney's thoughts. "Poor Tobias. I think he wanted to believe that Lady Willoughby had borne him a son. I wanted to tell him. Threatened to tell him. I was still foolish enough to love him—to think that he loved me. But Lady Willoughby made it quite clear that if I told him I would never see Jonas again. And the scandal would have ruined the Admiral's career."

"Surely, the Admiral must have known?"

"There were times when I was certain that he did. Hoped that he knew. Prayed that he knew that I was the one who had borne him a son. He never acknowledged knowing. His reputation and career were too important to him. And the prestige of Lady Willoughby's family name and wealth could not be ignored."

"What a selfish man."

"No, a proud man who worked hard to reach the top. Sir James wanted a son. Doted on him from a distance. He chided Lady Willoughby for years for not bearing him a child."

"It sounds like all he wanted was someone to carry on his legacy and walk in his footsteps."

"Tobias made plans for Jonas to follow in his footsteps before he was born. A Navy career. A family tradition." Her voice wavered. "Lady Helen threatened to keep my child from me. That was more than I could bear. Even so, for the first three months of Jonas's life I was ostracized—until that day he was baptized at St. Michael's. I was there watching, and I knew then that I would not allow her to keep me from my son any longer."

"How did she pull it off? You were the one pregnant."

"Tobias was often gone for months at a time. In the Far East. Deployed one place or the other. Long absences from each other did not seem to trouble them. Or perhaps it only troubled Lady Willoughby. When he was at sea, Lady Willoughby often traveled abroad. And that's what we did. For the last six months of my pregnancy, we lived in the French country-side in a rented villa."

"I thought Jonas was born in this country."

"He was, Sydney. My pregnancy was complicated. I was in my forties—facing the birth of my first child. My only child," she said sadly. "I insisted that the Admiral's child be born on British soil. And so we came back to England to a small maternity clinic in the North Country. I was quite ill by then and didn't know until afterwards that she had registered me in her name. And so my son was born and listed on the records as Helen's son."

She sighed. "When we left the clinic, Lady Willoughby carried the baby to the car. She drove into the next town, stopped the car, handed me some money, and told me that I was never to return to the manor again. Griselda guessed of course. But she has always been the loyal one. Lady Willoughby rarely flew down to meet her husband when his ship came in, fearing another woman being there. But people here in Stow-on-the-Woodland thought of them as the beautiful young Helen, the dashing naval officer, the devoted couple."

"Why the facade of a happy marriage?"

"James bowed under the public image. He wanted nothing to mar his career. Poor James. The Admiral had waited long years to pick a bride, and Helen was by far the most lovely to choose from. She owned the manor, had the social standing in London that appealed to him. Money was always on her side, but once she met the handsome naval officer, she determined to marry him.

"Even though he was much older, the Admiral was the envy of her friends. They guessed even then that he would go far in his career. Helen wanted to go with him. He remained rakishly handsome at forty-six when Jonas was born and still charming to other women."

She choked up as she said, "Lady Willoughby loved him and felt convinced that if she bore a child for the Admiral, he would never look at another woman again. When she found out I was pregnant with her husband's child, she wanted to thrash me. And then she offered to protect my reputation in the village where I had grown up; in exchange, the child would be raised as her own."

"She was young—healthy. Why not have her own child?"

"She had been thrown from a horse as a young child and severely injured. Complications eventually led to a hysterectomy. But the Admiral didn't know that."

Sydney touched Abigail's arm. "If Lady Willoughby took this secret to her grave, why have you risked sharing it with me?"

"I have to trust someone. Who better than Millicent Barrington's daughter? I think you will do right by my son if I die before my will is revised." She rested for a moment. "My health has been failing for some time, my heart flabby and undependable. When I went into Edmund's office some months before my last heart attack, he made offers to buy the property from me. He had some scheme for opening up the village to tourism. I had gone to his father all my life. When Edmund took over his father's clients, I thought I could trust him."

As the sun lowered on the horizon, the glare blinded them. They adjusted their chairs, drawing back into the shade. Sydney slipped a sweater around Abigail's shoulders. "Mr. Gallagher may be unscrupulous enough to carry it off. I've met him. He does have an elaborate plan to turn Stow-on-the-Woodland commercial, but the village would lose its quaint charm. It's time for you to trust my friend Jeff. Let's get your will written the way you want it. We'll have Edmund meet you here."

Abigail began to fidget with the button on her sweater. "Just weeks before my heart attack, I called for another appointment. Again Edmund offered to buy me out. When I refused, he put me off. He said he had to bring in some papers from London. I begged him not to delay—to help me get my affairs in order at once. He promised we would draw up the papers the next time we met."

"You should have seen another lawyer."

"When I told him I would travel to London and consult with one of his partners, Edmund threatened to reveal things about the Admiral and Jonas. I fear he may know that Jonas is my son. How, I cannot tell you, but we reached a shouting match that set my heart to racing. He told me I was a fool to keep the property for Jonas. Jonas had no interest in it."

Her voice weakened. "I hung up on Edmund, but before I did, I told him that you would manage the property for Jonas. After all, you were my friend's daughter."

"You didn't even know me, except when I was a child."

She closed her eyes for a moment. "But I wanted to trust you. My heart was just riding wild. I was desperate to right the wrong done so long ago."

"The wrong? Does that relate to the hold that you had over Lady Willoughby? Her property in exchange for your silence?"

"It was more than that, Sydney. With the property in my name, I could go on taking care of the children—and still be near Jonas. The Admiral wanted her to sell the property so they could move back to London. Tobias disliked the house filled with children when he came home. He had difficulty enough warming to his own son. I would have lost the right to care for the children. The right to see Jonas. So I went to Helen and threatened to tell the Admiral the truth. To tell him that Jonas was my son. I laid out my terms."

"What terms, Abigail?"

Her breathing seemed more rapid now, her eyes tired. "The property would go into my name for as long as I lived. At least one wing of the manor would always be kept for the children under my care. The Willoughbys would maintain the stables and the garden. And I would never be refused the right to see my son."

Abigail's lower lip had turned a bluish gray, but she went on. "The property was to go back to Helen at my death—I was so much older. And Helen would, of course, leave it to her son."

"And all that changed when Lady Willoughby died?"

"Yes," she whispered. "We must not speak of this again. But if I die before all of this is settled, promise me that you will make certain that Edmund Gallagher is not permitted to lay claim to Broadshire Manor. The land belongs to Jonas." Abigail looked exhausted. "You have been good for me, Sydney. And if that friend of yours can help us. . ."

"I'll have Jeff make the arrangements for tomorrow."

"If he doesn't come in time, the land is yours. I trust you to make certain that Jonas can lay claim to it." A smile lit her face. "There! Jonas is coming now."

The sight of him awakened Sydney's own senses, her longing to be needed, wanted by Commander Willoughby. His hair was still wet from the shower, his handsome face obviously just shaved. He was wearing tan slacks and a short-sleeve pullover shirt of blue chambray, a brilliant blue against his bronzed skin. Long-limbed and muscular, he strode briskly toward them. A confident, surefooted man. As he climbed the steps, the woody scent of his cologne was more pungent than the flowering shrub by the porch.

It was the same cologne he'd been wearing that night by the Windrush. His charm—the details of that night—surged back and forth in her mind like the rushes at the water's edge. She recalled the mesmerizing effect of his deep-set eyes meeting hers. Of admitting to him that she was cold in her bareback dress and having his arm slip around her, his soft cardigan sweater touch her bare back. She heard the thumping beat of his heart as he held her. Felt the strength of his arm and muscular body and was ready for the intensity of his warm lips as they sought hers.

But what had that moment at the Windrush meant to Jonas? She forced herself to look at Jonas now and traced his strong profile in her mind's eye. Saw again that stubborn jaw so much like the Admiral's.

He glanced at Abigail and in his deep, hypnotic voice said, "We'd better get you inside before the midges eat you alive."

His eyes were on Abigail, yet Sydney felt certain that he was simply biding his time, pacing himself, waiting for just the right moment to turn his attention her way.

He held Abigail's hand and helped her to her feet. Then he tucked her arm in his, leaving Sydney to follow behind them. And still Sydney felt certain that his own need of her had awakened the moment he found them sitting by the fountain.

They were into the main hallway before he turned back to her and smiled. "I was wondering, Syd, are you busy after supper?"

Her words jumbled in her throat. "I. Well, I usually—"

Abigail glanced back. "Of course she's free. I am well enough to put myself to bed and strong enough to at least read to the children until Griselda is ready to bathe them."

"What did you have in mind, Jonas?" Sydney asked shyly.

"Veronica's Tea Shoppe is closed by seven, so I thought we could walk down to Chutman's Pub."

"Isn't the pub for men only?"

"Not here in Stow-on-the-Woodland. It's a community affair where people gather to talk and drink."

"I don't drink."

"Not even tea?" he teased. "And they serve their bread-and-butter pudding, hot and creamy. We could skip supper here and have a light meal at the pub."

"No," Abigail warned. "Gregor is counting on sitting beside you at the table. You must not disappoint him."

"Oh, in the excitement I forgot."

He put his arm around Abigail, around his own mother without knowing, and moved down the corridor toward Griselda's kitchen.

But Sydney felt contentment. She would be with Jonas this evening. Out on their own. Walking the footpath to the pub and the Windrush with no one else with them. She looked again at his strong arm resting so gently on Abigail's shoulder and thought, with the pounding of her own heart and a flush of her cheeks, *Tonight, perhaps, his arm will be around me.*

Chapter 26

A bigail did not sleep after supper but rested in the comfort of her own room with its thick lace curtains on the windows and elegant seventeenth-century tapestry on the wall. Griselda had lit a fire in the fireplace and the crackling of burning logs added to the coziness. Keeley and Tesa sat at the quaint desk with its pigeonholes stuffed with their drawings, each girl laboriously sketching a picture of Keeley's Shetland pony.

Gregor poked his head in the door. "Miss Abigail, I want to go down to Chutman's Pub with Jonas."

"You've just had supper."

"I won't eat much."

"But Jonas is taking Sydney out for the evening."

His face shadowed. "They said I could come."

"You invited yourself?"

He refused to meet her eyes. His toes turned in, the way they did when he was making excuses. Her heart went out to him. "Gregor, give them some time alone."

"She hangs around him all the time."

Go gently with him, Abigail told herself. "Stay with me this evening. We haven't had a good visit for a long time."

"If you don't let me go, I can't catch up with them."

So he would be the uninvited guest. Firmly she said, "You are not to go this time. Try to understand." His dark eyes blazed as she said, "Why not work on one of your model planes in here? You could stay up until I retire."

"Jonas is helping me with the plane."

Jonas again. "Then let me rest a bit. After that we'll pay the Admiral a visit. Sir James likes it when you call on him."

"I saw him today. He was reading his *Navy News* and said Jonas's aircraft carrier is docking in Portsmouth soon."

"Gregor, was he reading or just looking at the pictures?"

"He tried to make out the words himself. Sometimes Sydney reads to him when I can't. She does everything for the Admiral that I used to do.

I wish she'd go home again."

"Jonas would feel bad if she went away."

He kicked the door, his boyish face anguished. "I know."

"Come here, Gregor. Jonas doesn't love you any less. He just wants to be with Sydney sometimes."

"I think he wants to marry her, and then he'll go away. I heard him tell the Reverend Rainford-Simms—"

"You followed Jonas down there? Were you eavesdropping?" As he reached her bedside, she cupped his sun-scaled cheeks. "Gregor, Griselda and I will be here for you if Jonas and Sydney get married."

"He'll send me off to Gordonstoun just to get rid of me."

"No, not to get rid of you. He's proud of you—like a son. He wants you to go there because it was his boarding school."

His lip quivered. "Do I have to go, Miss Abigail?"

"I thought you wanted to go. You'd meet so many boys your age. And have the chance to play so many sports."

"I'm not good in sports."

"Oh, but you run faster than anyone I know. And you are getting better in soccer."

"I might never come back to the manor."

"Of course you will." She had been too quick with her answer. He was still a little boy who needed her. "Would you rather go to the primary school here at Stow-on-the-Woodland?"

She tousled his hair. He smelled of shampoo, his breath minty from toothpaste. Sydney must have hugged him, for his shirt held the faint fragrance of her French perfume.

"I'll talk to Jonas," she said. "He wants to take you up to Gordonstoun for a visit. You will go, won't you? He'd be disappointed."

"He won't get in the car and go away without me?" Everyone he had known in Kosovo had left him.

"Jonas would never do that. I love you, Gregor. So does Jonas."

The boy nestled against her arm. "Are you going to leave us?"

"I don't want to, but I'm ill. Someday I'll have to go away, but I'll go on loving you. I just won't be here like I am now."

He seemed to understand. Seemed to accept. Gregor and the O'Reillys would be the last of her hidden children. The circle was closing in, the retreat from Dunkirk coming to a final close. Abigail Broderick at seventeen had been free-spirited, absolutely certain that she would live forever. But on the march to the burning city of Dunkirk, she had feared not living at all. Now she did not fear death, but where had the decades gone?

Was she really seventy-seven? Inside, she was still free-spirited; outside, dignified. Serene. She knew as she slipped her arm around Gregor's bony shoulders that her work was almost over. No one would pick up her dreams and run with them. The course she had run was her own. She wanted only to hear a "well done" when she reached the end of her journey.

Abigail kissed the top of Gregor's head. She wanted more than anything to be there for him as he grew up, to help him over the pitfalls, to perhaps go with him when he saw his own country again, but she knew she would not live long enough to do so.

"I want to rest now, Gregor. Would you take the girls down to Griselda? It's almost their bedtime."

He went obediently to the desk and folded Tesa's drawing book and lowered the rolltop. Tesa slipped off her chair and ran and flung herself at Abigail. Keeley stood shyly watching them.

"Sleep well, little ones. And count the sheep the minute your heads hit the pillow."

"I am done with counting sheep," Keeley announced. "Sydney told me I can count jasmine and roses instead."

She smiled. "Then tomorrow tell me how many you counted."

The door closed behind them. She lay against her pillows, listening to their voices as they walked down the hall. When their steps faded, the ringing of the bell at St. Michael's awakened her memories. She caught the scent of flowers outside her window and shut her eyes to search for sheep and jasmine and roses to count. The movie of her past was already in play, the reel spinning. Spinning a seventeen-year-old back to the long line of soldiers standing on the sands of Dunkirk. They stood there, shading their eyes, looking out on the choppy waters waiting for ships to rescue them.

And her hidden past played before her, bringing with it both joy and sadness. She remembered the coldness of the soldier's helmet on her head. But the face that she saw was not her own. *It was Sydney in the British uniform looking up at Neil Irwin and asking, "Why didn't you marry Abigail?"*

Neil's cheerful voice echoed in her memory. "Ah, mate, I'd have married my sweetheart after the war. But the battle of Normandy came along."

The reel kept spinning. Hermann and Isaac with grown-up faces, dressed in khaki undershirts and clinging to a dinghy. The long line of children who had come to her. Santos. Conan. Tyler. Rebecca.

The reel jammed, then started again. Herself—a woman in her thirties with rusty brown hair timidly gripping the knocker at the manor and looking up at a tall naval officer with smashing good looks. The beaches of Dunkirk were lost in a mist, and she was walking to the top of the golden hills in the Cotswolds, laughing up at the officer with the rakish smile. The dreadful realization that she was pregnant, the sin that almost destroyed her. But Charles Rainford-Simms had come to St. Michael's with his ministry of love and forgiveness.

The kaleidoscope of a lifetime. The changing patterns of her life. Dappled rainbows, checkered, twisted turns that had brought her to this moment. She saw the young Abigail Broderick. Saw the old Abigail. Watched herself go from rusty brown hair to silvery gray. Her dreams and destiny all one now. Woven into the pattern, she saw herself fleeing to the continent to Lady Willoughby's private French villa. Saw her body distorted with pregnancy and the beautiful Lady Willoughby planning for Abigail's child as though the baby had formed in her own womb. And the plan conceived that made the child forever a Willoughby.

There was no real sleep, only the drifting of the yesterdays in her memory. A pregnancy wrought with difficulties. A maternity clinic in the North Country. The reel of deception kept spinning. Jonas's birth recorded as Lady Willoughby's child. The nun wiring the Admiral that a son had been born. Then leaving the clinic on that sunless day and being told she was no longer needed. Ever.

The end of the reel spun off. Her return to the manor months later, refusing to be separated from her son another day. The threat to tell the truth. *The Admiral had stared at the child in Abigail's arms. For a moment it seemed like he knew, but he said nothing. Even now, Abigail saw Lady Willoughby thrusting the contract into the Admiral's hands. Saw the sadness in his eyes. "Abigail wants the manor. She wants to go on taking in children."*

He had glanced at Abigail. "Let her have anything, Helen."

The anguished voice of Helen: "You know, don't you, James?"

The cold, noncommittal "Know what, my dear Helen?"

"That you would lose everything if she told the truth." Helen had touched his cheek, having always loved him. "So, James, what you cannot openly admit, you cannot deny."

They signed, and Abigail, still holding Jonas, had said, "It will go no further. Ever. You can have your ships and Lady Willoughby this child. But I must watch him grow up."

Abigail's life had been capricious. Stimulating. Painful. Convoluted. Happy. Ever moving her forward. The many images all there. But even here in this room she was covered by an arc of forgiveness. It had all been part of growing up, growing old. The beginning tying in with the end. So dying was just a part of living, the capstone more glorious than the golden hills.

She was about to sew that last stitch on the unfinished quilt of her life. Was she to bury her secrets as Lady Willoughby had done? Was she to leave no visible legacy of love for Jonas? Abigail felt the heart flutter that came at unexpected moments. The lamps in her room formed shadows on the wall, highlighting the colors in the tapestry. She had one small hope. If her own courage failed her, then one day—and Sydney would know the right time—Sydney Barrington would tell Jonas the whole truth.

Chapter 27

The next morning Sydney sat alone on the top of the knoll. The happy cries of the children and the lamenting notes of Jonas's bagpipes wafted back toward her. As she thought of the pleasant evening at the pub with Jonas—of his strong arm around her—a shadow fell across her path.

She glanced up into the gaunt face of a stranger, a man younger than Jonas. If his cheeks were fuller, his skin less gray, she would have thought him attractive.

"You sent word that you wanted to see me," he said.

"And I'm surprised that you came. Sit down, please."

He held his ribs and eased down on the ground beside her. He took the apple she offered and bit into it. "Are my children living with you now?" he asked.

His accent was decidedly Irish, and she knew for certain that this was Keeley's father—the terrorist that she was supposed to fear. "We're all staying up at the manor."

"How are they, Miss Barrington?"

So Charles has told him my name. "All six of them are down there with Jonas Willoughby."

He winced at the name. "Yes. Who else but Jonas would be playing the bagpipes? Is he good to the Irish children as well?"

"He tries to be. Danny adores Mrs. Quigley."

"All of the children end up liking her. And Keeley?"

She turned and looked into his haunted eyes and pitied him. "She misses her father. Prays every night that he will come back. We've become good friends and often go riding together."

"I've seen you riding out on the hills. She seems happy with you. Please, take my children to America with you."

She laughed. "They have no passports."

His hand fell limply to his side. He had lost interest in the apple. Or perhaps he was too sick to even chew it. "I'll write a letter—giving you permission to take them. Will you?"

He was handing her the responsibility of his children. Had she come all the way to England for this stranger in his brooding silence to ask her help? Even on the open hillside, the odor of his festering wounds was strong.

"Do you want to stay and see the children?"

His cold pale eyes softened as he rubbed his whiskery chin. "I won't put them through another good-bye." He began to cough, a violent spasm that left fresh spots of blood on his shirt.

She reached out and touched his arm. "You're bleeding. I could send Dr. Wallis. You need medical attention."

"A friend is looking after me, Miss Barrington."

"Then go before Jonas and the children come back."

"Will you tell Jonas where I am?"

"I don't know for certain where you're staying. I'd only be guessing. And you haven't told me your name."

His smile twisted the gaunt lines in his face. "Which one of us are you protecting?"

He jerked to his feet. More drops of blood fell on the ground where he had been sitting. Far below, the lamenting wail of the bagpipes ceased. The children began racing up the hillside. Keeley stopped. Looked. And ran harder.

"You can barely stand. Let me help you?" Sydney offered.

He shook his head. "Someone is waiting for me."

"Next Sunday, I'll leave pictures of the children at the baptismal font. One of Keeley on her pony. One of both of them."

"I'll find them there. Thank you."

"Go," she said. "The children are coming."

Conan coughed as he slipped into the woods. And then the sound of him, the sight of him, disappeared.

Keeley stumbled into Sydney's arms. "Where did my papa go?" She pounded against Sydney's chest. "Where did he go?"

"I don't know for certain, Keeley."

Dear God, forgive me, she thought. *But Conan is right. He is too sick for them to see him this way.*

Keeley's sobs subsided as Sydney held her. "He didn't even wave."

"Maybe you just wanted it to be him, honey."

Jonas dragged up the hill with the other children clinging to him. "What's wrong with her?" he asked, bewildered.

"She misses her father."

Jonas knelt on one knee and pointed to his back. "Hop on. It's your turn for a free pony ride, Keeley."

"You're not my pony."

"I'm a make-believe one."

Shyly she climbed on his back, the other children standing around with envy in their eyes. Jonas supported her chubby legs. Keeley locked her arms around his neck. He shrugged her more securely on his back and then looked at Sydney with a penetrating gaze. "I won't ask any questions. We agreed to trust each other."

"I know. Thank you."

"Sydney, tomorrow we're going on a picnic of our own. Just the two of us. The children aren't invited."

Gregor scowled.

"No children," Jonas said, silencing his objection. "What do you say, Miss Barrington? Veronica at the tea shop promised to pack us a picnic box."

"I'd love to go with you. Just the two of us."

He went galloping off with Keeley clinging to him. Sydney covered Conan's drops of blood with her shoe. She felt grateful to Jonas for not asking questions that she could not answer. She had wanted to meet with Conan O'Reilly. She had met with a stranger.

Gregor slipped his hand in hers. "Don't look so sad, Sydney. You're the one going on a picnic with Jonas tomorrow."

"I know." She felt a lightness kick in, a momentary happiness that brought color to her cheeks, joy to her heart.

～

Sydney took the items of food from Veronica's basket as Jonas stretched contentedly on his back on the picnic rug. He peeked at her. "I'd like this time together to go on forever."

She pressed his hand against her cheek. "It can't. I have to go home. I have a company to run and they can't do the job without me."

"What a high-powered operative you are. Buying shipyards. Building carriers."

"That's not fair. I didn't ask to be the head of Dad's company when he died. I stumbled into that position, but I'm telling you, I conquered it with the Barrington spirit."

"Then why did you come to the Cotswolds if you were only going to turn around and leave me?"

"I think I came looking for a special place—a special person—and I found them both here."

The waters of the Windrush bubbled a few feet from them. "Jonas, I love being near water, listening to the sound of a waterfall or watching a river like this one coursing around the countryside." He laughed up at her, but she still said, "It's always the same—the sound of water makes me peaceful."

"I feel the same way. That's why I like going to sea."

"It's strange. Both sets of my parents died in water, yet I still find the sound of water peaceful."

He reached across the picnic rug and took her hand in his again. "Not strange at all. Water is symbolic of life. It keeps flowing endlessly. What I regret most is how untroubled I was when my ship was deployed to another crisis point. The Navy and going to sea were my life. I expected Louise to understand."

"Maybe you expected too much."

As Sydney took the rest of Veronica's surprises from the basket, she saw Lucas striding toward them with a young couple. The girl was short and pudgy with a pretty smiling face, the young man lean and whistling as he approached.

He winked at Sydney and gave Jonas a nudge with his boot. "On your feet, man. You have guests."

At the sound of his friend's voice, Jonas rolled to his side and scrambled to his feet. They pounded each other.

"Jock."

"Commander?" Jock glanced at Sydney. "I see we can finally stop our search for a London debutante."

"Sydney, this is Joseph Hollinsworth and his wife, Kathleen. Only we call him Jock." He pounded his friend's arm again. "I thought you'd be back on the carrier by now."

"I'm back with the squadron at Morayshire. We're expecting to be posted to the *Invincible* the next time she comes into port. But it won't be the same flying wingman for someone else."

Kathleen said shyly, "You're not flying wingman this time, Jock. If you don't tell Jonas, I will." Proudly, she said, "They've promoted Jock to squadron commander."

A cloud washed over Jonas's face, but he was quick to recover. "Getting liberal with their promotions, aren't they?"

"Desperate. You know I'd step aside if you were going back."

"Someday, Jock. What about you two joining us? Veronica packed plenty of food. What do you say, Sydney?"

"That Veronica thought we'd stay here for a week."

Jonas gave her a quick wink. "Don't I wish."

Jock dropped down beside them. "Jonas, I've been doing weekend flights in my uncle's Learjet while I'm waiting for the *Invincible* to come back. I solo now. So I can take her up alone." He chuckled. "My uncle's business is booming, particularly in the Scandinavian countries. We flew in here today—and my uncle is off to Finland, flying commercial. We have a flight scheduled next weekend. I'll meet my uncle in Helsinki. Head to Stockholm to pick up some passengers and back to London. If you're free, you could go along."

"Some other time, Jock." He seemed suddenly aware that Lucas was still hovering around. "No need for you to stand by, Lucas. My friends and I have a lot of visiting to do."

As Lucas stomped off, Sydney handed a plate to Kathleen. "What will you do now that your husband is going back to sea?"

"I'll be in London with my parents waiting for his return." Is that how it was? Waiting for a return, even before the ship left the harbor? Was that the kind of life she would have with Jonas Willoughby? A life where she would feel like an intruder on his time? But Kathleen was bubbling with joy, still flirting with Jock as though they had just married.

Between bites, Jonas teased, "Jock, did you reach the goals you set for your leave?"

Jock slipped his arm around his wife. "If you count Kathleen being sick to her stomach every morning—and sending me out at midnight for pickles just to get in practice when the obsession strikes her, everything went well."

Kathleen blushed. "But I never liked pickles," she admitted, taking a bite from the one that Sydney offered her.

Jock patted his wife's stomach. "This is my reason for taking on my uncle's jobs. Kathleen has a doctor's appointment in London next week. And," he said, "we might as well put in the request now. Jonas, we're going to want you to stand up with us when we have the baby christened." He stole a fresh glimpse toward Sydney. "And if you stay on board, you're invited, too."

Sydney and Jonas fell into an awkward silence.

"Look," Jock apologized, "we're not rushing you. We just thought, well, we thought you had something going here between you. Sorry."

∾

On Tuesday, as Edmund Gallagher knocked on the old oak door at the manor, Jeff VanBurien climbed the steps behind him. Edmund acknowledged the American with a curt nod and stepped into the great hall at Griselda's invitation.

"Mrs. Quigley, I have an appointment with Miss Broderick. Would you be so good as to tell her I've arrived?"

"Same thing," VanBurien said cheerily. "I have an appointment with Miss Broderick as well."

Griselda wiped her hands on her apron. "She's expecting you both. She's in the library waiting."

Edmund stalled. He glared at Jeff. "She sent for me regarding personal matters. I am her solicitor. So if you would be so good as to wait your turn—"

Griselda said, "She expects you both at the same time. She's in the library and doesn't like to be kept waiting."

Jeff extended his hand. "After you, Mr. Gallagher."

Edmund had just stepped into the massive library when he saw Sydney. The angry curve of his mouth tightened. He crunched his jaw, the crackling audible across the room. "So Dr. Wallis was right, Miss Barrington. You have settled in at Broadshire Manor."

Abigail sat with great dignity behind the Admiral's massive desk. She was wearing a blue velvet dress with a high collar that had always looked striking on her. Yet this morning the neckline seemed too big. She was indeed ill. Losing weight.

"Gentlemen," she said, and her voice was as strong as it had ever been, "we were getting worried that you might be late."

Jeff grinned. "I believe we're right on time, ma'am."

Edmund's annoyance blew out of control. "Abigail, I believe you made an appointment with me. I have other clients at the office. Can we get on with this?"

"Of course. But I have appointments with all of you. I believe you and Mr. VanBurien have met under different circumstances? And this is a dear friend of mine. Sydney Barrington." The smile lines at Abigail's eyes deepened. "Sydney, this is the solicitor I was telling you about. Edmund Gallagher."

"We've met," Sydney said coolly. "I believe he was urging me to sell the manor when I thought I was inheriting this place."

Edmund continued to bluff his way. "We have business to discuss, Abigail. Perhaps your friends could leave us alone?"

"No. As you know, Miss Barrington is presently my sole heir. You can understand her concern that her personal lawyer be present to defend her rights."

Jeff casually pulled up a chair and sat beside Sydney. Abigail flashed them a warm smile. "Mr. VanBurien and Sydney both know that I intend to change my will today. Edmund, if you refuse to cooperate, then Mr. VanBurien will arrange for one of your partners to journey here from London. Is that understood?"

Edmund's mouth grew taut, stretching his lips to a narrow line. He was tasting humiliation and he knew it—facing defeat and knew it. He cast a glance around the magnificent room and knew that his dream of ownership had slipped away.

"Is there a problem, Edmund?"

Sweat drenched his shirt. "Of course not."

"Then perhaps we should get started?"

Wallis had warned him. He had gone too far. Word would spread quickly through the village. He panicked, wondering how he could replace the funds he had misappropriated at the London office.

Edmund sank into the chair, the meeting already out of his hands, the taste of gall in his mouth.

~

Sydney left the library three hours later with a splitting headache. She had not enjoyed seeing Edmund Gallagher go down in defeat. The errors that he had made in Abigail's business matters had been pointed out and the legal implications spelled out by Jeff in a language that Edmund understood. In the end, Abigail insisted on a simple, handwritten will; and when it was done, Jeff and Sydney penned their names as witnesses. Sydney came from the room no longer the heir to 250 acres of land and six children, but she shared Abigail's joy. The Willoughby property would pass from generation to generation as it had always done.

Sydney headed toward her room, but Griselda stopped her. "Hurry, Sydney. That young man from America is on the phone."

Randolph again, she thought. How many times had he called since her arrival in England? Hadn't the day been bad enough? She built a fist around the receiver and said, "Hello. Sydney Barrington speaking."

"Syd, it's Randolph. When are you coming home? I miss you."

"I don't know."

"You don't know when you're coming, or whether I miss you?"

"A little bit of both."

"It's that Navy commander, isn't it? He's answered the phone several times when I called. Thinks I'm your business partner."

"You are."

"I should hate the guy. Whenever I ask him where you are, he says you're with the children or Abigail Broderick. You're different somehow, Sydney. In your letters, you seem happier than you've ever been."

"I am happier."

"When are you coming home?"

"You don't like the way I run things when I am there."

"I worry about the way you rush into big decisions. You're still trying to salvage Aaron's folly, and now Daron Emery tells me you've bid on another shipyard in Italy."

"Some of the European designers are so far ahead of us. We're in global competition. Remember?" She heard the competitive spirit in her own words.

"The only competition I'm worried about is that Navy commander. If you think the Europeans are so far advanced, maybe you'd better think about living abroad permanently."

She heard the bite in his words and felt defensive. "If I thought it meant taking Barrington straight to the top, then I would make this my permanent residence." *Or,* she thought reflectively, *if it means finding my castle in the air—my happiness—then, yes, I will change my address.*

"Don't do that. I'd miss you."

"You sound like I've already made the decision to stay."

"I think you have in your heart. Do you know what you will do with the house and the cabin?"

"Now you have my house up for sale! Those are things I would have to work out. But I think I want to keep the cabin. I want Keeley and Danny—"

"The kids?"

"Yes, I want them to spend some of their summers there. I loved that place. I want them to love it, too."

"You've changed, Sydney. Aaron's lost his hold on you."

"No, I've just found something I want more than Aaron's kingdom."

Chapter 28

The morning after the meeting with Gallagher, Sydney left for an emergency meeting at the Jarrow Shipyard. On returning days later she found the cottage closed and Jonas gone. Gregor was gone, too, and a black-and-white collie was spending most of her time beside the Admiral's bed.

It was lonely at the manor without them, but on Friday Sydney put on a cheerful face as she walked into a kitchen filled with the fragrant aroma of fresh baking. "Smells good in here, Mrs. Quigley."

Griselda beamed. "So you're awake, Sydney. There's a fresh pot of tea, and I will have something hot from the oven soon."

"Any word from Jonas? They've been gone a week. I thought they'd be home by now."

"Did you now?" Her eyes twinkled. "After Gordonstoun, he planned to take the boy to Morayshire to visit his old squadron."

"But I thought Jonas was taking me on that trip—at least that's what he told me."

"Guess he changed his mind—what with you off to that shipyard of yours without telling him."

"I left so early I didn't want to wake him."

"No matter. It's best this way. Gave Gregor a chance to have Jonas to himself. But Jonas practically has the boy signed up for the Navy and flying a Sea Harrier."

"I hope he won't pressure him about boarding school."

"Abigail won't let Jonas do that. Gregor is her boy. And she thinks he'll do best with another year or two at the village school. Jonas is like his father. Once he makes up his mind there's no stopping him. He wants Gregor to have the best preparation for going with the Royal Navy."

"Gregor is only nine."

"Jonas went away long before that. He went from his trainers into training for the Navy. And when he bid for flight school, I thought the Admiral would have a stroke."

"But the Admiral wanted his son in the Navy."

"Commanding a ship, not crashing on some flight deck."

It would never work out, Sydney thought. *A little boy and the Navy are stiff competition.* Yet she would gladly have gone to Gordonstoun and Scotland with them—to fill in those missing pieces of Jonas's life and to meet his Uncle Ian.

Sydney filled her cup as Griselda said, "Lucas was just here asking for you. He found your riding stick. It's over there." She nodded toward the table. "Said he kept meaning to give it back. Thought you might need it the next time you go riding."

It felt as if Griselda had punched her in the stomach. Sydney gripped the table and sat down, the cup rattling in the saucer as she put it on the table. "Did Lucas say anything else?"

"Just that you should be more careful next time. It upsets him if anything gets out of place in the stables. He doesn't like much, but he does like keeping a watchful eye on those horses. Those stallions are probably the only friends he has."

"You don't think much of Lucas, do you?"

"What's there to like?"

"He's good to the Admiral."

"It works best when he stays in the West Wing and I stay in the kitchen. Don't go getting yourself in trouble, Sydney. Not with Lucas. He's a private man. He doesn't like people overstepping their limits in the stables."

"I never intended to." She ran her finger moodily around the edge of her cup. "I'll be more careful next time I go riding. It's just—oh, never mind."

Mrs. Quigley turned from the old iron oven, mopping her brow. "Are you wanting to tell Griselda all about it?"

"I should talk to Jonas first. I just hope I'm here long enough to do so."

"You won't be if that young man of yours has his way. He called again this morning."

"Randolph called again? Was anything wrong?"

"Same thing today and yesterday and the day before and last week. The only thing wrong is he wants you back there to marry him. Usually Mr. Iverson just leaves a message for you. Takes care to spell his name one letter at a time, like as though I couldn't hear him. But this morning he told me to make it clear to you that he'll fly over here if you don't go home."

"He would. But Randolph is right. Daron Emery is doing a splendid job at Jarrow Shipyard. And Abigail is getting better. So I have no excuse to stay any longer."

Griselda's thick brows puckered. "None of us want you to go." Her voice cracked. She sniffed against her flour-white wrist. "Even the Admiral thinks you're part of the crew."

"I'm beginning to leave dust marks on the welcome mat." She met Griselda's steady gaze. "I hoped Jonas would get back so I could tell him good-bye."

The twinkle was back. "I thought you'd be more observant than that. He came back late last night."

Hot humiliation burned Sydney's cheeks. "Is he avoiding me?"

"Ask him," she called over her shoulder. "Poor boy doesn't know his own mind. And Gregor is certainly not going to volunteer the information. I can tell by your voice that you didn't know."

"I haven't seen Jonas since the picnic."

"That was more than a week ago. And he was upset when he didn't find you here for breakfast the morning you left for the shipyard."

"Didn't you tell him where I went?"

"Wasn't my job to tell him. That's between the two of you. Once you took off to that shipyard of yours, he moped around. I need to warn you. I think Jonas is trying to sort out his feelings about you, and you're not making it easy." She put her hands on her hips, a pack of wisdom wrapped behind her gruff manner. "Sydney, you are going to rub the design off that cup, so stop playing with it and get yourself another cup of tea."

"Would you like me to help you bake?" Sydney offered.

"Beautiful morning like this, and you have nothing to do except help me in the kitchen? The children are with Abigail. So go for a horseback ride. Enjoy yourself."

"I don't want to face Lucas right now. Not alone."

Mrs. Quigley mulled that one over with her arms deep in flour, forming dumplings and breakfast rolls. "Such problems you have. You could help Boris in the garden."

"I'd rather help Jonas." The words slipped out before she could retrieve them. "I don't know what made me say that."

"That's the trouble. You don't know your own heart." She took the loaves of nut bread from the oven, the aroma permeating the kitchen. Sydney's mouth watered.

"Now me, for instance—" Mrs. Quigley fanned her flushed face with the muslin cloth that served as her apron. "I knew right off with my husband, Arthur."

"You never talk about him."

"Can't without getting all choked up. I met him out there on the hills tending sheep for his uncle. Arthur was much like Jonas. Strong and tall, and a right handsome one. We were both young—me, I was just sixteen. I knew right off, once he showed up at Chutman's Pub. I chased him from the day I met him. Married him just past my eighteenth birthday. We settled here in Stow-on-the-Woodland so Arthur could farm the land."

"What happened to him?"

"Died with consumption—eight years after we married. Abby was my lifeline, what with me losing my Arthur like that."

"You should have married again."

The tired lines around Mrs. Quigley's eyes softened. "There can be only one Arthur in a lifetime."

There could be only one Jonas in a lifetime.

"Abby talked the Willoughbys into hiring me. When Lady Willoughby died, I stayed on. Wouldn't have 'cepting my friend Abigail was living at the manor by then. Even then, I thought I wouldn't stay on—not with the Admiral fussing like he did whenever he came home on leave and saw all them children."

"You're good with the children. That's what makes you and Abigail both so special."

Griselda set another baking pan in the oven and reset her timer. For a second Sydney thought Griselda's shoulders quivered. "Griselda, if I said something wrong, I'm sorry."

She snorted. "You'll be more sorry if you let Jonas go."

Sydney's cheeks burned. "I don't know what you mean."

Their eyes met again. "Been here all these weeks and don't know what I mean? Every time you look at him, you go scarlet."

Sydney put her hands to her cheeks to hide the burning. "I guess it's like you and Arthur—I've never known anyone like Jonas."

"Then go down to his cottage and tell him. Can't hurt. Might help. I did a bit of rushing after Arthur, once I met him."

"Gregor will be down at the cottage."

"Not this morning. This morning the children are with Abigail, and after that, Gregor promised me he would take the Admiral's noon meal to him. That means standing by and making certain the Admiral eats something. Since Gregor usually comes back with an empty tray, I figure he is doing most of the eating. But that boy understands the Admiral. Likes him. It's good for the children to have responsibility. Good for Gregor to be needed."

Sydney ran her finger around the rim of her cup again. "Griselda, you're deliberately keeping Gregor busy."

"I most certainly am. He's had Jonas to himself for a whole week. I didn't bake all these muffins and nut loaves just for the noon meal or for those young ones to snatch when they pass through my kitchen. I made some for Charles and for Jonas, too."

"May I go with you when you deliver them?"

"Most certainly not."

The scarlet crept back into Sydney's face; then she saw Griselda laughing at her.

"I intend to take milk and buns to Abigail's room so she and the children can have a party this morning. And I want you to take a treat down to Jonas. Kersten will be along later this morning for a cooking lesson. Although—God forgive me for judging her—the girl has no real talent with cooking as far as I can see. I'll just send the sweet rolls back to the vicarage with her."

"Whenever I see her, Kersten is quite curious about the O'Reilly children. You'd think she was writing a report on them."

Mrs. Quigley slapped the flour from her hands. "Don't get yourself involved, Sydney. But you're right about Kersten. She's a pretty little thing with a dozen questions about Danny and Keeley when she works with me here in the kitchen. I just go about my business as though I never heard her."

As she spoke, she deftly arranged some bread and muffins on a china platter. She stepped back to admire her own work before laying a linen cloth on top. "Jonas will think you baked these for him. It worked with Arthur."

"I've never baked in my life."

"Too busy running that corporation of yours, huh? Don't get too busy and miss the lasting things of life. Jonas likes his sweets with cream and jam. I put a little on the platter. Now get a scurry on you and get down to his cottage before he's out mending the fence or ordering the gardeners around."

Sydney's hand flew to her hair, finger-combing it.

"You look just fine. Now go on. And tell him you want tea to go with the muffins. He can put a kettle over that fireplace of his, and it will be quite cozy for the two of you. And don't you come back until you've talked things out."

As Sydney passed in front of the manor, she saw Griselda standing in the window, smiling.

Sydney had never gone inside the cottage before. Now, with her heart thumping and Mrs. Quigley's baked goods on a hand-painted china plate, she made her way over the flagstone path.

From the manor, she had a side view of the cottage, but approaching now, the whole place seemed concealed by overhanging branches and high hedges. Coming around the taller hedges, she had her first real glimpse of the weaver's cottage. Two chimneys jutted above its low thatched roof, and rambling roses framed the door. More flowers lined the walkway to the stone steps, the sunlight making their lavender and pink petals glow. Off to her left came the sweet smell of honeysuckle and a more intoxicating odor of fermented apples.

A black umbrella sat in a brass urn on the side of the steps, within easy reach should an afternoon rain squall hit while she was visiting. She reached out to tap the brass knocker and realized that the door stood ajar.

"Jonas, it's Sydney."

Silence. Not even TopGun sniffed at the door.

As she tapped gently, the door swung back. "Anybody home?"

She stepped into the cluttered room cautiously. A dirty cup and saucer had been left on the lamp table, newspapers were strewn all over the floor, and Jonas's night slippers lay by the chair. Still the room, peculiarly masculine, had a cozy, lived-in satisfaction with an iron fireplace on the far wall, a hearth rug in front of it, and a glittering sword in its sheath hanging above the mantel.

From where she stood, she saw an answering machine that was blinking with a message of its own. She was lured across the room by the framed photograph of a pretty young woman on the mantel.

"Oh, hello!" The greeting came from behind her.

She whirled around to face Jonas and his black-and-white collie. Jonas's gaze strayed to the mantel and back to Sydney.

"The door was ajar. I just came in," she said matter-of-factly.

His thick black brows arched. "I see that you did."

She held out the plate. "I'm sorry for barging in on you, but I brought a peace offering. Griselda said you'd make us tea."

"I can't think of anything I'd like better than having tea with you." He grinned, shut the dog out, and tossed his jacket on the chair. "I'll stir the fire and put the kettle on."

"Griselda said you'd do it that way."

"What else did Griselda tell you?"

"She said to pretend I baked the muffins myself."

He laughed, a deep pleasant chuckle, a happy sound like those moments together on the hillside. He came to her side in a few long strides and took the plate from her. As he peeked under the cloth, his eyes glowed. "Hmm. As though I wouldn't recognize her baking. Smells great! And she remembered the jam and cream."

Setting the plate down, he bent to strike a match to the kindling. "This won't take long."

"Jonas, where did that sword above the mantel come from?" The flames leaped around the kindling. He stood, his shoulder brushing hers. "That's the Admiral's ceremonial sword. It's the one he wore when he was in full dress uniform. When I was promoted to Lieutenant Commander, he gave it to me."

"You must be proud."

"I'm not likely to earn one myself. So, yes, I am proud to own it. And now with Dad ill—"

Her arm tingled at the twill of his sweater against it. "Don't underrate yourself." She looked up at him. "Abigail thinks you're as fine an officer as the Admiral."

Flecks of gray in his blue eyes overshadowed the sadness. "What else does Abigail say about me?"

Sydney laughed softly. "Over the last several weeks? That you're charming. Good looking. Intelligent. Trustworthy. That you'll go to the top. Even to a higher rank than your father."

"In other words, in Abby's eyes, I'm perfect?"

"Abigail tells me she has a thousand reasons for loving you."

He laughed. "Name just one."

"She's grateful to you for coming home."

"For the first time in my life, I think my dad needs me."

"He has always needed you. You just didn't know it."

"At first I thought about placing my father in a Navy residence. Now, I know I can't do it. I haven't worked out the details yet, but Dad has the right to live out his life here."

"I'm sure Lady Willoughby would want that."

He frowned. "And what do you know about Lady Willoughby?"

"Enough to know she would want you to take care of Abigail as well."

She moved away from him and inched her way along the wall, studying the pictures there. "If you keep the manor going for your father, does that mean you will have to give up the Navy?"

He followed her. "No. The Navy is my life. I'll make arrangements for others to come in and help Abigail and Griselda."

"And if Abby's heart gives out?"

"I would grieve for her, but there would be no regrets. With Dad I would grieve for an unhealed relationship. With Dad I never quite measured up, and now, with his health the way it is, we will never be able to set things right."

"When I'm with him, he talks about his son all the time."

"You seem to bring the best out of my father—and me. My father's plumb line was always ramrod straight—no bending, no allowance for error or deviation from the Willoughby standard. These days I no longer try to measure up."

"I don't believe that for a moment, Jonas. Coming home and sacrificing your chance to command a ship of your own is proof enough of that." She swallowed the rest of her curiosity and asked, "Were these all your ships?"

"Mine. Dad's. The other pictures were school photos taken at Gordonstoun and Dartmouth. And flying school."

She stopped by the picture from Gordonstoun. "You were really young there."

"I was head boy then. The lad on the playing field was our star rugby player. He won awards for rifle shooting." Jonas's face clouded. "I should have removed that picture, but he was one of Abigail's boys. He left a long time ago."

"Why?"

"I figured he left to fight with the IRA. It turned out that I was right."

She turned. "Is he Keeley's father? The missing Irishman?"

He said angrily, "Yes." He reached up to remove the picture.

Sydney put her hand on his arm. "Don't. Whatever politics came between the two of you, you were classmates and friends once. It's part of your past."

His voice was deep, his tone querulous. "You just don't understand the Irish question—the problem with the IRA."

"But I do understand the cry of a little girl. Someday you can show Keeley that picture. To Keeley he is not a terrorist. He's her father, and she loves him. She's just a frightened, lonely, five-year-old."

The kettle whistled persistently. He whirled to grab it. "I almost forgot. Get the muffins, would you? I'll pour the tea."

Moments later, Sydney gazed out the kitchen window with the teacup balanced in her hand. The magnificent English garden spread out from the house, past white marguerites that lay close to the ground. Far down the hill she could see an arbor of crimson roses. "The gardens are beautiful, Jonas."

"Abigail and my mother spent hours out there with the gardeners. Of course, Mother sometimes sat beneath one of the aspen or birch trees and watched Abigail work. But between them, they turned it into a place of beauty."

A place that she didn't want to leave behind. "Where were you when the work was being done?"

"Sitting on Mother's lap or spading the soil with Abigail."

"I'm going to hate leaving all of this."

"Then stay. Stay longer."

She laughed. "I have a corporation to run."

"I know. You keep reminding me."

Far to her left stood the stables and the grassland where the horses grazed. What had once been a moat in medieval times was a serene man-made lake now, a massive water tower beside it.

"The water tower mars this lovely setting," she observed.

"It's our reservoir for emergencies—a security factor in case of a dry season or fires. It's up to Lucas to keep the generator in mint condition. Boris is too old to tend it now."

Her eyes went back to the gardens. "Has it always been this lovely?"

"The gardens were overrun with weeds for a time during my long absence. And the manor was in a state of disrepair. I just wish Abby had told me she needed funds. But a year and a half ago someone left her money in a Swiss account, and she was able to get the manor repaired and the garden back the way she liked it."

The Broadshire Account. Mother and Dad's gift to Abigail.

"Fortunately, I have Dad's power of attorney now. Abby won't lack for funds ever again. Everything you see and everything out front belongs to us. Two hundred and fifty acres of it." He took her cup and set it aside. "All of this will belong to me someday, and I will have no one to share it with me if you go away. Sydney, I've been home for twelve hours trying to work up the courage to come and see you."

"Does it take courage?" she whispered.

"It takes courage to tell you what I want to tell you."

He was so close she could see the beat of his heart through his sweater. Could hear the thundering beat of her own.

"I don't want you to go away, Sydney. I love you."

He drew her closer and tilted her chin toward him. As he leaned down and his lips touched hers, the telephone rang.

A persistent ring like a trumpet blast, shattering their moment together.

Chapter 29

Captain McIntyre's voice roared over the wire. "Commander, there's a Learjet flying off course across Scotland with your friend Jock Hollinsworth in the pilot's seat."

Jonas snapped the television on:

"For those just tuning in, we are following the flight of a runaway corporate jet. . . . Identity of the pilot is being withheld. . . ."

"He's climbing erratically. That's not Jock's style."

"He's on automatic pilot. Air traffic requested escort when the jet veered off course. They've deployed two fighter jets."

"Are they from my old squadron?" Jonas asked.

"Yes, and they know Hollinsworth is on board. The wires into Northwood are jammed. The jets tracking him report no visible signs of life in the cabin and frosted windows in the cockpit."

"Then he's run out of oxygen. Is he flying alone?"

"He was scheduled to pick up two passengers in Stockholm. He was out of Helsinki on time but hasn't followed his flight pattern since leaving Stockholm. If the jet crosses over Ireland, they will shoot it down. Why the fool is logging hours on a commercial run, I'll never know."

"The privately owned aircraft en route to London veered west over Newcastle. . .unconfirmed reports coming in believe the chase planes are waiting for the order to intercept and destroy."

On the screen, the twin-engine plane with its long wings looked like a white eagle soaring. Jock had called it a beauty—white with burgundy stripes and burgundy leather seats inside. It hadn't been ten days since Jonas had stood with Jock, talking about the future. Now he was waiting for his plane to run out of fuel and crash. Or, with one word from the prime minister, the jet pilots would hear the order to fire and blow the Learjet out of the sky.

"The runaway jet is being tracked by fighter jets dispatched from a Scottish base. It is estimated that the plane drifting on automatic pilot will cross into Ireland within minutes. . . . The name of the Navy pilot is still being withheld."

"Captain, Jock's wife may be pregnant. She's in London."

"She's here at Northwood. . .waiting out the end with us."

When the call ended, Jonas looked at Sydney. "Jock is on board. They lost contact with him shortly after takeoff."

Sydney's face turned ghostly. In three strides he was at her side, his arm around her. "Sydney, nothing can be done. But Jock is not in pain. I promise you that. Within seconds, he'd be unconscious from oxygen starvation. A window blowout. A broken seal. Something caused decompression. Without oxygen, he would be euphoric one moment, disoriented and unconscious the next."

As he stood by her side, Jonas noticed the light blinking on the answering machine. He pushed the play button and heard "Friday, 9:25 a.m.," and then Jock's voice, "Commander, it's Jock. I have to talk to you. Where are you?"

Jock went on muttering. "I leave Stockholm at 9:10, en route to London. No. . .I think the plane took off with unwanted cargo. If I don't make it—" He started humming.

"Jonas, why would he spend half of a phone message humming a song? He knows your anger with the IRA. He's too close a friend to aggravate you with an Irish lyric," Sydney said.

"Jock did crazy things."

"But Kathleen is the one who would want to know when he was taking off—so she could meet him when he arrived in London. What did he mean unwanted cargo? Your friend wasn't transporting drugs, was he?"

Nettled, Jonas said, "Of course not. He did things like that—whistling, passing along jokes between us with a song. On some of our routine flights, Jock would hum some message. Something that just the two of us understood."

"But this time he sounded desperate. It sounds like the plane he was supposed to be flying took off without him. Jonas, he sang that same song at the picnic."

She tried to recall the lyrics as Jock had sung them and could only grab at a phrase or two. Something about green leaves in December and fragrant roses dying. And snows covering a land that had never known freedom. She remembered Jock telling them that the Irish thrived on laughter and music, yet their land did not know freedom, and only the fast-flowing rivers of their land ran free. She poked the replay button on Jonas's answering machine and listened to Jock again. In the middle of a sentence the message ended abruptly, as though someone had cut him off.

Jonas's voice cracked as he asked, "What difference does it make if he was humming an Irish lyric? Any moment, he'll never sing again. Whatever happened on board, he didn't have time to don an oxygen mask. That Learjet is on automatic."

"For how long?" she whispered.

"Until it crashes. But they'll shoot it down rather than risk a crash-landing in a populated city in Ireland. One word from the Prime Minister and they will blow Jock out of the sky."

"The runaway plane is over the Irish Sea, nearing the coast of the Emerald Isle."

"No, Jock. No." Jonas groaned as the jet lost its cruising altitude and plunged in a spiraling arc through the clouds toward earth, leaving a vapor trail behind her. It plunged into the sea, the twisted debris surfacing moments after the plane dove into its watery grave. The chase fighters lowered, circling above the sea. Then, as thousands of listeners watched, they changed course and headed back toward Scotland.

Jonas didn't move. Sydney switched off the television and hit the replay button on the answering machine again. "Friday, 9:25 a.m.," the mechanical voice said. And then Jock's voice, "Commander, it's Jock. I have to talk to you. Where are you? . . . Jonas, pick up that phone. . . I don't have long. . . We're still holed up in Stockholm. I may have lost the dart game. . . Scheduled to pick up two passengers in Stockholm, but the men who showed up—" The message ended abruptly.

"Jonas, what time did Jock's plane take off for London?"

"Nine-ten. And on schedule."

For the third time she hit the replay button and the mechanical voice with the nasal twang came through clearly. "Friday, 9:25 a.m."

He stared at her. "Jock called after the plane took off. If he wasn't on board, then someone commandeered that jet."

"So what happened?"

"Everything was normal out of Helsinki. Whatever happened took place in Sweden, where he was supposed to pick up two passengers."

"Was he telling you the destination—to a land that didn't have freedom where only the rivers ran free?"

He fixed his gaze on the BBC telecast, still repeating the same news. "Only a fool would try passing deliberately into Irish airspace—and refuse to respond to traffic control. He'd try bluffing first. Declare an emergency. No, whoever was in that cabin was unconscious. Jock may have been telling us that the theft was accomplished by Irish terrorists. A plane like that would be an asset to the IRA. You're brilliant, sweetheart."

He whirled around, grabbed his phone, and called McIntyre. "Captain," he said when McIntyre answered, "I don't think Jock Hollinsworth was on board that jet."

"Don't be a fool, Willoughby."

"He left a message on my answering machine fifteen minutes after the Learjet took off. Someone else was flying that plane."

"You sound certain."

"A gut reaction. There may be an Irish tie-in. When Jock and his wife visited us here in Stow-on-the-Woodland, we had dinner at Chutman's Pub. Jock challenged just about everyone to a game of darts—and he talked freely about his trip. Someone at the pub may have wanted that plane more than he did."

Sydney strained to hear the captain's answer. "You're crazy, Willoughby."

"Sir, the plane took off from Stockholm out of a private airstrip. We need to start looking there. Captain, may I have your permission to fly up there where Jock was last seen?"

"Is that wise, Willoughby?"

"He was my wingman—my best friend. Jock would do the same for me."

"All right. I've spoken to the chief inspector in the area. I told him I would send one of my own men to undertake an investigation. But if something goes wrong, we will deny sending you there. But, Willoughby, if you find him, accompany his body back to the base in Scotland."

"For proper burial?" he asked.

"No, for an autopsy."

"I don't intend to bring Jock back in a body bag. I expect to find him alive."

"There are reports that his uncle is under suspicion."

"Rodney Christopher wouldn't harm his nephew."

"Greed can be a strange bedfellow. Rumors have it that Christopher has Irish ties. For all we know, Jock Hollinsworth may have been scheduled to transport arms to the IRA."

⌇

Discovering Jock's body came within hours, more speedily than anyone expected. With the quick arrest and confession of Rodney Christopher, Jonas and the inspection team were led to an old warehouse close to the private airstrip in Stockholm where Jock was last seen. Jonas dropped down beside his friend's bruised and battered body. Jock lay in an embryo curl, blood crusted at his mouth. But he was alive.

Jonas gripped his hand. "Jock, you're going to be okay."

"My wife?"

"We'll get word to Kathleen right away. Sydney is with her."

"Did my uncle make it?"

"He wasn't flying the plane, Jock. Someone else was."

"Impossible. He'd never let anyone touch that plane." His voice faded. "I have to talk to him."

"No can do. They just arrested your uncle."

Jock tried to open his eyes. "For what?"

"For attempting to transport illegal arms into Ireland. And for conspiracy to transport his Learjet into the hands of the IRA—at the risk of your life."

"No, Jonas, he wouldn't do that."

"I'm sorry, old man. But we've always been up front with each other. Your uncle has already confessed."

He tried to lift his head and failed miserably. "Why?" he groaned.

"He was secretly involved in the Irish movement. But when I told him you were missing, he broke down. If he hadn't told us about the warehouse, we might not have reached you in time."

Jonas beckoned to the medical team. The medics tried to roll Jock to a more comfortable position. "Don't. Don't move me. I—I have to talk to Jonas. I told Uncle Rodney that something was wrong. The next thing I remember was a blow to my head."

Jock's body jerked as he was given an injection. He struggled to speak. "I think the plane was in the air when I called you. All I could do was leave a message on your machine. And then. . .two friends of my uncle broke in on me. The last thing I remember is being tossed in the back of the truck." His speech slurred. "You'll call Kathleen—"

"Right away."

As they lifted Hollinsworth on the stretcher, the Swedish inspector said, "He looks bad. Do you think your friend will make it?"

Jonas flashed a grim smile. "He'll make it. He has a score to settle with his uncle. And his reputation to salvage for working with that man."

"Can I give you a lift somewhere, Commander?"

"To the hospital. As soon as I know Jock is going to be all right, I'll head back to England. To his wife—and my girl."

In the days that followed, Jonas slipped into a brooding silence. As they walked together among the primrose bushes, Sydney said, "Now that I know that Jock will recover, I've made my reservation. I'm leaving Thursday, Jonas."

He whirled around to face her and gripped her arms. "Is there nothing I can do to make you stay?"

"Nothing. I think it's best for both of us. So much has happened—you need time to sort it all out. Abigail. Your dad. Jock."

"And you. You're the one who matters to me now."

"We'll stay in touch. We'll write—"

As they resumed walking, she linked her arm in his and pressed her head against his shoulder. "We knew I would go home someday."

"But I want you to stay." He leaned down and kissed her on the top of her head. "I love you. It won't be the same here without you."

"You won't be here, Jonas. You're going back to Northwood next week. Things will settle down to normal. And Dr. Wallis and Charles promised Abigail that they would arrange for more staff to help Griselda."

His fingers tightened around hers. "I'm grateful, Sydney."

As they reached the manor, Charles plodded up the stone steps. "Charles!" she called. "What are you doing here?"

He turned, his face old and tired, his blue eyes pale and heavy lidded. "I have come with bad news for Abigail."

"No, Charles," Jonas warned. "That Learjet crash and Jock's injuries have upset her enough."

Sydney nudged Jonas. "Charles, Jock is better, but you look as though you haven't slept for days."

"I haven't." He hesitated. "Jeff and Chandler insisted that I come now. It's about Conan O'Reilly."

Sydney's grip silenced Jonas. "What about Conan?" she asked.

"He's dead."

"Dead!"

Charles nodded. "You were right, Sydney, when you said he was staying in the vicarage with me." He peered over the tops of his glasses at Jonas. "I kept him in the Jacobean room. Abigail told me that you and the other boys played there when you were young, Jonas. Before my time at St. Michael's."

Jonas's gaze turned icy. "I trusted you, Charles. But you protected an Irish terrorist. You and Abigail?"

"She knows nothing. The last she saw of Conan was the night she had her heart attack. May I see Abigail alone, please?"

"Let him, Jonas. We'll be with you shortly."

Twenty minutes later, when Sydney and Jonas stepped into Abigail's room, Charles was putting the communion cups aside. Abigail held out a hand to each of them. "How is Jock?"

Jonas squeezed her fingers. "Better. Kathleen is with him."

"Charles took communion with me." She smiled, a serene look on her face. Turning to him, she said, "I'm ready to hear the bad news now that the children are with me. It's about Conan, isn't it?"

Charles nodded. "He's gone, Abigail. He was seriously injured, but he refused to see a doctor. He died from those wounds."

"Was he with you all that time?"

"I wasn't there the night he died. Friends buried him when I was in London with the archbishop."

"Then he was buried without a funeral."

Jonas turned livid. "He didn't deserve a funeral, Abigail."

~

Lucas Sullivan sat at his shortwave radio and twisted the dials. The crash of the Learjet just short of the Irish coastline had been a personal loss. What had gone wrong? What did he know of decompression and hypoxia? And what had become of Rodney Christopher? Had he been arrested? No matter where Lucas tuned in, the plane crash was stale news. Yesterday, Jock Hollinsworth's face had been sprawled across the television screen and his condition upgraded from critical to satisfactory. The investigation of the crash site was ongoing. How long would it take them to realize that weapons destined for the IRA were part of the debris?

Fools, he thought. *Better if it had been Hollinsworth dead, not two of my good men.*

Joseph Hollinsworth had outwitted him. Would he link the plane to Lucas? Not likely, but he might trace talks of his plane back to the picnic at

Stow-on-the-Woodland or the dart game at Chutman's Pub. Then Jonas Willoughby and Jock Hollinsworth would begin to put it all together. It seemed like everything began falling apart the day he found Sydney Barrington's riding stick in his room. What had she told Jonas? He had mistrusted her from the day she walked into the manor. He despised her now. But why had she chosen to keep silent about his shortwave radio set?

For his own safety he must move on. But first he would send one last message to Belfast. And then he would destroy the stables. He could not risk moving the technical equipment in time, and he regretted that his actions might cost the life of the Admiral. He had, after all, a fondness for the old man.

Conan was another burden. Convincing Charles that Conan was dead and buried was the best way to ward off any questions from Charles and the Church of England. He didn't care what they did with the dotty clergyman. They'd already put him out to pasture when they sent him to the smallest of flocks here in Stow-on-the-Woodland. What else could they do but retire him?

Lucas's plans for Stow-on-the-Woodland had failed, but his men were strong enough to start over somewhere else. Their cause was greater than any peace negotiations. He found satisfaction that the destruction of the stables would forever cut off the tunnel entry into the bottom floor of the manor. But he could not bring himself to destroy the splendid horses.

He had rescued the ammunition from the stockpiles hidden in the tunnel. The thought that the heat of fire would cause the tunnel entry to cave in gave him pleasure. He gathered up the discs from the computer and placed his gun collection in the back of the lorry. He would order the schoolmaster to drive the truck to the North Country. As the manor was slowly enshrouded in darkness, Lucas led the horses from the stable and tethered them one by one on a high hill.

He turned to the young sheepherder who met him there.

"Don't take Commander Willoughby's stallion."

"But he's a thoroughbred, Lucas."

"The stallion is as British as Jonas. Leave him." He rubbed the neck of the chestnut stallion, his favorite, and saddled him. "Take this one to the hills until I am ready to leave. O'Reilly may not live long enough to ride out with me, but take a second horse just in case."

"And the pony?"

"The pony belongs to Keeley O'Reilly."

At midnight he spread stacks of hay through the stables and around the circumference of his room. In the last half hour he sorted through his papers, stowed the most important ones in his briefcase, and left the others to burn. He saturated his mattress with gasoline and leaned it against the computer and wireless systems. He set fire to the wastebasket, knowing that it would smolder, giving him time to escape. Then, emptying the can of gasoline on the stairwell, he descended for the last time. Coils of smoke trailed from his room. He was going out in style. He struck another match to one of the stalls and fled.

Plumes of smoke darkened over Stow-on-the-Woodland as Lucas made his way stealthily to the primary school, where Conan was growing more restless than ever. He considered leaving him behind, letting him really die, but he could not do that to Keeley. The child's father was dying, but it was better for both of them to return to Ireland. He owed Conan O'Reilly that much.

Chapter 30

Barrington Enterprises won the Navy contract on the aircraft carriers, but the win did little to lift Sydney's sinking spirit. She stared down at the half-packed suitcases. Once she left the Cotswolds, she might never see Jonas again, not until the carriers slipped into the water at the Jarrow Shipyard in Tyne. He promised to be there for the launching, but going on without him now left her wobbly-kneed. Never had she loved anyone as she loved Jonas Willoughby. From that first day by the primroses, he had snipped at her heart strings with those pruning shears.

She flattened another blouse in the suitcase as someone banged repeatedly on her door. "Fire! Fire, Miss Barrington!"

She flung the door back. Boris's face flushed with excitement. "We have to get Miss Abigail to safety! The stables are burning; come, quickly!"

He shuffled off as close to a run as she had seen him do. She shoved her bare feet into her shoes and followed him.

"Where's Jonas? Where's Lucas?" she cried. "Is Lucas—"

"No one has seen Lucas, and Jonas went for his father."

"Boris, where are the fire trucks?"

He stared at her, dumbfounded. "We have no fire trucks. Just the water tower, if we can get it to work."

They found Abigail standing by her bed, trembling. Boris grabbed a coat from her closet and forced her arms in it.

"The children, Boris?"

"Griselda and Santos went for the children, Miss Abigail."

"Sit down," Sydney said gently. "Let me get your shoes on."

"No, get my riding boots from the closet. They should still fit me. Boris, grab blankets and wet washcloths for the children. They'll have trouble breathing."

"No," Sydney cautioned. "We have to get you outside."

They practically lifted her and ran. Abigail's booted toes dragged across the parquet to the front door. Plumes of smoke rose above the village as they rushed down the stone steps.

"I forgot my medicine." She coughed. "The Admiral! Sydney,

Boris—go for the Admiral. I'll be all right."

"Jonas went for his father," Boris assured her.

As they rounded the side of the house, they heard the crackling roar of the fire and saw the stables engulfed in flames. They found Griselda and the children in the primrose garden and gently lowered Abigail on a wooden bench.

Griselda stood in her flannel nightgown, an arm around two of the children. She stared transfixed at the shooting flames, unaware that the air had thickened with the smell of smoke. The schoolmaster and several stronger men had converged on the water tower, attaching hoses to the valves. As the water hit the fire, it sizzled into steam. Others beat the flames with towels and blankets, trying to halt the rapid spread of fire through the tall grass as the wind swept the burning embers toward the manor.

Keeley flew to Sydney. "My pony, Sydney. My pony."

Gregor's dark eyes were like neon lights in the flames. "Your pony's safe. The schoolmaster told me. He said someone turned the horses out of their stalls before the fire started."

Sydney was shocked. If someone had set the horses free, the fire was no accident. "Is Lucas fighting the fire?" she asked.

Gregor shrugged. "No one has seen him."

She put her free arm around him and thought of the terror he had known in Kosovo. "Are you all right, Gregor?"

He leaned against her, his dark eyes brimming with tears. "Griselda told me to be brave for the little children."

She ruffled his hair. "Gregor, have you seen Jonas yet?"

"Him and TopGun went back for the Admiral." He turned his head and cried out with delight, "There's Jonas!"

Jonas struggled toward them with his father's limp body in his arms and the dog close on his heels. He was breathing heavily as he reached them. Glaring at Abigail, he asked, "Did you have to go so far to protect Conan?"

"Don't even think that, Jonas." She made a place for the Admiral on the bench beside her, and Jonas eased his father down. Then he ran to join the other men.

Smoke drove the firefighters back. With a deafening rumble the roof and one wall of the stables caved in. The roar of the fire and the crackling of walls collapsing terrified Sydney. Above the popping explosions inside the stable, she heard the grinding gasp of the power generator nearby. The sound faded. Someone cursed. Boris tried to fire the generator again. It sputtered to action, and in minutes the water pump flowed freely.

The men from the village shouted as the flames leaped toward the manor. "Get the children farther back!"

"Griselda," Sydney urged, "we must get the children back!"

Jonas shrugged in disgust as he ran past them. "She doesn't hear you, Sydney. Even if she did, she wouldn't move away. This is her home. She'd have nowhere else to go."

"Griselda!" Sydney cried again. "Let's move farther back."

The woman was too dazed, paralyzed.

Abigail went to her and gently said, "Griselda, it's Abigail."

"It's like the London Blitz, Abby. Are the planes coming?"

"There are no planes, no bombs. The stables are on fire. We have to keep the children safe."

Danny's scream brought her to her senses. She gathered him to her and moved back as more plumes of smoke rose above them.

"I forgot my medicine," Abigail said, her voice raspy. "And the blankets for the children. The smoke is making it hard for me to breathe. We need wet cloths to put over our faces."

Moments later Sydney asked, "Where's Gregor?"

"Oh no. He must have gone for my medicine."

"I'll find him." The smoke burned Sydney's eyes as she ran back toward the house, slipping and sliding where the water had turned the ground to mud. She was near the West Wing now and saw tiny flames crawling up the side of the building toward the Admiral's room. She heard the shattering of glass as the windows blew. The flames licked higher, catching the eaves on fire.

"Jonas!" she screamed. "The house is on fire!"

They were dragging a hose toward the West Wing as she stumbled up the front steps and found Gregor on the top one, crying. He clutched Abigail's medicine bottle in one hand, a fistful of wet cloths in the other. He thrust the cloths at her. "I'm afraid, Sydney."

"We all are. It took a brave boy to go for her medicine." She took only a second to hug him against her, and then they were running through the smoke-filled night back to the others. As they reached them, the rest of the stable walls tumbled in and only the blackened silhouette of the old stables remained.

As the smoke rose, ash fell back on them. "The worst is over," Jonas said. "It'll take another two or three hours for the fire to die out. I've left the schoolmaster in charge."

Jonas looked exhausted, his face covered with soot. One sweater sleeve was torn away, the hairs on one arm singed. He squeezed Sydney's shoulder. "I'm glad you're all right. Thank God my forefathers were wise enough to set up a water system."

Abigail's hand still rested comfortably on the Admiral's arm, but his groggy indifference troubled Jonas. The old man's eyelids hung heavy, and his speech had slurred.

"Lucas?" the Admiral asked. "Is he safe? We have a ship to fire up. We're going on winter patrol off the coast of Ireland."

"Lucas is gone, Dad."

The vacant eyes stared at him in the darkness. "Did Lucas do this after all I've done for him?"

"Dad, why would you say that?"

He frowned, searching for his answer. "He stole money from my black box the other night. He thought I was sleeping."

Abigail patted the Admiral's hand. "Tobias, I'm still here to take care of you."

Jonas shook his head. "Don't worry, Abby. Dad's confused."

Sydney said, "Lucas is the only man in the whole village who missed the flames shooting in the air. Where was he? I think your father's right. Lucas had constant access to the stables. Who else would have saved Keeley's pony and your stallion?"

Jonas glanced where the stables once stood. "You don't think—"

"No, we would have heard him screaming. But you don't scream when you're setting a fire."

His anger roiled. "You're reading it wrong, Sydney. Lucas served with the Royal Navy. He's been Dad's steward for twenty years. He wouldn't do a thing like this."

Exasperated, she said, "Tomorrow ask your commanding officer and his intelligence team to sift through the ashes. You'll find evidence of a sophisticated computer system and a sender and receiver radio set. Why would the Admiral's caregiver need those? I know he had them. I was in his room once." When his eyes hardened, she said hastily, "I was with Keeley."

"He disliked children."

"But he felt a particular bond with Keeley and you know he loved horses. I think he let all the horses go free before he started the fire. You can stop blaming everything on Abigail. Abigail didn't burn the stables. She doesn't even have the strength to walk that far."

As they stared at the charred ruins, Sydney said, "I'm sorry, Jonas. It's just that Abigail loves you too much to ever hurt you. And you seem blind to her love."

He struggled to bring his eyes level with Sydney's. "We may never know how the fire started. Now help me. We must get my father back inside."

"Take the Admiral to my room," Abigail told him. "Tobias can sleep there, and I will sit with him. Griselda—"

The housekeeper stood shivering in her nightgown, a shawl thrown around her shoulders. The children huddled beside her.

"Griselda."

She turned and faced her old friend. "I'm here, Abigail."

"Would you take the children inside while Boris and Jonas assess the damage? And, Sydney, make some tea for all of us."

"That's my job, Abby," Griselda protested. "I made some sweet bread and cookies. Really, I should make the tea."

"Not tonight. Tonight I want you to be with the children. I want you to rest. Sydney will check in on you later."

$\sim$

An hour later Jonas discarded his ash-covered boots at the front door. The boots were waterlogged, the soles black from soot. He went directly to Abigail's room and found her spooning hot tea between the Admiral's lips.

Sir James swallowed, but his gaze remained vacant. There wasn't a flicker when Jonas entered. "Is Dad still dazed?"

"Lucas may have given him some sleeping medication—enough to keep him quiet when Lucas left the room."

Jonas's jaw jerked. "Griselda keeps his medicine in the kitchen."

Abigail smiled at him, her eyes sad. "Lucas knew his way around the kitchen. Now we'll say no more of it."

His gaze traversed the room, searching for Sydney. She came from the bathroom, a cup of scalding tea in her hands. She kissed his sooty cheek and handed him the tea. "Tell us what you've found, Jonas."

For a second he couldn't take his eyes from her. She was leaving soon, and he had done nothing to stop her from going away. He swallowed his pride, his yearning. "The stables are gone but still smoldering—and two of the stallions unaccounted for."

"Lost in the fire?" Sydney asked.

"We don't know. Some of the men offered to stay through the night.

They'll hose down anything that sparks again."

Her eyes still locked with his. "There's a wide patch of destruction between the house and stables. The walls of the kitchen were seared and some windows blown out from the heat."

He glanced back at his father asleep against Abigail's thick pillows. "The West Wing suffered considerable water damage. Some of Dad's Navy pictures are destroyed, and the rug is ruined. I'm glad he's resting. It would break his heart to see how close Lady Willoughby's property came to being destroyed."

Someone cleared his throat behind Jonas. He turned and saw Charles filling the doorway, a prayer book in his hands.

"How dare you come here!" Jonas exclaimed. "Wasn't the message you brought to us last night enough? Do you think I appreciated your telling us that Conan O'Reilly was gone?"

"I've come as your friend, Jonas."

"The friend of Her Majesty? The friend of Stow-on-the-Woodland? You hid a terrorist. Have you no conscience?"

"My conscience battled me all the while. But no matter what you think of me, I saw Conan O'Reilly as a prodigal in need of a Father."

Jonas's bitterness spewed out. "So you wanted to be his father? His own father failed him pitifully."

"I wanted God to be his Father."

"Charles," Abigail said, "you are welcome as long as I am here. But knowing you, Reverend, you always come with a purpose in mind. Perhaps even with a prayer."

"Abigail, I was thinking how fortunate we all are—"

"Fortunate?" Jonas exploded. "We just had a fire."

The catch in Charles's voice stilled him. "Dr. Wallis set up an emergency clinic on the south wing. Two of our villagers were overcome with smoke inhalation. One of the sheep farmers singed the hair on his face and arms. The pub owner has burns on both hands. They'll blister, but he'll be fine in a few weeks."

"So you expect me to be grateful?" Jonas asked.

"Jonas, the whole village turned out to help you, and my American houseguests were out there working hard beside the other men with no thought to their own safety."

"And Santos?" Abigail asked. "Where was he?"

"There as well, with smoke smudges on his cheeks and his clothes reeking of smoke. I saw a new Santos this evening, Abigail. A selfless man working hard to prevent the flames reaching the artwork at Broadshire Manor."

"Poor Santos. I never even thought of the art treasures."

"Just about your children," Charles said kindly. "They were always first in your mind, Abigail. You left an imprint on Santos's life as well. That's why he's here—why he stayed with the firefighters this evening instead of tearing down the tapestries from the walls or carrying paintings to safety." Charles's shoulders bent forward. "I've been with Griselda and the children. They're frightened, but she's with them. It was Griselda who said we all have need of healing in this house."

Jonas glared back. "No one from the manor was hurt."

"Since the night of Abigail's heart attack you have all been hurting. It's time to forgive one another. For past hurts." For a moment his eyes settled on Abigail and the Admiral. "To undo the past. To right the wrongs. The villagers—most of us—think Lucas was involved. I think the fire was more than a warning. More than the destructive act of one devious man. And until we know for certain—"

Jonas would have none of it. "All the sermons in the world can't erase the fact that you hid an IRA terrorist. What was wrong with you? The IRA killed your daughter."

"But I know Louise would not turn a wounded man out on the streets. I can understand if you cannot forgive me, Jonas, but I've come to ask you to hold a proper burial for Conan."

"Why didn't you give him a proper ceremony, as you call it?"

"I told you. I was in London with the archbishop, giving an accounting of harboring a wounded man in the vicarage."

"Were you completely honest with the archbishop, Charles?"

"I asked for time to consider the matter. And because of my long time with the church, he granted it. When I came back to the village, Lucas told me Conan was dead and buried."

"Lucas knew he was there?"

"Yes." Charles rubbed his hands distractedly. "Conan had a glimmering of faith in the end. He was born a Catholic. He'd forgotten all of that, but he still remembered Abigail praying for him. Louise was killed on his father-in-law's farm. That was shock enough, but when he learned that Louise was your fiancée, he was devastated. Even in illness, he wanted your friendship."

"I don't need your sermons, Charles."

"No, you need a Father's healing. A Father's restoration."

"My father never qualified."

"Because you wouldn't let him," Abigail defended.

"This morning as I walked about the village—knowing that my church will be taken from me—I climbed to the highest knoll and looked down on St. Michael's and knew that if I must, I will give it up. What I did for Conan came from my heart."

Abigail cried in alarm. "We won't let the archbishop send you away and close up St. Michael's again. If the archbishop fails us, no wonder Conan couldn't believe that a God of mercy was waiting to forgive him."

Jonas opened his mouth, but a look from Abigail silenced him. "Can't you understand? Jonas, both good and pain slip through God's fingers. You wanted to avenge Louise's death, but has it made you happy?"

"Where was God when Louise died?"

Charles said, "I must believe that a merciful God was in Ireland that day with my daughter—waiting for the angels themselves to carry her Home. The prophet Hosea says that God wants acknowledgment of Himself, Jonas. How long will you go on ignoring favor with a forgiving God?"

Jonas's eyes sought Sydney's again. She came to him and brushed back the ruffled strands of hair that the wind and fire had unsettled. "I think what Jonas really wants to know is whether your church will allow you to conduct a service for an enemy of this country?"

"Whatever objections they may have, it seems to me that every prodigal needs a listening ear—a gentle farewell."

Abigail's hand was motionless now. "Charles, if I had known that Conan was with you, you know I would have gone to him."

"I would have had to carry you there," he teased. "The Jacobean room is dark and airless. You would have wanted him removed from there at once."

"You did your best."

"The archbishop doesn't agree. I talked with him by phone once I knew that Conan was gone and admitted that I had broken the laws of the church protecting him. The church intends to retire me to the North Country. So what we do for Conan must be done quickly, Abigail."

In a flash of anger, she said, "I'll deal with the archbishop later. For now, Keeley and Danny O'Reilly are my concern."

Jonas steeled himself. Her words were directed to him now. "Conan was one of my boys. When I took his children in, I should have protected their father as well. But I didn't want to hurt you, Jonas. I haven't even found the courage to tell them that he's gone forever."

"I'll tell them," he offered huskily.

"No. I won't burden you with the children, Jonas."

Charles wrung his hands. "No matter what Jonas decides, Abigail, you and I will meet at Conan's grave—say, two days from now, and we'll have a memorial for a lost boy."

"I'll stay over long enough for the funeral," Sydney said. "And I think Jeff and Chandler will come."

"I'd have Kersten make us a funeral tea, Abigail, but I'm about to lose my house help. Last night she told me she is flying back to the States with Jeffrey."

The lamplight formed shadows on Abigail's frown. "Then something's going right. What will you do, Jonas?"

"I can't honor an enemy with a public funeral."

"Not honor, Jonas," Charles challenged. "Bury properly. Perhaps your conscience would let you do that. Have you called your commanding officer about Lucas yet? I can give them all the confirmation they need. Lucas was angry about the Northern Ireland agreements. Furious with his comrades for laying down arms." His expression held a measure of hope. "The cry for peace is much stronger than Lucas expected. But he's a strong leader. If he can get a small faction to follow him, one bombing would destroy everything."

Abigail pointed to a phone near her. "The lines are still open to Northwood. The fire didn't destroy the connection."

Jonas crossed the room with Sydney at his side. He wiped his palms on his trousers and took the phone. As he dialed in the number, she kissed him on the cheek. "Things will work out, Jonas. You can build the stables again."

"Better that I turn over the property to the National Trust and let them restore Broadshire Manor to its previous glory."

"We'll see. One step at a time."

"Will you stay with me, Sydney?" he asked. "Until Conan's funeral?"

"And after that?"

He was so close that the tweed of his torn sweater brushed her arm. His own smell of smoke and burning overpowered her usual French scent. She looked exhausted with rivulets of tears making uneven streams down her sooty face. Yearning for her gripped him.

"Yes—yes. Captain McIntyre? Commander Willoughby here."

He gave a brisk description of all that had happened. The fire. The possible betrayal of his father's steward. Conan's death.

"Is your father—and everyone else safe?"

"Captain, the Admiral is resting. Some of the firefighters were hurt, but no one at the manor was injured, although Lucas Sullivan must have intended harm to all of us."

"He was a classic sleeper, Commander. Living right there and using the manor as his headquarters."

"He always talked against the IRA dissidents."

"It's a small faction like Lucas who could ruin everything that has taken place at the conference table. Neither side wants any more violence in Northern Ireland. We don't want anything that will threaten the Ulster peace. That's why we wanted to find O'Reilly and that group still holding out with him."

And then Jonas—a proud, arrogant man as Charles had called him—said, "Sir, I'll resign my commission if it seems advisable. We had our man, Captain. A man I trusted and confided in, and I was too blind to see him. . . . He's gone, sir."

McIntyre's answer boomed back over the line. "We're not taking any resignations this year. Don't worry. Lucas Sullivan won't go far, Commander. We've been checking his background ever since my visit with the Admiral."

"You questioned his loyalty then?"

"Your father was alert enough to warn us. He told me when he was first retired a lot of gold braid came for visits. When the visitors dwindled, Mr. Sullivan didn't like it."

"But, sir, Sullivan was with the Royal Navy for years."

"He used the Service and your father to gain what he wanted. Stow-on-the-Woodland was a nice, quiet place for him to plan his war against any peace agreement. We believe now that Sullivan counted on the top brass from the Royal Navy dropping by for unexpected visits. He may have counted on being in on bits of information passed along whenever any of us visited the Admiral. Cordon off the area, Commander. We'll have military advisors there by morning. I want them to go through Sullivan's quarters."

"Sir, the stables were completely destroyed. Everything's in ashes. I should have known. You said it would be someone close at hand. Forgive me, sir, for not realizing that Lucas was using the Admiral and Broadshire Manor as headquarters."

He had used the words, and knew he was on the verge of seeking deeper forgiveness. He wanted inner peace. Tomorrow—or the next day—before

Sydney flew home, perhaps they could go to the vicarage together and talk with Charles. In spite of the heavy weight he was carrying this evening, Charles Rainford-Simms was a man of peace and joy. The peace and joy that Jonas needed. Something that he wanted for Sydney as well.

Captain McIntyre's blustery voice drew him back. "They'll sift through those ashes, Jonas. We have Sullivan's Navy records. His thumbprints. His photo. His history. We'll find him. And if he has sympathetic contacts there in the village, we'll find them. We're good at the waiting game. I just hope you're back to flying that Sea Harrier of yours or commanding your own ship by then. Good night, Commander."

Chapter 31

Sydney dressed in a striking dark suit for the walk down to St. Michael's churchyard. Somehow she could not bring herself to think of Conan O'Reilly as dead, not even with that memory of a gaunt young man on the hillside with an Irish twang and a catch in his voice when he spoke of his children. As sick as he was, she had thought him crafty enough to make his way safely out of Stow-on-the-Woodland. Was she the only one who questioned his sudden death and burial?

As she wandered down the wide hall, her high heels tapping against the parquet flooring, Jonas said, "Sydney."

She turned and met his smile. "Hi. You're not dressed for the memorial service yet."

"Come sit with me outside by the fountain."

She went gladly, happy that the white bench was too small for three people. "I've dreaded this day, Jonas. Mostly for the children and because Abigail is hurting."

"She's a strong woman."

"You say that when her heart is as weak as it is?"

"I'm talking about Abigail's inner strength. There's no flutter or missed beats to that one. No mother wants to bury her child, and Conan was as much one of hers as the rest of us."

You more than any of them.

"I have something to tell you," he said. "I won't be taking Edmund Gallagher to court. There's no need for that now."

"What happened?"

"I called his law offices in London this morning and spoke to the senior partners. Edmund Gallagher shot himself yesterday."

She felt a sudden chill. "Gallagher is dead?"

"Blackstone and Rentley threatened to have him disbarred. His career was over. What probably disgraced him even more was the loss of face here with old friends."

"Abigail would not push to that extreme."

"No, there were others who lost great sums through Edmund's

conniving. He tended to pick on widows with no immediate families. Thanks to your friend Jeff, Blackstone and Rentley were warned in time to correct these errors. They've combed through Edmund's files for days now. Once they told Edmund his career was over, he went back into his office and took his father's revolver out of the safe. For Edmund, greed was his downfall."

"Does Abigail know?"

"I just came from telling her. That on top of the memorial for Conan—and she's in for a rough day. But she's determined to walk down to the church on her own feet."

"We'll have to carry her back."

"Griselda is with her. They're old friends. But I don't know whether Keeley and Danny understand what's happening."

"Abigail and I talked with them last evening. Keeley cried so I took her to my room, and Danny stayed with Abigail."

"No wonder you both look exhausted, Sydney."

"Little children don't stay on their side of the bed."

He frowned. "This morning Abby said she had already lost a son, and losing Conan was more than she could bear. I'm not certain what she meant since he is the first of her hidden children to die."

She touched the back of his hand and ran her fingers gently over it. "Someday you'll understand." She glanced at his khaki shorts and cambric cloth shirt. "Are you going to the church, Jonas? You can walk down with me."

"You go along. I have something else to do."

"Your father is all right alone. He's so much better now."

"Boris has him up in the chair by the window so he can watch what's going on. He thinks it's a funeral at sea. He's commanding everything from his bridge. Last night when we talked, he finally remembered who Conan O'Reilly was. It's hard having Dad slip in and out of the present, but he had tears in his eyes when he told me, 'That boy and I used to walk by the Windrush.'"

"Did they?"

"Yes. A long time ago. Conan idolized my dad. I'm not sure why he and Dad hit it off so well, but they did. Abigail says Conan always wanted to be a Willoughby."

"You can't forgive Conan, can you, Jonas?"

He looked away, but she wasn't certain he was seeing anything beyond the fountain. Whatever had touched him—whatever he was struggling with inside—he would have to face his adversaries alone while the rest of them were gone.

She leaned over and kissed him warmly on the lips. "I love you, Jonas Willoughby. But Abigail is right. Until we forgive ourselves, we are never free to love anyone, not even ourselves. Later today I plan to go down to the vicarage and talk to Charles about forgiveness. I was hoping you would go with me."

He stared in disbelief. "I can't believe it. That's what I wanted to do—and have you go with me."

They stood up together.

"Syd, I don't think I really wanted to find Conan. My commitment—my duty to Her Majesty and to my country—was to track him down and turn him in. But I tried to look at his children through your eyes and Abigail's, and I thought, Dear God, how can I do it?"

From where they were, they heard Griselda say, "Come along, children. And, Gregor, take Abigail's arm."

As the door closed, Jonas resumed a familiar stance. Pensive. Distant. A handsome man with the sleeves of his shirt rolled up. His hands were flattened together, forefingers pressed to his lips, his eyes downcast. He seemed unaware that locks of his dark hair had fallen across his brow. Unaware of her.

"Jonas, I must go now. I'll be back."

He gave no indication of hearing her. "I felt all along that Abigail and Charles knew what was going on, but I never thought of Lucas. There's a loyalty to those of us with the Royal Navy."

"But you willingly blamed Abigail and Charles."

"They weren't wearing Navy blue." His smile was forced. "Don't make me feel any worse. Lucas could have destroyed us all in that fire—because I couldn't see through the color blue."

Did she dare leave him? "Stop blaming yourself, Jonas."

"Abigail told me that the war between Conan and me had to end sometime. I didn't think it would end this way. If I had known he was dying, I would have asked Dr. Wallis to see him. But I wouldn't be able to meet Conan as a friend. Whichever path I took I would betray someone: Conan, the children, Her Majesty. And all through that struggle, something inside told me that Louise would want me to forgive Conan."

"Let God forgive you."

His eyes met hers, the hazy blue like drifting clouds.

"I have to go, Jonas. I wish you were going with me."

Outside, she fled down the hill to catch up with the others. When she arrived at the churchyard, strangers in town were arguing with Charles. "This grave must be dug up."

He towered above them. "I forbid any tampering of this grave site. This is church property."

"The man was an Irish terrorist. We need to identify him, make certain it is Conan O'Reilly—"

"Your terrorist is dead, gentlemen. You must take my word for it. You can gain nothing by digging up O'Reilly's body. Let the man rest in peace. He had so little peace in his lifetime."

Charles with his snow-white hair made an imposing figure towering above the strangers. His collar seemed to pinch his neck; an impressive velvet robe flapped at his ankles. They backed off.

But would they come back in the stealth of night? Sydney wondered.

Conan lay in an unmarked grave, beneath a crudely carved cross bearing the words REST IN PEACE. Boris had helped the children nail the cross together and had himself painted the black letters against the wood. Clinging to Sydney's hand and her rag doll, Keeley stepped forward and placed a bouquet of hand-picked wildflowers on her father's grave. Many of the village folk who hunted him down had gathered to say farewell to Abigail's troubled Irish boy.

A slight breeze blew the vicar's hair. "Fly away, my son, like the dove," he intoned. "Conan O'Reilly, we must think of you as taking flight on the wings of a bird and finding shelter from your stormy life. Father, I believe he sought You in the end—"

As Charles spoke, the keening wail of bagpipes filled the air. Sydney glanced up and saw Jonas coming toward them in his Scottish kilt, coming steadily down the hill to the churchyard on those sturdy suntanned legs. The keening, lamenting wail of "Nearer, My God, to Thee" drifted out over the Cotswold Hills.

Sydney squeezed Keeley's shoulder and held tightly to Danny's hand. Suddenly Keeley pulled free and dropped her rag doll on the ground. She pointed toward the hills. "Papa. My papa."

Sympathy spread across the faces of the mourners, expressions that said "the child is grief stricken." But Sydney had seen her glancing off toward the golden hills. Surreptitiously, she looked and saw two men high on the hillside above the cemetery resting on saddled horses. She was certain that the thin young man on the hilltop was Conan O'Reilly. She glanced worriedly toward Abigail, but she stood serenely beside Griselda, a veil covering her face, her eyes fixed on the mound of dirt with its crudely shaped cross. Sydney glanced up again, but the sun blinded her. She saw nothing. No one. Not even a cloud of dust from horse and rider. A mirage? A phantom illusion? Her last desperate wish for life for Conan?

Her eyes strayed to Jonas. He met her gaze, unwavering.

She knew in that instant that he had looked toward the hills as well. He showed no anger, no fury. He gave her a quick nod, and she realized that the strangers at the graveside had drifted away from the mourners and were racing toward their car. She and Jonas would share their secret. It was best this way, allowing the children and Abigail this time in the churchyard for a proper good-bye.

❧

On Monday Sydney had her suitcases packed and sitting in one corner of the room with her laptop computer beside them. She and Jeff were leaving in the morning for Heathrow and the flight back home. She would come back someday. For now, the children at the manor would be safe with Abigail and Griselda and the newly hired staff.

With Jeff leaving, Blackstone and Rentley agreed to take on Sydney's long-term legal battle for custody of the O'Reilly children. But she braced herself for saying good-bye to Jonas. They would spend the afternoon together. Even now, he waited for her by the roses. As she ran down the steps, he plucked a vivid pink rose and handed it to her. Her garden! Her gardener!

"This is where it all began," she said. "The day I came back to Broadshire Manor, you were here pruning the roses."

"What did you think of me then?"

"That you were mighty handsome for a gardener. I was struck with how tall and strong you were. How tanned your skin was. How rugged you looked, yet how kind to Gregor you were. And when you looked at me over Gregor's head, your eyes were frosty blue."

"I wasn't doing a good job of pruning the roses. I kept watching you come up the hillside, looking poised and graceful." He pushed a stray strand of hair from her forehead. "I liked the way your hair was drawn back so I could see your face. I haven't been able to stop looking at you since you came. I think I knew the minute I saw you that you had walked into my life and I would fall in love again."

She remembered how their eyes had locked across the primroses and she blushed. "I'll miss you."

"Can we go for a walk?" he asked, catching her hand in his.

"Oh Jonas, I promised the children—"

His smile faded. "All right. They can come as long as they give us space of our own."

They walked down toward the Windrush, the children stumbling and screaming ahead of them. "Will it always be like this, Sydney? Me competing for your time with the children?"

"Will you mind?"

"Not as long as you come back to me."

"Don't, Jonas. Don't make leaving any harder. You know we agreed to give each other space. Time to sort out our feelings."

"I already know that I want you to be part of my life. But without you here, life will be empty. Have you ever thought about how much you would give up for the one you love?"

"I always think about how much I would gain."

Off to their right, the steeple of St. Michael's towered with the trees. "You attended the service on Sunday," he said.

You know I did. We sat together on that hard narrow bench. We stared at the same stained glass window. Heard the same music. Listened to the same message. But for most of that service Keeley wiggled beside me as I fixed my eyes on the baptismal font.

"Yes, I was there, Jonas."

"Do you remember what Reverend Rainford-Simms said?"

Her cheeks grew hot. She didn't remember one word of the sermon, only snatches of the parishioners rendering the morning reading from the Song of Songs. *"I belong to my lover and his desire is for me."*

The sermon was on the sanctity of marriage, and she sat there filled with remorse that she had broken the vows of purity with Randolph Iverson. How could God or Jonas ever forgive her? How could she forgive herself for not waiting? Now the words of the sermon tumbled around in her thoughts as she realized how deeply she cared for Jonas Willoughby.

Jonas stopped on the trail and ran his fingers gently over her cheek. "I think Charles spoke on marriage for our sake. He has been the wise one, long ago setting me free to fall in love again. I was the one holding on to Louise's memory."

"I thought you let her go," she whispered.

"I did when we took that trip to Ireland. You have to believe me. You're the one who fills my thoughts now."

"But if you knew the truth about me—"

"The past? I guessed long ago that Randolph was more than a friend, Sydney. We both have regrets. Let's start over from this moment in time. Let's accept God's forgiveness for the past." His eyes were pale blue this morning, full of love as he looked at her. "What do I have to do to get you to stay and marry me?"

You'd have to ask me.

"I can't stand the thought of you being on the other side of the pond. On Sunday, Charles quoted Solomon, saying that water can't quench love, nor rivers wash it away. Don't put an ocean between us. Having you here in England is what matters to me. I want to spend my life with you."

As they stood by the Windrush, the children ran circles around them. Jonas dug into his pocket for some money. "Gregor, Sydney and I have some serious business to discuss. I want you to take the children and buy some sweets at Veronica's Tea Shoppe."

Gregor's lower lip trembled. He scowled at the younger children. "Come on," he ordered.

"Gregor—son," Jonas called.

Gregor caught his balance, dug in with his toes turned in, his eyes cast down. "Yes."

"Whatever Sydney and I decide, Gregor, you will be part of our plans. We'll include you in any plans we make."

"You won't make me go to Gordonstoun right away?"

"Not until you're ready."

"What about Keeley and Danny?"

"Them, too."

"And the others—Tesa and Philip and Yasmin?"

"Abigail is making long-term arrangements for them when the National Trust comes in to restore the property. But we won't let them go unless it's a happy place."

He took Sydney's hand as the children ran off. "I'll ring you every week. Every day."

"Try e-mail," she said. "It's less expensive. Save your money for my ring."

"You'll have your ring. The biggest one I can find. But an ocean will separate us, Sydney—your country and mine. That's what worries me."

Beside them they heard the powerful rush of the river sweeping under the bridge and crashing over the rocks, and then flowing gently on. "There's no ocean here, Jonas. Just the River Windrush. And there's a bridge across that. We can bridge our differences, but we still need some time."

"What about your place on Lake Washington?"

"It's too big for one person. It was too big when my parents were alive, but it was home. I grew up in its rambling rooms, but I could let it go if I moved back here. But my retreat by the river—I can't let that go. I want to take the children back there every summer—or maybe at Christmas some time. Gregor will especially love it."

"I won't always be free to go with you."

"I know. You'll be at sea. But sometimes you can go with us. I want you to know and love that place as I do."

"And your job at Barrington Enterprises?"

"I worked out my options in case you invited me back. It's too soon for me to quit. We've just won the contract on the carriers. They won't even be launched until 2012."

"I can't wait that long—I'd be an old man."

She laughed. "Just a little older than you are now. But I'm talking about three months to make arrangements at home."

"And what do you have in that calculating mind of yours?"

"I'll keep the controlling interest in the company. I'll appoint someone else as CEO. In other words, I'll turn over the day-to-day operations."

"To Randolph Iverson?"

"He's the best man for the job. He wanted it in the first place. But I'll stay on as chairman of the board."

"What a business head you are. But how do you plan to juggle being a wife and mother with running Barrington Enterprises?"

"I'll plan quarterly board meetings—I'll fly over for those. And there's nothing to stop me from calling the board of directors to the Jarrow Shipyard. That would be convenient for me." She grinned. "I've had weeks working these details out in my mind in case you got around to asking me to marry you."

"Will you ever sell out—after you marry me?"

"Someday. I've had offers to merge. But I'm not stepping down until the carriers are commissioned. If you're going to be on board, I want them to be the best construction ever."

"They will be," he said, slipping his arm around her.

"I don't want to sell Barrington until we're the top defense company ever, and even then, I'll keep a controlling interest and remain a stockholder. Dad won't know, but if he did, I'd want him to be proud of the job I did and the choice I make when it's time to merge. Even when I sell, I'll only do so if the buyout keeps me on the board of directors for five or ten years."

"What about that option on a shipyard in Italy?"

"I'm still negotiating. I think it's to our advantage to have several plants here in Europe."

"You amaze me. But what guarantee do I have that you'll come back and marry me?"

They had been walking along the Windrush. She stopped and faced him. Standing on tiptoe she threw her arms around her Englishman's neck and hugged him.

"Is this guarantee enough?" she asked. She was laughing up at him, her lips parted, her eyes surely dancing.

He put his arms tightly around her and drew her closer. She was still smiling, laughing, as his lips came down hard on hers.

Epilogue

Abigail and the Admiral sat in the garden watching the mist rise as dawn spread its copper wings over the Cotswold Hills. Autumn had come to Stow-on-the-Woodland, brushing the land with patches of amber and jonquil yellow. The primrose bushes had been pruned back, and the ground lay russet like winter apples. Harvest dominated the countryside with farmers and combines already at work. Everything had changed with the season, everything but the constancy of the hills.

Abigail was grateful to see another sunrise when sunset was so close for both of them. Long after she and the Admiral were gone, strangers would come to sit in this quaint gazebo sheltered from the winds and dampness and find comfort, as she did, looking down on the meandering river and across at the hills bathed in coppery autumn hues. Their early morning ritual was always the same now. Griselda bundled them up in sturdy warm jackets and left them outside for an hour with lap robes snug around their legs to ward off the biting chill. Then she would hustle them inside to the drawing room where she served them tea and crumpets by the fire.

These autumn days brought color to the Admiral's cheeks, but Dr. Wallis fussed about Abigail sitting in the wind, fearing she would get her death of chill. She told him a woman on borrowed time needed the scent of fresh air and the sun on her face.

From her chair, she could see the ongoing facelift for St. Michael's. Inside the manor, the East and South wings resonated with hammering and shouting men as the National Trust began its restorations on Broadshire Manor. They had agreed to let Santos work in the gallery each morning to restore the vivid beauty to ancient works of art, one painting at a time.

Abigail folded her hands over the letter from Charles Rainford-Simms and thought of him in the North Country, content with a small plot of land of his own. When she wrote again, she would tell him about the new cleric at St. Michael's, the young man in his first pastorate, vibrant with ideas for enlarging his congregation. She would not mention the lively beat of the music or the cleverly worded sermons that parishioners forgot as they reached the door. But she would tell Charles about the autumn colors that covered the hillsides when Griselda walked down to put flowers on Louise's and Conan's graves. He always asked about the children—and she had told him they were back at the primary school.

She would miss her children, yet she had come to life's full circle—the hidden children of wars no longer came to her, but she had memories of dozens of boys and girls tucked away in her heart. A lifetime of treasures. Charles would not ask, but she knew he would wonder whether she had found the courage to tell Jonas the truth. Her silence still taunted her. She regretted Jonas not knowing that he was her son, and it saddened her that the girl she would have chosen for Jonas herself had gone back to her powerful position at Barrington Enterprises. But with Charles, she confided her sadness about the Admiral's continued decline, his memory wheel clogged more and more in the past.

But this is a good day, Abigail thought. *Tobias is fresh and alert.*

She sighed, and the Admiral rallied from his first nap of the day. He sent a swift glance her way, pleasure filling his face.

"My dear, is something wrong?"

"Nothing," she told him.

"What happened to that young woman who used to visit me?"

She had told him many times, but patiently she said, "Sydney went back to America. Remember?"

"I miss her. I thought Jonas really fancied her."

"He did."

He mulled that over, and she was certain that he had slipped back to the past, to the glory days of ships and sailing, back even to the day he was knighted by the Queen. He remembered that sometimes with great pride and his eyes bright with memory.

Instead he surprised her, saying, "I've worried about you, Abby. Where have you been?"

She patted his hand. "I told you yesterday." She regretted the sharpness in her tone and added, "I was ill, James, for a long time. But I'm better now."

"I thought you were gone—without Jonas knowing the truth."

Her heart fluttered. Skipped a bit. "The truth, Tobias?"

He covered her hand with his own. "I did love you. But I could not leave Helen. She needed me. I needed her."

Abigail nodded—allowing her hand to remain in his. "After she died, Tobias, I thought the two of us—"

"That would have been wrong, dear Abby. Jonas needed the memory of his mother. Abigail, what a mess I made of our lives." He closed his eyes and forced himself back to the moment. "My memory is not as good as it used to be. Where was I?"

"You were talking about Helen."

"No. No, I was talking about us. I never admitted to you that I knew about Jonas. I wanted nothing to mar my reputation or ruin my career."

She leaned against him. "I know. I've always known."

"Have you ever told Jonas?"

"No, there's no need to tell him now."

"But I know," Jonas said, coming out to the garden to join them. "I know that you are my mother."

She turned and watched her son coming toward her. *He knows. He knows he is my son.* She felt strength in his height, in his unwavering gaze. He stood with his hand resting on the rail of the gazebo. She longed to stand up and hug him—to dance with him. To tell him she had loved him forever.

"How?" she whispered, staring up at him. "How did you know?"

"Sitting with my father, night after night. The hours between midnight and dawn are long. He was always calling for you, and I began to wonder why."

"I'm so sorry."

"No, don't be. When I told Sydney that I knew, she told me I was lucky. I had two mothers who loved me. One who made a great sacrifice for me."

He crossed the lawn that separated them and put his hand firmly on her shoulder. "I've known for a long time that you've loved my father. You've sacrificed your life for him. Perhaps that is one of the reasons I was so angry at him."

"I wanted to be here in the manor so I could be close to you—to watch you grow up—to be here whenever you came home."

"You've always been here for me, Abigail."

"Oh Jonas. At last I can shout it to the world that you are my son. I don't have to go on pretending."

His face clouded. "We can't make a grand announcement. Stow-on-the-Woodland is a small town. And my uncle would never understand. I don't want to hurt him. The Willoughbys are a proud people. And Dad's reputation—his long Navy career—would be ruined. Can we go on as we've been?"

Silently? Robbed always of motherhood? She choked up. So close, but she was still to bear the secret to her grave. Her voice trembled. "Yes, if that's what you want. Yes."

"I can never tell the truth outside the manor—for the sake and reputation of the Willoughby family. I'll tell my commanding officer—I am obligated to do so."

"Oh Jonas, it could ruin you ever reaching the Admiralty."

"We'll let Captain McIntyre decide how it will affect my career." He leaned down and kissed the top of her head. "Abigail, you've been a good mother. I love you for that."

She held his hand against her cheek, kissed the palm, tears washing down her cheeks. "What will you do now?"

"I'm going back to sea soon. You and Dad will stay on here at the manor for as long as you want. Or I can move you to a residence where you will be well cared for. But Sydney will not hear of this—"

"We thought you would marry Sydney. And then she left."

"She's coming back, and she's determined to arrange for even more help for Griselda so you can live out your lives here."

"And the children?"

"You already know we've found homes for three of them. Tesa to distant relatives. And Blackstone and Rentley found a temporary home for Philip and Yasmin with an American couple in the northern Cotswolds."

Her throat constricted. She had never sent any of her children away willingly. "Will they treat them kindly?"

"Blackstone thinks so. The father is a photojournalist—the mother a biologist. They have a little girl of their own and an adopted son."

"But it's only a temporary home?"

He smiled. "Blackstone knows the family personally. He says once they see Yasmin and Philip, they'll never let them go. But we won't send them until after Christmas. You'll want that last Christmas together."

"You won't separate Danny and Keeley?"

"No. Sydney would not hear of it. Between the American embassy going to bat for her and the barrister in London making special arrangements, Sydney will be free to take them to America next summer."

"I was so hoping—"

"She's coming back, Abigail," he said with a grin. "I've asked her to marry me. Those trips to America with the children will be holiday times."

"And Gregor?" she asked with reprimand in her voice and the dreaded fear that Gregor would be lost and alone.

"Poor Sydney," he said, smiling even more. "When she gets me, she gets all three children. . .I think that will make you and Dad grandparents. Will you mind?"

Abigail tightened her grip over the Admiral's frail hand, her own vein-riddled one tissue-thin. "We will be very proud."

"From now on, Abby, I will think of you as my mother. But things must go on the way they have always been. You will always be the friend of the family. You do understand, don't you?"

"I didn't even deserve this much."

"But you do," the Admiral said. "You have deserved so much more than I ever gave you. Jonas—Abigail—can you forgive an old man his sin and selfishness? I have denied you both for so long."

Jonas—proud man that he was—embraced his father. "We'll go on from here, Dad. Next weekend, I will bring you a surprise, Abby. A celebration of motherhood and how much you mean to me."

"A surprise for me? Not the children?"

"They will enjoy my surprise as well. So will you, Dad."

He bent low and whispered gently in his mother's ear, "Thank you for all you've done for me. I love you, Abby. I'll see you both next weekend."

"Don't forget my surprise."

She watched this son of hers go in a brisk stride, confident in his own future, and, as he always did, he went away with her heart. She heard the engine of his car turn over and then he was racing toward London. Jonas Willoughby, her son.

"Who was that young man who just drove away?" the Admiral asked. "He's wearing the uniform of the Royal Navy."

"He's your son, Tobias. He followed in your footsteps."

He frowned, perplexed, grasping at the threads of memory. "You mean that little boy has grown up? I thought he was still away at Gordonstoun."

"That was many years ago."

"I'd forgotten. I'm glad he's with the Navy. He seems like a nice young man. Is he with the Admiralty?"

"Not yet. But he is a wonderful young man. He's your son. How could he be anything less?"

"If that's my son, I should have told him how proud I am of him. How much I love him. I wonder if he knows?"

"Why don't you tell him the next time he comes?"

The Admiral dozed again and moments later awakened to the present again, looking cheerful and alert. He threw aside his lap robe. "Abby, I am cold. I think we should go inside."

"Griselda will be along shortly to get us."

His old mischief curled the corners of his mouth into a smile. "But I'm inviting you to have tea with me, my lady."

He stood unsteadily and reached out his hand to her. They linked arms for balance and began the incredible task of climbing the stone steps. Abigail had forgotten how tall Tobias was; he was so much like his charming son, his hair still raven black with only fringes of gray at the temple. He gave her his rakish grin, and those once slate blue eyes, faded now, held a special glint in them for her.

Even his voice filled with laughter when he said, "Tomorrow I might not remember you, but today, my dear Abby, I do."

"Today is all that matters, Sir James."

And together they went up the last few steps and into the manor where the Admiral would have tea with his lady.

~

Jonas glanced at his watch. In another three hours he would hear Sydney's voice again and be able to tell her how much he loved her. She was flying high above the ocean, every second bringing her closer to the landing at Heathrow.

As he strode briskly toward the parking zone at Northwood, Captain McIntyre stopped him. "I wanted to catch you, Commander. So you're on your way to the airport already? And you're wearing your uniform to meet your girl?"

"Yes, she's never seen me in it, sir. I'm stopping off at the Hollinsworths' en route."

"Checking up on Jock again? He's had a rough recovery. But thanks to you, Commander, he's still alive."

"We'll both be flying again soon."

"You've earned wearing those wings again. I'll miss working with you at Northwood. Your stubbornness did your friend a favor. The disaster investigation would have delayed our search for him for months if you hadn't insisted that he wasn't on board."

"It still took too long before we found him."

"Tell Mr. Hollinsworth that they spotted Lucas Sullivan in Belfast. It's only a matter of time before he's in custody. According to his own men, he planned to commandeer that Learjet from the day Jock visited you in Stow-on-the-Woodland."

"Yes, I already told Jock. But no word on Conan?"

McIntyre's face clouded. "We've put off telling you. Sullivan dumped Conan O'Reilly off on his father-in-law's farm. Conan's in-laws took him in and arranged medical care for him."

"But Sean Callahan despises his son-in-law."

"True," McIntyre said philosophically. "But his wife was more merciful. She refused to turn the father of her grandchildren away again."

"That didn't bother Callahan before."

"Apparently a talk with the local priest persuaded him otherwise."

Jonas saw Sydney's dreams of mothering Keeley and Danny slipping from them. "Should I tell my fiancée and Abigail Broderick that he's been found alive?"

The captain rubbed his jaw with vigor. "It would only raise false hopes. We have a watch on the farm to keep abreast of the comings and goings. But the British won't even press charges against Conan. It's too late for that. When the lad reached his father-in-law's farm, his gunshot wounds were too infected. Conan O'Reilly won't live long. He's in and out of a coma—wouldn't even recognize his children if you took them to him. Best they remember him the way they last saw him."

Jonas shook the hand extended to him. "Then I'll be off, sir."

"Commander, I'm looking forward to meeting that fiancée of yours."

He patted the jewel box in his pocket. "So am I, sir."

⁓

After a brief visit with the Hollinsworths, Jonas reached Heathrow early and paced back and forth in the terminal until the announcement came that Sydney's plane was on the runway. His spine stiffened. He had an attack of the jitters. What if she changed her mind when she saw him? What if distance had changed them both?

The seconds ticked away. The minutes. Every welcoming speech he had prepared vanished. He had forgotten to pick up the flowers he had ordered that morning. He brushed his jacket with his hand for the third time. Checked his watch. Took his cap off and put it back on. She wanted to see him in full uniform.

His forehead felt damp, his collar too tight.

The passengers coming off the plane were detained behind a rope barrier while airline personnel consulted a passenger list.

He saw Sydney now and his fears vanished. Every fiber in his body came alive with longing to hold her. To not let her go.

Now she saw him and her smile matched his. She was more lovely than he remembered.

"Jonas."

He called back, "I thought your plane would never get here."

"We're four minutes early."

They were doing gymnastics trying to keep their eye on each other. He stretched, looking beyond the burly man in front of her. "I didn't think you'd be back so soon. My calendar is worn thin with counting the days."

She stood on tiptoe and steadied herself, grabbing the man's arm. "I didn't want to wait three months to see you again."

"Jump over the rope, sweetheart; I'll catch you!" he called.

"I'll toss her over," the burly man offered.

She laughed, her laugh as bubbly as the Windrush. "I love you, Commander Willoughby."

"I love you more, Sydney Barrington."

The people around them chuckled.

"I forgot the roses," he said.

"It doesn't matter. We have a lifetime to gather flowers."

The rope blocking their way was removed. The weary travelers pushed forward and then Jonas called out, "Barrel your way through, sweetheart. I love you. I'm waiting."

Suddenly the surging crowd fanned back, making a path for love. Jonas opened his arms wide as Sydney came running to him. He swept her up into his arms and whispered in her ear, "I love you, Sydney. And I will never, never let an ocean separate us again."

SUNRISE ON STRADBURY SQUARE

Dedication

To Amanda,
my honorary granddaughter.

A thing of beauty is a joy forever.

"If I should die," he wrote, "I have left no immortal work behind
me—but I have lov'd the principle of beauty in all things, and if I had
had time I would have made myself remembered."
—John Keats (1795-1821)

Prologue

Rachel McCully's stark encounter with her own mortality came at the most unexpected moment. At thirty-seven, she stood without question in the prime of her life, at the peak of her career as a university professor, and had come that morning fresh from the trails of a weekend mountain trip. She had bruises and blisters on her heels to prove it, a burn on her finger from the campfire when the marshmallow prong slipped from her hand, and a nasty snagged fingernail from changing her flat tire on the mountain turnout. But she came down the mountain with wonderful memories, eager to face her students and hand them their final exams.

On this last Monday in May, she walked tall—as she always did—with a brisk, vibrant step and an easy grace while cutting across the campus to McClaren Hall. The flush on her face came from the sun, its warmth invading her body. Contentment stole over her at the thought of another summer holiday abroad.

The heavens above her had formed a vault of powdery blue. Wispy white clouds played games with the sunshine. It was not the kind of day for disaster to dog her footsteps. The springtime air smelled fresh and clean, scented sweetly with the crimson and coral roses blooming against the university buildings. Students lazed on the freshly mown lawn between exams, some of them still cramming for their finals. Sprawling pepper trees dotted much of the campus, but a row of magnolias grew just over the footbridge on the walkway to McClaren. Rachel smiled to herself at the young couple huddled beneath the third magnolia—books open, arms around each other, the moment more important to them than their grade point average and graduation on Saturday.

She felt a twinge of envy, a tingle of memory. Her gaze veered from their happiness and stabbed at her own ghosts. The students sat on a white marble bench, its clawed legs stained from inclement weather. On a day much like this glorious, sun-filled morning, a moment on that bench beneath that same magnolia tree lay branded in Rachel's memory. The remembered snowy-white magnolia flower, the dark green leaves, the shaded sunlight on the somber face of the man beside her.

Rachel hurried past the young couple, but it was too late. Yesterday was there, the part of her that no one else remembered. No one else knew. She the English professor; he the visiting British don—serious-faced, broad-shouldered, lean.

~

She had been in her twenties and flattered by the visiting professor's attention. But that morning, as she looked into his dark eyes, she blushed under his gaze. They had become such good friends, constant companions. Flustered by his closeness, she said, "Sinclair, you do remember that I want you to speak to the Pen and Quill Club before you leave for London? I thought you could talk to them about C. S. Lewis—"

A scowl nettled his brows, his gaze piercing hers. "Must we talk about literature, Dr. McCully? I want to talk about us."

Her cheeks broiled in spite of the cool shade of the tree. "Us, Sinclair?"

Students walked past them as his fingers entangled hers. Tightened. "I want you to go back to England with me."

"I go abroad every summer," she had stammered.

He remained resolute. "I want you to go back as my wife."

She caught her breath, expecting his face to crease with that wry smile of his. She saw only his familiar studious expression, a handsome face if he would smile more. That morning—as with many mornings—his tie was askew on his otherwise perfect attire. Beneath his brown tweed jacket, he wore a thick, V-necked, Shetland sweater for what he considered to be the chill of spring. She wanted to reach out and straighten his tie. A playful gesture, a familiar one.

His knee brushed hers as he crossed his long, muscular legs. She drew away. He seemed unaware. He said a second time, "Will you marry me, Rachel?"

"You're joking of course."

"That hardly describes me."

True. Other words came to mind: conservative, professional. Committed, purposeful. *She admired his strength of character, but Sinclair was so unlike the carefree, jaunty men who took pleasure in mastering the mountains and skiing with her. What did the two of them have in common? Intellectual pursuits. Art and music. Literature. They talked about tradition—his as a schoolboy in England, as a student at Oxford, as a researcher on the life and works of C. S. Lewis. She boasted about her family tradition—the McCully name a legend at the university. They attended faculty doings as a couple. Walking and dining together. He played soccer and cricket. She favored hiking and skiing. Sinclair viewed mountain heights through a camera lens; she from the top of the mountain. He seemed distant, professional with his students. She entered into their lives. He was reserved. She took risks.*

He leaned closer. "Rachel, I am asking you to be my wife. I thought that's what you wanted."

"I do. But—my career means everything to me."

"You mean everything to me."

Other images blurred his features. Sinclair catching her eye across the crowded faculty room. The picnic in early spring with the bees buzzing overhead. He detested bees. She swatted at them playfully. He dared her to race across the narrow river, the water as cold as melting ice. They plunged in—his breaststroke powerful and even, his win four strides ahead of hers. But he was the one with a wretched cold and fever three days later. And the Thanksgiving break to his boyhood haunts in England. Meeting his family. Just tiny glimpses of the other Sinclair, the fun-loving man behind the studious expression.

He cupped her chin and forced her to look at him again. "Rachel, are you going to answer me?"

"I don't know what to say."

"Say yes."

A thousand crazy excuses ran through her mind. A thousand uncertainties. His reserve. His brilliance. The less restrained moments with his warm lips on hers. She wanted to ski and climb. To live. To be free. He wanted to marry and settle down and have lots of children. Three at least.

And what would they talk about for the next forty years? Shakespeare and Chaucer. Shakespeare's devotion to Anne Hathaway for breakfast. C. S. Lewis or the Lake Poets for supper. And in between poets, they would talk about sending their sons to Eton and the University of St. Andrews in Scotland.

She thought about the sleepless nights she had known since the day they met. The arguments she had with herself. The confusion that paralyzed her about childbearing—the fear of taking defective genes into a marriage, the fear of being a carrier of cystic fibrosis.

"Rachel, I thought you knew that I loved you."

Tears stung her eyes. "I didn't know for certain. How could I? I don't read minds or enjoy guessing games."

His smile was disarming, his quiet reserve unsettling. "But we talked about England and Stradbury Square. And living in Oxford. I told you that I wanted children. . .and marriage. We talked of marriage, Rachel."

"But not to each other."

I hoped. I wondered.

She had sat beside him at faculty meetings for two months, never tumbling to the idea that he had more than an intellectual interest in her. Then at the close of a heated discussion on dropping Victorian literature from the school program, this tall, striking Brit lingered at the back of the room waiting for her. "Would you be so good as to go to dinner with me, Dr. McCully?"

He spoke in the same crisp manner he used in the classroom. She thought him arrogant then, presumptuous. But at dinner and all the dinners that followed, she found him kind and caring. Utterly captivating. Delightful with his droll sense of humor. Never boring.

She expected him to pick a moderately priced restaurant that first evening; he chose the best, lavishing her with unexpected British charm and sending her into spontaneous laughter when he insisted on steaming Victorian tea in Chelsea Rose china. With cup in hand and eyes dancing, he saluted her. "Here's to rescuing you from the chaos of faculty meetings."

Sitting on that stone bench under the magnolia tree, he had said gently, "Rachel, I'm leaving at the end of the semester."

"I know," she whispered. "So am I."

"But you're traveling in Italy."

She ran her fingers over the back of his hand. "Would it help to know that I booked my return flight out of Heathrow?"

"That sounds as if you're willing to leave the door open." He stood and helped her stand. She was tall, but at six-one he was taller. He looked down at her, a twisted smile on his lips. "Perhaps you could reserve your answer until you reach London?"

When she responded, she was half teasing. Wasn't he? "We could meet under Big Ben. I'll give you my final answer then."

He whipped a pocket calendar from his jacket and scanned the pages, his Oxford pen poised. "Would noon on August seventh be good for you?"

~

Nine years! Had nine years really slipped by? Big Ben still chimed out the hour, but she and Sinclair had gone their separate ways. Back then, with Big Ben booming behind her, she had run away from her chance at happiness—foolish as it might be—with her secret fear of childbearing tucked deep inside her.

Yesterday and today merged. Just for a second, she turned back. Glancing across the footbridge, she gazed at the magnolia tree and the now empty stone bench. Rachel had always prided herself in controlling the calendar and the events of her life, something that her sister, Larea, could not do. Even now, nine years later, Rachel was the sum of many things, her life divided between teaching and sports, and her summers spent abroad. She juggled schedules and negotiated winding curves on mountain roads and the slopes of a ski run, but she could not control her sister's illness or this fresh emotional tug at her heartstrings at the awakening thoughts of Sinclair Wakefield.

As she neared McClaren Hall, two students waved. She sent back her winsome smile, anticipating the summer freedom as much as they did. She strolled on with purpose—her life, as always, disciplined and mapped out. So why, as she sprinted up the last two steps to the language arts building, did she suddenly feel such foreboding, such uncertainty, such pending doom?

Chapter 1

Shiny glass doors led into McClaren Hall and a mahogany paneled door into her office. She breezed into the room, smiling at her secretary.

"Dr. McCully, you are never late."

"I know. But I picked up a nail negotiating the mountain curves this morning. The trucker behind me almost ran me off the road before I could reach the safety of the turnout."

"Didn't he stop to change your tire?"

She laughed. "I did it myself."

"No wonder you look tired, rushing like that."

"A camping trip is worth it. The weather was perfect. You should go with me sometime, Elsa."

"I'd hate sleeping in a tent."

"You'd get used to it. Anything for me this morning?"

"A faculty meeting at four. . .and an appointment with your doctor at two this afternoon."

"Call him back and tell him I can't make it."

Elsa shrugged. "The nurse said you had to be seen."

"Why all the rush?"

"You're leaving for Europe after school is out."

"Good point."

"I told her this was finals week, but she insisted."

Rachel pocketed the pink memo without reading it. "Two o'clock. Anything else?"

"Jude Alexander wants to see you. She said she'll be back in a few minutes."

Rachel's brows puckered. "Why now? She skipped out on her last two appointments."

"I just posted some of your finals on the bulletin board."

"Oh! Then send her in when she comes back."

Rachel didn't feel chipper as she adjusted the blinds in her inner office, flooding the room with sunlight. In another ten years, she'd retire early, but at thirty-seven, retirement was on the back burner, the prospect rekindled only on bad days, and Jude could easily spoil an already harried schedule.

With a glance in the mirror, Rachel saw her mood mirrored there. Her uneasiness at a confrontation with Jude showed in the scowl ridges tightening around her mouth. She adjusted the silk scarf around her neck and slipped into her desk chair just as Jude swung the door open.

Jude stomped across the room, every fiber of her body vibrating as she dropped into the wing chair across from Rachel. "You flunked me, Dr. McCully."

Rachel met the girl's sullen gaze. She was a minister's daughter, but anger defined her. Jude was pretty, daring, defiant, a twenty-one-year-old on a crash course with the world.

Rachel saw herself reflected in the angry expression and remembered her own crash course with the world at eighteen. And the jolt that turned her life around.

More harshly than she intended, she said, "Jude, you set yourself up for failure."

"I barely squeaked by last semester in that Victorian lit class, and now, because of some dumb Lake Poets, I won't have enough credits to graduate."

Venting, she was like the hissing tire on Rachel's car, her words falling flat. "You can't do that to me, Prof. My parents are driving from Colorado for my graduation."

Rachel smiled patiently. "You knew the course objectives from the beginning of the semester. Five reports on the poets and *one* research paper of your own choosing. None of them out of reach—especially for an intelligent young woman like you."

What goes around, comes around. Her mother's voice saying, *"An intelligent young woman like you, Rachel McCully, wasting your life skiing. Dreaming of Olympic medals. They only last long enough to hang them on your wall—if you win one."*

Rachel straightened the plaque on her desk. *When I consider how my life was spent.*

Milton's words drove her to do her best at teaching. Most students respected Rachel; rarely did anyone cross her. She saw students as players on the world's stage and wanted them to find themselves before the curtain came down on their college career and forced them into the cold reality of life off campus. With some she succeeded. With Jude Alexander, she had failed.

"Jude, you turned in only three of the six projects."

Jude switched gears, mellowing her outburst to a plea. "Give me a D—give me anything, but let me graduate." The tears brimming in Jude's eyes quickly lost their remorse. "I don't care what Shakespeare did or what Wordsworth wrote."

"Shakespeare was not one of the Lake Poets."

Jude's lip trembled. "I'm just making a point. It's your fault, Dr. McCully, that I was forced to take these courses. What in the world will I ever do with Wordsworth?"

"Apparently nothing."

She leaned forward in the chair, her fist doubled. "I'm a political science major—I plan on foreign service. What am I supposed to do? Spout poetry to some foreign diplomat?"

The bitter circle kept going around in Rachel's head, kept coming back to confront her. Her own voice defiant like Jude's. "I plan to ski in the Olympics, Mother, and after that I'll be a ski instructor. I don't plan to bury myself in the classroom."

And her mother's controlled voice breaking. "Your sister would give anything to be able to stand up and teach—"

Over the years the stinging memory of coming in from the ski run to the classroom had mellowed Rachel. She understood with hindsight how desperately her mother had needed someone to blame.

"I didn't single you out, Jude. There are certain requirements for graduation. Fortunately, we discovered that you needed additional credits in English before your final semester."

Jude's shoulders sagged. "My parents will be here Friday."

Rachel pushed the box of tissues toward her. How many students had sat in Jude's place over the years? Some ready to quit their university studies. Some troubled over their campus romance. A few wanting to change their majors. She had counseled them, laughed with them, wept with them—especially Amanda Pennyman, the young woman whose fiancé had been killed the night before. For them, there had been sympathy and understanding, and often a prayer. But this morning Rachel made no attempt to blow out Jude's fire with a prayer.

Rachel felt her brows knit together, frowning when she should be showing mercy. "Jude, I'll recommend to the graduation committee that you be allowed to participate in the ceremony—for your parents' sake. But your diploma will be blank."

"What good will that do me?"

"It will get you through the rest of this week. You can make up this class during the summer."

"My folks won't put another dime on my education."

"Then earn the money. It's up to you, Jude."

"Well, I won't take your courses again."

"Under the circumstances, I think that's best. Now, I have another final to oversee. Why don't we talk some more after the graduation ceremony and see how things are going for you then?"

Smoldering eyes glared back. "If you don't pass me—"

"I've turned in your grades—with my recommendations. Now, dry your eyes, Jude. You do have a future and a hope—"

"You sound like my father. Always spouting about God's plan for my life."

"Your father is right. God does have a plan for you, Jude."

"Right now it looks like He has a plan to destroy me. Whatever He has in mind, I hope it's as far from you as I can get."

Rachel glanced at her watch. That sense of pending doom needled her again. Once before she had stood in the faculty room, begging her colleagues to give Jude another chance.

"I guess you think I owe you one, don't you, Doc, just because you kept me from being expelled once. You should have let me go. At least I could have told my parents you threw me out of the university. Now I have to tell them I flunked out."

"You can make up that one course. Life doesn't always toss us a bouquet of roses. Sometimes we get thorns along with them."

Jude's caustic words sliced the air. "I thought you and Wordsworth were into daffodils." She pushed herself to a standing position and gripped the edge of Rachel's desk, her knuckles bone-white. "You're the lucky one, Dr. McCully. You probably wouldn't recognize a thorn if you saw it. Everybody who knows you raves about you, except me. I think you're one tough lady."

Rachel leaned back in her chair as Jude stalked out, slamming the door behind her. Rachel saw herself as defiant and self-willed as Jude. For long moments, she sat brooding. When her office door flung open again, she expected to see Jude, but Nelson Rodgers, the department head, came in grinning.

"I just passed a tornado coming out of your office. What's wrong with Ms. Alexander this time?"

"It was just a misunderstanding."

"Your fault of course? I have to admire you, Rachel. You weather every storm. Why don't we have lunch together? We could celebrate the end of another collegiate battle with iced tea."

"I'm sorry, Nelson. I have an appointment at two."

"Then we'll catch lunch in the fall when you get back. You're okay with flying, right?"

"Not a problem for me."

He walked over to scrutinize the pictures on her wall. "This is a good one of your dad. And I recognize this one. And this one. But this—" He tapped the photo of Sinclair Wakefield standing beneath Big Ben. "Who's this man, Rachel?"

One of life's painful memories. One of life's special moments. She had taken the picture with a telescopic lens when Sinclair waited for her. She was grateful that the silk scarf around her neck hid the flush. "Don't you remember him? That's Sinclair Wakefield. He spent a sabbatical on staff nine years ago."

"Wakefield! Of course. A year before my time here. For a minute I thought he was my competition. So...when do you leave for England?"

"As soon I can tidy up my desk."

"I trust that's after the graduation ceremony."

"Yes, mid-June. I'll be gone two months this time."

He winked. "As long as you come back."

❧

At two, a nurse ushered Rachel into the plush office at the Blue Ridge Medical Center. With a noncommittal smile, she said, "Dr. Risner asked one of his colleagues to see you."

The nurse whipped out of the room, leaving Rachel to stare at the framed records of achievement and soothing seascapes on the wall. They did little to calm her. She was a stickler for time, and doctors were notoriously late. The minutes ticked away—and with them her patience.

2:10.

2:15.

2:20.

Rachel considered stepping back to the nurses' station and rescheduling when the door opened and Eileen Rutledge breezed into the room carrying a chart in her hand. A stethoscope bulged from the pocket of her white lab coat as she settled in the leather chair across from Rachel.

A tiny whipple of uncertainty caught in the pit of her stomach. Eileen had been one of her students in the early years of her teaching—an outstanding student who shared her love of Wordsworth. They were close in age. The last she knew, Eileen had finished medical school and gone on for a specialty in oncology.

Oncology.

Eileen folded her hands on top of the open chart. She offered a vague smile. "Surprised, Dr. McCully?"

"Yes, surprised to be on the opposite side of a desk. I had no idea you had moved back to the area, Eileen."

"A year ago. I moved back with my daughter." She slid a picture across the desk. "That's her school photo."

"She's lovely. Why, she looks like—"

"She does, doesn't she? Her name's Rebecca. She's eight."

Rachel stole a glance at the doctor's ringless left hand. Embarrassed, she said, "An eight-year-old? Has it been that long since you took my classes, Eileen?"

"Longer."

"I hoped we'd stay in touch after you graduated."

"After Rebecca came, it seemed best not to burden you with my problems." Her smile warmed. "Even though I didn't stay in touch, I remember the first class I ever took with you. You told us to put our pens and notebooks away, and for the next fifty minutes you made Keats and Byron and Wordsworth come alive for us."

"I loved those lecture periods. They were so much more fun than having my students frantically recording my every word."

"I fell in love with Wordsworth because of you—I still keep a book of his poems by my bed for those nights when sleep eludes me." She met Rachel's gaze. "Were you aware of how your eyes blazed with fire when we were late with our assignments?"

"I've been teased about it many times." The memory of Sinclair Wakefield pierced her, snatching away her joy. "Someone once told me that my eyes and my smile were my best features."

"They still are, Doc McCully. And I remember how you used to snack on celery and cold cuts at our Pen and Quill meetings. And you went wild over homemade fudge and black licorice."

"I thought only my closest friends knew that. But that isn't why I'm here this afternoon, is it? I expected to see Dr. Risner—I didn't know you were part of his clinic, Dr. Rutledge."

"He calls me in on consult frequently."

"Without consulting the patient?"

She thumbed through the chart. "He didn't call you with the test results?"

"No." The knot in Rachel's stomach tightened as she pulled the pink memo from her purse. "My secretary handed me this memo—*See Dr. Rutledge at two today*." She met the doctor's gaze again. "I didn't even read this. I thought I'd be seeing Dr. Risner."

Eileen took the picture of her child back. Gently, she said, "Let's back up and start over. Childhood diseases?"

"Measles, mumps. The usual."

"Hospitalizations?"

"None."

"Family history: heart disease? Diabetes? Cancer?"

"Cystic fibrosis. . .my sister died from it. My parents were killed in a fire."

"Yes. I remember." Eileen made her notations, then, with pen poised, said quietly, "Were you sick long before you saw Dr. Risner?"

"I'm never sick—except for an upper respiratory infection that sent me to the emergency room two weeks ago. The ER referred me to Dr. Risner for a follow-up."

"When Dr. Risner showed me your white count and chest film, I suggested more labs and a lung scan."

Rachel's lips felt parched. "What's going on, Eileen? Please, be up front with me."

"The way you were with your students? You wanted honesty and had little tolerance for excuses." She made a pretense of shuffling through the labs. "Your white count is much too high."

"There must be some mistake."

Eileen was an attractive young woman with alert eyes and a wholesome expression. An honest woman—the same brilliant student who had sat in Rachel's classroom, with the wisdom and experience of a few years thrown in. "Tell me, what kind of schedule have you been keeping lately? What's your energy level?"

"I just got back from a camping trip early this morning. I hiked without much difficulty." But this time she hadn't been the first one to the mountaintop; she had gone back to the campsite to rest.

"Any unusual bruises or bleeding?"

"You get bruised on the trail sometimes."

"Any fever?"

You should know, she thought, remembering the spiked fever in the emergency room. "It was 101 in the emergency room."

Eileen tapped the chart. "I'm at a disadvantage. I thought Dr. Risner had explained everything to you, Dr. McCully—"

"It's Rachel, please. I'm on this side of the desk now."

"I need to examine you thoroughly. We'll need more tests."

"Dr. Risner knows I'm going on a Rhine River cruise. I go abroad every summer. I can have the tests done when I get back."

"Rachel. . .there's a second concern. The radiologist found a shadow on your right lung."

She felt her heart skip a beat. "A shadow? I've never smoked."

"Your labs are abnormal. Your chest film abnormal. I can't let you go away until I know for certain what's going on."

Rachel focused on Eileen's shiny pierced earrings.

"If you're uncomfortable seeing me, Dr. McCully, we can call in another oncologist. But I offered to see you—you meant so much to me when I was your student."

In a voice that sounded like any but her own, Rachel said, "Be straight with me, Eileen."

"With your white count, we have to rule out leukemia."

The walls caved in on her. She took a deep breath. "Cancer?"

"I need to rule it out. If I'm right, God forbid, we'll have to decide on a course of treatment."

A shadow on her lung. Leukemia. These spelled medical tests and hospitalizations and treatments. She would not accept what her sister, Larea, had faced, her life cut short by an illness. No, this could not be happening again. As Eileen pushed back from her desk, her eyes sympathetic, Rachel heard herself rambling, "No. Stay where you are, Dr. Rutledge. Really, I'm fine. I just had the flu the night I went to the emergency room. That's how all of this got started."

Eileen's gaze held steady. "Please make an appointment with me before you leave the country. Let's make certain what's going on."

Inside, Rachel felt a wretched emptiness. This couldn't be happening to her. They had made a mistake. But she said, "If your diagnosis is correct, do you have a time frame?"

"Without treatment, possibly months. Traveling abroad first may be unwise."

"They do have doctors in England."

Dr. Rutledge took a book from her lab coat and consulted the back pages. "I have a friend in London. Timothy Whitesaul was a resident when I was in medical school. If you get in trouble—"

"I won't."

Yesterday, even an hour ago, Rachel stood at the edge of tomorrow. On the bend of a river. At the top of a mountain. This was not the time for dreams to be shattered. For hope to be swept away in the current.

She would not cave in to this diagnosis nor fall apart in front of a former student. Her hands shook as she pushed herself from the chair. She wanted to rage against Eileen, against God, against fate. She climbed mountains, didn't she? She had boundless energy, was envied by her friends. She wasn't going to let some error in the emergency room ruin her life.

Recouping her composure, she said, "Mark it down in your chart, Eileen. I intend to beat this thing, whatever it is."

In the car, her courage crumbled. *Cancer! I may have cancer.* She pounded the steering wheel. "No! I have no intention of being cut down before my time like Larea was. I'm still too young to die. God, don't You understand? I promised my sister that I'd do all those things we wanted to do together."

But it took Rachel several days before she stopped crying and set about to defy the odds. As she packed her suitcases, snippets of prose exploded in her mind. They narrowed down to two. She had miles to run and promises to keep—the one to her sister, Larea; the one to Sinclair Wakefield.

Chapter 2

Eight months later Eileen Rutledge sat at her desk at the Blue Ridge Medical Center and made a final notation in Rachel McCully's chart.

> *January 24: Patient has stopped all medication. She is leaving*
> *for London to complete the vacation that was interrupted*
> *several months ago. Am sending a copy of her medical records*
> *to Timothy Whitesaul in London, England.*

Eileen closed the chart and took out her own logbook. She thumbed past the weight and dosage charts to the back pages where she reviewed her own private record of Rachel McCully's progress.

May 29: Rachel McCully seen on consultation for Dr. Risner. Elevated labs and abnormal radiology films discussed with patient. Refuses additional tests or appointments at this time.

July 18: Phone call from London, England. Rachel McCully hospitalized after collapsing at Heathrow International. White blood count soaring. Arrangements made to evac her home.

August 8: Rachel had her first chemotherapy treatment today. She has told no one of her illness. How can I send her home to cope alone? That bond between student and professor is strong. I greatly admired Dr. McCully in my student days. Our roles have reversed. She must trust me now. After much soul searching, I took her home with me.

Rebecca took an immediate liking to Rachel. Rachel is already calling my bright-eyed little imp Becki. What have I done? I know better than to become involved with my patients. And now I have involved my own daughter.

September 5: Seven days post another chemo treatment. Rachel still violently ill. Will discuss change of dosage.

September 26: Rachel refuses to discuss her diagnosis. She views life from a literary landscape; I deal with science and research, cell division and coping. She scorns the emotional trauma of being dependent on the medical world. Today, for the first time, she spoke of her sister dying with cystic fibrosis. I tried to reassure her. She shouted back, "I don't like losing control. Or losing my hair. Or the thought of dying. Or having my students and colleagues know what's happening to me."

October 10: I opened the door to the bedroom where Rachel was resting. Rebecca was pillowed there with her. Rebecca's long shiny hair spread loosely over the pillow. Rachel's hair is already coming out in large clumps. They joked about Rachel going bald, and I heard my daughter say, "Don't feel sad. My dolls have wigs."

Last night they read *The Secret Garden.* Tonight Rachel is reading Beatrix Potter's *Peter Rabbit.* They are both much too old for Peter Rabbit, but they are content together. A gentle friendship. I remember what joy Dr. McCully gave me in my university classes, and now she is making literature live for my daughter. I think Rebecca reminds her of the child she never had. They adore each other. An eight-year-old and a thirty-seven-year-old. I closed the door with a lump in my throat.

October 31: Halloween. This evening, when I lost another patient, I wondered about the masks we humans wear. For Becki it is an innocent time, a problem no greater than deciding whether she will go about the neighborhood as Squirrel Nutkin or Jemima Puddleduck. She wants Rachel to go with her as Beatrix Potter. I tell her that Rachel is too ill this evening. For Rachel life is nightmarish. She is weakened by the very anticancer drugs that should secure a remission for her. "What is the use?" she asks me. "You are killing good cells along with the cancer." But she smiles when I tell her what Rebecca will wear for Halloween.

I wonder at times why Rachel never married. She is so good with Rebecca. Today while she was lying on the examining table, I asked her whether there was ever anyone special in her life, whether she had ever considered quitting the classroom for marriage and children. "You are still a young woman," I told her. "I decided against having children a long time ago," she said. She turned her face away, but not before I saw tears glistening in her eyes. "But not having a child mattered to me the day I turned thirty-five." And I wondered why that particular age and what memories had brought her to tears?

November 19: Dr. McCully has invited us to an early Thanksgiving dinner back at her place. Rebecca is adamant that we go. But she asked me why Thanksgiving is early this year. What should I tell her? Rachel will be having more chemo the day before Thanksgiving. She continues to tolerate the treatment poorly and is still in no condition to biopsy the shadow on her lung. What will I say to Becki if Rachel loses her battle with cancer?

November 28: Rachel challenges me with the inconsistencies of standard treatment, her desire for experimental drugs. "Dying does not fit into my schedule," she tells me.

We are fairly close in age, both too young to die. But I cannot promise Rachel a positive outcome, even if she changes doctors. She is bartering for time to live in an English village, *far from the madding crowd.* She speaks of it often. I focus on the immediate. I ask myself whether the shadow on her lung is a primary tumor. She is still too weak for a surgical biopsy. I wonder whether the cancer has metastasized to her brain. Is she imagining places? Or is she sending me a warning signal that she cannot continue in the program mapped out for her?

December 12: Rachel and Becki are poring over Christmas catalogues, planning surprises. Rachel insists that she will allow herself one shopping spree with my daughter. I have advised against it. Rachel's immune system cannot survive the crowded shopping mall. It's difficult enough knowing that she is still at the university part-time, forcing herself to keep her schedule. They ended the evening reading together. She calls my only child a beautiful gift and quotes John Keats: "A thing of beauty is a joy forever." If any good has come out of Rachel's cancer, it is this bond of friendship and the joy the three of us give one another.

December 20: There is no evidence of remission. For the first time, she asks me if she is dying. I repress my own fears. I remind her that she should consider a bone marrow transplant. She smiles and I know she will not complete the treatment program I laid out for her. I offer her the opportunity to see one of my colleagues for a second opinion. She speaks instead of going back to England, saying, "I have flunked your course, Dr. Rutledge."

No. Rachel McCully will always be at the head of the class.

January 1: We were having a quiet New Year's celebration, just the three of us, cocoa our only stimulant. My daughter looked up into the face of the woman who taught me so much about English literature. "Rachel, did you make a New Year's wish?" Becki asked.

"Yes, I asked God for the strength to go back to England."

Becki's face clouded. "Will you see Beatrix Potter?"

Rachel laughed, that rich melodious laugh of hers. "Miss Potter is gone—and, Becki, I will be gone someday, too. You understand that, don't you?"

Becki's lip trembled. "You mean heaven?"

"Yes. But you will remember, won't you? I will always love you. And when I go to England, I will take pictures of Miss Potter's Hill Top Farm and send them to you."

Above my daughter's head, our eyes locked. "It will be awhile before you can go," I told her.

"No, Eileen. I have my ticket. I'm stopping treatment."

It was impossible to argue with her in front of Rebecca. "You have a therapy appointment on the third."

"We'll see." And still smiling, she said, "Becki, what is your New Year's wish?"

"Two wishes. I want you to get well." She stole a glance at me. "And I really want to have a daddy. All my friends do."

I am afraid to look at my university professor. I think she knows who Becki's father is. Morrie Chadbourne's name will not pass between us. To even speak his name would make me cry. But Rachel knows. I am certain she knows. Yet it seems an unlikely time to tell her that Morris and I were once married. Divorced.

❧

It was mid-January—the eighteenth—when Rachel arrived at the Blue Ridge Clinic for her final appointment. Eileen had steeled herself for that moment, but she had not expected the tranquility on Rachel's pale, thin face.

"I can't change your mind about England?" she asked, stethoscope in hand.

Thoughtfully, Rachel said, "I'm at peace, Eileen. At peace with God and myself. For me, it's the right decision."

Eileen believed her. But this visit was harder on Eileen and even more painful when Rachel said, "I've been looking into experimental treatments for leukemia."

So had Dr. Rutledge, but she did not volunteer any information. Rachel shared hers. "There's a clinical trial going on in London and Switzerland. The drug they are using is highly specific. It attacks a protein enzyme. . .I have written to ask about it."

"That's a last-ditch effort, Rachel."

"Surely I qualify. My white count stays out of control."

"We don't have enough data on it."

"Enough to satisfy me, Doctor."

The doctor patted Rachel's arm and thought about Wordsworth's words: *"The world is too much with us."* She meshed his words with her own. *The medical world is too much with me. It has laid waste my power to separate the patient from the treatment. Rachel McCully knows the difference. But I am not Wordsworth. I cannot gather Rachel a host of golden daffodils. But I must let her choose her own path.*

Still she argued, "We should study the results longer."

Rachel squeezed her hand to reassure Eileen. "As you reminded me in the beginning, I might not have that long. But a number of those in the study have experienced complete remission."

"But for how long, Rachel?"

"Any amount of time is bonus time. You told me that your friend in London worked exclusively with experimental drugs."

"I should never have told you."

"If I can get in on his next clinical trial. . .Eileen, I'm praying that you will contact Dr. Whitesaul for me. He is being very selective."

Eileen couldn't fight prayer, not Dr. McCully's prayer. She tried another delay tactic. "They have the same research in Texas."

With that magnificent smile of hers, Rachel exuded confidence. "My dear Eileen, don't you realize that 'my heart still leaps up when I behold a rainbow in the sky'?"

Wordsworth again. She was choosing that part of the world so familiar to her in books. Eileen nodded, letting her go. She sat down on the stool and leaned against the counter. She was being forced to set aside her training as a physician—forced to view the options through Dr. McCully's eyes. McCully was looking for a cure—or for borrowed time. She had never known any patient who loved life more.

"Dr. McCully, what will I tell Becki?"

"That I love her. If I go into remission—and, Eileen, I intend to—then I want you to bring Becki for a visit. I already promised to take her to Beatrix Potter's Hill Top Farm."

Eileen knew that one way or the other they risked losing Rachel, either by progression of her illness or by her moving away. Her child should be outside playing with her friends, but Becki wanted Rachel to come over and read to her that evening. For a moment Eileen felt as though she had done her child a great disservice bringing Rachel into their lives. But no, Rachel had brought more than *The Secret Garden* and the Hill Top Farm into Becki's life. She had brought a special bond of love.

Again, their roles were reversed. Eileen was the student, Rachel her instructor in the course of life. At the office door, Rachel gave Eileen a quick hug. Like a child, Eileen felt sheltered in that embrace. Their two worlds collided. On parting, Rachel spoke of quality of life; Eileen countered with the latest research and the newest drugs being used here at home. Again she mentioned the possibility of a bone marrow transplant. But Rachel smiled the way she always did at the end of a semester.

Resigned, Eileen said, "I'll call Timothy Whitesaul this evening. He knows about you."

"Will he accept me in his program?"

"If I ask him—"

Rachel stood, adjusted her hairpiece, and gathered up her purse and jacket for the last time. "Will it take you long to send my medical records?"

Eileen tucked the chart under her arm and met Rachel's gaze. "If Timothy agrees, I'll air express them tomorrow."

Rachel flashed her radiant smile. "My colleagues at the university are throwing a farewell party for me on Tuesday. I want you and Becki to come. Will you?"

"Becki would never forgive me if we didn't. She loves grownup parties. And—she has a going-away present for you."

Dr. Rutledge watched her patient leave the clinic for the last time. Head high. Back straight. Her body much too thin. But Rachel left without regrets.

Dr. Rutledge had only one. She had failed Rachel McCully medically. But in her journal, she wrote:

I am not God. I am simply Rachel's friend, Rebecca's mother, and all of my training, all of my skills have not stopped the progression of

Rachel's illness. She is in God's hands. Or perhaps that is where she has been all along. Her strength, her faith are somehow rekindling my own.

Four days later Dr. Rutledge canceled two of her afternoon appointments and pulled into the faculty parking lot at the university. Hand in hand with her daughter, she went up the steps and into McClaren Hall.

Rachel McCully's dark lustrous eyes came alive when she lectured, danced when she laughed with friends, and sometimes teared when she quoted the Lake Poets. They were tearing now as the university president and the faculty from the English and history departments filed into her office.

"Bon voyage, Rachel," they chorused.

Nelson Rodgers walked in, balancing a cake with flickering candles. He looked smug as he placed the cake on her desk.

"What's this about, Nelson? It's not my birthday."

"That's what we want to know. We're not accustomed to a bon voyage party in the middle of the year."

Misty Owens's double chin quivered. "Quitting in the middle of the year doesn't make sense, not without an explanation. And not when so many students are clamoring to take your classes."

Rachel had to carry off her farewell with dignity, had to hide her fears from those who had known her for so long. She didn't want their pitying glances as the cancer took over. She laughed lightly. "Misty, I'm long past due for a sabbatical."

Nelson licked a bite of icing. "We should be celebrating your twelve years on our faculty, not sending you abroad."

Thirteen, she mused, *if you counted the two years part-time while I completed my doctoral studies and postgraduate courses abroad on a Fulbright Scholarship.*

He went on: "Rachel, you're at the pinnacle of success. We know you've had some trouble with your health this year, but why leave now? We're here for you."

They were, she knew. But she was going forward with her plans for a year abroad. By then, she'd be in remission. . .or dead. "I really am going to England next week," she managed.

Watching their smiles fade was like seeing the sun slip beyond the horizon. Brilliant one moment; thick dark clouds the next. She took in their expressions—these colleagues who admired her. A few envied her unequivocal success, her way of juggling schedules, but none of them wanted her to leave.

President Stokes caught her eye. "You'll be back before the year's over. Wait and see. We'll leave your room just as it is."

"But you are always scrambling for more space."

"This room has always been reserved for a McCully."

In the pause that followed, Nelson nosed around her bookcase and pulled out her high school annual. He flipped through the pages. "Listen to this. Your classmates thought you witty and wise. Fiercely competitive. Close to kindness, distant of heart. Rachel, does that ever describe you. It should say, next in line for department head—if I retired, that is."

Rachel swiveled her chair as he thrust the annual into her hands. Her full mouth and dark eyes were visible even in the black-and-white. Fiercely competitive? Yes. But on her last appointment with Eileen Rutledge, she had not even approached kindness of heart as they argued about her cancer treatment. Now as her colleagues broke ranks in the crowded office, she saw Eileen standing in the doorway, Rebecca by her side.

"I brought you a present, Rachel."

She smiled at the child. "That was very thoughtful of you, Becki."

Rebecca ran over and leaned against her.

"May I open your present?"

Becki nodded, then helped her tear the pink tissue, revealing a lampshade with tassels along its ridge and rabbits in blue and lavender. Rachel hugged Becki. "I'll cherish this forever."

President Stokes extended his hand to Eileen. "It's Dr. Rutledge now, isn't it? How nice of you and your daughter to join us."

"Someday I hope to send Rebecca here for her university studies."

"Dr. McCully will be back by then," he said with a catch in his voice. "It is a tradition here to have a McCully on staff."

As Eileen glanced across the crowded room, her eyes locked with Rachel's. "Rebecca and I hate to see her go. Rachel's grandfather was the president when I was a student. Her father with the history department—her mother here at McClaren."

"We're proud of Rachel living up to the family tradition."

Tradition? Rachel thought. *It was my sister who wanted to follow in our parents' footsteps, not me.*

Steve Swanson, her friend from the history department, focused his camera and snapped a picture as Rebecca and Rachel puffed their cheeks and blew out the candles. "I think you have one space left on your wall for this snap." He pointed to the spot near the photo of Sinclair and Big Ben. "I'll hang it up before you get back."

Rachel took a quick bite of cake and swallowed her answer. She didn't want to party or pretend. She wanted to go back in time and erase the last nine months of illness.

Steve was scrutinizing her life from the pictures on the wall. *Look closely enough,* she thought, *and you will know what shaped my life—family loyalty, the mountains, the works of great writers.* But the photos on the wall said nothing about her unfulfilled dreams.

"Rachel, are you listening?" Misty Owens asked. "I envy you. Dr. Rutledge has been boasting about how you awaken your own love of literature in your classrooms. And what you have done for Becki."

Rachel started to say it was her sister's love of literature that had influenced her, but how could she explain the ambiguity of where her sister's dreams left off and her own began. Rachel carried yesterday's pain with her—those growing-up memories that even now veiled her in an elusive, diaphanous mist.

Misty murmured her disapproval again. "Dr. Rutledge, can't you persuade Rachel to stay at home? Why all this nonsense about going abroad for a year?"

"It's something Dr. McCully has always wanted to do."

"Whatever for?"

Because of Sinclair Wakefield, Rachel thought. *Because for me, England is Sinclair.*

How strange it seemed to her, that after all these years, Sinclair remained fresh and alive in her thoughts. The dappled images of him always at the back of her mind. Even now, like a quick whisper from the past, her skin prickled at the remembered touch of his hand on hers, his lips sweet and minty lingering on her own.

She wanted time to find Sinclair Wakefield again and tell him why she had failed to meet him on that rainy summer morning under the shadow of Big Ben. She owed him the truth and for her own conscience needed to tell him that she had loved him even though she had sent him away. If he knew the truth, perhaps she could bear the death sentence hanging over her.

∾

In London, a month later, Sinclair Wakefield walked into the solicitor's office marked Blackstone and Rentley. He eased into the armed chair across from his old friend and stretched out his lanky legs. He had not felt so relaxed in a long time.

"So what's the good news you phoned me about, Bailey?"

"Your investments are holding steady in spite of a global market on a tailspin. With a few minor changes your losses will be minimal. We might even be able to increase your earnings."

"That's better than some of my friends are doing."

"You were always a cautious investor, a man with a strategy." He fingered his cuff link. "I have other good news. I took the liberty of leasing your cottage in the Lake District."

"Leased it?"

"It's part of your portfolio—"

"I was thinking about selling it."

"You're better off holding on to the property."

"Especially since you've already rented it."

"She's an American. She came to me on personal business. As we parted, she asked where she could find a rental in the North Country. She particularly asked me about Stradbury Square."

Sinclair reached up and straightened his tie, then clasped his hands again. "No one even knows that village is on the map."

"It isn't. That's why she surprised me. Once I told her about your place, that was it. She took it—sight unseen."

Wakefield felt a queasy sensation in his stomach. It passed quickly. "An American? What did she look like?"

Bailey leaned back in his chair. "Very attractive. But then, you always did have an eye for a beautiful woman."

"Is that how you see me, Bailey?"

"I'm sorry—that was in poor taste considering Mary and your boy."

"It's been two years."

"Right, old boy. Hard to believe. I tell you, I miss that little fellow. Blake used to come here and climb up in old Bailey's lap and look for sweets in my pocket."

"He was always asking when he could go back to see Bailey."

"I can't even begin to imagine your pain. I wish I could have done more after your wife and son were killed. Of course, I'm still handling the lawsuit against the railroad company."

"Your idea, not mine. It won't bring my family back. But this American, what can you tell me about her?"

Bailey flipped his pen, end over end. "She's a university professor on sabbatical. An English professor, I think."

Sinclair's palms went sweaty, his mouth dry. "You said she specifically asked about Stradbury Square?"

"Yes. The minute I told her about Wakefield Cottage, she leased it for a year. No questions asked. Money up front. She had funds transferred from the States." He scratched his head and checked his notes. "She won't be living there full-time until the end of April or early May. Said she had appointments to keep here in London."

"I'm glad you leased the property. It's best to have it occupied. Does the place need any repairs before she moves in?"

An amused smile caught the corner of Bailey's mouth. "The fence could do with a fresh coat of paint. And the fireplace should be checked. I'll call a friend in Grasmere. What about you, Sinclair?"

"I'm staying on in the house in Oxford. I feel closer to Mary and the boy there."

Bailey shifted uneasily. "And you're back to lecturing?"

"Two days a week on C. S. Lewis. And I started another degree. Art this time."

"Art?"

Sinclair stood, stretched. "I was always interested in the arts. It has filled the hours since—"

"Sinclair, you haven't asked me the name of your renter."

Rachel! Rachel with those magnificent dark eyes. "I think I already know who it is. We were supposed to meet under Big Ben once. Rachel McCully, right?"

Bailey's brows arched in surprise. Wakefield felt himself relaxing again, smiling. "She was long before Mary. I don't think she even knows I married and had a son."

Bailey whistled. "Should I tell her we've talked?"

"If she wanted to find me, she would. Whatever her reason for moving to Stradbury Square, I won't question it." He checked his watch. "I'm having dinner at the club. Would you care to join me?"

Bailey plucked his beard. "Sounds good. Are you staying a fortnight in London this time?"

"Just overnight. I'm driving back to Oxford in the morning."

Bailey put his calls on hold. He opened his desk drawer and took a pamphlet from it. "Miss McCully left this behind, quite accidentally, I think. It's a report on an aggressive anticancer drug being used here in London. Makes me think she's seriously ill."

Wakefield frowned as he read it. "If Miss McCully needs anything, make certain she gets it." He cleared his throat. "If she is ill, as you suggest, she may need a housekeeper. The woman who worked for Mother might be available."

"Audrey? I'll look into it."

Outside, as they strode in silent companionship toward the club, the deep chimes of the Clock Tower rang out. As the resonant bell tolled, Sinclair Wakefield glanced up at Big Ben. The light at the top of the Tower was lit, the House of Commons still in session. The gleaming splendor of The Houses of Parliament reflected in the River Thames, but the peace and calm that had engulfed him when he entered his solicitor's office had vanished. Just when he had reached that point in life when he was ready to pick up the missing pieces—just when he was beginning to come to terms with the loss of his beloved wife and son—he was forced to remember Rachel.

As the bell stopped tolling, Bailey asked, "So. . .what happened to your appointment with Miss McCully?"

"She never showed up."

"Maybe she was delayed in traffic."

"I waited for more than an hour. Three hours to be exact."

"You should have waited longer. She's a beautiful woman."

They had reached the club. Sinclair held the door open for Bailey and with another glance up at Big Ben, said, "A man's pride gets in the way. But God more than made up for my disappointment when he brought Mary and my son into my life. . .even if our time together was far too short."

Chapter 3

A spectacular spring morning lay before Rachel with the splendor of the purple-tipped hills and the serenity of a shimmering lake that was a striking hyacinth blue this morning. For years she had loved the North Country and the breathtaking Cumberlands from the words of the Lake Poets. Now she was drinking in the same beauty that Wordsworth and Coleridge had known. The meadowlands reflected myriad shades in emerald, russet, and gold from the surrounding hills, and that lavender patch high on the hillside above the lake must surely be heather in bloom, Rachel thought.

She longed to run along the footpath lined with brambles and wild Kiftsgate roses and foxgloves. To wander among the dancing daffodils. To catch an arced rainbow or a wispy cloud from the sky. She would give anything for the strength to climb the craggy heights, or even to walk along the zigzagging path on the lower hills. She dared not venture even a mile. But one day, when she licked this illness, she would run and climb again, and nothing would stop her.

This was the unspoiled English countryside Sinclair Wakefield had shared with her. Her senses quickened at the remembrance of his unexpected closeness. His woolly vest had prickled her cheek as he held her. The tantalizing scent of his aftershave lingered long after he leaned down to kiss her.

Three weeks after they had started dating, he had stood in her office in McClaren Hall, waving two round-trip plane tickets in his hand. "We don't celebrate your Thanksgiving at home," he had announced. "But we're going on holiday to England. Forget your turkey and dressing. I want you to meet my family."

They had taken their Thanksgiving break and padded it on both ends with added days. Still giddy with jet lag, they had driven north from London to his mother's house in Stradbury Square and the tiny village that had been his boyhood home. But Rachel's most lasting memory was standing on the lakeshore on that crisp, frosty morning in November, her arm linked with Sinclair Wakefield's. An early autumn had turned the hillside amber, the meadows in shadowed hues, the trees to patches of yellow. The lake barely rippled. Utter stillness.

In the shadow of the hills rising high above the switchback road, the windswept cliffs hung precariously over the lake. Standing there, Rachel and Sinclair had fallen victim to the allure of the Lakes and to each other. In that enchanting hour, she harbored the secret wish to come back to England with Sinclair when his year of teaching ended.

Sighing winds snatched away those dreams, buffeting her with the old fear of carrying the threat of cystic fibrosis into a marriage. Still she liked remembering that one moment in time when he had taken her back to his roots. Her no-nonsense, dignified professor totally different in a hooded jacket and casual corduroys, his shy smile showing his boyish side. He had been anxious for her to love his country. All she could think about then was loving him and knowing she could not destroy that love with defective genes.

This morning, standing once again on a tree-fringed lake, she wondered whether she had imagined Sinclair's love or only desired it. She snuggled into her thick sweater and checked the security of the scarf covering her soft, downy fuzz of hair.

The top branches of the trees reflected in the water. The high crags reflected there, too, rising in gentle slopes and stretching to rocky peaks. The lake mirrored more than hills and trees. It mirrored her soul, past and present, filling her with joy at just being alive. She felt keenly aware of yesterday—Sinclair a part of it—and keenly aware of today, where time was precious. The reflection of past and present cried out for her to catch a glimpse of eternity while still occupying a space on earth. The God of the cattle on a thousand hills did not count years as she did. God did not cling to the cycle of twenty-four-hour days as she had done.

During those first months of illness, her fists had knuckled in anger at Him for robbing her of health and time. At first she had it out with God, long nights of pacing in the empty bedroom, back and forth to the toilet bowl retching from the effects of chemo. Crying. Cajoling. Begging to not be faced with her sister's agonizing journey.

Now she felt an odd acceptance of what she could not change. Still she was left with a thousand questions and with so many unfinished dreams. What had she accomplished in life? What lingering impact had she made on her students? Had any of them been changed by the imprint of her life on theirs?

At times—like yesterday—she still had it out with God, but in a more amicable way she had reminded Him of those things she would still like to do. Browse the museums of Italy again. Sail a sloop off Hawaii with the wind in her face. Peek in on some of her students—especially Jude Alexander—to see whether they had measured up to her expectations. And simpler things like running or eating without feeling nauseous. Or skiing in Switzerland again or facing the challenge of climbing Mt. McKinley. And that cry of her heart for just one more glimpse of Sinclair! She realized that these thoughts didn't have spiritual ribbons attached to them, yet wasn't wanting the wind in your face and the sea on your skin and being free on a mountain slope part of knowing the creation? Knowing the Creator?

Rachel watched a song thrush take flight and followed its upward path toward the sun-bathed summit. The thrush had left its nest and flown. Wasn't that what she had done? Set a course of her own by spreading her wings and breaking with medical tradition? She had made the right choice. For what it was worth—and it might be costly—she was back in control, deciding on her own course of treatment. She did not encourage it for others, but it was the path for her—the choice to have quality of life, however brief.

These months of being too ill to climb would end, one way or the other. Like the thrush, she would take flight on an earthly journey, or perhaps on an eternal one. Until now, she had almost lost sight of looking ahead—of looking up—of being all she could be for a day, a week, a month, a year.

~

As Rachel ambled along the west end of the lake, she was aware of hikers on the hillside, marring her solitude. They had been there all along, blocked from her senses, but now she envied their freedom to scale the fells to the top and to come back down in the same steady gait with heavy rucksacks on their backs. She focused on a lone climber, a wiry man with a thick sweater tied around his waist, binoculars in his hand.

He paused, lifted the binoculars, and focused them on her. Then his pace increased, slipping and sliding past several hikers sitting on the rocks in front of him. He stopped a second time, eyeing her through the binoculars.

She thought it strange, but she was flattered nonetheless. In spite of the hiking boots, the man ran those last few yards toward her. Cupping his mouth, he hollered, "You look lonely as a cloud, Doc."

She frowned, pointing questioningly to herself.

"Yes, you," he laughed. "You look lonely as a cloud."

She heard the familiar ring to his voice. It had to be Morrie Chadbourne, one of those transplanted Americans who loved this country. He was pithy to the point of bluntness but so un-British. He skidded to a stop in front of her and whipped off his sunshades. "Hi, Prof."

"Morrie."

He grinned. "You remember me."

Why wouldn't she? After spending so many months with Eileen, who had once loved him, who probably still loved him, she expected him to say, *What are you doing here?*

Instead he dropped his rucksack to the ground and grasped both her hands. "I should have known you would end up at the Lakes."

"You don't seem surprised that I'm here."

"I called the university recently, trying to reach you."

"Me?"

"Yes, I wanted a quote or two from you for my next project."

Seeing him again, she thought him perhaps thirty-five, his dark hair silver-streaked at the temples and unruly as it had often been. Of the hundreds of students who had passed through Rachel's life, Morris Chadbourne proved one of the most promising and most successful. His latest scholarly work, a comparative study of Coleridge and Wordsworth, had been well-received in the literary world at Oxford and at the universities of London. She was certain it hadn't made him wealthy, but surely it had put him high in the literary ranks.

"Morris Chadbourne, you've done quite well for yourself."

"I don't exactly own the bank, Dr. McCully. But I lecture now, and that puts food on the table. And you?"

"I'm on sabbatical."

"Are you here on a study program? That's what professors do with sabbaticals, isn't it?"

"Not this one."

"Do you think the university would give me so much as a clue? Nothing. Even talked to President Stokes, and all he could promise was he'd let you know I was trying to reach you. Did he?"

"Possibly. My mail is piling up in London."

"At least he admitted that you were in England. Look, let's go somewhere and sit down. Treat's on me."

"I need to be getting back to Stradbury Square."

"So that's where you're hiding out. Any street address?"

"The Wakefield Cottage."

"You're not getting out of my sight until we sit down for a visit. You look exhausted."

"You're the one who was hiking."

He frowned, studying her. "You should be. You need some color in those cheeks of yours." He swung his rucksack over one shoulder and took her arm. "Hungry?"

"Not really."

"But you like quaint atmosphere. I know just the place."

He led her into a country inn with stone-flagged floors and gas lighting. He waved at the owner. "I brought my old university professor with me, Hanley. Be good to her."

"Chadbourne, the wife's making you a mint cake." He winked at Rachel. "From what I see, Chadbourne, she's not old."

"Just a matter of speaking. Will you add some open-faced sandwiches and cream tea? We'll take the table by the fireplace."

"Any word from Lord Somerset, Chadbourne?"

"He and his wife are still planning that world cruise."

As they settled by the small round table, Rachel glanced around, liking the warmth of the fire and the pub's atmosphere. A cast iron range with claw feet sat crookedly in one corner. A gas lantern swung from the ceiling above each table.

"You were right; this is a quaint place," Rachel acknowledged.

"I like it. A man can relax here. There are some tea shops where the proprietors don't appreciate dusty boots and sweaty hikers. It spoils their Victorian image. But Hanley welcomes climbers."

"I see that. Who is Lord Somerset?"

"One of the rich locals, if not the richest."

"He'd have to be for a world cruise."

"He's an art collector."

"You always had an interest in art—in stolen art, if I remember correctly." His eyes shadowed. "I still do."

She rested her chin on her folded hands. "I never knew why."

"Someday I'll tell you." He cracked his knuckles. "Are you feeling all right, Dr. McCully?"

"I'm fine."

She hoped the fire in the stone hearth would bring a rosy glow back to her cheeks. Her mirror had not lied this morning—her complexion was still pasty, the luster in her eyes not like the old days. She hoped that Morrie would not take notice, and if he did, that he would not comment again. But Morrie was always quick to express his concern when something worried him. How could she hide her illness when it was so evident now?

When Hanley delivered the sandwiches and cream tea, he asked, "So, Professor, are you staying with Chadbourne at Lord Somerset's?"

In spite of the pallor, she felt her cheeks burn. "Of course not. Morris and I just ran into each other moments ago. I don't even know Lord Somerset."

Hanley's sea green eyes pierced hers, amused, doubtful. "Have you not heard of Lord Somerset? He's the connoisseur of fine arts in the North Country."

"Quite knowledgeable," Morrie mumbled.

Hanley stood his ground. "Are you liking the Lakes?"

"Yes, it's been such a perfect day—and then running into Morrie here, that was special."

"He has never brought a fairer lady to my pub."

Again her cheeks burned. "My first visit here was in the fall some years ago. It was nice then, too, but much colder."

Hanley stroked his fleshy jaw. "Been here twenty years. April and May are good. We have more sunny periods, like today." He surveyed her, more amused questions in his glance. "You come to Hanley's Pub anytime. I'll be bringing my wife's cake shortly."

Morrie studied her as Hanley lumbered away. "Dr. McCully, I am sorry. Hanley's a bit of a romantic."

She rubbed her cheeks. "More embarrassing. Overbearing."

"You're not here on a study program, are you? You're ill."

"I'm better. But let's talk about you, Morrie. I've read several critical reviews on your study of Coleridge and Wordsworth. They were favorable. So what next?"

"A smaller study on the work of C. S. Lewis, and during my free time I'm researching lost art."

"World War II again?"

"Particularly a collection stolen in France. I'm on my own on that project, but I'm taking lectures at Oxford on Lewis."

Her cheeks flushed for the third time. "Have you studied under Sinclair Wakefield? He is well versed on Lewis."

"He just lectures two days a week. I'm petitioning for his seminars in the fall. How do you know him, Dr. McCully?"

"He was on faculty with us some years ago."

He held her gaze with a piercing glance. "Did you know Wakefield's wife and son were killed in a rail accident in France two years ago? Thankfully there were no other children—just the one boy, four or five when he died. But, of course, you would know that. You're staying in his cottage."

"I didn't know." *Why hadn't the solicitor mentioned it? Why had Audrey kept silent?* Pulling her sweater around her, she heard the tremor in her own voice. "I arranged for the cottage through a solicitor in London."

"You okay, Prof?"

"I'm all right." She straightened the tilt of her head scarf and wondered if the fuzz of hair showed.

He waved for the waitress. "Could you toss on another log? My guest is shivering with cold."

"You didn't have to do that, Morrie."

"The stone walls make it chilly." He took another sandwich and stowed it away in four bites. "I think I upset you. From the look on your face, you and Wakefield were more than colleagues."

"Good friends once." She touched the cuff of her sweater and checked the time. "I really should go."

"Not yet. Tell me about yourself."

Reluctantly, she settled back into her chair. "I finished my twelfth year of teaching a year ago. And then—well, we'll talk about that another time. What I really want to know is whether you still hear from Eileen Rutledge."

"We don't keep in touch. Do you?"

"She's been my doctor for the last several months."

He wiped his mouth. A flicker of understanding crossed his face. "Your doctor? Eileen is an oncologist."

"And a good one."

He reached across the table and squeezed Rachel's hand. "So that's why you're on sabbatical?"

"I told you, Morrie, I'm fine. I took a year off to take stock of my life as a teacher, wondering whether I left any lasting impression on the students who passed through my classes. You think about things like that when you've been ill."

"You were a good teacher. You know that, don't you?"

"I thought so."

"Don't get bogged down with that hay, wood, and stubble stuff you used to talk about when you graded our research papers."

She pushed her plate aside, the cake half eaten. "You touch their lives for a semester or two and they're gone. What I want to know now is whether they've succeeded."

"I turned out all right, didn't I?"

"But have all of your choices made you happy?"

"You mean Eileen?" he asked bitterly.

"I thought you two had something going between you."

"Just a college crush."

It was more than that, she thought. *There's a child. Do you know about Becki?* "I thought the two of you would marry."

"That affair with Eileen ended a long time ago. What happened to us after we left campus was not your problem. Your job was to teach the classics and you did a bang-up job."

She flashed a radiant smile. "I really must go, Morrie."

"I can't offer you a ride back to Stradbury Square, unless you want to ride on my handlebars."

"I have my own rental. But I'm surprised at you. You always had an old jalopy on campus."

"Part of my student image. I can't afford the luxury of a car here. I have a bike out behind the pub that gets me back and forth, and I depend on the underground or a taxi in the city."

They stood. "Doc, Stradbury Square is too far away. I have an extra room. Great spot to live. Spectacular scenery. A badminton court for when you're feeling better. Some private paths if you want to be alone. And, like Hanley suggested, an art collection that you won't believe."

"Then you're doing better in your writing than I thought."

"I make ends meet. But the art collection belongs to Lord and Lady Somerset."

His gaze shifted toward Hanley at the counter, who was nonchalantly wiping glasses. He lowered his voice. "I'd like to show you the Somersets' art treasures. The truth is, I'd give anything—do anything—to claim one of those masterpieces as my own."

Stolen art. For a second the look in his eyes troubled her.

"Doc, if you were close by, I could walk with you each day—help you gain some strength back. Maybe put some color back in your face." He looked boyish, eager. "If you won't share the house, there are guest cottages on the property. I'll arrange for you to stay in one of them. It's less isolated than Stradbury Square."

"I'm quite happy at the Wakefield Cottage."

He broke off a bite of the cake left on her plate and popped it into his mouth. "Will you come back soon?"

"We'll see."

"You'll have to do better than that. I want your word."

"All right. I will drive in someday. How's that?"

He caught her hand and smiled. "I'll count on it."

~

Morrie saw Rachel to her car and watched her pull out of the drive with a flick of her hand in farewell and that quick, warm smile. Old memories stirred with his first impressions of her when he was a collegian: striking, young, witty, desirable. And his own impudent belief that he could charm her, date her—he the young student from Kentucky besotted with his professor.

Now he wasn't certain whether it was his head or heart pounding—hammering, crushing his temples with its intensity. Years ago, back at the university, they seemed to move on the same wavelength. He could match her brilliance, and he knew it. But she had the confidence, the air of success, and he craved them both. She represented the position and popularity that he wanted.

In those early months on campus, he lingered after class or arrived early to engage her in conversation. He recalled sitting on the campus lawn a time or two, discussing the classics. All of that before Eileen Rutledge walked into his life.

Gripped by a fresh onslaught of loneliness, Morrie spun around, walked back into Hanley's Pub, and sat at the counter.

Hanley eyed him quizzically. "What will it be?"

"Another coffee. Black. And if Miss McCully comes back here again, no remarks. We are friends. Nothing more."

Hanley slapped an empty cup on the counter and filled it to the brim. "Just your old professor?"

Morrie gulped and felt the scalding drink going straight down. "Yes, that's it."

"She is much more a lady—more attractive than your other friends." He refilled Morrie's cup. "But you seem troubled at seeing her again."

"I didn't think it would matter, but I was wrong."

Hanley polished another wine goblet with his towel. "Another guest left a message for you."

Morrie glanced around, the coffee spilling on the counter as he turned back. "Who?"

"Didier Bosman, the museum curator from London. He was sitting in the far corner watching you and the lady, taking pictures, I think. He said to tell you he would call you later." Hanley slapped the towel across one shoulder and leaned across the counter. "Stay out of trouble, boy, especially if that woman is going to become important to you."

Morrie fell heir to a lot of Hanley's counsel. His own marriage was a battle zone, but he liked to match up others who came through his door. It added spark to his dull, routine days.

"The professor is ill, Hanley. That's my only concern."

But some of those old enamored longings taunted him. What was it about Rachel McCully that always lingered in the back of his mind? That she believed in him? Expected the best from him? Or perhaps it was her solitary way. For all of her love of the mountains, her personable way in the classroom, she was an enigma, a woman who felt comfortable alone, a woman who never quit climbing or dreaming. There was always another mountain to conquer. Now she was grounded and this God that Dr. McCully believed in had tossed her the challenge of her lifetime.

And he was about to throw her safety to the wind. The museum curator's plan had sounded so simple. Fill the Somerset Estates with guests—just a few would be ample. Disconnect the intricate alarm system. Unlock the side gate. And go to the caretaker's cottage and sleep. Sleep! All for a painting—not for money, but for the possession of an Asher Weinberger work of art.

Morrie would awaken the next morning the sane struggling scholar. And hate himself. But the Weinberger would finally be his. No, it had always been his right, his heirloom. No more legal hassles. Surely Dr. McCully would understand that.

Hanley took Morrie's empty cup and wiped the counter dry. "Looks like she is more than a professor to you, Chadbourne."

Had he been in love with her? Was he smitten again? No, he had been in love with Eileen Rutledge. Infatuated with Dr. McCully. Or was it that desperate need to prove himself to his professor once again?

Hanley whipped the towel from his shoulder and swiped the counter once more. "What is wrong, Chadbourne? A woman walks in here with you, and you fall apart."

"I must get back to the Somerset Estates."

"If you are responsible for them, you should. And take my advice, son.

No woman is worth this kind of fretting."

"Hanley," his wife bellowed from the kitchen.

As Hanley shambled off, Morrie slid off the stool and with half a chuckle left the pub. But he couldn't shake off Hanley's question. *What is wrong, Chadbourne?*

He was about to betray Rachel McCully—the one woman who thought him clever, scholarly. She was proud of him. Respected him. No matter what advice Hanley could dish out, or what the museum curator demanded, one thing Morrie knew for certain: He did not want Dr. Rachel McCully to be disappointed in him.

Chapter 4

Every day for eight weeks, except for those visits to the London clinic, Rachel awakened to a hermit thrush singing and to the happy patter of the housekeeper in the kitchen. She pushed herself to a sitting position, stretching her long legs beneath the cool sheets, and listened to the flutelike tones of the bird. Since coming to Wakefield Cottage, she shared the shyness of her feathered friend—its love of the woodland, its need for the privacy of her garden, its joy at awakening each morning. The bell-like music matched the song that quickened her own heart. Each time the sun burst over Stradbury Square, she felt pillowed by an eternal God, triumphant that she had beaten the odds by adding another day to her life, clearly defying the gloomy predictions of a year ago.

She ducked her head lower for a better view from her bedroom window. Stradbury Square was a peaceful village off the beaten trail where a few dozen or more thatched, whitewashed cottages and old stone houses nestled against the wooded gardens. Roads snaked around the countryside. A tranquil lake mirrored the hillsides and the church spire. Neighbors leaned over the picket gates to exchange gossip and homemade buns and jellies with Rachel in the same way that they had undoubtedly done in years gone by with Sinclair's mother.

Some of the neighbors remembered Rachel's visit almost ten years ago. They welcomed her back, and the housekeeper who had fretted over Sinclair as a boy had moved in once again to watch over Rachel. Audrey must be all of seventy, of sturdy stock, and stronger than Rachel. They never mentioned Sinclair, but pictures of him hung on the cottage walls, and the boyhood mementos that his mother had treasured lay on the bookshelves in the drawing room. On Fridays, faithful as the clock ticking in the corner of the room, Audrey dusted them with obvious pleasure.

Slowly, Rachel forsook the comfort of the old-fashioned bed, slipped into a new pair of slacks and a long-sleeve denim top, and grabbed her work gloves. As she stepped through the conservatory into the garden, she breathed in the sweet fragrance of the rambler roses and flowering shrubs—much easier on her queasy stomach than the sizzling sausage in the kitchen. She knew the pleasing aroma of the garden changed with the seasons—sometimes honeysuckle scented the air; sometimes the pungent spicy odor of the trailing arbutus or an intoxicating whiff of sweet peas tickled one's senses.

The sun filtered through the broadleaf evergreens and cut its path across the tapestry of flowers. She ambled over the pebbled path, cupping a pink camellia to her left, and stopping to trim a dead branch off her hollyhocks with her secateurs. Wakefield Cottage had become her sanctuary, her safe hideaway.

But it was not the haunts of poets that had drawn her to England. She had come here with a kaleidoscope of memories and fading portraits of Sinclair Wakefield. Treasured keepsakes. Vaporous shadows. Especially during her illness, she saw his face in the face of strangers. And now living in the cottage of his boyhood, she heard his voice in her dreams. Knowing that Sinclair had married and was now widowed, she resolved not to impose upon his grief. She had come to terms with the possibility of never seeing him again. Someday she would confide in Audrey, and if she lost this battle with cancer, Sinclair would one day know what really happened when he waited for her beneath Big Ben.

"Madam, you forgot your breakfast."

Would Rachel ever grow used to her housekeeper's greeting? She smiled. "Good morning, Audrey."

"Perfect morning," Audrey clipped. In truth, she was a soft-hearted woman who took pleasure in seeing to Rachel's needs. She wiped her red hands against the apron tied tightly around her ample middle. "You have a guest, Miss Rachel. Not too pleasant a man, I might add. Demanded admittance immediately."

"At this early hour?"

"Said he came for breakfast." She snorted, disgruntled again. "Said he knew you rose early. Such impudence."

That could only be Morrie Chadbourne. He was shamelessly bold—not a staid, polite British gentleman that Audrey would welcome. She pictured the two of them clashing at the door—Morrie demanding entry; Audrey reluctant to thrust company on Rachel before breakfast.

"What shall I tell him, Madam?"

"Is it Morrie Chadbourne?"

"He didn't give his name. Said you'd know right off."

Then it was Morrie—coming into town from Grasmere. He was lean as a rail, but his appetite would be ravishing. "Show him in, please. And, if you don't mind—"

"Will be no bother," Audrey said in her simple, country voice. "I'll crack another egg or two. Throw in more sausage."

"He can have my sausage and fried tomatoes." Rachel had no stomach for large meals; her poor appetite was an offense to Audrey. "And I think we'll just breakfast out here."

Audrey cast a glance at the rising sun. "As you wish, madam. But stay in the shade. No need to risk a sunburn."

She took Audrey's warning seriously. A hot sun could sap her energy or play havoc with the medicine that she was forced to take. "I will be careful. And, Audrey, Morrie likes plenty of toast and marmalade."

"Looks like he's never been fed before, but he won't go away from here hungry." She turned on her heels. "I'll see to that and have that breakfast for you both in a swift jiffy."

Rachel pocketed the shears, dropped her garden gloves on the workbench, and brushed the soil from her hands before tucking her short strands of hair beneath her scarf. As she heard Morrie's determined steps scrunching over the pebbled walkway, she squared her shoulders, standing tall as she had always done when she faced her students at the university.

A beguiling smile filled Morris Chadbourne's angular face as he came toward her, his dark-rimmed glasses making him look studious. "Hi, Doc McCully. Just getting in to see you was like the old days. I thought I was petitioning for a spot in your classroom."

She held out her hands. "Morrie, what a lovely surprise."

"You didn't keep your appointment—it's been three weeks since you promised to come see me."

"I have no excuse."

But she did. The trips to Timothy Whitesaul's clinic took time.

Morrie's nose crinkled at the heady fragrance in her garden. "Are you really sorry?"

"Yes, now that I'm thinking about it. . . Morris, what tore you away from the purple hills of Grasmere?"

"You." He wrapped his strong hands around hers and bent to kiss her cheek. "You didn't call on me like you promised."

"I thought you were just being polite."

"When I make a date with a lady, I expect her to keep it."

She teased. "I trust you didn't pedal all the way here."

"No, a friend offered to drive me here in his truck."

"A long, bumpy ride for a checkup."

"We did get an early start," he admitted.

"I still think you should buy a car."

He grinned down at her. "I never got the hang of driving on the wrong side of the road. Besides, one can almost do the thirty miles of the Lake District without wheels."

"You must be hungry."

"Famished. Haven't eaten since five this morning."

She slipped her arm in his as much to steady her gait as to show her affection for him. "We'll have breakfast out here," she said as they took their seats at the wrought iron table.

He crossed his gangly legs, a wiry, rawboned man like Wordsworth—his eyes wide and intense as he surveyed her garden. A red-breasted stonechat fed at the bird feeder, while a honeybee buzzed the delicate petals of the morning glories.

"I want you to go back to my place with me so we can go hiking again. There are several places I still want to show you."

Surely he understood. She had little strength for hiking. "I don't hike much anymore, Morrie."

"When I was a student, you were unbeatable on the mountain trails. The first to suggest a tennis match or a camping trip."

"Yes, I was all of that."

"So what happened? You said you were feeling better."

"I promised President Stokes I'd rest on my sabbatical. Hiking," she repeated, "I think not."

"Come on, Prof. It would be just what the doctor ordered."

"For now, I'm content tending my garden."

He glanced back at the garden gloves and spade lying on her workbench. "Let someone else do the digging and planting."

"That's what I've been telling her," Audrey snapped as she put their breakfast tray on the table. "Last week I persuaded her to hire another gardener, a local man. But look at her—still out here exhausting herself with gardening."

Rachel smiled as Audrey turned back to the kitchen. "Don't believe her. I mostly sit out here in my sun hat and tell the gardener what to do. I want my flower beds to be perfectly laid out for the people who live in this cottage next."

"I don't think the place is for sale."

"It will be someday."

She wondered, as she poured his tea, how much he knew about leukemia. How little she really knew about him. How much she imagined and admired. But there was the other side of Morrie that worried her. His anger at the mention of Eileen. The way his face clouded when he talked about the stolen masterpieces from World War II. The thing that troubled her most was Morrie perhaps not knowing that his daughter, Becki, existed.

A bemused smile formed around his mouth. Rachel did not think him handsome but kindly. He had so much to give, a charm and warmth all his own. She would gladly claim him as a lifelong friend, so attuned were they in their love for the outdoors, great literature, and England.

Yet they were vastly different—she fashion conscious even in her illness and still buying her clothes from exclusive women's shops. He a scholarly man, a literary genius, yet casual always, indifferent to the latest fads. Even today he was dressed in khaki slacks, newer than his frayed maroon shirt.

Morrie attacked his breakfast with a passion, but he was too busy a man to be dropping in for a carefree visit.

"What brought you in from Grasmere?" she asked softly.

"I wanted a decent breakfast. I'm a rotten cook, you know." He popped another bite of sausage into his mouth. "And when you didn't keep your promise to come see me, I worried about you."

Rachel set her demitasse cup down, her tapered fingers still wrapped around it as her gaze locked with Morrie's. "You must not worry about me, Morris."

"Then tell me the truth. How are you. . .really?"

"Sometimes my white count goes off the charts. But I'm responding to the new treatment here in England and may go into remission."

"Not a cure?"

"One can always hope for a five-year cure. Or ten years."

"No guarantee?"

"My doctor thinks there is real promise with the new revolutionary drugs he is using for leukemia. He makes no promise of a cure, but what he offers me most is hope."

How much easier to swallow one giant-sized pill a day, she thought, *than to face that dreaded chemo.* Eventually, if she responded to the treatment, she would remain on a maintenance dose. Already, in just a few weeks, her headaches were less frequent, her old energy creeping back.

Morrie leaned back, a piece of toast covered with marmalade balanced in one hand. "Come back to Grasmere with me. Then I'll take you into London for a second medical opinion."

"I have a physician in London."

"Come back with me. I'd be there to check in on you daily."

"Audrey does that."

"Rachel, you need a change."

"Before this disease takes me?"

"I didn't say that."

"Don't even think it. I'm going to beat this thing. I'll fight it all the way to the grave if I have to. That's better than surrendering. Giving up. Quitting."

"You were never a quitter."

"And I won't quit now. I'm not quite thirty-eight."

"Then you have three years on me. That's all." Frowning, he said, "In class you used to talk about eternity being in the hearts of men. I guess that goes for women, too?"

He had nailed her with what had once been her unswerving belief in meeting God's appointments without quibbling. But her thoughts remained earthbound, wandering slowly back to Sinclair. "Morris, I had unfinished business when I moved here—a friend I wanted to find again. Seeing him, I think, is not possible, so I can never patch up those last unsettled moments between us. If I could, then maybe I would give up battling this leukemia."

"You're not a quitter! This friend of yours, do I know him?"

She held back for a moment, then said, "You travel in the same circles. Lecture on the same circuits. He was a teaching colleague of mine back at the university."

Above the rim of his glasses, his brows knit together. "Wakefield! Why didn't you marry him, Rachel? A husband could comfort you now."

"I have Audrey for a companion."

He nodded. "You're friends but, I daresay, not confidants. Could I help you find him?"

She reached across the table and patted his hand. "It's too late, Morris. I should have taken care of this a long time ago."

The sun rose higher, rapidly reaching toward their shady corner. "Perhaps I can help in another way. The last time we met, you said you wanted to see some of your students again."

"Such a silly dream. I guess I just want to know whether I accomplished all I intended to in their lives."

"Wasn't a dozen years in the classroom enough?"

"Not if I failed to leave an imprint on their lives. I intended to. I prayed that I would."

"Have no regrets. You were a magnificent teacher."

"But I have no permanence, no one to carry on my name at the university. A McCully on campus has been a tradition for three generations."

"Your students are your legacy."

"A nebulous legacy," she said sadly. "I sat on the platform year after year and watched them march by in caps and gowns. They grabbed their diplomas and were out of my life."

"You found me again. Aren't you satisfied with the results?"

"Morrie, I am proud of you. Do you remember that lecture on Coleridge when we discussed living well? Persevering?"

He broke the stem of a flower from the bush. "Vaguely."

She knew by the changing shadows in his eyes that he remembered it well. Why wouldn't he? It was the day he met Eileen Rutledge. "We talked about Coleridge's qualities of greatness—about him not living up to his full potential."

"I'm not measuring up?" he scoffed. "The other day you bragged about my accomplishments."

"But something's troubling you. I think that's why you came here this morning."

"Come on, Doc. Just because I had a little run-in with your housekeeper when I barged in for breakfast?"

"When you came down the mountain the other day, you were full of charm and concern—the Morrie I remembered."

"And now?"

"You tell me. Back in the university, I told my students if they were ever in trouble, to call me. Collect, if they had to."

"I tried. But President Stokes wouldn't give me your forwarding address. I found you in spite of him. But I'm not your responsibility. So just to cheer you up, let's invite some other students back into your life for a big bash. A reunion of sorts. Doc, we'd be helping each other."

"You're serious." She saw by the intensity in his eyes that he was. "Oh, they'd be bored going back to the classroom. They may not remember me kindly. I didn't grade easily. And I know that I failed one—Jude Alexander—in more ways than one."

"I survived," he grinned impishly, "by transferring to Columbia's School of Journalism. It looked better on my résumé. You know, my views were too political, too liberal. I meshed better with the free spirits at Columbia."

"Was that your only reason for transferring?"

He stabbed at the last bite of sausage. "You want me to say Eileen Rutledge drove me away, don't you?"

"Only if it's true. I always thought the two of you were meant to be. I wanted you to work out your difficulties."

He snatched a dry piece of toast and smothered it with marmalade. "Working out a relationship is a tough call."

She waited until he met her gaze again. "I wish she knew about your success in the literary world. Was it Eileen's family that kept the two of you from marrying?"

"Didn't she tell you? We married and divorced two months later. Maybe she wanted to forget our little spring fling during my junior year. Eileen was in her second year at med school by then."

Rachel felt a crushing headache coming on as she thought of the brief exchange across the desk in Eileen's office.

"Eileen, the child looks like—"

"Yes, doesn't she?"

"Morris, why didn't you give your marriage a little longer?"

"Eileen's family didn't think I was good enough for her. I was just a poor, barefoot Kentucky boy who read Wordsworth down by the river." His words crackled. "How could I support her? I hadn't published my first article when I told Eileen I wanted to do literary research full-time. Her father threw away the welcome mat even before he met me."

"And Eileen's mother—was she a social snob, too?"

He looked chagrined. "No, Mrs. Rutledge was a good sort. She wanted her daughter to follow her heart."

"Why didn't you give Eileen a chance to do that?"

Morrie pushed his chair away from the table and squinted at the sun. "And why are you so stubborn about this class reunion?"

"The cottage isn't big enough. We'd have to rent a castle."

He gained time by sipping more tea. "There's nothing wrong with a castle, but I may come up with something better. You just get your invitation list written out—before we run out of time."

"If we have a reunion," she said softly, "I would put Dr. Rutledge's name on my list. And if she comes, she would want to see you."

He rose from the table. "She'd never come."

Thinking of Becki, Rachel smiled. "I rather think you are in for some surprises, Morris. Must you rush off?"

"My driver should be back by now. Maybe we can check out some castles on our way home."

"You are serious?"

"Where you are concerned, yes. Every good teacher deserves recognition." He pressed her shoulder, smiling. "No, don't get up. I can see myself out. Come for tea on Monday, and I'll show you the Somerset Estates."

"I have an appointment with my physician on Monday."

One brow arced as he looked at her, the eyes gentle as he was. "Do you want me to go into London with you?"

"That won't be necessary."

"But I have appointments in London myself. Wakefield and I are lecturing to a women's guild on Monday. If you're free in time, come and hear us."

She shook her head. "Not this time. But we could travel back from London together early Tuesday morning."

"No can do. I have another interview with an art dealer to discuss a painting I've had my eye on for a long time. The price he is demanding is still negotiable."

She reflected on Morrie's lifestyle, the job he held. Morrie had the quality of greatness but not the bank account to go with fame and fortune. "Morrie, neither one of us can afford to purchase a masterpiece."

His words sharpened. "Whatever it costs me—whatever I have to do—I want that Weinberger painting."

If she charted his breakfast mood swings on a graph, they would peak and dip, both ends shooting off the chart. This was not the Morrie she remembered sitting in the top row in her classroom, quietly debating, sometimes arguing the genius of literary giants. She remembered Morrie as a studious intellectual peering out on life through thick-rimmed glasses, pleasant to his classmates, yet preoccupied with rising above his boyhood limitations. He had been part of the basketball team but never a team player. Even then, he had been a solitary man, bedeviled with his obsession for art.

"Morrie, are you in trouble?" she asked.

The flecks of gray in his eyes darkened. "It's nothing I can't handle. Now, what about going into London together?"

"Protecting me again? Why are you being so good to me?"

He leaned down and brushed his lips gently across her cheek. "Because you are a remarkable woman, Rachel McCully."

Chapter 5

As he reached the swinging gate, Morrie Chadbourne's smile fragmented. He jammed his hands into his pockets and stumbled along to the truck with his eyes downcast.

"You took long enough," the driver said as Morrie hauled himself up into the passenger seat. "Did it go as planned?"

Morrie slouched lower and glared at the bearded driver beside him, a man younger than himself. "Not quite the way you expected, Chip. We didn't discuss having the reunion at the Somerset Estates. I can't do that to her. She trusts me."

"You'll get over it, Chadbourne. You're the one who wants that Weinberger painting. That means you figure out a way to deliver our share of the Somerset collection to us."

"I never meant to turn any of the collection over to you. It was all a joke on my part."

"Bosman isn't laughing."

Didier Bosman, the son of a European art dealer, was the museum curator he'd interviewed twice. Even his name threw Morrie into a tailspin. His image was easily recalled: medium height, rotund, thinning hair, respectably dressed, a nondescript face that would never be picked from the crowd. But the monetary value of each painting put a gleam in his eyes. After the interview, Bosman had tracked Morrie to Hanley's Pub, and was surely the sweat-togged figure prowling around the estates last evening.

Chip went on in his mocking tone. "A joke, was it? So you never wanted the Weinberger painting?"

Wanted it? Morrie could taste the desire. He knew the bitterness of trying to trace the ownership back to his great-grandmother in Paris. He had combed through sales records and art catalogs. Unless Morrie admitted who he really was, Weinberger's paintings would remain on museum walls and in private collections without restitution. And the others—those he could not trace—lost like the paper trail. How could he explain to anyone—even to Rachel McCully—why his interest in the works of Vermeer, Degas, and Monet was small in comparison? He had admiration for other artists, but he could live the rest of his life without a Rembrandt or a Goya or Matisse, if only he could lay claim to just one Weinberger painting.

"You tried the paper trail, Chadbourne. It didn't work."

His search had led him to the French-Swiss art connection, to the National Archives and Records in Washington, to the still-classified documents in France, and to the declassified documents in Germany. He could prove that the Chadbourne Collection had been well known in the city of Paris in the late 1930s—that it had hung on the walls of his great-grandmother's villa. But he could not prove he was the only heir.

"Cooperate with us. We can put that painting in your hands."

He hated the arrogance of the man. Chip was a bit of an actor. The acquired British accent was more midwestern American, as fraudulent as the man himself. Sometimes for the delight of it, he turned on an Irish brogue, claiming Ireland as his homeland. Morrie pegged him as more than a driver. Bosman gave the orders, but could he mastermind an art heist like this one?

"It won't work, Chip. Security is unbelievable. The gates electrified. The floor plan confusing. The alarm system—"

"Disable the system. We need two hours at most. Whatever you need, Bosman will get it. An electrician. A wire cutter. An explosives expert. The Millennium Dome heist failed. Bosman won't tolerate failure again." He swerved to avoid a rock in the road.

Morrie gritted his teeth. "I can't go through with it."

Chip shifted gears and took the hill at high speed. "It might cost you the professor if you back out on us now."

"Professor McCully is dying anyway."

The younger man's jaw clamped. "Dying? That's the end station for all of us. I didn't think she was that old."

"She isn't. She's sick. And whatever time she has left, I'm going to protect her. I'm going to see that she enjoys it."

"You're going soft for this woman?"

Once that might have been true—the university student infatuated with his professor. But not now. Morrie braced his foot on the floorboard as they took the narrow curves. He glanced back and could still see the Wakefield Cottage in the distance. He had been a fool to go there. Now Bosman knew where she lived.

"I'd say you can't protect her, short of marrying her. Maybe the wife can't testify against the husband. Either way, you wouldn't want anything to happen to her."

In cold fury, Morrie wanted to grab the wheel and take them both out on the next curve. "Leave Dr. McCully out of this."

The truck jerked forward. "Don't mess with us, Chadbourne. We need that Somerset house occupied in the next three weeks. And a better floor plan mapped out with the exact location for each painting—five from the drawing room, seven from the main gallery. Four from the library. The rest from the smoking room. See that you tag them and move the two Desmond oriental vases into the drawing room. Bosman has decided to take those as well. He already has a buyer."

He chortled. "Don't look so worried, Chadbourne. Somerset is heavily insured. He'll cut his losses with few questions asked."

"You underestimate him."

"No, my friend. You underestimate him. He wants no scandal."

He tossed a sheet of paper on Morrie's lap. "We want these two women invited to the reunion."

"Amanda Pennyman, Jude Alexander," Morrie read aloud. "How did you get these?"

"A museum contact back at the university. A simple matter."

"Forget Jude Alexander. She and Dr. McCully did not part on good terms."

"Then I'll take care of that one. You just make certain that Pennyman gets there. She has a live-in boyfriend. Kevin Nolan. Make certain he comes with her. That's an order. Just follow it."

"It's an irrational scheme. Just steal the paintings while the place is vacated—while the servants sleep and the Somersets cruise. There's no need for a reunion—"

"Scotland Yard is taking particular concern for private collectors on holiday. They would not expect a robbery with a house full of guests. For us, it will be a quick midnight entry. A quick exit. Nothing will happen to your guests."

"And innocent guests will be blamed for the art theft?"

"Right on. Knowing women guests, they will paw every vase and bronzed artifact within reach and leave their fingerprints."

Morrie choked on the lump in his throat. "Forget the Weinberger painting. I want no part of this."

"We know differently! Bosman doesn't question your motives, but I can't figure you out. The Weinberger must be worth two million. The rest of the collection much higher. Why were you willing to settle for just the Weinberger, Chadbourne?"

So they hadn't figured out Morrie's relationship to the Weinbergers. A distant relationship it was true, but his great-grandmother had married into the Chadbourne family in Paris. How long had she kept her Jewish heritage secret? Had it been her interest in the gifted Asher Weinberger that gave her away? Somewhere in the early '30s, Morrie's great-grandmother had added Asher's work to her vast collection. But the art plundering in Europe tore the paintings from Sophie Chadbourne's walls—and stole her soul. His soul. *Where,* Morrie reasoned, *was Rachel McCully's God when that happened? Was her God dead In the '30s? in the '40s?*

"You're a strange man, Chadbourne. Brilliant. Persuasive. Greedy. Your greed will cost you—or cost the women in your life. But you puzzle me—I thought you believed in our cause."

"Bosman told me he was researching the provenance issue—tracking the ownership of World War II paintings for the heirs. That's why I interviewed him. That was why I got involved."

"That was a nice little twist for Bosman. The caretaker for one of the largest collections in the north walked right into his office to interview him."

"I thought Bosman was legitimate until he boasted about his connection with the Millennium Dome jewel heist."

"We won't have another failure like that one, and we wouldn't give Somerset's paintings another thought if we didn't know their value. The Somersets are rich. We believe they are also heavily insured."

They were well informed. Morrie had been researching an article on the foiled robbery at the Millennium Dome when he met Bosman. As the truck rolled along, he ran it through his mind again. A dozen men had been arrested by Scotland Yard, and Didier Bosman was not among them. Bosman boasted a link to the robbery, but Morrie could not be certain he was not just a copycat thief, foolishly planning on bulldozers and smoke bombs and a boat waiting on the lake to whisk them away—and a number of followers like Chip willing to take the risk for the money involved.

"A robbery in the Lake District?" Morrie had joked. "I assume I can quote you in the article."

"Do that," Bosman said, "and you'll regret it."

Morrie repeated the same thought to Chip. "All that planning for $500 million worth of diamonds. It didn't work. It won't work at the Somerset Estates either."

"Bosman didn't spend all those years as a museum curator studying the value of paintings for nothing. Twenty paintings, that's all he wants.

Nineteen for us. One for you."

Twenty paintings out of three hundred. Morrie did not question the number. Bosman had done his homework. He had targeted the most valuable pictures in the collection. Those with the highest market value. Those most heavily insured. And four with questionable ownership and the least likely to be detected.

Considerate thieves? *No one loses that way,* he thought.

"Bosman has to be crazy. You can't put a boat on the Lakes for an escape route. And there's no way you can drive off with a truckload of stolen paintings without being caught before you reach Manchester or London."

"They'll be secure within an hour. When it's safe, we'll move them elsewhere, perhaps north to Scotland."

Thirty to sixty minutes' distance? Grasmere? Some other city. Some warehouse that Morrie was unaware of?

Chip's cockiness increased. "The Somerset Estates is just another practice run. A little drive in the country. The British Museum is next. There we won't settle for just twenty paintings."

He slammed on his brakes a block from the pub, jolting Morrie against the dashboard. "Out," he said, his sardonic smile as cutting as his tone. "I think you can walk from here."

As Morrie's feet hit the ground, Chip gave his final shotgun orders. "We'll be in touch. Bosman wants to place men and women in the area—and in the Somerset Estates. So we need the place occupied. Replace the security guards you have. And you'll need a butler for that reunion of yours, one of Bosman's choice."

Before Morrie could slam the door, Chip accelerated and made dust of the road as he drove away. There was no way for Morrie to redeem himself or to slip out of the net that surrounded him.

~

Back at Wakefield Cottage, Rachel lingered in the garden, watching a bee light on the crusty egg on her plate.

Why would Morrie even consider a school reunion, small as it would be? She questioned his motives.

He had betrayed Eileen.

Was she any safer under his spell?

At last she stood and carried the tray of dishes into the house. She found Audrey standing by the east window, her expression one of puzzlement. "So Mr. Chadbourne is gone? He is trouble, that one."

"Audrey, you don't know him."

Audrey turned, fire in her eyes. "I daresay you don't know him either. In our village, you park in front of the cottage when you come visiting. Not down the road, out of sight."

"His friend had errands to run."

"In Stradbury Square?" She shook her head. "His friend was parked down there the whole time. That's their truck in the distance." Her tone softened. "Come, see for yourself and give me that tray. Cleaning up is my job."

Audrey took the tray but remained rooted by the window. "There is no place in the world like Stradbury Square. That's why we don't want strangers coming about, ruining it for us."

Rachel gazed out on the landscape, a harmony of nature on ancient hillsides. Stradbury Square was a world to itself with its cobbled streets and secluded gardens and its narrow gravel roads snaking around the tapestry of color. In the distance the truck rambled over the winding road and disappeared from sight.

"You're certain that Morrie's friend simply waited for him?"

"Like he didn't want to be seen or remembered."

For want of words, Rachel said, "I've been meaning to ask you, Audrey. I don't recall this window from my first visit here."

"Mr. Sinclair had it put in when his mother took sick. He had to cut into the wall. Brought in contractors from London. Mrs. Wakefield had such happiness sitting here, once she couldn't walk about the village or work in her conservatory—but promise me, Miss McCully, that you won't be seeing that young man again."

"He wants me to have a reunion with some of my students."

The cups on the tray rattled. "A reunion here?"

Rachel laughed. "Not here. I suggested a castle."

"Don't take on anything extra right now. You need your rest. Get your strength back and then worry about parties and guests."

"Audrey—you know, I might not get better."

"All the more reason to save your strength. You have job enough just trying to get well. But if you are going to keep seeing that young man, then it's up to me to find out who the driver was. Once I offer a plate of scones to my neighbors, tongues will loosen. It's a country-style telegraph. We'll pass word along from cottage to cottage that we want to know about that truck and its driver." She looked determined. "If I pass enough scones along, we will have a description of that driver. It's my job to look after you. That's what the solicitor told me when he called to see if we needed any more repairs on the cottage."

"When I rented this place, he told me you went with the cottage. What a thoughtful man, looking after me like that!"

Audrey's throaty chuckle erupted. "Bailey Rentley just keeps the portfolio. It's the owner who pays for the repairs."

The owner. Sinclair. "How is Sinclair, Audrey?"

A fractional arc lifted the thick brow. "Still grieving for his wife and boy. But no one can tell that but me who knows him so well." Her shoulders heaved with a massive sigh. "I ought to tell him about your friend."

"Don't trouble Sinclair. He doesn't even know I'm here."

"I say he is fraught with learning, not stupid. If that solicitor Bailey knows you are living here, then Mr. Sinclair knows. There's not much that happens here in Stradbury Square that passes by Sinclair Wakefield."

"If he knows—is that why he doesn't come around anymore?"

The tired eyes sought Rachel's. "Mr. Wakefield always hoped you'd come back to Stradbury Square to live."

"I did."

"He didn't mean for you to come alone." Her expression grew stern. "That day Mr. Sinclair went into London to meet you, why did you not keep your appointment?"

Payback time. What goes around, comes around. Audrey could be her mother standing there, her gaze razor sharp. "I was there, Audrey. I just didn't let Sinclair see me."

A puzzled frown spread the wrinkles on the older woman's face. The momentary anger eased. "He changed after that—never mentioned you again. Then he met Mary. She was good for him. And that boy—I wondered why they didn't have more children. Mr. Sinclair used to talk about a big family. But Mary almost died when Blake was born. And Blake—God bless that little fellow—he was always frail, happy but frail—funny the way things come about."

She lifted her apron and dabbed her eyes. "He used to come and bring the wife and boy when his mother was still alive. Nice little boy. Loved to play with his father's toys." She gave a quick wave of her hands toward the bookshelves. "Little Blake would put them back in the same place when it was time to leave and come out to my kitchen and thank me for the cookies and tea. He never drank the tea, mind you. He was such a nice little boy. Shameful to be gone like that."

She turned and left the room, moving laboriously toward the kitchen, one hip higher than the other. "Seems to me that there's too much of yesterday's garbage and heartache still cluttering this place," she mumbled. "We ought to get it cleaned up, and I just might be the one to do something about it."

"Audrey, I never meant to hurt Sinclair."

She glanced back, her red-rimmed eyes watery. "I wish Mr. Wakefield knew that."

∽

Morrie's eyes focused on the gravel as he went to the back of the pub and unchained his bike. He considered going inside and pouring out his problems to Hanley, but he couldn't risk Hanley calling in Scotland Yard. Morrie had spent a lifetime working out his own problems, ignoring the need for God. Now it seemed impossible to call on a higher power to get him out of the mess he had walked into. With a helpless wave to Hanley in the doorway, he began the long ride back to the Somerset Estates.

He let himself in through the gate and entered the house through the back. He didn't turn on the lights until he reached the switch in the drawing room. As the room flooded with light, he moved to the stone fireplace, braced his hands against it, and stared up at the Weinberger painting that could ruin his life.

Morrie rarely grieved for his great-grandmother's violent death in Auschwitz. If he could lay claim to this one masterpiece, he rationalized, would he not be paying tribute to his great-grandmother and redeem a part of his own lost nature?

He only meant to right a wrong thrust on his Jewish family over sixty years ago. Now in a twist of events, he needed Rachel McCully, a Gentile, as his safety valve in the days ahead. If things went sour, Rachel would not suffer long. She was seriously ill, dying, wasn't she? No court in the land would lay the blame for an art heist on an innocent English professor on sabbatical.

That day when he had placed a call to the university to reach her, it wasn't the daffodils and rainbows in the sky that he needed. He wanted her wisdom about the straight and narrow, her personal integrity, her rock-hard way of facing life. Now, if he had it figured out right, he was on a fairly wide road to destruction. Perspiration dampened his brow. He never intended to be a thief. Still didn't. He just wanted to claim the painting that belonged in his family. How many museums had told him there were no heirs making claims against the Weinberger? A dead paper trail. They'd stolen more than an art collection from his great-grandmother in Paris. They had stolen her identity. His identity.

McCully could be his only hope. She had asked him about that lecture on Coleridge. His brain scrambled to remember that particular day at McClaren Hall. *McCully was in her second year at the university, a distracting figure in front of any classroom. Long-legged. Graceful. All of a hundred and twenty-five pounds. He remembered the quick swing of the hips as she turned from the chalkboard and faced the class with a brilliant smile.*

"That's it," she had said. "My goals for the semester."

He had expected scribbling on the Lake Poets, not five pert sayings in chalk. For the life of him, he remembered only one.

Living well is costly. Living without integrity, futile.

Not some sonnet or verse from the Lake Poets but her own rules to live by. It didn't take a genius to realize, young and attractive as she was, she intended to guide their minds beyond the classics to facing life beyond the campus. In her unassuming way, she had thrown God in as part of the package of learning.

"What if Coleridge had lived well?" she had asked that day. "At least better than he did. What if he had lived up to his full potential? To God's potential? What held him back?"

Someone had wisecracked, "Being the tenth son of a poor clergyman didn't help." Laughter. Agreement.

Bill Wong, the class joker, took up the mockery. "No wonder he had an albatross around his neck."

A more silky voice, a dreamer from the front row, said, "I think Coleridge was handsome, brilliant, talented, charming. Who else could have given us Christabel *and* Kubla Khan?"

Morrie cursed under his breath. Five points for you.

The same student added, "Being a charity pupil in school may have bothered him. Or maybe his impulsiveness stood in his way."

"Impulsiveness can be a good thing," Professor McCully had said. "And Samuel Coleridge did attend Cambridge."

"But he quit the university and joined the army," Morrie scoffed. "And his family and friends bought his discharge."

"So he bought his way out of trouble? Was that a good move for a man who possessed the qualities of greatness?" she asked. "He was gifted as a poet, as a literary critic, as a philosopher, but he left only a fraction of what he could have accomplished. What destroyed his creativity in the last years of his life?"

"Opium," someone suggested.

"Yes, he fell victim to that. Even his friend Wordsworth couldn't force that creative mind to go on producing when it was already dulled by drugs. What dulls your minds?" she asked.

Morrie, hearing the sadness in McCully's voice, realized that she was thinking beyond Coleridge to the students in front of her. She had made her point that day: You give your best. You don't buy your way out of trouble. The thought of his own creativity being destroyed worried him. Coleridge moved in acceptable circles with The Rime of the Ancient Mariner to his credit. What did Morrie have? One or two literary works that had placed him on the fringe of the literary world. Opium wouldn't destroy him, but he had allowed his smoldering resentment over the stolen art of World War II to lead him into wrong choices.

Morrie recalled that when the bell rang in McClaren Hall that day, students converged on the door, but he took his time gathering up his books. McCully had waited by the chalkboard as he came down the steps from the top row. He felt like he was entering the arena. Going for the death. "Prof," he said, "I can't worry about Coleridge digging himself out of trouble. I have problems of my own living down my childhood as a barefoot boy in Kentucky. No siblings—but rotten poverty. No opium—but reason enough to slip into oblivion."

"Forget about living down your boyhood. Live up to your potential. Don't waste any part of your life or your talents. You are a gifted young man, Morris Chadbourne. Very philosophical. A good debater. So find someone or something to live for."

At that moment, he thought McCully might be the one to live for. He had walked her to her office in McClaren Hall, rehashing the life and works of Samuel Coleridge.

When they entered her office, a young woman smiled at the professor and then turned to Morrie, the smile still on her lips. Attractive. Wholesome. As their eyes locked, her cheeks flushed.

"Mr. Chadbourne, this is Eileen Rutledge, one of my former students. One," she said with a twinkle, "living up to her potential. Someone who doesn't buy her way out of trouble."

Morrie recalled his toes curling inside his loafers, the way his bare toes had curled into the haystack back on the farm in Kentucky. He excelled in the classroom, did well on the basketball court, but he was reduced to awkwardness as Eileen Rutledge extended her slender hand to him. He shifted his books to his other arm and allowed his sweaty hand to tighten around hers.

So much of Morrie was wrapped up in that one brief moment—so much wrapped up in his life from those two women. The professor who influenced his *thinking and the young woman who walked into his life and grabbed his heart.*

Now he stood, head bowed beneath the Weinberger painting, and leaned against the mantel. "What have I done?"

Chapter 6

Sinclair Wakefield managed a quick handclasp with the young American as they made their way from the lecture hall at the University of London.

A strong grip, he thought. Not like he had expected.

Morris Chadbourne had such a casual way about him. He was a lanky man with that annoying American wit and a charming smile for the women. He didn't seem to have a care in the world. His features were firm, his handgrip solid, and whether Sinclair wanted to admit it or not, Chadbourne had a scholarly mind.

As they left the building the rain came down in torrents. Chadbourne pocketed his tie, raised the collar of his thin jacket, and shrugged good-naturedly. Sinclair belted his Burberry and balanced his briefcase as he shoved his bumbershoot open.

"Sir, how about supper together?" Morrie said. "We could wait out the storm that way. There's no need to drown running for the subway."

"Sorry, old chap, I have an evening appointment." He almost said, "Join us," but cut the invitation off at the impulse. His solicitor did not welcome uninvited guests. Besides, if Bailey Rentley's emergency call dealt with Sinclair's portfolio, he didn't want Chadbourne privy to his financial losses.

"Let's do supper the next time, sir?"

Sinclair didn't relish the idea at all. "Yes. Will do."

As he put his foot to the stairs, Chadbourne's casual farewell stopped him. "By the way, Don Wakefield, I ran into an old friend of yours near Grasmere a few weeks back."

Rachel! He disliked the jab in his midline. He turned, bent back his head and the umbrella. Rain washed his face. "Did you?"

"Rachel could do with a visit from an old friend, sir."

He was surprised at his own spark of jealousy. How well did this young man know Rachel McCully? Young? Why did he think of the American as young? There could not be more than six or seven years between them. But they were a world apart.

He ran down another three steps. "She's ill," Chadbourne called after him. "You know that, don't you, Wakefield?"

He disliked the American's constant use of contractions. Even more, he hated his confirmation of Rachel's illness. He paused when he reached the sidewalk and looked back up at the American. "Seriously ill?"

"I'd call leukemia touch and go. . . I'm not suggesting you stir up the old flames. You may not be capable of that."

Wakefield's anger flared. *How much did he know? How much had Rachel told him?*

"I'm sorry about your wife and son—but I think Rachel McCully could do with your encouragement."

Sinclair left Chadbourne, but impressions of the man and his message went with him. Was Morris Chadbourne spending time with Rachel in the Lake Districts? Was Chadbourne taunting him with her illness? Warning him? Mocking him? Or simply concerned?

She could do with a visit from an old friend.

Mary and the boy. *Dear God, what am I thinking? Rachel belongs to my past. I have no claims on her. Mary and the boy belong to—Mary and my son belong to my past.*

The rainy slime on the sidewalks of London splashed on Sinclair's trousers as he raced for the underground. He ran down another flight of steps to the tube, trying to decide whether he liked Chadbourne or disliked him. Even as he scrambled for a seat on the subway, he kept thinking about Chadbourne's casual invitation to dine together—the sardonic smile on his lips as he announced that Rachel could do with a visit from an old friend. Sinclair wanted to go to Rachel. To take her hand. To tell her he was sorry. But he could not bear the thought of someone else dying. The pain would be too intense; the loss of Mary and his son were still too raw.

He must return Audrey's phone calls, the ones he had ignored. He would ring her and ask how Rachel McCully was doing. But what if Rachel answered the phone? Pride stonewalled him as the toll of Big Ben resounded in his head.

Wakefield caged his pride by focusing on the afternoon lectures. *He had given his usual speech on C. S. Lewis, adding from personal experience his understanding of grief and its impact on the human soul. Chadbourne, on the other hand, came up with new approaches to presenting the works of Wordsworth and Coleridge, skillfully weaving in his passion for art. Take this afternoon for instance. He spoke on the greatest art forms—the men and women who paint with words, those who paint on canvas, and those who give us music.*

"They're all master craftsmen," Chadbourne had insisted.

Morris Chadbourne refused to separate the literary giants from the great musicians. He insisted on linking artist and author into the same mold. Invariably, his illustrations took his audience back to the looting of art during the Nazi regime. He stirred the listeners into a frenzy at the unfairness of heirs unable to claim what was rightfully theirs. Chadbourne's approach irritated Sinclair, boggled his mind.

Why? Sinclair wondered, did they continue to be booked on the same platform? And why not? He knew as the train rattled on toward his station that it was not the man or his subject that needled him. He braced his head against the muggy windowpane and felt the jolting to his neck as the train pulled into the next station. How could he seek out the woman he once loved? If Rachel McCully wanted to see him, she knew how to contact him. It was her move, not his. One who had been jilted did not rush in for a second rejection.

He reached the club twenty-five minutes later, feeling drenched from the rain and out of sorts with the world. He shook the rain from his umbrella and brushed his shoulders dry before pushing his way into the club.

The girl at the cloak check welcomed him. "Mr. Wakefield, what a miserable evening. The maitre d' said to tell you that Mr. Rentley will be late." She nodded up toward the private rooms on the balcony. "But Lord Somerset is already here."

"Lord Somerset? I wasn't expecting anyone but my solicitor."

"The table's set for four. There's the maitre d' now."

Leon approached with a bow. "We've set you up in a private room with a fireplace," he said, smiling. "That should help dry you out. Come, let me show you, Mr. Wakefield."

In the room, a lace curtain shielded the observation window. The window afforded a full view of the dining area, but those on the main floor would be unable to identify the guests inside.

Lord Somerset rose as he entered. "Sinclair, good of you to come. It's been far too long." His narrow green eyes remained unblinking beneath the gray-streaked brows. He said pointedly, "I haven't seen you since the funeral two years ago."

"My fault, James. Your wife sent me several invitations for dinner. I was not ready to socialize with others."

"Agnes understood. But I have no excuse for not meeting you at the club or driving into Oxford to see how you were doing."

"You were there for me, if I called. But I am surprised to see you this evening. I was told you were on a world cruise."

"My wife is. That's where I am supposed to be. If things go well this evening, I will join her at the next port."

"Problems?"

"Scotland Yard literally pulled me off the ship as I was about to board. That is what we are here to discuss."

"Scotland Yard? Am I part of the solution?"

"We hope so. Your solicitor should be along shortly. He told me to go ahead and order the evening's special for four."

"Lamb roasted in garlic, I trust."

They sipped coffee as they waited—one of those habits that Sinclair had developed in America, the year he met Rachel. He put the cup down and studied the man across from him. Lord Somerset's hair and sideburns were silver gray, his lips thick, but easily given to a smile. He had a ruddy face, and at seventy-four was developing a double chin and sagging neck folds. Usually guests were expected to wear ties at the club, but Lord Somerset had come this evening in a maroon turtleneck shirt and his tweed sport jacket, both giving him a more youthful appearance.

An amused smile crinkled his face. "Well, here comes Bentley now in his usual flurry—and with Inspector Farland in tow."

"Jon Farland? He specializes in art fraud."

"Right-o. The detective superintendent actually. He heads up the art fraud division. He usually gets his thief, as the saying goes, but someday, a thief is going to outfox that old boy." He stood, his grin broadening. "Good of you to join us, gentlemen."

The inspector gave a hearty laugh as he sat down. "It's the other way around, Lord Somerset. It is good of you to set your plans aside so willingly."

"I do have a personal interest in my art collection. I would hate to go on a world cruise and come home to an empty house."

"We don't think the house would be empty. Just some of the valuable paintings gone."

They were seated companionably when the dinner was served. Lord Somerset took a few bites and leaned back in his chair, his arms folded. "Well, Inspector, are we on a foxhunt, or just a false alarm?"

"We would not have troubled you, sir, if we were not concerned. I suggested that you meet us at the Yard, but Bailey thought it better to meet casually here at the club."

"A wise choice. That way I can slip out of town and out of sight as soon as we finish dinner. I understand from Bailey here that is what you expect me to do." He lit his pipe, drew on it. "But I am more inclined to skip this meal and race back to my estate to protect my possessions."

"Do that and the thieves get away."

"They may get away anyway. You're asking a lot of me, Inspector. I will spend the whole cruise thinking of my place being ransacked."

"We won't let that happen. We will stay in touch with you." The inspector rubbed his chin. "We would like to keep the illusion that you are at sea. You understand of course?"

Somerset gave a mocking bow. "Why don't you explain?"

"You no doubt read about that attempted diamond heist on the Millennium Dome some time ago?"

"Inspector, I am an Agatha Christie fan myself. The rest of my reading interests are limited to the financial page in newspapers and investment reports. But my wife was tied up in knots over the attempted diamond robbery. She insisted that we increase our insurance on our art collection immediately. That's why we left a caretaker in charge and increased our security before we left on what we expected to be a celebration of our fiftieth wedding anniversary."

"My apologies, sir."

Bailey Rentley flicked crumbs from his beard. With his mouth partially full, he asked, "How well do you know this caretaker?"

"My wife heard him lecture several months ago." He tapped the bowl of his pipe against the saucer and pointed the stem at Sinclair. "You share the same speaking lecture with Morris Chadbourne. My wife considers him quite gifted."

Sinclair nodded. "And quite charming with the women."

"Charming enough for my wife to convince me to give him a job as caretaker. I didn't mind. He seemed an amiable chap and quite committed to his research projects. A few brief inquiries and I knew he was not making a decent living with his books."

"James," Sinclair said, "you were always one to encourage ambitious young men to reach their goals. You encouraged me."

"Why not? Someone gave me a footing in the banking industry when I was young."

The inspector chuckled. "But you grew rich dabbling in the art world, an entrepreneur with his name on many charity bequests."

"Yes," he said, chest puffed. "I pulled myself up from the ground level and reached the top without the halls of higher learning as Sinclair has done. I earned respect and the right to friends in high places, including the monarchy. Yes, my wife and I were in full agreement to give Chadbourne a place to live. . .and the time needed to do his research."

The inspector turned to Sinclair. "Wakefield, you and Chadbourne were together at the University of London this afternoon. What can you tell us about him?"

"Outside of the lectures, nothing. We have no other contacts. But I agree with Lord Somerset. Chadbourne is ambitious. Brilliant. Committed to what he is doing."

"Committed enough for a robbery?" Farland asked.

Wakefield surprised himself by defending Chadbourne. "He is committed to art, not to stealing. We both have a great respect for artists. Past and present."

Bailey Rentley washed down his last bite of lamb with scalding tea. "Lord Somerset suggested we contact you when he found out the renter at Wakefield Cottage is a friend of Mr. Chadbourne's."

"There is no need to involve Rachel McCully. Mr. Chadbourne is a former student of hers. That's all." *But could her former student be in this kind of trouble?* Sinclair wondered. "Inspector, I think you have the wrong man."

"I agree," Somerset said. "We don't know too much about our caretaker, but we like what we know. So, Inspector Farland, how did this come about?"

"Let's back up to another robbery. When Scotland Yard was tipped off regarding the attempted jewelry heist at the Millennium Dome, we had time to replace the real diamonds with crystal fakes."

Lord Somerset chuckled. "A bit more difficult for me to replace the paintings on my walls with fakes."

"We understand that, but to the Yard's credit, we had more than a hundred men in that diamond operation. At least a dozen people were arrested. As far as we know, we arrested everyone involved."

"I have no 200-carat, Millennium Star diamond at risk, and you can hardly hide a hundred officers on my property."

"I daresay your Rembrandts and Monets and Italian vases and bronze statues are of untold value, Lord Somerset. Since the attempt at the Millennium Dome, there have been several copycat art thefts, many of them within a seven-month window. They use the same MO— *modus operandi*, as they call it. Bulldozers, smoke bombs, masks, and robbing museums or art shops near the river."

"Which means," Lord Somerset said, "that someone involved in that London robbery may have gone unnoticed."

"Or some clever gang has had ample time to plan another major heist. We have a man under surveillance, a rugby player by the name of Sean Larkins. Larkins has been in close proximity to two or three of these minor robberies, and he has a questionable record. MI5 Registry has a personal file on him here in London, and the CIA has a dossier in Langley, Virginia. Reason enough to watch Larkins's activities."

"Why not arrest him?"

"Lord Somerset, we cannot arrest him for being in the vicinity, nor can we arrest him for being seen in the company of Morris Chadbourne. But they hike together around Grasmere. They eat at the same pub. They were even seen together at the Norbert Museum in Bloomsbury recently, although that meeting may have been accidental. Larkins has let it be known that he has an interest in Lord Somerset's art collection—and Chadbourne is vocal in his lectures about wanting to own a Weinberger painting."

Somerset outstared the inspector. "My dear man, if you plan to rob someone, you don't go around announcing it."

"For me, the copycat robberies are announcement enough."

Somerset's green eyes were mocking. "I once told a museum curator that he invested too much time and money on security guards at night. I told him some clever thief will come along someday while the museum is full of Sunday visitors and walk off with a million-dollar painting."

"Impossible," the inspector snapped.

"I'm a mystery buff. Agatha Christie would come up with something like that."

"Agatha Christie is dead."

Somerset rubbed his hands together. "Think about it, Inspector. Get into the mind of the thief. Someone dressed in security garb politely removes a painting and disappears into the subterrain storage vaults. A delivery truck is waiting to whisk the thief and the painting away."

"In broad daylight—in a room full of people? Impossible."

"No. Quite possible, Inspector. Surprise is the key. Scotland Yard should be looking for the unexpected. Some foolhardy plan that will work because no one expects it to. I daresay, if the thief thought himself under surveillance, he would set another plan in motion."

"Only a madman would plan a robbery so openly, sir."

"A genius, Inspector, not a madman."

"I deal in facts, Lord Somerset. We are making a detailed check on the London museums, but it is time-consuming. Actually, there was an attempted robbery at the Norbert Museum some months ago. Foiled fortunately."

"Didier Bosman!" With care, Lord Somerset pocketed his pipe.

The inspector checked his notes. "Yes, Bosman is listed as the curator."

"I know for a fact that he prefers being called the Museum Director. Semantics of course. He's an insider in the art world, his advice much sought after. But he sees every painting for its monetary value. I was on the board at the Norbert Museum, but I resigned a year ago."

"A personal problem?" the inspector asked.

"Bosman and I got on well at first. I believed him capable of putting the museum on a profit basis once again. He did within months. He even negotiated the purchase of two expensive paintings that my wife wanted. She loves spending my money, but she dreads going to the auctions herself. Her heart, you know."

He retrieved his pipe again and dipped it into his tobacco pouch. "Later, I withdrew my funding and had Bosman's background searched. It seems he was accused of fraudulent art dealings at his last posting in Paris—before he came to London."

"I'll contact Paris on that one," Farland promised. "As it stands, Miss McCully, Chadbourne, and Sean Larkins have all visited the Norbert Museum."

"It's open to the public, Inspector. All three are interested in art."

"So is my fraud division at Scotland Yard. Have you seen Mr. Bosman since stopping your funding at the museum?"

Somerset drew on his unlit pipe. "Once at the club. He told me I would ruin him if art buyers found out I was no longer supporting the museum. I simply walked out on him."

The inspector nodded. "That gives us one more reason why your collection could be the actual target."

Sinclair's coffee had gone cold. His appetite vanished. "James, you and the curator may be at odds, but do you really believe he would enlist Chadbourne's help to steal one or more of your paintings?"

Once again, Somerset leaned back and folded his arms across his chest. "It is the inspector who anticipates a robbery. I am a wealthy man, or so my wife tells me, but I have no intention of allowing my collection to be stolen, if that is what the inspector is suggesting."

The inspector obviously resented the put-down. "Morris Chadbourne is well-positioned to oversee that theft."

A flicker of amusement crossed Somerset's face. "In my absence of course. This is a waste of time. The man is a scholar, a researcher. He dwells on the literary giants of the past and climbs the fells for exercise. He doesn't have time to mastermind a robbery while I'm away."

"That's why he must continue to think that you and your wife are at sea. Thankfully your wife can receive cables in your name until you are back on board."

"So I informed her. But she will never forgive me if I am delayed long in getting back to her. This was our fiftieth-anniversary celebration, gentlemen, preferably spent together."

Sinclair pressed his eyes with his thumb and forefinger, escaping Lord Somerset's steady, questioning gaze. Finally, he said, "I don't understand what you expect me to do. We haven't been in touch for two years, James." His tone took on a new edge. "And suddenly we are meeting together in a private room at the club calmly discussing the threat to your art collection."

"You heard the inspector. He promises me that nothing will go awry. I am personally holding him responsible for my Degas and Rembrandt and all of the other pictures that my wife treasures." Somerset's annoyance and sarcasm were evident in his voice. He was not as relaxed and unconcerned as he appeared. His anger was controlled, defensive, and Sinclair realized, he was depending on their friendship to fill the gap in his own absence.

Bailey leaned forward. "I told these gentlemen that you are studying art history and are acquainted with the major artists."

Sinclair's shoulder convulsed. "You know, I had to have something to do when I lost my wife and son."

Lord Somerset gripped Sinclair's arm. "Steady, man."

Even the inspector was silenced for a moment. "We are sorry about that, sir. But my department anticipates the possibility of a major art theft. Mr. Chadbourne could be involved. I have someone in every lecture hall where he speaks. I have an officer taking the same classes that he takes at Oxford. Unfortunately, my man is not scholarly. He's much more gifted for police work."

Sinclair looked at his watch. He had to call Audrey tonight and find out what relationship existed between Rachel and Chadbourne. Rachel would have every reason to be charmed by him. But at all costs, Sinclair had to protect her.

The inspector cleared his throat. "We have no problem with Miss McCully. But how well do you know her, Sinclair?"

"We taught together in America. She is ill now; I believe she has leukemia. Why are you following her every move?"

"We know about her illness. We know her schedule, Wakefield. She mostly stays close to the cottage, except for her trips to see the medical director at the Whitesaul Clinic in Bloomsbury. She drives herself into London." He consulted his notepad. "Stays at the same economic hotel near the clinic. Takes her meals there and only ventures out for medical visits and brief trips to the British Museum and, less frequently, to the Norbert Museum."

The inspector drummed his pen on the notepad. "I believe your mother was a patient at the Whitesaul Clinic, Sinclair."

"Yes, she died under Timothy Whitesaul's care."

"Unfortunately, Miss McCully does know Mr. Chadbourne."

"I told you, she was his university professor."

"When we spoke to her housekeeper about that relationship, she said that she wouldn't tolerate anyone coming into Stradbury Square and ruining it for the villagers. Or harming Miss McCully. Does she have reason to worry like that?"

"As far as I know the relationship between Miss McCully and Mr. Chadbourne is one of mutual respect."

"As you indicated, Miss McCully is ill. We know about her medical appointments with Dr. Whitesaul as soon as she does. We are very thorough, Sinclair."

Grudgingly, he admitted, "Mr. Chadbourne mentioned her illness this afternoon. I was unaware of it before."

"Chadbourne is planning a reunion for Miss McCully—this according to the housekeeper. With Lord Somerset away on a cruise, Chadbourne would be free to invite the guests to the Somerset Estates."

Somerset's arms tightened against his chest. "Pure speculation. And you are expecting me to sit back and allow a possible theft of my art collection to go on? What kind of a fool do you count me to be?"

The inspector went from stroking his chin to rubbing the back of his neck. "What we want is a place on your property to set up a Scotland Yard surveillance team."

The gray-streaked brows arched. "You really do expect trouble. But a place on my property is easily solved, Inspector. I have guest houses. One is occupied by a cleric friend of mine. The Reverend Charles

Rainford-Simms is a wise old chap."

"Then have him move out until after the reunion."

"No, but your men can move in. It will be crowded, but Charles will cooperate; a little excitement might offset his boring routine. A garden supply truck arrives at the estates every Monday."

"Good. Then I will send my men and equipment in that way, while Chadbourne is away lecturing. Sinclair can fill us in on that schedule. I'd like to add some of my own men to your security staff as well."

For a moment it looked like Somerset would refuse. Then he said, "I'll send word to Chadbourne that I have arranged for added security in my absence. He won't question that. He considers me an eccentric anyway."

He pushed back from the table. "We always have need for extra gardeners or kitchen staff. Just give me the word, Inspector, and I'll contact Charles to expect company, and I'll let Chadbourne know I've added on more gardeners and security staff for the summer. How many do you suggest?"

"Three or four on twelve-hour shifts. Eight total."

"And what do you want from Rachel McCully?" Sinclair asked.

"We want her to go ahead with the reunion. Since you were on faculty together some years ago, we want you on the guest list. And if her former student has made the wrong choices, we want you to help bring him up short."

"To turn him in?"

"You would do that for me, wouldn't you, Sinclair?" Lord Somerset asked. "It is hard enough for me to stay in the background—to even contemplate going back to the cruise ship. But if you would promise to be on hand. . . ."

"I can do that."

He would help a friend. But at all costs he would protect Rachel McCully first.

Chapter 7

S inclair shifted gears, stirring dust on the country road as he raced toward his boyhood home. In the distance, Stradbury Square looked as though it had been gouged from the imperial hillsides. Rugged drystone walls snaked across the countryside, dividing the fields into patches of Kendall green and golden wildflowers. Along the river's edge lay the old wool mill and the red sandstone ruins of the ancient Bruntwood Castle, places where he had played as a boy. Why had he stayed away so long and missed the richness of this familiar landscape?

He kept his focus on the fifteenth-century church spire that rose above the rooftops in Stradbury Square. The church lay dormant—its doors opened only when an itinerant bishop passed this way. The larger village just before Stradbury Square shared the visiting vicar, but Green Hills boasted its own English pub, a hotel that accommodated twenty guests, and the only grammar school for miles. Sinclair and Mary had considered sending Blake to the grammar school when he was old enough; he was too shy, too frail, to be sent away to a boarding school.

Ironic, he thought. *We never had to make that decision.*

The village grammar school had never been an option for Sinclair. He had grown up a social step above his playmates, financially positioned to be sent off to Weatherby School or Heatherdown Preparatory in Ascot. But as a boy, his infraction of the rules went against him when he was reported over and over for reading under his covers long after lights out. They took his flashlights away. He bought others. Embarrassed by his son's literary leanings, the older Wakefield insisted that his son attend Gordonstoun in Scotland to prepare for a military career. Sinclair refused. Instead, he embraced the traditions of Eton, proudly wearing its broad white collars and black-tail coats. But Sinclair, for all of his love of books, excelled in polo and cricket and horsemanship as well.

Just beyond the church, he spotted his mother's whitewashed house gleaming in the sun. He pulled off the road and stepped from the car. On his last visit Mary and Blake had been with him. He choked on the memory of his son's voice echoing over the wooded hills. *His beloved son crouching down by a bush and crying out in childish delight, "Oh, Daddy, there's a rabbit in there. I know there's a rabbit in there."*

What right did he have to shut out those moments of joy with Mary and Blake? Yes, they were gone, but death could not take away those good memories. He pocketed the car keys and moved toward the walkway. Until now, he had been hidden by the bushes and hedges, but he could still see someone working in the conservatory. Rachel?

He stopped again, steadying himself and allowing his eyes to run the length of the side of the house. The kitchen curtain parted. Sinclair saw the aged face of Audrey peering out. He put his finger to his lips. The curtain swept back in place.

Sinclair held his breath as the door to the conservatory opened. Rachel whipped the straw hat from her head and placed it on the hook inside the door. Then she stepped from the conservatory and turned toward the house with a bouquet of flowers in her hands. Her lovely hair was cut short, not at all as he remembered it. She wore light-colored slacks and a long-sleeved blouse with the sleeves rolled up.

You've lost weight, he thought. But there was a hint of that same sprint to her steps as she walked toward the front door.

The pounding of his heart thundered in his ears. *Take it easy,* he told himself. *Rachel is part of your past. Part of your pain.*

She was ill, but he would not allow himself to become involved emotionally. He braced himself against overt sympathy. He was here to help an old friend. End of commitment.

It was her voice, that lilting voice well remembered as she called out, "I'm coming, Audrey."

He began to walk again, striding briskly to overtake her.

～

As Rachel turned the doorknob, her attention was drawn to the man coming up the long walkway toward her. She shielded her eyes from the glare. His confident stride stirred her memory. She pushed the front door open, her eyes still focused on the stranger, an unsettling discomfort rising in her. He rounded the last hedge on the winding walkway, his steps as steady as ever, his handsome face more than familiar. Her breath caught when she recognized him—her heart thumping against her ribs the same way it had so many years ago when she first saw him at the garden luncheon on campus.

Recognizing him, she let the flowers she was carrying topple to the ground. Her hands fled to her short-cropped hair. Humiliation swept over her. Embarrassment. Resentment that he had come unannounced. "Sinclair!" she cried. "Sinclair Wakefield!"

"The same." He took another three steps and stopped. "I was afraid you might be out."

She touched her bobbed hair again. "I don't go out looking this way."

"You look fine."

"Until three months ago I was bald for a long time." She was afraid she would cry. She tugged at a tuft of hair. "Now I have this thick, wavy fuzz coming in. At least it no longer comes out in clumps."

"I like you with short hair. You look youthful and carefree."

"And I like just being alive."

He seemed at a loss for what to do with his hands. He slipped one hand in his tweed jacket. "You have had a rough time, but Audrey tells me you are getting better."

"That's what I tell her. I don't want her to worry."

His facial muscles twitched. "Is the treatment not working?"

"My white count is down, my doctor supremely cautious. He won't call it remission, not yet. But he's hopeful. So am I, Sinclair."

He seemed relieved and went the rest of the way to the steps. She looked down into that face she had once adored and whispered a quick prayer for strength. For the right words. She was walking a tightrope, but she was plucky, tenacious. She had to make it. If only he would smile.

"I should have come sooner, Dr. McCully."

"I didn't expect you to come." *I wanted you to come.* She laughed nervously. "Have you forgotten my name?"

"No, Rachel, I have not forgotten anything about you. I was afraid to come. I have no excuse. I've known you were here for several weeks. I didn't know about the leukemia until yesterday."

It was out in the open, and she felt overwhelming relief. No excuses. No lies. No shams. The illness called by its name. "I'm doing fine, Sinclair. Cancer sapped my energy, but even that is coming back. Come in, please."

He climbed the last three steps, his eyes holding hers. As he stood facing her, she reached up and straightened his tie.

"I meant to do that in the car," he said. "But then I thought you would have forgotten what a devil of a time I have knotting it."

"I haven't forgotten."

He took her hands and pressed them against his chest. She gave him her most captivating smile. "You'd better come inside. Audrey will want to see you."

Rachel watched him survey the room with pleasure, the expression on his face turning to joy. The drawing room still held its Victorian distinction, essentially the same way his mother had kept it. Her oak writing desk stood in the corner. Family portraits hung on the walls. The carvings and memorabilia from his boyhood, and the books he had treasured still filled the shelves. Except for the throw pillows that she had bought in London and an extra bookcase for the books she had brought with her, little had changed.

"You remind me of Wordsworth," she said. "Pensive. Contemplative."

He stroked his chin, the grin spreading wider over his face. "That bad, what say?"

Rachel thought back to that first time she saw him. She had not intended to go to the university luncheon that day, but she stood as they were introduced. She wondered now if her hand was as clammy as it had been back then as their hands clasped. That strong face, his features as chiseled as they had been ten years ago. The clipped accent, welcomed now. His eyes seemed sadder, yet his gaze held hers as he looked down at her.

He glanced away quickly and scanned the room again, his gaze settling briefly on the mantel, as though he were searching for a missing item. She took his hand—if for no other reason than to remove the serious expression that was creeping back; she led him down the narrow hall to the kitchen. "Audrey, I have a surprise."

Audrey's cheeks turned as red as her work-worn hands. She wiped them dry on her apron and went into Sinclair's open arms. "Oh Mr. Sinclair, you did come. I saw you from the window."

"And I saw the curtain fall back in place."

She laughed nervously. "But I didn't warn Rachel that you were here."

He wandered around the room and stopped in front of the water pump. Climbing ivy had wrapped around it. "Rachel, you could have had this old pump removed."

"I like its antiquity."

"Was the ivy your idea?"

"It gives the pump style."

He continued his inspection—lifting the lid from a cooking pot and peering into the oven. "Shepherd's pie, Audrey!"

"Made it just for you. And scones, too."

He glanced at Rachel. "I don't want to impose."

"You're not imposing, Sinclair. This is your home."

"Right now it's yours."

Audrey glared at them both. "Out of here, both of you. Go back and visit in the drawing room. I need space here. And you two need to remember that you are friends, not strangers."

"Come on, Rachel. I learned long ago that it's best to do what Audrey says. Do you have guests often?"

"Not often enough," Audrey told him. "And the last one was one of her former students—that Mr. Chadbourne."

Sinclair could tell that Morris Chadbourne had left a sour taste in Audrey's mouth. He followed Rachel back to the cozy comfort of the living room. For a moment they were silent, awkward in each other's company. She was still beautiful in spite of her illness, her smile unchanged. He remembered that warm smile the day he met her at the school luncheon. The two moments merged. She tugged his hand, inviting him to sit with her as they had done on the wide stone bench after the luncheon so long ago.

As he sat beside her, he said, "You have kept the cottage much like Mother left it."

"I changed the bedroom. I had a brand-new wardrobe and bedside stand brought in from London—I needed a spot for a very special lamp. And Bailey Rentley gave me permission to have the room painted. I like it bright and cheerful when I wake up."

"You could have changed the whole place. I had no idea you had moved to England until Bailey told me. Why didn't you contact me, Rachel? I would have come at once."

"I wanted to call you, Sinclair—but I thought it inappropriate."

"Because of Mary? She died two years ago."

"I'm so sorry."

"So am I. She was a wonderful woman."

"Sinclair, you asked about my illness. I have told you as much as I can. Now I want to talk about you and Mary and your son. It was a tragic way to lose them."

"Coming back here awakened all the memories. We used to come here to visit Mother. When she was gone, we came because Blake loved the old place."

"You haven't been back since you lost them?"

"Not after the funeral. I wasn't able to face it. Now I wonder why I didn't come. We were here the weekend before they were killed." He glanced back at the mantel, looking for the picture of Mary and the boy. "I had a picture of my wife and child; Mother kept it there on the mantel. . .I guess you packed it away when you moved in."

"I didn't know there was one."

They looked up as Audrey appeared with cups of tea. "I took it to my room, Mr. Sinclair. So Miss Rachel here wouldn't be troubled. I'll go get it."

"No. Leave it where it is. You were fond of them."

When Audrey left the room again, he talked about Blake running over the rolling hills and loving being where his daddy had grown up. "He was a sickly child, but when we brought him out here, he ran and played as though he didn't have to struggle for every breath."

For two years he had relived that rail crash in France, chiding himself brutally for not being with his family. After that, he had rejected the comfort of friends and buried himself in the study of art, in the writings of C. S. Lewis, and in teaching his classes back at Oxford. He admitted now that he had shut away the longing to return to Wakefield Cottage, living instead in Oxford in the house that he had shared with Mary and Blake.

As the hour elapsed, some of the grief poured from him. Some of the pain of death began to ease. He was home! The woman who had cared for him since he was a toddler was in the kitchen preparing him a simple meal, one of his favorites. And Rachel sat across from him—pale, thinner, burdened with her own illness, but those lustrous dark eyes were fixed on him. Listening.

"I find great comfort in the evening vespers at Oxford, sitting in an ancient cathedral, hearing God's voice in the music and in the things that are said. I didn't want human comfort."

"Nor did I when I was first told that I had cancer. That was like a death knell. Like dying, in a way."

"I'm sorry, Rachel."

"I'm not sorry that you came. We both needed this visit."

It was too late to tell her his real purpose in coming. Chadbourne and his problems could wait. From the kitchen the aroma of the shepherd's pie reached them. He felt as though a balm had been poured into his soul as Rachel listened to him. He told her about meeting Mary, about marrying her three months later. "She was a wonderful woman—a governess to the children of friends of mine."

"I went past your home in Oxford twice. But I never had the courage to knock. What would I have said? 'Oh Mrs. Wakefield, I'm an old friend of your husband's. Could I speak to him?'"

He laughed—deep, unbridled. "Mary knew about you. I wanted nothing between us. I told her you were my first love. Don't get me wrong. I adored my wife. She was special. If you had knocked on the door, Mary would have welcomed you."

"Once I found out what happened, I knew that I could never look you up." She paused, her brows knit. "Sinclair, you said that Blake was not a strong youngster. What did you mean?"

"He was perfect until he was two. He had colds and earaches, but we thought them normal. Then, just before his second birthday, he was in the hospital with pneumonia. At least we thought it was pneumonia. It turned out to be cystic fibrosis."

Rachel paled. "Cystic fibrosis?"

"It was my fault. I knew it was in my genetic history. But I ignored it. I wanted children—"

"Three. You always said three."

"Yes, but when I found out what I had passed on to my son, I knew there could never be another child."

"You are a carrier?" she whispered.

"I must have been the one. It had bypassed my generation. I was so certain it would not affect my children. But Mary and I were willing to take the risk. She knew how much I wanted a child."

Rachel clasped her hands, the color totally drained from her face.

"Are you all right, Rachel? I didn't mean to upset you."

"I think I need to get some air."

"Of course." He stood and extended his hand to her. "Would a walk in the garden do? Blake used to love it out there."

Rachel's hand was cold in his as they stepped into the yard. The scent of lavender and rosemary and honeysuckle seemed to revive her. Scalloped hedges formed the boundary line. His mother had often mingled her flower beds with peas and carrots and cabbage heads. But all he recognized were the begonias and roses.

Rachel brushed a slug from the drywall; then Sinclair steadied her as she bent to yank a weed from the ground. She seemed as at home in the yard as his mother had been.

She pointed to the south slope, brilliant with sprawling geraniums. "The spring snowdrops are almost gone."

"They'll come back," he said.

"Will they?"

They ducked beneath Audrey's clothesline. "Rachel, you are not overdoing?"

"How can I? The gardeners do all the work. Audrey wants us to develop the garden the way it used to be."

"Don't do that, Rachel. This is your garden. Grow it the way you want it to be."

"But I thought it would please you—"

She was like a child wanting to please him, wanting to show him everything at once. The color was coming back to her cheeks now. "Sometimes the yard is thick with butterflies." She turned suddenly. "Why didn't you come sooner, Sinclair? You knew I was here."

"I knew you had rented the cottage in Stradbury Square. But I thought, if you wanted to find me, you would. And then Morrie Chadbourne confronted me about not seeing you."

"Morrie. He forced you to come?"

"He gave me the excuse for coming. I'm glad I did."

"He's a good friend to me."

That tinge of jealousy hit again. "It sounds like you would defend Morrie Chadbourne to the death."

"If I have to, I will."

He had come here to warn Rachel against any reunion planned by Morrie Chadbourne. It was too late to warn her now.

An hour later the shepherd's pie had been eaten, the praises for Audrey sung, and now he must leave. He had not warned her about the threat to the Somerset art collection. He had not even mentioned that Scotland Yard would come at a moment's notice from him. Without knowing it, she was Scotland Yard's best bet to protect the Somerset collection.

"Sinclair, start visiting your friends again; won't you?"

"I'll give it a go. . .and you will tell me what comes of this plan for a reunion that you were talking about?"

"If you really want to know."

"I should be invited. My year at the university counts for something, you know." At the door he looked down at her. "Rachel, there's one thing we haven't talked about today."

"One thing?"

"Why didn't you meet me that day under Big Ben?"

Tears welled in her eyes. "I was there."

"But I waited three hours."

"I know. But I just couldn't face you and tell you it wouldn't work out between us."

He wanted to draw her to him. "I loved you—you know that."

She nodded. "It's because I loved you back then that I couldn't face you."

"But why? Why, Rachel?"

"My reason no longer matters." She reached up and touched his cheek, her hand cool against his face. "It was far kinder to you for me to go away."

Chapter 8

Rachel left Grasmere and drove the winding country roads for an hour, trying to follow Morrie's directions. His distance was as a crow flies, his left and right turns remembered from a man's perspective for a trip that required no map for him. She had tired from driving, her strength spent in the long ride from Wakefield Cottage. She decided on a U-turn on the narrow road and driving back to Grasmere for better directions from one of the local pubs—or giving up and going back to Stradbury Square.

Suddenly, in the distance, one mansion dominated the rolling hillsides—not to the right as Morrie had suggested but to her left. For a moment, she considered the Somerset Estates an isolated monstrosity, out of place in this countryside. It loomed ethereal with luminous gray clouds hanging low around it, like a scene from Daphne du Maurier's books, or a place where Agatha Christie would gladly send Miss Marple or Hercule Poirot to unravel a crime. There would be servants of course, especially a butler, but had Morrie mentioned anyone other than himself. Inside, the mansion would be a picture of wealth and beauty, incorporating style from more than one century. Today's weather fit the pattern for du Maurier, capturing the mansion in a gossamer mist. The thought of escaping into just such reading pleasure refreshed Rachel, taking her for a kilometer or two back to the delightful readings of her childhood.

The Somerset Estates dwarfed the neighboring villages, but as Rachel approached, the monstrosity became a magnificent work of art that possessed a character of its own with its stained glass windows and a leaf pattern in the stone facing on the front of the house. Turrets protruded from the corners of the building. The entire property covered a block square with a wrought iron fence on flagstone posts surrounding it. Grandiose. Lavish. But oddly placed on this country lane.

Many of the English country houses had been turned over to the National Trust in the economic fallout after World War II; others had fallen victims to an auction block. Lord Somerset had built his property in recent years, isolating it in the country—with the nearest neighbor a mile or more away. Rachel could see extensive gardens and outbuildings in the back. One of them had to be the caretaker's cottage. But cottage would hardly describe the place where Morrie lived. She parked in the circular drive on the side of the house and pushed the intercom button to the caretaker's cottage.

Morrie's voice boomed out: "Somerset Estates."

"Morris, it's Rachel McCully."

"Doc, I'll be right there."

Through the iron bars she saw him jogging toward her in a white T-shirt and tennis shorts, a towel around his neck.

He unlocked the gate and took her arm. "You didn't show up for my lecture in London."

"I stayed at the clinic for more tests."

His grip tightened. "Are you all right?"

"Dr. Whitesaul just wanted to make certain there were no side effects from the medicine. You know—liver, pancreas."

"And?"

"He'll call when the lab results come back."

"I have a confession to make. After the lecture, I told Wakefield about your leukemia."

"I know. He came to see me yesterday; but he has his own problems... I'm not one of them."

"I think he's beginning to see the end of his own tunnel. I told him you could do with an old friend in your life."

She threw back her head and laughed. "Is that how you see me, Morrie? As old?"

He gripped her shoulders. "No, I see you as beautiful. Desirable. I wish to God I could make you well."

She touched his lip. "Be careful how you express yourself, Morrie. God is my Friend—and I don't want His name abused."

"I'm sorry."

She smiled. "I hope you get in Wakefield's classes in the fall. I think you'll learn a lot about C. S. Lewis's God."

"That's not my purpose."

"But it is my prayer. Now what about that tour you promised me?"

"First I want you to see the caretaker's cabin."

When they reached the brick walkway, she looked back. The mansion rose three stories; the bedrooms all had balconies, and a sunroom faced south waiting for the morning sun to hit it. Ahead lay the gazebo and picnic table and the cricket and badminton courts on the other side of an arched bridge. Landscaped flower beds lay on both sides of the walk.

Rachel sensed Morrie's nearness as he led her toward the guest houses in the back and, startled, moved away to give herself more space.

An older man waved from the steps of the smaller guest cottage. "Good morning, Morris."

"Good morning, Charles." To Rachel, Morrie said, "That's Reverend Rainford-Simms."

"I noticed the clerical collar. Is he the vicar?"

"He was. The archbishop banished him to the North Country. Some squabble over defending an IRA terrorist in the Cotswolds."

"No wonder he was banned from the pulpit."

He squeezed her hand. "Charles is a nice sort. He cares about prodigals. Every man needs someone like that standing with him. But it means no parish. No funds to speak of. About all he does is putter and mutter in the flower beds."

"So he lives here permanently?"

"For now. The poor man's too old to work. Luckily, Lord Somerset set him up in the cottage." He grinned. "He's a peaceful sort. Takes life in his stride. We have great times running the gamut from politics to judgment."

When they entered Morrie's well-furnished cottage, Rachel took the soft chair and smiled at the untidy array of papers on his desk. He pulled another chair over close to her. "Are you still on for the reunion?" he asked.

She watched him, waiting for some sign of betrayal, then said lightly, "Of course, aren't you?"

"The castle is out."

She felt relieved. "Morrie, the idea was all I needed."

"I didn't say the reunion was out. I know just the perfect location. Great view of the rolling hills. Isolated from the crowds. Excellent accommodations. But more on that later."

His grin turned sheepish. "I started the guest list. I asked the alumni office to run a checklist and narrow it down to your classes on the Lake Poets. Then I asked for email addresses on any former students living abroad."

"Just like that they cooperated? Why all the rush, Morrie?"

"You're disappointed," he said.

"You did everything on your own."

He tensed. "I had to—believe me. I did have some help from your colleague Misty Owens. We wanted to conserve your strength."

He reached over and sifted through the mess on his desk, finally retrieving an email. "She really got things rolling."

"You've done all of this in just two or three days."

"Cyberspace," he said. "We're limiting the number of people to the first twenty—you being ill and all."

She ran her finger over the names. "Amanda Pennyman."

"She's living in London."

"I had no idea she was so close. Lenora Silverman."

"She's the lead singer in an opera in Rome."

"I know. I follow her career. And Sara and Lydia Arnold."

"Your friend Misty Owens suggested them. They'd have to fly in from the States. Nothing's confirmed."

"Sinclair Wakefield wants to be invited."

Morrie scowled. "Why him?"

"I told you. He spent a year at the university as a visiting professor." She looked up. "I don't see Eileen Rutledge's name."

His face hardened. "It would never work out," he warned. "I still come from the wrong side of the tracks."

Did he really see himself that way, this successful young man of hers?

"Stop it, Morrie. Once Eileen was your joy."

"I told you, that ended when I met her grandfather."

It was Rachel's turn to lift a quizzical brow. "Since when does a grandfather control what happens to a marriage?"

"He was the patriarch of the Rutledge family. Eileen took me home to meet him, and from the minute I crossed the threshold of that mansion of his, we were at odds."

"You told me that, but I think you've left a lot unsaid."

For a moment he was silent. Then with a lift of his hands, he said, "You won't let it go until I tell you; Eileen and I were waiting for her grandfather in the library, working up the courage to tell him we were married. I disliked the man before I met him. He had such a control over Eileen. It was important to her to please him. After all, he funded her schooling. I resented the opulence, the power play in that house. I stomped over the Oriental rug. Then, when I recognized the oil painting over his fireplace, I went ballistic."

"Over a painting?"

"That painting didn't belong there. It came from the Chadbourne Collection in Germany a long time ago. When I saw that picture hanging on his wall, I was convinced it was part of the art looted decades ago by Hitler or Goering." He looked away, his jaw chiseled in ice. "When her grandfather came into the room—a proud, stately old codger—I asked him outright where the painting came from, and before I knew it I was accusing him of harboring one of the lost works of art."

"Is there no way he could have come by it honestly?"

"How? Weinberger's paintings were confiscated during World War II. Eileen's grandfather was stationed in Germany at the end of the war—in command of one of those art recovery units."

"It doesn't account for the painting coming under his roof."

"Doesn't it? I told him that Weinberger painting belonged to my family. Instead of welcoming me into the Rutledge family, he ordered me from his house. Then he did the unthinkable. He had my background checked. Found out that I—"

Morrie nearly choked on the words. "Found out that I did have Jewish blood coursing through my veins."

Rachel studied him. "Morrie, is it true? Does it matter?"

"I was so far removed—four generations. A great-grandmother from a wealthy Jewish family, but it mattered to Eileen's grandfather. He forbid her to have anything more to do with me."

"And she agreed?"

"We were already married. I didn't give her a chance to explain it to him. I broke it off." He shook his head. "It was a week later before I saw her again. Eileen was doing her residency but traded shifts with a friend. She was absolutely beautiful that night. Glowing. I don't remember ever seeing her that way before. She told me she had something wonderful to tell me."

He swallowed. "And I put my finger to her lip and said, 'Not now, Eileen. I've come to say good-bye.' She told me it didn't matter what my heritage was. That she loved me."

" 'But it matters to your grandfather,' I told her. 'And I know how much your family means to you. You can have a divorce. They'll never know.' "

Becki! He doesn't know about his daughter.

He clenched his fists. "In the end, her grandfather had the wedding annulled—by some sleight-of-hand or a large-sized check, no doubt. In his sight we were never married.

"Eileen told me she wouldn't let me go over some dumb painting, and I caught her by the shoulders and said, 'That dumb painting is worth a few million. I've spent a lifetime trying to track down some of my family's possessions through the Swiss banks, through the art retrieval efforts. And to walk into your grandfather's house and find a part of my past hanging on his wall—it was too much.' "

"Morrie, did you ever see Eileen again?"

He turned with a sardonic smile. "Does it matter?"

"It does if you loved her. . .and sent her away."

"It's been over eight years—almost nine—since I heard from her. It's good that you kept in touch, Rachel."

"Eileen's the one who told me about my cancer."

He threaded his fingers through his unruly locks. "What a mess I've made of friends. I tried unsuccessfully to prove the painting belonged to my family and lost Eileen because Jewish blood flowed through my veins. And now I'm living in a house with one of Weinberger's last works of art on the wall."

"Here at the Somerset Estates? Then let me see the work of the artist who destroyed your lives."

"It's in the main house. That's where we will hold the reunion, now that the Somersets have boarded their cruise ship."

She smiled, trying to ease the anger that stood between them. "Which means your first obstacle is out of the way?"

"Everything is fine about using the place. Trust me."

"That's my weak point. I'm not certain what your motives really are." She patted his arm. "Morrie, whatever is going on in your mind, please rethink it."

He led her to the house. It was more magnificent than she had imagined. Murals and paintings filled the walls. A copper statue stood in the smoking room. Two porcelain vases sat on the sideboard in the dining room. She fingered them both. When Rachel and Morrie reached the drawing room, he went straight to the painting hanging above the fireplace.

She tried to see it from Morrie's eyes—tried to picture the empty canvas as Asher Weinberger picked up his brush. He had been born after the impressionist artists in France. But like them, he lived in France and had obviously been influenced by painters like Claude Monet and Renoir. Weinberger's painting caught some of the shimmering effects of light used by the Impressionists, but he had chosen a swollen river, not a garden or rural scene.

"When did he paint this one, Morrie?"

"In 1939 as the threat of the Third Reich moved in. You can feel the uncertainty in his painting—see it in the darkness of the river and in the face of the man entering the water."

"Symbolic?"

"I think so. His earlier paintings were happier ones. The last ones symbolic of his deep need to find a way of escape from what was happening as Hitler rose to power. In this painting, he didn't capture the movement, the quality of the Impressionists that he tried to imitate. That impulsive brush stroke is missing."

"Still there's a special quality to this work."

"Lord Somerset recognized Weinberger's genius and paid a great sum to own it. I've spent years trying to prove my right to Weinberger's paintings. I want to turn my research into a book."

"That will take years."

"I have time."

Rachel smiled at his confidence. A year ago she had felt the same way. Now she was buying every minute, savoring each new day. But it was the wrong time to lecture Morrie. His expression was pained as he stood beneath the Weinberger masterpiece.

"This reunion—this whole plan of yours—it's about the Weinberger painting, isn't it?" she asked.

He kept his back to her. "You don't understand. The Somersets have no right to this painting."

"And you do? Sometimes I'm not sure when you're joking, Morrie. Haven't the Weinberger paintings cost you enough unhappiness already?"

"Sometimes it's too late to turn back."

He didn't sound like Morrie Chadbourne, the student who had sat on the high tier in her classroom at McClaren Hall. He sounded like someone she didn't know, and the niggling doubts that Audrey had expressed became her own. But she had spent a lifetime defending the weak links in the chain. Her own sister. Students who struggled to get a C. Mountain climbers who couldn't go the distance. And now Morrie. A gifted scholar, yes. But an angry man inside, and somehow the painting hanging above them was a clue to his bitterness.

"If you needed my help, would you admit it, Morrie?"

"I think not. I respect you too much to disappoint you."

"Then if you don't trust me, find someone else to help you."

"I could do that. But, Rachel, I need your friendship."

"You have it, Morrie."

"I want to protect you."

"Protect me from what?"

"You and I need each other."

"It can never be any more than a friendship."

"The old distance between professor and student?" He ruffled his dark hair and, with a sly smile, said, "Marry me, Prof."

She smiled. "So you can be a young widower?"

He leaned forward and placed his hand on hers. "I want to take care of you. You don't have to take this journey alone."

"I'm not," she reminded him.

"What do you mean?"

"God is with me."

"Charles could marry us."

"You're jesting of course?"

"No, I'm serious. What about this weekend?"

"Not this weekend, Morrie. Nor next weekend. I'm not in love with you, and I would have so little time to offer."

"I'd like you to spend that time with me."

She felt pity for him, for herself. "You realize, don't you, that beneath this scarf of mine, my hair is just growing in."

"Big deal."

She threw back her head, and the sun coming in the window shimmered against her long silken neck. He took a firmer grip of her hand. "Please marry me, Prof."

She met his gaze. "I think you are stark raving mad. But it's a wonderfully kind madness." She pulled her hand free. "I'm fine with the way things are. I'm happy at Stradbury Square."

"I'd do my best to make you happy."

"Oh Morrie, I don't know whether to laugh or cry. You were always so impulsive."

"You know I've always respected you."

"Marriage takes more than that," she said gently. "Now, I really must go."

She knew she was ill as she drove home, the flush of her cheeks more likely fever than distress over her visit with Morrie. It was almost dusk when she reached the cottage.

Audrey looked alarmed when she saw her. "You go on to bed, Miss Rachel. I'll bring you tea. I will call Sinclair—"

"Please don't. You were right about Morrie Chadbourne. He is a troubled man. I don't know how to help him."

"Would anyone?"

She thought of Eileen. Eileen and Morrie should face each other once again. "Give me a minute alone, Audrey. Please."

Rachel went to her rolltop desk, each step an effort. She sat down and took out a piece of pink stationery and wrote her first invitation:

My dear Eileen,

Would you consider taking Becki out of school early? I am having a celebration in a magnificent mansion here in the Lake District. You and Becki must come as my guests. I want to keep my promise to Becki and take her to Hill Top Farm. But more, I need your help, Eileen, and all I can promise is a special surprise for you.

She sealed the envelope and was grateful to find Audrey standing there as she turned toward her bedroom. "Give me your arm, Audrey. I feel rather weak this evening." She was shivering as Audrey helped her into bed. "I must go into London in the morning," she managed.

"To post a letter?"

"That, yes. But I need to see the doctor."

"You have overdone today," Audrey scolded. "Driving in to see that Mr. Chadbourne."

"You tried to warn me. . .and I wasn't listening. Would you believe, he asked me to marry him?"

Audrey's hands fluttered to her chest. "No."

"That's what I told him."

"Rest now. Tomorrow I'll drive into London with you."

"Do you drive the motorway?"

A grin crinkled Audrey's tired face. "It's been awhile, but it must be like riding a bike again. Once I get my foot to the pedal, we'll do all right."

∽

It was 3 a.m. in London when Audrey finally reached Sinclair Wakefield. He sat on the edge of the bed in his room at the club, the phone gripped in his hand, his sleep-dazed mind trying to sort Audrey's jumbled words.

"It's Miss Rachel. . .in bed. . .fever."

Sinclair felt his heartbeat in his throat. "Slow down, Audrey. I am still half asleep. What's wrong?"

"Rachel is burning with fever."

"Try sponging her."

"I've *been* sponging her—I can't get her to stop thrashing or being sick to her stomach."

"Is she having difficulty breathing?"

"When the fever goes up, she breathes fast."

He was alert now. "Pain. Is she having pain, Audrey?"

"Some, I think."

"I'll see what I can do. Give me her doctor's number."

He scribbled the information on the paper by his bedside as he burrowed his bare feet into the rug. Why was he getting involved? Why? Because she still mattered to him. "Stay with Rachel, Audrey," he said, his voice raspy. "Do not leave her side."

"I won't, sir. I am here right now, holding her hand."

I should be. He went through the operator and declared an emergency. Minutes later, he heard a calm, reassuring voice: "Whitesaul Clinic. Timothy Whitesaul speaking."

"Timothy, Sinclair Wakefield here."

"Wakefield! You just caught me on my way out the door."

"Rather late to be leaving your office."

"I had some patients I wanted to check on. And some charts to tidy up. I'm off for the weekend. Wakefield, I haven't seen you since your mother was a patient of mine. How are you?"

"I'm concerned about my friend, Rachel McCully."

"You're acquainted? She's due in my clinic this week."

"She's sick, Timothy."

"Most of my patients are. What seems to be the problem?"

"Weakness. Vomiting."

"It goes with the disease."

"The housekeeper says she's burning up with a fever."

"She may have an infection. That's one of the risks."

"I know. She knows the risks. And I know what the results can be sometimes. We lost Mother that way. I don't want what happened to my mother to happen to Rachel."

"Your mother had age against her and a weak heart. McCully is a young woman."

"Timothy, I'm well aware that you take patients who are risks, young or old. White counts soaring. Failure to respond to the usual anticancer drugs. You're a risk taker."

"So is McCully. That's why I agreed to take her on in one of my clinical trials."

"Please, put my mind to rest. Drive up to the Cumberlands to see her?"

"At three in the morning? You know I don't make house calls. If she's not having trouble breathing, bring her down to London right away."

"I'm in London myself overnighting at the club."

Another calculated pause. "Then it would waste precious time for you to drive up there and back. Find someone to drive her here. We may have to hospitalize her, and I want her under my care." His voice was tight. "Not everyone approves of my using experimental drugs, but it's Rachel McCully's only chance." He seemed to be thumping on the phone. "I don't understand. In these first few weeks, she responded well."

"Until now—can't you break the rules and go to her? The only person available to drive her is a housekeeper who's in her seventies. What if Rachel refuses to come with her?"

"That's foolishness. Is Miss McCully depressed?"

"I have never seen her happier. She's surrounded by—"

"She's out in public?"

The hour left them both irritable. They were baiting each other, each defensive of Rachel for his own reason.

"Our agreement was for her to stay isolated there in Stradbury Square, Sinclair. To live quietly."

"Doctor, she voted for quality of life."

"We're selective in choosing our patients."

"She's grateful."

The doctor's control slipped. "Noncompliant is not acceptable."

"Neither is dying."

Finally, Whitesaul relented. "The best I can do is cancel my plans for the weekend. I'll wait here at the clinic. If she gets in trouble en route, they should go to the nearest hospital."

Wakefield slammed the receiver down. He couldn't drive up to the Lake District to pick Rachel up. They'd lose too much time. He had to depend on Audrey. He forced calm into his voice as he called her. "Find someone to help you drive Rachel into London. Dr. Whitesaul is waiting for her."

"Oh dear. That means driving on the motorway. I don't think I can do it. I'll take her to someone here."

He heard panic in her voice. "Audrey—" His words dangled, lost in memories.

"I am still here, Mr. Sinclair."

"Audrey, I don't want to lose her. I just found her again."

There was a quick sob on the other end—Audrey having one of her romantic gasps. "All right. We'll come, but tell me how to get there."

He gave directions and could only pray that she had written them down. "How is Rachel now?"

"She doesn't look good, Mr. Sinclair. She did fall asleep moments ago though. But driving all that distance on the motorway—what if something happens to her?"

"It won't. I will meet you at the clinic."

Chapter 9

Rachel awakened in a different bed, in a strange room, in an unfamiliar setting, her arm attached to an intravenous feeding. Groggy, she searched her surroundings. Audrey was sitting by her bedside, patting her hand. Sinclair was standing at the foot of her bed.

His presence became a reality when she heard his deep voice. "Welcome back, Rachel. We have been worried about you."

"Where have I been?"

"Asleep for two days."

"You can't be serious."

"From what I know of Wakefield here," Timothy Whitesaul announced from the doorway, "this man of yours rarely jokes."

Man of mine. She focused on Timothy, looking professional in his white lab coat with a stethoscope around his neck. "I don't remember coming into London, Doctor."

Audrey sighed with relief. "Oh, wonderful. Then you don't remember my neurotic driving on those hairpin curves?"

"You drove me here, Audrey?"

"That I did. I sponged you all night long like I used to do for Mr. Wakefield when he was a little boy. But when your temperature went higher, I called him, even though you told me not to. I was so afraid for you."

"I was in London—at my club. I told Audrey to bring you right in. I thought she would ask a neighbor to do the driving."

"It wasn't like the bicycle," Audrey said nervously. "I kept closing my eyes to block out the headlights."

Through the grogginess, Rachel recalled with sudden clarity the blaring of horns. "Didn't I offer to take the wheel?"

"That's when I pretended I didn't hear you."

Whitesaul strolled across the room. "You arrived at my clinic without a dent in your car, but you gave us a fright with your high fever," he said as he reached for his stethoscope. "Fortunately, it turned out to be flu—a setback for you, but you'll be out of here in another three days."

He put the stethoscope to her chest. "Deep breath. Again."

"I'm still alive."

"That's how I prefer my patients."

"What about the shadow on my lung?"

"According to the X-ray, it's still there. But it hasn't grown."

"Doctor, Miss Rachel is not strong enough for any surgery."

He gave Audrey a gentle smile. "But Dr. McCully knows that we will have to remove it once she is strong enough."

"When will that be?. . . Never mind." Rachel's voice faded. "Did I really sleep for two days?"

He tapped the IV bag. "With a little help from me. So what have you been doing—one of those exhausting spring cleanings?"

"I drove into Grasmere one day—and forgot my medicine."

He scowled. "You remember the agreement when you came on my clinical trial."

"Yes. But it was just one day."

"Fortunately for you, Dr. Rutledge made me promise that you would not be thrown out of the program."

"I'm grateful."

"One missed dosage should not exhaust you like this, Dr. McCully. Don't forget, I agreed to you living in Stradbury Square for its isolation. I thought it would do you good."

"It's been perfect."

"Then what happened?"

Sinclair stirred at the foot of the bed. "She tends to overdo. Now she is planning a reunion with some of her students."

Whitesaul sat on the edge of Rachel's bed. "Eileen Rutledge called me this morning. I keep her abreast of your treatment. She received your overnight letter—and your invitation."

"Is she coming?"

"This weekend." A sparkle lit in his eyes. "I look forward to seeing her."

"Oh, so do I."

Whitesaul arced one eyebrow. "Ever since I met Eileen, I've tried to persuade her to spend a year at my clinic."

"She has a daughter."

"I know. I was in residency at the medical center when Rebecca was born. Eileen doesn't go anywhere without her daughter." He pocketed his stethoscope. "I think the child could be happy in England, and Eileen would be so helpful here in the clinic."

"Is she considering it?"

"I like to think that she is. There is a postgraduate medical school in London. I want Eileen to attend there and prepare to work for me in cancer research and clinical trials."

"She likes what she's doing."

"We work with patients. She wouldn't lose out on that. She could make such a contribution to cancer research. She's good."

"She'd have to have a reason for making such a change."

He smiled ruefully. "She could marry me. Rebecca could do with a father."

He doesn't know about Morrie, she thought, and felt an overwhelming sadness. In wanting to bring Morrie and Eileen together, she was exposing all of them to even deeper pain.

Whitesaul tapped Audrey on the shoulder. "Time for you to get some rest. I'll send you back to the hotel in a cab." He turned to Sinclair. "We'll leave you two alone."

Alone with Sinclair, all the old feelings came back. Rachel had to contain them, not add to his pain. Her pain. Grappling for words, she asked, "Sinclair, when did they send for you? Was it Audrey's doing? She shouldn't have bothered you."

"Whitesaul let me know the minute he admitted you."

She blushed under his steady gaze. "You didn't have to come."

"I wanted to come. Isn't that what old friends are for?"

He took the chair that Audrey had vacated, and the familiar scent of his cologne flooded her with memories of what might have been. She tried desperately to hold them at bay, to cage them. He was here as her friend. Nothing more.

They fought silence for a while. She smiled wistfully, without speaking, admiring the man that he was. His strength, his strong muscular frame were two of the things she most liked about him. He had such a keen mind, but it was his masculinity that struck her now. His strength comforted her. And then she laughed as he reached up to straighten his tie.

"What's funny, Rachel?"

"That tie of yours. And I feel uncomfortable when you don't say anything."

"Since my wife's death, I have come to appreciate the discipline of silence. That's why I spend so much time at the vespers at Oxford. I find them comforting and peaceful."

She placed her hand over his. "You miss her."

"I loved her."

His hand felt warm under hers. *You loved me once,* she thought. *And I walked away from that love.* "Sinclair, I was afraid of the silence when I learned about my cancer. I felt so alone, like you must have felt when you lost Mary and your son."

"But I have come to terms knowing that they did not die alone. God doesn't run out on tragedy. For different reasons, we were both frightened by our losses, Rachel."

"You lost the two people dearest to you." She waited a moment before speaking again. "I lost my dignity and my hair. And I lost control of my life—I hated that."

"I think we were both afraid that God had forgotten us."

"I'm learning," she said, "that He is always there."

"That is what brought me through the loss of my wife and son. Now you're faced with not knowing what's going to happen."

"With this cancer? I keep telling Morrie that I intend to lick this illness."

"For him?" Sinclair's voice had tightened.

She searched his face for double meaning. "You don't like him, do you?"

"The truth is, I don't trust the man. And I trust him less because of his involvement with you."

"We're just friends."

He placed his other hand on top of hers and rubbed her wrist with his thumb. "That's what you tell me."

She closed her eyes, not wanting him to see the mist forming there. *I need you,* she thought. *That's why I came back to England. But right now I need you for a different reason.*

❧

Sinclair took one of those moments of silence to watch her. Even in illness, those dark eyes were brilliant, not with fever but with her love of life. A year ago her long hair would have fallen softly over the pillows. Now there was just a short cropping of silky dark curls covering her scalp. Her face was finely shaped, her features gentle.

Was he trapped with sympathy for her because she was ill? Or was that the old stirring inside of him, a love that had been shattered when she failed to meet him under Big Ben?

Take it easy, he told himself. He had stayed at her bedside for the last forty-eight hours, sitting in the silence of this room listening to her breathing, watching the IV fluid drip into her body. He had agonized at the thought of her never getting well again. Even when Whitesaul entered the room and placed his hand firmly on Sinclair's shoulder, he was afraid to ask. Finally, the doctor had taken him out of the room for a cup of coffee and a lecture.

"I don't know what your plans are, Wakefield, but I can tell you that I believe Dr. McCully will go into a remission."

"Then she will get well?"

"She will get better. We're trying an experimental drug; you know that. She'll probably be on the medicine the rest of her life. But I can't tell you how long she will live."

"You just promised me a remission."

"I can't promise you how long it will last. She has that other problem—possibly a benign tumor on her lung. Again, no guarantees." He wrapped his stethoscope around his fingers. *"I have watched you watching her. Does she know how you feel?"*

"I don't even know how I feel myself."

He unraveled the stethoscope a second time. *"Don't make a commitment you can't live up to, Sinclair. Your mother was my patient and we lost her—and I know about your wife and son—the loss of someone else would not be easy."*

"But you believe in a remission."

"But I don't believe in a broken heart."

Then you didn't know about Big Ben, *Sinclair thought. But he had shaken hands with the doctor and considered the grip strong and therapeutic. He didn't know his own heart and mind as he went back to Rachel's bedside. Some wounds were still too raw.*

Rachel interrupted his thoughts. "Will you really come to the reunion at the Somerset Estates?"

"Yes, but why are you so persistent about this reunion?"

"I'm going through with it to protect Morrie from doing something that could ruin his life." Tears fell gently down her cheeks. "There's a magnificent painting at Lord Somerset's that Morrie wants at all costs."

"Valuable? Nothing in Somerset's collection is inexpensive."

"Sinclair, Morrie is one of my most successful students, but he could never afford to purchase a Weinberger masterpiece. If he goes ahead with the reunion at the Somerset Estates, I will be there for him, perhaps to reason with him and to keep him from doing something rash. As a personal friend of Lord Somerset, perhaps you will be there to protect the paintings on his wall."

No, I will be there for you.

Rachel skirted the truth, repressing her fears, alluding to robbery.

"I have never been very good at parties, Rachel."

"You are good at helping people who are lost."

For a second he wanted to tell her about Lord Somerset and Scotland Yard. The betrayal of confidence bothered him. He found his voice. "Mr. Chadbourne and I are acquainted at the professional level only. I find him an arrogant man. In his lectures, he frequently talks about the art theft and looting in World War II. This is a controversial topic in art circles. He knows that, but he won't back off."

"He's Jewish, Sinclair."

"Jewish? That's not a problem for me."

"It is the reason for his interest. One of the art collections stolen during Hitler's era belonged to his family."

"How would you know that?"

"Morrie told me." She hastened to defend him. "The Asher Weinberger paintings belonged to his great-grandmother."

"Is Chadbourne the heir then?"

"He hasn't been able to prove his ownership. He traced one of the Weinberger paintings to the walls of a retired banker back in the States. Now Morrie is convinced that your friend Lord Somerset has another of the Weinberger paintings in his possession. He said he's going to prove ownership at any cost."

"There are legal channels."

"Morrie claims he has tried them all. There are gaps in the ownership records over the last sixty years. Now he says those paintings will never be his, short of stealing them."

"A lot of art was lost and destroyed in Germany. Some was squirreled away and ended up in the hands of the wrong people. But Lord Somerset has been a legitimate collector for years."

"Morrie can't let it go. I wish Lord Somerset kept his collection in a vault—then I wouldn't be so worried."

Sinclair laughed. "He is not that kind of man, Rachel. He leaves the paintings on the wall for his guests to enjoy."

"I wish Lord Somerset knew about Morrie's plans for a party. I know the reunion is ridiculous. I don't know whether Morrie can pull it off. People just can't pack up and fly to England. And I don't have a legitimate reason to invite them."

"What better reason than a visit with you, Rachel?"

"That's what Morrie told me. But is that enough?"

If he was to help her, he had to ease her concern. For her health's sake, they had to approach this reunion with a light heart. Wasn't that what Rachel wanted? What she needed? In that year in America she had taught him the freedom of laughter. She loved life, laughed often.

He tapped his fingers, grinning unexpectedly, and saw her pleasure as his smile widened. "Rachel, we could turn this party of yours into a literary reunion, a learning experience. We could take your guests on side trips to Shakespeare's birthplace and Anne Hathaway's cottage in the village of Shottery."

"And stop and have lunch in Stratford-upon-Avon? But I would still be betraying Morrie."

"I think Mr. Chadbourne really wants to do something special for you. That is not fake. He's genuine there."

"It did start out with my wanting to know whether I had left an imprint on the lives of my students. Whether my life had counted. That's when Morrie came up with this plan."

He nodded solemnly. *That may be when Morrie found that you fit into his plans.* "I know you are worried about Morrie. But in fairness to the others who are coming, we will turn this reunion into something special. Can you do it, Rachel?"

She warmed to his plan. Her thoughts chased his. "We could walk in the Lake District where Wordsworth lived. . .at least you could walk with them."

"I will find you a white marble bench to rest on."

She looked away, but the sparkle had come back into her expression. "A bench like the one under the magnolia tree?"

"Would you like that?"

"I'd like it better if you would sit there with me."

"I might be too busy taking your guests to the site where Coleridge penned *The Rime of the Ancient Mariner.* Or herding them on a boat so they can sail on Lake Windermere. We'll work it out."

He met those lustrous eyes of hers, wondering whether she was still thinking about the bench under the magnolia tree. Or was she envisioning the vast lake as Wordsworth must have seen it—shimmering, glimmering, sparkling with sails?

Her excitement seemed unstoppable. "Oh Sinclair, what a marvelous classroom. My students would love walking momentarily in the shoes of the Lake Poets and literary giants. Nothing will go wrong. Nothing.

Maybe I'm only imagining Morrie ruining his reputation. Illness does that to you. We'll just keep him busy."

Had he been too lighthearted? She was overly confident now—foolishly confident—that nothing would go wrong, that nothing could threaten a reunion like that if she kept Morrie busy.

"Can I bill you as the visiting professor from Oxford?"

He saluted her. "I'd be honored."

"You won't forget the Dove Cottage in Grasmere? Everyone could pen their names in the guest book there." She sighed happily. "Morrie has a favorite pub—he knows the owner well. Perhaps we could all have lunch there."

The game they were playing strengthened her. "For those who dislike poetry and museums, Morrie can arrange to take a group for a strenuous hike in the fells of Lakeland," he suggested.

"In the steps of John Peel," she laughed without mirth. "Oh, how I wish I could climb again. But you must be careful. I don't want any of my students falling from some pinnacle."

"You are more concerned about the young man who may fall from grace."

It was obvious Chadbourne's entanglement with this family painting worried Rachel. But Morrie's redemptive journey concerned Sinclair more than Lord Somerset's art collection. He strangled a sigh. Scotland Yard and Lord Somerset would never see it that way.

"For those with the child still in them, I can take them to the farm where Beatrix Potter wrote about Peter Rabbit and Mrs. Tittlemouse. You could go, too, Sinclair. I promised Becki Rutledge I would take her there."

"You have color back in your cheeks just talking about it. I think things will work out for you, Rachel."

He leaned over and kissed her on the cheek. "Rest now."

"You, too."

He met Timothy Whitesaul in the hall. "So you are leaving?"

"I will be back this evening. Can I use your phone?"

"For a toll call?"

"Scotland Yard."

If Whitesaul was shocked, he didn't show it. His broad hand spread toward his office. "I trust my patient is not in trouble."

"Only medically, Doctor."

Sinclair walked into Whitesaul's office alone and across the room to the desk. He picked up the receiver and dialed. He was massaging his temples when a clear, efficient voice on the other end jarred him. "May I help you?"

"Inspector Farland, please—yes, he's expecting my call."

Chapter 10

Eileen Rutledge turned her travel-weary body toward the plane window. A pitch-dark sky loomed outside, black as night, like a web tightening around her and leaving her lost in its emptiness and space. She disliked flying and liked it less on this long journey abroad. But it was not the apprehension of hijackers or terrorists that kept her awake. It was Rachel's invitation to England that crowded her thoughts.

She tried to read between the lines of Rachel's invitation and came up with uncertainty. Rachel could be worse, dying; maybe she wanted to say good-bye. Rachel was better; she wanted to share her good news in person. Rachel was counting her days but wanted to keep her promise to Becki. She scolded her thoughts and sent them winging.

Back at the clinic, she had faced a mad rush for an early holiday, hurriedly transferring her patients to the care of her colleagues and writing detailed notes that revealed her own personal interest in each case. Within hours of leaving for the airport, she had spent two hours with a critically ill patient. Holiday scheduling rarely fit into a patient's life span. In Eileen's profession, someone was always losing the battle.

As midnight stretched into the wee hours of the morning, all she could see beyond the plane window were utter darkness and tiny blinking lights like glittering diamonds on the wings of the plane. All she could hear was the rumbling in the belly of the jet and the annoying snores of passengers around her. She didn't risk slipping away to the lavatory for fear that Rebecca would awaken and be frightened in her strange surroundings.

Rebecca slept in the first-class seat beside her, looking angelic rather than an impish, soon-to-be third grader. Eileen stroked the child's long red-brown curls, the lump in her throat rising with a spontaneous burst of love. What a treasured, undemanding time this trip would be for the two of them.

Eileen's hand moved from the child's hair to the soft cheek and lingered there. Her life was too busy, robbed of moments like this. Eileen loved being a physician, but motherhood never agreed with her scheduling. Too often Rebecca was left with the live-in housekeeper, often picked up by her from the private school she attended, and all too often bedded down by this woman called Amy. Not by a woman called *Mommy*.

She smiled over the lost argument on what they should bring for Rachel. Rebecca had insisted that *The Secret Garden* and *The Tale of Peter Rabbit* would make Rachel happy.

"Oh honey," Eileen had protested in the midst of overflowing suitcases, "those are little children's books."

"Oh no, Mommy. Rachel told me these are her favorites."

There was no dissuading her. Twice in flight when they slipped from her lap, Eileen tried to rescue them. Both times Rebecca stirred and closed her hands more tightly around them. The bond was there between Rachel and Rebecca, and for this reason alone, Eileen was taking the trip to England.

Both times as the books slipped from her possession, Rebecca cried out, "Are we almost there, Mommy?"

"We've a long way to go."

"Will we never get there?"

Rebecca was sizing up time, untroubled about her mode of transportation. For Eileen, with each flight, she considered the potential of not reaching her destination, but she shoved these fears aside, knowing there would always be unfinished tasks and dreams at the end of her journey. But God had not brought her safely this far without a purpose. She longed to visit England, but England stirred uncertainties from her past. Morrie lived there. Rachel, with her spontaneous love of life, was happy at the Wakefield Cottage. And Timothy Whitesaul, the Brit who had taken part of his residency at the medical center where she trained, lived and worked in London. They had remained friends through correspondence and phone calls, but there was a sense of embarrassment at seeing him again—this doctor who had been there in the birthing room, offering her his support and friendship the night Rebecca was born.

As the night wore on, the plane turned crisp and cool inside. The couple across from her kitted down with more blankets.

The attendant turned her way and smiled. "Pillows? Blankets?"

Eileen took two blankets. One to place gently over Rebecca's legs, the other to throw across her own lap. Rebecca had nestled against the airline pillow once again and drifted into a deep, even breathing. Eileen saw Morrie in the sleeping child and thought of Morrie's head on the pillow beside her during their honeymoon, looking rumpled and boyish as he slept, a relaxed, contented twist to his mouth.

Rebecca had Morrie's facial features—the firm dimpled chin, the high cheekbones. She also had his impulsive nature and insecurities. Were these Eileen's fault?

Why not admit it? She had brought her child into the Rutledge family with its high social snobbery, and under the care of the family patriarch, a dominating great-grandfather. The old man was ancient now and grumpy, tottering around the Rutledge mansion, still controlling the disbursement of his stocks and bonds. He spent his time reading the financial pages of three newspapers and watching the ticker tape slithering across the bottom of his TV screen, but he couldn't always remember where he put his car keys or false teeth. Little pleased him, not even the valuable paintings on his walls, nor Eileen's success as an oncologist—a dream he had shared with her. A dream he had funded.

Eileen had once been his pride and joy, Rebecca second fiddle—rejected because she was Morrie's child. With time, their roles would reverse because Rebecca adored her great-grandfather, grump and all. She had insecurities like Morrie—but what could Eileen expect for a child with an unforgiving great-grandfather, a missing father, and a working mother? Her child was surprisingly independent in spite of everything, and a good student.

Since Rachel McCully had gone away, Rebecca asked for little from her mother, save for chocolate-covered raisins and that promised trip to Hill Top Farm. When the invitation from Rachel came, Eileen grabbed the opportunity for three weeks where she could spend every breathing minute with her daughter, a desperate move to make up some of the missed times when she had been needed by her patients.

Maybe Timothy Whitesaul was right. Working at the Whitesaul clinic might offer her more time with Rebecca. With every report he sent on Rachel, he extended to Eileen his invitation to leave the security of her job in the States for the challenge of cancer research. At times the thought appealed to her, but perhaps sometime in the future when a drastic move like that would not uproot Rebecca from her private school and sheltered life. She laughed to herself—maybe that would be twelve years from now.

The flight attendant walked the aisle again, coming back for her periodic check on her first-class passengers. She dropped a hot towel into Eileen's hand. Eileen pressed it against her face and felt refreshed as she held it against her sleep-deprived eyes. As she washed her hands and inspected them, she was glad at the prospect of twenty-one days abroad, a chance for her betadine-scrubbed skin to be smooth again.

The attendant stood at her side, whispering, "We're going to serve breakfast soon for those who want it."

"It's so early."

"I know. But we want the trays cleared before we land."

She checked her wristwatch. "Breakfast at three-thirty in the morning? I think not. I promised my daughter we could eat at the hotel."

Eileen closed her eyes for what seemed only a moment, but when she opened them again the ribbons of sunrise glowed on the silver wings of the jumbo jet. The sky blushed in shades of begonias, from a pale pink to waves of coral and salmon. The plane drifted along on a bed of billowy white clouds that separated now and then for a glimpse of the glistening channel below.

She considered waking Rebecca, but the child was such a grump in the morning. Again, so like Morrie. So like her great-grandfather. Eileen let her sleep and rested her own head against the soft cushion to welcome the sunrise. The distant horizon still appeared faint, like a morning mist, but nature kept tossing its deceptive images at her. As the plane descended, she saw the island called England, surrounded by water. Now patched pieces of land beneath them appeared as lava-colored ridges, wave after wave of rolling lowlands peaking like distant mountains.

"Mommy."

She touched the soft cheek again. "Good morning, sleepyhead."

Rebecca stirred and stretched as she pushed her cramped body into a sitting position. "Where's my coat, Mommy?"

"In the closet." Crushed and wrinkled, no doubt, along with her own raincoat.

Rebecca rubbed some of the sleep from her eyes. "Are we almost there?"

"Almost."

"Will Rachel be there?"

"I don't know, but someone will meet us. I'm sure."

But forty-five minutes later when they cleared customs and entered the crowded lobby, Eileen was startled to see Timothy Whitesaul waiting for them.

He stood, smiling down at her. He was a strapping man, over six feet tall and well-muscled. His face was as handsome as ever, and his hazel eyes still held that certain glow.

She offered her hand. "It's been a long time, Timothy."

"Much too long. I came early so I wouldn't miss your plane. A man can get lost in the crowd at Heathrow."

"Kind of like Kennedy back home."

"More like O'Hare International. That's the real nightmare."

He seemed reluctant to let her hand go. She was even more surprised when he pulled her to him and hugged her, but not half as startled as Rebecca. The child scowled up at him. "Who are you?"

"A friend of your mother's. And aren't you the young lady? All grown up now."

The scowl deepened. "I'm eight years old."

"I haven't seen you since you were eight pounds, one ounce."

"This is Timothy Whitesaul, sweetheart. He was at the hospital when you were born. He's the one who sends all the presents." Eileen patted her daughter's head, then turned her attention to Timothy once again. "Where's Rachel McCully?"

"Waiting for you at the Wakefield Cottage in Stradbury Square. I'll be driving you up there tomorrow."

"That's thoughtful of you, but I plan to rent a car. . . . I want to spend time with Rebecca and drive up there with her."

His smile caved. "Will you have any time for me this trip?"

"We'll see. I'm certain something can be arranged. I didn't sleep much on the plane. I really need to get to the hotel."

He hurried them along to the baggage claim and when the cart was loaded, he grinned wickedly and whipped Rebecca on top. He was strong as an ox, his hands broad, his smile broader. "You can direct traffic from there, Rebecca. Clear the path so we can get to the car. Your mother is worn-out."

"And I'm hungry."

To avoid Timothy inviting them to breakfast, Eileen said, "Sweetheart, I'll order our meal in the room. Tomorrow when we're rested, we'll drive up to Rachel's place."

Balancing on top of the luggage cart seemed to please Rebecca. "Clear the way. Clear the way," she announced, and surprisingly the path cleared for them.

Eileen put one hand on the handle, her fingers touching Whitesaul's. "I'll be more pleasant after I've rested," she said.

"I know. We'll be in touch. Can I call you? Would it bother your daughter?"

"Yes, to both questions. I assume you have Rachel's number?"

"And she has mine. She's planning some university reunion. She shouldn't be putting herself under such stress."

"There's no changing her if she's made up her mind."

"Clear the way. Clear the way. Look, Mommy, everybody is moving for us!" Rebecca observed.

"Yes, I see that." To Timothy she said, "How is Rachel?"

"The bout with flu set her back, but not for long. I think she is making progress. . .the shadow on her lung is another question."

"Then she's not in a crisis? This isn't an emergency visit?"

"No. She really wants to see you."

"What if the leukemia goes into an acute stage?"

He glanced at her as he maneuvered the luggage cart. "Eileen, you know the answer to that. A bone marrow transplant would be the only option then."

Her voice sounded professional, belying the ache inside. "She has no siblings, no immediate living relatives at all. That narrows her chance for a bone marrow match."

"Then let's not buy trouble ahead of time."

They were out of the terminal and moving toward his parked car. "Rachel insisted on the Ritz Hotel for you."

She stared up at him. "That's out of the question. Rachel can't afford that."

"Don't snub an opportunity like that. The French-styled rooms are grand. Rachel has already made arrangements. You can't rob her of that pleasure. And, Eileen, don't force Rebecca to have breakfast in the room. I won't stay."

She felt her neck turn scarlet. "I'm sorry."

"I'm not. You were always honest with me. I wouldn't want you to miss tea in the Palm Court. Rebecca will love the scones and jams."

He was silent a moment. "I don't suppose you've given any serious thought to moving abroad? To working with me in cancer research?"

"Every time I have a rough day—or lose a patient, I think about it."

"Then I'll pray for more rough days."

"You'd better pray for my daughter. Rebecca may not like England."

"How can she help but like it? Rachel McCully is here, and I am, too. And I want you both to come back and live here. I'd take good care of you," he promised.

Chapter 11

North, in the Lake District, Rachel sat in the drawing room at the Wakefield Cottage, her ringed hands clasped as she looked at the two men sitting across from her.

Sinclair nodded to his companion. "Rachel, this is Jon Farland. His chief interest is art fraud."

And you've betrayed me, she thought. *Bringing him here without asking me.* "I don't understand."

"Someone broke into the cottage during your trip to London."

"During my medical confinement, you mean. But, Sinclair, nothing was stolen. We haven't noticed anything missing."

She thought of Morrie and flew to his defense. Without naming him, she said, "If you are into art fraud, I don't know how you can help us. As Sinclair knows, there are only four paintings here at the cottage, none of them of interest to an art thief. It had to be a stranger passing through the village."

Sinclair countered in his deep voice, "Rachel, you know strangers don't come here. We're not even on the map."

"I found my way."

"No, I brought you here the first time, Rachel." When Farland's thick brows arched, Sinclair said, "You were my guest, Rachel. Mother's guest. Not a stranger. Why don't you tell Jon what you found when you got back? Let him sort it out for us."

Reluctantly she said, "We were gone several days, Mr. Farland. When we came back, the front gate was open."

"Is that unusual?"

"That would be unusual. I just thought in our haste to leave Audrey might have left it that way."

Although he looked calm, Sinclair sounded provoked. "Audrey said you didn't leave by way of the gate."

Of course, that made sense. The car was parked in the back. They would have gone through the garden. But she couldn't decide whether Sinclair was annoyed with her or with Audrey. Or was it his precious property that he wanted protected? She felt victimized by an intruder in the house, and Sinclair was incensed at the idea of a stranger passing through Stradbury Square.

Didn't he understand? She was sick, and Audrey was frantic when they left the cottage. The gate in the garden had been open, too, and some of the flowers crushed and in need of replanting. She wanted to tell him she would pay for the repairs, to just leave her alone. She hadn't sent for him anyway, and she certainly hadn't asked his friend Jon to come. She was about to speak her mind, but the look in his somber eyes was concern, not anger.

"I was sick when we left, Mr. Farland. I didn't take notice of anything." Her voice held a tremor. "I feel so violated, knowing that someone came in while we were gone."

Sinclair leaned forward and placed his hand on hers. "Stradbury Square has always been safe, Rachel. I don't think it will happen again. The neighbors will be watching closely, making certain you are safe. They've given me their word."

"Whatever happened, Audrey refuses to go to Lord Somerset's for the reunion. She insists she must stay here to protect the place. I can't let her stay here alone."

A prankish smile spread over Farland's square face. "She could handle it. I surprised her when I walked into her kitchen, and she had a heavy pot in her hand in a flash. She would have hit me with that thing if I hadn't told her who I was."

"And who are you?"

"A friend of Sinclair's."

Sinclair was less humorless. "I'll talk to Audrey. You will need her at Lord Somerset's. I want her there to watch over you."

"And you. She still thinks of you as a little boy."

He grinned sheepishly. "Much to my dismay."

"Go step by step," Farland said. "What was the first thing you noticed when you came back to the cottage?"

"The open gate. Then the trampled flowers in my garden. A flowerpot was knocked from the top of the dry wall and broken."

"Yes, we think the intruder scaled the wall there, then forced the gate open when he—they—left."

"That's what I decided. The minute we came home, I went out to the garden for some fresh flowers. That's when I noticed—"

Farland scratched his temple. "Animals might have trampled the flowers." He didn't seem convinced as he jotted notes in his little black book.

"Then why the human footprints?" she asked. "A rubber sole crushed one of my pink camellias. I know that for certain. And I think somebody in a great hurry broke off my hollyhocks just brushing past them." She sighed. "I take great care in my garden, Mr. Farland. It's been my refuge during my illness."

From the quick exchanged glances with Sinclair, she knew he was aware of just how sick she had been. Had Sinclair used her leukemia to persuade Farland's personal interest in the problem?

"While I was in the garden cutting some roses, I heard Audrey scream. I found her in my bedroom, indignant at the shattered glass all over my rug. She kept saying, 'Mr. Sinclair will speak his piece, once he sees that broken window.'"

Farland's eyes sparkled, but he kept his voice businesslike. "The day after you left for London, your neighbor saw two strangers driving away in a red truck."

Her stomach tightened. She knew it was not the flu this time. Two men. Morrie and a man with a beard had driven into Stradbury Square in a red truck. She felt heartsick. Maybe Morrie was concerned about her. Maybe he had—

She met Sinclair's searching gaze and glanced away. "One of your former students came here in a truck, didn't he, Rachel?"

"Please don't quiz me like that, Sinclair. Whoever broke into the house didn't even take the money lying on my dresser."

Farland stroked his chin. "Perhaps they were just surveying the place for a future robbery."

"Really, old man," Sinclair snapped. "I want to encourage Rachel, not frighten her. I don't want to lose a good renter."

Is that all I am—a good renter?

Farland pulled them back to the break-in. "I checked your bedroom, Miss McCully. I'm quite certain that's how they entered the cottage. Once they came over the garden wall, they forced the window open and accidentally shattered the glass."

"So why did they leave a brick in the middle of the floor for a calling card?"

"Rachel, I will have the window repaired. Just try to remember. Are you certain that nothing is missing?"

"Don't press her, Wakefield. If she can recall anything important, she'll call us. Won't you, Miss McCully?"

She turned angrily on Farland. "I don't know who you are. You want me to tell you the truth, so be honest with me."

He brushed his flattop with his broad hand. "I'm *Inspector* Jon Farland. I'm with the art fraud division at Scotland Yard."

Scotland Yard? He had come with prying questions and a quick friendly smile. His pale eyes looked sleep deprived, his jacket less than pressed, and he smelled of stale cigarettes. She had noted his big, well-padded hands when he sat down, and thought him a repairman ready to suggest a paint job on the cottage. As they talked about art, she had imagined him an art dealer or an intellectual acquaintance of Sinclair's from Oxford. But an inspector from Scotland Yard—here to cover a break-in? Surely something more urgent brought him to Stradbury Square.

Aggravated, she said, "Mr. Farland, I brought no real valuables to England with me—just my jeweled watch and my mother's diamond ring. I was wearing them. The rest of my jewelry was untouched. There is nothing here of value to a thief."

"You may be the one of value to them. Perhaps someone you met in London. Or at the clinic. Someone from your past who thinks you can endanger them."

"That's foolishness. A former student and Sinclair are the only ones from my past who know I'm staying here. Tell me, Inspector, have there been other break-ins in Stradbury Square or the neighboring villages?"

He shrugged. "London is my jurisdiction. But Sinclair and I are friends. I've posted my men in the village. When you are at Lord Somerset's, they will keep an eye on your place." He laid a mobile phone on the end table. "That's coded in to my direct line. Call anytime. Someone will always be at that number."

"Is all this necessary?" she asked.

He stood. "Sinclair thinks so."

"You must be a good friend to go out of your way for a village off the beaten path."

"The truth is, we are concerned about you, Miss McCully. You are a guest in our country."

"One of thousands, Inspector."

"But the only one of importance to Sinclair Wakefield."

She blushed and fell silent. Inspector Farland patted her hand awkwardly. "Miss McCully, you just go and enjoy that reunion at Lord Somerset's."

Sinclair asked, "Have you heard from Somerset?"

"Not since he rejoined his cruise ship. Let me see, I believe their next port of call is New Zealand."

"Will you be in touch then?"

"Not unless there is something to report. No use worrying him. And you, Miss McCully, have nothing to worry about either."

"Did Sinclair tell you? I have guests coming tomorrow."

Again a whimsical smile covered the inspector's face. "I know. They are staying at the Ritz this evening. You should have seen my men scrambling for that duty."

Apprehension ripped through her. "You're worried about their security, even there at the Ritz?"

"Yes, because they will be guests in this cottage. They are driving up here with Timothy Whitesaul. Right, Sinclair?"

"That's the plan."

Farland hesitated on the front steps as Audrey came hurrying to them. "Phone call for you, Mr. Sinclair."

"For me? No one knows I am here, except the inspector."

"It sounds like Dr. Whitesaul," she whispered. "He said Rachel's guests are driving up from London by themselves. He wants to know whether that will be a problem for you."

Farland frowned. "Let me talk to him."

～

Early that morning, Morrie Chadbourne climbed to the top of Old Man of Coniston, a rocky projection still snowcapped at the top and isolated enough to give him time alone. The Coniston, old as the surrounding hills, was rumored to shelter goblins, fairies, and ghosts. He had ghosts of his own: a failed marriage, his planned betrayal of Lord Somerset, and his Jewish heritage. Charles Rainford-Simms had told him to be proud of his heritage. Morrie had a legal right to an Asher Weinberger painting, but legality was as close as he would get.

When he reached the memorial to the airmen killed in a navigational exercise in the fall of '44, he slumped to the ground and took some trail food and a slice of goat cheese from his backpack. He quenched his thirst with bottled water. He'd been here before and pitied the young British airman and seven Canadians who died when their Halifax bomber crashed into the mountain.

Morrie took a bite of the cheese. He wondered whether any of the victims' families had ever climbed to this spot, to sit as he was doing to mourn for them. Below him, the village of Coniston rose above the water's edge. He figured that some of the old-timers still remembered the smoke rising when the plane crashed. He imagined some of them making the journey to the crash site to leave flowers on the unmarked graves of somebody's son. Somebody's husband.

At the foot of Old Coniston the day had begun warm and sunny, the air hinting to midsummer. High in the fells, the late spring seemed more like midwinter with its crisp chill. Trouble had dogged Morrie to the craggy top. He found isolation climbing alone, but he envied the airmen who had found oblivion. What had gone wrong with his own life? He was a successful scholar, yet he still blamed others for his miserable boyhood and Eileen's rejection. He still felt anger at Asher Weinberger for dying young and Lord Somerset for being so stinking rich. Morrie was good at climbing—better at running out when the going got rough.

The brooding rocks were as barren as his own pleasure. Far to his north lay the simmering firths of Scotland, a land scented with heather. To the south lay the bustling city of London. He was trapped between the two, caught in the shadow of the mountains. Toward dusk, Morrie came down the last few yards of the fells, half running. The good hike and climb on Old Coniston had cleared his mind and made him feel good inside. But the sight of the man standing there waiting for him churled his stomach.

Didier Bosman showed his anger in the way he stood guard over Morrie's bicycle—feet spread, legs rigid, shoulders squared, clenched hands jammed in his pockets.

"Bosman, what are you doing here?" Morrie asked, unchaining his bike from the tree.

"I waited for you at Hanley's Pub. When you didn't arrive, I came here to meet you. I'm staying at The Old England Hotel on Lake Windermere. We could eat there. Prince Philip and Prince Charles found it a charming enough place to visit."

"I'm not dressed for that."

"Should we drive back to Hanley's Pub and have supper?"

He didn't want Hanley to see him in company with this man. "Whatever you have to say, Bosman, say it to me here."

Didier Bosman was sixty-ish with thinning silver gray hair that left him with a high forehead. His face was full without flabby skin. Wide, black-rimmed glasses magnified the shrewd green eyes. Behind the sharp gaze lay the brilliant mind of an insider from the art world.

"We had everything worked out, Morris, but Chip tells me you were joking about helping us. You know I am not a joking man."

That art theft at Lord Somerset's had been Bosman's plan. Now with Rachel McCully's safety in question, Morrie was in too deep to pull himself free. For a second, he wanted to lure Bosman to the top of Old Coniston and leave him there with a smashed skull. Do that and he would never be at peace and never discover who was really behind this intricate plan to steal another man's treasures. Bosman took credit, but was he discreet and clever enough to work out the details on the theft of the century?

Sweaty from hiking, Morrie felt shabby compared to Didier in his tailored clothes. Bosman probably had a dozen suits in shades of tan, with muted ties as blanched as his face. "Bosman, let it go. Just enjoy the paintings at your museum. There's no risk that way."

"No one notices me there. Even when I try to give the guests historical facts on the artists and their work, people don't listen to me. They make senseless comments and go back to their brochures for answers. I won't be ignored any longer."

"Change jobs then."

"Once we market the Somerset collection, I plan to retire."

"You're already a successful man," Morrie reminded the older man. "Curator at two major museums on the continent. You rescued the Norbert Museum from bankruptcy and put Norbert back in the tourist guides as a must-see museum on fine arts."

Gloomily, he said, "But it takes all my earnings to keep my ex-wives in high-rise apartments. What I need is money they cannot touch. Gold they know nothing about."

"It won't work. The escape route is impossible."

"We go down. You go down. And my ex-wives are cut off without a sixpence. I like the thought of them moving to more economical accommodations. My two divorces have been most costly."

"Why steal the Somerset collection? The museum vaults are full of priceless paintings. You can market them."

"Too risky. Some of them date back to the Hitler era. I don't want Jewish families discovering them on the market and having the theft traced back to me because of some Jew."

Morrie raged at the prejudice. As he picked up the bicycle chain, his fingers trembled. "I won't help you, Bosman."

Bosman whipped a hand recorder from his pocket and thrust it in Morrie's face. He clicked the ON button. Morrie heard himself saying, "I have been the caretaker for nine months now. I know the Somerset Estates inside and out."

"Well enough to plan a robbery?"

He had laughed in Bosman's face, then, pressed for an answer, said, "Robbing the place would be a snap for a smart thief."

Morrie remembered Bosman snapping back, "I am that smart thief. I have been locked away in musty museums far too long. So what would you do if you planned to rob the Somerset Estates?"

For humor's sake, Morrie had flipped to a clean sheet of paper and sketched a map of the Somerset property. He pointed to the side gate. "This would be your safest entry."

Bosman's eyes had narrowed behind those rimmed glasses. "What would it cost for you to help me, Chadbourne?"

Without thinking, he bantered, "Promise to put the Asher Weinberger painting permanently in my hands."

Bosman roared with delight. "You'd hang the Weinberger in the caretaker's cottage—right under the nose of Lord Somerset?"

The tape kept running with Bosman's rambling thoughts and every one of Morrie's suggestions for a successful robbery. "Mr. Chadbourne, I don't intend to remain poor and unknown any longer. Sometimes I want to tear the pictures from the museum walls. But that has been my life for twenty years. People who love art come to gawk and admire. They have that right. But Somerset owns far more paintings than one man should; don't you agree?"

To humor him, Morrie had said, "Of course."

Bosman clicked the recorder's OFF button. "We will go through with the plans, and for the safety of your guests, you will turn off the alarm system for us." Didier held up the recorder. "Do you have any doubts about helping us, Chadbourne?"

Morrie's own words condemned him. The salty taste in his mouth was more like fish oil.

"Most of your guests are of little interest to us. But this American, Rachel McCully—you seem to have an interest in her. I want those paintings, Chadbourne, at any cost. We know your schedule. Your every move. You won't be free to protect Miss McCully every minute; you do understand what I'm saying?"

Morrie understood. As he cycled back to the Somerset Estates, he sought for a way to fight back. But how could he leave for London early in the morning with his every move being observed?

He didn't know much about the wide and narrow roads, but pedaling through the countryside, he knew he was on the wide one with a deep chasm on either side. Somerset was worth millions. Billions, if his wife kept bidding for paintings. Bosman wanted only twenty select paintings. The most insured? The least known for marketing? No, he had targeted a Rembrandt, a Monet, and a van Gogh. Morrie could take off, run out. He was good at that. Eileen had warned him often enough that his introspection and bursts of anger and impulsiveness would ruin him one day.

Morrie didn't know for certain who his enemies were, but he could trust Charles Rainford-Simms. Charles dealt with prodigal sons. He found Charles at the back of the property, kneeling in front of a flower bed—his clerical collar smudged, his sleeves rolled up, his hands a mixture of soil and fertilizer. His lined face broke into a grin. "I missed our Sunday tea, young man."

Pushing to his feet, his knees cracked. Even with stooped shoulders, Rainford-Simms towered above Morrie, a kindly man with thick, snow-white hair, and translucent blue eyes that twinkled behind his glasses. His gaze neither probed nor threatened.

"I spent the day up on Old Coniston, Charles."

"Thinking? Praying?"

"Arguing with myself mostly. You should have gone with me."

"Ask me next time. I'd enjoy a good chat with you up there."

"You'd have me cornered, all right. By the way, Charles, could you get me off this property without my absence being noted?"

The bushy brows meshed. "The garden supply truck comes again the day after tomorrow. I've asked for extra supplies so I can have the gardens looking superb when your guests arrive."

"But we have gardeners."

"They have assignments. These flower beds are my joy."

"You're certain the truck can't come sooner?"

Charles smiled. "The rest of the staff would notice."

"That will have to be soon enough. Do you think the driver could bring an extra jumpsuit, large enough for me to wear?"

He sized him up, eyes amused. "I'll call and ask him."

"No questions asked?" Morrie was eager now.

"You have argued with yourself all day. I will not add to your burden. I'll tell the driver to count on a passenger when he leaves the grounds.

How far do you need to go, Morris?"

"I want to catch the rail into London that morning."

Charles wiped his hands and slipped an arm around Morrie's shoulders. "I think we'd better have that cup of tea now."

Chapter 12

Jude Alexander left her desk at the American embassy in London and walked out the front entry, between what she called the Samson pillars. For a second she stood a stone's throw from a row of cement planters and directly beneath the bronzed eagle with the American flag fluttering above it. She had an indescribable, unexpected moment of homesickness. But she couldn't go home, not to the parsonage where her parents lived.

She had followed part of her dream into foreign service, but the glamour she had expected escaped her. Life was, after all, pretty routine. Jude was little more than a member of a secretarial pool, and if her clearance rating could be tagged, it would be at the lowest level. She hadn't seen one confidential report cross her desk in the twelve months she had been here. She had wanted so much more. Her last evaluation came as a warning. Failure to improve on the job meant closed doors to any other embassy assignments.

She was doing better, trying harder, and running faster away from her father's God. She glanced around, eyes wide with expectation. The stranger on the phone had told her he was Sean Larkins. He spoke with a charming voice and an Irish accent, but he said he was American born, running free as she was doing. If he expected her to recognize his name, she didn't. Adjusting her hair, Jude recalled the rest of their conversation.

"I think we went to the same university. Different classes of course. I've just seen the list for the Rachel McCully reunion. We're invited to the same party."

Party. Reunion. McCully. She didn't have a clue, but she recognized the name McCully and froze.

"Miss Alexander, are you still there?"

"I'm listening."

"It's a university reunion in the Lake District. We'll be honoring our old prof. Kind of nice, what say?"

She could barely say anything. She didn't want to honor McCully and never wanted to see that woman again. "I didn't do well in McCully's

744

classes, Mr. Larkins. I don't think she'd like to see me put in an appearance."

"I hardly squeaked by myself. But she was a nice lady. Be good to see her again. You'll love the Somerset Estates where we're staying. I'm a soccer and rugby man myself, but they have a badminton court on the grounds. I'll challenge you to a game."

If he expected her to be a pro at badminton, she wasn't. "I don't have any holiday time coming."

"Then take a sick leave. Say, could we get together this evening? Talk, maybe have dinner? If we're going to drive up to the reunion together, we'd better get acquainted."

"I—I haven't been invited."

"That doesn't make sense. Maybe Morrie Chadbourne used the wrong e-mail address—he's the one throwing the party. Well, never mind. I'll bring you a copy of my invitation. You're definitely on the list. That's how I got your name."

"I really have to go." *I'm being watched. On probation. You sound intriguing, but I can't lose my job over you.*

"I'll wait for you. What time do you get off?"

"In thirty minutes. But you don't know where I work."

"Don't I? The operator said, 'American embassy' when she answered." Jude laughed. "You are crazy."

"Crazy about finally meeting you. Do you have a favorite restaurant?"

"Surprise me."

"My kind of gal. I'm in Hyde Park right now, using my cell phone. I can reach Grosvenor Square by the time you walk out the door. I'll be waiting for you near one of those cement pillars."

She liked the laughter in his voice. "How will I know you?"

"If they don't arrest me for loitering, I'll be the tall, good-looking one with a polka dot handkerchief in my pocket."

"I have blond hair."

"I know. You wear it pulled back from your face, but one lock of it falls over your right brow. You like dangling earrings and bright lipstick. And I already know you have big brown eyes."

She shoved her apprehension aside. "Be seeing you."

She saw him now doing exactly what he said he would be doing: waiting near the cement pillars. He was definitely tall and good-looking, his deep-set eyes shadowed, his pale lower jaw looking as though he had recently sacrificed a beard. She walked toward him, taking note of his polka dot handkerchief as he rose to meet her.

He took her hand and smiled captivatingly. "I didn't think you would be this beautiful, Miss Alexander."

∼

In the tiny bedroom in their London apartment, Kevin Nolan booted up Amanda's computer. She wanted him to bring her e-mails when they met for lunch. With Mandy's workload in advertising, even a short lunch was a coveted time together. He decided to propose again today and knew what the answer would be. She ran scared when it came to marriage, to any commitment.

Amanda's only e-mail was a fancy graphic design announcing a reunion in the Lake Districts with her old English professor. With Mandy's tendency toward sentimental journeys, he considered deleting the invitation. But he ran the risk of making her mad and putting a locked bedroom door between them. Kevin didn't like life this way. He wanted marriage—he wanted to spend the rest of his life with Amanda Pennyman as husband and wife. But he didn't want to go to some crazy reunion with Amanda's professor.

Going off to the North Country for even an overnight lacked the excitement of going to the steeple races. Now that was excitement—the horses running neck and neck. Where was this reunion being held? He scanned it a second time: *The Somerset Estates.* Kevin felt such a revulsion that he cupped his mouth. Not at Lord Somerset's! James Somerset?

He'd had a run-in with the man, and once was enough. Somerset was a retired president, still holding office at the bank. Kevin was the boyish-looking auditor saying politely, "We have a problem here, sir. The books have been tampered with."

Somerset had faced him with his arms folded across his chest, his massive frame making Kevin shrink under his glare. "Look again, Mr. Nolan. I'm certain *you* have made the mistake."

They met a second time, but that time Kevin had the upper hand. "The bank has sixty days, sir, to correct this error."

Sixty days, or else, he had implied.

Kevin crushed the e-mail in his hand and raced out the door. Amanda didn't like him running late. Not even for a lunch. He loved her. It was as simple as that. He had been a bachelor when he met her. She had told him right off: no drinking, no smoking. She had been less emphatic with his love of horses, but another few months at the support group and even that urge to put a little money on the race would be chiseled away. He needed to save every shilling for the day he married his little Asian princess—the beautiful girl with cinnamon skin and honest eyes who used her gentle humor and a dozen beautiful hats to make herself feel comfortable anywhere. She was one-fourth Chinese, just enough to make her long hair a silky brown and to give a slight slant to her dark eyes. His princess.

Amanda wanted the elegance of Georgian housing, but he feared they were stuck in this apartment for the next thirty years. Cramped as it was, it was busting their wallets. But it lay in the heart of London in close proximity to the museums and art galleries that Amanda loved; he felt drawn to Trafalgar Square with its political rallies and public meetings.

Public meetings sparked another unwanted memory of his last encounter with Lord Somerset: the betting line at the racetrack. He had stood in line behind a tall, overbearing man arguing with the bookie. The man turned, their eyes locking, freezing. Kevin had given him a quick nod. "Good afternoon, Lord Somerset."

Under his breath he had said, "See you here the next time."

On his way to meet Amanda, he stopped at the department store to buy a bouquet of flowers. Balancing the flowers and Amanda's invitation in his hand, Kevin stepped out of Harrods and started down the sidewalk seconds before the bomb exploded in the art shop down the street. As he pitched forward, he remembered that Amanda was waiting for him on the next corner at the lunch cafe.

He lay sprawled on the street, the crumpled invitation to Dr. McCully's reunion skittering from his limp fingers, caught by a frolicsome spring breeze.

As he drifted in and out of consciousness, a policeman knelt beside him. "Lie still, son. The ambulance is coming. I think this is yours," he said, tucking McCully's invitation into his pocket.

When he woke in a sterile hospital room, Amanda was at his bedside. He tried to tell her about the shards of splintered glass blowing against him. He felt the sting on his face, looked at his bandaged hand, felt his swollen lips.

Amanda's soft voice reassured him. "You're going to be all right, Kevin. There was a bombing in an art shop near Harrods. The clerk there was killed. Thankfully. . ." Her voice broke.

"Oh honey, I missed our luncheon date."

"It doesn't matter." She rested her fingers on his bandaged hand. "I love you, Kevin."

"Then marry me."

747

"Someday."

"No, as soon as I get out of here. When are they going to release me?"

"Not until tomorrow. By the way, I found this in your pocket."

"The invitation came via e-mail; I was taking it to you. Who is she anyway?"

"The English professor who was kind to me the day Lee died."

Lee, the dead fiancé—the reason Amanda feared another commitment.

"Will you go with me, Kevin?"

"I don't care to go, but if you want to go to this reunion by yourself, okay."

"No, we both go. Or we both stay home. Dr. McCully prayed for me the day Lee died—"

"Wait! This isn't going to be a religious retreat, is it?"

"No, Kevin. Just a reunion. I really want to go, but Dr. McCully would be disappointed to know we're living together."

He took her fingers and kissed them with swollen lips. "Then marry me, Mandy."

She avoided his eyes. "We'll probably talk about great literature at the reunion."

"Sounds boring."

"She's anything but boring. Will you go with me, Kevin?"

He felt trapped. "Give me one good reason why I should."

"Because you'll like her. She's very classy. And very compassionate. I remember the day I sat in her office and told her about Lee. She came around and put her arms around me and held me until I stopped sobbing. I always had the feeling she knew what it was like to lose someone."

A moody silence hung between them.

"Kev, when I heard about the accident near Harrods, I couldn't get to you fast enough."

He turned his bruised face on the pillow and touched her cheek with his bandaged hand. "And all I could think about was you coming. But this reunion—I'm not sure, Mandy. Spending several days with strangers."

❧

In the dressing room in Rome, Lenora Silverman turned on her agent. She blessed him in English, a peppery blasting of words that accompanied a quick stomp of her foot. Realizing what she was doing, she switched to a fiery Italian. She could as easily have scolded him in German or French.

"No, you listen to me, Tomas." She waved her invitation to Rachel McCully's reunion in the air. "I want to go to that gathering in England. I could leave after the Sunday performance. Please book me on the midnight flight. On any flight."

He threw up his hands. "Your fans expect you to sing in *Madame Butterfly*. You have the lead part. You are Cho-Cho-San."

Cho-Cho-San, the lovely geisha girl. The opera in its beauty and tragedy was one of her favorites. She loved the part of the young Japanese girl married to the American navy lieutenant. No matter how many times she had heard it, she teared when he promised to come back "when the robins nest again."

"I have a stand-in. She is very good. She longs for the opportunity to prove herself. Please let her take my place."

He nodded reluctantly. "Perhaps she will make a better Cho-Cho-San."

Offstage, Lenora felt unattractive—stocky and too short. But when she filled her lungs and sang, her chest rising with the volume, she felt beautiful. She escaped into the parts she sang, regardless of the language, and for months now, had been Cho-Cho-San in *Madame Butterfly*.

"I would only miss five performances."

His hands shot in the air again. "Five too many."

She closed her eyes and tried to think back to her classes at the university. She barely remembered the other students, but she remembered her English professor, Rachel McCully, saying, *"Lenora, you don't want to teach. You want to sing."*

"But I am afraid to tell my parents. I'm afraid I'll fail."

"You won't know unless you try. Change your major."

"But I won't be able to take any more of your classes."

"The world won't disintegrate if you stop your English classes. But if you don't change your major to music you will never sing professionally. You were born to sing. You have the gift of languages. The gift of music."

Lenora had sung in all the great works, feeling the power of drama and music in grand opera. She had sung at all of the great opera houses—minor parts and lead soprano—in Paris, Rome, Vienna, Budapest, and at the Royal Opera House in London.

She looked at Tomas and stomped her foot again. "I must go, Tomas. I wouldn't even be here if it weren't for the influence of Rachel McCully on my life. She taught me more than English literature. She taught me to believe in myself. To follow my dreams."

~

Two hours across the Canadian border sat the sprawling Tallard farm, visible from the motorway. It spread over rolling hills with a whitewashed farmhouse and barn and Guernsey cattle grazing lazily in the morning sun. Seven years before Janet Tallard had made the decision to throw her education to the winds and marry the Canadian widower with three young sons.

The three boys needed a mother. No, they needed mothering, and that burly man, her gentle giant in jeans and boots, needed a wife. Someone to share his heart and hearth and faith. She never looked back. Her ready-made family delighted her, and three young boys who had barely known their own mother found in Janet someone who could fill that empty void: Paul, Mickey, and Jared. Four, seven, and nine back then. Eleven, fourteen, and an awkward sixteen now. She loved them the day she married Tad, loved them even more when she discovered that she could not bear a child of her own.

It had not been seven years of smooth sailing. They argued over the boys sometimes. Argued about the sermons they heard on Sunday mornings. Argued about the long hours it took to make a go of the farm with so few hired hands. Farming was new to her. Pitching hay deplorable. Rising at dawn exhausting. The needs of three small boys bewildering. The kitchen had been a safer haven, but even there she was a novice. Tad had come to her rescue. He didn't buy cookbooks but taught her the recipes he loved.

"Give a man his meat and potatoes seven days a week," he told her, "and he will rise up and call you blessed."

It took some doing on her part to convince the boys, and finally their father, that they couldn't eat and run. Dinnertime would be family time, and the vegetables and fruit were not to be left on their plates as garbage.

Janet had pitched in, side by side with Tad, because she was determined to prove her love and the wisdom of marrying an older man—she twenty and he thirty-five on the day of their wedding. She had no regrets even now as she made her way to the postal box hugging the motorway. Her ponytail flapped against the small of her back as she crossed the tractor-mowed lawn in her boots and jeans, the jeans too tight now, Jared had told her. But the boys needed new school clothes, and new shoes for church and Sunday school, and the mission project for starving children was more urgent than a new pair of work pants.

She yanked open the lid to the metal mailbox and pulled out the ads and bills and junk mail. And the good mail—a card from an old college friend and a letter from home. And a thick envelope marked *Airline Ticket Enclosed.*

She tore the envelope open; the ticket bore her name.

The departure flight was days away. Destination: London, England.

What kind of a lottery was this? What kind of a joke? It had to be Tad, always planning special surprises. Her whole life she had wanted to travel to England, but it was one of the dreams she had set aside to become Mrs. Tad Tallard.

The ticket looked legitimate. She had to tell Tad. Racing across the property toward the barn was almost an impossibility in heavy boots. Her feet felt weighted to the ground. Her heart raced. She burst into the barn. "Look at this," she cried.

Four pairs of eyes looked up from their work. Tad and the boys. Tad and his three look-alikes.

"I just got the mail," she announced.

The boys exchanged glances, smiling. Tad put the feed bucket on the barn floor and wiped his big hands on the sides of his overhauls. "Anything for me?" he asked.

"Bills. And the cattle magazine. There's an article on a new kind of feed. And more on the cattle disease in England."

"And?" he pressed.

"An airline ticket for me. It's from you, isn't it? Oh Tad, I love you. I love you."

"You never gave me cause to doubt it."

"But why a holiday just for me?"

He pointed back to the boys and waved them closer. "Their idea. You had an invitation to a reunion in England. It came by e-mail. Jared here thought we should surprise you."

"We even put in some of our spending money," Paul said.

Tears brushed her eyes. "Are you trying to get rid of me?"

"Naw," Mickey admitted. "We'll be stuck with Dad's cooking."

Jared poked him. "Dad can handle it. We just wanted to thank you for being our mother."

Janet Tallard. Twenty-seven. The mother of three. The proudest mom in Canada. "I wanted to be your mother. . . This ticket says I leave this week. Tad, why aren't you going with me?"

"Somebody has to tend the farm. You won't be gone that long, but I miss you already."

"Where am I going exactly?"

"To the Lake Districts for a class reunion with your old English professor."

"Rachel McCully?"

Days before she left the university in her sophomore year, she had convinced herself that marriage to a dairy farmer didn't need a university degree, but her counselor—an energetic English prof named McCully—had disagreed. But once Janet's decision was final, she had come to the wedding and sat on the bride's side.

"What is she doing in England? Oh, I remember. She always traveled abroad in her summers."

"She's living there now," Tad said quietly. "She's ill, Janet. I don't know how seriously."

She looked down at the ticket, faced him again. "Ill? Not Dr. McCully. You remember her, Tad. She came to our wedding. She has boundless energy."

"The truth is I don't remember her. Only that you talk about her. At our wedding I had three kids to keep in tow. And a beautiful bride coming down the aisle to me."

"Dr. McCully took the boys off your hands at the reception."

"Yeah, I remember her," Jared said. "She grabbed me two pieces of wedding cake just to keep me quiet."

"Dad doesn't dig the computer world, so I e-mailed an answer back to the man throwing the party." Mickey was an exact replica of his father: sandy hair, big grin, burly. Muscled and tenderhearted. "The man who is throwing the party told me your friend has leukemia. We want you to go, Mom."

"Leukemia! Oh, not Dr. McCully."

Tad cleared his throat. "The first twenty invitations accepted were on their way. We just got in under the wire." Awkwardly, he said, "You'll need some dresses for the trip."

Janet looked at this beloved family of hers. Knew that Paul needed shoes. He couldn't go on wearing hand-me-downs. And she was secretly pinching pennies from her grocery money so the boys could go to summer camp. "I don't need any dresses, Tad. I'll make do, but I could use a new pair of shoes."

"That and a new hairdo. The boys made an appointment for you. They want you to have your nails done too."

She looked down at her work-worn hands.

"They have those fancy, make-believe nails. They glue them on, I think," Mickey informed her. "At least I think that's what the lady at the beauty parlor told us."

Tad couldn't take his eyes off her; he was looking at her the same way he had on their wedding day. "I love you, Janet. It will be the first time we've been apart, but I want you to go. And if your professor is ill, maybe you can help her."

He opened his arms, and she went into them. He smelled of the barn and the farm, but it was like a sweet fragrance to her.

~

In the Los Angeles Race for the Cure, Lydia Arnold, a high school teacher, stood waiting for her sister to finish the race. The pack of runners streamed toward her. She still could not pick Sara from the sea of faces, but she knew Sara was there, running her heart out for another social cause. Why had she chosen to run the marathon against breast cancer? Lydia could not be certain. But she was grateful. Until two years ago, a mastectomy had always been someone else's battle.

Exhausted runners were crossing the line now, and there was Sara, young, vibrant, determined, her strong legs stretching toward the finish line. Her tank top was wet with sweat, her hair damp from running. She crossed the line and stopped on the edge of the crowd to catch her breath. She bent over, hands to her knees trying to fill her lungs with air.

You did it for me, Lydia thought, *but you don't know that.*

It was another five minutes before she could reach twenty-two-year-old Sara. "Great job, sis. I'm proud of you."

"You sound like an old mother hen, but I didn't win."

"Was that the goal? I thought you ran in the race against cancer. I have my car. Can I drive you home? We could go out for breakfast first."

"Dressed like this? Lydia, don't be such an idiot. Drop me off at my apartment. What I need is a hot shower and a long nap."

And to be as far away from me as you can get.

"What about dinner this evening?"

"I have other plans."

As they made their way toward the parked car, Lydia asked, "Sara, do you remember Rachel McCully?"

"Of course. She turned the dull poets of yesteryear into music. I loved her classes."

It was one of the few things they had in common.

"What made you think of her, Lydia?"

"They're throwing a party for her in England. The invitation came by e-mail. It's for both of us. It looks like marvelous scenery in the Lake Districts."

"And a crowded tour bus and rotten accommodations."

Like the only trip we ever took together. "No, we'd be staying in an old mansion. Will you go, if I pay the way?"

She whipped the sweatband from her forehead and wrung it out. "A free trip to England? First class or nothing."

"First class then. I called my travel agent. She's working on a booking. I'll tell her to make it first class."

"You'd blow a whole wad on me?"

I'd do anything to win your favor. Your love. Your respect. "The money is yours when I die. Might as well spend it now."

"Why cross the ocean to see a teacher?"

"You know why. McCully was special to me. I was in her first creative writing class. Older than the teacher. But I learned so much from her. . . and I always wanted to go to England."

"Then go. You don't need me tagging along. We don't always get on, you know. We're sisters all right, but we had a crazy set of parents. They doted on you, and I came along nineteen years later. Unexpected, you know."

"Don't be cruel, Sara. Mom and Dad are good to you."

"I know. But they're more like my grandparents. Right now, I don't seem to have much in common with them, and you and I are practically strangers."

"Not my choice." Lydia bit her tongue, thinking, *They are your grandparents. Someday I will have to tell you the truth, and then I will lose you forever.*

She had never told anyone the truth about Sara until that year in the creative writing class. She had written about a child, a lost child. About an empty womb, a dead heart. And Professor McCully had written across her paper, *Lydia, you shouldn't bear your pain alone. My office door is always open.*

It was wide open the day Lydia went to her. McCully glided across the room and told her secretary, "Hold my calls." Then she closed the door and said, "Lydia, where is that lost child?"

They emptied a box of tissues that day, the two of them. The next semester, when Lydia ran out of funds and was leaving the university, she went to Rachel McCully to tell her good-bye. "I have no funds or scholarship to go on with my studies."

"You have to finish. You have the child to think about."

"I think about her all the time."

That night Rachel McCully took her out to dinner and handed her a thousand dollars. "This should keep the registrar happy until we can find you some scholarship funding. I've already started the ball rolling."

Lydia had shoved the money back across the table. "Oh you can't do that, Dr. McCully."

"Oh but I can. Call it a loan if you feel better about it. If you can't pay it back, we'll just consider it an investment."

She paid it back three years later during her first year of teaching. As she started the car she said, "Sara, read the small print at the bottom of the invitation. It looks like Rachel McCully has cancer."

"Cancer? Then she didn't send her own invitation, Lydia. She'd never tell us something like that. She took on our problems, but she'd never share her own."

"I know. That's why I want to go. She gave me a lifetime of memories. That invitation just asks me to give her back a few days. Will you go with me, Sara?"

"I'll sleep on it."

But Lydia knew she would go. She had just run a marathon in the race against cancer. Yes, Sara, for all of her outward indifference, had a tender heart. She would turn this holiday into a continued race, this time in the fight against leukemia.

～

In New Zealand, the sleek, white cruise ship bobbed gently in the bay as a stretcher was carried down the gangplank. Few passengers noticed. Those who did showed little interest.

"Just another elderly passenger," an American deckhand said to the steward standing beside him. "Those old ones wait too long to travel like this. A rich diet does them in. Sets the old heart pumping."

The steward saw it differently. The Somersets had tipped generously, especially the woman. *He had been making up their bed for them when she clutched her chest and said, "I need the ship's doctor."*

He tried to help her. Things like this happened on board. Heart attacks. Broken ankles. Even deaths. He tried to ease Mrs. Somerset into a chair, think-ing, Where is Lord Somerset when he is needed?

At the slot machines, *he was certain.*

"You'll be all right, Mrs. Somerset," he promised.

But he knew from her ashen face that it was serious. He watched now, feeling a personal sadness for her. He turned away from the rail, unable to watch the proud man following the stretcher down the ramp. *Worthless man. Wealthy man*, he thought.

Ah! If he, the Italian steward from Milan, could lay his hands on even a fraction of that man's investments. He was too busy to know how sick his wife really was.

~

An hour later, Lord Somerset ran alongside the stretcher as it was taken toward the medical evac plane standing on the tarmac. He smiled down at his wife, her small hand in his, and whispered, "We did it. You really fooled them. Thank you, my dear, for getting me off that cruise ship. I need to be getting back to the mansion."

"Trouble?" she whispered.

"Nothing for you to worry about, my dear."

She was silent again, her eyes closed. Slowly she opened them. It was then he realized how chalky and clammy her skin was. Her eyes were listless, her hand limp in his.

"I'm not pretending, James," she managed, as they settled her inside the plane. "I really did have another heart attack." She struggled for each breath. "A mild one, the doctor said."

"But you told me—he told me—"

"He told you what I instructed him to say. James, you always told me that a man would tell you anything for a price. But that's your world, not mine. I'm so ashamed, James—"

"It's all right. We can go on another cruise as soon as you're better."

"You'll have to go without me. I'll never be well enough to risk it again."

"Nonsense, Agnes. We've spent fifty years together. We're not going to quit now."

"You told me that's a long time for spending your money."

I can't make it fast enough. . . You'll put me in the poorhouse. . . Not another painting, Agnes? No, I'm spending evenings at the club just to get away from you. Didn't she realize he was joking? That he couldn't live without her? That she was his strength, the only woman he'd ever wanted to come home to? He lifted her hand to his lips and kissed it.

Her eyes closed, the long lashes glistening with tears. Lord Somerset hated himself for forcing her to take this trip. What had he done to her?

"James."

"I'm here."

She tried to cup his cheek. Her hand dropped to her side. "I'll be all right, James. I want to rest now."

He wanted to say "Happy anniversary, darling," but the words strangled in his throat.

Chapter 13

Morrie Chadbourne stood beneath the squeaking gilded sign with the face of Mona Lisa engraved on it. COVENTRY ART THEFT REGISTRY, it read. He didn't know whether he had the strength to walk up the long narrow steps to the second floor. Walk them and he might be throwing his career to the winds. He hesitated. How could he face the people upstairs? Should he barge in and announce the biggest heist in Lake District history? Who would believe him? His motives were mixed. *Steal the Weinberger painting first. No.* His stomach turned sour at the thought.

The eyes of the *Mona Lisa* made him squirm, and he did what he always did. He ran off, ran toward the River Thames to the hub of London and the melting pot of people who would swallow him into oblivion. His legs cramped on the second block. Before him, the broad sweep of the Thames rippled and glistened. He couldn't miss the Houses of Parliament and Big Ben across the river. The Union Jack fluttered from the Victoria Tower. Beyond them lay St. James Park and Buckingham Palace. There would be police constables, mounted and walking, and somewhere in the maze of London, Scotland Yard. He'd given the Yard little thought until now and repressed it. Better to risk his confession to a stranger at the Coventry Registry.

He turned back, retraced his steps, and scowled up at the squeaking sign as he went up the stairs to the second floor. A framed copy of the *Mona Lisa* hung in the Coventry office. It was balanced on a ledge above the company motto: ART INVESTIGATORS: RECOVERING MISSING MASTERPIECES.

Art gawkers had stared up at da Vinci's masterpiece for decades, trying to figure out what the lady herself was thinking. He was struck by her hands, her eyes, her low-cut dress. But he was mostly annoyed by the gaze she fixed on him as though she had deliberately turned his way. If the investigators at the registry were anything like Mona Lisa, they could put a thief in his corner and have a confession with that same scrutinizing gaze.

Right now, with Mona Lisa's eyes on him, the only loss Morrie wanted to report was a man who had lost his way. That kind of problem was best dealt with in the company of Charles Rainford-Simms or at St. Paul's Cathedral or Westminster Abbey, places where he sometimes felt more dead than alive, places where he was constantly drawn back again.

The irony of it struck him. The art registry investigated and tracked down the loss and theft of some of the most valuable art treasures in the world, yet they obviously worked under a tight budget of their own. Everything looked practical, efficient: no plush chairs, no rich carpeting, no gilded frames with Claude Monet or Pierre Renoir paintings.

Why wouldn't an art theft registry have at least copies of Rembrandt's *Portrait of an Old Man* or Seurat's *Seascape*? There was no still life, no Henry the VIII glaring down at him, no troubled mental distortions by Picasso to break the plainness of the paneled walls. No angels or religious paintings at all to remind him of his Jewishness and to cause him to wonder.

Not even a secretary to man the front desk.

What had he walked into, an office full of modern-day sleuths? One wall was covered with an orderly display of black-and-white photos of famous paintings. The one nearest him was a lost Matisse drawing. Another section was marked: MISSING ART 1939-1945 with names like Goya, Cezanne, Van Eyck, Vermeer. Under another picture, it said, FROM THE DAVID-WEILLS COLLECTION. The whole display was made up of art lost, stolen, stashed away in the vaults of some museum or possibly even stowed away at Lord Somerset's. And this registry seemed bent on finding them.

Several rooms shot off from the main lobby, the larger office to his right with the door ajar and the sound of angry voices coming from it. He could see two men: one blustery, the other a more easygoing chap with his smile more tolerant than the man behind the desk. The director of the registry and a client, no doubt.

Morrie's wait seemed eternal, but in truth he had been there less than ten minutes, long enough to hear some of the exchange from the director's office and the man with heavy jowls shouting, "No, I will not release Jillian for that assignment in Brazil."

"She's the best investigator we have."

"That's your usual claim. She is the most attractive, so I am not sending her to South America with you."

"We're friends. I have the bravo. She has the brains."

"Sorry, Joel. Jillian asked for the desk job until she gets restless being hunkered down in London or quits glowing like a schoolgirl when her bridegroom walks in. Whichever comes first."

"They've been married two years."

"They don't know it. Those foolish kids act like honeymooners."

"That job in Brazil deals with a VanStryker painting. It needs a woman's touch."

"Choose another woman."

As they continued to ignore him, Morrie's thoughts drifted, but he spun around at the sound of light footsteps and caught sight of a flesh and blood Mona Lisa walking briskly his way. What Morrie saw on a quick head-to-toe glance was elegant legs and lively eyes, tawny hair lying smoothly over narrow shoulders, and a beguiling blush of innocence when she smiled at him. He was about to trust his life and career—to say nothing of his heart—to this attractive young woman in a trim navy suit.

"Hello, I'm Jillian Reynolds. May I help you?"

"I wasn't expecting you."

She laughed. "Nor I you."

Her voice matched his first impression of lighthearted. "I'm sorry. Our secretary must be out for a moment."

"A long moment," he told her.

Now that she was closer, her eyes were perceptive and definitely blue, brilliant like sapphires. It was easier to keep eye contact with her than the *Mona Lisa*.

"I saw your sign outside."

"Most people come looking for it. This is an art theft registry. You've either lost a great painting and come to report it, or—"

He didn't let her finish. "I want to stop a robbery."

"That's a switch. But how would you know about that?"

"I'm Morris Chadbourne, and I'm involved."

"You should talk to Scotland Yard."

"No, I won't do that. You record lost works of art, don't you? I want to register twenty paintings before they are stolen."

"Are you certain they are of value?"

He noted the large diamond on her hand. "Yes, Mrs. Reynolds, there's a Rembrandt and Monet and Weinberger among them."

"Not one of them worth less than two mil. Mr. Chadbourne, I think you'd better talk to Brooks Rankin. He's in charge here." She glanced toward the director's office.

"They've been raking you over the coals," he said.

"I'm fair game. Most of the Coventry investigators are men. I broke that tradition. But it looks like Brooks and Joel will be another hour ironing out their differences."

"I can't wait that long. I'm already changing my mind—"

"Then you'd better come into my office."

He followed her and sank into the chair across the desk from her. For the next twenty-five minutes he told her about the planned robbery. How they were going to pull it off. How deeply involved he was. She jotted notes but said nothing. So far he had not mentioned Didier Bosman or Chip by name. He did so now with a hollow sound to his voice.

"Not Didier Bosman from the Norbert Museum? I know him."

Now for the first time she seemed to doubt him. He hastened to explain the school reunion for Rachel McCully. The mess he was in. The Asher Weinberger painting that involved him. "Weinberger is my particular interest."

"My particular interest is all of World War II," she said. "That's my specialty now. I spend my time tracing the paper trail, particularly the loss of art under Hitler. Even Picasso hid some of his work during that time. We're still trying to find it. There are so many gaps in the ownership. And now so many dispossessed owners. So many frustrated heirs."

"I'm only interested in that one painting," he said.

She pulled a thick notebook from her shelf. "According to our records several of Weinberger's paintings were destroyed."

"Because he was a Jew."

She smiled as though she knew. Understood. "Perhaps. But we don't have a record of any of his work surviving the war. And we have no living heirs listed here, unless—"

"I've seen two of his paintings, Mrs. Reynolds."

"Genuine? Then they may be the only two not destroyed."

"Are you no longer searching for them, Mrs. Reynolds?"

"I never stop looking."

He liked this girl.

"Morrie—may I call you that? I recognize your name now. My husband writes music and art reviews. He did an article on one of your lectures on Wordsworth and Coleridge. In the article, Chandler wrote about your interest in artists like Weinberger, men who were lost along with their art. You're quite a scholar."

"All I am now is a thief, ma'am."

"You're just thinking about being one. I want to help you. You want to stop the theft without hurting your guests. In recent art thefts, people have been injured. One man killed. Can you really pull off this reunion without someone being hurt?"

He nodded.

"Morrie, you have told me everything about this robbery but the exact location. Am I to guess that?"

"Are you familiar with the Somerset collection?"

The delft blue eyes glowed. "Lord Somerset from the Lake District— that eccentric old gentleman? He's worth millions."

"Several. His property alone makes him a wealthy man."

"Coventry asked permission to view his collection. Somerset refuses every time. He tells us that he won't have Coventry coming into his place and ripping the paintings from his wall."

"That implies some illegal ownership beyond the Weinberger."

"I don't think so. He's just very possessive of his collection. He would never deliberately acquire a stolen painting or a vase—or whatever—not knowingly. He's quite a man of integrity, or so we've been informed."

"Do you know him?"

"I met him at an auction and a second time at the British Museum when he was browsing for his own pleasure. The only time he spared me ten minutes of his time was at a banquet in London."

"Lord Somerset and his wife are away on a world cruise. I can get you in to see the collection in his absence."

"You can! What's the exchange rate?"

"Your promise to come to the reunion that I'm holding there. Can you pretend to be one of Dr. McCully's former students?"

"Hardly. I did most of my university studies in Europe and took my degree in Rome."

"What about this scenario? You started a course under Dr. McCully and left for Rome three weeks later."

She seemed amused. "A possibility, but if I'm going to help you, I need to know the whole truth. Are you trying to stop a jewel heist like London's Millennium Dome robbery?"

"No, the theft of fifteen or twenty paintings from the Somerset collection."

"He must own three hundred paintings or more. Why such a few paintings?"

"For quick disposal."

"Why is this so important to you, Morrie?"

"I'm the caretaker at the Somerset Estates. Lord Somerset trusts me."

Again she nodded toward the director's office. "I will have to talk to Brooks and Joel Gramdino. They may not want to get involved without notifying Scotland Yard."

"Please don't."

"If they decide to help you, how will I let you know?"

He pulled a copy of the invitation to the reunion from his pocket. "This is your personal invitation to Dr. McCully's reunion. The second sheet is a list of the guests. Just show up."

"Brooks may turn these papers over to Scotland Yard."

"I will have to trust you. But if you and your husband show up for the party, I'll know you are going to help me. You'll be helping yourself as well. It will be a close-up view of Lord Somerset's entire collection."

"That excites me. But what happens when Dr. McCully and I meet? You can't recognize someone who never sat in your class."

"I'll tell her what's happening—not about the art heist, but about you. I'll tell her I need your help—that I owe you one for an old favor. Rachel won't like it, but if anyone can pull it off, she will."

"Can you pull it off, Mr. Chadbourne? If we stop the robbery, you will be involved. Most likely arrested. I won't pad the Coventry reports. There will be consequences."

"I know. Maybe I will feel more at peace when it is over."

$\sim$

Thirty minutes later, Jillian looked up to see Chandler standing in the doorway and wondered how long he had been there. He gave her that special smile that he reserved only for her. She still thought him a handsome man—this husband of hers—with his dark red-brown hair and Grecian features with a finely chiseled mouth. Those smoky-blue eyes would absolutely dance when she told him about the positive pregnancy test. But do that now and he would never agree to the Lake District reunion. She was torn with telling, but would two more weeks make that much difference?

"I wondered when you would notice me, Jillian."

"I was just thinking about you. You wrote an article on the man I interviewed this afternoon—Morris Chadbourne. Come see, Chan. I've been putting my notes on the computer."

Chandler was a music critic but had expanded his reviews to include all arts. At times, he served as a consultant with Central Intelligence, assignments that she dreaded. He grinned. "You're using that code of yours that drives your boss crazy."

"As long as it doesn't drive you crazy. Honey, we've been invited to a university reunion in the Lake District. Here, take a look. Our names are already on the list that says Mr. Chadbourne was really sure of himself."

He scanned the invitation. "An American university? You went to school in Rome. So who is this Dr. McCully? It says she was your teacher. You've never mentioned this woman before."

"I'll be amazed if Professor McCully remembers me."

"No one who meets you ever forgets you, Jillian Reynolds."

"That's where the lie comes in. I'm to tell the professor I took one of her classes for three weeks before moving to Rome."

He frowned at the guest list. "Looks like I'll go with you."

"Why the sudden interest? I imagined this would bore you."

"But Langley might want me there with Sean Larkins on the guest list. I doubt he ever attended an American university."

"Neither did I. Does that make me of CIA interest, too?"

"I'll vouch for you. Larkins is a rugby player. On his last visit to America, he was asked to pack up and leave quietly."

"Did he do something wrong?"

"It's the company he keeps. He's always a stone's throw away from trouble. Kevin Nolan here presents a different problem. You may remember the name—he was in the vicinity of that bombing near Harrods where a London art clerk was killed. Nolan was injured. Now he's going to a reunion where a valuable art collection is on display? It may not be significant. . .but wherever Sean Larkins is, trouble could be just behind him."

"So we have our separate agendas at the reunion?"

"Yes, and I won't let you out of my sight. But why the lie, Jillian? This pretense of knowing McCully—it's not like you."

"It may prevent an art theft."

❧

The third phone call came to Hanley's Pub early in the afternoon. Hanley's wife was out of earshot when he put his lips close to the mouthpiece. "Hanley's Pub."

"Is Morris Chadbourne there yet?"

He recognized the caller. Who wouldn't after three calls? The man was from the North Country, but was this a toll call? The static on the line was more long distance. But he'd play the man's game. "Not yet."

"You will let Bosman know the minute he walks in?"

Hanley didn't need any more trouble. He was already worried about the use of the sheds behind his property. If his wife discovered what he was up to, his life would be more miserable than ever. "Of course—soon as he walks in."

But he liked Chadbourne and wouldn't betray him, not unless the price for his services was right. He needed a break. He'd like his expenses paid to the French Riviera, especially if his wife agreed to man the pub while he was gone.

He yanked the towel from his shoulder and wiped the countertop. The bike hadn't been chained behind the pub all day. Wherever Morrie Chadbourne had gone, he hadn't started out on his cycle. It wasn't often that a man as smart as Chadbourne had time for the likes of Hanley. But Hanley knew fishing and the Lake Districts and how to listen when a man was down. They were good friends, but he felt sorry for Morrie. He seemed unhappy, ever since that old professor of his showed up at the pub.

Morrie had told him once that it didn't take Oxford to make a man intelligent. He would be surprised at how cunning Hanley had become. It wasn't every day that old Hanley could outsmart the art critics of the world.

〜

At the Wakefield Cottage that evening Rachel and her guests were in the drawing room, enjoying cups of cocoa when Audrey appeared. "Miss Rachel, that Mr. Chadbourne is on the line."

Eileen's color drained. "Not Morris? Rachel, you tricked me into coming here?"

"No, Eileen. I invited you because I wanted you to come."

"Does Morris know I'm here?"

"He will soon enough."

"Mommy, who is Morris?"

"An old friend, honey. Rachel, he'll be—he'll be furious."

Audrey fidgeted in the doorway. "Miss Rachel, you know Mr. Chadbourne doesn't like waiting."

With a faint smile for Eileen, she picked up the extension. "Morris, this is Rachel. Where have you been?"

"In London. I just spent six miserable hours in a bus on the motorway. Are you all right, Rachel?"

"I'm fine."

"Good. The party is a go. The details are finalized."

"I can't believe anyone will come."

"I had to turn people away. But I'll keep the final list a surprise. I have friends coming, a man and a woman, and I need you to pretend that the woman spent time in one of your classes."

She felt an upsweep of rage. "You turned away some of my former students for strangers? Why the deception, Morris?"

"Please, Rachel, just help me."

She watched Eileen whisper something to Becki, and then she was on her feet rushing from the room. "Yes. Yes, I am listening, Morris. And who is this student that I am to remember?"

"Jillian Reynolds. Jillian Ingram in your classroom."

He spent the next few minutes describing her. "Really attractive. Quite a number. Oh yes. The specifics. About your height, Rachel. Brownish hair. Blue eyes. Really blue."

His description annoyed Rachel. *Your ex-wife is here, as lovely as ever, and you're thinking about someone you just met.*

"The rest of the guest list will be a surprise."

I can count on that, she thought. Strangers, perhaps.

"Morrie, I will need two bedrooms with a connecting door."

"For you and Wakefield?" he teased.

If he had been standing in front of her, she would have slapped him. "You can house Sinclair Wakefield wherever you want. My rooms are for personal friends. And I want comfortable housing for Audrey."

"She's the housekeeper, Rachel."

"And you were a barefoot boy in Kentucky. Find Audrey a room as nice as the one you have chosen for yourself."

"I'll be staying out in the caretaker's cottage."

"Very well furbished. Put Audrey as close to me as possible. I may need her if I have a sleepless night."

He did not ask the names of her guests, and thankfully not their ages. A guest of eight would not please him.

"Everything is set for next week. Wakefield and I have mapped out some tours. He'll take our guests to Oxford and Stratford-upon-Avon. You can grab a free day and rest up."

There he was switching back and forth between conniving and kindness. "I'll enjoy a rest day."

"Rachel, you and your guests should arrive just before dinner. That way everyone else will be settled in, and you won't have any extra work."

"That's asking too much for you."

"You're the guest of honor, remember. It's going to be a special party. Trust me, Rachel."

She glanced at Becki, who was sitting in a chair much too big for her. She looked frail and diminished, a Beatrix Potter book still in her hand. "Morrie, we will see you around five on Sunday."

She hung up and leaned down to kiss the top of the child's head. "Where's your mother, Becki?"

"She went outside—she's crying."

"Wait here. I'll just be a minute."

"You'll be in trouble. Mommy wants to be left alone."

"I'll risk it."

She found Eileen in the garden, staring up at the stars. "I'm so sorry. I should have told you, Eileen."

"I should have guessed. I knew I would have to face him someday. I won't spoil your party, Rachel. It means too much to you."

"You won't mind? In spite of seeing Morrie again?"

Eileen wiped away her tears. "I never told him about Becki. He never liked children."

"Once he sees her—" No, she was not certain what would happen. "He loves you. I'm certain of that, Eileen."

"He loves himself more."

She tried again. "He needs our help, Eileen."

"Yours, perhaps. He always liked you." As Rachel watched, the moon caught Eileen's lovely face in shadows. She folded her arms across her chest, warding off whatever blows lay ahead.

But before Rachel could apologize again, Eileen said, "Poor Morris. He has always needed somebody's help. Perhaps that is why I fell in love with him. He needed me back then."

Chapter 14

Sinclair ran the back of his fingers over the bristly growth on his chin. He had shaved poorly this morning, shaved and showered in haste because his alarm clock had failed to ring. He'd raced through the whole day, played center forward in a rough soccer game between faculty and undergraduates in midafternoon, and was back in time for his last lecture with a deep gash on his finger and his muscles aching from soccer abuse.

Yet the whole day put together had been one of unexpected pleasantries: young scholars prepared for a definite exchange on thought and purpose. A light lunch at a favorite corner café. A personal triumph—as though he had arranged it—when the rain of the dismal gray morning gave way to a cool afternoon. And that sense of renewed physical strength participating in a hard-fought soccer game, with the faculty winning.

From the window of his office, he looked out on the town and hills that he had come to love. Oxford, situated between two rivers, had been home for Sinclair since his undergraduate days. Even this glimpse reminded him of his life here. The morning rush to lectures. The town and gown rivalry. History and tradition. Medieval towers and cloisters. Ancient spires and narrow streets crowded with students on bicycles—he had been one of those students once—and the leisurely movement of boats on the rivers. Given the opportunity, he could still enter the annual rowboat competition on the Thames and come in first place. Then came the end of the day with its reluctant stride home to an empty house.

He was not quite forty-two, yet he had spent years here. Four years of studying the classics, his honors high enough to stay on and research for his doctorate in literature. After years of browsing through the libraries—Bodleian was one of his favorites—he still delighted in stretching his mind. His boyhood choice to pursue an intellectual career proved even now to be the right one for him. He would have made a poor soldier or captain of a ship; he found challenge in stirring minds, not winning battles.

Life had not been all cranial pursuits. He excelled in sports and still did. He'd earned the title of *blue* in rowing and rugby competition with

Cambridge and could still fit into his dark blue blazer that represented those matches. Much to his credit on the social level, he had friends among the townspeople.

He heard the distant sound of the chapel bells calling the listeners to evensong. Until this moment, busyness had marked his day, allowing him to send any thoughts of Rachel and Mary scudding to the background. Should he skip vespers to go home to his seventeenth-century house with its frontage flush with the sidewalk? He still slept on the third floor, waiting for total exhaustion before wending his way nightly to the room he had shared with Mary.

The vesper bells kept ringing. Was it always to be the ring of bells that tore at his soul? Big Ben in London, reminding him of Rachel's rejection. The pealing of church bells in Stradbury Square on the morning he said farewell to his wife and son. The vesper bells at Oxford—calling him to evening prayers, offering him hope. As the tolling continued, he set his books aside and in the long flowing robe of an Oxford don, strode toward the cathedral, his aching muscles stretching the distance with him.

Inside, daylight still filtered through the thirteenth-century stained-glass windows. He sat alone toward the back of the sanctuary, willing that no one would come near him. Daring God to be the only one. The boys' choir came first, somber and singing a cappella; they looked like well-scrubbed cherubs and sang like angels. At least the way Sinclair imagined angels could sing. It was a long procession of children and adults in white robes with red bows, with hymnbooks held reverently in their hands.

After the first reading in the Psalms, Sinclair took his pen and notepad from his pocket and balanced it on his knee. As the sanctuary filled with the choir's anthem, he wrote:

> *My beloved Mary, life is so empty here without you. No flesh and blood for me to see, to touch. Just memories. And I find myself still blaming God for robbing me of my happiness. But, Mary, I find myself blaming you for taking our son away.*

He crossed the last line out, feeling guilty for having written it. The pen twirled in his fingers, rubbing painfully against the miserable gash from the soccer game.

> *Oh Mary, do you remember how you loved the soccer games and went to cheer me, with Blake on your lap? I miss that.*

Mary as honest as the promises of God, "a little nobody," as she called herself, finding him when he most needed her. She berated herself that she had not gone to university. Sinclair insisted that their marriage was built on love, not on higher learning or scholastic prerequisites. In her plainness, she was beautiful to him. In her simple, easygoing way, she filled his life with boundless happiness. Laughter had died for a little while after Rachel, but Mary had brought it back into his life.

He put pen and paper together again.

Without you here, I have difficulty seeing the beauty in a sunrise. I have only recently been back to Stradbury Square, twice since losing you and Blake, but I remember how much you loved the sunrise there. On Easter I rose early from a sleepless night and went out on the rolling hills behind Oxford. I watched the sun rise, and for the first time since I lost you, I really found you again.

In a way I let you go that morning. Now I am struggling again, wanting you back, needing you to protect me from falling in love again. For six years, you were the sunrise in my life, the flesh and blood that became one with me, the union that gave us Blake. You would tell me to go on with living. But, my beloved Mary, it is Rachel who has come back into my life, not you.

She is here in England. But she is ill, and I cannot separate first love from sympathy. Every time I want to reach out and take her hand, I think of you and my longing for you. I cannot separate my longing for you—my longing for her. But you are dead. She is here. She is as beautiful as ever. But time is against her. Dear Mary, I cannot bear the thought of losing someone else. Sitting here in the evening vespers, I admit to myself that I have loved you both.

~

Mary had come to him in the most unexpected moment, at a time when he had decided to remain a bachelor. She was walking ahead of him on the rolling hills behind Oxford. Flowers in bloom. The sky a peacock blue. The beginnings of an evening wind whipping against his face. Suddenly a hardball careened into his chest, winding him, angering him. A young woman and three children charged toward him and stopped dead in front of him.

Clenching the ball in his fist, he said with what dignity he could muster, *"Madam, you should teach your children how to pitch a ball properly."*

"They're not mine," she said, *looking at him unabashed. He held the ball up, his fingers still gripping it. "Not yours? Then perhaps one of those sheep tossed it my way."*

With an amused smile she eyed the condemned sheep grazing nearby. "The ball is ours. The children are not mine. I'm their governess. If you are so concerned about pitching the ball properly, then you teach them."

His jaw locked.

"Mary, why is he wearing that funny robe?" This from the smaller of the three, all of five years old, Sinclair concluded.

"He's from the university—a teacher like your daddy."

"You're our teacher, and you don't wear funny clothes."

The child was right. Mary was attractively dressed: flannel slacks. Cool blouse. A brilliant scarf at her neck. Long lashes shielded pale blue eyes. Her makeup was modest, her face ordinary. But when she smiled, he said, "Don't go. I apologize for my robe, but I came straight from my lecture. A good walk clears my mind after a long day."

Walking delays going back to an empty room. *"When one cooks like I do, Mary, there is little to rush home to."*

"Mary will cook for you," the older boy informed him, the boy named Darrel.

For the first time, her composure slipped. To tease her more, Sinclair said, "I look forward to testing your cooking."

"May we have the ball back?" she asked. "It truly is ours."

"But I need it to teach the boys how to pitch."

They walked back to the campus together, the three urchins running ahead of them, his flowing robe over his arm. In front of the house where the children belonged, she said good-bye.

"May I see you again, Mary?" he asked.

"Not without knowing your name."

They married three months later. "Someone had to rescue you from the children," he said.

But it was Mary who had rescued him, filled his life, completed it.

❧

Another anthem filled the cathedral. He took his pen and wrote again. One word: *Rachel.* And the scribbled notation: *My beloved Mary, I feel that Rachel is coming between us.*

He capped and recapped the pen. Silence engulfed him. The sanctuary had emptied. He was the only one left in the pew.

"Don Wakefield! Remember me?" a young man asked. "I'm Darrel Moreland. Mary was my governess."

"The boy who slammed that hardball into my chest?"

"Afraid so. I'm at the university now as an undergraduate."

"Has it been that long ago that I met you?"

"Yes sir. . .and I was at the funeral—"

"Yes, I remember. We named our son after your younger brother."

"That was a point of contention between us for a long time."

Sinclair chuckled dryly. "I warned Mary that it might not sit well with you, you being the oldest son. And then, of course, we never had another child."

A grin cut across the young man's face and lingered there. "It's a good thing, sir. I never liked the name Darrel."

"That's what I told Mary about my name when she wanted to name our son after me."

He felt suddenly peaceful inside, uplifted. His colleagues at the college never broached the subject of Mary and Blake. Yet here was this under-graduate talking about them as though they had just this minute stepped from the chapel. It was good to discover that someone else remembered his wife and son had lived.

He clapped Darrel on the back as they walked down the aisle toward the chapel door. "Darrel, if you need help—have problems, or any ques-tions on your tutoring, in fact if you just want to talk or pitch a hardball, come see me."

"I was afraid to impose on your grief, sir."

"No, Darrel. If you had not tossed that ball, I would never have met Mary."

They were actually laughing as they stepped into the cool of the eve-ning. He could not recall a word from the evensong, not even a phrase from the anthems sung, but he remembered Mary and Blake with great pleasure and a new sense of freedom. Sinclair parted from Darrel out-side the cathedral and made his way to the empty house, his thoughts on tomorrow's commitment and deception.

Tomorrow he would drive to the Somerset Estates and walk and live in the company of Rachel McCully for the next several days.

He wanted to go. He dreaded going.

∽

The following afternoon, Eileen helped Rachel pack the car for their trip to the Somerset Estates. Rachel seemed distracted as she turned the keys over to the young constable from London.

It was the same policeman who had followed Eileen to the Lake District. "Doctor's orders," Timothy Whitesaul had said.

So far, no one had explained the cause for alarm, but Eileen remained on guard. Now, with a police guard left at the cottage, something was seriously wrong. Rachel had said that Morrie was in trouble. From the caution taken at the Wakefield Cottage, Eileen dreaded what lay ahead.

She buckled Becki into the backseat. "Mommy, I can do that myself. I'm not a little child."

"I know. I'm sorry, sweetheart."

Eileen offered to drive, but Rachel took the wheel. She was backing out when the constable stopped her. "You forgot this." He thrust the cellular phone through the window. "Sorry, Miss McCully. Farland's orders."

"Yes, I know. It's coded direct to his desk in London."

"Don't worry, Miss McCully. Everything will work out. The inspector has men stationed at the Somerset Estates."

She put her finger to her lips.

"I'm sorry. My error. I forgot the child was with you."

"I'm not a child, and Mommy says I have big ears. So there."

He grinned. "We'll take good care of the cottage, Miss McCully. And you have a good trip, Miss Becki."

Grumbling from the backseat, Audrey said, "Keep the kitchen clean. I'm not coming back to a bunch of dirty dishes."

He saluted her and grinned again. "We'll leave the place spotless. Now you go on. We're sending an escort behind you."

Sitting in the backseat beside Audrey, Becki giggled. "If you don't want him to leave the dirty dishes, Audrey, why did you let him take care of the house?"

Rachel turned and exchanged glances with Audrey. "We—we just don't like to leave the house empty."

The age lines on Audrey's forehead deepened further. "You just don't want the flowers in your garden crushed again. Nor the gate left ajar. None of it my doing."

"Audrey, that's enough."

Eileen checked the passenger's side mirror as they drove away. Nothing was said until they reached the main turnoff and the car behind them followed at a polite distance.

"We do have company, Rachel."

"I know. Get used to it."

"I feel like we're going to a policeman's ball."

Rachel sighed. "That might be more fun. Stop fretting, Eileen. I don't know any more than you do. Sinclair guarantees our protection. Morrie swears that we're going to have fun."

"Am I risking my daughter's safety? If so, find me a phone. I'll call Timothy Whitesaul to come and take us back to London."

"No, Mommy, Rachel promised to take me to Hill Top Farm."

Rachel caught Becki's eye in the mirror. "I plan to keep that promise on Wednesday, Becki. We'll have a grand time."

As they drove on in silence, Eileen took note of Rachel's soft hands relaxed on the steering wheel. There had been a big change in Rachel in these weeks in England. She did look better; even her skin had taken on a more rosy glow. Her profile was as strong as ever, her eyes bright again. She was still much too thin but glamorous enough in her choice of clothes and makeup; it was unlikely her guests would guess how sick she had been.

"Do I pass inspection, Doctor?" Rachel asked.

"Yes. You look great."

"As long as I don't look older. Before the party ends, I'll be thirty-eight."

They had been driving for an hour when a smile spread across Rachel's face. She pointed to the pretentious gate, swung wide for their arrival. "There it is. Our home for the next several days."

"Wow!" Becki exclaimed. "Is it a castle?"

"Sort of."

"It's certainly impressive," Eileen agreed.

The Somerset Estates appeared like an ominous-looking structure high on a rocky hill, with sloping emerald-green hills that reached lazily toward the river behind it. It reminded Eileen of a castle on the Emerald Isle—one she had seen a long time ago. Before Morrie. Before Becki.

"Rachel, it's magnificent. And, Becki, you have to be careful. You mustn't touch a thing."

"Good. Then I won't have to wash my hands or help Audrey in the kitchen."

"You know what I mean, young lady."

"Eileen, she'll do just fine. I'm so nervous about seeing some of my former students that I'm more apt to be the one who breaks something."

"Then we'll both be in trouble, Rachel."

As Rachel parked in the front drive, Becki wrapped her arms around Rachel's neck. "I like your wig. You look just like you. And that's very pretty."

She patted the child's hand. "With Becki's vote of confidence, I think I'm ready."

"It's beautiful," Eileen observed.

"Me or the house?"

Eileen poked her playfully. "Both."

"Wait until you see the inside. Let's go in."

"Rachel, I feel a bit ill. Just nerves, I think."

"I guarantee—Morrie won't bite."

"Does he really live here?"

"Not in the main house, in the caretaker's cottage in the back. But don't feel sorry for him. It is well furbished. He has three bedrooms and lots of work space."

"It's more than he ever had."

"Then be glad for him."

"Do you think he's happy here, Rachel?"

"Has Morrie ever been truly happy?"

"I don't think so."

She took the keys from the ignition. "Not even in those two months when you were married?"

Eileen frowned as she glanced back at Becki. But Becki was busily piling out of the car, talking excitedly with Audrey.

"Rachel—I'd almost forgotten those two months. They were the happiest of my whole life."

They went up the seven flagged steps, Becki walking between them and Audrey lagging behind. Before Rachel could ring the chimes, the double doors swung back.

A balding, dignified man welcomed them into the domed, marble hallway. "I'm Mr. Freck. Do come in," he said.

Awestruck, Becki whispered, "Do people really live here?"

"Yes, miss." The butler smiled, patted her head, and then said to Rachel, "Mr. Chadbourne and the rest of your guests are waiting for you in the drawing room. Your luggage will be delivered to your rooms."

"Don't forget my books," Becki told him.

"They'll be in your room, miss."

"The rest of you go on," Audrey told Rachel. "I'll see to the kitchen."

With the same warm smile he had showered on Becki, the butler led them to the drawing room, into what was obviously one of the Somersets' favorite rooms. It spelled comfort and coziness, splendor and magnificence. The room went silent as they entered. Rachel scanned the group and was delighted with the familiar faces and the tapestry of memories they stirred.

She was tempted to say, "Put down your pen and papers, class," but all she could do was smile at them.

Before Rachel could find her voice, one couple rose and came toward her. They made a handsome couple crossing the room. He was tall and muscular with a dimpled grin, she vibrant like a fashion model in her Italian suit. Her radiant blue eyes met Rachel's. *Morrie's friend, no doubt,* Rachel thought.

"Dr. McCully, I hope you remember me."

How can I? We have never met.

She took a quick survey of this student who had never been her student—a lovely girl with a lively step and an enchanting smile. Long tawny hair swept across her shoulders. She held out her hands to Morrie's friend. "Jillian Ingram. Of all people."

There! She hoped she got it right.

"It's Jillian Reynolds now," the young man said, taking her hand. "I'm Chandler, Jill's tagalong husband."

Chandler Reynolds had a guileless smile, his gaze direct and friendly. Rachel liked him immediately—she didn't have to remember him from her classroom.

"My wife and I are grateful you invited us."

"The pleasure is mine, Chandler."

His eyes danced with merriment as he talked to her, but she knew those alert eyes would not miss a thing. He was sizing up her guests, acquainting himself with Somerset's art treasures.

"Were you in class with some of the others, Jillian?"

She blushed. "So far I haven't recognized anyone."

But Rachel did. Misty Owens, her colleague from the university, and Elsa, the last secretary that she had on campus. Bill Wong, who had gone on to be a chaplain in the army. Her eyes settled on the Arnold sisters. She ached, wondering if they had ever settled their differences.

"Oh Lydia and Sara, what a joy to see you."

Feeling weak in all the excitement, she linked her arm with Eileen's and felt the tremor in Eileen's body. She didn't dare look at Morrie. Not yet. Instead she said, "Amanda Pennyman." It netted a quick wave from Amanda, and a supportive hug from the young man beside her. "Amanda, what are you doing these days?"

"Kevin and I are living in London. I'm in advertising."

That was the job Amanda's fiancé had wanted, the young man who was killed on a motorcycle. Lee. Lee something. She turned to Kevin. "Are you in advertising, too?"

"I used to be into horse racing until I met Mandy," he said, as though a confession were expected of him. "Now I've settled down with a real job—"

"He's a bank auditor." Amanda sounded unsure of herself, nervous to have the attention of the room drawn to them.

Slowly Rachel looked from face to face. She caught her breath when she recognized Jude Alexander sitting alone, the girl's gaze burning with resentment as their eyes met.

She groped for another name or two. Remembered others, especially the girl with the golden voice. "Lenora, I thought you were doing the opera *Madame Butterfly* in Rome. Lead soprano."

"I am—thanks to you. My stand-in is filling in for me."

Janet Tallard stood by the piano, looking as calm and sure of herself as the day she went down the aisle to marry her beloved widower. Her face still glowed. "Hello, Dr. McCully."

"You came all the way from Canada, Janet—without Tad? Just for this reunion?"

"I left Tad home with the boys—tending the farm and milking the cows."

The room broke into laughter. From the corner of her eye Rachel saw Morrie stumble to his feet, glaring angrily at his past. Taking Eileen's arm and Becki's hand she crossed the room to meet him. "Morrie, dear. You remember Eileen—"

He looked ashen, gray like his temples. That he still cared about the woman standing in front of him, Rachel had no doubt.

He gave her a quick hug. "It's been a long time, Eileen."

"A few years. This is—my daughter, Becki."

"I didn't know you married again."

"I didn't."

His expression twisted. "Neither did I, Eileen."

"Becki, this is Mr. Chadbourne," Eileen said.

Becki offered her hand.

Rachel nudged him. "Aren't you going to say hello to Becki?"

Words seemed to lodge in his throat. He brushed back his unruly lock of hair. Timidly, Becki drew back her hand.

He murmured, "She's a bit young for a university reunion."

$\sim$

Afterwards—after dinner and dessert—the guests settled back in the drawing room where Asher Weinberger's masterpiece was central to the room. It hung above the fireplace in solemn beauty, its darkness overshadowing the reunion. Seeing it, Rachel hesitated in the alcove and held her breath. This was the painting that could hang like an albatross around their necks—the painting that could ruin Morrie's life.

Morrie moved to the front of the room, dimmed the main lights, and pressed a panel beneath the stone mantel. It threw a cataclysmic effect over the painting, spotlighting the brush strokes of the gathering black clouds and the last ribbons of sunlight.

An eerie silence fell over the room, a silence broken by Becki. "That's kind of pretty, Mr. Chadbourne. Did you paint it?"

A quizzical frown spread over his face. "No, I didn't."

"My great-granddaddy has a painting like that."

Sinclair came to stand beside Rachel in the alcove where their voices were muted, and where his steadying hand comforted her. "It's amazing how light changes the face on that picture."

"It's frightening what Morrie is trying to do."

"Everything is going to work out."

"Not between Morris and Becki," she whispered.

"Everyone else finds her a charming child."

Morrie's voice demanded their attention. "Lord Somerset developed an intricate lighting system in order to mute or brighten or cast shadowy images on the artwork on his walls. Somerset's art collection is one of the most valuable ones in England. There are paintings in every room—even in the rooms where you're staying. You can look, but don't touch. That goes for you too, smidgen," he said, glancing down at Becki.

"I can't touch. I'm not that tall. And my name is Rebecca."

"That was my mother's name."

More of Rachel's happiness stole away. "Sinclair, the guests should retire, but someone should stay up and make sure—"

"Nothing will happen this evening. I'm certain of that."

"Do you have Inspector Farland's word on it?"

"Farland has it covered. You concentrate on your guests, Rachel. Especially Jude Alexander. I sat with her at dinner, and I don't think you are her favorite person."

"I told Morrie she would be unhappy. . .that if he invited her, she could make the rest of us miserable."

"According to the invitation list, she was definitely invited: *Jude Alexander and guest.* But she came alone." He shrugged. "I challenged her to a game of badminton tomorrow. She was dead on the button with her answer. She told me she had no time for batting a feathered shuttlecock across the net with an older man."

Rachel smothered her chuckle against his shoulder. "At least I like older men," she teased.

Morrie stood beneath the Weinberger, his voice modulated as he said, "Weinberger's earlier works imitated the Impressionist painters. Bright and full of sunlight. But in 1939 his paintings began to show the darkness that was descending over Europe." He pointed toward another painting, his smile warm when he gazed at Amanda or Jude, shadowed and wounded when he looked at Eileen. "The smaller painting over there by Eileen is a work by Degas. The one by the piano a Claude Monet, and that one by you, Jude, is a Cezanne. But the Asher Weinberger overshadows them all simply by a flick of this switch."

He turned the dimmer, forcing the light changes to highlight the picture. "Note the shimmering effects of light in the far corner of the canvas as though the sun just set." But there were darkness and rage in the swollen river, fear in the face of the boatman as he tried to push away from the shore.

"Sinclair, what is Morrie trying to do?"

"Maybe he's sending a signal to one of the guests—letting that person know which paintings to target—which ones to steal."

She looked away to hide the hurt in her eyes. As she turned, Morrie glanced her way, and she saw rage and darkness in his expression—as though Asher Weinberger had painted Morrie's portrait and hung it on the wall.

Chapter 15

Rachel slept with the curtains open, using daylight like an alarm clock. But greeting the first streak of dawn as it cracked the darkness was not to her liking even in this luxurious bedroom. What had awakened her? The wind? Someone prowling in the corridors outside her door? Light steps? Heavy ones? Bare feet?

Listening, she finally distinguished Becki's steps pattering to their adjoining bathroom, and Eileen saying, "No, Becki, we are not going to Hill Top Farm today. That's Wednesday. So come back to bed before you wake Rachel."

Rachel turned and twisted for another fifteen minutes before tossing the bedding aside and standing up. Sleepless nights often made her argue with herself about the outcome of her cancer treatment. Mostly, she was optimistic, determined to go on with living, to prove the doctors liars. The next moment she felt uncertain about the outcome. Unhappy about this reunion. This was not her gathering. It was Morrie's.

But this miserable battle with cancer was her own, and she had no intention of it spoiling the week for Morrie or anyone. She thrust thoughts of her sister's early death aside. This didn't happen twice in one family, did it? Whatever the label—cancer, cystic fibrosis—it seemed unfair.

I'm still young. Days shy of thirty-eight, she thought.

No, she had already lived twice as long as Larea—and lived it to the fullest for both of them. She went to her dresser, uncapped her medicine bottle, and tapped out one pill. *Timothy's miracle cure.*

This morning she cupped it in her hand. "Okay, wave of the future, Timothy Whitesaul believes in you. I'd like to believe in you, too." She rolled the pill over before popping it into her mouth. "Are you living up to your rave reviews and blasting those cancer cells so I can get back to mountain climbing?"

Not letting her hopes wander beyond that, she pushed her fresh grief for Larea and the longings for Sinclair back into the darkness as she picked up the glass schooner and, like a chaser, sent the water and the pill down her throat.

Sunrise on Stradbury Square

At the first real glimmerings of day, Rachel dressed and made her way down the long cascade of steps on the spiral staircase, running her hand over the polished balustrade with its oak leaf motif and pressing her feet into the thick red carpet. The house lay quiet except for the murmur of voices coming from the kitchen and the whispering of wind coming through the open windows and stealing down the long marble corridor.

Even the silent hallway was an art gallery with murals of battlefields on both sides of the corridor. Standing guard beneath each mural was a life-sized ivory statue with the carved features of the monarchy and the world's political giants: Queen Victoria, King George IV, Churchill, Roosevelt, Lord Nelson.

She switched on the lights as she entered each room, switched them off as she left. The clock in the main gallery said five. It coincided with Rachel's jeweled watch. The gallery with its graceful domed ceiling was as magnificent as the cathedrals in London. Portraits of the Somersets hung on the end wall—Lord Somerset with an arrogant smile and his arms folded across his massive chest. *A vain man,* she decided, yet the eyes looking down at her twinkled in the morning light. His wife seemed more regal in her deep lavender gown, a diamond necklace at her breast, but Rachel saw unhappiness in her eyes.

You own all of this, and you have missed joy.

The rooms teemed with art treasures, the opulence the vanity of one man. The Somerset Estates had imperial grandeur but no heirs. The owners had a legacy of affluence and excess, but they had squandered so much of their wealth on themselves, yet had built their name with charitable giving. In a museum she would find the display awesome, but here it brought her sadness. The Wakefield Cottage was serene in comparison, the home she had grown up in on faculty row near campus ordinary and livable. Her own well-furnished condo had not been elaborate.

She made her way from the smoking room back to the drawing room, knowing that the Asher Weinberger drew her there. She looked up at it in the darkened room and longed for the picture to reveal its secrets, its control over Morrie.

"Good morning, Dr. McCully."

She whirled around. "Chandler Reynolds, you frightened me."

Jillian's husband stepped from the shadows in a navy jogging suit. "I thought I was alone, too. Did you take the grand tour?"

"Yes. I had trouble sleeping."

Turning to the tapestry drapes, he opened them, allowing early daylight to steal into the room. Grinning at her, he said, "There, that puts the Weinberger back in the limelight."

"Morrie. . .Morrie is obsessed with that painting."

"Are you? That picture says volumes, Dr. McCully, but I don't think it has the answers you're looking for."

They took turns focusing their attention back on the painting. "I'm not certain I know the questions yet. But why are you up so early this morning?"

"I've been out for my morning run."

"I envy you. I used to be a mountain climber and could sleep anywhere. Campsites. In the cramped space in the back of my van. Today in this luxurious setting with its oak bedposts and headboard, the tapestries over the windows, a bathroom bigger than my bedroom at the cottage—I woke up at four. Maybe the seventeenth-century bed kept me awake."

"Jill and I got an eighteenth-century mattress like my army cots."

"You were in the military?"

"Army intelligence—stationed with the American troops in Bosnia. I considered reenlisting and then I met Jillian in Vienna. But after talking with Chaplain Wong about this latest unrest in the Middle East, I would be willing to serve again."

"As a chaplain?"

"No, with intelligence. Or with the Army Rangers. My wife goes ballistic at the thought of my going army again. But I still have a mind for trouble."

"So do I."

"Then did you notice anything different about this room, Dr. McCully?"

She looked around, perplexed. The dirty cups and saucers from the night before had been cleared away. The cushions on the chairs fluffed. Dear Audrey's hands at work again. "No, I don't see anything unusual."

"Look again. Look over here on this wall where Eileen Rutledge was standing last evening, where I'm standing now."

Her gaze shot to the empty space where the light from the window cast its morning rays across the cream walls. She stared in disbelief. "One of the paintings is gone, Chandler."

"That's right. The small Degas."

"Why would anyone take that painting?"

"It has a nice monetary tag. At least a million. I doubt that Lord Somerset's alarm system can detect his paintings walking, not if someone has free access at the gate. But we have time and that alarm system on our side. No one goes out those locked gates without permission or a code key in hand."

She felt a jumbled mistrust of Chandler. Last night she had thought him guileless, trustworthy. Betray that first impression and she shared his guilt of being the only ones in the drawing room before the other guests awakened. Or should she go with her instincts? He had been with army intelligence. Was he intelligent enough to unravel this mess?

"Chandler, we must tell Morrie."

"Not yet."

"He's the caretaker. Either you go find him or I will."

"Let Chadbourne discover the loss. That gives us time to find out who else had a case of insomnia this morning."

"And it gives the thief time to get away."

"You, my dear lady, have nothing to worry about. You are no thief. And don't look at me that way." He held up his hands. "I'm wearing a jogging suit. No backpack. I didn't take the painting."

As she moved toward the door, he strolled across the room and blocked her way. "Don't sound the alarm. We'll be having breakfast in a very short while."

"Are we to pick the thief from the way he chews sausage?"

He held up a handkerchief. "Or if someone claims this."

Jude's! Her stomach tightened. With effort, she maintained her dignity but raged inside. "None of my former students would take that painting."

"That leaves Becki," he said, eyes twinkling. "But she told us she is too short to touch any of Somerset's treasures. So, dear lady, that leaves someone outside of your classroom. Someone like me. But I'm an art and music critic. Not a thief. I'm your friend. You have to trust someone."

"Everyone at the reunion claims me as a friend." *Except, perhaps, Jude Alexander,* Rachel thought.

Chandler's lips curled. He glanced past the empty spot on the wall to the dangling Claude Monet. "One of those *friends* of yours attempted to take that painting as well."

The Monet hung catawampus, tilted sideways, askew like Sinclair Wakefield's ties. A clammy chill started at the base of Rachel's spine. She rubbed her arms to ward off the goosebumps. "Please, straighten it, Chandler."

"And leave my fingerprints? I daresay the person ahead of us wore gloves. Last evening Chadbourne told us we could look at any of the paintings in this mansion but not to touch them."

He urged her to sit down on the French settee. "You must not get involved," he cautioned. "Whoever moved that Monet must go on trusting you. Now, just think about the missing painting. It may trigger your memory. Something you saw or heard. Something or someone who awakened you."

Becki had awakened her. Perhaps the wind. But they were not connected. She tried to remember what the Degas painting looked like. She knew more about the artist.

Edgar Degas. She searched her mind and placed him in Paris, born into a wealthy Parisian family. Surely that meant an Impressionist painter. A man with a high brow and searching dark eyes. Beardless, if she remembered his self-portrait correctly. "He was an Impressionist painter, wasn't he? Sunlit landscapes."

He smiled. "More neoclassical. He chose jockeys and ballet dancers and ordinary women for his subjects. Did you know Degas lived to a ripe old age, unusual for that time in history? I'd buy all of those years if I could spend them with Jillian."

He was back on track when she said, "I'm sure you're aware that Degas was known for his sculptures of horses and ballet dancers. There's a horse sculpture in the smoking room—a marvelous craftsmanship."

"Then I'm sure we both have our fingerprints on it. Morris warned us against touching things, but he may have been tempting us to do just that. We expect to find his fingerprints in the mansion. But if something goes wrong at this reunion, suspicion will fall on any of us who left a print on a vase or sculpture."

He eased into a chair and stretched his long legs. "Degas had his own style; his color and compositions influenced the art world of his day. But he broke with the Impressionists in midlife and later became a recluse. I suspect that will ultimately happen to the Somersets. Since his wife's heart condition, they have become virtual recluses here in the Lake District."

"Recluses? They are on a world cruise right now."

"Oh! Well, likely they'll touch ports where they can acquire another masterpiece to hang on these walls. And for what? No moving van will follow their hearse to the grave. The Somersets will check out empty-handed, like the rest of us."

Rachel stormed from the room with Chandler close behind her. In the dining room, she wrapped her arms around her chest as she stared out the glass doors toward the gardens and guest cottages.

"I'm sorry, Dr. McCully. That Degas may date back to World War II. My wife is interested in the art thefts of that era."

"You sound like Morrie. He believes the Weinberger painting was stolen from his great-grandmother back then."

"If he's an heir, let him lay claim to it. But what if he's an ordinary thief planning to use all of us here at the reunion?"

She whirled on him. "Many of those collectors in World War II were Jewish like Morrie. He can't come up with the sales records and art catalogues demanded of him. The paper trail stopped there for Morrie."

"He'd lose anyway. Lord Somerset would never hang a painting on his wall if he thought it was stolen. It would be stowed away in the subterranean vaults."

The thought of a subbasement on the property came as a surprise. But why not a temperature-controlled room for his paintings? "Maybe that's where the Degas is now."

"As small as it is, the Degas could be anywhere. In one of the rooms upstairs. In the trunk of one of the vans parked outside. In a guest cottage—or in the toolsheds out back."

She shivered. "Or in your room, Chandler."

"Or yours." He smiled. "Don't get involved. Let Jillian and I handle it for you. Mr. Chadbourne told us you were ill."

"Is nothing sacred with Morrie? Maybe he was afraid no one would come if he didn't play on their sympathies."

"He told my wife the Somersets don't need the Weinberger painting. I'd keep my eye on that if I were you, Dr. McCully."

"I don't understand you, Chandler. You're friends."

"Friends with Chadbourne? I just met him yesterday."

You are playing with my mind, trying to make me mistrust my guests. Playing the devil's advocate and asking me to trust you. And now I find you are not even Morrie's friend.

"My wife and Chadbourne have mutual interests. History, for one. And art." He seemed suddenly amused, this guileless man mocking her. His deep chuckle filled the room. "Jillian is not a thief, Dr. McCully, but if my wife finds a sculpture or painting she's been searching for, she simply picks it up or takes it off the wall and goes on with her business."

"What is her business?"

"She dabbles in magnificent paintings like the Weinberger and the missing Degas."

Rachel's attention was drawn toward a stranger making his way from the back of the property toward the main house. The man was wearing a raincoat on this warm sultry morning. "Who is that, Chandler? For a moment I thought it was Morrie."

The stranger passed the badminton courts and drew closer. Slightly taller and better looking than Morrie, he carried a metal briefcase, large enough to hide a million-dollar painting.

"That man was not with us last evening—and he is definitely not one of my former students."

Chandler said quietly, "His name is Sean Larkins."

"You know him?"

"I know of him. He's a popular rugby player from Ireland. He usually sports a beard. People who know him call him Chip. That man should never have been invited here. If you'll excuse me, Dr. McCully, I think I'd better shower and change for breakfast. My wife was sleeping when I left the room."

The stranger slipped behind the side bushes to the front entry. Moments later the musical chimes at the front door sent the butler running. Rachel cut across his path. "I'll get it, Mr. Freck."

"But, madame..."

"It is most likely one of my guests."

She opened the door and smiled up at the stranger. He was handsome, in a sullen sort of way, with height to his credit and a cleft chin to distinguish him. He flashed a winsome smile. "Well, the saints be praised—the professor herself. I would know you anywhere, Dr. McCully. Just as full of beauty as ever."

She considered matching his blarney. "And who might you be?"

"It's Sean. Surely you remember me? Sean Larkins." His hurt was as forced as his accent. "I'm a friend of Jude Alexander's."

Warning enough, she thought.

"She did tell you I was coming late?"

"Jude really hasn't said anything to me."

"Shy as ever, that girl."

Hardly the description for Jude. "I was the lad in the top row in your Chaucer class," he said.

"Were you now?"

This was not a face she remembered. His bone structure was well chiseled, chin firm and determined. He was most presentable in his gray suit and tie, his raincoat slung over his arm now. His deep-set eyes blazed as he waited for Rachel's appraisal to simmer. One thing she knew for certain.

He had never been in her classroom.

"Mr. Larkins, I never taught Chaucer."

Undaunted, he said, "Really? Well, it was *one* of those challenging classes of yours. Luck runs with me. If you don't remember me, at least I'm not in trouble."

You are in more trouble for trying to deceive me.

"I'm looking for Mr. Chadbourne," he announced.

"So was I."

"But I'll settle for Jude. I'm here as her guest."

It's everybody's party, Rachel thought.

As she stood back, Sean stepped inside and gawked up at the magnificent gold pillars and domed ceiling. "I think I'm going to like this place. As lovely as the castles of Ireland."

"Well, Mr. Larkins," Rachel said graciously, "if you want to freshen up for breakfast, Mr. Freck will show you to a room with a balcony. I'm certain you'll enjoy your accommodations."

The butler frowned his disapproval. "Follow me, sir."

Rachel walked down the hall and found Morrie in the dining room. "It's turned into quite a gathering, Morrie," she commented.

"I'm glad you like it."

"I didn't say that. It may be my reunion, Morris, but many of the guests are strangers to me. The young man on his way upstairs is Sean Larkins, a friend of Jude's."

Morrie managed a quick glance from the doorway, a sudden rage filling his eyes. "Chip Larkins? Your friend Jude is keeping poor company. How long has she known him?"

It was the wrong time to tell him about the missing Degas. She didn't trust the Morrie looking at her now. She said cautiously, "Would it matter how long they've known each other?"

"He is someone I'd rather see outside the gates. I'm going to keep my eye on him, Rachel. Inviting him was a big mistake."

"I didn't send the invitations."

"Someone sent his."

She didn't argue but admitted, "I've made some mistakes with Jude Alexander. This is the first I've seen her since she failed one of my classes. She still despises me."

His mood mellowed. "If someone didn't pass, was it your fault, Dr. McCully?"

"I feel that I let her down. That one course kept her from graduating.

Jude meant to go into foreign service."

"She did. She works at the American embassy. Your friend Jude is just lucky she isn't waiting tables in some restaurant. Hanley could do with an attractive waitress at his pub."

"At Hanley's? Jude would probably make more on tips than I did teaching at the university." She smothered a sigh. "Until last evening I wasn't certain what happened to her. She's a minister's daughter. Angry with everyone." *Angry like you are.* "What grieves me the most is she put God on the back burner."

"With me, Rachel, God isn't even on the back burner."

"Then I failed you, too, Morris."

Chapter 16

The guests left in separate cars for Windermere and Grasmere, leaving Rachel alone to fret over the missing Degas. She found no time to snatch a few moments alone with Sinclair before he was out the door with the others. Even as they moved toward each other after breakfast, Morrie had whisked him away to the drawing room. Sinclair cupped her chin in passing, "I'll see you this evening. Are you certain you want to stay home alone?"

"Certain," she had told him and wondered whether he heard the uncertainty in her voice. Maybe even the tremor.

When the massive front door closed behind her guests, Rachel went upstairs to her room to mull over her own stubbornness behind a locked door. She didn't have Audrey to confide in. With the beds already made up, the floors swept, the bathroom tiles scoured clean again, the shower stalls wiped dry, the staff would be resting.

She was already tense as a circus wire. How many more paintings would slip from the walls of the mansion in the next several days? With her old indomitable spirit, she had tackled a gathering that directly opposed Timothy Whitesaul's cautious approach to recovery. Timothy constantly urged her to avoid a crowd for the sake of her immune system, to get plenty of rest, good food, fresh air, and exercise. His parting words were always, "Keep the stress level at a minimum, Rachel; just relax."

Didn't he understand? With Rachel, it was grabbing at time, reaching out to help Morrie, reaching beyond that to help herself. Had her choices in the classroom prepared any of her students for life in the real world? Had she been prepared for it herself? The delight of seeing some of her former students took a nosedive. Could she face several more days when even the next few hours seemed daunting, crushing, insurmountable?

Rachel opened her purse, took the cell phone, and pressed the coded number to Inspector Farland's office in London. *"Someone will always be at that number,"* he had promised.

A polite voice informed her, "Your party is unavailable at this time. Leave your name and number; he will return your call."

Before another painting disappeared? She snapped the OFF button and tossed the phone back into her purse. Outside her room, she heard footsteps in the corridor. Whispers. Doors opening quietly, closing again. Her breath came in tight gasps as she unlocked her door and cracked it open. Someone had just disappeared into a room across from her. Kevin's room? Sean's? Chaplain Wong's. No, she had seen all three of them leave.

The door opened again. The butler slipped on to the next room and went stealthily inside. Rachel did not wait for him to reappear but went quickly downstairs. Even there came the whispering sounds of someone in the drawing room. Determined, she stepped inside and startled Jillian and Chandler Reynolds.

Jillian had a camera in her hands. "Jillian, I saw you leave less than an hour ago! What are you doing?"

"Taking pictures."

"I can see that. But this is a private collection."

Jillian went on snapping the Weinberger from varied angles.

"Stop her, Chandler. We're here to protect Lord Somerset's collection, not photograph it. We have trouble enough."

"We have more trouble than you think." Chandler stood by the piano pointing to where the Monet had tilted only hours ago. Like a mockery to Morrie's Jewishness, a copy of van Ruisdael's *Jewish Cemetery* hung in its place. "I tried to tell you earlier, Dr. McCully. My wife is here on official business."

"What happened to the Monet painting, Chandler?"

"It's anyone's guess. Someone took it while we were all straggling in and out for breakfast. With two paintings missing, everybody at this reunion falls under the umbrella of suspicion. Jillian is starting in this room—getting as many pictures as possible. That way we will know when something else is missing."

Rachel clutched her jaw. "There are over three hundred paintings. It's impossible for Jillian to photograph them all."

"We have to start somewhere. And do so quickly. Dr. McCully, we're both here trying to help Morrie Chadbourne." Jillian's eyes went back to the Weinberger. "I need pictures to compare with the ones we have at the Coventry Art Theft Registry."

"Dr. McCully, my wife is an art fraud investigator."

Her camera clicked again. "This could be one of the masterpieces confiscated in 1939—and lost for all these years. If it is a genuine Weinberger, it is listed at the Registry."

Rachel calmed. "You know inspector Jon Farland?"

"We've worked together in the past. They respect the work the Registry does. We have a comprehensive list of art missing from all over the world. We're constantly adding to our records. But I need proof that this is a genuine Asher Weinberger. Lord Somerset has refused all requests to view his collection."

"Surely Lord Somerset is a cautious investor. He will have legitimate documentation to prove his purchase."

"That only makes proof of rightful ownership harder. We thought all the Weinberger paintings were lost. Now Morrie may be right. Three or four of the originals may have survived the war."

"You seem so sure of yourself, Jillian."

She faced Rachel, the camera at her side. "It's my job. Name any of the great artists and their names are no doubt on our registry. Some painting missing. Some drawing. An unfinished canvas. An unclaimed Spanish tapestry. A charcoal sketch. Wood panels. Sculptures. Rare books."

"You make it sound like everything was stolen."

"Thousands of works were. So many of the paintings smuggled out of Germany are still unaccounted for. A pastel by Degas is still missing. Bruegel's *Enchanted Island*. A Rembrandt drawing. One of the Vermeer paintings from the Rothschilds' collection. Even a Gutenberg Bible—at least an excellent fake—is missing."

"Maybe they were destroyed by bombings."

"Dr. McCully, more were destroyed by violence and greed. Some were deliberately demolished because the artists or owners were Jewish. In the last days of the war, truckloads of stolen property were transferred to underground shelters and the salt mines of Austria. And heaven knows where else."

Jillian gave an elegant sweep of her hair back from her face and turned with the sparkle of a fashion model, her perceptive eyes lively as she looked at Rachel. Gently she said, "Dr. McCully, gaps in ownership—that's the problem today. A lot of marketing went on during the war—the sale of property that belonged to somebody else. Now, these decades later, heirs are dying or dead. The newer generation has little interest in lost or stolen art."

"We'll have to tell Morrie what's going on when he gets back—"

"By the time he gets back the film will be on its way to the Registry. But Morrie really did ask for my help, Dr. McCully."

The cell phone in Rachel's purse rang. She took it out, pressed it to her ear. "Inspector, I'm glad you called back." She nodded as she listened. Relief spread over her. "Yes, they're here with me. Lunch? Yes, I could drive in there to meet you."

She smiled at Jillian and Chandler when the call ended. "That was Inspector Farland. He said for you to be careful. I'm sorry; I didn't realize—" She gave them an apologetic shrug. "I've been invited out. Charles will be the only one having lunch with you today. He's the older gentleman who works in the gardens for love of it. Poor man. He lost his parish when the Archbishop of Canterbury banned him to the North Country."

It was Chandler's turn to be surprised. "Not Charles Rainford-Simms? I stayed at his rectory in the Cotswolds. He is really a nice old man. He took a raw beating protecting an Irish prodigal." He looked at her. "You may not be able to trust any of us, Dr. McCully, but you can trust Charles Rainford-Simms."

When Rachel left, she found Charles kneeling by a flower bed near the side gate. He rose to meet her. His stooped shoulders had cut him down to six-two, but he still towered above her.

Soft ridges had been chiseled into his face through kindness. "Don't look so unhappy, my dear," he said.

"I'm just worried about Lord Somerset's art collection."

"Everyone seems to be. I wouldn't worry, my dear. Mr. Chadbourne doubled the staff before the reunion. Even the butler was a last-minute replacement."

"Mr. Freck is a replacement? That worries me. He was just up on the second floor going through the rooms."

He brushed his brow with the back of his hand, streaking his snow-white hair with soil. Thick bushy brows tented as he seared her with his brilliant blue eyes. "There you go adding another care to your narrow shoulders. Next thing you'll be telling me about the missing paintings. Morrie told me as he left this morning. I may even know who took them."

She stared at him. "And you're doing nothing about it?"

"I'm gardening. It's a wonderful vantage point."

He could be dotty, forgetful. His imagination was in overplay. The crook in her neck tightened as she looked up at him. "One of them was stolen before dawn. The other during breakfast."

"Two thieves," he said calmly. "Those paintings are still on the grounds; I'm certain of it. So are you running away needlessly, my dear?"

"I'm just going to lunch."

"With Morrie, I trust? He admires you, Miss McCully."

"No, with someone else. Morrie was one of my most gifted students. That's why I agreed to this reunion. But I worry about his obsession with art."

"Can you fault a man for his love of art?"

"If it forces him to steal."

"I see."

"Charles, can you stop him from whatever he's going to do?"

His blue eyes shone with merriment. "Morrie may be a prodigal son, but I don't like to interfere with the Lord's business unless He wants me there."

"Morrie doesn't even know that Becki is his child."

He considered that. "I thought so. She looks like him. But a man on a redemptive journey doesn't need interference from me; he needs someone running alongside of him. Guiding him a little."

"Like you did for that Irish terrorist in the Cotswolds?"

"So you know about young Conan O'Reilly?"

"Even hearing about it made Morrie angry with the Church of England for taking your parish away."

Amusement twinkled his eyes. "Tell Morrie I broke the rules of the church; that's why the parish was given to a younger man."

She kicked a pebble from the walkway. "You know Morrie doesn't believe in our God."

"Neither did the Irish lad. But, like that boy, perhaps Morrie believes in God more than we realize." He let his hand rest comfortingly on her shoulder. "I think you need someone running alongside of you, too. If you need me, Rachel, I'll either be at my cottage or at one of these flower beds." He took a crumpled handkerchief from his pocket and wiped the tears from her eyes. "You seem to be searching for answers yourself," he said.

"That's how all this reunion came about. I have leukemia—"

"I know."

He sounded as though it were merely a headache or the nuisance of a runny nose. Seeing it from that perspective, she smiled at him. "I had eternity in mind."

"So did God when He created you. I see from your guests that you have touched more lives than you will ever know. You are well esteemed. Let that be enough. Whatever accolades are due you will be waiting for you when the time comes."

"I may not have long to wait."

He wiped the soil from his hands and chuckled merrily. "Take me, my dear. I'm more than halfway there. Or three-fourths. Or maybe I will simply go back to this flower bed and get that call Home. Time is important but not a cause for fretting."

"Chandler Reynolds said you were a wise old man."

Another chuckle erupted. "And did he put the emphasis on the old or on the wise?"

~

Sinclair Wakefield drove four of the guests into Grasmere for the day so they could explore Wordsworth country. Excusing himself for a business appointment, he pointed the four women in the direction of Dove Cottage and suggested that they have lunch at The Swan, an oak-beamed restaurant with an excellent view.

They synchronized their watches and agreed to meet late in the afternoon for the drive back to the Somerset Estates for a late dinner. He waited until they slipped into the crowd, then drove to Hanley's Pub to meet Inspector Farland. He considered the pub a poor meeting spot to discuss stolen art when the inspector's blustery voice could easily echo across the room.

Coming in from the bright sunshine, he allowed his eyes to adjust to the darkness. Inspector Farland sat in the far corner with his back to him. There would be no noisy greeting to draw everyone's attention to them. He crossed the room and took the seat across from him. "Good morning, Inspector."

"Jon will do."

Sinclair took the rebuke in stride and scanned the menu as the pub's owner lumbered over to their table. A man that size was a heart attack waiting to happen, his skin gray as he faced the inspector. Sinclair settled on trout; Farland took smoked ham.

When Hanley walked away, Sinclair asked, "Does he know who you are?"

"I think so, and I don't think Hanley takes to strangers."

"He took to me quickly enough."

"Right. He takes to the climbers and the locals. He's always crowded, but he seems ill at ease with me this morning."

"How would you know that with your back to him, Jon?"

"That mirror by the fireplace lets me watch him when he doesn't know it. So what's this about missing paintings?"

"Two of them. A Degas and a Monet."

He whistled. "And how is Chadbourne handling that?"

"He was expecting trouble, but not one painting at a time."

Hanley was back. When he lingered, the inspector frowned. "That's all. Thank you." His voice carried too loudly, trailing behind Hanley. "I don't feel comfortable with that man."

"You'd do better not letting him hear you," Sinclair cautioned.

Grudgingly he lowered his voice. "So Chadbourne admits that he's expecting more trouble. Do you think he's involved?"

"Inspector, I think today took him by surprise. But remember, we are acquainted at the professional level. Not close associates. He won't be confiding in me."

"Because of Dr. McCully? She's a beautiful woman."

He leaned forward. "Then don't cheapen her. I am there at the reunion to make certain that no harm comes to Rachel."

"Lord Somerset believes you are there on his behalf."

"Then I've already failed him with the missing paintings."

～

Hanley wiped the glasses on the counter for a third time, then took the wet towel and rubbed the countertop with vigor. His wife screamed for him from their back kitchen. Long ago he had tired of her whining. Now he hated the sound of her voice. But, he had to admit, her cooking pleased their guests: Cumberland cheese and sausage. Trout from the streams or the cucumber sandwiches preferred by some guests. And her mint cake drew others who would prefer the more picturesque tea shops.

Yesterday his wife questioned him about the phone calls that kept coming to him ever since that reunion started over at the Somerset Estates. *"I know who that caller is, Hanley."*

Acid fear ate at his gut. Did she really know the name of the caller? Had she listened on the extension?

She had put her hand on his and begged, *"We should close the pub for a month and go away—we don't need the money, Hanley."*

But he tasted the money, savored the prospect of more. He longed for the time when he would have wealth in his pocket, extra money that she knew nothing about. Money that would not be recorded in the expense record or taxed by the government. Money that would guarantee him the chance to leave her forever.

Go away? Go away with her? Did she think that they would be safe by going away? Didier Bosman was not a man to be crossed. Now Hanley had discovered that Chip was part of the reunion at Somerset Estates, so

Bosman had a man on the inside and boasted there were others. *"Someone to keep an eye on Morrie Chadbourne."*

Hanley worked out the truth after recognizing that arrogant voice on the other end of the phone. A theft had been planned right under his nose. All along, he credited the planning to Didier Bosman and Morrie Chadbourne. Now he had pinpointed the mastermind behind the Somerset robbery. He celebrated his discovery with a burst of uncontrollable laughter, suppressed with a schooner of beer. There were those—like Scotland Yard—who might pay for his knowledge. But old Hanley knew how to keep still. When to keep still. The adrenaline pumped through his body every time the phone call came. But he valued living, treasured keeping his knowledge under wraps until just the right time.

The sun reflected through the goblets on the shelf. He rearranged them and still the light caused shimmering pictures in his mind. He could pack tonight. Take some of the earnings from the week and fly to the Riviera. Stay in some hotel on the beach. Watch the sunbathers. Maybe find the courage to take his own oversized body into the warm water. He could still float. Still let the warm Mediterranean flow between his toes. How cheaply he had been bought—and how wealthy he could become. He would wait. Take pictures of the paintings in the shed. And someday—

He slung the wet towel over his shoulder and leaned against the shelves. His body trembled so that the crystal behind him rattled. No one was buying his silence. He chose to be silent for his own safety. He would keep the pub open long after midnight on Saturday as he had been ordered to do. That was all. That meant nineteen paintings would be stored in the sheds behind the shop. For how long? Maybe he could forget to unlock the sheds. Then Bosman and the others might head for the motorway to Manchester or London—and never come back to Hanley's Pub.

His thoughts raced back to his younger, thinner days when he could swim. That was how he met his wife on the beaches of France. For the first time in many years he needed her again. Needed the woman she once was when they were both young, and she the strong one, certain that he could make a go of the pub. He glanced down at his rotund belly, the white apron snugly around it. His hands too chubby, his jaws too fleshy. A fat man too heavy for his stature. His wife had not fared much better. But they had made a go of their pub—twenty years of making a go at it. Clients liked them. The locals came often. Two generations of customers. They had a thriving business. Everybody liked old Hanley. Everybody tolerated his wife for her cooking.

Their favorite guest was the American, Morrie Chadbourne. Hanley kept his friendship with Chadbourne under wraps. He wanted to warn Morrie of the danger, but not at the cost of his own safety. He prayed that the man would not come again, that he'd never park his bike behind old Hanley's pub again.

Hanley stood with his feet planted on the cold, stone-flagged floor, pain radiating through the calves of his legs, the clogged vessels kicking up a fuss again. He glanced toward the table by the window. The two men had been there for hours. When he refilled their coffees, he heard snatches of their conversation. Wakefield, the one man had been called. And Inspector Farland, the one smelling of cigarettes. Scotland Yard was sitting in the far corner of his pub, and Hanley felt trapped.

Now he stiffened even more. Coming through the front door was the lovely professor McCully, walking sprightly, smiling at him. The empty goblet in his hand crashed to the stone floor as the two men at the table by the window rose to meet her.

Chapter 17

By the third evening, a spirit of pretense hovered over the guests. They agreed on a formal dinner with candlelight and pre-dinner music and no open discussion on the missing paintings. Most of them had spent leisurely side trips to Ambleside and Derwent Waters. Now, in spite of the tensions over the thefts, they appeared an amicable lot as they gathered to listen to the music.

Eileen arrived first in a slim-fitting turquoise evening dress, the color of Becki's eyes. When she saw her name tag beside Morrie's, she quickly rearranged the place settings.

"Oh Eileen," Rachel protested.

"It's best this way."

As the guests took their seats, Chandler played his mother's Stradivarius, a faraway look in his smoky-blue eyes as he tucked the high-glossed violin under his chin. Skillfully he glided the bow across the strings, filling the room with waltz music and ending with the lively notes of "The Blue Danube" waltz.

Sinclair held out his hands. "Dance with me, Rachel."

She went happily into his arms. Soon others joined them. Even Jude and Sean seemed lost in the music, and in spite of his bandaged hand, Kevin was light on his feet and more than content with Amanda's head on his shoulder.

"Mommy, dance with Morrie," Becki urged.

"Yes, dance with me," Morrie said.

When the waltz ended, they silently took their seats again, their faces flushed, the paintings truly forgotten.

Amanda had come in her Georgette gown, her lap computer in her hand. Now she slipped the laptop beneath the table and smiled apologetically at Rachel. "As soon as dinner is over, I'm going to finish designing an advertisement page on hideaway estates in Britain. Once my boss learns I'm staying at the Somerset Estates, he'll like my idea. Kevin has given me some graphic arts ideas; I'd so love to see him work at my advertisement agency."

"I thought Kevin was content with the job as an auditor."

She blushed. "Rachel, if we worked together, he'd be too—"

Kevin shot Rachel a lopsided grin. "Too busy for betting at the horse races. I can't convince her I'm a reformed man."

"You don't mind my bringing the computer to the table?"

What I mind is how blind you are to Kevin's love, she thought. *How tempted you are to mold him into your dead fiancé. Oh Amanda, you have to learn to trust Kevin. Or lose him.* She smiled at Kevin, liking his boyish appearance, his sincerity.

"It won't do any good to argue with Amanda, Professor. That laptop is my biggest competition." He sounded bitter, but there was a gentleness as he held the chair for Amanda. Once she was seated, he leaned down and kissed her on the cheek. Rachel liked Kevin Nolan, but in just these few days she was well aware that the Reynolds were watching him closely. But why? What had he done?

Even Sean had appeared at the last minute in a borrowed tuxedo, looking handsome and guarded. His churlish expression made his eyes seem even more shadowed. He stood in that familiar stance, one hand in a pocket, the other resting on Jude's shoulder. Rachel tried to catch Jude's eye, to reassure her, but Jude and Sean had their own agenda.

Sinclair took his place at the end of the table, opposite from her, and she was grateful for his presence, his strength. The loss of his wife and child had left deep ridges by his eyes, and he had a tightness around his mouth that she did not remember, but he looked more handsome than ever, his white dress shirt a direct contrast to his coppery skin. He smiled across the flickering candles—a brightness to his brown eyes. Strands of silver had crept into his dark hair, but they only made him more distinguished.

Sinclair lifted the ornate dinner bell and rang it. Rachel's thoughts leaped back to Big Ben tolling. "Reverend Rainford-Simms agreed to have the meal with us—and offer a dinner prayer."

Charles, a cleric without a parish, stood like a gentle giant with a slight stoop to his shoulders. "Methinks," he said, eyes twinkling, "that it would be better to sing an old Welsh song." Promptly he began to sing in a deep, resonant voice:

"Lord of the hills and lakes, bring peace and calm.
For friends beside us, all around us,
Let us offer You our hymn of praise."

An age tremor struck his voice midway, but he went on singing, his fingers tented, pensive. His eyes remained wide open, full of merriment with secrets of his own.

"Oh Lord of the hills,
We ask for hearts that see You everywhere.
We give Thee thanks.
We give Thee praise."

Rachel decided that the Very Reverend Rainford-Simms had made up the words as he sang them. But who could question his honest face? His sagelike appearance? He had sized up his divided company and had directed their attention toward the Lord of the hills. Whether her guests saw the hills would be an individual matter. Whether they found peace at this reunion would depend on what they did with the Lord of the hills.

"Are you my other grandfather?" Becki asked as the song ended and the food was passed.

Charles caught her eye as grandfathers do and said, "Perhaps we could talk about it after dinner."

The adults smothered their laughter. One eight-year-old bobbed her head. Happiness welled up in Rachel. The conversation passed easily at first, but then Jude challenged them with the Weinberger painting in the sitting room. "Morrie here tells me that the Weinberger is a stolen masterpiece."

Morrie's eyes smoldered. "I said, 'What if it were stolen from the Jews during the war?'"

Rachel glanced at Eileen and saw that she had retreated into silence. She sat, eyes downcast.

Charles Rainford-Simms's voice boomed across the room to her. "Didn't you tell me that your father owned one of the Weinberger paintings, Dr. Rutledge?"

She barely lifted her eyes to meet his. "My grandfather has a very large collection; Weinberger's work is just one of them."

"Great-granddaddy doesn't like the Jews," Becki announced, her mouth full of sliced lamb.

"Hush, Rebecca."

"But it's true, Mommy. He told me that himself. He went to war. He was a soldier. And when he came home he hated the Jews."

"But we don't," Eileen assured her daughter.

Morrie's gaze searched the face of the child, and then her mother's. "Tell me, Dr. Rutledge, why did he keep such an expensive painting when Weinberger is a Jewish artist?"

"I don't share my grandfather's prejudices, Morris. And neither does my daughter. In fact when I was in med school I went with a young man who had Jewish blood. But my grandfather destroyed our relationship."

Rachel felt the icy chill passing between Morrie and Eileen. She wanted to slap Morrie's hand, wanted to wrap her arms around Eileen. But what had Eileen said? *"A young man who had Jewish blood."* She didn't identify him as Morrie.

Chandler Reynolds leaned forward. "My wife has made a study of the lost art from World War II."

"Much of it looted and destroyed when the Nazis took over," Morrie snapped.

"You're right, Morrie," Jillian said. "But even now, a number of good organizations are still searching for those missing masterpieces."

"How well I know! But they're turning them over to the Louvre and other museums around the world when they find them," Morrie insisted.

"Never intentionally." Jillian stared Morrie down, forcing him to lower his eyes. "Imagine how difficult it is to trace the original owners. Proving ownership is like fitting a jigsaw together, piece by piece. It's a painstaking search. So many of the victims died. There are no records to prove ownership."

Calmly Sinclair said, "The Rothchilds and Rosenbergs and Weinbergers were only three of the collections stolen in France during the war. The looting went on all over Europe. But it was that five-hundred-million-dollar jewel heist in London's Millennium Dome that sparked my own interest in studying art history."

Jillian flashed him a warm smile. "Then you do know that paintings by Rembrandt, Monet, van Gogh, and Vermeer were ripped from the walls of art collectors and private collections by the Third Reich? The whereabouts of works like Cezanne's *Snow Scene* are still unknown. But we'll go on searching."

Once disgruntled, Morrie could not shake it. "We know that wartime partnerships existed between neutral countries. Nazi depositors used money and art stolen from innocent victims. Strangers gained financially with other people's possessions. And still do. We know all of that, yet today the heirs are rebuffed by officials who fail to return these assets to rightful owners."

He turned his anger and frustration on Eileen. "I still want to know how that Weinberger painting found its way into your grandfather's private collection."

"My grandfather came by that painting honestly."

"Did he?"

Charles propped his elbows on the table. "Young man, do you think any of us in this room approve of stolen art? Not even the heart of a thief—should one exist."

"I'm not a thief," Becki declared.

Expressions around the table masked. Feet shuffled. Hands reached for half empty water goblets. Sinclair kept his eyes on Rachel, his lips sealed.

Rainford-Simms remained himself. "I'm glad you're not a thief, Becki. But it is the people behind those paintings that matter to me. Great artists. Collectors. Individual families who loved the masterpieces. And the twisted thinking of those who looted them. It's what happened to them that matters." He tapped his chest. "What matters is what's going on inside of us. We cannot hang those paintings back on the walls, not sixty-plus years after they were looted."

Morrie challenged him. "Charles, don't you understand? Nazi gold was stolen from slaughtered Jews. Billions in money and property never restored."

Charles looked from Morrie to the faces around the table. "I understand. But stealing another painting will not right the injustices already done." He glanced at Jillian. "It is the same with art, is it not, Mrs. Reynolds? Someone has already stolen the Degas from the walls of this mansion. We must be on our guard. But what do we know about Weinberger? I think that is the painting that most concerns Morris."

"He could have been a great artist," Jillian said.

"But he died in Auschwitz," Morrie snapped.

She stared him down. "Some of Weinberger's work was destroyed. But, according to you, some of his paintings are still out there. He just didn't live long enough to be well-known."

"Jillian, if that painting in the sitting room is a genuine Weinberger, what then?" Jude asked.

"Then we'd better treasure it."

"I rather think it would be fun to steal it."

"Jude," Rachel said.

"Oh come on, Professor. You never could take a joke."

"Stealing is not a joke."

Jillian's soft voice took control again. "At least we get a glimpse of the heart of Asher Weinberger. He could have been a great artist. Could have known world acclaim. He didn't live long, but he lived long enough to paint his heart on canvas."

Audrey appeared from the kitchen carrying a tray of steaming plum pudding. She shuffled around the table, placing a china bowl in front of each guest. Last of all she put a small portion in front of Rachel and smiled. With that smile, Rachel knew that this woman's rough hands had painted her heart for all of them in the meal she had prepared.

"Thank you, Audrey," she whispered.

At the last bite of plum pudding, the guests began to excuse themselves, one by one, leaving half empty crystal goblets and sticky china bowls. Candles flickered. The stereo played softly. When the last guest left the room, Sinclair walked the length of the table to sit beside her. "Are you all right, Rachel?"

"The arguments about art and Nazi gold unnerved me."

"Why don't you take Eileen and Becki and go back to Wakefield Cottage before something awful happens?"

"And leave Audrey and my other guests?"

"The missing Degas was merely a warning. It won't stop there. Send the guests into Grasmere. Cancel this reunion."

"And disappoint Morrie? You don't like him, do you?"

"I believe him capable of anything. He's not the same lighthearted man who lectures with me. Whatever is going on in his life is related to that painting that's worth two or three mil."

"I think it's worth more than that to him." As her cheeks flushed, she started to rise. He cupped her hand. "Don't go."

"I should help Audrey clear up this mess."

"I arranged for additional help in the kitchen. Audrey will supervise. She's quite capable, you know."

He lifted the bell and shook it. When Audrey appeared, he said, "I'm trying to keep Rachel from tiring herself."

"Try putting a lid on an active volcano. It's in her to work." Audrey gave Rachel an affectionate pat on the shoulder. "You have a full-time job just entertaining your guests."

"We plan an easy day tomorrow. Sinclair is taking our guests to Oxford for the day. And I'm taking Becki to Hill Top Farm."

Audrey blew out the candles. "Mr. Sinclair, you need to walk off that dinner. You two should catch some fresh air before evening sets in."

Rachel started to stand. Sinclair put his hand over hers again. "Don't go, Rachel. Stay here with me," he urged.

"But we should spend time with our guests."

"*Our* guests have things pretty much in hand."

She glanced out the wide window. Jude and Sean had separated from the others and now stood against the iron fence. Sara and Lydia sat on the stone bench watching the badminton game. Janet Tallard looked at peace with her world, her head thrown back in laughter, as she talked with Lenora. *High society and a pretty farm girl together.*

She searched, but Morrie and Eileen were not together. Would they ever be? "Sinclair, I look at all those students, and Janet is the most content. The same happy girl who sat in my classroom. The same young woman I tried to counsel against dropping out of school to marry. And do you know what she told me?"

"I won't know until you tell me."

"She said all she ever wanted to be was a wife and mother."

A shadow clouded his eyes. "Mary was content like that. She made my life complete."

In a way I never could have done. "I wish Eileen and Morrie would get back together again. Did you see them dancing?"

"I was too busy watching you, Rachel. You can't force a couple back together. Becki, as dear as she is to you, is not your responsibility."

"In a way she is. What Becki wants more than anything else in the world—"

"Is for you to get well."

"More than that. She wants a daddy like her friends have. Eileen never told Morrie about Becki." She turned to face Sinclair and confided, "They met at the university and were married briefly and divorced. Actually, Eileen's grandfather had the wedding annulled."

"Don't meddle, Rachel. The child would only be hurt."

"Morrie is angry because he thinks Eileen bore a child out of wedlock."

"Then he doesn't think very highly of her!"

"It's a long story."

"I have all night," he said as Audrey scooped up the last stack of dishes. "We can turn on the electric log in the fireplace."

"You do that, Mister Sinclair," Audrey suggested. "Take Rachel into the drawing room, and I'll bring you some hot tea. And don't worry about

Becki. I'll go for her soon and give her a bath."

"Tell her I'll be in to read to her."

She glanced at Sinclair. "Not tonight, Miss Rachel. I'll do the reading. You two just enjoy each other."

Moments later, Sinclair's eyes darkened as he pushed himself to his feet and stared down at the fireplace. "Rachel, I haven't been totally honest with you. I expected trouble at the reunion. That's why I'm here, but Inspector Farland and I were both surprised at how quickly the Degas and Monet were stolen."

"Morrie didn't take those paintings! I'm certain of it."

"But someone may attempt to steal more paintings while we are here. That's why Inspector Farland is keeping an eye on us."

"Is half of Scotland Yard here?"

"Several officers are mingling with the staff. They will be ready for anything."

"Then nothing will go wrong. Does Morrie know?"

"No. And he is not to know. Are you aware that Jillian Reynolds works for the Coventry Art Theft Registry?"

"Yes."

"Then you know that the registry is committed to recovering stolen masterpieces, no matter where they've been taken."

"Yes, Jillian has been sizing up the Weinberger. But why would Morrie invite them here?"

"You invited me."

"I'm glad you came. I needed you here."

He cocked his head at a rakish angle. "If you hadn't invited me, I would have invited myself."

The firm jaw relaxed into a smile. The lights in the room caught his rugged good looks. And for the tenth time since he stood at the gatepost at Stradbury Square and came up the walkway back into her life, she regretted breaking her promise. If she beat this cancer—if she went on living—she would never think of Big Ben or hear it chime again without aching inside.

"What are you thinking about, Rachel?"

"About the day we were to meet at Big Ben."

He took a step toward her. "Are you ready to tell me what happened? I waited there for you. A long time."

"I know. I watched you."

He took her hands. "Tell me what happened."

Behind them they heard the labored footsteps of Audrey coming with her tea. Rachel pulled free and smiled wanly. "I think this is the wrong time."

"But soon?"

"Soon," she promised.

Chapter 18

As the ferry took them across the lake to the village of Sawrey, Rebecca's excitement mounted. "Oh Rachel, I wish Beatrix Potter would be there today. I wish she hadn't died so soon."

Rachel smiled. "Shall we pretend she's there?"

"Mommy and Morrie will think we're foolish."

"Then we shall be foolish."

"Why did Morrie have to come with us?"

"To be with your mommy, I think. Do you mind his coming?"

"He's not much fun. I don't like him."

"Because he calls you smidgen?"

"I don't call him names." She ran ahead for a moment, then came back and slipped her hand in Rachel's.

The springtime fragrance of lilacs filled the air. Castle Cottage stood across the street. A few Herdwick sheep grazed in the meadows. Spruce trees grew in the woods. Rushes lined the edge of Esthwaite Water. Rachel pulled Becki back from the water's edge, but she broke free and ran through the rolling countryside, her feet trampling the wildflowers.

She went back and clutched Rachel's hand again. They half ran, searching for the sand bank where Flopsy, Mopsy, Cottontail, and Peter had lived. They discovered a big fir tree, but only a squirrel scampered for cover. They looked for the farm where Jemima Puddleduck lived and found instead a nest of robins. Crossing the stone bridge hunting for Jemima's woods, they found only fields of radishes, lettuce, and parsley. They hunted for rabbits, toads, and mice. Rebecca wanted to find Squirrel Nutkin sailing on a raft and saw only a nightingale in the orchard.

"I wish Ribby the cat was still alive. And Tom Kitten and Samuel Whiskers and Pigland Bland," Rebecca mused.

"But they are. Remember, we're pretending. If we find Ribby the cat, Duchess the dog will be right behind."

"Mommy said Miss Potter married when she was middle-aged. So don't worry, Rachel. You can still marry Sinclair Wakefield."

"I'd have to wait for him to ask me."

"Mommy thinks he already asked you."

A long time ago, she thought.

Finally they went past the stone wall at the bottom of the garden, through the wicket gate. Rachel held tightly to Rebecca's hand as they went up the sloping path to the cottage. Hill Top Farm overlooked the village, keeping watch on a sprawling acreage of land. It was just as Beatrix had lived it, just as Rachel remembered it from her last trip, just as Rebecca dreamed it would be. Ahead of them lay Miss Potter's two-story house with a weather vane on the chimney and ivy vines growing up one wall. Pots of geraniums sat on the windowsill. Rhododendrons grew in the yard. The garden was filled with some of her favorite colors: pink foxgloves, yellow snapdragons, blue larkspurs.

Inside were the carved oak furniture and the stairs leading to the small cozy rooms on the second floor where Beatrix Potter wrote with her quill pen. Rebecca whispered that the pantry in the large kitchen surely held nibbles for the squirrels in the neighborhood; Rachel whispered that she smelled veal pie baking.

Together they pictured Beatrix Potter—a plump woman in her long tweed skirt sitting at her desk with a quill pen in hand and writing her animal stories. They pictured her going down the long, narrow stairs and putting on her wide-brimmed straw hat before lumbering along in her clogs out to her Herdwick sheep.

"Mommy said she had rheumatic fever when she was twenty."

"I'd forgotten that, Becki."

"Her hair came out in clumps—like yours did."

"I haven't forgotten that. Did you know she had lively blue eyes like yours, Becki?"

Morrie and Eileen lagged behind them, but Rachel could hear them talking and knew it was not going well.

Moodily, Morrie said, "I should have gone to Stratford-upon-Avon with the others instead of coming to a kids' farm."

"Why didn't you, Morrie?" Eileen asked him.

Rachel heard the wretchedness in his voice, the longing. "I wanted to be with you, Eileen. Like old times. I thought the two of us could go off and spend the day together. Rachel and the smidgen don't need our company."

"I'm not leaving. . . Morrie, did you know Beatrix Potter died during World War II—just before Christmas?"

"Did she now? Do you think Rachel will live to Christmas?"

"Of course. She's getting better."

He tried again. "Rachel is good with your daughter. I guess it's easy. She's such a happy little girl."

"Her father was that way a long time ago."

His voice cracked, cleared. "I've been wanting to find the courage to ask you. Who was he?"

"Rebecca's father? Surely you have guessed by now?"

Rachel felt her heart pounding and wondered whether Becki was listening, too, and knew that she was.

Eileen's voice was sad and soft as she said, "Morrie, you are Rebecca's father."

~

As they went back through the side gate at the Somerset Estates, Eileen tugged at Becki's hand and dragged her away without a word. Before they reached the main house, Becki glanced back and gave an uncertain wave intended for her father.

Morrie toed the ground, his eyes downcast.

"She's your daughter, Morrie. Are you going to let her walk away?" Rachel asked.

His jaw tightened. "A child I've never seen before drops into my life and—" He ran his hands despairingly through his thick hair. "Don't you understand, Rachel? It's too late. I'm a scholar, not a father. I wouldn't know what to do with a child."

"Give yourself a chance to know her. Let her know you."

"I'd be a disappointment, Rachel. You can see how I disappointed Eileen. Like Eileen told me this afternoon, I'm more interested in the Weinberger painting than in an eight-year-old I never knew existed."

"So you are punishing Eileen?"

"She should have let me know. I had a right—"

"Did you leave a forwarding address or simply vanish?"

"That's what her grandfather wanted. I didn't measure up. If she wanted me to know about the child, she could have reached me through the alumni office."

"The child has a name, Morrie. Rebecca Lynne."

"My mother's name."

"So it's the past then? Not today? A war over sixty years ago, not your child? Oh Morrie, be careful what choices you make."

"What happened back then affected my life."

Your reason. Your feelings, she thought. "What happened just now will affect your daughter for the rest of her life. She's eight, Morrie. Vulnerable. Don't hurt her."

He started to walk away and called back, "I don't want to hurt Rebecca. But tell Eileen it would be best if she packed up now and took her away."

"I won't do that—unless I leave with them."

"It would be safer for you as well."

"You're being destroyed by what happened all those years ago."

He cracked his knuckles. "I'm being destroyed by what might happen this week. There's a tie-in with that war and Eileen's family. Eileen's grandfather was in the military, involved in the postwar art restitution. It seemed strange that I found one of those missing paintings hanging on his wall. And now the one in Somerset's possession. You can tell how he values it by the place he has given it in his home. The value I place on it."

"You don't really believe Becki is your child! You are more willing to believe that a painting belongs to you than your own child."

"I know for a fact that my family accumulated an art collection before Hitler came to power. In the case of Asher Weinberger, he was a distant relative; my family purchased many of his paintings along with works by Degas and Claude Monet and Cezanne. All looted from my great-grandmother's estate in Paris. Those facts I believe in. But to say that I'm a father? I don't have much time, Rachel. I only have the time left before Somerset gets back to prove that painting belongs to me."

"Do you plan to steal it?"

He looked smitten. "I didn't take the Monet or Degas."

"Someone did."

"I don't make much as a lecturer, but if I could own the Weinberger, I could sell it and send the money to Eileen."

She stared at him. Something he had wanted to possess for years, and he would sell it for Rebecca? "You'd do that for Becki? Is supporting her more important than knowing your child? Oh Morris, what has become of the caring student I once knew?"

"An art historian I read about said he was tracing a thread back through time. That's what I'm doing. And I think that's what you're doing, too. Tracing your own life span. You want to help Rebecca because she belongs to one of your students."

"To two of them. Your thoughts are evocative, Morrie. But not quite accurate. I know where I've been. What I've done. Right now I want to know where the threads knotted. Where the tapestry was marred. Whether

I can unravel some of the past and change the tapestry of my life. Or the lives of my students."

"Isn't that what I want to do? Prove that thread of ownership. Get some of these masterpieces back in the right hands. Provide for my—for my daughter. I call it righting a wrong. You call yours the tapestry of life."

"You've lost me."

"What I'm saying is we're no different, Rachel." He stomped off, angry with himself. Angry with her. Angry with the world.

～

Jude and Amanda passed Morrie on the walkway. When they reached Rachel, Amanda asked, "Is something wrong, Dr. McCully? Mr. Chadbourne looked upset."

"That's how she affects people," Jude said.

"We were just discussing the tapestry of life." She smiled at them both, then said quietly to Jude, "I'm glad you came to the reunion."

"And I'm wondering why I came. I'm not part of your legacy, you know."

Amanda turned on her. "Don't talk to Professor McCully like that, Jude."

Amanda fell in step with Rachel, allowing Jude to saunter on ahead of them, sulking. "Professor, I'm sorry about Jude."

"She's not your problem. Do I dare tell you that I'm glad that you and Kevin are here?"

"We know. You didn't have to tell us. I've been wanting to talk to you alone—about Kevin and me. Do you think we'll have time on the cruise on Lake Windermere?"

"We'll make time, Amanda."

～

Eileen sat down at the desk in their room as Becki kicked off her shoes and flung herself on the bed. "I'm sorry, Rebecca."

"It's no big deal."

"You've wanted to know your father for so long."

"No big deal." She rolled on her stomach. "Did you bring me here to meet him?"

"No."

"Did Rachel?"

"I'm afraid so."

"Then I hate them both."

"You don't mean that. Not after you and Rachel had such a lovely time at Hill Top Farm. The two of you are the best of friends."

"She can't be my best friend and Morrie Chadbourne's friend, too." She grabbed a book and buried her face in it.

Eileen had brought her black logbook to England with her, the one with weights and dosage charts, the one where she kept the diary pages about Rachel. She reached for it now and wrote: *Rebecca met her father today. And I may have lost my child. . . .*

The tears kept her from writing more. She brushed them away and turned back to the notes she had written since arriving in England.

Sunday—May 26: Our first day in England: Timothy Whitesaul met us at Heathrow. Surprised us, I should say. I had forgotten how ruggedly attractive he is. How kind. He welcomed Rebecca as he would his own child. But then I had forgotten how involved he was in my pregnancy, how caring, never asking me who my child's father was. Never knowing I had been married. And he was there when she was born—more father to her than Morrie would ever have been.

Monday morning—May 27: I am waiting for the bellboy to carry our luggage down to the car. Rebecca has gone off with Timothy to see the sidewalks of London, whatever that means.

Timothy surprised us by arriving at the Ritz for breakfast. He insisted on treating us before we left for Wakefield Cottage. I asked about Rachel. He is optimistic. He couldn't take his eyes from me at the table. I blushed like a schoolgirl and Rebecca asked me why my face was red. I remember that same look when Timothy held Rebecca in the delivery room, those wide eyes of his filled with love. He asked me again if I had given any thought to moving to England and becoming part of the Whitesaul Clinic. How blind I have been. Corresponding with him all these years. Enjoying the unexpected phone calls from him. Calling back to thank him for Rebecca's birthday presents, and Christmas presents, and just special-day presents. His invitation goes beyond cancer research. Without couching his desire into words, he is asking me to become part of his life, part of Rebecca's life. I am flattered, but is this what I really want?

Monday noon—May 27: Driving on the left side of the road is a challenge, especially on the motorway. I soon had my heeled foot to the pedal, and kept abreast of the wildest of drivers. Thankfully, Rebecca was absorbed with the countryside, the crowded towns, but even more with the expectation of seeing her friend Rachel again. I did not tell her that the car behind us was there for our protection, that the young man behind the wheel belonged to Scotland Yard.

Late Monday—May 27: What joy to see Rachel so happy in Wakefield Cottage. She is at home here. She is still much too thin, her once gorgeous complexion sallow. But those eyes and that smile will never change. Seeing her now, I am confident Timothy is right. Rachel will lick this battle with cancer. Or am I being selfish, not wanting my child to lose her friend? Not wanting to lose her myself. I feel like a student again—looking up to her professor. Learning from her.

Tuesday—May 28: Rachel has betrayed me and I am angry. This reunion that she plans is with Morrie Chadbourne. "I meant to tell you," she said. Had she told me, Rebecca and I would never have flown to England. I wanted to call Timothy Whitesaul and beg him to drive up here and take Rebecca and me back to Heathrow. That was my plan until I saw Rachel and Rebecca talking about going to Hill Top Farm. I won't take this dream from my child.

Sunday—June 2: Today I saw Morrie Chadbourne for the first time in nine years. I have never stopped loving him. Could he possibly feel the same about me?

Tuesday—June 4: Rachel amazes me. She is everywhere at once, the gracious hostess. Yesterday she walked across the grounds with Janet Tallard, arm in arm and laughing—as though they had secrets of their own. Of all the guests, Janet is the most at peace, the most calming on Rachel after her argument with Jude Alexander at breakfast. Is Jude capable of stealing the paintings? Does she dislike Dr. McCully that much?

Tuesday afternoon—June 4: Amanda Pennyman seems to be avoiding any time alone with Rachel ever since the name Lee passed between them. I suspect that she and Kevin are not married. That Amanda's past has been awakened by being here again. But knowing Rachel, she will find time to spend with Amanda. At least that is her plan. Time alone with each of her former students to encourage them—to leave another imprint on their lives. Kevin enjoys talking to Rachel—he talks about horses and she about the gardens here on the property.

Wednesday at breakfast—June 5: I saw it again today. Rachel's eyes light up whenever Sinclair Wakefield walks into the room. He is an attractive man. And I remember that day back in the clinic when I asked her whether there had ever been anyone special in her life. When I asked her why she never married and had children, she turned away with tears in her eyes. Could Sinclair be the reason for those tears?

Wednesday evening—June 5: Hill Top Farm. Becki could not have been happier. She and Rachel pretended the whole trip. Seeing rabbits and squirrels and imagining Beatrix Potter still tending her sheep. It would have been perfect if Morrie had not gone with us—for today he discovered that Rebecca is his child. What should have brought him joy left him staring at Becki. "You mean the smidgen is mine, Eileen?"

Eileen closed her logbook where she had made her Hill Top entry. She brushed the burning tears from her eyes, forced a smile on her face, and steeled herself against the pain inside. The pain Becki must surely be feeling.

"Rebecca," she said cheerfully, "let's—"

But Becki was gone.

Chapter 19

Becki wanted the pain and hurt to go away. She didn't like Morrie Chadbourne. She didn't like him one bit. Her tummy felt like it did when she got sick. Her cheeks felt hot, like they did when she had a fever and her mother stayed home from the hospital to take care of her. She squirmed for several minutes before she rolled over on her stomach. Her eyes kept filling with tears as she propped herself on her elbows and balanced her book on the pillow.

Today had been the best day of her life. Today had been the worst day of her life. Hill Top Farm with Rachel—that was the best part. When they walked toward the meadows in the village of Sawrey, Rachel promised that she would get well.

Rachel loved animals as much as Becki did. That's what she liked about her. "I never had an animal," Becki had confided, leaning against the fence.

"Neither did I, Becki. My sister was ill all her life. She had trouble breathing, so we could never have animals in the house."

But they had a host of imaginary animals at Hill Top Farm. And live ones, too. The sheep grazing. The cat scampering across their path. The squirrel in the hedge on the stony path up to Beatrix Potter's cottage. Right now Becki would like to sit on the sandbank and maybe cry a little. Maybe cry a whole lot.

Becki wished now that Rachel had let her fall into the Esthwaite Water on their trip today. She'd be gone now, not hurting like this. She wanted to be Squirrel Nutkin sailing away on a raft so that no one would ever find her again. She risked another side glance at her mother, the moment stolen between pages from the book she was reading. *No big deal,* she had said.

But that had been a lie. It stung more than when she had skinned her ankle on the playground. It hurt more than those times when her classmates teased her about the daddy who was never there. It made her sadder than when Great-granddaddy shouted about the man who ran out on her mother.

"So where is your daddy?" the kids would ask her.

And that smarty-pants Emily, saying, "I bet you never had a father. That's what my mother thinks."

"Oh, he's away. He'll be back someday."

She had come up with wonderful excuses, pretending as she had done all day today at Hill Top Farm. Excuses like, "My father is on a secret mission for the president." Or, "My father is an army general. He'll come home when the war is over."

No one thought to ask her, "Which war?"

Great-granddaddy said there was always a war, people killing each other for no reason. He didn't like anybody outside his country either. And he always seemed unhappy about the blood that ran in her veins.

The lump in her throat was familiar. Usually it came when she was mad at her classmates, peeved at the sitter, or just plumb annoyed with her great-granddaddy. Her eyes ached from fighting back the tears. She wouldn't let her mom see her cry. Not over Morrie Chadbourne. When she was naughty or slow to obey, her mother told her, "You are just like your father. Good-looking. Smart as a whip like he is. And stubborn and proud."

Rebecca thought about that. Morrie was tall. He knew a lot about art and books. He always won at badminton—she liked sitting out on the bench watching him. The other guests liked him, especially Jude and Rachel. And he really liked that dumb painting in the drawing room. He liked it better than he liked her. He called the painting "a masterpiece"; he called her "smidgen."

Just a week ago she had wanted to be like her father because the imaginary father was perfect. But not the real father. She liked Sinclair Wakefield so much better than Morrie. Sinclair was kind to her and told her about his son, Blake. Sinclair still loved Blake, the way she wanted her daddy to love her. And Kevin Nolan talked to her about horses and called her by her proper name. *"Stay in England long enough, Rebecca, and Amanda and I will teach you to ride one of our favorite stallions."*

Of all the people in England, Becki liked Timothy Whitesaul the best because he always sent her presents. The next time the kids at school asked her about her father, she would tell them that he was a famous doctor who lived in England and was fighting cancer. She thought about Chaplain Wong and decided that his children were lucky because he missed them all the time; she liked it when he told her about Jesus loving children. Morrie Chadbourne didn't seem to know anything about loving anyone.

Now what she had longed for all of her life—finding her father—turned out to be the worst day of her life. She stole another glance at her mother, who was still leaning over her black logbook. Wet tissues lay on the desktop. Her mom reached for another tissue. Then she started writing again, a fountain pen clutched in her hand, the one she called her lucky pen because Timothy Whitesaul had sent it to her from England.

The Secret Garden caught Becki's attention again. She longed for a secret garden of her own with friends to hide away with. She was angry at Rachel for being Morrie's friend. Hill Top Farm had been such a wonderful day of pretending.

All of that turned into the worst day of her life when her mother's words thundered in her ears. *"Morrie, you are Rebecca's father."*

The man who called her smidgen.

She had dreamed of meeting her daddy one day, always picturing him as someone strong and brave. Someone handsomer than any of the dads she knew. He would come back into her life and say, "I'm here. . .for always."

Sometimes she talked to her imaginary, perfect dad. And told him secrets. And made up stories about what they would say to each other. But Morrie Chadbourne didn't want to talk to her. He didn't want her to be his daughter.

Mommy seldom talked about her daddy and never in front of Great-grandpa. He called him "the miserable scoundrel." That always made Mommy cry. Suddenly, Rebecca felt very angry at the miserable scoundrel. Without a word, she pushed herself to her feet and ran into the adjoining bathroom. She flushed the toilet and turned on the faucet. Splashing her face with cold water, she felt hot tears merge with the water. She grabbed a towel—Rachel's towel, she thought—and wiped her face dry. Dropping the towel on the sink, she peered into Rachel's room. Rachel was gone.

Quietly she went through the room, out Rachel's door, and down the long, curving stairway. The balustrade no longer looked like a marvelous slide. Nothing mattered except finding her father and telling him she hated him for making her mom cry. *A smidgen, am I? I'm sure that's better than being a scoundrel.*

She wandered through the empty hallway into the kitchen. Audrey dropped the potato peeler and opened her arms wide. Becki flew into them.

"There, there, child." She wiped Becki's tears with her apron. "What's wrong?"

"I have to find Mr. Chadbourne."

"From the looks of you, I wouldn't want to be in his shoes. So why don't you tell old Audrey all about it?"

"I can't right now. Mommy always says we talk to the person who makes us mad first. Then we won't tattle to others."

"Wise, that mother of yours. Do you want some scones and milk first? Then you can get your thoughts together."

"If you please, I'll come back for the scones and milk. I have to see Mr. Chadbourne first."

Audrey glanced at the wall clock. "All right. Off you go then." She put two cookies in Becki's hand. "One for you and one for Morris." Her eyes twinkled. "A peace offering. He should be out in his cottage right now. Should I call him and check?"

"No. I want to surprise him."

With a quick hug, Audrey let her go. Once outside, Becki ran toward the back of the property, not even stopping to pick one of the flowers that she loved. She was racing past the first guest cottage when Charles called out to her. "Where are you going in such a hurry, little one?"

I'm not a little one, she thought. *I'm not a smidgen.* "I'm Rebecca Lynne Rutledge, and I'm looking for my father."

He tented his fingers to his lips. "I see. That is an important mission. But you won't find him at the cottage."

"Audrey said he was there."

He shook his head. "I know for a fact that he went out to the toolshed about thirty minutes ago. Would you like me to go with you? The shed is kind of a creepy old place."

She considered his offer, some of her bravado wearing thin. "No," she said politely. "I want to talk to him by myself."

The door to the shed creaked as she pushed it open. A stale, musty smell hit her nostrils. The room was much bigger than she expected, but it was dark inside, with one lightbulb dangling from the ceiling. Shovels and garden hoes hung on hooks on each side of the room.

"Morrie," she called.

No answer.

She walked in slowly. The door slammed behind her, sending a cold breeze across her bare legs. It took a minute before she could force her feet to keep moving. She crossed to the end of the room and found a staircase leading down toward a cellar.

A heavier door blocked her entry. She tugged at it and finally opened it wide enough to slip in. Here the corridor was lit much brighter. She tried to call Morrie's name again but managed only a squeak. The corridor branched off into several tunnels, a basement playground. It was cold here, and very dark. She listened and then walked toward the sound of a phone ringing.

Closed doors lay on one side of the tunnel. Seeing another light toward the middle of the hallway, she followed it, running her hand along the damp wall so she would not stumble. She felt terrified that she had come this far without Charles. She wanted to run back and find him when her father stepped into the hall and said, "What are you doing here?"

~

Morrie stared down at his daughter, feeling as cold and empty as the corridor in which he was standing. She looked small and vulnerable, yet her chin stuck out defiantly.

"What are you doing here, smidgen?"

"Looking for you."

He pointed to the door he had come from. "Come in then. In here. We need to keep the door closed. This is a temperature-controlled room."

She shivered as she stepped inside. "You don't seem surprised to see me."

"Not really. Charles called and said you were on your way."

"I heard the phone ringing. That's how I found you. It's scary down here."

"That's why we don't invite people down. But now that you're here, look around. These are the chambers where Lord Somerset keeps his extra paintings and the ones not catalogued as yet."

He felt hopelessly unable to strike up a conversation with a child. What did he know about what children liked? He knew nothing about this child. Not her birthdate. Not her favorite colors or what grade she was in. Finally he mumbled, "Did you enjoy the trip to Hill Top Farm today?"

"Yes—until I found out you were my father."

"I was just as surprised as you were."

Her lip quivered. "Are you really my father?"

"That's what your mother says."

"She never tells a lie. You made her cry."

"I didn't mean to. Go back to your room, and don't tell anyone you followed me here."

"Audrey knows. And Charles told me you came in here."

"Good. Announce it to the world. So what do you want?"

She was a plucky sort. "I want to know why you dislike me so. I always dreamed my daddy would be a nice man."

He choked at the thought of shattering her dreams. "I never dreamed about you. I never knew you existed until today."

"Don't you like my mommy?"

The kid could hold her own, the way he used to debate in school, winning verbal wars, throwing his knowledge about as a weapon. As a cry for acceptance. *Like* Eileen? Always.

"I loved your mother from the day I met her."

She frowned. "Great-granddaddy says you had a funny way of showing your love."

"So he's still alive?"

"Mommy says he's too mean to die."

"Do you believe that?"

She shrugged. "I like him. I think he's a nice old man, but not as nice as Charles."

"Maybe you and your great-granddad are two of a kind."

"No, Mommy says I'm like you—like my daddy. But I would never run away from Mommy. So why did you run away?"

He could think of a hundred reasons, but only the truth mattered to this child. "Your great-grandpa sent me away."

"He said you could never afford to take care of my mom."

"Well, she won't have to worry. She'll be a rich woman when he dies."

"No," she said matter-of-factly, "I'll be rich. He's leaving all his money to me." She seemed to be crooking her neck looking up at him. "I don't care if he does or not. Money hasn't made him happy. Besides, he might spend it all before he dies."

He raged. "He's leaving nothing to Eileen?"

"Just a dumb painting."

"The one in his living room?"

"You know about that?"

"It's a long story."

She was looking around the room again with those curious blue eyes of hers. She cocked her head to stare into the vault, then ran her wrist over the pile of soft cloth used to protect the paintings. A quizzical frown arced her brows as she looked at the metal container that stood like an oversized briefcase—leaning with the Degas painting against the table leg.

"I think that's one of the stolen paintings," she said. "So where is the other one?"

"I don't know, but I assure you, smidgen, I didn't take it."

"I know. But I saw who did."

He lunged for her and grabbed her arms. "What are you talking about?"

Her fist tightened. "I saw the man who took the painting."

A man. So a man had stolen it. What kind of lies did this child tell? "Don't say anything like that."

"But I did see him with my own eyes. I woke up when it was still dark out. I went downstairs by myself."

"You expect me to believe that?"

"I'm used to visiting my great-granddad in a big old house. So I wasn't afraid to go downstairs alone. I was in the drawing room when I heard the man coming—so I hid behind the drapes."

He shook her, not violently, but born of the fear inside him for the safety of this child of his. "Don't tell anyone what you just told me. Don't tell your mother. Don't tell Rachel—"

"You're the first person I told. I saw the man, and I saw him go out the doors with that metal box in his hands." She pointed. "That metal box right there."

"Out through the French doors?"

"I don't know what kind of doors they are. He just pushed them open and went out."

"You're wrong. You have to be wrong."

Fear clouded her face. "I don't like you. You don't want to be my daddy. You don't even believe me when I tell you the truth."

With forced unkindness he said, "My life is too busy for a child's vivid imagination." He was being deliberately cruel, desperate to protect this child of his. "I want you to go back to the main house. I wouldn't mention this visit to your mother. It would just upset her to know you had been down in these tunnels." His voice cracked. His fist doubled against his weakness. "Eileen is always careful to protect you. She's a good mother. Now go before I send you packing."

She flung one of the crushed cookies at him and ran, her footsteps echoing in the hollow corridor. Morrie did not follow but stood in the tunnel blindly watching her go. But it was all right. Charles would be waiting for her at the top of the stairs.

~

"That was quite a touching scene."

Morrie did a double take as Sean Larkins stepped from the inner vault, a teacup in his hands. Larkins eyed the Degas. "The child said she knows who took the painting. I am sorry to hear that, Morrie."

"She's just a child. She has a wild imagination. You should have seen her at Hill Top Farm today."

"You went with her?"

"I'm her father."

"You amaze me, Morrie. You have endless surprises up your sleeve."

You can't even begin to imagine what surprises I have for you and Bosman before this reunion ends. He would be glad to see Scotland Yard cuff them and lead them away.

"What are you doing down here, Chip?"

"Checking the place out, tagging a few more paintings Bosman may want to collect. If he doesn't want them, I do. By the way, Morris, I suggest that you stop calling me Chip at this reunion."

"It's the name I know you by."

"My name is Sean Larkins."

"I know that now—your name as Irish as your fake brogue."

"I am Irish, third generation back. It gave me an in with the rugby team."

"You made a good name for yourself on the team."

"That I did. I'm still negotiating a new contract so I can play professionally again."

"I would think a famous name would be good enough for you. Why get yourself messed up with Didier Bosman?"

"I'm like you, Morris. Greedy for both fame and fortune." He looked around at the uncatalogued paintings. "It seems to me that it would be a simple matter to remove one or more of these magnificent paintings from the vault and go undetected for some time. Long enough to market them. If Bosman is not interested, I am. What say we work on this together?"

"You're forgetting the elaborate alarm system we have here."

Larkins flashed a cocky grin. "How effective a robbery can be when it's far removed from a major city!"

"You're forgetting our staff is well-trained, efficient."

"Would you raise the battle cry with cooks and gardeners? Or did you bring a special detail from Scotland Yard for this unique gathering?"

"I should have thought of that."

His cocky grin remained. "Maybe someone did. But don't forget. Make certain that alarm system is off Saturday night."

"Saturday then?"

"That's right. The robbery is set for Saturday. By the way, is Kevin

Nolan's room the first or second door on the left?"

"What do you want with Nolan?"

"It's payback time. We have a surprise for him. He lucked out at the bombing near Harrods. If he hadn't stopped and gone shopping for his girl, he would have been by the art shop when the bomb went off."

"You and Bosman were involved in that? Kevin was the intended victim? You are mad, Chip. An innocent clerk was killed that day."

"Plans are sometimes costly," he said.

"What about Jude Alexander? How did you rake her in?"

"You told me you wouldn't invite her. I had to work around that invitation myself. I make a dandy escort, don't you think?"

"Is the girl involved, Chip?"

"She pleases me. I find her most attractive and useful. She dislikes McCully enough to do anything we ask. All that points in her favor." Larkins put the teacup on a shelf. "I am delighted to know your daughter, Morris. For the child's safety, I suggest that you keep her from announcing to others that she observed a robbery. I'll see you at dinner. . .and don't forget. Have the decks in the main house cleared by midnight Saturday. Bosman and the truck will be here around one."

He sauntered off and was whistling as he reached the stairs. Morrie stared at the metal container with the Degas painting leaning against it. He wondered where the Monet had been hidden. Wondered who had taken it.

But Rebecca was more important than the paintings. Rebecca, his child! Yesterday he did not care what happened to her. Now, her safety was in his hands. With a despair he couldn't control, he kicked at the Degas painting and left an irreversible tear in the canvas, cutting its value from four million to two.

Chapter 20

Rachel stood stock-still, motionless by the French windows that overlooked the lovely gardens. The Somerset house lay quiet all around her, a strange stillness echoing in its vastness. The house seemed undisturbed—the morning mute, all noise suspended in the vaulted ceilings above her. Though she strained to hear, she heard not even the muffled sounds of the staff in the kitchen. Even the wind sent no whispers across the corridor. She wanted to hear the whimper of a voice. A murmur behind one of the closed doors upstairs. The rustle of the leaves in the gardens. The swish of a maple leaf tumbling to the ground.

She wanted last evening back with Sinclair whispering old promises as he blew a breath across the tip of her ear, stirring old memories. Old longings.

She thought back to those marvelous camping days in the woods back home, to her contentment before cancer, before chemo and her hair coming out in clumps, before her move to England. She had loved the quietness of an early morning in the woods. The awakening of birds. The canopy of the sky, with moss and fallen leaves for the carpet beneath her feet. She liked the memory of a rucksack on her back as she started up the mountain. The water cascading over the cliff. A tossed rock rippling the water. The smell of the pines and wildflowers. The feel of her boundless energy going higher. What had happened to all of that? Tomorrow she would be thirty-eight, not old in the sequence of time, but her body, struggling to regain its old strength, would not be able to scale the smallest fells. And never Scafell Pike as the rest of her guests would do on Saturday morning.

Today, the guests were left to find their own excitement. She was left to spend the day alone. They had made it five days into the reunion with two paintings missing, one attempt to remove another one, and Morrie stirring a ruckus when he found the Desmond vases sitting on either side of the fireplace in the drawing room. But perhaps the major threat was over. Perhaps the fears had been imaginary and Scotland Yard needlessly concerned.

Sunrise on Stradbury Square

Opening the French windows, she had a better view of Chaplain Wong. He was sitting alone with his back braced against one of the landscape boulders, a writing pad on his knee. She smiled to herself, remembering him as the class joker with a quick laugh and a love for poetry. He still had his quick wit, but poetry had taken second place to his two sons. Back on campus, would she have guessed him destined for the chaplaincy and fatherhood?

And where were the others this morning? Kevin and Amanda had gone off to browse through the Windermere Steamboat Museum on the banks of Lake Windermere. The women traveling on their own had taken a picnic down by the lake. Jude and Sean had escaped to the hills above the Somerset property, and even now could be seen off to her left in what could only be described as the beginnings of an argument. Eileen and Rebecca took off without her this morning and were walking in the gardens. But were they aware they were walking in the direction of Morrie's cottage?

Rachel turned from the window and went wearily up the great curving staircase. What she had meant for good had backfired. The differences between Eileen and Morrie kept escalating, trapping Rebecca between them. And she, Rachel McCully, had expected the miracle of reconciliation by bringing them together. Timothy Whitesaul's arrival this evening would light the fuse even more.

Rachel paused at the top of the steps. She had ventured little on the upper floors of the mansion, staying mostly to her own elegantly furnished bedroom at the top of the stairs. Now she strolled toward the end of the hallway—past Lydia and Sara's room, beyond the room that Lenora and Janet were sharing.

At the end of the corridor, Rachel discovered double doors in an arched alcove near Jude's room. They led her into a smaller hall with a spiraling staircase at the far end where a skylight flooded the stairwell with sun. The sound of organ music reached her. She started up the stone-flagged steps and paused to listen again. Following the notes to a landing, she saw a sign that read SOMERSET CHAPEL.

From all she had heard, Lord Somerset was not a man given to religion. Whatever he did seemed only to magnify his wealth and position. Inside the chapel, she saw Sinclair sitting at the organ, his back to her. Not wanting to disturb him, she slipped into a pew and took in the magnificence of the carved, vaulted ceiling and the stained glass windows. The chapel was a miniature cathedral patterned in the shape of a cross with the organ at one transept, the baptistery at the other, and a semicircular apse with a highly carved pulpit and a cross that was at least eight feet high. Somerset had spared no money in this chapel, but for what purpose? There was the damp, musty smell of a room seldom used and a faint coat of dust along the top of the highback cushioned pews.

She realized that this was the high spot on the mansion, the oblong-shaped building that she had viewed from the gardens. The turrets and towers on the corners of the building intrigued her, the spire on the roof puzzled her. Now she knew it rose above the chapel. Had Somerset built this sanctuary to please his wife? Or his own ego? Did Charles even know it existed, or had he been brought onto the property as Lord Somerset's personal priest?

Her mind raced. The guests had agreed to spend Sunday sharing the great writings of the poets of the Lake District. In the early afternoon, they would gather on the stone benches and feast on the picnic prepared by Audrey and cheer the ongoing men's competition on the badminton court. With Rachel's discovery of the Somerset Chapel, they could really make it a proper Sunday. She would ask Sinclair to play the organ, Chandler to play his violin again, Lenora to sing. Perhaps "Ave Maria," since that was her favorite. And Charles, the man banished to the North Country, could stand behind a pulpit, and Chaplain Wong could offer the benediction.

The organ music stopped. Sinclair turned and discovered her sitting there. "Rachel. I thought I was alone."

"Don't stop playing on my account."

He grinned. "My playing leaves a lot to the imagination."

"I didn't know you played."

He came down the aisle and sat beside her. "Mary tried to teach me a song or two."

"Sinclair, I have a plan for Sunday."

"Do you now?"

And so she told him. He nodded in agreement. "But Chaplain Wong and Miss Silverman are leaving early Saturday morning before the Scafell hike. One of Inspector Farland's men is driving them into Heathrow."

"I'd forgotten in the excitement. That means Lenora is going back to being Cho-Cho-San in *Madame Butterfly*."

"And Wong is heading back to his post in the Gulf."

"You liked them, didn't you, Sinclair?"

"Especially Wong. He makes good company. But you need to know,

Inspector Farland intends to have their luggage thoroughly inspected at Heathrow."

"That's awful."

"That's necessary. He wants their forwarding addresses."

"Try Rome and the army."

He smiled. "Don't be offended. I'd rather they be cleared that way, wouldn't you? Neither Farland nor I expect any problem for Wong or Miss Silverman. It's a safeguard really."

"Then why all the fuss?"

"There will be a reckoning day when Lord Somerset gets back and finds paintings worth millions missing. We're personal friends—I should have told you, but I was backed against a retaining wall. I wanted to be at the reunion with you. But I promised Somerset I would be here to watch over his art collection."

"A heart divided," she said. "What is Somerset like?"

"James? He's very wealthy, of course, protective of his art collection. Less protective of his wife, Agnes—although he provides for her liberally and would be lost without her."

She turned to a safer topic. "Why did you come up here?"

"I was looking for the missing paintings."

"Sinclair, you shouldn't wander off alone like that."

He laughed. "And what brought you up to the chapel?"

"Curiosity."

"Mine went wild, too. I can't believe those paintings left the property. How could they, do you think?"

"What about the garden supply truck that came on the grounds the morning after we arrived? And Audrey tells me there have been two food deliveries."

He slapped his forehead with his broad hand. "The garden truck! That's how Inspector Farland brought in his men. Of course, two paintings could go out the same way."

"But it doesn't make sense. We've been gone for hours each day, plenty of time for someone to break in. Why not rob the mansion when it's empty? Why fill it up with so many guests?"

He scowled severely. "Because one of your guests may be involved. Or—and I've mulled this over in my sleep—one of the guests may be planted here deliberately, in an act of vengeance."

She shuddered. "That kind of thinking points back to—"

He touched her lips, a sadness suddenly touching his expression.

"Whatever happens, a friend may be involved. Your friend or mine."

She allowed his comforting caress. "I wish we had canceled this reunion."

Gently he pulled away, cupped her chin, looked down into her face. "That's like wishing away our chance to know each other again. That's what is important to me right now. But as far as I'm concerned, you pulled it off, Rachel. Your guests seem happy. You're holding up—I hope Timothy thinks so when he sees you. I asked him to join us when we climb the fells on Saturday."

"Don't let anything happen to you, Sinclair."

"I won't. That's why I asked Timothy to join us. I think it wise to have a doctor along. He's an excellent climber as well."

"You are expecting trouble on the mountain?"

"Aren't you? I'm just sorry you can't take the climb with us. You love climbing. You won't mind being left here alone?"

"Audrey will be here with her pots and pans to defend me. And surely Eileen won't take Becki on a climb like that. Don't worry. It's the art collection that's in danger. Not me. I still think everything is going to be all right. Maybe Inspector Farland has wasted his time sending men here."

"Wasted?" he challenged. "Someone did take those paintings."

"But nothing horrible as I expected. No gang of thieves breaking in on us."

"Rachel, anyone who knows our schedule so far knows that we will be gone on Friday and Saturday. I think I should stay here when you take the Lake Windermere cruise tomorrow."

She clasped his hand. "No, I want you there with me."

He sighed, expelling the air from his lungs. "Are you up to talking about Morrie, as in where did he go this morning?"

She pushed her fears aside. "He went off on his bicycle quite early. The Reynolds left right after that. I'm certain they weren't together. I don't think Morrie really wants to face Eileen and Becki again this morning. The child is really upset."

"Perhaps that was just an excuse."

"Now you're trying to worry me again."

"Morrie and Sean Larkins are obviously at odds. And Sean and his girlfriend, Jude, are not the adoring couple that he wants us to believe. What kind of a student was he, Rachel?"

"Sean? He was never my student."

"What? He told me he took your Chaucer class."

"And I told him I never taught Chaucer."

He squeezed her hand. "Sean is looking for an excuse to avoid the climb on Saturday, but I want him where I can keep my eye on him. You're not to be here alone with him on Saturday."

"Inspector Farland's orders?"

"No, mine."

The sun shining through the stained glass windows formed its own shadowed reflection on Sinclair's handsome face. She wanted to talk about them, to forget everything else. "It has been a strange reunion," she said. "Will any good come out of it?"

"Haven't you discovered your answers yet? I've watched you these last few days, and I'm convinced that as a teacher you left a deep impression on your students."

"Sinclair, did you know I never intended to be a teacher?"

"You didn't?"

"Being a university professor was my sister's goal. Apart from Larea, I would have left the great books of literature on the shelf in my parents' study. But Larea was ill, and I would read to her for hours at a time. The Brontë sisters and Milton. George Eliot. Dickens. Thackeray. We'd laugh about the styles and the way people talked in the Victorian period. We spent so much time reading together that I started loving literature."

His somber eyes grew serious. "What did you want to do?"

She squinted as she glanced up at the windows. "Honestly?"

"Honestly."

"I wanted to climb mountains. Swim rivers. Win Olympic medals. Be famous in the sports world. I didn't want to follow the McCully tradition at the university."

"In my year on campus with you, I envied your popularity with the students. To me, you were a born teacher. What changed your mind about the mountains and rivers and medals?"

"My sister's illness. . .her death."

Their eyes locked. "I could never get you to talk about her."

"When I do, the pain seems raw again."

"Rachel, no one knows we're up here in the chapel. We can stay here the rest of the day if we have to. There are no demands on our time. It seems a good place to talk about what happened. I've waited a long time for some answers."

"Big Ben?" she whispered.

"You told me it no longer mattered. It does to me, Rachel."

She managed to get her words beyond the lump in her throat. "You wanted children; I didn't. It is as simple as that."

"I don't believe that. You adore children. I've watched you with Rebecca. You would have made such a wonderful mother."

She shook her head. "I decided against children long before I met you. I could never bring myself to tell you why, not when being a father was so important to you. I planned to tell you the truth when we met under Big Ben. Do you remember telling me that Blake had cystic fibrosis?"

She watched his expression change from firmness to bewilderment. From confusion to understanding. "Not meeting me under Big Ben has something to do with cystic fibrosis?"

"It ran in my family, too."

"What? You should have told me."

"My sister died from complications from that miserable disease. I could have been a carrier—"

"We could have talked about it."

"You would have tried to convince me that it didn't matter. It did to me, Sinclair."

"Genetic defects should have mattered to me, too," he said. "But I wanted a son so desperately that I risked being a father. Blake suffered from that. After that, Mary and I decided against more children. Rachel. . .I want to know more about your sister."

She nodded and found her voice. "It was a terrible struggle growing up with a sick sibling. Even at the university, few people knew what was going on. Mother considered Larea's illness a private affair. Mother didn't intend for it to become a shameful matter for me, but I decided it was my fault. I felt guilty that I was well and Larea wasn't. So I started spending long hours reading to her. I knew she would never be well enough to follow her dream. We both tried to protect our parents, pretending that Larea would get well."

"You tucked all that inside?"

"I was younger, but I was the strong one—off skiing and climbing and swimming. And she wanted to know all about it. We spent hours on her bed just talking. We were great friends."

"She certainly changed your life."

"I hated losing her, but my sister never lost hope. She believed she would one day be well enough to run and climb and teach. She was determined to carry on the family tradition and make it a third generation of McCully teachers on campus."

"Is that why you took up her dream?"

"Partly."

"Did you ever qualify for an Olympic team?"

"Yes, I did. I'd been away for a week at one of our training bases. When I got home from skiing, I burst into the house, anxious to share my time with Larea—she lived for those times. I can still remember crying out, 'Larea, I'm home.'"

He slipped his arm around the back of the chapel pew, barely touching her shoulders. She felt comforted by his nearness. "I kept shouting, and there was no answer. I started up the steps and saw my mother at the top of the stairs leaning over the banister. 'Your sister is dead, Rachel. And if you had been home two days ago, like you promised, you would have been here in time.'"

He stiffened. "What a cruel way to tell you."

"Mother was hurting. Devastated. I ran up the stairs and brushed past her into Larea's room—and it was empty."

"And right then you gave up your own plans?"

"Circumstances changed my plans. By the time the funeral was over, I had missed the ski camp and the chance for the team. Back then the games were every four years. By then I could have my university degree in English, and that's what I did. If it hadn't been for Larea's love of literature, I would never have found my way down the mountain slopes into the classroom."

"She really influenced your life, didn't she?"

Her words came slowly. "Larea could rarely attend church and never climbed mountains. She thrived on good books and music and taught me so much about life and God from the limitations of her own room. And sometimes from her hospital bed."

"I grew up alone, the only child. At least, as a growing lad, I didn't have to lose someone as close as your sister."

You lost Mary and Blake, she thought.

"I hope being a teacher pleased your parents."

"It pleased me. I found I was good at teaching. I figured I'd spend fifteen or twenty years in the classroom and then start traveling and seeing and doing some of the things I dreamed of doing. Then, a year ago, I was diagnosed with leukemia."

"Tell me, did Larea's illness and death have something to do with not meeting me at Big Ben?"

Sitting in the quiet of the Somerset Chapel, Rachel pictured the

Parliament buildings glimmering as they had done that day. She recalled Big Ben ringing out the hour from the Clock Tower. She had stood there, watching him and crying, then caught a boat up the Thames past the Parliament buildings. Big Ben had boomed out in resonant tones again. She could almost feel the spray of the Thames on her face as she had felt it that day.

Now a tear was stealing down her cheek. "Sinclair, I was going to tell you I couldn't marry you."

"Were you going to tell me why?"

"No. It sounded so cold to say I wouldn't marry you because I didn't want to take defective genes into my marriage. I wouldn't bear you any children. Whenever you told me you wanted children, I would go home and cry myself to sleep."

She reached out and straightened his crooked tie as he said, "We missed so much time, didn't we? And yet, if you hadn't walked out of my life, I would never have known Mary. I've been very fortunate. I have loved two women. Rachel, I'm still in love with you."

"I'm a poor risk. This leukemia—I can't make any promises."

"I'm willing to take the risk."

"Sinclair, you haven't been listening to me. It's too late now. I'm a health risk. A remission will only buy me time."

His eyes turned brilliant as he slid closer to her. His arms tightened around her. "I've been listening to my heart. Rachel, I am still in love with you," he repeated. He went on happily, "This Somerset reunion won't last forever."

"Neither will I, Sinclair."

But suddenly she felt utter freedom. Time didn't matter. She went willingly into his arms and lingered there, comforted, content, free to love him again.

∽

Hanley had come to the point that he was hearing the phone ringing even in his sleep. He was fully awake now and winced as it rang again. He took the receiver and gripped it in his hand on the third ring. "Hanley's Pub."

He heard the croak in his own voice and the cold indifferent answer on the other end. "Are they there?"

A lie would net him nothing. "Morrie and Chip arrived a few minutes ago. They're at the table with Bosman now."

Hanley didn't like Didier Bosman, a decolorized man with a devious plan that could ruin all of them. They would end up on the run, and all Hanley wanted was a trip to the Riviera. He had no hankering to hang a Rembrandt in his cramped lodgings. Hanley had less to lose than the rest of them. Take Bosman for instance. What was wrong with being the administrator at the Norbert Museum? If you listened to the man, his stewardship as keeper of famous works of art had failed him. Hanley figured his greed, his revenge, would be his downfall.

But Chadbourne really worried Hanley. Morrie had dragged into the pub, pale and listless, looking like he hadn't slept in a month. He had stalked across the room to Bosman's table without even a nod to Hanley. But then, he didn't know Hadley was working with them.

"Freck is here, too," he announced over the phone. "He said to tell you he took care of the painting."

"Which one? The Monet?"

"Should I ask?"

"No, just tell Bosman I want no mix-up on Saturday night."

Hanley digested the warning personally. How was he to slip away from his wife at the midnight hour? Better to leave the toolsheds unlocked and stay away from the property to save his own skin.

"Sir, Bosman was talking about using the delivery trucks on Monday, maybe driving north into Scotland."

There was an explosion on the other end. He held the phone away from his ear. "Tell Bosman the plans are made. No changes. No delivery trucks."

Hanley pressed the mouthpiece closer again. "My wife—"

"You deal with your wife. Nothing will go wrong."

Hanley's hand trembled as he cradled the phone. He set four goblets on the countertop and filled them. The man on the other end had instructed no liquor, but Hanley needed a chaser, and from the looks of the men at the table, they could do with a bracer themselves.

Especially Chadbourne.

As Hanley lifted the tray to carry it to them, a young couple came through the door and stopped by the counter.

"We're pushing our luck, Jillian, coming in here."

"Morrie came in moments ago. I saw him. You know he recommends this place for lunch, Chandler."

The tray in Hanley's hand shook.

The girl eyed him with a smile. "I'm looking for a friend. He comes here frequently. Oh never mind. There he is over there. Is the tray for them?"

Hanley nodded.

"Chandler, you take it. Help this poor man." She sashayed across the room. Hanley stayed on her heels and heard her say, "Morrie, we've been looking everywhere for you. We wanted to talk to you about the Weinberger painting."

"What about it?" Sean Larkins asked.

What about it? Hanley wondered.

Without a hint of a surprise, she smiled at Sean and brightened as she recognized Didier Bosman. "Mr. Bosman, remember me? I'm Jillian Reynolds from the Art Theft Registry in London."

Bosman half stood and smiled politely. He peered at her through his wide, black-rimmed glasses. His thin lips were tight as he answered, "We meet again. So you like eating at Hanley's, too? I often drive up for a meal myself."

Hanley felt as though he had been punched in the pit of his stomach. No one ever drove six hours to Hanley's, Pub. Bosman would hang them all if he said another word.

But the girl kept talking. "I haven't been to the Norbert Museum since that attempted robbery."

"Thanks to you, we've had no more problems. Would you and your husband care to join us?"

Chandler placed a glass in front of each man and then sat down beside his wife and acknowledged the balding butler. "Mr. Freck, no wonder you didn't help serve breakfast this morning. It must be your day off. The coffee lost its flavor without your expertise."

Hanley hovered behind Bosman's chair, waiting for recognition or dismissal. He had to get the message across to Bosman and hit on a feeble plan. "My wife was asking—can you all come back for a midnight supper Saturday?"

Bosman drummed his fingers on the goblet, his gaze sharp. "If you'd be so good as to tell me what's on the menu on Saturday."

Twenty paintings from Lord Somerset's collection, Hanley thought. "My wife's special."

"If we can't make it by twelve, what about one? Would that be convenient, Hanley?"

"I'll check. And you, Mr. Chadbourne?"

Morrie shoved back his chair. "I have other plans."

Chapter 21

Hills and dales surrounded Lake Windermere with the higher blue-green mountains rising in the north and the gentle rolling hills to the south filled with spring daffodils. An early morning mist had risen, leaving the lake an electrifying blue like Becki's eyes. The sun glistened across the tranquil waters, turning the crest of the ripples into glittering diamonds.

The Daffodil, their sleek luxurious motor yacht, lay anchored at the end of a long wooden dock—Twenty-five tons of grace with a resident chef and an area for sunbathing. As they waited to board for an all-day cruise, Rachel turned to Jillian. "Jillian, you're not worried about seasickness, are you? I promise, the lake is so calm."

"It's another kind of sickness. I've been ill every morning since we arrived at the Somerset Estates."

"You don't mean? Oh dear. Does Chandler know?"

"I didn't dare tell him before we came; but once I do, he'll be ecstatic. He wants to be a father."

"I think he will make a wonderful parent."

"That's what I think about you, watching you with Rebecca. You should have been a mother, Dr. McCully."

"Even if I had married, there would have been no children."

"You're so adamant!"

She moistened her lips. "My sister was ill with cystic fibrosis all her life. When she died, I vowed I would never have a child. Treatment is much better today. Patients live longer. But my parents knew their pregnancies would be high risk. They took the chance—I wouldn't do that to a child of mine."

Jillian placed her hand gently on Rachel's arm. "It is strange," she mused. "This exact same group will never meet again. But we will always hold good memories, won't we?"

"Interesting ones, albeit tainted with stolen art."

"Morrie was afraid of something like that. That's why he came to the Art Theft Registry and asked for our help."

"He did?"

"Yes, he said he wanted to stop a robbery. It will take months to prove it, but initial checks at the registry indicate that Morrie is right about the Weinberger. We're petitioning the courts to take that painting. That means Lord Somerset may have to find a replacement picture for over his fireplace."

Her gaze went to the group again. "Tuesday we'll be going our separate ways. But, Dr. McCully, I have a feeling there's one person here who won't be slipping out of your life again."

Rachel felt her checks blaze. "I don't see him yet. Maybe he's off buying my birthday cake."

"I rather thought it would be difficult to surprise you. At least pretend. Sinclair is planning a birthday party for you at dinner. You mustn't disappoint him. The cake—that's when everything fell into place for me about the two of you." She laughed, her sapphire eyes glowing. "It's funny, Dr. McCully. I never noticed Don Wakefield during my three weeks in your classroom."

Rachel bantered back. "In a way, Jillian, I really wish you had been in my classroom."

"In a way, I feel like I have been. I hated using a lie to gain entry into the Somerset Estates. But in my line of work, we do use devious ways to track down missing masterpieces."

❦

The Daffodil launched at nine, only moments after Sinclair and the cake were safely on board. They navigated around islands of trees in the center of the lake, glided past acres of gardens along the lakeshore, passed bustling market towns and villages perched on the banks of the lake, and to Becki's delight, glided past Hill Top Farm on the western shore.

Rachel strolled casually along the rail, talking to her guests, knowing that one of them could be an art thief. Any one of them could leave the Somerset Estates with a framed two mil in a suitcase or be led away by Inspector Farland at Heathrow and booked as a common criminal. That was the agreement with Lord Somerset, should a robbery occur: No one would be taken into custody at the mansion. A scandal would be avoided at all costs.

As Rachel moved along the rail, she thought how pleasant it was being with these young adults. She would spend the day with them, marveling at the scenery, conversing with them as they sunbathed or swam, and eat beside them on the flying bridge. Only a few years—twelve at most—had passed since they had left her classroom, but Rachel clearly remembered their faces. Yet the details of how they acted or dressed on campus seemed vague, except for Amanda in her hats, Chaplain Wong in his baggy khakis, and Sara like a walking model. Wong was the class joker. Jude, the rebel. Lydia, the poor girl working her way through university. And Janet, her gifted, happy-go-lucky poet.

How quickly Rachel had slipped back into her teacher's role, expounding on Wordsworth and Coleridge in the evenings, reminding them of how often she had prayed for them, and discovering that they had left an imprint on her own life. They had come into her life for brief periods, and now her only commitment to them was friendship. Even Becki would soon put away the Beatrix Potter books, their charming moments with rabbits and squirrels almost gone.

Since the robbery, she had dreamed about Scotland Yard mug shots. All of their faces were there, young as they had been on campus. She wanted them to be the carefree, frolicsome students that she remembered. Even the glare of the sun on their faces now—mature faces with the air of innocence gone—were important to her.

Sleep had been troublesome during her illness, but the stolen Monet and Degas had given her fitful nights of dreaming as she flitted through the mansion in a negligee and gown searching for missing paintings and discovering a sonnet or haiku or simple message hanging in their place: *Something of beauty is gone forever. The Tales of the Missing Monet. The Rhyme of the Lost Museum.* She tried to shake free of her worries. She wanted to take mental snapshots of her students and guests back to Wakefield Cottage. Suddenly she laughed at herself. She sounded ancient, not thirty-eight.

And still laughing, she heard Sara Arnold say, "Why not share your joke with me, Dr. McCully?"

She slipped her arm around Sara's slim shoulders. "And why don't you tell me what you have been doing since graduation?"

"Running marathons in the fight against cancer. I ran the last one for Lydia—maybe I'll do one for you someday."

Not thirty minutes later, while they were waiting for the lunch bell, Rachel found Lydia leaning against the rail watching a sailboat moving effortlessly across the water with its sails into the wind.

"It's so beautiful here, Rachel. It reminds me of John Keats: 'A thing of beauty is a joy forever.'"

"That was always one of your favorite lines, and mine. Did you recall that Keats died as a young man? He wrote of beauty, Lydia, but he also feared dying. Feared he would cease to be. He was afraid of leaving no immortal work behind him. I have wrestled with thoughts like that since I knew about my leukemia."

"Are you afraid?" she whispered.

"Only of not being all I could be and of not being here next week, next year."

"I had cancer, too."

"I know. Sara told me. She said she ran the Los Angeles marathon in the fight against cancer."

"Yes, I was proud of her."

"She said she ran it for you, Lydia."

"For me? She knows? She knows I had a mastectomy?"

"And she knows that you paid her tuition at the university. Your parents told her."

"Why? They agreed we would never tell her."

"They were afraid you might die with your cancer. They wanted Sara to know the truth. The whole truth, Lydia."

"How can I tell her who I am? We're constantly at odds."

"Why do the two of you keep on pretending? If you run out of time, Lydia, she may never know who she really is. Who you are. This reunion could be a time of healing for both of you."

∽

The crew served their three-course lunch on the aft deck with a choice of smoked salmon smothered with mint and seasonal vegetables or chunks of Lakeland lamb with an apricot-almond sauce for their main dish. Jude and Sara were still in their swimsuits; Jude with her skin turning pink, Sara with an even tan. They had just come back on board from waterskiing. Kevin, who had gone with them, was toweling himself down, his thick, blond hair clinging to his scalp. Amanda stood by his side, holding out his T-shirt and fretting that swimming had not been good for his facial wounds.

As the afternoon lake winds died down, dusk crept in slowly, eerily. The setting sun hovered on the horizon. The hills turned to purple-rimmed shadows. And then they feasted again, this time on smoked trout and new potatoes and curried chicken with ginger and garlic. Dressed to the nines, they ate in the dining room with its wide viewing windows.

Sinclair sat on Rachel's right, Kevin on her left, wearing his bright yellow dress shirt. Morrie remained distant, moody, his eyes on Becki. Rachel tried to draw him back as the others jostled about campus life and teased her about her love of hiking.

Amanda smiled at Kevin. "You should have been at university with us. Dr. McCully always made learning fun."

He gave Amanda a boyish grin. "I like the sound of her mountain trips better than a class on poetry."

"Kevin, the minute my classes were over on Friday, I headed right for a campground or a mountain trail," Rachel said. "Eileen and Amanda went with me a couple of times. Several students did."

"But why take students with you?" Sean asked. "I would have thought you'd like to be alone."

"They were my life. The classroom went with us. We'd sit under giant redwoods and talk about great writers and thinkers and preachers. Sometimes we didn't get back for evening chapel."

"That's what some of the students liked about her, Sean," Sinclair told him. "Rachel was willing to take her faith beyond the pew and the school chapel."

She laughed. "Sinclair, you know some of the faculty opposed my unorthodox ways. Just ask Misty Owens here. But students opened up. The mountains and the rivers set them free to discuss their fears. Their hopes. A lot of sonnets came out of those trips. I still have copies of the poems Lydia wrote."

"Lydia wrote poetry?" Sara asked.

"Poems about you, Sara. You should ask her about them."

Sara stared at her sister. "What were they about, Lydia?"

Rachel waited, prayed.

From deep inside, Lydia found her strength. Without wavering, she said, "About a lost child. An empty womb. A dead heart."

Sara gave an impatient shrug. "Oh that sounds morbid, Lydia."

"No, I wrote them out of my love for you."

To break the silence that fell over them, Kevin turned to Rachel and said privately, "I didn't want to come to this reunion. I didn't think I'd be welcomed here after I had a run-in with Lord Somerset over a banking incident."

"But I am glad you came. You're very fond of Amanda."

"Yes, but I'm tired of my mother asking me if I've found the right girl yet. I've found her, but I don't dare let them meet. She'd be so busy lecturing us on immorality that I'd have a tough time convincing Mother that the one thing I want to do is to get married and spend the rest of my life with Amanda Pennyman."

"And your mother would disapprove of that?"

"Not about—"

Before he could finish his sentence, Timothy Whitesaul slipped into the chair that Sinclair had vacated. "Happy birthday, Rachel."

She patted his hand. "You made it possible with your miracle pills! It's been such a long journey. But I've always known that even in death, I would have a refuge."

"It will be awhile before you take that refuge."

"Is that a promise, Timothy?"

"It's a known fact." His broad face creased with a smile. "Your white blood count is coming down. Way down. Normal, in fact. Sinclair convinced me to save the news for a birthday present. So. . .happy birthday, Rachel."

"You mean—"

"Your leukemia is in remission. But we'll keep watching that shadow on your lung. Like I tell all my patients, now is the time to go skydiving or to take up the Argentine Tango."

She was too happy to cry. "I won't get that radical."

She glanced up as Sinclair placed the cake in front of her. Their eyes locked.

"I love you," he mouthed. "Happy birthday, darling."

As Dr. Whitesaul munched his first bite of cake, he turned to Sara and Lydia Arnold. "Rachel tells me you are sisters."

Sara gave him a defiant toss of her head. "We're trapped in the same bloodline—actually we're trapped in Lydia's lies." Tears brimmed. "She doesn't have the courage to admit who I really am."

"No, you're wrong, Sara." All eyes turned on Lydia. She glanced at Rachel and then said, "We're not sisters. You are much more important to me, Sara. You are my daughter."

Sara turned chalk white, her lower lip trembling. Finally she stumbled to her feet and moved toward Lydia. "Mother," she whispered.

"Forgive me, Sara." Lydia held out her hands.

Sara gripped them and, weeping, the two embraced.

Dusk kept slipping away as the rising moon sent new streamers of light across the rippling lake. Rachel was still slicing the birthday cake when a sudden wind squall hit without warning. Rain clouds swept in.

Dusk turned to a blackened sky, and rain pelted against the boat, rocking it unsteadily. The yacht tilted precariously starboard as plates full of birthday cake slid across the table and crashed to the floor.

On the deck, crew members ran toward the bow of the yacht. The captain barked his orders over the intercom. Kevin and Morrie were on their feet at once, running out of the dining room, Sean and Jude on their heels. Sinclair shoved back his chair and whispered to Rachel, "Wait in here."

Along the shoreline, Rachel could see the villagers hurrying to batten down their thatched roofs. Leaves blew like tumbleweeds. Tree limbs swayed, splintered, crashed. The sheep were skittish in the pasture, running blindly into the fences.

The storm whipped across the lake, turning the tranquil waters into rolling waves. Sailboats dipped with the waves, cutting the surface with their riggings. Rachel stood frozen by the window, watching the frantic move to lower the sails.

The Daffodil listed with the wind, tossed about without a rudder. As the captain fought the mechanical difficulties, he attempted to radio his position. Static filled the airwaves. Another violent gust of wind swept over them. Another rolling wave stirred the lake waters. The next swell lifted the yacht and sent it crashing against a rowboat, capsizing it. The occupants sank beneath the waters, struggled to the surface.

Screams erupted, "Man overboard! Man overboard!"

Rachel saw Amanda leaning over the rail, crying pitifully. She made her way toward the deck. "Go back, Rachel," Sinclair cried. "Stay inside the cabin. I'll come back for you."

Rachel shook her head and slid across the deck until she reached them. "What did we hit, Sinclair?" she demanded.

"A rowboat. Two or three passengers. At least that many heads bobbing. I've never seen a squall like this one—now take Amanda and go back inside."

Rachel shivered in the drenching rain and stared down into the semidarkness as the crew dragged the injured on board. Rachel pulled Amanda against her. "What is it, Amanda?"

"Kevin is gone. I saw him go overboard."

Beyond the damaged rowboat, a long figure bobbed facedown in the water. Rachel recognized the yellow shirt, the blond hair. She pointed. "There! That has to be Kevin!"

Sinclair stripped to his waist, kicked off his shoes, and dove off the front of the yacht. They watched him surface, gulp in more air, and plunge beneath the waters again. When he surfaced this time, he had locked his arm around the chest of a man and was towing him toward the yacht. Willing hands reached out to hoist Kevin Nolan and Sinclair back on board the rocking vessel.

But the cheer of the rescue caught in their throats.

Kevin lay on the deck—limp, pale, waterlogged.

Chapter 22

Rachel was up early to watch the mountain climbers gather in the lobby. The men were going in full force, but she was surprised to see Amanda Pennyman hurrying down the stairs in her hiking boots, sun goggles around her neck.

"Amanda, are you going on the climb, too?" she asked her.

"I have to be there for Kevin. I don't want anything to happen to him again today."

"It won't. Sinclair said that yesterday's storm was unusual. Try to focus in on a twenty-four-hour day. That means no looking back—no rushing ahead."

"I can't forget what happened yesterday. I almost lost Kevin on Lake Windermere."

"I know. That was such a tragic accident."

"I don't think you understand. It was no accident, Dr. McCully. Last night, Kevin told me someone pushed him overboard."

"But, Amanda, everything happened during the storm."

"No, Dr. McCully. Someone deliberately pushed Kevin overboard. We're determined to find out who did it."

The reality hit Rachel. She forced herself to remain calm. To tread lightly. Surely, Amanda was overreacting. Surely—no, she knew that Amanda had told the truth. She formed her words carefully, safely. "I think Kevin means a lot to you."

"He does."

"But you're not married yet?"

She flicked her hair back from her cheek. "You knew?"

"You're still talking about Lee. A bride doesn't talk about another man like that."

Her cheeks flushed. "I wanted Kevin to measure up to Lee."

"Kevin can't measure up to an imagined perfection. Lee was a wonderful young man, Amanda, with his whole future ahead of him. I remember how you grieved for him, but he was the kind of person who would have wanted you to go on with your life."

"How can I? I still blame myself for his death."

"Amanda, did you tell Lee to break the speed limit? Or cut corners too quickly on his motorcycle? You know he was careless behind the wheel. Lee was brilliant, but he took too many risks."

"We quarreled that morning."

"I thought so. We don't get to choose what our last words are with someone we love. Lee would have understood that."

"I think he took his anger out on the motorcycle."

Rachel had known Lee. Known them both. He was an easygoing young man, spirited down to his boots. A risk taker and an honor student. A young man who made friends easily and who had swept Amanda off her feet.

The diamond came three weeks later, just one more of Lee's impulsive decisions. But the motorcycle always came first. He kept it polished even at the cost of keeping his dates on time. But for Amanda, Lee could do no wrong.

In her eyes, he was just about perfect. And in many ways he was. But it was Kevin who mattered now. Amanda had to choose. Or she had to set Kevin free. She had to set both men free.

"Kevin is his own man, Amanda. He loves you, but he can never wear another man's shoes. What is it you like about Kevin?"

She seemed perplexed with the question, as though Rachel McCully of all people would see the qualities in him. "He's honest and kind. He tries to please. He's a hard worker—"

"He's boyish and funny, and very much in love with you. But he feels that Lee is like an albatross around his neck."

"I never meant for that to happen. But, Rachel, he gambles."

"So did Lee in his own way. I thought Kevin was going to a support group, getting help for his gambling."

"He is. Ever since we came to the Somersets', Kevin keeps telling me that Lord Somerset should be in a support group, too."

"With Kevin getting help, you're running out of excuses. I watched you last evening when you thought he wasn't going to wake up."

"I thought he was dead. It was like losing Lee again."

"Amanda, let Lee go, before you force Kevin to walk out on you. He likes being an auditor. You know that, don't you?"

"I want him to do something more glamorous."

"Do you want a makeover or someone who loves you?"

Her voice cracked, trailed. "I'm afraid of commitment. Of something happening to Kevin again."

"Nothing will happen. I promise you. Sinclair and Timothy will be there. And Morrie is an experienced guide in these fells. Go on. Everyone is ready to leave, and Morrie hates waiting for people. If you get tired, stop and rest."

"And if Kevin gets tired?"

"He probably will. It's a demanding climb, and he's still traumatized from yesterday, and still wearing scars from that bombing near Harrods. That's a heavy plate for any young man. So if he gets tired, stop and rest and talk about your future together."

Her smile turned impish. "Dr. McCully, you said I should just think about twenty-four hours at a time."

"I'll make an exception—just this once."

Amanda gave her a quick hug and ran to catch the others. "Wait for me!" she cried.

When Rachel turned, she saw Becki standing by the window with her face pressed to the windowpane.

"Will my daddy be all right?"

She had called Morrie "Daddy." Was there still hope for Eileen and Morrie? Was there hope for the three of them? Becki turned from the window, waiting for her answer.

"Your daddy is a very good climber."

"Somebody tried to hurt Kevin yesterday."

"Oh Becki, who told you that?"

"Timothy Whitesaul."

Rachel thought of the buffeting winds on the high hills. The brooding peaks. The slippery trails. The amateurs climbing with the group today. The weather could change at a moment's notice, change without warning as it had done on the lake yesterday. Another wind-driven rain on the craggy heights could be deadly.

"Everyone will be fine," she said, trying to convince herself.

Becki looked up and shared her secret. "Morrie told me he would sit with me at dinner tonight."

She felt rage. Morrie intended to have the climbers stop off at Hanley's Pub for a late supper. Had he heard Becki correctly? Had he lied deliberately? Rachel swallowed her anger and said gently, "If Morris gave you his word, then he'll certainly get down the mountain safely. Sinclair and Timothy went with him. Nothing will happen."

"Did Sinclair promise to have supper with you, Rachel?" Becki asked.

"Not tonight. He doesn't always remember his appointments, not if he's lost in one of his books. A long time ago, I persuaded him to go on a camping trip with the hiking club."

"Did he keep his promise?"

"He forgot. When I arrived at his apartment, I expected him to be out on the sidewalk with his camping gear, but he was sitting at his kitchen table, reading a book on art restoration. All he could say was, 'Oh Rachel, I forgot.' But I didn't stay mad at him forever."

"You don't think Morrie will keep his promise, do you?"

"I don't know, Becki."

"Did Sinclair make you cry when he didn't keep his promise?"

"A little."

"Maybe I'll cry, too."

Maybe, Rachel thought, *you'll cry a whole lot. Morrie will not be home for dinner.* "Come, why don't we walk in the garden?" she suggested.

❧

Since moving to the Lake District, Morrie had spent many an hour scaling the craggy hills, seeking their grandeur and isolation at a trout stream or within sight of a herd of deer watering by a brook. After yesterday's near tragedy on Lake Windermere, a somber mood swept over the guests. But Morrie determined to keep his promise to the men game enough to tackle the strenuous climb on Scafell Pike. Reaching the summit was the only way for these men to enjoy the true beauty of Lakeland. That was the place for mountaineers and backpackers, for the rock climbers and the locals accustomed to reaching the heights. Today he must inspire these men to break away from the thick gray mist that hovered over the reunion and shrouded the Somerset Estates in darkness.

He was resolute that nothing in the high steep fells of Lakeland would keep the men from climbing. He wanted them to reach the summit, even knowing that one of the guests might not want them all to reach there safely. The pinnacles bred rugged men. Perhaps the climb would unveil the uninvited guest as well, but as he joined the men at the appointed hour, he was shocked to see Jude Alexander standing there in her shabby hiking boots with a backpack slung over her shoulders, and Amanda, smartly dressed and ready for the hike.

Kevin looked less prepared. His face was still colorless from yesterday's mishap. He would keep his eye on Kevin. Until now he had considered Kevin a possible problem. Now he believed differently. Before that first wave hit their yacht, he had seen Kevin tumbling headfirst into the water.

Someone had helped him over the side.

"So the three of you are going with us?" he asked and headed for the cars without waiting for their answers.

They rode through rural countryside on the way to the peaks, over a grassy slope, past a remote river valley, and on to the wooded lowlands and high tarns. The easy part was over as they stepped out of the cars and checked their shoelaces and trail food.

"If you're going to turn back, do so now," Morrie warned them. "Once we start, we keep going."

At his signal, they adjusted their backpacks and began the single file ascent toward the sun. They climbed steadily toward England's highest peak, up toward the crags and cliffs.

Taking a trail break two hours later, they looked up and saw the jagged promontory, a rough, bouldery summit.

"Jude, a person could take quite a fall from there," Sean said.

"You frighten me with your crazy remarks," she said, replacing the cap on her water bottle.

The trail led the group across a footbridge, past a well-kept sheepfold, and up a zigzagging path toward steep fellsides. They took another break at the watercourse where a stream of silvery water tumbled between the gleaming walls of rock.

"Are you still with us?" Morrie asked Amanda.

Amanda shook her head. Her heels had blistered. The pounding of her heart hindered her climb. She looked at Kevin, and he nodded his agreement. "Morrie, Amanda and I are going to wait here until you get back. We've decided to call it a day. We'll wait on the boulders where we saw a herd of red deer watering at the tarn."

Sean eyed them contemptuously. "You're quitting already? We might come down a different trail."

"Then we'll make our own way back."

"No," Sinclair said. "If the others choose another route down, Whitesaul and I will come back this way for you."

Amanda looked exhausted, Kevin even more peaked. Sean shook his head. "What's wrong, Nolan? You can't swim. You can't climb."

"Leave them alone," Morrie warned. "If they can't get to the top, that's no disgrace. Look how far they've come."

Sean shifted his rucksack and started climbing again as Kevin told her, "Amanda, I've lost my wallet."

"Where?"

"I don't know. It was in my rucksack."

"And Sean was walking behind you."

Morrie overheard them. "I'll keep my eyes open. We'll settle this back at the Somersets."

"But what would he want with my wallet?"

"I'm wondering the same thing."

Sinclair gave them a reassuring smile. "Do you have enough water? Trail food?"

"We're set. We're just sorry we can't push any farther."

Sinclair nodded. "You've made a wise choice. Maybe even a safe one." He shaded his eyes to watch the others pushing ahead; then he shook hands with Kevin and followed Morrie up the path.

Progress was slow as they clambered to the heights and stepped from boulder to boulder, but Jude was gutsy, sticking close behind Sean. It was rough work crossing the boulder fields. Sean Larkins was leading the climb now, taking over in his mocking way. Morrie fell behind him, scowling. The man had a volcanic nature, like his own. *They were two of a kind,* he admitted to himself. *Time bombs walking through volcanic ridges.*

Their ascent path to Scafell Pike rose southwestward into the thickly wooded fells, and higher to the barrenness of Scafell Pike. By the last twenty feet, the weather turned. Tempers soared. Sighing winds whipped around the precipitous cliffs. Looking down a kilometer away was another tricky path crowded with hikers.

Looking back, they could see for miles, but a mountain mist was rapidly closing in on them. "The rest of you get started down," Morrie told them after they had rested and eaten. "I want to have a talk with Sean."

Wakefield and Whitesaul had gone only a short distance when they heard the cries of other climbers. They looked back and saw Morrie and Sean wrestling on the edge of the promontory. They ran back up the hill as Morrie's head cracked against the rock. Fists flew. The two toppled, rolled closer to the edge. Morrie was on top now, blood pouring from his temple. He jammed his hand angrily against Sean's jaw, backing him closer to the precipice.

It took both Wakefield and Whitesaul several minutes before they could tear the two men apart. They dragged them to their feet. "What's wrong with you fools?"

"Just a friendly argument, Sinclair." Morrie winced as Whitesaul examined the jagged cut on his temple.

Sinclair shoved Sean ahead of him. "That's a pretty angry scuffle over a friendly argument," he said.

~

Becki and Rachel were waiting for the climbers when they arrived back at the mansion. Morrie was the last one to come through the door. "Morrie," Becki cried.

He turned and frowned. "What are you doing up, smidgen?"

"We were going to have supper together. You promised."

He put his hand to his wound, as though he were willing himself to remember. "I'm sorry. We'll have to make that another time. I am sorry. It was your mother's idea, not mine."

Timothy Whitesaul caught Rebecca on the run, picked her up, and carried her upstairs.

Rachel watched them go and then turned angrily on Morrie. "What has happened to you, Morrie? Must you hurt that child at every turn?"

"I'm trying to protect her, Rachel. We have problems. The safest spot for that child is with her mother."

She retreated. "Morris, you should let Eileen look at that wound."

"I can take care of it." He tried to smile, but the swelling on his face stopped him. "Charles scheduled a chapel service for us tomorrow. So it's up to you to have our guests in bed before midnight," he urged.

"I can't ask them to retire at a certain time. They aren't children. They're on holiday with just a little more time together. The reunion is almost over."

"Thankfully," he said.

"It was your idea to hold the reunion here."

"And it's my job to protect Lord Somerset's property. I didn't think about that enough before the reunion. I've thought a great deal about it since I met my daughter." He fixed his weary eyes on her. "Just help me, Rachel. Make sure the guests retire early. It's important. I'll be staying in the main house this evening in Wong's old room, if you need me."

She shook her head. "The guests have formed some special friendships. Chandler and Kevin have a chess competition going that goes past midnight. The women like sitting up and chatting by the fireside, beneath your Weinberger painting, I might add."

Morrie winced. "It isn't mine yet. It may never be mine. But someone took the Monet and Degas paintings, and now a Rubens is missing. I can't risk something else coming off the walls."

He strolled off, but at the foot of the stairs, he turned back. "Rachel, I'm grateful for what you tried to do. But you do know, don't you, that it will never work out for Eileen and me?"

She bit into her lower lip. "And Becki?"

"I could never be permanent in her life."

~

Charles found Rachel sitting alone in the garden. She was holding a cup of tea and sipping it.

"Good evening," he said. "I see the climbers are back."

"Yes, and they're an irritable lot. Morrie was injured. He didn't say how. And he broke his promise with his daughter so Timothy carried her upstairs."

"I don't like to tell you, but another painting was taken off the wall in the drawing room."

"That's what Morrie said. That narrows it down, doesn't it? Most of the men were gone all day climbing the Scafell Pike."

"But the painting was taken before dawn this morning."

"Then Morrie knew before he left for the climb? So someone is really laughing in our faces."

"No, someone is trying to distract us. To keep us from suspecting anything major."

"And I'm just worried about Morrie and the man he has become. He has a child, and it doesn't seem to matter to him."

Charles sat beside her. "I gather he just isn't very keen on God either. He doesn't like sermons, so I can't practice mine on him."

"And I try to engage him in discussions on Michelangelo's Sistine Chapel and on the Italian Renaissance. Maybe through the paintings, he may discover the truth for himself."

"My dear child, 'more things are wrought by prayer—'"

She laughed lightly, grateful for Charles and his wise ways. Together they quoted Alfred Lord Tennyson, 'Than this old world dreams of.'"

"So you see, my dear, I know the poets, too."

"Charles, you have one of those hearts of gold."

He threw back his head, stretching the flabby skin of his neck, and roared with laughter. "Sometimes, dear child, I still see myself as a man with a heart of stone."

"You're much too kind for that. Maybe a polished stone with one side of the stone stamped 'to Ireland with love.' Or with Conan O'Reilly's name. I still marvel at all you did for him. Most people would shun an Irish terrorist."

"Did you know my daughter died in Ireland at the hands of terrorists?"

"Oh Charles."

"So you see, my dear, God has a lot of polishing to do on this hard heart of mine. The rough edges are being hewn away. Hacked sometimes. I miss my parish, but I have the sky and earth for my sanctuary. And little ones like Rebecca as a friend."

"And the rest of us as part of your flock?"

His eyes met hers again, blue as the larkspurs. "One prodigal at a time. I am a fortunate man. And you are a fortunate woman."

"How so?"

"Chaplain Wong and I have had some good chats. You left a great impression on him."

"On Bill? Really? He was the class joker at the university. He took my classes just to meet graduation requirements."

"I daresay life is more serious for him now. Did you know that he credits you for choosing the chaplaincy?"

"Me? We never discussed his becoming an army chaplain."

"But you told him there was more to life than daffodils and sonnets."

"I had to, Charles. Bill was not all that keen on studying literature— except he liked writing poetry."

"Oh, he enjoyed your classes at least in retrospect. But what he most remembers—so he tells me—is that day on the mountain trails when you prayed with him. He did a turnaround after that. Said you told him to choose a career that would put him in the thick of ministry."

"But we never discussed the army."

"But you told him to be a good soldier for Jesus Christ."

Her eyes misted. "When he leaves here, he is going on reassignment— hopefully, home to his wife and children."

Charles brushed the soil from his hands and touched her arm. "No, his posting is back to the Gulf."

"On the front lines? Surely not with the ground forces or the Army Rangers?"

"If there are covert operations still going on, he would want to be with them. He's parachuted in with them before. I had that privilege in World War II. Jumping with British commandos as their chaplain. I understand Bill."

"Charles, he might get killed."

"He wants to be with the soldiers—in the thick of ministry." Charles knuckled a tear from her cheek. "He wants to leave a safe and goodly heritage for his children. He told me that if anything happens to him that I was to thank you for touching his life and leading him to Jesus."

"Nothing has happened to him yet, Charles."

"I know. But my memory gets shabby now and then, and I might forget my promise—should it ever be needed."

Over the lump in her throat, she said, "Thank you for telling me. Charles, I will miss you when this reunion is over. I hope you will come to Wakefield Cottage to see me."

"I'd like that."

"There's a centuries-old church there. Rarely used. A cleric visits once in a while, but not since I've been there. Why don't you—"

"The banished shepherd?" he interrupted.

"You could come. It doesn't have to be in an official capacity. The villagers would repay you in food and lodging."

"That's how I began my ministry. Perhaps I could end it in the same way. Have they had any wedding ceremonies there lately?"

"No, and no young couples planning one that I know of."

"I have a couple in mind."

"Amanda and Kevin!"

"That would be good," he said. "But I have someone even more special in mind. I think the laws and my licenser would still permit me to marry someone. They banished me to the North, but they didn't strip away my rights."

"You mean me." She flushed scarlet. "Charles, it's ever so beautiful when the sun comes up over Stradbury Square."

"I'd be up to meet it."

"You could have your own garden, or help me with mine."

"But once you're well, you'll be going home again."

"No. I want to stay there forever. But you probably won't want to leave the Somerset Estates or these lovely gardens."

A dark cloud crossed his face, veiled his kindly expression. "Perhaps when this is all over, the property will be vacated or turned over to the National Trust."

"Why would you say a thing like that? The Somersets have no plans to leave."

He smiled. "Mrs. Somerset is not well. She finds this forced isolation deplorable. But I have no right to put an added burden on you. You don't even know them."

She stood and looked around her. "Nor envy them. It's magnificent here but not cozy like my Wakefield Cottage."

He tucked her arm in his, and they walked down the bricked pathway toward the main house. "You have brought a measure of sunshine to this place. I wish Mrs. Somerset could have been part of it. She is such a lonely old woman. Old like I am."

Rachel walked a few more steps and stopped. She was worried and didn't know why. How could she explain the brooding premonition to Charles? She looked up at the magnificent mansion and felt nothing but dark, shadowed oppression. "Morrie wants me to have all of the guests in bed tonight before midnight. He's adamant about it," she said.

"So that is the hour? Take his advice. Do what he says."

"Then our lives are at risk?"

He squeezed her hand. "Only if you interfere. Our prodigal son is merely hours from disaster. But there are so many twists and turns for a man on a redemptive journey. We have to believe that, in the end, he will make the right choices."

Chapter 23

Midnight! Rachel listened for the sounds of silence, wanting them. Wanting everyone to be safely asleep. She heard instead the whisper of the wind, the roll of distant thunder, the rumble of a heavy truck on the country road so seldom heard at this hour. She strained to hear the hollow sounds of the mansion, the creaking of steps, the mumble of voices, and would have welcomed some outcry, some din or racket, the clatter of a dish to reassure her that she did not keep vigil alone.

At the scratching of a tree branch against her windowpane, she caught her breath and slipped through the darkness to her open window. Crickets sang. A possum rattled across the top of the balcony rail. Two shadowy figures stole across the back of the property. They stepped cautiously. Halted. Drew back into the chimerical darkness of the pine trees. She strained her eyes, waiting. Then movement again as they skirted the flower beds.

Clammy fear tugged at her. She hurried through the adjoining bathroom into Eileen's room. "Eileen. Eileen, I need your help."

Only Becki lay in a curled knot on the big bed. She went over and kissed the damp brow of the sleeping child. *Where? Where is your mommy?* she wondered.

She cracked the door. Across the corridor came an uneven snore. Down the hall the flush of a toilet, the running of water. And midway down the corridor she saw someone. Eileen. Her hand on the doorknob to Morrie's room. Impulsively, Rachel darted out, closing the gap between them.

"Eileen, that is not the way to win him back."

Eileen's grip on the doorknob slackened.

"Morrie is in trouble, Eileen. You can't help him that way."

"What way, Rachel? I know how it must look, but I want to have it out with him. I'm sick of the way he's treating Becki."

"Dear Eileen, you can't force him to love her."

"That's what you intended when you invited us to come."

Rachel felt stunned. "I know. . .and I was wrong. I am so sorry."

"It hurts. He doesn't believe that Becki is his own child—"

"He knows. But he's not the Morrie we knew. Not the young man who came down the hills just weeks ago, running over to me there at the lake. Carefree. Jaunty. Laughing. He is so ill-tempered now—and worried and obsessed with that painting."

"He was always vulnerable, but he's become a puzzle to me."

"To both of us, Eileen. You were married to him. Can you trust him for one more thing?"

"As Becki's father? No."

"I mean, can you still trust his judgment? Can you trust him to stop whatever mischief is going on at this reunion? We need to talk to Morrie. Confront him for his own sake."

A grumpy, sleepy voice said, "I told you that man is trouble. Told you that from the beginning, Miss Rachel."

Startled, they turned and saw Audrey peeking out her bedroom door, her cotton nightie rumpled, her upper teeth missing. She covered her mouth and mumbled, "Miss Rachel, are you all right?"

"I'm fine. I just have to find Morrie."

Audrey glanced apologetically at Eileen. "He's been prowling around all night. Sneaking some old lady up the stairs. Older than me," she explained.

Puzzled, Rachel asked, "A stranger? Not one of our guests?"

"Came in thirty minutes ago. Mr. Chadbourne had me make up the master bedroom—said he could trust me to help him. Wasn't to my liking. But he has been nice to me these last few days. Making it a point to thank me for my meals and for being friends to Becki and to Miss Eileen here. Who wouldn't be nice—"

"The woman," Rachel said impatiently. "Tell me about her."

"Not much to tell. We had to help the poor soul up the stairs. She stopped almost every step to catch her breath. 'Course that helped me breathe, too, what with not knowing what I was into with that Mr. Morrie. He's a charmer with all that flattery." She looked disgusted with herself. "I even get taken by it."

"Audrey, who is the woman?"

"She didn't give any name. About dug the skin off my hand, she held so tight. Just said she was glad to be home again. Sweet face. Tried to smile. Acted like the lady of the house—fancy enough clothes." She paused. "Touched the things on the dresser, like they were hers. Ran her hands over the bedpost. Fluffed her pillow like she'd done it before. I've done right by her. I've been looking in on her. She's still breathing."

Worry clouded Eileen's face even more. "Rachel, do you think it's Lord Somerset's wife?"

"Impossible. The cruise ship is halfway around the world."

"Makes no matter to me, Miss Rachel. After I helped her into bed, I asked Mr. Chadbourne about her. He just stomped off back downstairs."

Eileen stared at his closed door. "He's not in his room?"

"His room is empty. No one has slept in that bed," she huffed, forgetting to keep her nearly toothless mouth covered. "See for yourself, if you don't believe me."

Rachel touched Audrey's shoulder. "We believe you. I'm going downstairs and have a look around. Morrie can't be far."

"I'll go with you," Eileen offered.

Rachel suppressed a chuckle. "In that robe and slippers? Go back to the room and stay with Becki. And take Audrey with you."

"I am not going anywhere, not without my teeth."

"Then get them. Eileen, maybe you should look in on the woman. Make certain she's all right. After that, let her rest."

Rachel went down the grand staircase and followed the light into the smoking room. The drapes were drawn back from the wide French windows, and the vast backyard eerily lit with the night lanterns that surrounded the property.

Chandler and Kevin were bent over the chessboard in the far corner. At the sight of her, Chandler grinned. "Kevin is winning so we can stop if you want us to, Dr. McCully," he offered.

She crossed the room to them, feeling exhausted inside. "It looks like we're all suffering from insomnia this evening."

Chandler nodded. "Sinclair asked us to keep a watch here. He's out patrolling the property. Whitesaul is with him."

Rachel gave a sigh of relief. "Then it was Sinclair and Timothy I saw out in the garden." She glanced at their game board. "Please. Go on with your chess game."

"Actually we don't even remember whose turn it is. Do we, Chan? We're busy keeping an eye on Mr. Freck. The old butler's been busy dusting the paintings. Going from room to room."

"At this hour, Kevin?"

"It may be more than dusting, Rachel." Chandler pointed to the painting of Lord Nelson on the wall above them. He picked up a flashlight and beamed it on an iridescent marking on the gilded frame. For a second, it glowed.

"What a strange thing to do to an expensive frame."

"Not odd, if you are tagging it for easy identification."

She braced her hand on the table, her uneasiness growing. Kevin patted her hand. "Don't worry, Dr. McCully. The marking will wash off. So far we've found three paintings in this room marked that way. As soon as Freck decides to call it a day, we're going to check the other rooms."

"So it hasn't been just chess that keeps you up late."

"No. Jillian asked us to help out this way. She had to go into the Art Theft Registry yesterday with more pictures."

"A long drive."

"The inspector arranged for a private plane. She'll be back later this morning." He grinned. "By the way, I insisted that she make an appointment with an obstetrician while she's in London. I want Jillian and our baby to have the best of care."

She felt the smile creep along her cheek. "You know then?"

The roar of a truck on the country road caught their attention. Rachel glanced at her watch: *Twelve-fifty*. She had forgotten the truck. Thought it long past the mansion. Had it parked on the lonely road and waited? Yes, it was definitely coming closer, turning on the corner by the side of the mansion.

Chandler glanced out the windows. "Company?"

"We'll know soon. It's driving our way without headlights. I have to find Morrie."

"You can stop looking, Rachel." Chandler pointed to his cell phone. "Charles called. Morrie went out the side gate just before you came downstairs."

"Then he's—" Hot tears burned her eyes. "Why didn't Sinclair or Charles stop him?"

"I don't know, but back home we would say the ball is set in motion. We have to let it keep spinning."

She nodded at the windows. "If you see anyone moving along the side of the house toward the drawing room, one of you go upstairs as quickly as possible. We'll want someone up there to protect Becki and Eileen and the others."

Kevin stumbled to his feet. "I'm going to Amanda now."

"Sit down," Chandler said calmly. "Do what Rachel says."

Rachel heard the engine die. The truck doors open. The side gate creak. From where she stood, she saw the outside lights dim, go out. An uncanny darkness settled around the house. The interior lights in the smoking room and hall flickered. Darkened. Flicked on again. Something was wrong.

She raced for the door. "No," Chandler warned. "Stay right where you are, Rachel."

She dashed ahead of him and came to a running stop in the great hallway. Four men in black ski suits and balaclava masks were positioned inside the hall. One man was coming out of the drawing room with a painting in each hand, a handgun tucked in his waistband. He froze at the sight of Rachel.

The black-clad man closest to the main door stood beneath the statue of Winston Churchill. He was of medium height; his mask stretched skin-tight over a high forehead. In his right hand, he brandished a .45 semi-automatic, the sight of it forcing Rachel to remain motionless.

The powerfully built figure by the French windows was silent, yet he seemed to be in charge. His gray-streaked brows showed through his mask. "Get her out of here and get those paintings in the truck," he demanded.

Near Rachel, the tall and lean thief fastened his eyes on her. They were Morrie Chadbourne's eyes. A nausea worse than the kind she experienced on chemotherapy hit her. Her skin prickled. Her knees locked. She was about to utter his name when from the corner of her eye she saw a sudden movement. It was Jude, a pajama-clad Becki beside her. They started down the stairs together. They stopped, immobile at the sight of the strangers.

"What's happening, Rachel?" Jude asked.

"Jude, take Becki back to her room."

"But, Rachel, we want milk and cookies. Don't we, Jude?"

"Go back to your mommy, sweetheart."

Jude took another step down. One of the masked intruders glared up at her. He leaned the paintings he was holding against the wall and grabbed his Beretta. The dim lights in the hall reflected off the gun as he harked, "Go back to your room, Jude."

"Sean? Is that you, Sean?"

He shrank back. Jude took another step. "Sean. I know it's you. I know your voice."

She was running now, down the grand staircase, leaving Becki standing on the first landing, her small hand gripping the rail.

"Sweetheart, please go back to your mommy," Rachel cried.

Her voice was drowned out by Sean's: "Don't force me to hurt you, Jude." He aimed the Beretta, his finger tightening on the trigger.

"Sean, you were going to the pub with Morrie. What are you doing here?"

"Taking a little of a rich man's treasures."

The man in charge raged, "Shut up, you fool."

"Don't call me a fool. What I know could cost you a hundred years, if you had that many left." Sean tore off his mask. "Go back, Jude. I care about you. I don't want to hurt you."

"I can't let you do this, Sean."

"You can't stop me."

She was seven steps from the bottom when the gun exploded.

"Oh no. No." Sean's voice broke with a strangled cry. "I didn't mean it, Jude. I'm sorry."

For a second, her eyes stared widely, questioningly at him. She balanced on the step. Swayed. Then toppled headfirst down the stairs, leaving a bloody trail on the thick carpet.

From another direction, three shots fired wildly. The statue of Winston Churchill toppled. A Desmond vase on a pedestal splintered. The hall mirror cracked. The glass in the French windows shattered.

Becki screamed. She stared at Jude's crumpled form and cried, "Help me."

Morrie stood immobilized in the shadows. But at her second cry, *"Help me, Daddy,"* he stumbled toward her and caught her in his arms. He loosened her grip from the balustrade and threw them both on the floor. "It's okay, smidgen. I'm here."

She rasped, "Why are you wearing funny clothes, Daddy?"

As Jude moaned, Rachel braved a halting step toward her. The man in charge boomed out, "Dr. McCully, not another step."

He was a tall man, barrel-chested, strands of gray hair showing beneath his cap.

"My friend is hurt, sir."

"And we don't want the same thing to happen to you." He pointed to the man by the door. "Bosman, deal with her if she crosses us. Sean, snap out of it."

Sean's voice agonized, "But my girl is hurt."

"Forget her. You and Freck get the rest of the tagged paintings from the other rooms."

Boldly, he crossed Rachel's path as she crept toward Jude. He jerked her unmercifully. Behind his mask, his eyes were cold and mocking. "You could ruin everything. Where is Kevin Nolan?" He pressed the nerves in her upper arm. "Where is he?"

She tried to break free. He squeezed harder, the pain excruciating. "He's playing chess."

Becki screamed again. A piercing wail. "Let Rachel alone!"

Morrie tucked his daughter's face in the crook of his arm. "Lie still, smidgen. Everything will be okay."

She protested with a muffled cry, "He's hurting Rachel."

Freck and Sean reappeared, each carrying two paintings. Sean stared at Jude lying helplessly on the floor, then glared at Morrie. "I have the Weinberger for you."

"Put it back. I no longer have any need for that painting."

The powerful grip on Rachel's arm slackened. "Mr. Freck, that's the wrong picture. They both are."

For a second Freck looked confused. "They're tagged, sir." As Jude moaned, the man turned his fury on Morrie. Without warning, he cracked the butt of his revolver across Morrie's cheekbone. Blood gushed out. "You betrayed us, Chadbourne. You marked the wrong paintings."

"I had to stop you somehow."

"Daddy, you're bleeding. . . I want my mommy."

From the stairwell, Eileen cried, "I'm coming, sweetheart."

"Another step," the man warned, "and you'll need a doctor."

Morrie caught her eye. "Go back, Eileen. These men intend to take what they want. Becki is okay."

"Morrie, I can't let Jude bleed to death. I'm a doctor."

"Don't come. She'll be okay."

"No, I'm coming down to our child—and to help my patient."

Something snapped inside the stranger. "This child is yours, Chadbourne?"

"Yes. . .she's my daughter."

He laughed ruefully. "Confound it. Then it's over. All over. I've lost." He moved with surprising speed toward the French doors. Before anyone could stop him, he crashed through the shattered glass. Fell. Rolled. Was on his feet again, running. Darkness swallowed him up as he raced toward the back of the property.

～

Sinclair waited outside the French doors with Inspector Farland's iron grip on his arm, "Inspector, I'm going in for Rachel. There's already been one round fired."

"We negotiate first. Panic them, and there will be more gunfire.

More injuries. My men have the property surrounded. As soon as Morris Chadbourne gives the signal, we go in."

"You still think you can trust Chadbourne?" Sinclair asked.

"I have no choice. I am counting on that child making an honest man of him. We know he deliberately tagged the wrong paintings. His idea—"

As he spoke, the masked figure ran from the mansion and raced toward the back of the property. "Let him go, Wakefield. He won't get beyond the gate."

Sinclair shook himself free. "I'm not waiting, Inspector."

Farland smiled in the darkness. "I'll send one of my men with you."

Sinclair knew the truth before he reached the musty toolshed. The sense of betrayal overwhelmed him. The man's breach of faith. His corruption. How long had they known each other? Sickened, he kicked in the door to the shed. It sprang back. He went down the narrow steps and into the tunneled basement—into the vaulted room filled with art.

The room was temperature-controlled, but Sinclair felt a naked emptiness inside, a glacier-chill to his bones. His old friend stood there facing him, a revolver in his hand. His face was ruddy, his thick lips parted, his silver gray hair slicked back. The black turtleneck shirt caught him at the double chin. He was surrounded by what he had treasured all of his life. Masterpieces. Paintings in every size. Sculptures. Framed paintings. Unframed canvases. The Degas. His mask lay on the table, his pipe pouch beside it.

"Lord Somerset." Even saying the name pained Sinclair.

"I've been expecting you, Sinclair. It was not like you to be sleeping on the job. How long have you known?"

"Long enough, James, to keep hoping I was wrong. Thank goodness my wife, Mary, never lived to see this."

Somerset looked unperturbed. "I never meant for you to be involved. Actually your solicitor and the inspector forced me to seek your help. I liked the idea of a town and gown mentality with a distinguished academician like you. In my absence, you would defend my name and property to the last kilometer."

"What happened to you? You are a wealthy man. Why mastermind this insane robbery, James? Why target Kevin Nolan?"

Lord Somerset leaned against one of the musty crates. "Surely you guessed I'm in debt. Heavy gambling debts mostly. And I left errors on the bank books. I was safe until young Kevin Nolan did that last bank audit. Unfortunately, we gambled at the same racetracks. It didn't take him long to learn about my gambling losses. I had to destroy him before he ruined me. But it looks like I've botched this whole affair."

"Perhaps you never wanted to succeed."

He slapped the revolver against the palm of his hand. "That's good of you to suggest, Sinclair. Yes, a game maybe? I was bored with retirement. Frustrated with being useless. I thought I could play my curtain call like Hercule Poirot."

"Put the gun down, James."

Somerset's mouth twisted into a sardonic grin. "You think me mad, my friend? You're young enough to be my son, but you represented success to me. You probably don't have an extra shilling to your name, but you had the academic life—the acceptance of everyone at Oxford; I coveted that." His arrogance melted into desolation. He put the gun down. "My poor wife! Agnes will be devastated by all of this. All she ever wanted to do was spend my money and grace the walls of our home with beauty. But do you know how difficult it is to live with a woman for fifty years, Sinclair?"

"Mary and I never had that opportunity."

Somerset turned as Inspector Farland entered the vault. "Ah! Inspector, we meet again, under less favorable conditions."

Farland plucked at his bristly jaw. "I've come to arrest you, old friend."

Somerset folded his arms across his hulking chest. "I daresay when we had dinner at the London club, I expected you to arrest me then."

"I never guessed how deeply involved you were until later. You must have thought us gullible fools that night."

"Yes, I almost changed my mind seeing you again, Sinclair. You had gone through so much with the loss of your wife and son, yet nothing changed your character. The financial mess that I faced only pointed out my own weaknesses. In the past, what was money? My wife and I had only ourselves to please."

"Lord Somerset, you could have sold your paintings—and pulled yourself out of debt."

"For how long, Inspector? Agnes would go on buying paintings. I would go on gambling. Sell them, and my wife would rant and rave at me. But a robbery? She would be furious at the thieves, not at me." He gave the inspector a mocking smile. "She'd comfort me at our loss, and the insurance would bail me out. Young Nolan was my solution. Once the robbery happened—Nolan's past gambling addiction would mark him as a suspect."

For the first time, Sinclair saw Lord Somerset as elderly, confused, his features ridged with years. The more Sinclair heard his old friend try to explain himself, the more he pitied him.

"I had willing conspirators, Inspector. A museum curator and Mr. Larkins were unlikely thieves. Chadbourne walked into our hands. And that butler," Lord Somerset said with contempt. "A greedy little cur. And old Hanley over at the pub was pure putty; all he wanted was a trip to the Riviera—a chance to get away from his wife. Poor bloke. Prison won't have the same appeal."

His chest heaved involuntarily. "Agnes constantly bid on a Rembrandt or Rubens. But without wealth, how welcome would I be in the clubs in London? Or esteemed in Grasmere and the Lake District? How easily we'd be forgotten if we could no longer support our favorite charities. How often would I have an invitation to have tea with Her Majesty and Prince Philip?"

"Was all of this worth it, Lord Somerset?"

He shook his hoary head. "I will have to face my wife's humiliation, Sinclair, and risk her turning against me. She stood at my side for fifty years—and now my wife will have nothing."

Grief for an old friend rocked Sinclair. "I could speak to my solicitor, James. He could contact the National Trust. It might salvage the property. Agnes deserves more, but that's the best I can offer."

The gray-streaked brows knit together. "When I learned of my wife's heart condition, I would have bought her the world to please her." He choked out the words. "All I had to do was bluff my way financially for a year or two, and then Agnes would be gone. It wouldn't matter what happened to me after that."

Behind them, Rachel and Morrie had crowded into the vault. She glanced at the powerful figure with his arms crossed.

"Sit down," Somerset invited.

"Where would you suggest, sir?"

"The crates are quite comfortable. I'm Lord Somerset. You must be Dr. McCully, the one who kept Morris from being a thief."

"I thought you and your wife were on a world cruise."

"My wife took sick. We came home early."

As Sinclair slipped his arm around Rachel, Somerset glowered at Morrie. "Chadbourne, trusting you was one of my biggest mistakes. You betrayed me. You intended to stop this robbery."

"I have to live with myself, Lord Somerset. But most of your paintings are safe, except for the Rubens and the Monet and that Degas. I thought a mathematical genius like you would appreciate the final tally."

"Three out of three hundred. A fair score," he agreed. "But what about the injured girl, Morrie?"

"It's touch and go for her. Dr. Whitesaul is transferring Jude to the nearest medical facility. They'll airlift her to London." He rubbed his eyes. "The bullet penetrated her abdomen. It fragmented. Ricocheted off the bone."

"I'm sorry," he said wearily. "Perhaps Charles could—"

"Right now, Charles is with your wife."

Somerset's eyes misted. "I should be."

Inspector Farland moved closer and led Somerset toward the stairs. "I just had word that your wife wants to see you."

His face twisted. "May I go to her?"

The inspector nodded. "As soon as I can arrange to send some of my men with you. She's waiting in the master bedroom."

~

Pushing his way ahead of the inspector, Morrie strode from the basement without a backward glance. Outside, the men from Scotland Yard waited for him. A June rainstorm had darkened the sky. Black clouds hovered low over the mansion. The distant thunder and lightning inched closer.

"Daddy." The voice out of the darkness seared him.

He bent down and engulfed Becki in his arms, holding tightly to this flesh and blood that he had never cradled as an infant. "I'm sorry, smidgen."

"Are they going to take you away, Morrie?"

"They have to."

"I won't let them. Mommy and I won't let them hurt you."

He felt her hot tears on his neck and saw Timothy Whitesaul standing in the downpour with his arm around Eileen. More pain, like burning fuel, licked at his skin. He knew he didn't deserve Eileen. Whitesaul did. Morrie had no one to blame but himself.

He hugged his child tighter. "Becki, listen to me. If they don't take me away, I'd only run away. I always go off alone."

"Don't you want to be with Mommy and me?"

The emptiness was an ache deep inside him. An impossible longing. How long would it last? Today. Tomorrow. He'd run again.

A voice boomed across the night: "Let Chadbourne go."

Lord Somerset filled the door of the toolshed with his massive frame. His black sweat top was skintight, his wrists cuffed. "The child's father was a pawn in my hands. Let him go."

The inspector massaged his scrubby jaw. "We have evidence to the contrary—and Chadbourne's own confession."

"The man is a fool, but, Inspector Farland, you would need me to file complaints against him. I won't do that. As my caretaker, he has done an impeccable job. He rescued the very thing I would have destroyed. He kept the art collection at the estates. You have the others—Bosman, Larkins, Hanley, and Freck. Deal with them. And, Inspector, you have me."

❦

Sinclair and the men from Scotland Yard waited respectfully outside the door to the master bedroom as Lord Somerset, hands uncuffed by his request, spent a few minutes alone with his wife.

Five minutes. Ten. Twenty.

"Should we go in, Inspector?" one of the men asked.

Farland scowled at his watch. "Give him five more minutes."

The commotion and weeping in the room erupted seconds later. A frail voice cried out, "No, James. No, darling. Not that way."

A long wail. A crushing thud. Sounds they could hear even in the hallway.

Sinclair shouldered the door open.

Agnes Somerset lay weeping against her pillow, her finger pointing toward the open glass door that led to the balcony.

Sinclair knew before they crossed the room to peer over the balcony rail that Lord Somerset had taken matters into his hands one final time.

❦

In the aftermath, Rachel considered it incongruent that in the midst of the turmoil inside the mansion and the death of Lord Somerset, Janet Tallard came down the bloodstained stairs with that warm, congenial smile and suitcases in her hands.

She stopped when she saw Rachel and Sinclair standing together. Her eyes grazed the room. Men from Scotland Yard moved efficiently through the chaos. Others bore the shrouded form of Lord Somerset through the garden toward the gate.

"What happened, Sinclair—not one of our—?"

"No one you knew, Janet. It's been a nasty ruckus. An unprovoked robbery. Thankfully, we didn't disturb your sleep."

"I use earplugs," she said, embarrassed. "I can sleep through anything."

He smiled, his serious face handsome. "You just did."

At a signal from Sinclair, Kevin was at her side, taking her luggage into his own hands. "I'm driving you as far as the train station. Are you ready to go, Mrs. Tallard?"

Rachel hugged her. "Kevin will explain everything. Go. And try to remember the good times we had these last few days."

"I can hardly wait to share it all with Tad and the boys."

With another quick hug and a puzzled frown, she stepped gingerly through the shattered glass and debris and out through the main door of the mansion.

Rachel squeezed Sinclair's arm. "I envy Janet's happiness, Sinclair. She is heading home, back to her uncomplicated life with Tad on the dairy ranch in Canada—where Guernsey cows graze contentedly and three growing boys call her Mom."

Epilogue

Rachel awakened in time to watch the sunrise over Stradbury Square and to hear the first flutelike tones of the thrush greeting the morning. She padded barefoot to the window, dropped to her knees, and propped her elbows on the windowsill. The sun spread its path across her tapestry of flowers. A gentle breeze caught the pungent scents of lavender and honeysuckle.

Everything was as she had left it. The sky as blue as the crescent lake. The garden and the birch and aspen trees in full bloom. She let her gaze run along the dry stone walls to the hills dressed in imperial purple and dotted with yellow wildflowers. The neighbor's sheep grazed. Winding roads snaked around the countryside. She was eager to get her hands in the soil and to trim back her rambling roses. The smell of baking came from her kitchen. Sausage to please Sinclair. Scones to please her.

There were good memories from Somerset Estates. She would keep those. The painful images she would sort through in the months ahead. She had a long time. She had forever. She pitied the fragile hold that Lord Somerset's wife had on life. In time, Rachel would find it in her heart to be charitable toward James Somerset's memory, a man who needed forgiveness from all of them and went without it. The few guests from the reunion who had not flown home were staying on at the hotel a few miles from Stradbury Square. And dear Audrey, with her starched apron and swollen legs and as faithful as the ticking clock, was back in her kitchen, doing what she had done for decades, pleasing Mr. Sinclair.

Just beyond the neighbor's whitewashed cottage stood the ancient church with its fifteenth-century spire stabbing the sky; its empty pulpit would surely appeal to Charles. He was right! The first wedding would be her own. Rachel was certain of it.

As she thought of Sinclair, Becki burst into the room and latched her arms around Rachel's neck. "Oh Rachel, don't let Mommy take me home today."

She pulled Becki down beside her. "You can come back someday."

"Promise?"

Was it a promise Rachel could keep? She said, "We'll see. And if you can't, Sinclair and I will come and visit you."

"It won't be the same that way."

It would never be exactly the same. "If we're to get to Heathrow in time, we'd better get dressed, Becki."

"Mommy said Morrie is taking us, so you can stay home."

There was a flicker of hope and then despair. "But, Becki, I thought Inspector Farland wanted Morris to stay in the area?"

"Inspector Farland made him promise that he'd come back." She sounded so grown up, so matter-of-fact. Had the truth caught up with her that this daddy of hers would not be going home with them? Ever?

Rachel forced back her despair and said quite cheerily, "Up. I'll race you for the shower."

"Audrey said we can have breakfast in the garden."

"Oh, that will be grand, Becki. Now off with you."

"You said we were racing—"

"I changed my mind. You're my guest. So you go first."

At the door, Becki turned back. "We found Kevin's wallet."

"You did? I bet it was in his suitcase all the time."

"No, in your garden. Inspector Farland said it was planted there." She shrugged as Eileen came up behind her. "Mommy said Jude and Sean wanted to hurt Kevin. Didn't you, Mommy?"

Eileen tousled Becki's hair. She met Rachel's inquiring glance. "Becki seems to know everything, Rachel. Did she tell you we found the Monet painting behind the hedge?"

"One of the stolen paintings? Here at Wakefield Cottage?"

"They intended to put the blame on you and Kevin."

She shuddered. "Jude's parents are coming. They'll stay as long as they have to—in order to take her home with them."

"It may be awhile. Timothy said her wounds will heal, severe as they are. She can function on one kidney, but it will take longer for her to change inside. Although Timothy said she's asking for you, Rachel. I think that's a good sign."

"I told her I would stand by her."

"You're a remarkable woman, Dr. McCully."

She touched her throat. "Someone else told me that once."

"Morrie?" Eileen shooed Becki off toward the shower. "Don't look at me that way, Rachel. It will never work out between us."

"But Becki said he's driving you to Heathrow."

"I owe her a chance with her father. Inspector Farland agreed. He said with Lord Somerset dead, they have little to hold Morrie on, except his conscience. He did stop the robbery." She shook her head. "Morrie had so much potential. But he resented my coming from a wealthy family. Unless Becki told him, he doesn't know that my grandfather intends to leave his wealth to Becki—his Weinberger painting to me."

"And what will you do with the Weinberger, Eileen?"

"I know what it's worth, but I'd like to give it to Morrie. It's rightfully his. That painting would be too painful for me to keep. I would always think of him. Do you understand?"

"Yes."

❧

As Morrie unloaded the luggage at Heathrow, Eileen exclaimed, "Morrie, what are you doing with suitcases? You promised Inspector Farland that you would go right back after you saw your daughter off safely. You're not running away again?"

He did what he always did. He flashed a dimpled grin to cover his insecurities. Becki had his impulsive nature—and his eyes, blue and piercing. "I just need time alone, Eileen."

"You're breaking your word to the inspector."

"I broke my word to you, too, a long time ago. I promised you 'until death do us part.'"

"What you broke was my heart."

They stood on opposite sides of the car now, their gazes meeting across the rooftop of the rental. "I love you, Eileen."

"I know."

"I never meant to hurt you."

"I know."

"Will you be all right?"

"Will you, Morrie?"

He nodded. "I'm catching a plane to Paris. Once we're inside the terminal, can you and Becki make it to your departure gate without me?"

We've made it for eight years! This was the same Morrie she had fallen in love with. The vulnerable Morrie who had needed her was running away again. "Of course we'll be all right. We can go on from here."

"Will you tell that old codger that you saw me?"

"Why upset my grandfather?"

"That's right. He might cut you right out of the will for lining up with this old Jewish boy."

"Stop it, Morrie. Becki is going to be proud of her Jewish heritage."

"You're going to do that for me?"

"I'm doing it for Becki. And just for the record, my grandfather has tried to make it up to me ever since you went away. He didn't realize how much I cared about you until you were gone."

His eyes darkened behind the glasses. "He told you that?"

"He shows it in the way he showers Becki with his love. Don't worry, Morrie. Granddad is not leaving me any inheritance."

"Because of me?"

"He never says. But everything he has will go to Becki when she's of age. . .except the Weinberger painting. That will be mine."

He flinched. "Becki told me. So, it's payback time. You win after all, Eileen."

He picked up the heavier suitcases, and they started walking, side by side. Like it had once been. Like it would no longer be. Rebecca ran ahead of them toward the tiled concourse. Morrie watched her go and said sadly, "I feel like I've lost everything. When you board that airplane, I have nothing left."

"God will always be there for you, Morrie."

"God? I'd like to believe that. Charles kept urging me to consider eternal matters before it was too late."

"Is it too late, Morris?" Eileen whispered.

"I don't know. I hope not. That's one of the reasons I'm going away. To sort everything out. I posted a note to Inspector Farland, telling him I'd be back." He glanced at her, looked away again. "I can't believe God would love me. Forgive me. I've made such a mess of things."

"He wants you just as you are, Morrie."

"Without you?"

"Your choice."

Rebecca was peering around the crowd. "Mommy, hurry or we'll miss the plane."

"I'm coming, darling. Morrie, aren't you at least going to say good-bye to her?"

"I don't know what to say."

"You'll think of something. You're always good with words."

He walked over awkwardly, set the luggage down, and knelt by his daughter. "I'll miss you, smidgen. Maybe your mommy will bring you back someday, and we can spend some time together."

"Don't make her promises that you won't keep, Morrie."

He embraced Becki, almost crushing her. "I'm sorry, smidgen. I wish it could have been different."

"No big deal," she said, catching her breath, but there were tears in both of their eyes.

He straightened, grabbed his own luggage. "I'll leave you here. I hate long good-byes. Have a safe journey, Eileen. Write sometime. Send me pictures of Rebecca Lynne. Of yourself."

As they entered the terminal alone, Timothy Whitesaul was waiting for them. He stooped down and Becki flew into his arms. He held her tight. "Go ahead and cry, honey. I know it hurts."

Eileen wanted to burst into tears. Timothy was everything that Morrie could never be, a man with unexpected tenderness.

He looked up at Eileen. "Rachel called. She said Morrie was driving you in to Heathrow."

"He did."

"Will you be coming back to him?"

She shook her head. "It's over. Really over. He's running away, Timothy."

"I saw him racing in with his luggage. He ran past me. Never noticed me. Where is he going?"

"To Paris, I think."

"He's trying to find himself. Rachel McCully has deeply influenced him. And then—discovering Becki, I think he'll be back. He'll do what's right. Charles Rainford-Simms said he's on a redemptive journey so Morrie can't run far. You know him, Eileen. You loved him. There has to be some good in him."

And so much good in you, she thought. She compared the two men: Morrie, charming and beguiling, Timothy, practical. Morrie fought the world he lived in; Timothy lived to improve his world, quietly pursuing his cancer research with little praise from his colleagues. In a crowd, should he choose, Morrie—her first love—could be the center of attention; they often met in a crowd, their eyes catching across the auditorium. In that same crowd, Timothy would stand on the sidelines, or engage in a quiet conversation with one or two. She had met Timothy on an emergency room rotation—she the intern, he the resident-on-call. In the chaos, he remained calm.

In the chaos, they discovered each other.

Becki walked between them now, her hand securely in Timothy's. She was the center of their lives. It was as if she belonged there. As though she were really his.

"Will you come back to me someday, Eileen?" he asked. "My offer is still good."

She glanced up as he guided them through the crowd. "Do you mean that job at your research clinic?"

"No, the one by my side."

When they reached the departure gate, he said, "I want you to marry me. I want to make a home for you and Becki here in England." He touched her cheek gently, the feel of his broad hand comforting. "I have always loved you. And I think you know that for me—in a very real way—Becki has always been mine."

She managed to surmount the lump in her throat. "I know. You're so good to us."

"Will you come back, Eileen?"

"Will you give me time to sort out my feelings?"

He smiled, their eyes locking above Becki. "You can have all the time in the world as long as you come back into my world."

～

Kevin Nolan and Amanda Pennyman watched Rachel and Sinclair walk out through the garden gate at Wakefield Cottage and down the country lane. "I envy them," Kevin said.

"They are happy, aren't they? It seems so funny seeing Dr. McCully radiantly happy like that. I just never thought about her that way."

"What way is that?"

"You know, silly goose. Romantic and all."

"She's a wonderful person, Amanda. I liked her from the start. Thanks for inviting me to the reunion."

"I almost got you killed."

"I don't think that was in your plans," he teased.

"How do you feel, Kevin? Really?"

"With all that's happened?" He patted the wallet in his pocket. "Like a sacrificial goat."

"Kevin."

"Hmmm?"

"You haven't asked me to marry you lately."

"I did two weeks ago. And the week before that. And in April, when I was afraid Mother was coming to visit us."

"But not lately. Lately, you haven't wanted to make an honest woman of me."

He looked at her. Everything had changed except his deep longing to marry Amanda. He looked away, fixing his eyes on Dr. McCully and Don Wakefield. They were not much older than Kevin himself. He watched them walk leisurely over the stone-flagged path, side by side at first, then hand in hand. He envied the joy they had found in discovering each other again.

Amanda nudged him. "Kevin, ask me to marry you again."

He turned, met her anxious gaze, and gave her a crooked smile. He tried to quiet the drumbeat of his heart. "I won't take the risk of you turning me down again."

"Maybe I won't this time. What if I propose to you?"

Don't mock me, he thought. "Things have changed, Amanda."

"Forever?"

"It has the forever quality to it."

"I don't want to lose you. I want us to stay together."

He felt pained. "Not without a permanent commitment."

"When that bomb exploded near Harrods—when I heard it on BBC—I was so afraid, Kevin. I knew you were in the area, waiting for me. I was certain something had happened to you."

"Something did." How could he tell her?

"I was afraid you were dead."

"Like Lee?"

"No, like you. I thought I had lost *you.*" A tear tracked down her cheek. "I love you, you big galoot."

"So you've told me for three years. You still wouldn't marry me."

Her gaze strayed down the path. "Dr. McCully told me that true love only comes along once in a lifetime."

"What about Lee?"

"He was my first love." She brushed at her tears. "I was strong-willed back in college, always living on the edge. I don't think Lee and I would ever have married."

"You were engaged."

"I know. But I've grown up in the last ten days. I know what I want now. Rachel told me not to let you get away because God brought us together."

"It's not that easy, Amanda. It's that religious jargon, isn't it?" he challenged.

"It's more than jargon, Kevin."

"I know." His brow arced. "You don't have to explain. I knew all of that as a boy. Threw it over as a teenager. Blocked it out when you moved in with me. In these last few days, I knew that I couldn't go on without God in my life. That's why I went off fishing with Sinclair yesterday. I knew he had something I didn't have. We talked about it."

"You certainly didn't catch any fish."

"But I caught hold of eternity for a time. That was better than trout. I haven't felt this peaceful and clean in a long time, Amanda."

"God forgave you even after we broke His laws."

"He's in the business of forgiving, Amanda."

"That's what Dr. McCully told me when you fell overboard in Lake Windermere. Everybody thought it was an accident—that you had been goofing off, standing on the rail. I knew differently. I told Dr. McCully that someone pushed you in."

"It happened so fast, but I think it was Sean. I hit my head on the way down so I couldn't be certain with my senses dulled."

"Dr. McCully and I had a long talk after you were hurt. That's when I told her we weren't married."

"There was never anyone else for me. I look at the professor and Wakefield and marvel at how little time they may have left to spend together. But no complaints. They're content. Happy."

"They're in love, Kev."

"They wasted all those years. I won't go on wasting mine."

"Then you won't marry me, Kevin?"

He grinned finally. "You haven't asked me yet."

～

As they turned back toward the garden at Wakefield Cottage, Rachel smiled when she caught sight of Kevin and Amanda.

"Sinclair, do you think we have given them enough time?"

"From the way he's kissing her, I rather think so. If they don't watch out, they will break off your hollyhocks."

"They were damaged when the house was invaded, remember?"

"Inspector Farland put a tag on that one, as he calls it. Sean's fingerprints match up. I think they had Plan A and Plan B. If they couldn't defame Kevin at the reunion, then they planned to leave his wallet and the Monet painting here at the cottage."

"Poor Somerset. Trying to destroy the man who audited his books.

And poor Morrie. Involved with him just for a painting."

"At least Amanda is one of your success stories, Rachel. And Kevin—he's a poor fisherman, but a jolly good man. Now let's walk back toward the lake and give them more time together," he said with a rakish grin.

She slipped her arm in his. "That suits me fine. I like being alone with you. Eileen called from Heathrow. Morrie is not coming back. He boarded a plane to Paris."

"He'll come back. He'll do it for Rebecca. Thanks to the challenges in your classroom, he is an intelligent young man. Now, dear Rachel, let's talk about us."

She knew he was about to propose. She was created for this moment in time. Not to fill her sister's role as a university professor—although she had filled the role well. Not to go down in history as an Olympic gold medalist, nor just to leave an imprint on other lives, but to find her soulmate, her companion, her lover, her fulfillment in God's choice for her. All else had come to this moment when she could let someone else love her for herself.

"You fought a good fight in your battle with cancer, Rachel. I think you've been laying up treasures in heaven some that will surely bear the names of your students, but now it's time to think about us. I want to marry you, Rachel."

"I'm on bonus time. There's no guarantee on my remission."

"There's no guarantee on anyone's tomorrow. Let's just enjoy every moment we have. Will you marry me, Rachel?"

"Can I give you my answer tomorrow?" she teased.

"I won't wait until tomorrow. I want my answer today."

She tilted her head and met his gaze. "And Audrey would be furious if I didn't say yes."

"Then say yes."

"Yes—but people will think you foolhardy marrying me."

"I've been accused of being self-sufficient. Independent."

"I rather liked that about you."

They made their way back along the country lane, over the pebbled path that led into the garden. "Rachel, I promise you, tomorrow—for all of our tomorrows—we'll spend as much time as we can at Wakefield Cottage. You're happy here, aren't you?"

"Radiantly happy, Sinclair."

"I'll go into Oxford three days a week for my classes."

"But you will come home to me again. There will be many days to watch the sunrise over Stradbury Square. We did that when we first came here together, ever so long ago."

"You remembered?"

"You told me it was the only place we could be alone."

He said thoughtfully, "Mary would be pleased about us."

"That's an odd thing to say."

"No, Mary knew about you. Sometimes she said that a corner of my heart and a nugget of my memory would always be yours. She was right, you know. I adored Mary, loved her. She made my life complete, but part of me always remembered you. Can you understand that, Rachel?"

She felt vibrant and alive like the day they met. "I think so. And all those years, you were always in my mind. A kaleidoscope of portraits and shadowy images. The sound of your deep, rich voice whispering in my ear, shouting in my dreams. Somehow you were always there even when you weren't." Her voice lowered. "But you know there can never be any children. Timothy Whitesaul doesn't want me to risk it, not after my cancer and my family history of cystic fibrosis."

"But there *can* be children."

She leaned her head against him. "It would be too risky."

His fingers tightened around hers. "Charles told me about a little girl from his last parish at St. Michael's. Tesa was sent away to live with distant relatives, but it didn't work out. She's unhappy there. He wants to find a permanent home for her."

"A little girl of our own?"

"She's younger than Becki. Shy and bright-eyed and small for her age. I already plan to add another wing to the cottage—a couple of small bedrooms and a small bath. Tesa would have a room of her own."

"Won't it be too much for Audrey?"

"She can be Tesa's nanny. We'll hire help in the kitchen."

"Audrey won't like that."

"But she will love Tesa."

"Oh Sinclair. A little girl of our own? I will adore her. When can we go and get her?"

"Slow down, love. We could arrange for Charles and Audrey to go for her while we are on our honeymoon. But we can stop and see her on our way, so she will be comfortable with us—and so we will have someone special to come home to."

"I love you, Sinclair Wakefield."

He smiled, his eyes teasing. "How gratifying."

Even as they stopped on the cobbled path, she knew as he took her in his arms, his lips on hers would be sweet and tender. She went gladly into his embrace, and time no longer mattered.

About the Author

DORIS ELAINE FELL writes with a sensitive pen, a tender heart, and a spirit of laughter—taking you into a world of adventure touching lives, touching rebels.

Her multifaceted career as teacher, missionary, nurse, freelance editor, and author, has taken her all over the world and inspired her novels. She is the best-selling author of 17 novels with Simon & Schuster's Steeple Hill/Love Inspired imprint, Fleming Revell, Harvest House, Howard, Crossway, and OakTara. Doris was a Christy Award finalist in 2000, a 2003 SPU (Seattle Pacific University) Medallion Award winner, and received the 2004 Silver Angel Award, Excellence in Media (EIM).

Don't miss her exciting Seasons of Intrigue series (*Always in September, Before Winter Comes, April Is Forever, The Twelfth Rose of Spring, To Catch the Summer Wind, The Race for Autumn's Glory*, or her Fields of Valor series (*Betrayal in Paris, The Trumpet at Twisp, In the Shadow of Catherine*).

Seven of her titles were published in large print with Thorndike Press, and two books have editions in German and Italian, with another as a special limited edition in Australia. Her short stories also appear in Multnomah's *The Story Tellers' Collection Book 2* and the ChiLibris publication *What the Wind Picked Up*. Doris is also the author of two nonfiction books, *Lady of the Tboli* (Christian Herald Books), *Give Me This Mountain* (Jungle Camp devotional), and articles in mainstream and inspirational publications, such as "Mom and the Talking Bears" (*Focus on the Family*), *Tapestry: Walk Thru the Bible Ministries, Missouri Synod Lutheran Publication, Adventist Review*), "Brat Boy" (*RN Magazine*), "A Seed for Tomorrow" (*Home Life*), "Bells, Bearhugs, and Mixed Blessings" (*Journal of Christian Nursing*), and Sunday school publications such as *Evangel* and *Standard*.

Doris Elaine Fell writes from her home in Southern California.

FELL, DORIS ELAINE   2016

THE RECONCILED HEARTS TRILOGY

F 2010 PB   A

DATE DUE			
4-23-16